PETER F. HAMILTON

THE NEUTRONIUM ALCHEMIST

PART 1: CONSOLIDATION

ASPECT®

D0057642

WARNER BOOKS

A Time Warner Company

WARNER BOOKS EDITION

Aspect is a registered trademark of Warner Books, Inc.

Cover design by Don Puckey and Carol Russo
Cover illustration by Jim Burns

Warner Books, Inc.
1271 Avenue of the Americas
New York, NY 10020

Visit our Web site at
www.warnerbooks.com

Ⓦ A Time Warner Company

Printed in the United States of America

First Warner Books Printing: April, 1998

10 9 8 7 6 5 4 3 2

THE NEUTRONIUM ALCHEMIST

PART 1: CONSOLIDATION

CAST OF CHARACTERS

SHIPS

LADY MACBETH

Joshua Calvert	Captain
Melvyn Ducharme	Fusion specialist
Ashly Hanson	Pilot
Sarha Mitcham	Systems specialist
Dahybi Yadev	Node specialist
Beaulieu	Cosmonik

OENONE

Syrinx	Captain
Ruben	Fusion systems
Oxley	Pilot
Cacus	Life support
Edwin	Toroid systems
Serina	Toroid systems
Tyla	Cargo officer

VILLENEUVE'S REVENGE

André Duchamp	Captain
Desmond Lafoe	Fusion specialist
Madeleine Collum	Node specialist
Erick Thakrar	Systems specialist/CNIS undercover agent

UDAT

Meyer	Captain
Cherri Barnes	Cargo officer

FAR REALM

Layia	Captain
Furay	Pilot

| Endron | Systems specialist |
| Tilia | Node specialist |

ARIKARA

Meredith Saldana	Rear-Admiral, squadron commander
Grese	Lieutenant, squadron intelligence officer
Rhoecus	Lieutenant, voidhawk liaison
Kroeber	Commander

BEEZLING

| Kyle Prager | Captain |
| Peter Adul | Alchemist team physicist |

HABITATS

TRANQUILLITY

Ione Saldana	Lord of Ruin
Dr Alkad Mzu	Inventor of the Alchemist
Parker Higgens	Director Laymil project
Oski Katsura	Laymil project electronics division chief
Kempster Getchell	Laymil project astronomer
Monica Foulkes	ESA agent
Lady Tessa	ESA head of station
Samuel	Edenist intelligence agent
Pauline Webb	CNIS agent
Father Horst Elwes	Priest, refugee
Jay Hilton	Refugee
Kelly Tirrel	Rover reporter
Lieria	Kiint
Haile	Juvenile Kiint

VALISK

Rubra	Habitat personality
Dariat	Horgan's possessor
Kiera Salter	Marie Skibbow's possessor
Stanyon	Council member
Rocio Condra	Possessor blackhawk Mindor

Bonney Lewin	Hunter
Tolton	Fugitive
Tatiana	Fugitive

ASTEROIDS

TRAFALGAR

Samual Aleksandrovich	First Admiral Confederation Navy
Lalwani	Admiral, CNIS chief
Maynard Khanna	Captain, First Admiral staff officer
Motela Kolhammer	Admiral, 1st Fleet commander
Dr Gilmore	CNIS research division director
Jacqueline Couteur	Possessor
Murphy Hewlett	Confederation Marine lieutenant

KOBLAT

Jed Hinton	Deadnight
Beth	Deadnight
Gari Hinton	Jed's sister
Navar	Jed's half sister

AYACUCHO

Ikela	Owner of T'Opingtu company, partizan leader
Liol	Owner of Quantum Serendipity
Voi	Ikela's daughter
Prince Lambert	Captain starship *Tekas*
Dan Malindi	Partizan leader
Kaliua Lamu	Partizan leader
Feira Ile	Ayacucho SD commander, partizan leader
Cabral	Media magnate, partizan leader
Mrs Nateghi	Lawyer
Lodi Shalasha	Garissan radical
Eriba	Garissan radical
Kole	Socialite
Shea	Prince Lambert's girlfriend

JESUP

| Quinn Dexter | Messiah of the Light Bringer sect |

Lawrence Dillon	Disciple
Twelve-T	Gang lord
Bonham	Disciple
Shemilt	Disciple, SD commander
Dwyer	Disciple, systems specialist

PLANETS

NORFOLK

Louise Kavanagh	Refugee
Genevieve Kavanagh	Refugee
Luca Comar	Grant Kavanagh's possessor
Marjorie Kavanagh	Louise's mother
Mrs Charlsworth	Kavanagh sisters' nanny
Carmitha	Romany
Titreano	Possessor
Celina Hewson	Louise's aunt
Roberto Hewson	Louise's cousin

OMBEY

Ralph Hiltch	ESA head of station, Lalonde
Cathal Fitzgerald	Ralph's deputy
Dean Folan	ESA G66 division
Will Danza	ESA G66 division
Kirsten Saldana	Princess of Ombey
Roche Skark	ESA director
Jannike Dermot	ISA director
Landon McCullock	Police commissioner
Diana Tiernan	Police technology division chief
Admiral Farquar	Royal Navy, Ombey commander
Nelson Akroid	Armed Tactical Squad captain
Finnuala O'Meara	Rover reporter
Hugh Rosler	DataAxis technician
Neville Latham	Exnall's chief inspector
Janne Palmer	Royal Marine colonel
Annette Ekelund	Possessor
Gerald Skibbow	Refugee
Dr Riley Dobbs	Royal Navy personality debrief psychology expert

Jansen Kovak	Royal Navy medical institute nurse
Moyo	Possessor
Stephanie Ash	Possessor
Cochrane	Possessor
Rana	Possessor
Tina Sudol	Possessor

NEW CALIFORNIA

Jezzibella	Mood Fantasy artist
Leroy Octavius	Jezzibella's manager
Libby	Jezzibella's dermal technology expert
Al	Brad Lovegrove's possessor
Avram Harwood III	Mayor of San Angeles
Emmet Mordden	Organization lieutenant
Silvano Richmann	Organization lieutenant
Mickey Pileggi	Organization lieutenant
Patricia Mangano	Organization lieutenant
Gus Remar	Rover reporter
Kingsley Pryor	Lieutenant commander, Confederation Navy
Luigi Balsmao	Commander Organization fleet
Cameron Leung	Possessor blackhawk *Zahan*
Oscar Kearn	Captain Organization frigate *Urschel*

KULU

Alastair II	The King
Simon, Duke of Salion	Chairman security commission
Lord Kelman Mountjoy	Foreign Office minister
Lady Phillipa Oshin	Prime minister
Admiral Lavaquar	Defence chief
Prince Howard	Kulu Corporation president
Prince Noton	Ex-president Kulu Corporation

NYVAN

Gelai	Possessor, Garissa genocide victim
Ngong	Possessor, Garissa genocide victim
Omain	Possessor, Garissa genocide victim
Richard Keaton	Data security expert

| Baranovich | Organization lieutenant |
| Adrian Redway | ESA head of station |

OTHERS

CONFEDERATION

Olton Haaker	Assembly President
Jeeta Anwar	Chief presidential aide
Mae Ortlieb	Presidential science aide
Cayeaux	Edenist ambassador
Sir Maurice Hall	Kulu Kingdom ambassador

EDENISTS

Wing-Tsit Chong	Edenism's founder
Athene	Syrinx's mother
Astor	Ambassador to the Kulu Kingdom
Sinon	Syrinx's father

It seemed to Louise Kavanagh as though the fearsome mid-summer heat had persisted for endless, dreary weeks rather than just the four Duke-days since the last meagre shower of rain. "Air from the devil's cookhouse," the old women of the county called this awful unbreathable stillness which blanketed the wolds. It complemented Louise's mood perfectly. She didn't feel much of anything these days. Destiny had apparently chosen her to spend her waking hours doing nothing but wait.

Officially, she was waiting for her father, who was away leading the Stoke County militia to help quell the insurrection which the Democratic Land Union had mounted in Boston. The last time he'd phoned was three days ago, a quick, grim call saying the situation was worse than the Lord Lieutenant had led them to believe. That had made Louise's mother worry frantically. Which meant Louise and Genevieve had to creep around Cricklade manor like mice so as not to worsen her temper.

And there had been no word since, not of Father or any of the militia troops. The whole county was crackling with rumours, of course. Of terrible battles and beastly acts of savagery by the Union irregulars. Louise tried hard to close her ears to them, convinced it was just wicked propaganda put about by Union sympathisers. Nobody really knew anything. Boston could have been on another planet as far as Stoke County was concerned. Even bland accounts of "disturbances," reported on the nightly news programs, had ceased after the county militias encircled the city—censored by the government.

All they could do was wait helplessly for the militias to triumph as they surely would.

Louise and Genevieve had spent yet another morning milling aimlessly around the manor. It was a tricky task; sitting about doing nothing was so incredibly boring, yet if they drew attention to themselves they would be given some menial domestic job to do. With the young men away, the maids and older menservants were struggling with the normal day-to-day running of the rambling building. And the estate farms outside, with their skeleton workforce, were falling dismayingly far behind in their preparations for the summer's second cereal crop.

By lunchtime, the ennui had started to get to Louise, so she had suggested that she and her sister go riding. They had to saddle the horses themselves, but it was worth it just to be away from the manor for a few hours.

Louise's horse picked its way gingerly over the ground. Duke's hot rays had flayed open the soil, producing a wrinkled network of cracks. The aboriginal plants which had all flowered in unison at midsummer were long dead now. Where ten days ago the grassland had been dusted with graceful white and pink stars, small shrivelled petals now skipped about like minute autumn leaves. In some hollows they had drifted in loose dunes up to a foot deep.

"Why do you suppose the Union hates us so?" Genevieve asked querulously. "Just because Daddy's got a temper doesn't mean he's a bad man."

Louise produced a sympathetic smile for her younger sister. Everyone said how alike they were, twins born four years apart. And indeed it was a bit like looking into a mirror at times; the same features, rich dark hair, delicate nose, and almost Oriental eyes. But Genevieve was smaller, and slightly chubbier. And right now, brokenly glum.

Genevieve had been sensitive to her moodiness for the last week, not wanting to say anything significant in case it made big sister even more unaccountably irritable.

She does idolize me so, Louise thought. Pity she couldn't have chosen a better role model.

"It's not just Daddy, nor even the Kavanaghs," Louise said. "They simply don't like the way Norfolk works."

"But why? Everybody in Stoke County is happy."

"Everybody in the county is provided for. There's a difference. How would you feel if you had to work in the fields all day long for every day of your life, and saw the two of us riding by without a care in the world?"

Genevieve looked puzzled. "Not sure."

"You'd resent it, and you'd want to change places."

"I suppose so." She gave a sly grin. "Then I'd be the one who resented them."

"Exactly. That's the problem."

"But the things people are saying the Union is doing . . ." Genevieve said uncertainly. "I heard two of the maids talking about it this morning. They were saying horrible things. I ran away after a minute."

"They're lying. If anybody in Stoke County knew what was going on in Boston, it would be us, the Kavanaghs. The maids are going to be the last to find out."

Genevieve shone a reverent smile at her sister. "You're so clever, Louise."

"You're clever too, Gen. Same genes, remember."

Genevieve smiled again, then spurred her horse on ahead, laughing gladly. Merlin, their sheepdog, chased off after her, kicking up whirling flurries of brown petals.

Louise instinctively urged her own horse into a canter, heading towards Wardley Wood, a mile ahead. In summers past the sisters had claimed it as their own adventure playground. This summer, though, it held an added poignancy. This summer it contained the memory of Joshua Calvert. Joshua and the things they'd done as they lazed by the side of the rock pools. Every outrageous sexual act, acts which no true well-born Norfolk lady would ever commit. Acts which she couldn't wait for them to do again.

Also the acts which had made her throw up for the last three mornings in a row. Nanny had been her usual fuss the first two times. Thankfully, Louise had managed to conceal this morning's bout of nausea, otherwise her mother would have been told. And Mother was pretty shrewd.

Louise grimaced forlornly. *Everything will be fine once Joshua comes back.* It had become almost a mantra recently.

Dear Jesus, but I hate this waiting.

Genevieve was a quarter of a mile from the woods, with Louise a hundred yards behind her, when they heard the train.

The insistent tooting sound carried a long way in the calm air. Three short blasts, followed by a long one. The warning signal that it was approaching the open road crossing at Collyweston.

Genevieve reined her horse in, waiting for Louise to catch up with her. "It's coming into town!" the younger girl exclaimed.

Both of them knew the local train times by heart. Colsterworth had twelve passenger services a day. This one wasn't one of them.

"They're coming back!" Genevieve squealed. "Daddy's back!"

Merlin picked up on her excitement, running around the horse, barking enthusiastically.

Louise bit her lip. She couldn't think what else it could be. "I suppose so."

"It is. It is!"

"All right, come on then."

Cricklade manor lurked inside its picket of huge geneered cedars, an imposing stone mansion built in homage to the stately homes of an England as distant in time as in space. The glass walls of the ornate orangery abutting the east wing reflected Duke's brilliant yellow sunlight in geometric ripples as the sisters rode along the greensward below the building.

When she was inside the ring of cedars, Louise noticed the chunky blue-green farm ranger racing up the long gravel drive. She whooped loudly, goading her horse to an even faster gallop. Few people were allowed to drive the estate's powered vehicles. And nobody else drove them as fast as Daddy.

Louise soon left Genevieve well behind, with an exhausted Merlin trailing by almost a quarter of a mile. She could see six figures crammed into the vehicle's seats. And that was definitely Daddy driving. She didn't recognise any of the others.

Another two farm rangers turned into the drive just as the first pulled up in front of the manor. Various household staff and Marjorie Kavanagh hurried down the broad steps to greet it.

Louise tumbled down off her horse, and rushed up to her father. She flung her arms around him before he knew what was happening. He was dressed in the same military uniform as the day he left.

"Daddy! You're all right." She rubbed her cheek against the coarse khaki-green fabric of his jacket, feeling five years old again. Tears were threatening to brim up.

He stiffened inside her manic embrace, head slowly tipping down to look at her. When she glanced up adoringly she saw a look of mild incomprehension on his strong ruddy face.

For a horrible moment she thought he must have found out about the baby. Then a vile mockery of a smile came to his lips.

"Hello, Louise. Nice to see you again."

"Daddy?" She took a step backwards. What was wrong with him? She glanced uncertainly at her mother who had just reached them.

Marjorie Kavanagh took in the scene with a fast glance. Grant looked just awful; tired, pale, and strangely nervous. Gods, what had happened in Boston?

She ignored Louise's obvious hurt and stepped up to him. "Welcome home," she murmured demurely. Her lips brushed his cheek.

"Hello dear," Grant Kavanagh said. She could have been a complete stranger for all the emotion in his voice.

He turned, almost in deference, Marjorie thought with growing bewilderment, and half bowed to one of the men accompanying him. They were all strangers, none of them even wore Stoke County militia uniforms. The other two farm rangers were braking behind the first, also full of strangers.

"Marjorie, I'd like you to meet Quinn Dexter. Quinn is a . . . priest. He's going to be staying here with some of his followers."

The young man who walked forwards had the kind of gait Marjorie associated with the teenage louts she glimpsed occasionally in Colsterworth. Priest, my arse, she thought.

Quinn was dressed in a flowing robe of some incredibly black material; it looked like the kind of habit a millionaire monk would wear. There was no crucifix in sight. The face which smiled out at her from the voluminous hood was coldly vulpine. She noticed how everyone in his entourage was very careful not to get too close to him.

"Intrigued, Father Dexter," she said, letting her irony show.

He blinked, and nodded thoughtfully, as if in recognition that they weren't fooling each other.

"Why are you here?" Louise asked breathlessly.

"Cricklade is going to be a refuge for Quinn's sect," Grant Kavanagh said. "There was a lot of damage in Boston. So I offered him full use of the estate."

"What happened?" Marjorie asked. Years of discipline necessary to enforce her position allowed her to keep her voice level, but what she really wanted to do was grab hold of Grant's jacket collar and scream in his face. Out of the corner of her eye she saw Genevieve scramble down off her horse and run over to greet her father, her delicate face suffused with simple happiness. Before Marjorie could say anything, Louise thrust out an arm and stopped her dead in her tracks. Thank God for that, Marjorie thought; there was no telling how these aloof strangers would react to excitable little girls.

Genevieve's face instantly turned woeful, staring up at her untouchable father with widened, mutinous eyes. But Louise kept a firmly protective arm around her shoulder.

"The rebellion is over," Grant said. He hadn't even noticed Genevieve's approach.

"You mean you rounded up the Union people?"

"The rebellion is over," Grant repeated flatly.

Marjorie was at a loss what to do next. Away in the distance she could hear Merlin barking with unusual aggression. The fat old sheepdog was lumbering along the greensward towards the group outside the manor.

"We shall begin straightaway," Quinn announced abruptly. He started up the steps towards the wide double doors, long pleats of his robe swaying leadenly around his ankles.

The manor staff clustering with considerable curiosity on top of the steps parted nervously. Quinn's companions surged after him.

Grant's face twitched in what was nearly an apology to Marjorie as the new arrivals clambered out of the farm rangers to hurry up the steps after their singular priest. Most of them were men, all with exactly the same kind of agitated expression.

They look as if they're going to their own execution, Marjorie thought. And the clothes a couple of them wore were bizarre. Like historical military costumes: grey greatcoats with broad scarlet lapels and yards of looping gold braid. She strove to remember history lessons from too many years ago, images of Teutonic officers hazy in her mind.

"We'd better go in," Grant said encouragingly. Which was absurd. Grant Kavanagh neither asked nor suggested anything on his own doorstep, he gave orders.

Marjorie gave a reluctant nod and joined him. "You two stay out here," she told her daughters. "I want you to see to Merlin, then stable your horses." While I find out just what the hell is going on around here, she completed silently.

The two sisters were virtually clinging together at the bottom of the steps, faces heavy with doubt and dismay. "Yes, Mother," Louise said meekly. She started to tug on Genevieve's black riding jacket.

Quinn paused on the threshold of the manor, giving the grounds a final survey. Misgivings were beginning to stir his mind. When he was back in Boston it seemed only right that he should be part of the vanguard bringing the gospel of God's Brother to the whole island of Kesteven. None could stand before him when his serpent beast was unleashed. But there were so many lost souls returning from the beyond; inevitably some dared to disobey, while others wavered after he had passed among them to issue the word. In truth he could only depend upon the closest disciples he had gathered.

The sect acolytes he had left in Boston to tame the returned souls, to teach them the real reason why they had been brought back, agreed to do his bidding simply from fear. That was why he had come to the countryside, to levy the creed upon all the souls, both the living and the dead, of this wretched planet. With a bigger number of followers inducted, genuinely *believing* the task God's Brother had given them, then ultimately their doctrine would triumph.

But this land which Luca Comar had described in glowing terms was so empty, kilometre after kilometre of grassland

and fields, populated by dozing hamlets of cowed peasants; a temperate-climate version of Lalonde.

There had to be more to his purpose than this. God's Brother would never have chosen him for such a simple labour. There were hundreds of planets in the Confederation crying out to hear His word, to follow Him into the final battle against the false gods of Earth's religions, where Night would dawn forevermore.

After this evening I shall have to search myself to see where He guides me; I must find my proper role in His plan.

His gaze finished up on the Kavanagh sisters who were staring up at him, both trying to be courageous in the face of the strangeness falling on their home as softly and inexorably as midwinter snow. The elder one would make a good reward for disciples who demonstrated loyalty, and the child might be of some use to a returned soul. God's Brother found a use for everything.

Content, for the moment, Quinn swept into the hall, relishing the opulence which greeted him. Tonight at least he could indulge himself in decadent splendour, quickening his serpent beast. For who did not appreciate absolute luxury?

The disciples knew their duties well enough, needing no supervision. They would flush out the manor's staff and open their bodies for possession: a chore repeated endlessly over the last week. His work would come later, selecting those who were worthy of a second chance at life, who would embrace the Night.

"What—!" Genevieve began hotly as the last of the odd adults disappeared inside the manor's entrance.

Louise's hand clamped over her mouth. "Come on!" She pulled hard on Genevieve's arm, nearly unbalancing the younger girl. Genevieve reluctantly allowed herself to be steered away.

"You heard Mother," Louise said. "We're to look after the horses."

"Yes, but . . ."

"I don't know! All right? Mother will sort everything out." The words brought scant reassurance. What *had* happened to Daddy?

Boston must have been truly terrible to have affected him so.

Louise undid the strap on her riding hat, and tucked it under an arm. The manor and its grounds had become very quiet all of a sudden. The big entrance-hall doors swinging shut had acted like a signal for the birds to fall still. Even the horses were docile.

The funereal sensation was broken by Merlin who had finally reached the gravel driveway. He barked quite piteously as he nosed around Louise's feet, his tongue lolling out as he wheezed heavily.

Louise gathered up the reins of both horses and started to lead them towards the stables. Genevieve grabbed Merlin's collar and hauled him along.

When they reached the stable block at the rear of the manor's west wing there was nobody there, not even the two young stable lads Mr Butterworth had left in charge. The horses' hooves made an almighty clattering on the cobbles of the yard outside, the noise reverberating off the walls.

"Louise," Genevieve said forlornly, "I don't like this. Those people with Daddy were really peculiar."

"I know. But Mother will tell us what to do."

"She went inside with them."

"Yes." Louise realized just how anxious Mother had been for her and Genevieve to get away from Daddy's friends. She looked around the yard, uncertain what to do next. Would Mother send for them, or should they go in? Daddy would expect to talk with them. The old daddy, she reminded herself sadly.

Louise settled for stalling. There was plenty to do in the stables; take the saddles off, brush the horses down, water them. She and Genevieve both took off their riding jackets and set to.

It was twenty minutes later, while they were putting the saddles back in the tack room, when they heard the first scream. The shock was all the more intense because it was male: a raw-throated yell of pain which dwindled away into a sobbing whimper.

Genevieve quietly put her arm around Louise's waist.

Louise could feel her trembling and patted her softly. "It's all right," she whispered.

The two of them edged over to the window and peered out. There was nothing to see in the courtyard. The manor's windows were black and blank, sucking in Duke's light.

"I'll go and find out what's happening," Louise said.

"No!" Genevieve pulled at her urgently. "Don't leave me alone. *Please*, Louise." She was on the verge of tears.

Louise's hold tightened in reflex. "Okay, Gen, I won't leave you."

"Promise? Really truly promise?"

"Promise!" She realized she was just as frightened as Genevieve. "But we must find out what Mother wants us to do."

Genevieve nodded brokenly. "If you say so."

Louise looked at the high stone wall of the west wing, sizing it up. What would Joshua do in a situation like this? She thought about the layout of the wing, the family apartments, the servants' utility passages. Rooms and corridors she knew better than anyone except for the chief housekeeper, and possibly Daddy.

She took Genevieve by the hand. "Come on. We'll try and get up to Mother's boudoir without anyone seeing us. She's bound to go there eventually."

They crept out into the courtyard and scuttled quickly along the foot of the manor's wall to a small green door which led into a storeroom at the back of the kitchens. Louise expected a shouted challenge at any moment. She was panting by the time she heaved on the big iron handle and nipped inside.

The storeroom was filled with sacks of flour and vegetables piled high in various wooden bays. Two narrow window slits, set high in the wall, cast a paltry grey light through their cobweb-caked panes.

Louise flicked the switch as Genevieve closed the door. A couple of naked light spheres on the roof sputtered weakly, then went out.

"Damnation!" Louise took Genevieve's hand and threaded her way carefully around the boxes and sacks.

The utility corridor beyond had plain white plaster walls

and pale yellow flagstones. Light spheres every twenty feet along its ceiling were flickering on and off completely at random. The effect made Louise feel mildly giddy, as if the corridor were swaying about.

"What's doing that?" Genevieve whispered fiercely.

"I've no idea," she replied carefully. A dreadful ache of loneliness had stolen up on her without any warning. Cricklade didn't belong to them anymore, she knew that now.

They made their way along the disconcerting corridor to the antechamber at the end. A cast-iron spiral staircase wound up through the ceiling.

Louise paused to hear if anyone was coming down. Then, satisfied they were still alone, she started up.

The manor's main corridors were a vast contrast to the plain servant utilities. Wide strips of thick green and gold carpet ran along polished golden wood planks, the walls were hung with huge traditional oil paintings in ostentatious gilt frames. Small antique chests stood at regular intervals, holding either delicate objets d'art or cut crystal vases with fragrant blooms of terrestrial and xenoc flowers grown in the manor's own conservatory.

The outside of the door at the top of the spiral stairs was disguised as a wall panel. Louise teased it open and peeped out. A grand stained-glass window at the far end of the corridor was sending out broad fans of coloured light to dye the walls and ceiling with tartan splashes. Engraved light spheres on the ceiling were glowing a lame amber. All of them emitted an unhealthy buzzing sound.

"Nobody about," Louise said.

The two of them darted out and shut the panel behind them. They started edging towards their mother's boudoir.

A distant cry sounded. Louise couldn't work out where it came from. It wasn't close, though; thank sweet Jesus.

"Let's go back," Genevieve said. "Please, Louise. Mummy knows we went to the stables. She'll find us there."

"We'll just see if she's here, first. If she's not, then we'll go straight back."

They heard the anguished cry again, even softer this time.

The boudoir door was twenty feet away. Louise steeled herself and took a step towards it.

"Oh, God, *no*! No, no, no. Stop it. Grant! Dear God, help me!"

Louise's muscles locked in terror. It was her mother's voice—Mother's scream—coming from behind the boudoir door.

"Grant, no! Oh, please. *Please*, no more." A long, shrill howl of pain followed.

Genevieve was clutching at her in horror, soft whimpers bubbling from her open mouth. The light spheres right outside the boudoir door grew brighter. Within seconds they glared hotter than Duke at noon. Both of them burst apart with a thin *pop*, sending slivers of milky glass tinkling down on the carpet and floorboards.

Marjorie Kavanagh screeched again.

"Mummy!" Genevieve wailed.

Marjorie Kavanagh's scream broke off. There was a muffled, inexplicable thud from behind the door. Then: "RUN! RUN, DARLING. JUST RUN, NOW!"

Louise was already stumbling back towards the concealed stairway door, holding on to a distraught, sobbing Genevieve. The boudoir door flew open, wood splintering from the force of the blow which struck it. A solid shaft of sickly emerald light punched out into the corridor. Spidery shadows moved within it, growing denser.

Two figures emerged.

Louise gagged. It was Rachel Handley, one of the manor's maids. She looked the same as normal. Except her hair. It had turned brick-red, the strands curling and coiling around each other in slow, oily movements.

Then Daddy was standing beside the chunky girl, still in his militia uniform. His face wore a foreign, sneering smile.

"Come to Papa, baby," he growled happily, and took a step towards Louise.

All Louise could do was shake her head hopelessly. Genevieve had slumped to her knees, bawling and shaking violently.

"Come on, baby." His voice had fallen to a silky coo.

Louise couldn't stop the sob that burped from her lips. Soon it would become a mad scream which would never end.

Her father laughed delightedly. A shape moved through the liquid green light behind him and Rachel.

Louise was so numbed she could no longer even manage a solitary gasp of surprise. It was Mrs Charlsworth, their nanny. Variously: tyrant and surrogate mother, confidante and traitor. A rotund, middle-aged woman, with prematurely greying hair and an otherwise sour face softened by hundreds of granny wrinkles.

She stabbed a knitting needle straight at Grant Kavanagh's face, aiming for his left eye. "Leave my girls alone, you bloody fiend," she yelled defiantly.

Louise could never quite remember exactly what happened next. There was blood, and miniature lightning forks. Rachel Handley let out a clarion shriek. Shattered glass erupted from the frames of the oil paintings down half the length of the corridor as the blazing white lightning strobed violently.

Louise crammed her hands over her ears as the shriek threatened to crack open her skull. The lightning died away. When she looked up, instead of her father there was a hulking humanoid shape standing beside Rachel. It wore strange armour, made entirely of little squares of dark metal, embossed with scarlet runes, and tied together with brass wire. "Bitch!" it stormed at a quailing Mrs Charlsworth. Thick streamers of bright orange smoke were belching out of its eye slits.

Rachel Handley's arms turned incandescent. She clamped her splayed fingers over Mrs Charlsworth's cheeks, teeth bared in exertion as she pushed in. Skin sizzled and charred below her fingertips. Mrs Charlsworth mewed in agony. The maid released her. She slumped backwards, her head lolling to one side; and she looked at Louise, smiling as tears seeped down her ruined cheeks. "Go," she mouthed.

The grievous plea seemed to kick directly into Louise's nervous system. She pushed her shoulders into the wall, levering herself upright.

Mrs Charlsworth grinned mirthlessly as the maid and the burly warrior closed on her to consummate their vengeance. She raised the pathetic knitting needle again.

Ribbons of white fire snaked around Rachel's arms as she grinned at her prey. Small balls of it dripped off her fingertips, flying horizontally towards the stricken woman, eating eagerly through the starched grey uniform. A booming laugh emerged from the clinking armour, mingling with Mrs Charlsworth's gurgles of pain.

Louise put her arm under Genevieve's shoulder and lifted her bodily. Flashes of light and the sounds of Mrs Charlsworth's torture flooded the corridor behind her.

I mustn't turn back. I mustn't.

Her fingers found the catch for the concealed door, and it swung open silently. She almost hurled Genevieve through the gap into the gloom beyond, heedless of whether anyone else was on the stairs.

The door slid shut.

"Gen? Gen!" Louise shook the petrified girl. "Gen, we have to get out of here." There was no response. "Oh, dear Jesus." The urge to curl into a ball and weep her troubles away was strengthening.

If I do that, I'll die. And the baby with me.

She tightened her grip on Genevieve's hand and hurried down the spiral stairs. At least Genevieve's limbs were working. Though what would happen if they met another of those . . . people-creatures was another question altogether.

They'd just reached the small anteroom at the bottom of the spiral when a loud hammering began above. Louise started to run down the corridor to the storeroom. Genevieve stumbled along beside her, a low determined humming coming from her lips.

The hammering stopped, and there was the brassy thump of an explosion. Tendrils of bluish static shivered down the spiral stairs, grounding out through the floor. Red stone tiles quaked and cracked. The dimming light spheres along the ceiling sprang back to full intensity again.

"Faster, Gen," she shouted.

They charged into the storeroom and through the green door leading to the courtyard. Merlin was standing in the wide-open gateway of the stable block, barking incessantly. Louise headed straight for him. If they could take a horse they'd be free. She could ride better than anyone else at the manor.

They were still five yards short of the stables when two

people ran out of the storeroom. It was Rachel and her father (except it's not really him, she thought desperately).

"Come back, Louise," the dark knight called. "Come along, sweetie. Daddy wants a cuddle."

Louise and Genevieve dashed around the gates. Merlin stared out at the yard for a second, then turned quickly and followed them inside.

Globules of white fire smashed into the stable doors, breaking apart into complex webs which probed the woodwork with the tenacity of a ghoul's fingers. Glossy black paint blistered and vaporised, the planks began to blaze furiously.

"Undo the stall doors," Louise called above the incendiary roar of the fire and the braying, agitated horses. She had to say it again before Genevieve fumbled with the first bolt. The horse inside the stall shot out into the aisle which ran the length of the stable.

Louise rushed for the far end of the stables. Merlin was yapping hysterically behind her. Fire had spread from the doors to straw bundled loosely in the manger. Orange sparks were flying like rain in a hurricane. Thick arms of black smoke coiled insidiously along the ceiling.

The voices from outside called again, issuing orders and promises in equal amounts. None of them were real.

Screams were adding to the clamour in the courtyard now. Quinn's disciples had inevitably gained the upper hand; Cricklade's few remaining free servants were being hunted and possessed without any attempt at stealth.

Louise reached the stall at the end of the stables, the one with Daddy's magnificent black stallion, a bloodline geneered to a perfection which nineteenth-century sporting kings could only dream of. The bolt slid back easily, and she grabbed the bridle before he had a chance to arrow into the aisle. He snorted furiously at her, but allowed her to steady him. She had to stand on a bale of hay in order to mount him. There was no time for a saddle.

The fire had spread with horrendous speed. Several of the stalls were burning now, their stout old timber walls shooting out wild sulphurous flames. Merlin was backing away from them, his barking fearful. Over half a dozen horses were milling in the aisle, whinnying direly. Flames had cut them off from the stable doors, the noisy inferno pressing them back from their one exit. She couldn't see Gen.

"Where are you?" she shouted. "Gen!"

"Here. I'm here." The voice was coming from an empty stall.

Louise urged the stallion forwards down the aisle, yelling wildly at the panicking horses in front of her. Two of them reared up, alarmed by this new, unexpected threat. They began to move en masse towards the flames.

"Quick!" Louise yelled.

Genevieve saw her chance and sprinted out into the aisle. Louise leaned over and grabbed her. At first she thought she'd miscalculated the girl's weight, feeling herself starting to slide downwards. But then Genevieve snatched at the stallion's mane, causing it to neigh sharply. Just as Louise was sure her spine would snap, or she'd crash headfirst onto the aisle's stone flagging, Genevieve levered herself up to straddle the base of the stallion's neck.

The stable doors had been all but consumed by the eerily hot fire. Their remaining planks sagged and twisted on the glowing hinges, then lurched onto the cobbles with a loud bang.

With the intensity of the flames temporarily reduced, the horses raced for the door and their chance of freedom. Louise dug her heels into the stallion's flanks, spurring it on. There was an exhilarating burst of speed. Yellow spires of flame splashed across her left arm and leg, making her cry out. Genevieve squealed in front of her, batting frantically at her blouse. The stench of singed hair solidified in her nostrils. Thin layers of smoke stretching across the aisle whipped across her face, stinging her eyes.

Then they were through, out of the gaping door with its wreath of tiny flames scrabbling at the ruined frame, chasing after the other horses. Fresh air and low sunlight washed over them. The hefty knight in the dark mosaic armour was standing ahead of them. Streamers of bright orange smoke were still pouring from his helmet's eye slits. Sparks of white fire danced across his raised gauntlets. He started to point a rigid forefinger at them, the white fire building.

But the posse of crazed horses couldn't be deflected. The

first one flashed past stark inches from him. Alert to the danger they presented, even to someone with energistic power, he began to jump aside. That was his mistake. The second horse might have missed him if he'd stayed still. Instead, it struck him almost head on. The screaming horse buckled on top of him, forelegs snapping with an atrocious *crack* as inertia sent it hurtling forwards regardless. The knight was flung out sideways, spinning in the air. He landed bonelessly, bouncing a full foot above the cobbles before coming to a final rest. His armour vanished immediately, revealing Grant Kavanagh's body, still clad in his militia uniform. The fabric was torn in a dozen places, stained scarlet by the blood pumping from open wounds.

Louise gasped, instinctively pulling the reins to halt the stallion. Daddy was hurt!

But the flowing blood swiftly stanched itself. Ragged tears of flesh started to close up. The uniform was stitching itself together. Dusty, grazed leather shoes became metallic boots. He shook his head, grunting in what was little more than dazed annoyance.

Louise stared for a second as he started to raise himself onto his elbows, then spurred the horse away.

"Daddy!" Genevieve shouted in anguish.

"It's not him," Louise told her through clenched teeth. "Not now. That's something else. The devil's own monster."

Rachel Handley stood in front of the arched entrance to the courtyard. Hands on hips, aroused wormlet hair threshing eagerly. "Nice try." She laughed derisively. A hand was raised, palm towards the sisters. The awful white fire ignited around her wrist, wispy talons flaring from her fingers. Her laugh deepened at the sight of Louise's anguish, cutting across Merlin's miserable barking.

The bullet-bolt of white fire which caught Rachel Handley an inch above her left eye came from somewhere behind Louise. It bored straight through the maid's skull, detonating in the centre of the brain. The back of her head blew off in a gout of charred gore and rapidly dissipating violet flame. Her body remained upright for a second, then the muscles spasmed once before losing all tension. She pitched forwards.

Bright arterial blood spilled out of her ruined, smoking brain-pan.

Louise twisted around. The courtyard was empty apart from the woozy figure of her father still clambering to his feet. A hundred empty windows stared down at her. Faint screams echoed over the rooftops. Long swirls of flame churned noisily out of the stable block's wide doors.

Genevieve was shaking violently again, crying in convulsive gulps. Concern for the little girl overcame Louise's utter confusion, and she spurred the stallion once more, guiding it around the vile corpse and out through the courtyard's entrance.

From where he was standing beside the window of the third-floor guest suite, Quinn Dexter watched the girl riding the superb black horse hell-for-leather over the manor's greensward and towards the wolds. Not even his awesome energistic strength could reach the fleeing sisters from this distance.

He pursed his lips in distaste. Someone had aided them. Why, he couldn't think. The traitor must surely know they would never go unpunished. God's Brother saw all. Every soul was accountable in the end.

"They'll head for Colsterworth, of course," he said. "All they're doing is postponing the inevitable for a couple of hours. Most of that poxy little town already belongs to us."

"Yes, Quinn," said the boy standing behind him.

"And soon the whole world," Quinn muttered. And then what?

He turned and smiled proudly. "It is so nice to see you again. I never thought I would. But He must have decided to reward me."

"I love you, Quinn," Lawrence Dillon said simply. The body of the stable lad he had possessed was completely naked, the scars from the act of possession already nothing more than faint, fading pink lines on the tanned skin.

"I had to do what I did on Lalonde. You know that. We couldn't take you with us."

"I know, Quinn," Lawrence said devoutly. "I was a liability. I was weak back then." He knelt at Quinn's feet, and beamed up at the stern features of the black-robed figure. "But I'm not anymore. Now I can help you again. It will be like before, only better. The whole universe will bow before you, Quinn."

"Yeah," Quinn Dexter said slowly, savouring the thought. "The fuckers just might."

• • • •

The datavised alert woke Ralph Hiltch from a desultory sleep. As an ESA head of station, he'd been assigned some temporary quarters in the Royal Navy officers' mess. Strange impersonal surroundings, and the emotional cold turkey from bringing Gerald Skibbow to Guyana, had left his thoughts racing as he lay on the bunk after a three-hour debrief session last night. In the end he'd wound up accessing a mild trank program to relax his body.

At least he hadn't suffered any nightmares; though Jenny was never very far from the surface of his mind. A final frozen image of the mission: Jenny lying under a scrum of man-apes, datavising a kamikaze code into the power cell at her side. The image didn't need storing in a neural nanonics memory cell in order to retain its clarity. She'd thought it was preferable to the alternative. But was she right? It was a question he'd asked himself a lot during the voyage to Ombey.

He swung his legs over the side of his bunk and ran fingers through hair that badly needed a wash. The room's net processor informed him that Guyana asteroid had just gone to a code three alert status.

"Shit, now what?" As if he couldn't guess.

His neural nanonics reported an incoming call from Ombey's ESA office, tagged as the director, Roche Skark, himself. Ralph opened a secure channel to the net processor with a sense of grim inevitability. You didn't have to be psychic to know it wasn't going to be good.

"Sorry to haul you back to active status so soon after you arrived," Roche Skark datavised. "But the shit's just hit the fan. We need your expertise."

"Sir?"

"It looks like three of the embassy personnel who came

here on the *Ekwan* were sequestrated by the virus. They've gone down to the surface."

"*What?*" Panic surged into Ralph's mind. Not that abomination, not loose here in the Kingdom. Please God. "Are you certain?"

"Yes. I've just come out of a Privy Council security conference with the Princess. She authorized the code three alert because of it."

Ralph's shoulders slumped. "Oh, God, and I brought them here."

"You couldn't have known."

"It's my job to know. Goddamn, I grew slack on Lalonde."

"I doubt any of us would have done anything different."

"Yes, sir." Pity you couldn't sneer with a datavise.

"In any case, we're right behind them. Admiral Farquar and my good colleague Jannike Dermot over at the ISA have been commendably swift in implementing damage limitation procedures. We estimate the embassy trio are barely seven hours ahead of you."

Ralph thought about the damage one of those *things* could inflict in seven hours and put his head in his hands. "That still gives them a lot of time to infect other people." Implications began to sink through his crust of dismay. "It'll be an exponential effect."

"Possibly," Roche Skark admitted. "If it isn't contained very quickly we may have to abandon the entire Xingu continent. Quarantine procedures are already in place, and the police are being told how to handle the situation. But I want you there to instill a bit of urgency, kick a bit of arse."

"Yes, sir. This active status call, does that mean I get to go after them in person?"

"It does. Technically, you're going down to advise the Xingu continent's civil authorities. As far as I'm concerned you can engage in as much fieldwork as you want, with the proviso that you don't expose yourself to the possibility of infection."

"Thank you, sir."

"Ralph, I don't mind telling you, what this energy virus can do scares the crap out of me. It has to be a precursor to something, some form of invasion. And safeguarding the Kingdom from such threats is my job. Yours too, come to that. So stop them, Ralph. Shoot first, and I'll whitewash later if need be."

"You've got it, sir."

"Good man. The admiral has assigned a flyer to take you down to Pasto city spaceport, it's leaving in twelve minutes. I'll have a full situation briefing datapackage assembled ready for you to access on the way down. Anything you want, let me know."

"I'd like to take Will Danza and Dean Folan with me, and have them authorized to fire weapons on the surface. They know how to deal with people who have been sequestrated. Cathal Fitzgerald too; he's seen the virus at work."

"They'll have the authorization before you land."

•　•　•　•

Duchess had risen above the horizon by the time Colsterworth came into view. The red dwarf sun occupied a portion of the horizon diametrically opposite Duke, the two of them struggling to contaminate the landscape below with their own unique spectrum.

Duchess was winning the battle, rising in time to Duke's fall from the sky. The eastward slopes of the wolds were slowly slipping from verdant green to subdued burgundy. Aboriginal pine-analogue trees planted among the hedgerows of geneered hawthorn became grizzled pewter pillars. Even the stallion's ebony hide was darkening.

Duke's golden glow withdrew before the strengthening red tide.

For the first time in her life, Louise resented the primary's retreat. Duchess-night was usually a magical time, twisting the familiar world into a land of mysterious shadows and balmy air. This time the red stain had a distinctly ominous quality.

"Do you suppose Aunty Daphnie will be home?" Genevieve asked for what must have been the fifth time.

"I'm sure she will," Louise replied. It had taken Genevieve a good half hour to stop crying after they'd escaped from Cricklade. Louise had concentrated so hard on comforting her sister, she'd almost stopped being afraid herself. Certainly it was easy to blank what had happened from her mind. And she wasn't quite sure exactly what she was going to say to Aunt Daphnie. The actual truth would make her sound utterly mad. Yet anything less than the truth might not suffice. Whatever forces of justice and law were dispatched up to Cricklade would have to be well armed and alert. The chief constable and the mayor had to believe what they faced was deadly real, not the imaginings of a half-hysterical teenage girl.

Fortunately she was a Kavanagh. People would have to listen. And please, dear Jesus, make them believe.

"Is that a fire?" Genevieve asked.

Louise jerked her head up. Colsterworth was spread out along a couple of miles of a shallow valley, growing up from the intersection of a river and the railway line. A somnolent little market town with ranks of neat terrace houses set amid small, pretty gardens. The larger homes of the important families occupied the gentle eastern slope, capturing the best view over the countryside. An industrial district of warehouses and small factories cluttered the ground around the wharf.

Three tall spires of filthy smoke were twisting up from the centre of the town. Flames burned at the base of one. Very bright flames. Whatever the building was, it glowed like molten iron.

"Oh, no," Louise gasped. "Not here, too." As she watched, one of the long river barges drifted past the last warehouse. Its decks were alight, the tarpaulin-covered cargo hold puffing out mushrooms of brown smoke. Louise guessed the barrels it carried were exploding. People were jumping off the prow, striking out for the bank.

"Now what?" Genevieve asked in a woeful voice.

"Let me think." She had never considered that anywhere other than Cricklade was affected. But of course her father and that chilling young priest had stopped at Colsterworth first. And before that . . . A midwinter frost prickled her spine. Could it all have started at Boston? Everyone said an insurrection was beyond the Union's ability to mount. Was the whole island to be conquered by these demons in human guise?

And if so, where do we go?

"Look!" Genevieve was pointing ahead.

Louise saw a Romany caravan being driven at considerable speed along one of the roads on the edge of town below them. The driver was standing on the seat, striking at the cob horse's rump with a whip. It was a woman, her white dress flapping excitably in the wind.

"She's running away," Genevieve cried. "They can't have got to her yet."

The notion that they could join up with an adult who would be on their side was a glorious tonic for Louise. Even if it was just a simple Romany woman, she thought uncharitably. But then didn't Romanies know about magic? The manor staff said they practised all sorts of dark arts. She might even know how to ward off the devils.

Louise took in the road ahead of the racing caravan with a keen sweep, trying to work out where they could meet it. There was nothing directly in front of the caravan, but three quarters of a mile from the town was a large farmhouse.

Frantic animals were charging out of the open farmyard gate into the meadows: pigs, heifers, a trio of shire-horses, even a Labrador. The house's windows flashed brightly, emitting solid beams of blue-white light which appeared quite dazzling under the scarlet sky.

"She's heading straight for them," Louise groaned. When she checked the careering caravan again it had just passed the last of Colsterworth's terraced houses. There were too many trees and bends ahead for the driver to see the farmhouse.

Louise sized up the distance to the road, and snapped the bridle. "Hang on," she told Genevieve. The stallion charged forwards, dusky red grass blurring beneath its hooves. It jumped the first fence with hardly a break in its rhythm. Louise and Genevieve bounced down hard on its back, the younger girl letting out a yap of pain.

A jeering crowd had emerged on the road behind the caravan, milling beneath the twin clumps of geneered silver birch trees which marked the town's official boundary. It was almost as if they were unwilling, or unable, to venture out into the open fields. Several bolts of white fire were flung after the fleeing caravan—glinting stars which dwindled away after a few hundred yards.

Louise wanted to weep in frustration when she saw people

walking out of the farmhouse and start down the road towards Colsterworth. The Romany woman still hadn't noticed the danger ahead.

"Shout at her! Stop her!" she cried to Genevieve.

They covered the last three hundred yards bellowing wildly.

It was to no avail. They were close enough to the caravan to see the foam coating the nose of the piebald cob before the Romany woman caught sight of them. Even then she didn't stop, although the reins were pulled back. The huge beast started to slow its frantic sprint to a more reasonable trot.

The stallion cleared the hedge and the ditch running alongside the road in an easy bound. Louise whipped it around to match the caravan's pace. There was a tremendous clattering coming from inside the wooden frame with its gaudy paintwork, as if an entire kitchen's worth of pots and pans were being juggled by malevolent clowns.

The Romany woman had long raven hair streaming out behind her, a brown face with round cheeks. Her white linen dress was stained with sweat. Defiant, wild eyes stared at the sisters. She made some kind of sign in the air.

A spell? Louise wondered. "Stop!" she begged. "Please stop. They're already ahead of you. They're at that farmhouse, *look*."

The Romany woman stood up, searching the land beyond the cob's bobbing head. They had another quarter of a mile to go until they reached the farmhouse. But Louise had lost sight of the people who had come out of it.

"How do you know?" the woman called out.

"Just *stop*!" Genevieve squealed. Her small fists were bunched tight.

Carmitha looked the little girl over, then came to a decision. She nodded, and began to rein back.

The caravan's front axle snapped with a prodigious crunching sound.

Carmitha just managed to grab hold of the frame as the whole caravan pitched forwards. Sparks flew out from underneath her as the world tilted sharply. A last wrenching *snap* and the caravan ground to a halt. One of the front wheels trundled past her cob horse, Olivier, then rolled down into the dry ditch at the side of the road.

"Shit!" She glared at the girls on the big black stallion, their soot-stained white blouses and grubby desolate faces. It must have been them. She'd thought they were pure, but you just couldn't tell. Not now. Her grandmother's ramblings on the spirit world had been nothing more than campsite tales to delight and scare young children. But she did remember some of the old woman's words. She raised her hands *so* and summoned up the incantation.

"What are you *doing*?" the elder of the two girls yelled down at her. "We have to get out of here. Now!"

Carmitha frowned in confusion. The girls both looked terrified, as well they might if they'd seen a tenth of what she had. Maybe they were untainted. But it if wasn't them who wrecked the caravan . . .

She heard a chuckle and whirled around. The man just appeared out of the tree standing on the other side of the road from the ditch. Literally out of it. Bark lines faded from his body to reveal the most curious green tunic. Arms of jade silk, a jacket of lime wool, big brass buttons down the front, and a ridiculous pointed felt hat sprouting a couple of white feathers.

"Going somewhere, pretty ladies?" He bowed deeply and doffed his hat.

Carmitha blinked. His tunic really was green. But it shouldn't have been, not in this light. "Ride!" she called to the girls.

"Oh, no." His voice sounded indignant, a host whose hospitality has proved inadequate. "Do stay."

One of the small kittledove birds in the tree behind him took flight with an indignant squawk. Its leathery wings folded back, and it dived towards the stallion. Intense blue and purple sparks fizzed out of its tail, leaving a contrail of saffron smoke behind it. The tiny organic missile streaked past the stallion's nose and skewered into the ground with a wet thud.

Louise and Genevieve both reached out instinctively to pat and gentle the suddenly skittish stallion. Five more kittledoves were lined up on the pine's branches, their twittering stilled.

"In fact, I insist you stay," the green man said, and smiled charmingly.

"Let the girls go," Carmitha told him calmly. "They're only children."

His eyes lingered on Louise. "But growing up so splendidly. Don't you agree?"

Louise stiffened.

Carmitha was about to argue, maybe even plead. But then she saw four more people marching down the road from the farmhouse and the fight went out of her. Taking to her heels would do no good. She'd seen what the white fireballs could do to flesh and bone. It was going to be bad enough without adding to the pain.

"Sorry, girls," she said lamely.

Louise gave her a flicker of a smile. She looked at the green man. "Touch me, *peasant*, and my fiancé will make you eat your own balls."

Genevieve twisted around in astonishment to study her sister. Then grinned weakly. Louise winked at her. Paper defiance, but it felt wonderful.

The green man chortled. "Dearie me, and I thought you were a fine young lady."

"Appearances can be deceptive," she told him icily.

"I will enjoy teaching you some respect. I will personally see to it that your possession takes a good many days."

Louise glanced briefly in the direction of the four men from the farmhouse who were now standing beside the placid cob. "Are you quite sure you have mustered sufficient forces? I don't want you to be too frightened of me."

The green man's laboured smile vanished altogether, as did his debonair manner. "Know what, bitch? I'm going to make you watch while I fuck your little sister in half."

Louise flinched, whitening.

"I believe this has gone far enough." It was one of the men who'd arrived from the farm. He walked towards the green man.

Louise noticed how his legs bowed outward, making his shoulders rock slightly from side to side as he walked. But he was handsome, she acknowledged, with his dark skin and wavy jet-black hair tied back in a tiny ponytail. Rugged; backed up by a muscular build. He couldn't have been more than about twenty, or twenty-one—the same age as Joshua. His dark blue jacket was dreadfully old-fashioned, it had long tails which came to a point just behind his knees. He wore it over a yellow waistcoat, and a white silk shirt that had a tiny turned-down collar complemented with a black ruff tie. Strange apparel, but elegant, too.

"What's your problem, boy?" the green man asked scornfully.

"Is that not apparent, sir? I find it difficult to see how even a gentleman of your tenor can bring it upon himself to threaten three frightened ladies."

The green man's mouth split into a wide smile. "Oh, you do, do you?" White fire speared out of his fingers. It struck the newcomer's blue jacket and flared wide into clawing braids. He stood calmly as the coils of incandescence scrabbled ineffectively across him, as if he wore an overcoat of impervious glass.

Unperturbed by his failure, the green man swung a fist. It didn't connect. His opponent ducked back with surprising speed. A fist slammed into the side of the green man's torso. Three ribs shattered from the enhanced blow. He had to exert some of his own energistic strength to stave off the pain and repair the physical damage. "Fuck," he spat, shocked by this inexplicable recalcitrance on the part of someone who was supposed to be a comrade. "What the hell are you doing?"

"I would have thought that obvious, sir," the other said from behind raised fists. "I am defending the honour of these ladies."

"I don't believe this," the green man exclaimed. "Look, let's just get them possessed, and forget it. Okay? Sorry I mouthed off. But that girl has the devil's own tongue."

"No, sir, I will not forget your threat to the child. Our Lord may have deemed me unworthy to join Him in Heaven. But, still, I count myself as more than a beast who would commit rapine upon such a delicate flower."

"Delicate . . . You have got to be fucking joking."

"Never, sir."

The green man threw his hands in the air. He turned to the other three who had accompanied his opponent from the farm. "Come on, together we can boil his crazy brain and send him back to the beyond. Or maybe you can ignore them pleading to be let back into the world," he added significantly.

The three men exchanged an uneasy glance.

"You may indeed best me," the man in the blue jacket said. "But if I have to return to that accursed nowhere, I will take at least one of you with me, possibly more. So come then, who will it be?"

"I don't need any of this," one of the three muttered. He pushed his way past the other two and started to walk down the road towards the town.

The man in the blue jacket gave the remaining two an inquiring look. Both of them shook their heads and set off down the road.

"What is it with you?" the green man shouted furiously.

"I believe that is a rhetorical question."

"Okay, so who the hell are you?"

For a moment his handsome face faltered in its resolution. Pain burned in his eyes. "They called me Titreano, once," he whispered.

"Okay, Titreano. It's your party. For now. But when Quinn Dexter catches up with you, it's going to be the morning after like you've never fucking believed."

He turned on a heel and stalked off along the road.

Carmitha finally remembered to breathe again. "OhmyGod!" Her knees gave out, and she sat down fast. "I thought I was dead."

Titreano smiled graciously. "You would not have been killed. What they bring is something far worse."

"Like *what*?"

"Possession."

She gave him a long, mistrustful stare. "And you're one of them."

"To my shame, my lady, I am."

Carmitha didn't know what the hell to believe.

"Please, sir?" Genevieve asked. "What should we do now? Where can Louise and I go?"

Louise patted Gen's hands in caution. This Titreano was

one of the devils after all, no matter how friendly he appeared to be.

"I do not know this place," Titreano said. "But I would advise against yonder town."

"We know that," Genevieve said spryly.

Titreano smiled up at her. "Indeed you do. And what is your name, little one?"

"Genevieve. And this is my sister, Louise. We're Kavanaghs, you know."

Carmitha groaned and rolled her eyes. "Christ, that's all I need right now," she mumbled.

Louise gave her a puzzled frown.

"I regret I have not heard of your family," Titreano said in what sounded like sincere regret. "But from your pride, I venture it is a great one."

"We own a lot of Kesteven between us," Genevieve said. She was beginning to like this man. He'd stood up to the horrors, and he was polite. Not many grown-ups were polite to her, they never seemed to have the time to talk at all. He was very well spoken, too.

"Kesteven?" Titreano said. "Now that is a name I do know. I believe that it is an area of Lincolnshire. Am I correct?"

"Back on Earth, yes," Louise said.

"Back on Earth," Titreano repeated incredulously. He glanced over at Duke, then switched to Duchess. "Exactly what is this world?"

"Norfolk. It's an English-ethnic planet."

"The majority," Carmitha said.

Louise frowned again. What ever was wrong with the Romany woman?

Titreano closed his eyes, as if he felt some deep pain. "I sailed upon oceans, and I thought no challenge could be greater," he said faintly. "And now men sail the void between stars. Oh, how I remember them. The constellations burning so bright at night. How could I ever have known? God's creation has a majesty which lays men bare at His feet."

"You were a sailor?" Louise asked uncertainly.

"Yes, my lady Louise. I had the honour to serve my King thus."

"King? There's no royal family in the Earth's English state any more."

Titreano slowly opened his eyes, revealing only sadness. "No King?"

"No. But our Mountbatten family are descended from British royalty. The Prince guards our constitution."

"So nobility has not yet been overthrown by darkness. Ah well, I should be content."

"How come you didn't know about old England?" Genevieve asked. "I mean, you knew about Kesteven being a part of it."

"What year is this, little one?"

Genevieve considered protesting about being called "little one," but he didn't seem to mean it in a nasty way. "Year 102 since settlement. But those are Norfolk years; they're four Earth years long. So back on Earth it's 2611."

"Twenty-six hundred and eleven years since Our Lord was born," Titreano said in awe. "Dear Heaven. So long? Though the torment I endured felt as if it were eternal."

"What torment?" Genevieve asked with innocent curiosity.

"The torment all us damned souls face after they die, little one."

Genevieve's jaw dropped, her mouth forming a wide O.

"You've been dead?" Louise asked, not believing a word of it.

"Yes, Lady Louise. I was dead, for over eight hundred years."

"That's what you meant by possession?" Carmitha said.

"Yes, my lady," he said gravely.

Carmitha pinched the top of her nose, wrinkling her brow. "And how, exactly, did you come back?"

"I do not know, except a way was opened into this body's heart."

"You mean that's not your body?"

"No. This is a mortal man by the name of Eamon Goodwin, though I now wear my own form above his. I hear him crying inside me." He fixed Carmitha with a steady eye. "That is why the others pursue you. There are millions of souls lost in the torment of beyond. All seek living bodies so they may breathe again."

"Us?" Genevieve squeaked.

"Yes, little one. You. I'm sorry."

"Look, this is all very interesting," Carmitha said. "Complete drivel, but interesting. However, just in case you haven't caught hold, right now we are drowning in deep shit. I don't know what you freaks really are, possessed zombies or something nice and simple like xenocs with psychic powers. But when that green bastard reaches Colsterworth he's going to be coming back with a lot of friends. I've got to unhitch my horse, and we three"—her gesture took in the sisters—"have got to be long gone." She arched an eyebrow. "Right, Miss Kavanagh?"

"Yes." Louise nodded.

Titreano glanced at the passive cob, then the stallion. "If you are serious in your intent, you should travel together in your caravan. None of you has a saddle, and this mighty beast has the look of Hercules about him. I'll wager he can maintain a steady pace for many hours."

"Brilliant," Carmitha snorted. She hopped down onto the hard-packed dirt of the road and slapped the side of her ruined caravan. "We'll just wait here for a wheelwright to come along, shall we?"

Titreano smiled. He walked over to the ditch where the wheel had fallen in.

Carmitha's next acidic phrase died unspoken as he righted the wheel and pushed it (one-handed!) up out of the ditch, treating it as though it were a child's hoop. The wheel was five feet in diameter, and made of good, heavy tythorn wood. Three strong men would struggle to lift it between them.

"My God." She wasn't sure if she should be thankful or horrified at such a demonstration. If all of them were like him, then hope had deserted Norfolk long ago.

Titreano reached the caravan and bent down.

"You're not going to . . ."

He lifted it by the front corner—two, three feet off the road. Carmitha watched as the broken axle slowly straightened itself. The splintered fracture in the middle blurred, then for a brief moment the wood appeared to run like a liquid. It solidified. And the axle was whole again.

Titreano jemmied the wheel back onto the bearing.

"What are you?" Carmitha whispered weakly.

"I have already explained, my lady," Titreano said. "What I can never do is bring you to believe what I am. That must come of its own accord, as God wills."

He went over to the stallion and held his arms up. "Come on, little one, down you come."

Genevieve hesitated.

"Go on," Louise said quietly. Plainly, if Titreano had wanted to harm them, he would have done it by now. The more she saw of these strange people, the more her heart blackened. What could possibly fight such power?

Genevieve smiled scampishly and swung a leg over the stallion. She slithered down his flank into Titreano's grip.

"Thank you," she said as he put her down. "And thank you for helping us, too."

"How could I not? I may be damned, but I am not devoid of honour."

Louise got most of the way down the stallion before she accepted his steadying hand. She managed a fast, embarrassed grin of thanks.

"I'm sore all over," Genevieve complained, hands rubbing her bottom.

"Where to?" Louise asked Carmitha.

"I'm not sure," the Romany replied. "There should be a lot of my folk in the caves above Holbeach. We always gather there if there's any kind of trouble abroad. You can hold those caves for a long time; they're high in the cliffs, not easy to reach."

"It would be a short siege this time, I fear," Titreano said.

"You got a better idea?" she snapped back.

"You cannot stay on this island, not if you wish to escape possession. Does this world have ships?"

"Some," Louise said.

"Then you should try to buy passage."

"To go where?" Carmitha asked. "If your kind really are after bodies, exactly where would be safe?"

"That would depend on how swiftly your leaders rally. There will be war, many dreadful battles. There can be nothing less. Both our kinds are fighting for their very existence."

"Then we must go to Norwich, the capital," Louise said decisively. "We must warn the government."

"Norwich is five thousand miles away," Carmitha said. "A ship would take weeks."

"We can't hide here and do nothing."

"I'm not risking myself on some foolhardy errand, girl. Fat lot of good you precious landowners will be, anyway. What has Norfolk got which can fight off the likes of him?" She waved a hand towards Titreano.

"The Confederation Navy squadron is still here," Louise said, her voice raised now. "They have fabulous weapons."

"Of mass destruction. How's that going to help people who have been possessed? We need to break the possession, not slaughter the afflicted."

They glared at each other.

"There's an aeroambulance based at Bytham," Genevieve said brightly. "That could reach Norwich in five hours."

Louise and Carmitha stared at her. Then Louise broke into a grin and kissed her sister. "Now who's the clever one?"

Genevieve smiled around pertly. Titreano made a face at her, and she giggled.

Carmitha glanced down the road. "Bytham's about a seven hour journey from here. Assuming we don't run into any more problems."

"We won't," Genevieve said. She took hold of Titreano's hand. "Not with you with us."

He grinned halfheartedly. "I . . ."

"You're not going to leave us alone," a suddenly stricken Genevieve asked.

"Of course not, little one."

"That's that, then."

Carmitha shook her head. "I must be bloody mad even thinking of doing this. Louise, tether your horse to the caravan."

Louise did as she was told. Carmitha climbed back up on the caravan, regarding it suspiciously as she put her weight on the driver's seat. "How long is that repair going to last for?"

"I'm not quite sure," Titreano said apologetically. He helped Genevieve up beside Carmitha, then hoisted himself up.

When Louise clambered up, the narrow seat was cramped.

She was pressed against Titreano, and not quite sure how she should react to such proximity. If only it were Joshua, she thought wistfully.

Carmitha flicked the reins, and Olivier started forwards at an easy trot.

Genevieve folded her arms in satisfaction and cocked her head to look up at Titreano. "Did you help us at Cricklade as well?"

"How's that, little one?"

"One of the possessed was trying to stop us from riding away," Louise said. "She was hit by white fire. We wouldn't be here otherwise."

"No, Lady Louise. It was not I."

Louise settled back into the hard seat, unhappy the mystery hadn't been solved. But then by today's standards it was one of the lesser problems confronting her.

Olivier trotted on down the road as Duke finally disappeared below the wolds. Behind the caravan, more of Colsterworth's buildings had started to burn.

* * *

Guyana's navy spaceport was a standard hollow sphere of girders, almost two kilometres in diameter. Like a globular silver-white mushroom on a very thin stalk, it stuck out of the asteroid's rotation axis; the massive magnetic bearings on the end of the connecting spindle allowed it to remain stationary while the colossal rock rolled along its orbital track. The surface was built up from circular docking bays linked together by a filigree of struts and transit tubes. Tanks, generators, crew stations, environmental maintenance machinery, and shark-fin thermo dump panels were jumbled together in the gaps between bays, apparently without reference to any overall design logic.

Narrow rivers of twinkling star-specks looped around it all, twining in elaborate, interlocked figure-eights. The rivers had a current, their points of light drifting in the same direction at the same speed; cargo tugs, personnel commuters, and MSVs, firing their reaction drives to maintain the precise vectors fed to them by traffic control. Ombey's code three defence alert had stirred the spaceport into frantic activity for the second time in twenty-four hours. But this time instead of preparing to receive a single craft, frigates and battle cruisers were departing. Every few minutes one of the big spherical Royal Kulu Navy ships would launch from its docking bay, rising through the traffic lanes of smaller support craft with an arc-bright glare of secondary fusion drives. They were racing for higher orbits, each with a different inclination; Strategic Defence Command positioned them so they englobed the entire planet, giving full interception coverage out to a million kilometres. If any unidentified ship emerged from a ZTT jump within that region, it would be engaged within a maximum of fifteen seconds.

Amid the departing warships a lone navy flyer rose from the spaceport. It was a flattened egg-shape fuselage of dark blue-grey silicolithium composite, fifty metres long, fifteen wide. Coherent magnetic fields wrapped it in a warm golden glow of captured solar wind particles. Ion thrusters fired, manoeuvring it away from the big frigates. Then the fusion tube in the tail ignited, pushing it down towards the planet seventy-five thousand kilometres below.

The one-gee acceleration sucked Ralph Hiltch gently back into his seat, making the floor stand to the vertical. On the seat next to him, his flight bag rolled over once to lie in the crook of the cushioning.

"This vector will get us to Pasto spaceport in sixty-three minutes," Cathal Fitzgerald datavised from the pilot's seat.

"Thanks," Ralph replied. He widened the channel to include the two G66 troopers. "I'd like you all to access the briefing that Skark gave me. This kind of information could be critical, and we need all the breaks we can get around here."

That earned him a grin and a wave from Dean Folan, a non-committal grimace from Will Danza. They were both sitting on the other side of the aisle. The sixty-seater cabin seemed deserted with just the four of them using it.

None of his little team had complained or refused to go. Privately he'd made it quite clear they could pull out without any indiscipline action being entered on their file. But they'd all agreed, with varying degrees of enthusiasm. Even Dean

who had the best excuse of all. He'd been in surgery for seven
hours last night; the asteroid's navy clinic had to rebuild sixty
per cent of his arm. The boosted musculature, ruined by the
hit he'd taken in Lalonde's jungle, had to be completely replaced with fresh artificial tissue, along with various blood
vessels, skin, and nerves. The repair was still wrapped in a
green sheath of medical nanonic packaging. But he was looking forward to levelling the score, he'd said cheerfully.

Ralph closed his eyes and let the briefing invade his mind,
neural nanonics tabulating it into a sharply defined icono-
graphic matrix. Details of the Xingu continent: a sprawl of
four and a half million square kilometres in the northern
hemisphere, roughly diamond-shaped, with a long mountainous ridge of land extending out from its southern corner. The
ridge crossed the equator; and Ombey's broad tropical zones
meant the entire continent was an ideal farming region, with
the one exception of the semi-desert occupying the centre. So
far only two-fifths of it was inhabited, but with a population
of seventy million, it was the second-most prosperous continent after Esparta, where the capital Atherstone was situated.

After Xingu came the embassy trio, Jacob Tremarco,
Savion Kerwin, and Angeline Gallagher. Their career files
contained nothing exceptional, they were all regular Kulu
Foreign Office staffers: loyal, boring bureaucrats. Visuals,
family histories, medical reports. It was all there, and none of
it particularly useful apart from the images. Ralph stored them
in a neural nanonics memory cell, and spliced them with a
general characteristics recognition program. He hadn't forgotten that strange image-shifting ability the sequestrated had
demonstrated back on Lalonde. The recognition program
might give him a slight edge if one of them attempted a dis-
guise, though he didn't hold out much hope.

The most promising part of the datapackage was the series
of measures Admiral Farquar and Leonard DeVille, Xingu's
Home Office minister, had implemented to quarantine the
continent and trace the embassy trio. All civil traffic was
being systematically shut down. Search programs were being
loaded into the continent's data cores, watching for a trail of
unexplained temporary glitches in processors and power circuits. Public-area security monitor cameras had been given

the visual pattern of the trio, and police patrols were also being briefed.

Maybe they'd get lucky, Ralph thought. Lalonde was a backwards colony on the arse edge of nowhere, without any modern communications or much in the way of civil authority. But Ombey was part of the Kingdom, the society he'd sworn to defend with his life if need be. Years ago at university, when he'd discreetly been offered a commission in the agency, he'd considered Kulu a worthwhile society. The richest in the Confederation outside Edenism, it was strong economically, militarily; a technology leader. It had a judicial system which kept the average citizen safe on the streets, and was even reasonably fair by modern standards. Medical care was socialized. Most people had jobs. Admittedly, ruled by the Saldanas, it was hardly the most democratic of systems, but then short of the Edenist Consensus few democratic societies were truly representative. And there were a lot of planets which didn't even pretend to be egalitarian. So he'd swallowed any niggling self-suspicion of radicalism, and agreed to serve his King until his death.

What he'd seen of the galaxy had only served to strengthen his conviction that he'd done the right thing in taking the oath. The Kingdom was a *civilized* place compared to most; its citizens were entitled to lead their lives without interference. And if that meant the ESA occasionally having to get its hands dirty, then so be it, as far as Ralph was concerned. A society worth having is worth protecting.

And thanks to its own nature, Ombey should definitely be able to cope better than Lalonde. Although the very systems which made it more able also gave the enemy a greater opportunity to spread its subversion. The virus carriers had been slow to travel on Lalonde. Here they would suffer no such restrictions.

Cathal Fitzgerald cut the flyer's fusion drive when they were two hundred kilometres above Xingu. Gravity took over, pulling the flyer down. Its magnetic field expanded, applying subtle pressures to the tenuous gases pushing against the fuselage. Buoyant at the centre of a sparkling cushion of ions, the flyer banked to starboard and began a gentle glide-spiral down towards the spaceport below.

They were a hundred and fifty kilometres high when the flight computer datavised a priority secure signal from Roche Skark into Ralph's neural nanonics.

"We might have a problem developing," the ESA director told him. "A civil passenger flight from Pasto to Atherstone is having trouble with its electronic systems, nothing critical but the glitches are constant. I'd like to bring you in on the Privy Council security committee to advise."

"Yes, sir," Ralph acknowledged. The datavise broadened to a security level one sensenviron conference. Ralph appeared to be sitting at an oval table in a plain white bubble room with walls at an indeterminate distance.

Admiral Farquar was sitting at the head of the table, with Roche Skark and the ISA director Jannike Dermot flanking him. Ralph's neural nanonics identified the other three people present. Next to the ISA director was Commander Deborah Unwin, head of Ombey's Strategic Defence network; Ryle Thorne, Ombey's national Home Office minister, was placed next to her. Ralph found himself with Roche Skark on one side, and Leonard DeVille on the other.

"The plane is seven minutes from Atherstone," Deborah Unwin said. "We have to make a decision."

"What is the plane's current status?" Ralph asked.

"The pilot was instructed to turn back to Pasto by my flight controllers as part of the quarantine procedures. And that's when he reported his difficulties. He says he'll be endangering the passengers if he has to fly all the way back to Pasto. And if it's a genuine malfunction he will be."

"We can hardly go around using our SD platforms on civil aircraft just because they have a dodgy processor," Ryle Thorne said.

"On the contrary, sir," Ralph said. "In this situation we have to maintain a policy of guilty until proven innocent. You cannot allow that plane to land in the capital, not under any circumstances. Not now."

"If he has to fly back to Xingu he may well kill everyone on board," the minister protested. "The plane could be downed in the ocean."

"Atherstone has a high proportion of military bases in the surrounding district," Admiral Farquar said. "If necessary the plane can simply sit on a landing pad surrounded by marines until we work out a satisfactory method of detecting if the virus is present."

"Is the pilot using his neural nanonics to communicate with flight control?" Ralph asked.

"Yes," Deborah said.

"Okay, then it's a reasonable assumption that he's not been sequestrated. If you can guarantee a landing pad can be guarded securely, I say use it. But the plane must remain sealed until we find out what's happened to the embassy trio."

"Good enough," Admiral Farquar said.

"I'll put the marines at Sapcoat base on active status as of now," Deborah said. "That's over a hundred kilometres from Atherstone. The plane can reach it easily enough."

"A hundred kilometres is a safe enough distance," Ryle Thorne said smoothly.

Ralph didn't like the minister's attitude; he seemed to be treating this as if it were a minor natural incident, like a hurricane or earthquake. But then the minister had to go back to his constituents every five years and convince them he was acting in their best interests. Ordering SD platforms to fire on their fellow citizens might be hard to explain away in public relations terms. That was one of the reasons the royal Saldanas had a parliament to advise them. An insulating layer around the blame. Elected politicians were always culpable and replaceable.

"I'd also suggest that once the plane's landed you use an orbital sensor satellite to mount a permanent observation on it," Ralph said. "Just in case there's any attempt to break out. That way we can use the SD platforms as a last resort; sterilize the entire area."

"That strikes me as somewhat excessive," Ryle Thorne said with elaborate politeness.

"Again, no, sir. On Lalonde the enemy were able to use their electronic warfare capability to interfere with the LDC's observation satellite from the ground; they fuzzed the images to quite a degree. I'd say this fallback option is the least we should be doing."

"Ralph was brought in because of his experience in combating the virus," Roche Skark said, smiling at the minister.

"He got off Lalonde precisely because he instigated these kinds of protective measures."

Ryle Thorne gave a short nod.

"Pity he didn't protect *us* from the virus," Jannike muttered. Except in a sensenviron context nothing was really sotto voce; all utterances were deliberate.

Ralph glanced over at her, but the computer-synthesised image of her face gave nothing away.

Chapman Adkinson was getting mighty tired of the continual stream of datavises he was receiving from flight control. Worried, too. He wasn't dealing with civil flight control at Atherstone anymore; they'd gone off-line eight minutes ago. Military protocols were being enforced now, the whole planet's traffic control being routed through the Royal Navy operations centre on Guyana. And they were none too sympathetic to his condition.

Esparta was rolling by below the plane, one of the lush national parks which surrounded the capital. A jungle scarred only by the occasional Roman-straight motorway and dachas belonging to the aristocracy. The ocean was five minutes behind them.

His neural nanonics were accessing the external sensors, but the visual image was only being analysed in secondary mode, mainly to back up the inertial guidance system which he no longer wholly trusted. He was concentrating on schematics of the plane's systems. Twenty per cent of the onboard processors were suffering from random dropouts. Some had come back on-line after a few seconds, others remained dead. The diagnostic programs he ran simply couldn't pinpoint the problem. And, even more disturbing, in the last fifteen minutes he'd been experiencing spikes and reductions in the power circuits.

That was what had made him argue with the military controllers. Processor glitches were an acceptable menace; there was so much redundancy built into the plane's electronic architecture it could survive an almost total shutdown; but power loss was in a different hazard category altogether. Chapman Adkinson had already decided that if they did try to force him to fly back over the ocean he was going to ditch there and then, and to hell with the penalties they'd load into his licence. The biohazard in Xingu couldn't be that lethal, surely?

"Chapman, stand by for some updated landing coordinates," Guyana's flight controller datavised. "We're diverting you."

"Where to?" Chapman asked sceptically.

"Sapcoat base. They're prepping a clean reception area for you. Looks like the passengers are going to have to stay on board for a while once you're down."

"As long as we get down."

The coordinates came through, and Chapman fed them directly into the flight computer. Twelve minutes to Sapcoat. He could accept that. The plane banked gently to port, and began to curve away from the city which lay somewhere beyond the horizon's black and silver heat shimmer.

It was a signal for the glitches to quadruple. Circuits began to drop out at a frightening rate. A quarter of the system's schematics flicked to a daunting black, leaving only ghostly colourless outlines where functional hardware had been a moment before. Power to the two rear starboard compressors failed completely. He could hear the high-pitched background whine deepening as the blades slowed. The flight computer's compensation program went primary, but too many control surfaces had shut down for it to be truly effective.

"Mayday, mayday," Chapman datavised. Even his primary transmitter had failed. Backup processors were activated. The fuselage began to vibrate and judder, as if the plane were ploughing through a patch of choppy air.

His neural nanonics reported a stream of datavises from the passenger cabin, querying the shaking and sudden loss of in-flight entertainment processors. He called up a procedural file and shunted it into what was left of the plane's entertainment circuits. Seatback holoscreens should be playing a placebo message about clear air turbulence and the precautions their pilot was now instigating.

"What is it?" flight control asked.

"Losing power and height. Systems failure rate increasing. Shit! I just lost the tail rudder databus." He datavised an emergency code into the flight computer. A silvery piston slid out of the horseshoe console in front of him, a dull chrome-red pistol grip on the end. It reached his lap and rotated silently through ninety degrees. Chapman grabbed it. Manual control. *Christ, I've never used one outside of Aviation Authority simulations!*

The datavise bandwidth to the flight computer started to shrink. He prioritized the schematic to display absolute essentials. Holographic displays on the console came alive, duplicating the information.

"Find me a flat patch of land, now, damn it!" How he was going to bring the plane down in VTOL configuration with both the starboard compressors out wasn't something he wanted to think about. Maybe a motorway, and use it like a runway?

"Request denied."

"What?"

"You may not land anywhere but the authorized coordinate."

"Fuck you! We're going to crash."

"Sorry, Chapman, you cannot land anywhere outside Sapcoat."

"I can't *reach* Sapcoat." His datavised control linkage to the flight computer began to fail. The pistol grip shifted slightly in his hand, and he felt the plane tilt in tandem.

Careful! he told himself. A firm pressure on the grip, and the nose began to edge back. The holographic horizon graphic showed he was still in a shallow dive. More pressure, and the descent rate slowed.

The door into the cockpit slid open. Chapman Adkinson was wired too tight to care. It was supposed to be codelocked, but the way hardware was crashing . . .

"Why have you altered course?"

Chapman shot a quick glance over his shoulder. The guy was dressed in a cheap suit, five years out-of-date. He wasn't just calm, he was serene. Incredible! He must feel the plane's buffeting.

"Technical problem," Chapman managed to gasp. "We're putting down at the nearest landing pad that can handle an emergency." The pistol grip was fighting his every movement. And now the holographic displays were wobbling. He wasn't sure if he could trust them anymore. "Get back into your seat now, fella."

The man simply walked up behind the pilot's chair and slid his head over Chapman's shoulder, peering out of the narrow curving windscreen. "Where is Atherstone?"

"Look, pal—" Pain lanced deep into his thigh. Chapman grunted roughly at the shock of it. The man's left index finger was resting lightly on his leg, a small circle of his uniform's trouser fabric was burning around it.

Chapman swatted at the small blue flames, eyes blinking away sudden tears. His thigh muscle was smarting abominably.

"Where is Atherstone?" the man repeated. "I have to go there."

Chapman found his calmness more unnerving than the plane's failure. "Listen, I wasn't joking when I said we had technical problems. We're going to be lucky if we make it over this sodding jungle. Forget about Atherstone."

"I will hurt you again, harder this time. And I will keep on hurting you until you take me to Atherstone."

I'm being hijacked! The realization was as staggering as it was improbable. Chapman gagged at the man. "You have got to be kidding!"

"No joke, Captain. If you do not land in the capital, I will see to it you don't land anywhere."

"Holy Christ."

"Atherstone. Now where is it?"

"To the west somewhere. Christ, I'm not sure where. Inertial guidance has packed up."

A mirthless smile appeared on the man's face. "Then head west. It is a big city. I'm confident we'll see it from this height."

Chapman did nothing. Then winced as the man reached past him. He put his hand on the windscreen, palm flat. Horrifyingly deep white cracks splintered outward.

"Atherstone." It was an order.

"Okay. Just take your goddamn hand off that." The windscreen was artificial sapphire for God's sake. You couldn't crack it by *leaning* on it. A neural nanonics status check showed him half his synaptic augmentation had crashed, and virtually all the memory cells had shut down. But there was enough capacity for a datavise. "Code F emergency," he shot at the flight computer. Followed by a small prayer that it hadn't glitched completely yet.

"ISA duty officer," came the response. "What's happening?"

Chapman used the last of his neural nanonics' capacity to issue a metabolic override, keeping his face perfectly composed. He must not betray the silent conversation by a twitch of emotion. "Attempted hijacking. And the plane's falling apart around me."

"How many hijackers?"

"Just one, I think. Can't access the cabin cameras."

"What does he want?"

"He says he wants to go to Atherstone."

"What sort of weapon is he using?"

"Not sure. Nothing visible. Some kind of implant. Maybe a thermal induction field generator. He burnt my leg and damaged the windscreen."

"Thank you. Hold please."

Like I can do something else, Chapman thought acidly. He flicked a curious glance at the man who was still standing to one side of the chair. His face was as emotionless as Chapman's.

The plane rocked alarmingly. Chapman tried to damp it down by swaying the pistol grip to compensate for the erratic motion. On a plane with fully responsive control surfaces it might have worked, here it just slewed the tail around. He noticed the nose had dropped a couple of degrees again.

"If you don't mind me asking, what's so bloody important in Atherstone that you've got to pull this crazy stunt?"

"People," the man said blandly.

Some of the man's calmness was infiltrating Chapman's own mind. He pulled back on the pistol grip, easing the nose up until they were level again. Nothing to it. At least there were no more systems dropping out, the malfunctions appeared to have plateaued. But landing would be a bitch.

"Chapman," the ISA duty officer datavised. "Please try and give us a visual of the hijacker. It's very important."

"I'm down to about two kilometres altitude, here. Seventy

per cent of my systems have failed, and all you want is to see what he *looks* like?"

"It will help us evaluate the situation."

Chapman gave the man a sideways glance, loading the image into one of his remaining three functional memory cells. His datavise bit rate was now so low it took an entire second to relay the file.

Ralph Hiltch watched the pixels slowly clot together above the bubble room's table. "Savion Kerwin," he said, unsurprised.

"Without a doubt," Admiral Farquar acknowledged.

"That plane left Pasto ninety minutes after their spaceplane landed," Jannike Dermot said. "They obviously intend to spread the virus as wide as possible."

"As I've been telling you," Roche Skark said. "Ralph, do you think he's infected anyone else on the plane?"

"Quite possibly, sir. The flight computer and Chapman's neural nanonics are obviously being assaulted by a very powerful electronic warfare field. It might be several of them acting in unison, or it could just be Savion Kerwin's proximity to the electronic systems, after all the flight computer is housed below the cockpit decking. But we really can't take the chance."

"Agreed," Admiral Farquar said.

Chapman Adkinson waited for fifteen seconds after he'd datavised the visual file. The crippled flight computer reported the communications channel was being maintained. Nothing happened, there was no update from the ISA officer.

A Royal Kulu Navy reserve officer himself, Chapman knew of the response procedures for civil emergencies. Rule of thumb: the longer it took to come to a decision, the higher up the command structure the problem was being bumped. This one must be going right to the top. To the people authorized to make life or death decisions.

Intuition or just a crushing sense of doom, Chapman Adkinson started laughing gleefully.

The man turned to give him a strange look. "What?"

"You'll see, fella, soon enough. Tell me, are you the biohazard?"

"Am I a—"

The X-ray laser struck the plane while it was still eighty kilometres away from Atherstone. Ombey's low-orbit SD platform weapons could hit combat wasps while they were still two and a half thousand kilometres distant. The plane was a mere three hundred kilometres beneath the platform which Deborah Unwin activated. Oxygen and nitrogen atoms in the lower atmosphere simply cracked into their sub-atomic constituents as the X ray punched through the air, a searing purple lightning bolt eighty kilometres long. At its tip, the plane detonated into an ionized fog which billowed out like a miniature neon cyclone. Scraps of flaming, highly radioactive wreckage rained down on the pristine jungle below.

2

He was actually born in the United States of America, though few people ever liked to admit that particular fact, then or afterwards. His parents were from Naples; and Southern Italians were universally looked down on and despised even by other poor immigrant groups, let alone the superior intellectuals of the time who openly stated their hatred of such an inferior breed of humans. As a consequence, few biographers and historians ever admitted the simple truth. He was, above all, a bona fide made in America monster.

His birthplace was Brooklyn, on the chilly winter's day of January 17, 1899, the fourth son of Gabriele and Teresina. At that time the district was home to a seething mass of such burgeoning immigrant families trying to build fresh lives for themselves in this new land of promise. Work was hard, labour cheap, the infamous city political machine strong, and the street gangs and racketeers prominent. But among all these difficulties his father managed to earn enough to support his family. And as a barber he did so independently and honestly, rare enough in that time and place.

Gabriele's son never followed that route; there were just too many odds stacked against him. The whole Brooklyn environment seemed designed to turn its young male population from the good.

After being expelled from school at fourteen for fighting with his (female) teacher he began running errands for the local Association chief. He was one of the lowest of the low. But he learned: of men's vices and what they would do to obtain them, of the money to be made, of loyalty to his own, and most of all what people gave the Association's leader: respect. Respect was the key to the world, a commodity no one ever showed him or his father. A man who was respected had everything, a prince among men.

It was during this criminal apprenticeship that the ultimate seeds of his destruction were sown, ironically by himself. He contracted syphilis in one of the many seedy brothels which local boys of his age and background visited on a regular basis. Like most people he survived the first stage, the boils on his tender genitalia healing within a couple of weeks. Nor did the second stage disturb him to any great extent; an equally short time spent suffering what he convinced himself was a bad case of flu.

Had he visited a doctor he would have been told that it is the tertiary stage which proves lethal in a fifth of those infected, eating away at the frontal lobes of the brain. But once the second stage has passed, the malicious disease becomes dormant for a long time, sometimes measurable in decades, lulling its victim into a false sense of security. He saw no reason to share the humiliating knowledge.

Paradoxically, it was this very disease which contributed to his inexorable rise over the next fifteen years. Because of the nature of its attack on the brain it amplified its victim's personality traits: traits which in his case had been forged in turn-of-the-century Brooklyn. They comprised contempt, hostility, anger in tandem with violence, greed, treachery, and guile. Excellent survival qualities for that particular dead-end district, but in a more civilized environment they set him apart. A barbarian in the city.

In 1920 he moved to Chicago. Within months he was heavily involved with one of the major syndicates. Until that era the syndicates ran the rackets and the brothels and the gambling joints, and raked in a good deal of hard currency. And at that relatively insignificant level they might well have remained. But that was the year when Prohibition came into effect throughout the nation.

The speakeasies opened, the back alley breweries flourished. Money flooded into the coffers of the syndicates, millions upon millions of easy, dirty dollars. It gave them a power base they had never dreamed of before. They bought the police, they owned the mayor and most of city hall, they intimidated the crusading newspapers and laughed at the law.

But money brought its own special problem. Everybody could see how vast the market was, how profitable. They all wanted a cut.

And that was where he finally came into his own. Whole districts of Chicago degenerated into war zones as gangs and syndicates and bosses fought like lions for territory. With the neurosyphilis gradually eroding his rationality he emerged from the ranks of his contemporaries as the most ruthless, the most successful, and the most feared gang boss of them all. Quirks became vainglorious eccentricities; he opened soup kitchens for the poor; for slain colleagues he threw funeral parades which brought the entire city to a halt; he craved publicity and held press conferences to promote his magnanimity in giving people what they really wanted; he sponsored broke jazz musicians. His flamboyance became as legendary as his brutality.

At its height his tyranny was sufficient to be raised at cabinet meetings in the White House. Nothing the authorities did ever seemed to make the slightest difference. Arrests, inquiries, indictments; he bought his way out with his money, while his reputation (and associates) kept witnesses silent.

So government did what government always does when confronted with an opposition which can't be brought down by fair and legal means. It cheated.

His trial for tax evasion was later described as a legal lynching. The Treasury made up new rules, and proved he was guilty of breaking them. A man who was both directly and indirectly responsible for the deaths of hundreds of people was sentenced to eleven years in jail over delinquent taxes to the total of $215,080.

His atrocious reign was ended, but his life took another sixteen years to wither. In his latter years, with the neurosyphilis raging in his head, he lost all grip on reality, seeing visions and hearing voices. His mind now roamed through a purely imaginary state.

His body ceased to function in a peaceful enough manner on January 25, 1947, in a big house in Florida, surrounded by his grieving family. But when you are already utterly insane, there is little noticeable difference from your very own delusory universe and the distorted torment of the beyond into which your soul slips.

Over six hundred years passed.

The entity which emerged from the beyond into the fractured, bleeding body of Brad Lovegrove, fourth assistant manager (urban sanitation maintenance division) of the Tarosa Metamech Corp of New California, didn't even realize he was back in living reality. Not to start with, anyway.

The first possessed being to reach New California did so on a cargo starship from Norfolk, one of the twenty-two insurgents Edmund Rigby had helped possess in Boston. His name was Emmet Mordden, and as soon as he reached the planet's surface he began the process of conquest; snatching people off the streets and the autoways, inflicting agonizing injuries to weaken their spirits and open their minds to receive the souls in the beyond.

A small band of possessed filtered unobtrusively through the boulevards of San Angeles in the days which followed, slowly building up their own ranks. Like all of the possessed emerging across the Confederation they had no distinct strategy, simply a single driving impulse to bring more souls back from the beyond.

But this one among them was of no use to the cause. His mind shattered, he could relate to no external stimuli. He shouted hysterical warnings to his brother Frank, he wept, he delivered huge monologues about his shoe factory where he promised he'd give them all work, tiny spits of energy would fly from him without warning, he giggled constantly, he shat his pants and started slinging it about. Whenever they brought him food his energistic ability would turn it to the image of hot spicy pasta which gave off an appalling stink.

After two days, the growing cabal simply left him behind in the disused shop they'd been using as a base. Had they bothered to check him before they left they would have noticed that the behaviour was slightly more moderate, the talk more coherent.

Psychotic thought patterns which had formed in the early 1940s and run on unchecked for six centuries had finally begun to operate within a healthy neurone structure once more. There were no chemical imbalances, no spirochaete bacteria, not even traces of mild alcohol toxicology, for Love-grove didn't drink. His sanity gradually returned as thought processes began to move in more natural cycles.

He felt his mind and memories coming together as though he were emerging from the worst cocaine trip ever (his long-time vice back in the 1920s). For hours he simply lay on the floor trembling as events tumbled through his expanding consciousness. Events which sickened the heart, but which belonged to him nonetheless.

He never heard the shop's service door open, the surprised grunt of the realtor agent, the heavy footsteps marching towards him. A hand closed around his shoulder and shook him strongly.

"Hey, dude, how did you get in here?"

He flinched violently and looked up to see a man in a very strange helmet, as if glossy green beetle wings had folded over his skull. Blank, golden bubble eyes stared down at him. He screamed and spun over. The equally startled realtor took a pace backwards, reaching for the illegal nervejam stick in his jacket pocket.

Despite six hundred years of technological development he could still recognize a hand weapon when he saw one. Of course, the real giveaway was the expression of superiority and nervous relief on the realtor's face; the one every fright-ened man wears when a piece has suddenly swung the odds back in his favour.

He drew his own gun. Except it wasn't exactly a draw—no holster. One second he wanted a gun, the next his fingers were gripping a Thompson submachine gun. He fired. And the once-familiar roar of the weapon nicknamed a trench broom hammered his ears again. A curiously white flame emerged from the barrel as he trained it on the cowering figure of the realtor, fighting the upwards kick.

Next, all that was left was a mangled, jerking body pump-ing gallons of blood onto the bare carbon-concrete floor. The craterous wounds were smoking, as if the bullets had been in-cendiaries.

Bulge-eyed and horrified, he stared at the corpse for a mo-ment, then vomited helplessly. His head was whirling as though the eternal nightmare was returning to clasp him once more.

"Christ no," he groaned. "No more of that crap. Please." The Thompson submachine gun had vanished as mysteriously as it had appeared. Ignoring the nausea which sent shivers down every limb he staggered out through the door and into the street. Crazy images mugged him. His head slowly tipped back to view the pulp-magazine fantasy into which he had emerged. Low wispy clouds scudding in from the ocean were sliced apart by the chromeglass sword-blade skyscrapers which made up downtown San Angeles. Prismatic light gleamed and sparkled off every surface. Then he saw the naked crescent of a small reddish moon directly overhead. Starship exhausts swarmed casually across the cobalt sky like incandescent fireflies. His jaw dropped in absolute bewilderment. "Goddamn, what the hell *is* this place?" demanded Alphonse Capone.

Ombey's rotation had carried the Xingu continent fully into the centre of the darkside as the Royal Navy flyer Ralph Hiltch was using passed over the outskirts of Pasto. The city was situated on the western coast, growing out from the Falling Jumbo seaport in a sustained hundred-year development spree. It was flat country, ideal for urbanization, placing minimal problems in the path of the ambitious civil engineers. Most of the level districts were laid out in geometric patterns, housing estates alternating with broad parks and elaborate commercial districts. Hills, such as they were, had been claimed by the richer residents for their chateaus and mansions.

Accessing the flyer's sensor suite, Ralph could see them standing proud in their own lakes of illumination at the centre of large sable-black grounds. The narrow, brightly lit roads which wound around the hills were the only curves amid the vast grid of brilliant orange lines spread out below him. Pasto looked so beautifully crisp and functional, a grand symbol of the Kingdom's economic prowess, like a merit badge pinned on the planet.

And somewhere down there, amid all that glittering regimented architecture and human dynamism, were people who could bring the whole edifice crashing down. Probably within a couple of days, certainly no more than a week.

Cathal Fitzgerald angled the flyer towards the big cube-shaped building which was the Xingu police force headquarters. They landed on a roof pad, at the end of a row of small arrowhead-planform hypersonic planes.

Two people were waiting for Ralph at the bottom of the airstairs. Landon McCullock, the police commissioner, was a hale seventy-year-old, almost two metres tall, with thick crew-cut ginger hair, dressed in a midnight-blue uniform with several silver stripes on his right arm. Beside him was Diana Tiernan, the police department's technology division chief, a fragile, elderly woman dwarfed by her superior officer, a contrast which tended to emphasise her scholarly appearance.

"I appreciate you coming down," Landon said as he shook hands with Ralph. "It can't have been an easy choice for you to face this thing again. The datapackage briefing I've had from Admiral Farquar gave me a nasty jolt. My people aren't exactly geared up to cope with this kind of incident."

"Who is?" Ralph said, a shade too mordantly. "But we coped on Lalonde; and we aim to do a little better here."

"Glad to hear it," Landon said gruffly. He nodded crisply to the other three ESA agents coming down the airstairs; Will and Dean carrying their combat gear in a couple of bulky bags. His lips twitched in a memory-induced smile of admiration as he eyed the two G66 division troopers. "Been a while since I was at that end of an operation," he murmured.

"Any update on the plane which was shot down?" Ralph asked as they all walked towards the waiting lift.

"Nobody survived, if that's what you mean," Diana Tiernan said. She gave Ralph a curious look. "Was that what you meant?"

"They're tough bastards," Will said curtly.

She shrugged. "I accessed a recording of Adkinson's datavise. This energy manipulation ability Savion Kerwin demonstrated seemed quite extraordinary."

"He didn't show you a tenth of what he could do," Ralph said.

The lift doors closed, and they descended to the command centre. It had been designed to handle every conceivable civil emergency, from a plane crash in the heart of the city to out-right civil war, a windowless room which took up half of the floor. Twenty-four separate coordination hubs were arranged in three rows, circles of consoles with fifteen operators apiece. Their access authority to the continent's net was absolute, providing them with unparalleled sensor coverage and communications linkages.

When Ralph walked in every seat was taken, the air seemed almost solid with the laserlight speckles thrown off by hundreds of individual AV projection pillars. He saw Leonard DeVille sitting at Hub One, a raised ring of consoles in the middle of the room. The Home Office minister's welcoming handshake lacked the sincerity of McCullock's.

Ralph was quickly introduced to the others at Hub One: Warren Aspinal, the Prime Minister of the Xingu continental parliament; Vicky Keogh, who was McCullock's deputy; and Bernard Gibson, the police Armed Tactical Squad commander. One of the AV pillars was projecting an image of Admiral Farquar.

"All air traffic was shut down twenty minutes ago," said Landon McCullock. "Even police patrol flights are down to a complete minimum."

"And the crews of those that are still in the air have been required to datavise files from their neural nanonics to us here," Diana said. "That way we can be reasonably certain that none of them have been infected by Tremarco or Gallagher."

"There was an awful lot of traffic using the city roads when I flew over," Ralph said. "I'd like to see that shut down now. I can't emphasise enough that we must restrict the population's movement."

"It's only ten o'clock in Pasto," Leonard DeVille said. "People are still on their way home, others are out for the evening and will want to return later. If you shut down the city's ground traffic now you will cause an astounding level of confusion, one which would be beyond the police force's ability to resolve for hours. And we must have the police in reserve to deal with the embassy people when we detect them. We thought it made more sense to allow everyone to go home as normal, then introduce the curfew. That way, the vast majority will be confined to their houses come tomorrow morning. And if Tremarco and Gallagher have started infecting them, any outbreak will be localized, which means we should be able to isolate it relatively easily."

Sit down and make an impact, why not? Ralph thought sourly. I'm supposed to listen and advise, not barge in and act like a loudmouth arsehole. Damn, but Kerwin and the plane has me hyped too hot.

Trying to hide how foolish he felt, he asked: "What time will you introduce the curfew?"

"One o'clock," the Prime Minister said. "Only die-hard nightbirds will still be out and about then. Thank heavens it's not Saturday night. We really would have been in trouble then."

"Okay, I can live with that," Ralph said. There was a quick victory smile on DeVille's face, which Ralph chose to ignore. "What about the other cities and towns; and more importantly the motorways?"

"All Xingu's urban areas are having their curfew enacted at one o'clock," McCulloch said. "The continent's got three time zones, so it'll be phased in from the east. As for the motorways, we're already shutting down their traffic; so cities and major towns are going to be segregated. That wasn't a problem, all motorway vehicles are supervised by the Transport Department route and flow management computers. It's the vehicles on the minor roads which are giving us a headache; they're all switched to autonomous control processors. And even worse are the farm vehicles out there in the countryside, half of those bloody things have manual steering."

"We estimate it will take another three hours to completely shut down all ground traffic movement," Diana said. "At the moment we're setting up an interface between Strategic Defence Command and our police traffic division. That way when the low-orbit SD sensor satellites locate a vehicle moving on a minor road they'll perform an identification sweep and catalogue it. Traffic division will then datavise the control processor to halt. For manually operated vehicles we'll have to dispatch a patrol car." A hand waved lamely in the air. "That's the theory, anyway. A continent-wide detection and identification operation is going to tie up an awful lot of processing power, which we really can't spare right now. If we're not very careful we'll wind up with a capacity shortfall."

"I thought that was impossible in this day and age," Warren Aspinal interjected mildly.

Diana's humour became stern. "Under normal circumstances, yes. But what we're attempting to do has no precedent." She offered the others sitting at Hub One a reluctant shrug. "My team has got three AIs in the basement and two at the university which are attempting to access and analyse every single processor in the city simultaneously. It's a refinement of Admiral Farquar's idea of tracking the energy virus through the electronic distortion it generates. We've seen it demonstrated on Adkinson's plane, so we know the approximate nature of the beast. All we have to do is perform the most massive correlation exercise ever mounted. We find out which processors have suffered glitches during the last eight hours, and cross-reference the time and geographical location. If it happened to several unrelated processors in the same area at the same time, then it's a good chance the glitch was caused by someone who has the virus."

"Every processor?" Vicky Keogh queried.

"Every single one." Just for a moment, Diana's dried-up face wore an adolescent's smile. "From public net processors to streetlight timers, AV adverts, automatic doors, vending machines, mechanoids, personal communications blocks, household supervisor arrays. The lot."

"Will it work?" Ralph asked.

"No reason why not. As I said, there's a possible capacity problem, and the AIs might not manage to format the correlation program within the time frame we need. But when the program comes on-line it should provide us with the electronic equivalent of seeing footprints in snow."

"And then what?" Warren Aspinal asked quietly. "That's what you were really brought down here for, Ralph. What do we do with these people if we find them? There is something of a political dimension involved in using the SD systems every time we locate one of the afflicted. I don't dispute the necessity of eliminating Adkinson's plane. And people will certainly agree to us using force to obliterate the threat to start with. But ultimately we have to find a method of eradicating the energy virus itself, and without damaging the victim. Not even the Princess can go on authorizing such destruction for ever, not when it's aimed against the Kingdom's own subjects."

"We're working on it," said Admiral Farquar. "Gerald Skibbow is going into personality debrief right now. If we can find out how he was infected, and how he was purged, then we ought to be able to come up with a solution, some kind of countermeasure."

"How long will that take?" Leonard DeVille asked.

"Insufficient information," the admiral answered. "Skibbow isn't very strong. They're going to have to go easy on him."

"Yet if our preparations are to mean anything," Landon McCullock said, "we have to catch the embassy duo tonight, or tomorrow morning at the latest. And not just them, but anyone they've come into contact with. This situation could escalate beyond our ability to contain. We must have a policy ready for dealing with them. So far the only thing we know that works is overwhelming firepower."

"I've got two things to offer," Ralph said. He looked at Bernard Gibson, and gave him a penitent smile. "Your squads are going to have to take the brunt of this, especially to start with."

The police AT Squad commander grinned. "What we get paid for."

"Okay, here it is then. First off, contact with someone who is carrying the energy virus doesn't necessarily mean you contract it yourself. Will and Dean are excellent proof of that. They captured Skibbow, they manhandled him, they were in very close proximity to him for hours, and they're both fine. Also, I was on the *Ekwan* with the embassy trio for a week, and I wasn't infected.

"Secondly, despite their power they can be intimidated into submission. But you have to be prepared to use ultraviolence against them, and they have to know that. One hint of weakness, one hesitation, and they'll hit you with everything they've got. So when we do find the first one, it'll be me and my team which heads the actual assault. Okay?"

"I'm not arguing so far," Bernard Gibson said.

"Good. What I envisage is spreading the experience of an assault in the same fashion the virus is spread. Everyone who is with me on the first assault will be able to familiarise themselves with what has to be done. After that you assign them to head their own squads for the next round of captures, and so on. That way we have your whole division brought up to speed as swiftly as possible."

"Fine. And what do we do with them once we've subdued them?"

"Shove them into zero-tau."

"You think that's what got rid of Skibbow's virus?" Admiral Farquar asked sharply.

"I believe it's a good possibility, sir. He was extremely reluctant to enter the pod in *Ekwan*. Right up until then he was quite docile. When he found out we were going to put him in the pod, he became almost hysterical. I think he was frightened. And certainly when he came out of the pod at this end the virus was gone."

"Excellent." Warren Aspinal smiled at Ralph. "That course of action is certainly more palatable than lining them all up against a wall and shooting them."

"Even if zero-tau isn't responsible for erasing the virus, we know it can contain them the same way it holds ordinary people," Ralph said. "We can keep them in stasis until we do find a permanent solution."

"How many zero-tau pods have we got available?" Landon asked Diana.

The technology division chief had a long blink while her neural nanonics chased down the relevant files. "Here in the building there are three. Probably another ten or fifteen in the city in total. They tend to be used almost exclusively by the space industry."

"There's five thousand unused pods in the *Ekwan* right now," Ralph pointed out. "That ought to be enough if this AI correlation program works. Frankly, if we need more than that, we've lost."

"I'll get some maintenance crews to start disconnecting them straight away," Admiral Farquar said. "We can send them down to you in cargo flyers on automatic pilot."

"That just leaves us with forcing infected people into them," Ralph said. He caught Bernard's gaze. "Which is going to be even worse than capturing them."

"Possible trace," Diana announced without warning as she received a datavise from one of the AIs. Everyone sitting at Hub One turned their attention on her. "It's a taxi which left the spaceport twenty minutes after the embassy trio's spaceplane arrived. The vehicle's processor array started suffering some strange glitches five minutes later. Contact was lost after a further two minutes. But it can't have been a total shutdown, because traffic control has no record of a breakdown in that sector this afternoon. It simply dropped out of the route and flow control loop."

The warehouse which housed Mahalia Engineering Supplies was sealed up tight, one of twenty identical buildings lined up along the southern perimeter of the industrial park, separated from its neighbour by strips of ancient concrete and ranks of spindly trees planted to break the area's harshness. It was seventy metres long by twenty-five wide, fifteen high; dark grey composite panels without a single window. From outside it looked inert; innocuous if somewhat spurned of late. Furry tufts of Ombey's aboriginal vegetation were rooting in the gutters. Denuded chassis of ancient farm vehicles were stacked three or four deep along one wall, sleeting rust onto the concrete.

Ralph focused his shell helmet's sensors on the broad roll-up door in the centre of the end-wall fifty meters in front of him. It had taken him and his team four minutes to get here from police headquarters in one of the force's hypersonics, following the city-wide trail of route and flow processor dropouts located by Diana and the AIs. Three police Armed Tactical Squads had also been dispatched to the industrial park, under orders from Bernard Gibson. In total, eight of the little planes had landed, encircling the warehouse at a five-hundred-metre distance.

There wasn't a single crack of light leaking around the door. No sign of life. Infrared didn't reveal much, either. He scanned along the side of the building again.

"The conditioning unit is on," Ralph observed. "I can see

the motor's heat, and the grille's venting. Someone's in there."

"Do you want us to infiltrate a nanonic sensor?" Nelson Akroid asked. He was the AT Squad's captain, a stocky man in his late thirties, barely coming up to Ralph's shoulder. Not quite the image one expected from someone in his profession, but then Ralph was used to the more bulky G66 troops. Ralph suspected Nelson Akroid would be a healthy opponent in any hand-to-hand fighting, though; he had the right kind of subdued competence.

"It's a big building, plenty of opportunities for ambush," Nelson Akroid said. "We'd benefit from positioning them exactly. And my technical operators are good. The hostiles would never know they'd been infiltrated." He sounded eager, which could be a flaw given this situation. Ralph couldn't imagine him and his squad seeing much active duty on Ombey. Their lot was more likely endless drills and exercises, the curse of any specialist field.

"No nanonics," Ralph said. "We could never depend on them anyway. I want the penetration team to deploy using standard search and seizure procedures. We can't believe any information from a sensor, so I want them going in fully alert."

"Yes, sir."

"Diana?" he datavised. "What can the AIs tell me?"

"No change. There are no detectable glitches in the warehouse processors it can access. But there's very little electronic activity in there anyway, the office and administration systems are all switched off, so that doesn't mean much."

"What's the taxi's maximum capacity?"

"Six. And the Industry Department says Mahalia employs fifteen staff. They service and distribute parts for agricultural machinery right across the continent."

"Okay, we'll assume the worst case. A minimum of twenty-one possible hostiles. Thanks, Diana."

"Ralph, the AIs have discovered another two possible glitch traces in the city's route and flow network. I instructed them to concentrate on vehicle traffic around the spaceport in the period after the embassy trio arrived. Another taxi suffered a lot of problems, and the other's a freight vehicle."

"Shit! Where are they now?"

"The AIs are running search routines; but these two are proving harder to find than the first taxi. I'll keep you updated."

The channel closed. Ralph reviewed the AT Squad as they closed in on the warehouse, black figures who seemed more mobile shadows than solid people. They know their job, he admitted grudgingly.

"Everyone's in place, sir," Nelson Akroid datavised. "And the AIs have taken command of the security cameras. The hostiles don't know we're here."

"Fine." Ralph didn't tell him that if Tremarco or Gallagher were in there they'd know for sure that the AT Squad was outside. He wanted the squad charged up and professional, not shooting at phantoms.

"Stand by," Ralph datavised to the Squad. "Status of the assault mechanoids, please?"

"On-line, sir," the AT Squad's technical officer reported.

Ralph gave the roll-up door another scan. Like Pandora's box, once it was open there would be no going back. And only he, Roche Skark, and Admiral Farquar knew that if the virus carriers got past the AT Squad, then the industrial park would be targeted by SD platforms.

He could *feel* the low-orbit observation satellite sensors focusing on him.

"Okay," he datavised to the squad. "Go."

The assault mechanoid which Ombey's AT Squads employed looked as if the design team had been accessing too many horror sensevises for inspiration. Three metres high at full stretch, it had seven plasmatic legs, resembling tentacles with hooves, which could move it over the most jumbled terrain at a sprint that even boosted humans couldn't match. Its body was a segmented barrel, giving it a serpentine flexibility. There were sockets for up to eight specialist limb attachments, varying from taloned climbing claws to mid-calibre gaussrifles. Control could be either autonomous, operating under a preloaded program, or a direct waldo datavise.

Five of them charged across the parking yard outside the

warehouse, covering the last thirty metres in two seconds. Long, whiplike cords lashed out from the top of their bodies, slashing against the door's centimetre-thick composite. Where they hit, they stuck, forming a horizontal crisscross grid four metres above the ground. A millisecond later the cords detonated; the shaped electron explosive charge was powerful enough to cut clean through a metre of concrete. The ruined door didn't even have time to fall. All five assault mechanoids slammed against it in a beautiful demonstration of synchronized mayhem. What was left of the door buckled and burst apart, sending jagged sections tumbling and bouncing down the warehouse's central aisle.

With a clear field of fire established, the mechanoids sent a fast, brutal barrage of short-range sense-overload ordnance blazing down the length of the building. Sensors instantly pinpointed the designated-hostile humans flailing around in panic, and concentrated their fire.

Behind the assault mechanoids, the AT Squad flashed through the smoking doorway. They scuttled for cover between the stacks of crates, scanning the deeper recesses of the warehouse for hidden hostiles. Then, with the mechanoids taking point duty down the central aisle, they began to fan out in their search and securement formation.

Mixi Penrice, proprietor of Mahalia Engineering Supplies, had been struggling to remove the linear motor from the stolen taxi's rear axle when the assault mechanoids crashed into the warehouse door. The noise of the shaped electron explosive charges going off was like standing next to a lightning strike.

Shock made him jump half a metre in the air, not an easy feat given he was about twenty kilos overweight. Terrible lines of white light flared at the far end of the warehouse, and the door bulged inwards briefly before it disintegrated. But he wasn't so numbed that he didn't recognize the distinctive silhouette of the assault mechanoids sprinting through the swirl of smoke and composite splinters. Mixi shrieked and dived for the floor, arms wrapping around his head. The full output of the sense-overload ordnance struck him. Strobing light which seemed to shine through his skull. Sound that was trying hard to shake every joint apart. The air turned to rocket exhaust, burning his tongue, his throat, his eyes. He vomited. He voided both his bladder and his bowels; a combination of sheer fright and nerve short-out pulses.

Three minutes later, when pain-filled consciousness returned, he found himself lying flat on his back, shaking spastically, with disgustingly thick liquids cooling and crusting across his clothes. Five large figures wearing dark armour suits were standing over him, horribly big guns trained on his abdomen.

Mixi tried to clasp his hands together in prayer. It was the day which in his heart he'd always known would come, the day when King Alastair II dispatched all the forces of law and order in his Kingdom to deal with Mixi Penrice, car thief and trader in stolen parts. "Please," he babbled weakly. He couldn't hear his own voice; too much blood was running out of his ears. "Please, I'll pay it all back. I promise. I'll tell you who my fences are. I'll give you the name of the bloke who wrote the program which screws up the road network processors. You can have it all. Just, please, don't kill me." He started sobbing wretchedly.

Ralph Hiltch slowly pulled back his shell helmet's moulded visor. "Oh, *fuck!*" he yelled.

* * *

The white plaster and stone interior of Cricklade's family chapel was comfy and sober without the exorbitant lavishness prevalent throughout the rest of the manor. Its history was cheerful, anyone walking into it for the first time was immediately aware of that; you only had to close your eyes to see the innumerable christenings, the grand marriage ceremonies of the heirs, Christmas masses, choral evenings. It was as much a part of the Kavanaghs as the rich land outside.

Now though, its gentle sanctity had been methodically violated. Icon panels defaced, the dainty stained-glass windows broken, the statues of Christ and the Virgin Mary smashed. Every crucifix had been inverted; red and black pentagrams daubed on the walls.

The despoiling soothed Quinn as he knelt at the altar. Before him an iron brazier had been set up on top of the thick stone slab. Avaricious flames were busy consuming the Bibles and hymn books it contained.

His body's lusts satiated by Lawrence, fed on gourmet food, and overindulged on the bottles of vintage Norfolk Tears from the cellar, he felt miraculously calm. Behind him, the ranks of novices stood to attention as they waited to be inducted into the sect. They would stand there, motionless, for all of eternity if necessary. They were that scared of him.

Luca Comar stood in front of them, like some masterful drill sergeant. His dragon armour glinted dully in the firelight, small plumes of orange smoke snorting from his helmet's eye slits. He had worn the guise almost continually since possessing Grant Kavanagh's body. Compensating for some deep psychological fracture, Quinn thought. But then everyone returning from beyond was flaky to some degree.

Quinn allowed his contempt to rise, the raw emotion bubbling into his brain. The hem of his robe gave a small flutter. Here on Norfolk such pitiful masquerades would triumph, but on few other worlds. Most Confederation planets would fight back against the incursions of the possessed, and those were the planets which counted. The planets where the real war would be fought, the universal war for belief and devotion between the two celestial brothers. Norfolk was irrelevant to that struggle, it could contribute nothing, no weapons, no starships.

He lifted his gaze above the flames darting out of the brazier. A vermillion sky was visible through the gaping rents in the broken window. Less than a dozen first magnitude stars twinkled above the wolds, the rest of the universe had been washed out in the red dwarf's sullied glow. The tiny blue-white lights seemed so delicate and pure.

Quinn smiled at them. His calling was finally revealed. He would bring his divine gift of guidance to the lost armies which God's Brother had seeded throughout the Confederation. It would be a crusade, a glorious march of the dead, folding the wings of Night around every spark of life and hope, and extinguishing it for ever.

First he would have to raise an army, and a fleet to carry them. A frisson of his own, very personal desire kindled in his mind. The serpent beast speaking right into his heart. Banneth! Banneth was at the very core of the Confederation, where the greatest concentration of resources and weapons lay.

The obedient novices never moved when Quinn rose to his feet and turned to face them. There was an amused sneer on his snow-white face. He jabbed a finger at Luca Comar. "Wait here, all of you," he said, and stalked down the aisle. Dark magenta and woad moire patterns skipped across the black fabric of his robe, reflections of his newfound determination. A click of his fingers, and Lawrence Dillon scurried after him.

They passed quickly through the ransacked manor, and down the portico's stone steps to the farm rangers parked on the gravel. A smudge of smoke on the horizon betrayed Colsterworth's position.

"Get in," Quinn said. He was on the verge of laughter.

Lawrence clambered into the front passenger seat as Quinn switched the motor on. The vehicle sped down the drive, sending pebbles skidding onto the grass verge.

"I wonder how long they'll stay in there like that?" Quinn mused.

"Aren't we coming back?"

"No. This crappy little world is a dead end, Lawrence. There's nothing left for us here, no purpose. We have to get off; and there aren't many navy starships in orbit. We've got to reach one before they all leave. The Confederation will be waking to the threat soon. They'll recall their fleets to protect the important worlds."

"So where are we going if we do get a frigate?"

"Back to Earth. We have allies there. There are sects in every major arcology. We can gnaw at the Confederation from within, corrupt it completely."

"Do you think the sects will help us?" Lawrence asked, curious.

"Eventually. They might need a little persuading first. I'll enjoy that."

The AT Squad had the exclusive shop completely surrounded. Moyce's of Pasto occupied a more hospitable section of the city than the Mahalia warehouse. The building's design was an indulgent neo-Napoleonic, overlooking one of the main parks. It catered to the aristocracy and the wealthy, trading mainly on snob value. The shop itself was only a fifth of the business; Moyce's main income came from supplying goods and delicacies to estates and the upwardly mobile clear across the continent. There were eight separate loading bay doors at the back of the building to accommodate the fleet of lorries which were dispatched every night. Their feed roads merged into a single trunk road which led down into a tunnel where it joined one of the city's three major underground ring motorways.

At ten past midnight its distribution centre was normally busy loading lorries with the day's orders. Nothing had emerged in the four minutes it had taken the AT Squad to deploy. However, there was one vehicle parked outside the end loading bay, obstructing the road: the taxi which the AI cores had traced from the spaceport. All its electrical circuits had been switched off.

Fifteen assault mechanoids dashed up the slope to the loading bay doors, their movements coordinated by the Squad's seven technical officers. Three of the doors were to be broken down, while the others were to be blocked and guarded. One had been assigned to the taxi.

Six of the assault mechanoids lashed out with their electron explosive whips. Squad members were already running up the feed roads behind them.

Not all of the whips landed on target. Several detonations chopped into support pillars and door joists. Brick-sized lumps of stone came flying back down the feed roads. Two of the assault mechanoids were hit by the chunks, sending them cartwheeling backwards. The entire central loading bay collapsed, bringing with it a large section of the first-storey floor. An avalanche of crates and cylindrical storage pods tumbled down onto the road, burying a further three assault mechanoids. They started to fire their sense-overload ordnance at random; flares and sonic shells punching out from the wreckage amid huge fountains of white packaging chips.

Crumpled kitchen units and patio furniture skittered down the mound.

The AT Squad members dived for cover as another two mechanoids started to gyrate in a wild dance. Their ordnance sprayed out, slamming into walls and arching away over the park. Only three of the remaining assault mechanoids were actually firing ordnance into the two loading bays which had been broken open.

"Pull them back!" Ralph datavised to the technical officers. "Get those bloody mechanoids out of there."

Nothing happened. Sense-overload ordnance was squirting out everywhere. The assault mechanoids continued their lunatic dance. One pirouetted, twining its seven legs together, and promptly fell over. Ralph watched a dozen flares shoot straight upwards, illuminating the whole area. Black figures were lying prone on the feed roads, horribly exposed. A sense-overload flare speared straight into one of them; then it expanded strangely, creating a web of rippling white light. The suited figure thrashed about.

"Shit," Ralph grunted. It wasn't a flare, it was the white fire. They were in the distribution centre! "Shut down those mechanoids now," he datavised. His neural nanonics reported that several of his suit systems were degrading.

"No response, sir," a technical officer replied. "We've lost them completely, even their fallback routine has failed. How did they do that? The mechanoids are equipped with military-grade electronics, a megaton emp couldn't glitch their processors."

Ralph could imagine the officer's surprise. He'd undergone it himself back on Lalonde as the awful realization struck. He stood up from behind the parapet on top of the tunnel entrance, and lifted the heavy-calibre recoilless rifle. Targeting graphics flipped up over his helmet's sensor image. He fired at an assault mechanoid.

It exploded energetically, its power cells and ordnance detonating as soon as the armour-piercing round penetrated its flexing body. The blast wave shifted half of the precariously tangled wreckage in front of the collapsed loading bay. More crates thumped down from the sagging first-storey floor. Three assault mechanoids were sent lurching back down the feed roads, plasmatic legs juddering in fast undulations. Ralph shifted his aim and took out another one just as it started to lumber upright.

"Squad, shoot out the mechanoids," he ordered. His communications block informed him that half of the command channels had shut down. He switched on the block's external speaker and repeated the order, bellowing it out across the feed roads at a volume which could be heard above the detonating mechanoids.

A streak of white fire lanced down from one of Moyce's upper windows. The threat response program in Ralph's neural nanonics bullied his leg muscles with nerve impulse overrides. He was flinging himself aside before his conscious mind had registered the attack.

Two more mechanoids exploded as he hit the concrete behind the parapet. He thought he recognized the heavy-calibre gaussrifle which the G66 troops used. Then an insidious serpent of white fire was coiling around his knee. His neural nanonics instantly erected analgesic blocks across his nerves, blanking out the pain. A medical display showed him skin and bone being eaten away by the white fire. The whole knee joint would be ruined in a matter of seconds if he couldn't extinguish it. Yet both Dean and Will said smothering it like natural flames made hardly any difference.

Ralph assigned his neural nanonics full control of his musculature, and simply designated the window which the white fire had emerged from. With detached interest he observed his body swivelling, the rifle barrel swinging round. His retinal target graphics locked over a window. Thirty-five rounds pummelled the black rectangle, a mixed barrage of high explosive (chemical), shrapnel, and incendiary.

Within two seconds the room had ceased to exist, its carved stone frontage disintegrating behind a vast gout of flame and showering down on the melee below.

The white fire around Ralph's knee vanished. He pulled a medical nanonic package from his belt and slapped it on the charred wound.

Down on the feed roads most of the AT Squad had switched to their communications block speakers. Orders, warnings, and cries for help reverberated over the sound of multiple explosions. A vast fusillade of heavy-calibre rifle fire was pounding into the loading bays. Comets of white fire poured out in retaliation.

"Nelson," Ralph datavised. "For Christ's sake, make sure the troops out front don't let anyone escape. They're to hold position and shoot to kill now. Forget the capture mission; we'll try it back here, but nobody else is to attempt anything fancy."

"Yes, sir," Nelson Akroid answered.

Ralph went back to the speaker. "Cathal, let's try and get in there. Isolation procedure. Separate them, and nuke them."

"Sir." The cry came back over the parapet.

At least he's still alive, Ralph thought.

"Do you want stage two yet?" Admiral Farquar datavised.

"No, sir. They're still contained. Our perimeter is holding."

"Okay, Ralph. But the second there's a status change, I need to know."

"Sir."

His neural nanonics reported the medical package had finished knitting to his knee. The weight load it could take was down forty percent. It would have to do. Ralph tucked the heavy-calibre rifle under his arm, then bending low, he ran for the end of the parapet and the steps down to the trunk road.

Dean Folan signalled his team members forward, scurrying around the side of the big mound of crates and into the loading bay area. Flames had taken hold amid the fragments piled outside.

It was dark inside the loading bays. Projectile impacts had etched deep pocks into the bare carbon-concrete walls. Rattail tangles of wire and fibre-optic cable hung down from the fissured ceiling, swaying gently. Through the helmet's goggle lenses he could see very little, even with enhanced retinas on full sensitivity. He switched his shell helmet sensors to low light and infrared. Green and red images merged to form a pallid picture of the rear of the loading bay. Annoying glare spots flickered as small flames licked at the storage frames which lined the walls. Discrimination programs worked at eliminating them.

There were three corridors leading off straight back from the rear of the bay, formed by the storage frames. Metal grids containing crates and pods ready for the lorries, they looked like solid walls of huge bricks. Cargo-handling mechanoids had stalled on their rails which ran along the side of the frames, plasmatic arms dangling inertly. Water was pouring out of five or six broken ceiling pipes, spilling down the crates to pool on the floor.

Nothing moved in the corridors.

Dean left his gaussrifle at the head of the middle corridor, knowing it would be useless at close range, the electronic warfare field would simply switch it off. Instead, he drew a semi-automatic rifle; it had a feed loop connected to his back-pack, but the rounds were all chemical. The AT Squad had grumbled about that at the start, questioning the wisdom of abandoning their power weapons. Nobody had complained much after the mechanoids went berserk, and their suit systems suffered innumerable dropouts.

Three of the team followed him as he advanced down the corridor, also carrying semi-automatics. The rest of them spread out around the bay and edged down the other two corridors.

A figure zipped across the end of the corridor. Dean fired, the roar of the semi-automatic impressively loud in the confined space. Plastic splinters from the crates ricocheted through the air as the bullets chiselled into them.

Dean started running forwards. There was no corpse on the floor.

"Radford, did you see him?" Dean demanded. "He was heading towards your corridor."

"No, Chief."

"Anybody?"

All he got was a series of negatives, some shouted, some datavised. No doubt the hostiles were about, his suit blocks were still badly affected by the electronic warfare field. His injured arm was itchy, too.

He reached the end of the corridor. It was a junction to another three. "Hell, it's a sodding maze back here."

Radford arrived at the end of his corridor, semi-automatic sweeping the storage frames.

"Okay, we fan out here," Dean announced. "All of you: keep two other squad members in visual range at all times. If you lose sight of your partners, then stop immediately and reestablish contact."

He picked one of the corridors leading deeper into the shop and beckoned a couple of the Squad to follow him.

A creature landed on top of Radford; half man, half black lion, features merged grotesquely. Its weight carried him effortlessly to the floor. Dagger claws scraped at Radford's armour suit. But the integral valency generators had stiffened the fabric right from the moment of impact, protecting the vulnerable human skin inside. The creature howled in fury, thwarted at the very moment of triumph.

Radford's suit systems as well as his neural nanonics began to fail. Even his shocked yell was cut off as the communications block speaker died. The suit's fabric started to give way, slowly softening. One of the claw tips screwed inwards, hungry for flesh.

Even amid his frantic twisting and bucking to throw off the creature Radford was aware of a whisper which bordered on the subliminal. It had surely been there all his life, but only now with the prospect of death sharpening his perception was he fully conscious of it. It began to expand, not in volume, but in harmony. A whole chorus of whispers. Promising love. Promising sympathy. Promising to help, if he would just—

Bullets smashed into the flanks of the creature, mauling the fur and long muscle bands. Dean kept his semi-automatic steady as the thing clung to Radford's body. He could see the armour suit fabric hardening again, the claws slipping and skidding.

"Stop!" one of the team was shouting. "You'll kill Radford."

"He'll be worse than dead if we don't," Dean snarled back. Spent casings were hurtling out of the rifle at an astounding rate. Still the beast wouldn't let go, its great head shaking from side to side, emitting a continual wail of pain.

The team was rushing en masse towards Dean down the narrow corridors between the storage frames. Two more were shouting at him to stop.

"Get back!" he ordered. "Keep watching for the rest of the bastards." His magazine was down to eighty per cent. The rifle didn't have the power to beat the creature, all the thing had to do was hang on. Blood was running down its hind legs, the fur where the bullets struck a pulped mass of raw flesh. Not enough damage, not nearly enough.

"Someone else fire at it for Christ's sake," Dean yelled frantically.

Another rifle opened up; the second stream of bullets catching the creature on the side of its lycanthrope head. It let go of Radford, to be flung against the storage frame. The rampant wail from its gaping fangs redoubled.

Dean boosted the communications block's volume to its highest level. "Surrender or die," he told it.

It might have had a beast's form, but the look of absolute hatred came from an all-too-human eye.

"Grenade," Dean ordered.

A small grey cylinder thumped into the bloody body.

Dean's armour suit froze for a second. His collar sensors picked up the detonation: explosion followed by implosion. The outline of the beast collapsed into a middle-aged man, colour draining away. For a millisecond the man's frame was captured perfectly, sprawled against the storage frame. Then the bullets resumed their attack. This time, he had no defence.

Dean had seen worse carnage, though the limited space between the storage frames made it appear terrible. Several of the AT Squad obviously didn't have his experience, or phlegmatism.

Radford was helped to his feet and mumbled a subdued thanks. The sound of other teams from the AT Squad shooting somewhere in the building echoed tinnily down the corridors.

Dean gave them another minute to gather their composure, then resumed the sweep. Ninety seconds after they started, Alexandria Noakes was calling for him.

She'd discovered a man hunched up in a gap between two crates. Dean rushed up to find her prodding the captive out of his hiding place with nervous thrusts of her rifle. He levelled his own rifle squarely on the man's head. "Surrender or die," he said.

The man gave a frail little laugh. "But I am dead, señor."

Eight police department hypersonics had landed in the park outside Moyce's of Pasto. Ralph limped wearily towards the one which doubled as a mobile command centre for the AT Squad. There wasn't that much difference from the rest, except it had more sensors and communications gear.

It could have been worse, he told himself. At least Admiral Farquar and Deborah Unwin had stood down the SD platforms, for now.

Stretchers with injured AT Squad members were arranged in a row below a couple of the hypersonics. Medics were moving among them, applying nanonic packages. One woman had been shoved into a zero-tau capsule, her wounds requiring immediate hospital treatment.

A big crowd of curious citizens had materialized, milling about in the park and spilling out across the roads. Police officers had thrown up barricades, keeping them well away.

Nine bulky fire department vehicles were parked outside Moyce's of Pasto. Mechanoids trailing hoses had clambered up the walls with spiderlike tenacity, pumping foam and chemical inhibitors into smashed windows. A quarter of the roof was missing. Long flames were soaring up into the night sky out of the gap. Heat from the inferno was shattering the few remaining panes, creating more oxygen inflows.

It was going to be a long time before Moyce's would be open for business again.

Nelson Akroid was waiting for him at the foot of the command hypersonic's airstairs. His shell helmet was off, revealing a haggard face; a man who has seen the ungodly at play. "Seventeen wounded, three fatalities, sir," he said in a voice close to breaking. His right hand was covered by a medical nanonic package. Scorch marks were visible on his armour suit.

"And the hostiles?"

"Twenty-three killed, six captured." He twisted his head around to stare at the blazing building. "My teams, they did all right. We train to cope with nutters. But they beat those *things*. Christ—"

"They did good," Ralph said quickly. "But, Nelson, this was only round one."

"Yes, sir." He straightened up. "The final sweep through the building was negative. I had to pull them out when the fire took hold. I've still got three teams covering it in case there are any hostiles still in there. They'll do another sweep when the fire's out."

"Good man. Let's go see the prisoners."

The AT Squad was taking no chances; they were holding the six captives out on the park, keeping them a hundred metres apart. Each one stood in the centre of five squad members, five rifles trained on them.

Ralph walked over to the one Dean Folan and Cathal Fitzgerald were guarding. He datavised his communications block to open a channel to Roche Skark. "You might like to see this, sir."

"I accessed the sensors around Moyce's when the AT Squad went in," the ESA director datavised. "They put up a lot of resistance."

"Yes, sir."

"If that happens each time we locate a nest of them, you'll wind up razing half the city."

"The prospects for decontaminating them aren't too good, either. They fight like mechanoids. Subduing them is tricky. These six are the exception."

"I'll bring the rest of the committee in on the questioning. Can we have a visual please."

Ralph's neural nanonics informed him that other people were coming on-line to observe the interview: the Privy Council security committee over in Atherstone, and the civil authorities in Pasto's police headquarters. He instructed his communications block to widen the channel's bandwidth to a full sensevise, allowing them to access what he could see and hear.

Cathal Fitzgerald acknowledged him with the briefest nod as he approached. The man he was guarding was sitting on the grass, pointedly ignoring the semi-automatics directed at him. There was a slim white tube in his mouth. Its end was alight, glowing dully. As Ralph watched, the man sucked his cheeks in, and the coal glow brightened. He removed the tube from his mouth and exhaled a thin jet of smoke.

Ralph exchanged a puzzled frown with Cathal, who merely shrugged.

"Don't ask me, boss," Cathal said.

Ralph ran a search program through his neural nanonics

memory cells. The general encyclopedia section produced a file headed: Nicotine Inhalation.

"Hey, you," he said.

The man looked up and took another drag. "Sí, señor."

"That's a bad habit, which is why no one has done it for five centuries. Govcentral even refused an export licence for nicotine DNA."

A sly, sulky smile. "After my time, señor."

"What's your name?"

"Santiago Vargas."

"Lying little bastard," Cathal Fitzgerald said. "We ran an ident check. He's Hank Doyle, distribution supervisor for Moyce's."

"Interesting," Ralph said. "Skibbow claimed to be someone else when he was caught: Kingsford Garrigan. Is that what the virus is programmed to do?"

"Don't know, señor. Don't know any virus."

"Where does it come from? Where do you come from?"

"Me, señor? I come from Barcelona. A beautiful city. I show you around sometime. I lived there many years. Some happy years, and some with my wife. I died there."

The cigarette glow lit up watery eyes which watched Ralph shrewdly.

"You died there?"

"Sí, señor."

"This is bullshit. We need information, and fast. What's the maximum range of that white fire weapon?"

"Don't know, señor."

"Then I suggest you run a quick memory check," Ralph said coldly. "Because you're no use to me otherwise. It'll be straight into zero-tau with you."

Santiago Vargas stubbed his cigarette out on the grass. "You want me to see how far I can throw it for you?"

"Sure."

"Okay." He climbed to his feet with indolent slowness.

Ralph gestured out over the deserted reaches of the park. Santiago Vargas closed his eyes and extended his arm. His hand blazed with light, and a bolt of white fire sizzled away. It streaked over the grass flinging out a multitude of tiny sparks as it went. At a hundred metres it started to expand and dim, slowing down. At a hundred and twenty metres it was a tenuous luminescent haze. It never reached a hundred and thirty metres, evaporating in midair.

Santiago Vargas wore a happy smile. "All right! Pretty good, eh, señor? I practice, I maybe get better."

"Believe me, you won't have the opportunity," Ralph told him.

"Okay." He seemed unconcerned.

"How do you generate it?"

"Don't know, señor. I just think about it, and it happens."

"Then let's try another tack. Why do you fire it?"

"I don't. That was the first time."

"Your friends didn't have any of your inhibitions."

"No."

"So why didn't you join them? Why didn't you fight us?"

"I have no quarrel with you, señor. It is the ones with *passion*, they fight your soldiers. They bring back many more souls so they can be strong together."

"They've infected others?"

"*Sí.*"

"How many?"

Santiago Vargas offered up his hands, palms upwards. "I don't think anyone in the shop escaped possession. Sorry, señor."

"Shit." Ralph glanced back at the burning building, just in time to see another section of roof collapse. "Landon?" he datavised. "We'll need a full list of staff on the nighttime shift. How many there were. Where they live."

"Coming up," the commissioner replied.

"How many of the infected left before we arrived?" he asked Santiago Vargas.

"Not sure, señor. There were many trucks."

"They left on the delivery lorries?"

"*Sí.* They sit in the back. You don't have no driver's seat these days. All mechanical. Very clever."

Ralph stared in dismay at the sullen man.

"We've been concentrating on stopping passenger vehicles," Diana Tiernan datavised. "Cargo traffic was only a secondary concern."

"Oh, Christ, if they got on to the motorways they could be halfway across the continent by now," Ralph said.

"I'll reassign the AI vehicle search priority now."

"If you find any of Moyce's lorries that are still moving, target them with the SD platforms. We don't have any other choice."

"I agree," Admiral Farquar datavised.

"Ralph, ask him which of the embassy pair was in Moyce's, please," Roche Skark datavised.

Ralph pulled a processor block from his belt, and ordered it to display pictures of Jacob Tremarco and Angeline Gallagher. He thrust it towards Vargas. "Did you see either of these people in the shop?"

The man took his time. "Him. I think."

"So we've still got to find Angeline Gallagher," Ralph said. "Any more city traffic with glitched processors?"

"Three possibles," Diana datavised. "We've already got two of them located. Both taxis from the spaceport."

"Okay, assign an AT Squad to each taxi. And make sure there are experienced personnel in both of them. What was the third trace?"

"A Longhound bus which left the airport ten minutes after the embassy trio landed; it was a scheduled southern route, right down to the tip of Mortonridge. We're working on its current location."

"Right, I'm coming back to the police headquarters. We're finished here."

"What about him?" Nelson Akroid asked, jerking a thumb at the captive.

Ralph glanced back. Santiago Vargas had found another cigarette from somewhere and was smoking it quietly. He smiled. "Can I go now, señor?" he asked hopefully.

Ralph returned the smile with equal honesty. "Have the zero-tau pods from *Ekwan* arrived yet?" he datavised.

"The first batch are due to arrive at Pasto spaceport in twelve minutes," Vicky Keogh replied.

"Cathal," Ralph said out loud. "See if Mr Vargas here will cooperate with us for just a little longer. I'd like to know the limits of the electronic warfare field, and that illusion effect of theirs."

"Yes, boss."

"After that, take him and the others on a sightseeing trip to the spaceport. No exceptions."

"My pleasure."

•   •   •

The Loyola Hall was one of San Angeles's more prestigious live-event venues. It seated twenty-five thousand under a domed roof which could be retracted when the weather was balmy, as it so frequently was in that city. There were excellent access routes to the nearby elevated autoway; the subway station was a nexus for six of the lines which ran beneath the city; it even had seven landing pads for VIP aircraft. There were five-star restaurants and snack bars, hundreds of rest rooms. Stewards were experienced and friendly. Police and promoters handled over two hundred events a year.

The whole site was an operation which functioned with silicon efficiency. Until today.

Eager kids had been arriving since six o'clock in the morning. It was now half past seven in the evening. Around the walls they were thronging twenty deep; scrums outside the various public doors needed police mechanoids to maintain a loose kind of order, and even they were in danger of being overwhelmed. The kids had a lot of fun spraying them with soft drinks and smearing ice creams over the sensors.

Inside the hall every seat was taken, the tickets bought months ago. The aisles were filled with people, too, though how they had got in past the processor-regulated turnstiles was anyone's guess. Touts were becoming overnight millionaires, those that weren't being arrested or mugged by gangs of motivated fourteen-year-olds.

It was the last night of Jezzibella's Moral Bankruptcy tour. The New California system had endured five weeks of relentless media saturation as she swept across the asteroid settlements and down to the planetary surface. Rumour, of AV projectors broadcasting illegal activent patterns during her concerts to stimulate orgasms in the audience (not true, said the official press release, Jezzibella has abundant sexuality of her own, she doesn't need artificial aids to boost the Mood Fantasy she emotes). Hyperbole, about the President's youngest daughter being completely infatuated after meeting her, then sneaking out of the Blue Palace to go backstage at her concert (Jezzibella was delighted and deeply honoured to meet all members of the First Family, and we are not aware of any unauthorized entry to a concert). Scandal, when two of the band, Bruno and Busch, were arrested for violating public decency laws in front of a senior citizens holiday group, their bail posted at one million New California dollars (Bruno and Busch were engaged in a very wonderful, sensitive, and private act of love; and that bunch of filthy old perverts used enhanced retinas to spy on them). Straight hype, when Jezzibella visited (as a private citizen—so no sensevises, please) a children's ward in a poor district of town, and donated half a million fuseodollars to the hospital's germ-line treatment fund. Editorial shock at the way she flaunted her thirteen-year-old male companion, Emmerson (Mr Emmerson is Jezzibella's second cousin, and his passport clearly states he is sixteen). A lot of spectator fun, and official police cautions, derived from the extraordinarily violent fights between her entourage's security team and rover reporters. The storm of libel writs issued by Leroy Octavius, her manager, every time anyone suggested she was older than twenty-eight.

And in all those five weeks she never gave an interview, never made a single public utterance outside of her stage routine. She didn't have to. In that time, the regional office of Warner Castle Entertainment datavised out thirty-seven million copies of her new MF album *Life Kinetic* across the planet's communications net to worshipful fans; her back catalogue sold equally well.

The starship crews who normally made a tidy profit from selling a copy of an MF album to a distributor in star systems where they hadn't been officially released yet cursed their luck when they arrived on planets where Jezzibella had passed through in the last eighteen months. But then that was the point of being a touring artist. A new album every nine months, and visit ten star systems each year; it was the only way you could beat the bootleggers. If you weren't prepared to do that, the only money you ever got was from your home star system.

Few made the transition from local wonder to galactic mega-star. It took a lot of money to travel, and entertainment companies were reluctant to invest. The artist had to demonstrate a colossal degree of professionalism and determination before they were worth the multimillion-fuseodollar risk. Once they'd breached the threshold, of course, the old adage of money making more money had never been truer.

High above the costly props and powerful AV stacks on-stage, an optical-band sensor was scanning the crowd. Faces merged into a monotonous procession as it swept along the tiers and balconies. Fans came in distinct categories: the eager exhilarated ones, mostly young; boisterous and expectant, late teens; impatient, already stimmed-out, nervous, fearfully worshipful, even a few who obviously wanted to be somewhere else but had come along to please their partner. Every costume Jezzibella had ever worn in an MF track was out there somewhere, from the simple to the peacock bizarre.

The sensor focused on a couple in matching leathers. The boy was nineteen or twenty, the girl at his side a bit younger. They had their arms around each other, very much in love. Both tall, healthy, vital.

Jezzibella cancelled the datavise from the sensor. "Those two," she told Leroy Octavius. "I like them."

The unpleasantly overweight manager glanced at the short AV pillar sticking out of his processor block, checking the two blithesome faces. "Roger dodger. I'll get on it."

There was no quibbling, not the faintest hint of disapproval. Jezzibella liked that; it was what made him such a good manager. He understood how it was for her, the things she required in order to function. She needed kids like those two. Needed what they'd got, the naivete, the uncertainty, the delight at life. She had none of that left, now, not the sweet side of human nature. The eternal tour had drained it all away, somewhere out among the stars; one energy which could leak out of a zero-tau field. Everything became secondary to the tour, feelings weren't allowed to interfere. And feelings suppressed long enough simply vanished. But she couldn't have that, because she needed an understanding of feelings in order to work. Circles. Her life was all circles.

So instead of her own emotions, she familiarised herself

with this alien quality which others owned, examining it as if she were performing a doctoral thesis. Absorbed what she could, the brief taste allowing her to perform again, to fake it through yet one more show.

"I don't like them," Emmerson said petulantly.

Jezzibella tried to smile at him, but the whole charade of pandering to him bored her now. She was standing, stark naked, in the middle of the green room while Libby Robosky, her personal image consultant, worked on her dermal scales. The bitek covering was a lot more subtle than a chameleon layer, allowing her to modify her body's whole external texture rather than simply changing colour. For some numbers she needed to have soft, sensitive skin, a young girl who quivered at her first lover's touch; then there was the untainted look, a body which was naturally graceful without workouts and fad diets (like the girl she'd seen through the hall's sensor); and of course the athlete/ballerina body, supple, hard, and muscular—big favourite with the boys. It was the feel of her which everyone out there in the hall wanted to experience; Jezzibella in the flesh.

But the tiny scales had a short lifetime, and each one had to be annealed to her skin separately. Libby Robosky was an undoubted wizard when it came to applying them, using a modified medical nanonic package.

"You don't have to meet them," Jezzibella told the boy patiently. "I can take care of them by myself."

"I don't want to be left alone all night. How come I can't pick someone out of the audience for myself?"

As the reporters had been allowed to discover, he really was only thirteen. She'd brought him into the entourage back on Borroloola, an interesting plaything. Now after two months of daily tantrums and broodiness the novelty value had been exhausted. "Because this is the way it has to be. I need them for a reason. I've told you a hundred times."

"Okay. So why don't we do it now, then?"

"I have a show in a quarter of an hour. Remember?"

"So what?" Emmerson challenged. "Skip it. That'll cause a real publicity storm. And there won't be any backlash 'cos we're leaving."

"Leroy," she datavised. "Take this fucking brat away before I split his skull open to find out where his brain went."

Leroy Octavius waddled back over to where she stood. His bulky frame was clad in a light snakeskin jacket that was an optimistic size and a half too small. The tough, thin leather squeaked at every motion. "Come on, son," he said in a gruff voice. "We're supposed to leave the artists to it this close to a show. You know how spaced out they get about performing. How about you and I have a look at the food they're laying on next door?"

The boy allowed himself to be led away, Leroy's huge hand draped over his shoulder, casually forceful.

Jezzibella groaned. "Shit. Why did I ever think his age made him exciting?"

Libby's indigo eyes fluttered open, giving her a quizzical look. Out of all the sycophants, hangers-on, outright parasites, and essential crew, Jezzibella enjoyed Libby the most. A grandmotherly type who always dressed to emphasise her age, she had the stoicism and patience to absorb any tantrum or crisis with only the vaguest disinterested shrug.

"It was your hormones which went a-frolicking at the sight of his baby dick, poppet," Libby said.

Jezzibella grunted, she knew the rest of the entourage hated Emmerson. "Leroy," she datavised. "I paid that hospital we visited enough fucking money; have they got a secure wing we could leave the juvenile shit in?"

Leroy gave a backwards wave as he left the green room. "We'll talk about what we're going to do with him later," he replied.

"You fucking finished yet?" Jezzibella asked Libby.

"Absolutely, poppet."

Jezzibella composed herself, and ordered her neural nanonics to send a sequence of encoded impulses down her nerves. There was an eerie sensation of wet leather slithering on the top of her rib cage, all four limbs shivered. Her shoulders straightened of their own accord, belly muscles tightened, sinuous lines hardened under skin that was turning a deeper shade of bronze.

She dug deep into her memory, finding the right sensation

of pride and confidence. Combined with the physique it was synergistic. She was adorable, and knew it.

"Merrill!" she yelled. "Merrill, where the fuck's my first-act costume?"

The flunky hurried over to the big travelling trunks lined up along a wall and began extracting the requisite items.

"And why haven't you shitheads started warming up yet," she shouted at the musicians.

The green room abruptly became a whirlwind of activity as everyone found legitimate employment. Private, silent datavises flashed through the air as they all discussed the impending frailty of Emmerson's future. It diverted them from how precarious their own tenures were.

* * * *

Ralph Hiltch accessed various reports as he flew back over the city. The priority search which Diana Tiernan's department had initiated was producing good results. According to the city's route and flow road processor network, fifty-three lorries had left Moyce's that evening. The AIs were now chasing after them.

Within seven minutes of Diana assigning the lorries full priority, twelve had been located, all outside the city. The coordinates were datavised into the Strategic Defence Command up in Guyana, and sensor satellites triangulated the targets for low-orbit weapons platforms. A dozen short-lived violet starbursts blossomed across Xingu's southern quarter.

By the time Ralph's hypersonic landed another eight had been added to the total. He'd stripped off his damaged lightweight armour suit in the plane, borrowing a dark blue police fatigue one-piece. It was baggy enough to fit over his medical nanonic package without restriction. But for all the package's support, he was still limping as he made his way over to Hub One.

"Welcome back," Landon McCullock said. "You did a good job, Ralph. I'm grateful."

"We all are," Warren Aspinal said. "And that's not just a politician speaking. I have a family in the city, three kids."

"Thank you, sir." Ralph sat down next to Diana Tiernan. She managed a quick grin for him. "We've been checking up on the night shift at Moyce's," she said. "There were forty-five on duty this evening. As of now, the AT Squads have accounted for twenty-nine during the assault, killed and captured."

"Shit. Sixteen of the bastards loose," Bernard Gibson said.

"No," Diana said firmly. "We think we may have got lucky. I've hooked the AIs into the fire department's mechanoids; their sensors are profiled for exploring high temperature environments. So far they've located a further five bodies in the building, and there's still thirty per cent which hasn't been covered. That accounts for all but eleven of the night shift."

"Still too many," Landon said.

"I know. But we're certain that six of the lorries zapped so far contained a shift member. Their processors and ancillary circuits were suffering random failures. It matched the kind of interference which Adkinson's plane suffered."

"And then there were five," Warren Aspinal said quietly.

"Yes, sir," Diana said. "I'm pretty sure they're in the remaining lorries."

"Well I'm afraid 'pretty sure' isn't good enough when we're facing a threat which could wipe us out in less than a week, Chief Tiernan," said Leonard DeVille.

"Sir." Diana didn't bother to look at him. "I wasn't making wild assumptions. Firstly, the AIs have confirmed that there was no other traffic logged as using Moyce's since Jacob Tremarco's taxi arrived."

"So they left on foot."

"Again, I really don't think that is the case, sir. That whole area around Moyce's is fully covered by security sensors, both ours and the private systems owned by the companies in neighbouring buildings. We accessed all the relevant memories. Nobody came out of Moyce's. Just the lorries."

"What we've seen tonight is a continuing pattern of attempted widespread dispersal," Landon McCullock said. "The embassy trio have been constant in their attempt to distribute the energy virus as broadly as possible. It's a very logical move. The wider it is spread, the longer it takes for us to contain it, and the more people can be infected, in turn making it more difficult for us to contain. A nasty spiral."

"They only have a limited amount of time in the city,"

Ralph chipped in. "And the city is where we have the greatest advantage when it comes to finding and eliminating them. So they'll know it's a waste of effort trying to spread the contamination here, at least initially. Whereas the countryside tilts the balance in their favour. If they win out there, then Xingu's main urban areas will eventually become cities under siege. Again a situation which we would probably lose in the long run. That's what happened on Lalonde. I imagine that Durringham has fallen by now."

Leonard DeVille nodded curtly.

"The second point," said Diana, "is that those infected don't seem able to halt the lorries. Short of them using their white fire weapon to physically destroy the motors or power systems the lorries aren't stopping before their first scheduled delivery point. And if they do use violence against a lorry the motorway processors will spot it straightaway. From the evidence we've accumulated so far it seems as though they can't use their electronic warfare field to alter a lorry's destination. It's powerful, but not sophisticated, not enough to get down into the actual drive control processors and tamper with on line programs."

"You mean they're trapped inside the lorries?" Warren Aspinal asked.

"Yes, sir."

"And none of the lorries have reached their destination yet," Vicky Keogh said, with a smile for the Home Office minister. "As Diana said, it looks like we got lucky."

"Well thank God they're not omnipotent," the Prime Minister said.

"They're not far short," Ralph observed. Even listening to Diana outline the current situation hadn't lifted his spirits. The crisis was too hot, too now. Emotions hadn't had time to catch up with events; pursuing the embassy trio was like space warfare, everything happening too quick for anything other than simplistic responses, there was no opportunity to take stock and think. "What about Angeline Gallagher?" he inquired. "Have the AIs got any further leads?"

"No. Just the two taxis and the Longhound bus," Diana said. "The AT Squads are on their way."

* * *

It took another twelve minutes to clear the taxis. Ralph stayed at Hub One while the interception operations were running, receiving datavises from the two Squad commanders.

The first taxi was laid up beside one of the rivers which meandered through Pasto. It had stopped interfacing with the route and flow processors as it drew up next to a boathouse. Road monitor cameras had been trained on the grey vehicle for eleven minutes, seeing no movement from it or the boathouse.

The AT Squad members closed in on it, using standard leapfrog advancement tactics. Its lights were off, doors frozen half-open, no one inside. A technical officer opened a systems access panel and plugged his processor block into it. The police AI probed the vehicle's circuitry and memory cells.

"All clear," Diana reported. "A short circuit turned the chassis live, blew most of the processors, and screwed the rest. No wonder it showed up like one of our hostiles."

The second taxi had been abandoned in an underground garage below a residential mews. The AT Squad arrived just as the taxi company's service crew turned up to take it away on their breakdown hauler. Everyone at Hub One witnessed the scenes of hysterics and anger as the AT Squad took no chances with the three service crew.

After running an on-the-spot diagnostic, the crew discovered the taxi's electron matrix was faulty, sending huge power spikes through the on-board circuitry.

"Gallagher has to be on the bus," Landon McCullock said as he cancelled his datavise to the AT Squad, the service crew's inventive obscenities fading from his borrowed perception.

"I can confirm that," Diana said. "The damn thing won't respond to the halt orders we're issuing via the motorway route and flow processors."

"I thought you said they couldn't alter programs with their electronic warfare technique," Leonard DeVille said.

"It hasn't altered its route, it just won't respond," she shot back. An almost uninterrupted three-hour stint spent interfacing with, and directing, the AIs, was beginning to fatigue her nerves.

Warren Aspinal gave his political colleague a warning frown.

"The AT Squad teams will be over the bus in ninety seconds," Bernard Gibson said. "We'll see exactly what's going on then."

Ralph datavised a tactical situation request into the hub's processor array. His neural nanonics visualized a map of Xingu, a rough diamond with a downward curling cat's tail. Forty-one of Moyce's delivery lorries had been located and annihilated now, green and purple symbols displaying their movements, the locations when they were targeted. The bus was a virulent amber, proceeding down the M6 motorway which ran the length of Mortonridge, the long spit of mountainous land which poked southwards across the equator.

He switched to accessing the sensor suite on the lead hypersonic. The plane was just decelerating into subsonic flight. There was nothing any discrimination filter program could do about the vibration as it aerobraked. Ralph had to wait it out, impatience heating his blood feverishly. If Angeline Gallagher wasn't on the bus, then they'd probably lost the continent.

The M6 was laid out below him in the clear tropical air. The hypersonic's shaking damped out, and he could see hundreds of stationary cars, vans, buses, and lorries parked on the motorway's service lanes. Headlights illuminated the lush verges, hundreds of people were milling around, some even settling down for midnight picnics by their vehicles.

The static pageant made the bus easy to spot, the one moving light source on the motorway, heading south at about two hundred kilometres an hour. It roared on past the riveted spectators lining the lane barrier, immune to the priority codes being fired into its circuitry from the motorway's route and flow processors.

"What the hell is that thing?" Vicky Keogh voiced the unspoken question of everyone accessing the hypersonic's sensor suite.

The Longhound Bus Company had a standardized fleet of sixty-seaters made on the Esparta continent, with a distinct green and purple livery. They were used all over Ombey, stitching together every continent's cities and towns with an extensive, fast, and frequent service. The principality didn't yet have the economy or population to justify vac train tubes linking its urban areas like Earth and Kulu. So the Longhound buses were a familiar sight on the motorways; more or less everyone on the planet had ridden on one at some time in their lives.

But the runaway vehicle speeding down the M6 looked nothing like a normal Longhound. Where the Longhound's body was reasonably smooth and trim, this had the kind of sleek profile associated with the aerospace industry. A curved, wedge-shaped nose blending back into an oval cross-section body, with sharp triangular fin spoilers sprouting out of the rear quarter. It had a dull silver finish, with gloss-black windows. Greasy grey smoke belched out of a circular vent just behind the rear wheel set.

"Is it on fire?" a disconcerted Warren Aspinal asked.

"No, sir." Diana sounded ridiculously happy. "What you're seeing there is its diesel exhaust."

"A what exhaust?"

"Diesel. This is a Ford Nissan omnirover; it burns diesel in a combustion engine."

The Prime Minister had been running his own neural nanonics encyclopedia search. "An engine which burns hydrocarbon fuel?"

"Yes, sir."

"That's ridiculous, not to mention illegal."

"Not when this was built, sir. According to my files, the last one rolled off the Turin production line in 2043 AD. That's the city of Turin on Earth."

"Have you a record of any being imported by a museum or a private vehicle collector?" Landon McCullock asked patiently.

"The AIs can't find one."

"Jenny Harris reported a phenomenon similar to this back on Lalonde," Ralph said. "She saw a fanciful riverboat when I sent her on that last mission. They'd altered its appearance so it seemed old-fashioned, something from Earth's pre-technology times."

"Christ," Landon McCullock muttered.

"Makes sense," Diana said. "We're still getting a correct identification code from its processors. They must have thrown this illusion around the Longhound."

The hypersonic closed on the bus, sliding in over the motorway, barely a hundred metres up. Below it, the omnirover was weaving from side to side with complete disregard for the lane markings. The ceaseless and random movement made it difficult for the pilot to stay matched directly overhead.

Ralph realized what had been bothering his subconscious, and requested a visual sensor to zoom in. "That's more than just a holographic illusion," he said after studying the image. "Look at the bus's shadow under those lights, it matches the outline."

"How do they do that?" Diana asked. Her voice was full of curiosity, with a hint of excitement bleeding in.

"Try asking Santiago Vargas," Vicky Keogh told her sharply.

"I can't even think of a theory that would allow us to manipulate solid surfaces like that," Diana said defensively.

Ralph grunted churlishly. He'd had a similar conversation back on Lalonde when they were trying to figure out how the LDC's observation satellite was being jammed. No known principle. The whole concept of an energy virus was a radical one.

"Possession," Santiago Vargas called it.

Ralph shivered. His Christian belief had never been that strongly rooted, but like a good Kingdom subject, it was always there. "Our immediate concern is what do we do about the bus. You might manage to land AT Squad teams on the thing if they were equipped with airpack flight suits, but they can hardly jump down from the hypersonic."

"Use the SD platforms to chop up the motorway ahead of it," Admiral Farquar suggested. "Force it to stop that way."

"Do we know how many people were on board?" Landon McCullock asked.

"Full complement when it left Pasto spaceport, I'm afraid," Diana reported.

"Damn. Sixty people. We have to make at least an effort to halt it."

"We'd have to reinforce the AT Squads first," Ralph said. "Three hypersonics isn't enough. And you'd have to stop the bus precisely in the centre of a cordon. With sixty possible hostiles riding on it, we'd have to be very certain no one broke through. That's wild-looking countryside out there."

"We can have reinforcements there in another seven minutes," Bernard Gibson said.

"Shit—" It was a datavise from the pilot. A big javelin of white fire streaked up from the bus, punching the hypersonic's belly. The plane quaked, then peeled away rapidly, almost rolling through ninety degrees. Bright sparkling droplets of molten ceramic sprayed out from the gaping hole in its fuselage to splash and burn on the motorway's surface. Its aerodynamics wounded, it started juddering continuously, losing height. The pilot tried desperately to right it, but he was already too low. He came to the same conclusion as the flight computer and activated the crash protection system.

Foam under enormous pressure fired into the cabin, swamping the AT Squad members. Valency generators turned it solid within a second.

The plane hit the ground, ploughing a huge gash through the vegetation and soft black loam. Nose, wings, and tailplane crumpled and tore, barbed fragments spinning off into the night. The bulky cylinder which was the cabin carried on for another seventy metres, flinging off structural spars and smashed ancillary modules. It came to a jarring halt, thudding into a steep earthen bluff.

The valency generators cut off, and foam sluiced out of the wreckage, mingling with the mud. Figures stirred weakly inside.

Bernard Gibson let out a painful breath. "I think they're all okay."

One of the other two hypersonics was circling back towards the crash. The second took up position a respectful kilometre behind the bus.

"Oh, Christ," Vicky Keogh groaned. "The bus is slowing. They're going to get off."

"Now what?" the Prime Minister demanded. He sounded frightened and angry.

"One AT Squad can't possibly contain them," Ralph said.

It was like speaking treason. I betrayed those people. My failure.

"There are sixty people on that bus," an aghast Warren Aspinal exclaimed. "We might be able to cure them."

"Yes, sir, I know that." Ralph hardened his expression, disguising how worthless he felt, and looked at Landon McCullock. The police chief obviously wanted to argue; he glanced at his deputy, who shrugged helplessly.

"Admiral Farquar?" Landon McCullock datavised.

"Yes."

"Eliminate the bus."

Ralph watched through the hypersonic's sensor suite as the laser blast from low orbit struck the fantasm vehicle. Just for an instant he saw the silhouette of the real Longhound inside the illusory cloak, as if the purpose of the weapon was really to expose truths. Then the energy barrage incinerated the bus along with a thirty-metre-diameter circle of road.

When he looked around the faces of everyone sitting at Hub One, he saw his own dismay and horror bounced right back at him.

It was Diana Tiernan who held his gaze, her kindly old face crumpled up with tragic sympathy. "I'm sorry, Ralph," she said. "We weren't quick enough. The AIs have just told me the bus stopped at the first four towns on its scheduled route."

3

Al Capone dressed as Al Capone had always dressed: with
style. He wore a double-breasted blue serge suit, a paisley
pattern silk tie, black patent leather shoes, and a pearl-grey
fedora, rakishly aslant. Gold rings set with a rainbow array
of deep precious stones glinted on every finger, a duck-egg
diamond on his pinkie.

It hadn't taken him long to decide that the people in this future world didn't have much in the way of fashion sense. The
suits he could see all followed the same loose silk design, although their colourful slimline patterns made them appear
more like flappy Japanese pyjamas. Those not in suits wore
variants on vests and sports shirts. Tight-fitting, too, at least
for people under thirty-five. Al had stared at the dolls to start
with, convinced they were all hookers. What kind of decent
gal would dress like that, with so much showing? Skirts
which almost didn't cover their ass, shorts that weren't much
better. But no. They were just ordinary, smiling, happy, every-
day girls. The people living in this city weren't so strung up
on morality and decency. What would have given a Catholic
priest apoplexy back home didn't raise an eyebrow here.

"I think I'm gonna like this life," Al declared.

Strange life that it was. He seemed to have been reincarnated as a magician: a real magician, not like the fancy trick-
sters he'd booked for his clubs back in Chicago. Here,
whatever he wanted appeared out of nowhere.

That had taken a long while to get used to. Think and . . .
pow. There it was, everything from a working Thompson to a
silver dollar glinting in the hot sun. Goddamn useful for
clothes, though. Brad Lovegrove had worn overalls of shiny
dark red fabric like some kind of pissant garbage collector.

Al could hear Lovegrove whimpering away inside him,

like having a leprechaun nesting at the centre of his brain. He was bawling like a complete bozo, and making about as much sense. But there was some gold among the dross, twenty-four-karat nuggets. Like—when he first got his marbles together Al had thought this world was maybe Mars or Venus. Not so. New California didn't even orbit the same sun as Earth. And it wasn't the twentieth century no more.

Je-zus, but a guy needed a drink to help keep that from blowing his head apart.

And where to get a drink? Al imagined the little leprechaun being squeezed, as if his brain were one giant muscle. Slowly contracting.

A macromall on the intersection between Longwalk and Sunrise, Lovegrove squealed silently. There's a specialist store there with liquor from every Confederation planet, probably even got Earth bourbon.

Drinks from clear across the galaxy! How about that?

So Al started walking. It was a lovely day.

The sidewalk was so wide it was more like a boulevard in itself; there were no paving slabs, instead the whole strip had been made from a seamless sheet, a material which was a cross between marble and concrete. Luxuriant trees sprouted up through craters in the surface every forty yards or so, their two-foot sprays of floppy oval flowers an impossible shade of metallic purple.

He spotted a few trashcan-sized trucks trundling sedately among the walkers enjoying the late-morning sunshine, machinery smoother than Henry Ford had ever dreamed of. Utility mechanoids, Lovegrove told him, cleaning the sidewalk, picking up litter and fallen leaves.

The base of each skyscraper was given over to classy delis and bars and restaurants and coffee shops; tables spilled out onto the sidewalk, just like a European city. Arcades pierced deep into the buildings.

From what Al could see, it was the same kind of rich man's playground setup on the other side of the street, maybe a hundred and fifty yards away. Not that you could walk over to be sure, there was no way past the eight-foot-high glass and metal barrier which lined the road.

Al stood with his face pressed to the glass for some time,

watching the silent cars zoom past. Big bullets on wheels. All of them shiny, like coloured chrome. You didn't even have to steer them no more, Lovegrove told him, they did it themselves. Some kind of fancy electrical engine, no gas. And the speed, over two hundred kilometres an hour.

Al knew all about kilometres; they were what the French called miles.

But he wasn't too sure about using a car that he couldn't drive himself, not when it travelled that fast. And anyway, his presence seemed to mommick up electricity. So he stuck to walking.

The skyscrapers gave him vertigo they were so tall, and all you could see when you looked up at them was reflections of more skyscrapers. They seemed to bend over the street, imprisoning the world below. Lovegrove told him they were so high that their tops were designed to sway in the wind, rocking twenty–thirty metres backwards and forwards in slow motion.

"Shut up," Al growled.

The leprechaun curled up tighter, like a knotted snake.

People looked at Al—his clothes. Al looked at people, fascinated and jubilant. It was a jolt seeing blacks and whites mixing free, other types too, light-skinned Mediterranean like his own, Chinese, Indian. Some seemed to have dyed their hair completely the wrong colour. Amazing.

And they all appeared so much at ease with themselves, owning a uniform inner smile. They had a nonchalance and surety which he'd never seen before. The devil which drove so many people back in the twenties was missing, as if the city elders had abolished worry altogether.

They also had astonishingly good health. After a block and a half Al still hadn't seen anyone remotely overweight. No wonder they wore short clothes. A world where everyone was in permanent training for the big game, even the seventy-year-olds.

"You still got baseball, ain't you?" Al muttered under his breath.

Yes, Lovegrove confirmed.

Yep, paradise all right.

After a while he took off his jacket and slung it over his

shoulder. He'd been walking for a quarter of an hour, and it didn't look as if he'd got anywhere. The massive avenue of skyscrapers hadn't changed at all.

"Hey, buddy," he called.

The black guy—who looked like a prizefighter—turned and gave an amused grin as he took in Al's clothes. His arm was around a girl: Indian skin, baby blonde hair. Her long legs were shown off by a pair of baggy culottes.

Cutie pie, Al thought, and grinned at her. A real sweater girl. It suddenly struck him that he hadn't hit the sack with a woman for six centuries.

She smiled back.

"How do I call a cab around here?"

"Datavise the freeway processors, my man," the black guy said expansively. "City runs a million cabs. Don't make a profit. But then that's what us dumb taxpayers are for, to make up the shortfall, right?"

"I can't do the data thing, I ain't from around here."

The girl giggled. "You just get off a starship?"

Al tipped the rim of his fedora with two fingers. "Kind of, lady. Kind of."

"Neat. Where you from?"

"Chicago. On Earth."

"Hey, wow. I never met anyone from Earth before. What's it like?"

Al's grin lost its lustre. Je-zus, but the women here were forward. And the black guy's thick arm was still draped over her shoulder. He didn't seem to mind his girl making conversation with a total stranger. "One city's just like another," Al said; he gestured lamely at the silver skyscrapers, as if that was explanation enough.

"City? I thought you only had arcologies on Earth?"

"Look, you going to tell me how to get a fucking cab, or what?"

He'd blown it. The moment he saw the man's expression harden, he knew.

"You want us to call one for you, *buddy*?" The man was taking a longer, slower look at Al's clothes.

"Sure," Al bluffed.

"Okay. No problem. It's done." A phony smile.

Al wondered exactly what it was the man had actually done. He didn't have no Dick Tracy wrist radio to call for a cab or anything. Just stood there, smiling, playing Al for a sucker.

Lovegrove was filling Al's head with crap about miniature telephones in the brain. He had one fitted himself, he said, but it had packed up when Al possessed him.

"Going to tell me about Chicago now?" the girl asked.

Al could see how worried she was. Her voice, mannerisms, the way she had merged into her man's encircling arm. They all telegraphed it, and he knew how to read the signs. Fear in other people was wholly familiar.

He thrust his face forwards toward the black guy, snarling at the wiseass bastard. Just for an instant three long scars pulsed hotly on his left cheek. "Gonna remember you, cocksucker. Gonna find you again. Gonna teach you *respect*, and, buddy, it's gonna be the real hard way to learn." The old rage was burning in his body now, limbs trembling, voice rising to a thunderous roar. "Nobody shits on Al Capone! You got that? Nobody treats me like some dog turd you stepped in. I fucking ruled Chicago. I owned that city. I am not some asswipe street punk you can take for a ride. I. Deserve. RESPECT."

"Bastard Retro!" The man swung a punch.

Even if Lovegrove's body hadn't been enhanced with the energistic power which possessing souls exuded in the natural universe Al would probably have beaten him. His years in Brooklyn had pitched him into countless brawls, and people had quickly learned to steer clear of his awesome temper.

Al ducked instinctively, his right fist already coming up. The blow was focused, mentally and physically. He struck the man perfectly, catching him on the side of his jaw.

There was an ugly sound of bone shattering. Dead silence. The man flew backwards five yards through the air, hitting the sidewalk in a crumpled sprawl. He slid along the carbon concrete composite for another couple of yards before coming to rest, completely inert. Blood began to splatter from his mouth where serrated bone had punctured his cheek and lip.

Al stared, surprised. "Goddamn!" He started to laugh delightedly.

The girl screamed. She screamed and screamed.

Al glanced around, suddenly apprehensive. Everyone on the broad sidewalk was looking at him, at the injured black guy. "Shut up," he hissed at the loopy broad. "Shut up!" But she wouldn't. Just: scream, and scream, and scream. Like it was her profession.

Then there was another sound, cutting through her bawling, rising every time she took a breath. And Al Capone realized it wasn't just handguns he could recognize after six hundred years. Police sirens hadn't changed much either.

He started to run. People scattered ahead of him the way kittens ran from a pit bull. Cries and yells broke out all around.

"Stop him!"

"Move!"

"Stinking Retro."

"He killed that dude. One punch."

"No! Don't try to—"

A man was going for him. Beefy and hard-set, crouched low for a pro football tackle. Al waved a hand, almost casually, and white fire squirted into the hero's face. Black petals of flesh peeled back from the bone, sizzling. Thick chestnut hair flamed to ash. A dull agonized grunt, cutting off as pain overloaded his consciousness, and the man collapsed.

Then all hell really did hit the fan. Anxious people became a terrified mob. Stampeding away from him. Fringe onlookers got caught and bowled over by thudding feet.

Al glanced back over his shoulder to see a section of the road barrier fold down. The squad car glided over it towards him. An evil-looking black and blue javelin-head, airplane-smooth fuselage. Dazzlingly bright lights flashed on top of it.

"Hold it, Retro," a voice boomed from the car.

Al's pace slackened. There was an arcade ahead of him, but its arching entrance was wide enough to take the squad car. Goddamn! Alive again for forty minutes and already running from the cops.

What else is new?

He stopped, and turned full square to face them, silver-plated Thompson gripped in his hands. And—oh, shit—another two squad cars were coming off the road, lining up directly towards him. Big slablike flaps were opening like wings at their rear, and *things* came running out. They weren't human, they weren't animal. Machine animals? Whatever, they sure didn't look healthy. Fat dull-metal bodies with stumpy gun barrels protruding. Far too many legs, and all of those rubber, no knees or ankles.

Assault mechanoids, Lovegrove said. And there was a tinge of excitement in the mental voice. Lovegrove expected the things to beat him.

"They electric?" Al demanded.

Yes.

"Good." He glared at the one taking point, and cast his first sorcerer's spell.

Police patrol Sergeant Alson Loemer was already anticipating his promotion when he arrived at the scene. Loemer had been delighted as his neural nanonics received the updates from the precinct house. With his outlandish clothes, the man certainly looked like a Retro. The gang of history-costumed terrorists had been running the police department ragged for three days, sabotaging city systems with some new style of plasma weapon and electronic warfare field. Other acts too. Most officers had picked up strong rumours of snatches going down, people being lifted at random from the streets at night. And not one Retro had been brought to book. The news companies were datavising hive loads of untamed speculation across the communications net: a religious group, a band of offplanet mercenaries, even wackier notions. The mayor was going apeshit, and leaning on the police commissioner. Smooth people from an unnamed government intelligence agency had been walking around the corridors at the precinct house. But they didn't know anything more than the patrol officers.

Now he, Sergeant Loemer, was going to nail one of those suckers.

He guided the patrol car over the folded barrier and onto the sidewalk. The crim was dead ahead, running for the base of the Uorestone Tower. Two more precinct cars were riding with Loemer, closing on the crim, hemming him in. Loemer deployed both of his patrol car's assault mechanoids, and datavised in their isolate and securement instructions.

That was when the patrol car started to glitch, picking up

speed. The sensors showed him frightened citizens in front, racing to escape; one of the assault mechanoids wobbled past, shooting wildly. He fired shutdown orders into the drive processor. Not that it made much difference.

Then the Retro started shooting at the patrol cars. Whatever the gun was, it ripped straight through the armour shielding, smashing the axles and wheel hubs. Metal bearings screeched in that unique, and instantly recognizable, tone which heralded imminent destruction. Loemer thumped the manual safety cut out, killing power instantly.

The patrol car slewed around and bounced off the road barrier to smack straight into one of the Regree trees planted along the sidewalk. The internal crash alarm went off, half deafening an already dazed Loemer, and the emergency side hatch jettisoned. Loemer's bubble seat slid out along its telescoping rails. The translucent bubble's thick safety-restraint segments peeled back, allowing him to drop, wailing, to his knees as the air around him spewed out a terrible volley of sense overload impulses. His neural nanonics were unable to datavise a shutdown code into the crazed assault mechanoids. The last thing he saw as he fell onto the ground was the ruined Regree tree starting to keel over directly above him.

Even Al was bruised by the wild strafing of the sense-overload ordnance. The manic glee as he watched the patrol cars skid and smash was swiftly curtailed by the onslaught of light, sound, and smell. His energistic ability could ward off the worst of it, but he turned and began a stumbling run towards the arcade's entrance. Behind him the assault mechanoids continued to deluge the street with their errant firepower, lumbering about like drunks. Two ran into each other, and rebounded, falling over. Legs thrashed about in chaos, beetles flipped on their backs.

The sidewalk was littered with prone bodies. Not dead, Al thought, just terribly battered. Je-zus but those mechanical soldier contraptions were nasty pieces of work. And unlike real police, you wouldn't be able to buy them.

Maybe New California wasn't quite paradise after all.

Al staggered his way along the arcade, caught up in the flow of people desperate to escape the havoc. His suit faded away, the sharp colour and cut reverting to Lovegrove's original drab overall.

He picked up a little girl whose eyes were streaming tears and carried her. It felt good to help. Those goddamn brainless pigs should have made sure she was out of the way before they came at him with guns blazing. It would never have happened back in Chicago.

Two hundred yards from the arcade entrance he stopped among a group of anxious, exhausted people. They'd come far enough from the sense-overload ordnance to be free of its effects. Families clung together, others were calling out for friends and loved ones.

Al put the little girl down, still crying, which he thought was due to the Kaiser gas rather than any kind of injury. Then her mother came rushing up and hugged her frantically. Al was given profuse thanks. A nice dame. Cared about her children and family. That was good, proper. He was sorry he wasn't wearing his fedora so he could tip it to her.

Just how did people express that kind of formal courtesy on this world anyhow? Lovegrove was puzzled by the question.

He carried on down the arcade. Cops would be swarming all over the joint in a few minutes. Another hundred and fifty yards, and he was out on the street again. He started walking. Direction didn't matter, just *away*. This time he kept Lovegrove's overalls on. No one paid him any attention.

Al wasn't entirely sure what to do next. Everything was so strange. This world, his situation. Mind, strange wasn't the word for it, more like overwhelming. Or just plain creepy. Bad to think that the priests had been right about the afterworld, heaven and hell. He never went to church much, much to his momma's distress.

I wonder if I've been redeemed, paid my celestial dues. Is that why I'm back? But if you got reincarnated didn't you start off as a baby?

They weren't the kind of thoughts he was used to.

A hotel, he told Lovegrove, I need to rest up and think about what to do.

Most of the skyscrapers had some sort of rentable accommodation, apparently. But it would have to be paid for.

Al's hand automatically went to a leg pocket. He drew out

a Jovian Bank credit disk, a thick, oversize coin, sparkly silver on one side, magenta on the other. Lovegrove obediently explained how it worked, and Al put his thumb on the centre. A hash of green lines wobbled over the silver side.

"Goddamn!" He tried again, concentrating, wishing. Doing the magic.

The green lines began to form figures, crude at first, then sharp and regular. You could store an entire planet's treasury in one of these disks, Lovegrove told him. Al's ears pricked up at that. Then he was aware of something being not quite right. A presence, close by.

He hadn't really thought about the others. Those who had been there when he came into Lovegrove's body. The same ones who had deserted him in the disused shop. But if he closed his eyes, and shut out the sounds of the city, he could hear the distant babelesque clamour. It came from the nightmare domain, the pleas and promises to be brought forth, to live and breathe again.

That same perception gave him a most peculiar vision of the city. Walls of thick black shadow amid a universal greyness. People moved through it all, distorted whispers echoing all around, audible ghosts. Some *different* from others. Louder, clearer. Not many of them among the multitude.

Al opened his eyes and looked down the road. A section of the barrier was folding down neatly. One of the bullet cars drew to a halt beside it. The gull-wing door slid up, and inside was a proper car, a genuine American çonvertible wearing the streamlined image of the New California vehicle like a piece of clothing. It was low-slung, with a broad hood and lots of chrome trim. Al didn't recognize the model, it was more modern than anything in the twenties, and his memory of the thirties and forties wasn't so hot.

The man in the red leather driving seat nodded amicably. "You'd better get in," he said. "The cops are going to catch you if you stay out on the street. They're a mite worked up about us."

Al glanced up and down the sidewalk, then shrugged and climbed in.

Inside, the image of the bullet car tinted the air like a stained soap bubble.

"The name's Bernhard Allsop," the man behind the steering column said. He swung the car out into the road. Behind them the barrier rose up smoothly. "I always wanted me an Oldsmobile like this beauty, never could afford it back when I was living in Tennessee."

"And this is real now?"

"Who knows, boy? But it sure feels real. And I'm mighty grateful for the opportunity to ride one. You might say I thought it had passed me by."

"Yeah. I know what you mean."

"Caused a bit of commotion back there, boy. Them pigs is riled good and proper. We were monitoring what passes for their radio band these days."

"I just wanted a cab, that's all. Someone tried to get smart."

"There's a trick to riding around this town without the police knowing. Be happy to show you how sometime."

"Appreciate it. Where are we going?"

Bernhard Allsop grinned and winked. "Gonna take you to meet the rest of the group. Always need volunteers, they're kinda hard to come by." He laughed, a high-pitched stuttering yodel reminding Al of a piglet.

"They left me behind, Bernhard. I don't have anything to say to them."

"Yeah, well. You know how it was. You weren't altogether there, boy. I said we should have taken you along with us. Kin is kin, even though it ain't exactly family here, know what I mean? Glad to see you came through in the end, though."

"Thank you."

"So what's your name, boy?"

"Al Capone."

The Oldsmobile swerved as Bernhard flinched. His knuckles whitened as he tightened his grip on the wheel; then he risked an anxious sideways glance at his passenger. Where before there had been a twenty-year-old man dressed in a set of dark red overalls, there was now a debonair Latin-ethnic character in a double-breasted blue suit and pigeon-grey fedora.

"You shitting me?"

Al Capone reached into his suit and produced a miniature baseball bat. A now highly apprehensive Bernhard Allsop watched it grow to full size. It didn't take much imagination to figure out what the black stains around the end were.

"No," Al said politely. "I'm not shitting you."

"Holy Christ." He tried to laugh. "Al Capone."

"Yeah."

"Holy Christ. Al Capone in my car! Ain't that something?"

"That's certainly something, yeah."

"It's a pleasure, Al. Christ, I mean that. A real pleasure. Hell, you were the best, Al, the top man. Everybody knew that. Run a bit of moonshine in my day. Nothing much, a few slugs, is all. But you, you ran it for a whole city. Christ! Al Capone." He slapped the steering wheel with both hands, chortling. "Damn, but I can't wait to see their faces when I bring you in."

"Bring me in to what, Bernhard?"

"The group, Al, the group. Hey, you don't mind if I call you Al, do you? I don't want to give no offence, or nothing. Not to you."

"That's okay, Bernhard, all my friends call me Al."

"Your *friends*. Yes siree!"

"What does this group of yours do, exactly, Bernhard?"

"Why, get larger, of course. That's all we can do for now. Unity is strength."

"You a Communist, Bernhard?"

"Hey! No way, Al. I'm an American. I hate the filthy Reds."

"Sounds like you are to me."

"No, you got it all wrong. The more of us there are, the better chance we stand, the stronger we are. Like an army; a whole load of people together, they got the strength to make themselves felt. That's what I meant, Al. Honest."

"So what does the group have in mind for when they get big and powerful?"

Bernhard gave Al another sideways glance, puzzled this time. "To get out of here, Al. What else?"

"To get out of the city?"

"No. To take the planet away." He jabbed a thumb straight up. "From that. From the sky."

Al cast a sceptical eye upwards. The skyscrapers were flashing past on either side. Their size didn't bother him so much now. Starship drives still speckled the azure sky, streaked flashbulbs taking a long time to pop. He couldn't see the odd little moon anymore. "Why?" he asked reasonably.

"Damn it, Al. Can't you feel it? The emptiness. Man, it's horrible. All that huge nothing trying to suck you up and swallow you whole." He gulped, his voice lowering. "The sky is like *there*. It's the beyond all over again. We gotta hide. Someplace where we ain't never going to die again, somewhere that don't go on for ever. Where there's no empty night."

"Now you're sounding like a preacher man, Bernhard."

"Well maybe I am a little bit. It's a smart man who knows when he's beat. I don't mind saying it to you, Al. I'm frightened of the beyond. I ain't never going back there. No siree."

"So you're going to move the world away?"

"Damn right."

"That's one fucking big ambition you've got there, Bernhard. I wish you a lot of luck. Now just drop me off at this intersection coming up here. I'll find my own way about town now."

"You mean you ain't going to pitch in and help us?" an incredulous Bernhard asked.

"Nope."

"But you gotta feel it, too, Al. Even you. We all can. They never stop begging you, all those other lost souls. Ain't you afraid of going back there?"

"Can't say as I am. It never really bothered me any while I was there first time around."

"Never bothered . . . ! Holy Christ, you are one tough sonofabitch, Al." He put his head back and gave a rebel yell. "Listen, you mothers, being dead don't bother Al Capone none! Goddamn!"

"Where is this safe place you're taking the planet to, anyhow?"

"Dunno, Al. Just follow Judy Garland over the rainbow, I guess. Anywhere where there ain't no sky."

"You ain't got no plans, you ain't got no idea where you're going. And you wanted me to be a part of that?"

"But it'll happen, Al. I swear. When there's enough of us, we can do it. You know what you can do by yourself now, one man. Think what a million can do, two million. *Ten* million. Ain't nothing going to be able to stop us then."

"You're going to possess a million people?"

"We surely are."

The Oldsmobile dipped down a long ramp which took it into a tunnel. Bernhard let out a happy sigh as they passed into its harsh orange-tinged lighting.

"You won't possess a million people," Al said. "The cops will stop you. They'll find a way. We're strong, but we ain't no bulletproof superheroes. That stuff the assault mechanoids shoot nearly got me back there. If I'd been any closer I'd be dead again."

"Damn it, that's what I been trying to tell you, Al," Bernhard complained. "We gotta build up our numbers. Then they can't never hurt us."

Al fell silent. Part of what Bernhard said made sense. The more possessed there were, the harder it would be for the cops to stop them spreading. But they'd fight, those cops. Like wild bears once they realized how big the problem was, how dangerous the possessed were. Cops, whatever passed for the federal agents on this world, the army; all clubbing together. Government rats always did gang up. They'd have the starship weapons, too; Lovegrove burbled about how powerful they were, capable of turning whole countries to deserts of hot glass within seconds.

And what would Al Capone do on a world where such a war was being fought? Come to that, what would Al Capone do on any modern world?

"How are you snatching people?" he asked abruptly.

Bernhard must have sensed the change in tone, in purpose. He suddenly got antsy, shifting his ass around on the seat's shiny red leather, but keeping his eyes firmly on the road ahead. "Well gee, Al, we just take them off the street. At night, when it's nice and quiet. Nothing heavy."

"But you've been seen, haven't you? That cop called me a Retro. They even got a name for you. They know you're doing it."

"Well, yeah, sure. It's kinda difficult with the numbers we're working, you know. Like I say, we need a *lot* of people.

Sometimes we get seen. Bound to happen. But they haven't caught us."

"Not yet." Al grinned expansively. He put his arm around Bernhard's shoulder. "You know, Bernhard, I think I will come and meet this group of yours after all. It sounds to me that you ain't organized yourselves too good. No offence, I doubt you people have much experience in this field. But me now . . ." A fat Havana appeared in his hand. He took a long blissful drag, the first for six hundred years. "Me, I had a lifetime's experience of going to the bad. And I'm gonna give you all the benefit of that."

* * *

Gerald Skibbow shuffled into the warm, white-walled room, one arm holding on tightly to the male orderly. His loose powder-blue institute gown revealed several small medical nanonic packages as it shifted about. He moved as would a very old man in a high-gravity environment, with careful dignity. Needing help, needing guidance.

Unlike any normal person, he didn't even flick his eyes from side to side to take in his newest surroundings. The thickly cushioned bed in the centre of the room, with its surrounding formation of bulky, vaguely medical apparatus didn't seem to register on his consciousness.

"Okay, now then, Gerald," the orderly said cordially. "Let's get you comfortable on here, shall we?"

He gingerly positioned Gerald's buttocks on the side of the bed, then lifted his legs up and around until his charge was lying prone on the cushioning. Always cautious. He'd prepared a dozen candidates for personality debrief here in Guyana's grade-one restricted navy facility. None of them had exactly been volunteers. Skibbow might just realize what he was being prepped for. It could be the spark to bring him out of his trauma-trance.

But no. Gerald allowed the orderly to secure him with the webbing which moulded itself to his body contours. There was no sound from his throat, no blink as it tightened its grip.

The relieved orderly gave a thumbs-up to the two men sitting behind the long glass panel in the wall. Totally immobilized, Gerald stared beyond the outsized plastic helmet that lowered itself over his head. The inside was fuzzy, a lining of silk fur which had been stiffened somehow. Then his face was covered completely, and the light vanished.

Chemical infusions insured there was no pain, no discomfort as the nanonic filaments wormed their way around his dermal cells and penetrated the bone of the skull. Positioning their tips into the requisite synapses took nearly two hours, a delicate operation similar to the implanting of neural nanonics. However these infiltrations went deeper than ordinary augmentation circuitry, seeking out the memory centres to mate with neurofibrillae inside their clustered cells. And the incursion was massive, millions of filaments burrowing along capillaries, active superstring molecules with preprogrammed functions, knowing where to go, what to do. In many respects they resembled the dendritic formation of living tissue in which they were building a parallel information network. The cells obeyed their DNA pattern, the filaments' structure was formatted by AIs. One process designed by studying the other, but never complementary.

Impulses began to flow back down the filaments as the hypersensitive tips registered synaptic discharges. A horribly jumbled montage of random thoughtsnaps, memories without order. The facility's AI came on-line, running comparisons, defining characteristics, recognizing themes, and weaving them into coherent sensorium environs.

Gerald Skibbow's thoughts were focused on his apartment in the Greater Brussels arcology: three respectably sized rooms on the sixty-fifth floor of the Delores pyramid. From the triple glazed windows you could see a landscape of austere geometries. Domes, pyramids, and towers, all squashed together and wrapped up within the intestinal tangle of the elevated bhan tubes. Every surface he could see was grey, even the dome glass, coated with decades of grime.

It was a couple of years after they had moved in. Paula was about three, totter-running everywhere, and always falling over. Marie was a tiny energetic bundle of smiles who could emit a vast range of incredulous sounds as the world produced its daily marvels for her.

He was cradling his infant daughter (already beautiful) in

his lap that evening, while Loren was slumped in an armchair, accessing the local news show. Paula was playing with the secondhand Disney mechanoid minder he'd bought her a fortnight ago, a fluffy anthropomorphized hedgehog that had an immensely irritating laugh.

It was a cosy family, in a lovely home. And they were together, and happy because of that. And the strong arcology walls protected them from the dangers of the outside world. He provided for them, and loved them, and protected them. They loved him back, too; he could see it in their smiles and adoring eyes. Daddy was king.

Daddy sang lullabies to his children. It was important to sing; if he stopped, then the hobgoblins and ghouls would come out from the darkness and snatch children away—

Two men walked into the room, and quietly sat down on the settee opposite Gerald. He frowned at them, unable to place their names, wondering what they were doing invading his home.

Invading . . .

The pyramid trembled as if caught by a minor earthquake, making the colours blur slightly. Then the room froze, his wife and children becoming motionless, their warmth draining away.

"It's okay, Gerald," one of the men said. "Nobody is invading. Nobody is going to hurt you."

Gerald clutched at baby Marie. "Who are you?"

"I'm Dr Riley Dobbs, a neural expert; and this is my colleague, Harry Earnshaw, who is a neural systems technician. We're here to help you."

"Let me sing," a frantic Gerald yelled. "Let me sing. They'll get us if I stop. They'll get us all. We'll be dragged down into the bowels of the earth. None of us will ever see daylight again."

"There's always going to be daylight, Gerald," Dobbs said. "I promise you that." He paused, datavising an order into the AI.

Dawn rose outside the arcology. A clean dawn, the kind which Earth hadn't seen for centuries; the sun huge and red-gold, casting brilliant rays across the dingy landscape. It shone directly into the apartment, warm and vigorous.

Gerald sighed like a small child, and held his hands out to it. "It's so beautiful."

"You're relaxing. That's good, Gerald. We need you relaxed; and I'd prefer you to reach that state by yourself. Tranquillizers inhibit your responses, and we want you to be clearheaded."

"What do you mean?" Gerald asked suspiciously.

"Where are you, Gerald?"

"At home."

"No, Gerald, this is long ago. This is a refuge for you, a psychological retreat into the past. You're creating it because something rather nasty happened to you."

"No. Nothing! Nothing nasty. Go away."

"I can't go away, Gerald. It's important for a lot of people that I stay. You might be able to save a whole planet, Gerald."

Gerald shook his head. "Can't help. Go away."

"We're not going, Gerald. And you can't run from us. This isn't a place, Gerald, this is inside your mind."

"No no no!"

"I'm sorry, Gerald, truly, I am. But I cannot leave until you have shown me what I want to see."

"Go away. Sing!" Gerald started to hum his lullabies again. Then his throat turned to stone, blocking the music inside. Hot tears trickled down his cheeks.

"No more singing, Gerald," Harry Earnshaw said. "We're going to play a different game. Dr Dobbs and I are going to ask you some questions. We want to know what happened to you on Lalonde—"

The apartment exploded into a blinding iridescent swirl. Every sensory channel splice into Gerald Skibbow's brain thrummed from overload.

Riley Dobbs shook himself as the processor array broke the direct linkage. In the seat next to him Harry Earnshaw was also stirring.

"Sod it," Dobbs grumbled. In the room through the glass, he could see Skibbow's body straining against the webbing. He hurriedly datavised an order into the physiological control processor for a tranquillizer.

Earnshaw studied the neural scan of Skibbow's brain, the huge electrical surge at the mention of Lalonde. "That is one very deep-seated trauma. The associations are hotwired into almost every neural pathway."

"Did the AI pull anything out of the cerebral convulsion?"

"No. It was pure randomization."

Dobbs watched Skibbow's physiological display creep down towards median. "Okay, let's go in again. That trank should take the edge off his neurosis."

This time the three of them stood on a savanna of lush emerald-green knee-high grass. Tall snowcapped mountains guarded the horizon. A bright sun thickened the air, deadening sounds. Before them was a burning building; a sturdy log cabin with a lean-to barn and a stone chimney.

"Loren!" Gerald shouted hoarsely. "Paula! Frank!" He ran towards the building as the flames licked up the walls. The roof of solar cell panels began to curl up, blistering from the heat.

Gerald ran and ran, but never got any nearer. There were faces behind the windows: two women and a man. They did nothing as the flames closed around them, simply looked out with immense sadness.

Gerald sank to his knees, sobbing.

"Wife Loren, and daughter Paula with her husband Frank," Dobbs said, receiving their identities direct from the AI. "No sign of Marie."

"Small wonder the poor bastard's in shock if he saw this happen to his family," Earnshaw remarked.

"Yeah. And we're too early. He hasn't been taken over by the energy virus yet." Dobbs datavised an order into the AI, activating a targeted suppression program, and the fire vanished along with the people. "It's all right, Gerald. It's over. All finished with. They're at peace now."

Gerald twisted around to glare at him, his face deformed by rage. "At peace? At peace! You stupid ignorant bastard. They'll never be at peace. None of us ever will. Ask me! Ask me, you fucker. Go on. You want to know what happened? *This*, this happened."

Daylight vanished from the sky, replaced by a meagre radiance from Rennison, Lalonde's innermost moon. It illuminated another log cabin; this one belonged to the Nicholls family, Gerald's neighbour. The mother, father, and son had been tied up and put in the animal stockade along with Gerald.

A ring of dark figures encircled the lonely homestead, distorted human shapes, some atrociously bestial.

"My God," Dobbs murmured. Two of the figures were dragging a struggling, screaming girl into the cabin.

Gerald gave a giddy laugh. "God? There is no God."

•   •   •

After nearly five hours of unbroken and mercifully uneventful travel, Carmitha still hadn't convinced herself they were doing the right thing in going to Bytham. Every instinct yelled at her to get to Holbeach and surround herself with her own kind, use them like a fence to keep out the nemesis which prowled the land, to be safe. That same instinct made her queasy at Titreano's presence. Yet as the younger Kavanagh girl predicted, with him accompanying them nothing had happened to the caravan. Several times he had indicated a farmhouse or hamlet where he said his kind were skulking.

Indecision was a wretched curse.

But she now had few doubts that he was almost what he claimed to be: an old Earth nobleman possessing the body of a Norfolk farmhand.

There had been a lot of talk in the last five hours. The more she heard, the more convinced she became. He knew so many *details*. However, there was one small untruth remaining which bothered her.

After Titreano had spoken about his former life to the fascination of the sisters, he in turn became eager to hear of Norfolk. And that was when Carmitha finally began to lose patience with her companions. Genevieve she could tolerate; the world as seen through the eyes of a twelve-(Earth)-year-old was fairly bizarre anyway, all enthusiasms and misunderstandings. But Louise, now; that brat was a different matter. Louise explained about the planet's economy being built around the export of Norfolk Tears, about how the founders had wisely chosen a pastoral life for their descendants, about how pretty the cities and towns were, how clean the countryside and the air were compared to industrialized worlds, how nice the people, how well organized the estates, how few criminals there were.

"It sounds as though you have achieved much that is worthy," Titreano said. "Norfolk is an enviable world in which to be born."

"There are some people who don't like it," Louise said. "But not very many." She looked down at Genevieve's head, cradled in her lap, and smiled gently. Her little sister had finally fallen asleep, rocked by the gentle rhythm of the caravan.

She smoothed locks of hair back from Genevieve's brow. It was dirty and unkempt, with strands shrivelled and singed from the fire in the stable. Mrs Charlsworth would have a fit of the vapours if she saw it thus. Landowner girls were supposed to be paragons of deportment at all times, Kavanagh girls especially.

Just thinking of the old woman, her sacrifice, threatened to bring the tears which had been so long delayed.

"Why don't you tell him the reason those dissidents don't like it here," Carmitha said.

"Who?" Louise asked.

"The Land Union people, the traders flung in jail for trying to sell medicine the rest of the Confederation takes for granted, the people who work the land, and all the other victims of the landowner class, me included."

Anger, tiredness, and despair spurted up together in Louise's skull, threatening to quench what was left of her fragile spirit. She was so very tired; but she had to keep going, had to look after Gen. Gen and the precious baby. Would she ever see Joshua again now? "Why are you saying this?" she asked jadedly.

"Because it's the truth. Not something a Kavanagh is used to, I'll warrant. Not from the likes of me."

"I know this world isn't perfect. I'm not blind, I'm not stupid."

"No, you know what to do to hang on to your privileges and your power. And look where it's got you. The whole planet being taken over, being taken away from you. Not so smart now, are you? Not so high and mighty."

"That's a wicked lie."

"Is it? A fortnight ago you rode your horse past me when I was working in one of your estate roseyards. Did you stop for a chat then? Did you even notice I existed?"

"Come now, ladies," Titreano said, uneasily.

But Louise couldn't ignore the challenge, the insult and the vile implication behind it. "Did you ask me to stop?" she demanded. "Did you want to hear me chat about the things I love and care about the most? Or were you too busy sneering at me? You with your righteous poverty. Because I'm rich I'm evil, that's what you think, isn't it?"

"Your family is, yes. Your ancestors made quite sure of that with their oppressive constitution. I was born on the road, and I'll die on it. I have no quarrel with that. But you condemned us to a circular road. It leads us nowhere, in an era when there is a chance to travel right into the heart of the galaxy. You shackled us as surely as any house would. I'll never see the wonder of sunrise and sunset on another planet."

"Your ancestors knew the constitution when they came here, and they still came. They saw the freedom it would give you to roam like you always have done, like you cannot do on Earth anymore."

"If that's freedom, then tell me why can't we leave?"

"You can. Anyone can. Just buy a ticket on a starship."

"Fat bloody chance. My entire family working a summer cupping season couldn't raise the price of one ticket. You control the economy, too. You designed it so we never earn more than a pittance."

"It's not my fault you can't think of anything other than grove work to do. You have a caravan, why don't you trade goods like a merchant? Or plant some rose groves of your own? There's still unsettled land on hundreds of islands."

"We're not a landowning people, we don't want to be tied down."

"Exactly," Louise shouted. "It's only your own stupid prejudices which trap you here. Not us, not the landowners. Yet we're the ones who you blame for your own inadequacies, just because you can't face up to the real truth. And don't think you're so unique. I want to see the whole Confederation, too. I dream about it every night. But I'll never be able to fly in a starship. I'll never be allowed, which is much worse than you. You made your own prison. I was born into mine. My obligations bind me to this world, I have to sacrifice my entire life for the good of this island."

"Oh, yes. How you noble Kavanaghs suffer so. How grateful I am." She glared at Louise, barely noticing Titreano, and not paying any attention to where the cob was trotting. "Tell me, little Miss Kavanagh, how many brothers and sisters do you think you have in your highborn family?"

"I have no brothers, there's only Genevieve."

"But what of the half-bloods?" Carmitha purred. "What of them?"

"Half-bloods? Don't be foolish. I have none."

She laughed bitterly. "So sure of yourself. Riding high above us all. Well I know of three, and those are just the ones born to my family. My cousin carried one to term after last midsummer. A bonny little boy, the spitting image of his father. Your father. You see, it isn't *all* work for him. There's pleasure, too. More than to be found in your mother's bed."

"Lies!" Louise cried. She felt faint, and sick.

"Really? He lay with me the day before the soldiers went to Boston. He got his money's worth of me. I made sure of that; I don't cheat people. So don't you talk to me about nobility and sacrifice. Your family are nothing more than titled robber barons."

Louise glanced down. Genevieve's eyes were open, blinking against the red light. Please don't let her have heard, Louise prayed. She turned to look at the Romany woman, no longer able to stop her jaw from quivering. There was no will to argue anymore. The day had won, beaten her, captured her parents, invaded her home, burned her county, terrorized her sister, and destroyed the only remaining fragment of happiness, that of the past with its golden memories. "If you wish to hurt a Kavanagh," she said in a tiny voice. "If you wish to see me in tears for what you claim has happened, then you may have that wish. I don't care about myself anymore. But spare my sister, she has been through so much today. No child should have to endure more. Let her go into the caravan where she can't hear your accusations. Please?" There was more to say, so much more, but the heat in her throat wouldn't let it come out. Louise started sobbing, hating herself for letting Gen see her weakness. But allowing the tears to flow was such an easy act.

Genevieve put her arms around her sister and hugged her fiercely. "Don't cry, Louise. Please don't cry." Her face puckered up. "I hate you," she spat at Carmitha.

"I hope you are satisfied now, lady," Titreano said curtly.

Carmitha stared at the two distraught sisters, Titreano's hard, disgusted face, then dropped the reins and plunged her head into her hands. The shame was beyond belief.

Shit, taking out your own pathetic fear on a petrified sixteen-year-old girl who'd never hurt a living soul in her life. Who'd actually risked her own neck to warn me about the possessed in the farmhouse.

"Louise." She extended an arm towards the still sobbing girl. "Oh, Louise, I'm so sorry. I never meant to say what I did. I'm so stupid, I never think." At least she managed to stop herself from asking "forgive me." Carry your own guilt, you selfish bitch, she told herself.

Titreano had put his own arm around Louise. It didn't make any difference to the broken girl. "My baby," Louise moaned between sobs. "They'll kill my baby if they catch us."

Titreano gently caught her hands. "You are . . . with child?"

"Yes!" Her sobbing became louder.

Genevieve gaped at her. "You're pregnant?"

Louise nodded roughly, long hair flopping about.

"Oh." A small smile twitched across Genevieve's mouth. "I won't tell anyone, I promise, Louise," she said seriously.

Louise gulped loudly and looked at her sister. Then she was laughing through her tears, clutching Genevieve to her. Genevieve hugged her back.

Carmitha tried not to show her own surprise. A landowner girl like Louise, the highest of the high, pregnant and unmarried! I wonder who . . .

"Okay," she said with slow determination. "That's another reason to get you two girls off this island. The best yet." The sisters were regarding her with immense distrust. Can't blame them for that. She ploughed on: "I swear to you here and now, Titreano and I will make sure you get on the plane. Right, Titreano?"

"Indeed, yes," he said gravely.

"Good." Carmitha picked up the cob's reins again and gave them a brisk flip. The horse resumed its interminable plodding pace.

One good act, she thought, a single piece of decency amid the holocaust of the last six hours. That baby was going to survive. Grandma, if you're watching me, and if you can help the living in any way possible, now would be a good time.

And—the thought wouldn't leave her alone—a boy who wasn't intimidated by Grant Kavanagh, who'd dared to touch his precious daughter. A lot more than just touch, in fact. Foolhardy romantic, or a real hero prince?

Carmitha risked a quick glance at Louise. Either way, lucky girl.

• • •

The longbase van which nosed down into the third sub-level car park below City Hall had the stylized palm tree and electron orbit logo of the Tarosa Metamech Corp emblazoned on its sides. It drew up in a bay next to a service elevator. Six men and two women climbed out, all wearing the company's dull red overalls. Three flatbed trolleys, piled high with crates and maintenance equipment, trundled down obediently out of the rear of the van.

One of the men walked over to the elevator and pulled a processor block out of his pocket. He typed something on the block's surface, paused, then typed again, casting a nervous glance at his impassive workmates as they watched him.

The building management processor array accepted the coded instruction which the block had datavised, and the elevator doors hissed open.

Emmet Mordden couldn't help the way his shoulders sagged in sheer relief as soon as the doors started to move. In his past life he'd suffered from a weak bladder, and it seemed as though he'd brought the condition with him to the body he now possessed. Certainly his guts were dangerously wobbly. Being in on the hard edge of operations always did that to him. He was strictly a background tech; until, of course, the day in 2535 when his syndicate boss got greedy, and sloppy with it. The police claimed afterwards that they'd given the gang an opportunity to surrender, but by then Emmet Mordden was past caring.

He shoved the processor block back into his overalls pocket while he brought out his palm-sized tool-kit. Interesting to see how technology had advanced in the intervening seventy-five years; the principles were the same, but circuitry and programs were considerably more sophisticated.

A key from the tool-kit opened the cover over the elevator's small emergency manual control panel. He plugged an optical cable into the interface socket, and the processor block lit up with a simple display. The unit took eight seconds to decode the elevator monitor program commands and disable the alarm.

"We're in," he told the others, and unplugged the optical cable. The more basic the electronic equipment, the more chance it had of operating in proximity to possessed bodies. By reducing the processor block functions to an absolute minimum he'd found he could make it work, although he still fretted about the efficiency.

Al Capone slapped him on the shoulder as the rest of the work crew and the flatbeds squeezed into the elevator. "Good work there, Emmet. I'm proud of you, boy."

Emmet gave a fragile grin of gratitude, and pressed the DOOR CLOSE button. He respected the resolve which Al had bestowed on the group of possessed. There had been so much bickering before about how to go about turning more bodies over for possession. It was as though they'd spent ninety per cent of their time arguing among themselves and jockeying for position. The only agreements they ever came to were grudgingly achieved.

Then Al had come along and explained as coolly as you like that he was taking charge now thank you very much. Somehow it didn't surprise Emmet that a man who displayed such clarity of purpose and thought would have the greatest energistic strength. Two people had objected. And the little stick held so nonchalantly in Al Capone's hand had grown to a full-sized baseball bat.

Nobody else had voiced any dissension after that. And the beauty of it was, the dissenters could hardly go running to the cops.

Emmet wasn't sure which he feared the most, Al's strength or his temper. But he was just a soldier who obeyed orders, and happy with it. If only Al hadn't insisted he come with them this morning.

"Top floor," Al said.

Emmet pressed the appropriate button. The elevator rose smoothly.

"Okay, guys, now remember with our strength we can always blast our way out if anything goes wrong," Al said. "But this is our big chance to consolidate our hold over this town in one easy move. If we get rumbled, it's gonna be tough from here on. So let's try and stick to what we planned, right?"

"Absolutely, Al," Bernhard Allsop said eagerly. "I'm with you all the way."

Several of the others gave him barely disguised glances of contempt.

Al ignored them all, and smiled heartily. Je-zus, but this felt good; starting out with nothing again apart from his ambition. But this time he knew the moves to make in advance. The others in the group had filled him in on chunks of history from the last few centuries. The New California administration was a direct descendant of the old U.S. of A government. The feds. And Al had one or two old scores to settle with those bastards.

The elevator doors chimed gently as they opened on the one hundred and fiftieth floor. Dwight Salerno and Patricia Mangano were out first. They smiled at the three staff members who were in the corridor and killed them with a single coordinated blast of white fire. Smoking bodies hit the floor.

"We're okay, they didn't get out an alarm," Emmet said, consulting his processor block.

"Get to it, people," Al told his team proudly. This wasn't the same as the times with his soldiers like Anselmi and Scalise back on Cicero's streets. But these new guys had balls, and a cause. And it felt righteous to be a mover again.

The possessed spread out through the top floor. Tarosa Metamech uniforms gave way to clothes of their own periods. A startlingly unpleasant variety of weapons appeared in their hands. Doors were forced open with precisely applied bolts of white fire, rooms searched according to the list. Everyone following their assignment to the letter. Capone's letter.

It was six o'clock in the morning in San Angeles, and few of the mayor's staff were at work. Those that had turned up early found Retros bursting into their offices and hauling them out at gunpoint. Their neural nanonics failed, desktop blocks crashed, net processors wouldn't respond. There was no way to get a warning out, no way to cry for help. They found themselves corralled in the deputy health director's office, seventeen of them, clinging together in panic and mutual misery.

They thought that would surely be the worst of it, crammed into the one room for hours or maybe a couple of days while negotiations for their release were conducted with the terrorists. But then the Retros started taking them out one at a time, summoning the toughest first. The sound of screams cut back clean through the thick door.

Al Capone stood by the long window wall of the mayor's office, and looked out at the city. It was a magnificent view. He couldn't remember being so high off the ground in his life before. This skyscraper made the Empire State Building look puny for God's sake. And it wasn't even the tallest in the city.

The skyscrapers only occupied the central portion of San Angeles, fifty or sixty of them bunched together to form the business, finance, and administration district. Beyond that the vast urban sprawl clung to the shallow folds of the land, long grey lines of buildings and autoways, interspaced with the equally regular squares of green parks. And to the east was the brilliant glimmer of the ocean.

Al, who had always enjoyed Lake Michigan in the summer, was fascinated by the glistening turquoise expanse as it reflected the first light of a new day. And the city was so clean, vibrant. So different from Chicago. This was an empire which Stalin and Genghis Khan would both envy.

Emmet knocked on the door, and popped his head around when he didn't receive an answer. "Sorry to bother you, Al," he ventured cautiously.

"That's okay, boy," Al said. "What've you got for me?"

"We've rounded up everyone on this floor. The electronics are all fucked, so they can't get word out. Bernhard and Luigi have started to bring them to possession."

"Great, you've all done pretty goddamn good."

"Thanks, Al."

"What about the rest of the electrics, the telephones and math-machine things?"

"I'm getting my systems plugged into the building network now, Al. Give me half an hour and I should have it locked down safe."

"Good. Can we go to stage two?"

"Sure, Al."

"Okay, boy, you get back to your wiring."

Emmet backed out of the office. Al wished he knew more about electrics himself. This future world depended so much on their clever mini-machines. That had to be a flaw. And Al Capone knew all about exploiting such weaknesses.

He let his mind slip into that peculiar state of otherness, and felt around for the rest of the possessed under his command. They were positioned all around the base of City Hall, strolling casually down the sidewalk, in cars parked nearby, eating breakfast in arcade diners.

Come, he commanded.

And the big ground floor doors of City Hall opened wide.

It was quarter to nine when Mayor Avram Harwood III arrived in his office. He was in a good mood. Today was the first day in a week when he hadn't been bombarded with early morning datavises from his staff concerning the Retro crisis. In fact there hadn't been any communication from City Hall at all. Some kind of record.

He took the express elevator from his private car bay up to the top floor, and stepped out into a world which wasn't quite normal. Nothing he could clarify, but definitely wrong. People scurried past as usual, barely pausing to acknowledge him. The elevator doors remained open behind him, the lights inside dying. When he tried to datavise its control processor there was no response. Attempting to log a routine call to maintenance he found none of the net processors were working.

Damn it, that was all he needed, a total electronics failure. At least it explained why he hadn't received any messages.

He walked into his office to find a young, olive-skinned

man lounging in his chair, a fat soft stick in his mouth with one end on fire. And his clothes . . . Retro!

Mayor Harwood spun around, ready to make a dash for the door. It was no good. Three of them had moved in to block the opening. They were all dressed in the same kind of antique double-breasted suits, brown hats with broad rims, and carrying primitive automatic rifles with circular magazines.

He tried to datavise a citizen's distress call. But his neural nanonics crashed, neatly tabulated icons retreated from his mind's eye like cowardly ghosts.

"Sit down, Mr Mayor," Al Capone said munificently. "You and I have some business to discuss."

"I think not."

The Thompson's butt slammed into the small of Avram Harwood's back. He let out a cry at the pain, and the world went dizzyingly black for a second. One of his big armchairs hit the back of his legs, and he fell down into the cushions, clutching at his spine.

"You see?" Al asked. "You ain't calling the shots no more. Best you cooperate."

"The police will be here soon. And, mister, when they arrive they are going to fillet you and your gang. Don't think I'll help you negotiate, the commissioner knows my policy on hostage situations. No surrender."

Al winked broadly. "I like you, Avvy. I do. I admire a man who stands up for himself. I knew you wouldn't be no patsy. It takes smarts to get to the top in a city like this, and plenty of them. So why don't you have a word with that commissioner of yours. Clear the air some." He beckoned.

Avram Harwood twisted around as Police Commissioner Vosburgh walked into the office.

"Hi there, Mr Mayor," Vosburgh said blithely.

"Rod! Oh, Christ, they got you too . . ." The words shrank as Vosburgh's familiar face *twisted*. A feral-faced stranger sneered down at him; hair was visibly sprouting out of his cheeks. Not a beard, more like thick prickly fur.

"Yeah, they got me too." The voice was distorted by teeth which were too long for a human mouth. He burst into a wild laugh.

"Who the hell are you Retro people?" an aghast Avram Harwood asked.

"The dead," Al said. "We've come back."

"Bullshit."

"I ain't arguing with you. Like I told you, I'm here to make a proposition. One of my guys—comes from just after my time—he said people took to calling it an offer you can't refuse. I like that, it's great. And that's what I'm making here to you, Avvy, my boy. An offer you can't refuse."

"What offer?"

"It's like this: Souls ain't the only thing I'm resurrecting today. I'm gonna build up an Organization. Like I had me before, only with a shitload more clout. I want you to join it, join me. Just as you are. No catch; you have my word. You, your family, maybe a few close friends, they don't get possessed. I know how to reward loyalty."

"You're crazy. You're absolutely berserkoid. Join you? I'm going to see you destroyed, all of you deviant bastards, and then I'm going to stamp on the pieces."

Al leaned forwards and rested his elbows on the desk, staring earnestly at the mayor. "Sorry, Avvy. That's one thing you ain't gonna do. No fucking way. See, people hear my name, and they think I'm just a bigshot hoodlum, a racketeer who made good. Wrong. I used to be a fucking king. King Capone the first. I got the politics tied up. So I know which strings to pull in City Hall and the precinct houses. I know how a city works. That's why I'm here. I'm launching the biggest heist there's ever been in all of history."

"What?"

"I'm gonna steal your world, Avvy. Take the whole caboodle from under your nose. These guys you see here, the ones you called Retros, they didn't know what the Christ they were doing before. Because just between you and me shutting off the sky like it's some kind of window with thick drapes is a bit of a wacko idea, you know? So I've straightened them out. No more of that bullshit. Now we're playing straight hardball."

Avram Harwood lowered his head. "Oh, Christ." They were insane. Utterly demented. He began to wonder if he would see his family again.

"Let me lay it out for you here, Avvy. You don't take over a society from the bottom like the Retros were trying to do. You know, little bit at a time until you're in the majority. Know why that's a crappy way to get on top? Because the goddamn self-righteous majority is gonna find out and fight like fuck to stop you. And they get led by people like you, Avvy. You're the generals, the dangerous ones, you organize the lawyers and the cops and the special federal agents to stop it happening. To protect the majority that elects you from anything which threatens you or them. So instead of an assways first revolution, you do what I'm doing. You start at the top and work down." Al got up and walked over to the window wall. He gestured at the street far below with his cigar. "People are coming into City Hall, Avvy. The workers, the police captains, the attorneys, your staff, tax clerks. All of them; the ones who'd lead the fight against me if they knew what I was. Yeah. They're coming in, but they ain't going out again. Not until we've made our pitch to each and every one of them." Al turned to see Avram Harwood staring at him in horror. "That's the way it is, Avvy," he said softly. "My people, they're working their way up from the ground floor. They're coming all the way up here. And all the people sitting in their offices who would normally fight against me—why, they're going to be the ones who lead our crusade out into the world. Ain't that right, guys?"

"You got it, Al," Emmet Mordden said. He was hunched over a couple of processor blocks at one end of the desk, monitoring the operation. "The first twelve floors are all ours now. And we're busy converting everyone on thirteen to eighteen. I make that approximately six and a half thousand people possessed so far this morning."

"See?" Al waved his cigar expansively. "It's already begun, Avvy. Ain't nothing you can do about it. By lunch I'm gonna own the entire city administration. Just like the old days when Big Bill Thompson was in my pocket. And I got even bigger plans for tomorrow."

"It won't work," Avram Harwood whispered. "It can't work."

"Course it will, Avvy. The thing is . . . returned souls. They ain't altogether marbles intacto. *Capisce*? It's not just an Organization I'm building. Shit. We can be honest in here, you and me. It's a whole new government for New California. I need people who can help me run it. I need people who can run the factory machines. I need people who can keep the lights on and the water flowing, who're gonna take the garbage away. Fuck, if all that goes down the pan, my citizens, they're gonna come gunning for me, right? I mean, that's what the Retros didn't think about. What happens after? You still gotta keep things running smoothly." Al sat on the arm of Avram Harwood's comfy chair and put a friendly arm around his shoulder. "Which is where you come in, Mr Mayor. Plenty of people want to run it. Everyone in this room, they all want to be my lieutenants. But it's the old problem. Sure they're keen, but they ain't got the talent. But you, you my boy, you have got the talent. So how about it? Same job as before. Better salary. Perks. Fancy girl or two on the side if you like. So what do you say? Huh, Avvy? Say yeah. Make me happy."

"Never."

"What? What was that, Avvy? I didn't hear too good."

"I said NEVER, you psychopathic freak."

Very calmly, Al rose to his feet. "I ask. I go down on my fucking knees and ask you to help me. I ask you to be my friend. You, a wiseass I ain't never even seen before. I open my goddamn heart to you. I'm bleeding across the floor for you here. And you say no? No. To me!" Three scars burned hot and bright on his cheek. Everyone else in the office had retreated into a daunted silence.

"Is that what you're saying, Avvy? No?"

"You got it, shithead," Avram Harwood shouted recklessly. Something wild was running free in his brain, a mad glee at confounding his adversary. "The answer is never. Never. Never."

"Wrong." Al flicked his cigar onto the thick carpet. "You got it way wrong, buddy. The answer is yes. It is always yes when you talk to me. It is yes fucking please Mr Capone Sir. And I'm going to fucking well hear you say it." A fist thumped on his chest for emphasis. "Today is the day you say yes to me."

Mayor Avram Harwood took one look at the stained baseball bat which had materialized in Al Capone's hands, and knew it was going to be *bad*.

* * *

Duke-dawn failed. There was no sign of the primary sun's comforting white light brushing the short night before it as the bright disk rose above the wolds. Instead, a miscreant coral phosphorescence glided out over the horizon, staining the vegetation a lustreless claret.

For a harrowingly confused moment Louise thought that Duchess was returning, racing around the underside of the planet after it had set scant minutes ago to spring up ahead of the lumbering Romany caravan. But after a minute's scrutiny she realized the effect was due to a high haze of reddish mist. It really was Duke which had risen.

"What is it?" Genevieve inquired querulously. "What's wrong?"

"I'm not sure." Louise scanned the horizon, leaning around the corner of the caravan to check behind them. "It looks like a layer of fog really high up, but why is it that colour? I've never seen anything like it before."

"Well I don't like it," Genevieve announced, and folded her arms across her chest. She glared ahead.

"Do you know what's doing that?" Carmitha asked Titreano.

"Not entirely, my lady," he said, appearing troubled. "And yet, I sense there is a rightness to it. Do you not feel comforted by its presence?"

"No I bloody don't," Carmitha snapped. "It's not natural, and you know it."

"Yes, lady."

His subdued acknowledgement did nothing to alleviate her nerves. Terror, uncertainty, lack of sleep, not having eaten since yesterday, remorse, it was all starting to add up.

The caravan trundled on for another half a mile under the brightening red light. Carmitha steered them along a well-worn track below a forest. Here, the land's gentle undulations were gradually increasing to form deeper vales and rolling hills. Dried up streambeds crisscrossed the slopes, emptying into the deeper gullies which ran along the floor of each valley. There was more woodland than out on the open wolds, more cover from, and for, prying eyes. All they had to go on was Titreano's strange sixth sense.

Nobody spoke, too tired or too fearful. Louise realized the birds were missing from the air. The characterless forest loomed up like a shaggy cliff face mere yards away, bleak and repellent.

"Here we are," Carmitha said as they rounded a curve in the track. It had taken longer than she thought. Eight hours at least. Not good for poor old Olivier.

Ahead of them the slope dipped down to expose a broad valley with heavily forested sides. The alluvial floor was a chessboard of neat fields, all marked out by long dry-stone walls and geneered hawthorn hedges. A dozen streams bubbling out from the head of the valley funnelled into a small river which meandered off into the distance. Red sunlight glinted off a narrow sliver of water running along the centre of its baked clay banks.

Bytham was situated about three miles down the valley; a cluster of stone cottages split in half by the river. Over the centuries the community had grown outwards from a single humpbacked stone bridge. At the far end, a narrow church spire rose above the thatched roofs.

"It looks all right," Louise said cautiously. "I can't see any fires."

"Quiet enough," Carmitha agreed. She hardly dared consult Titreano. "Are your kind out there?" she asked.

His eyes were closed, yet his head was thrust forwards, as though he were sniffing the air ahead. "Some of them," he said, regretfully. "But not all of the village has been turned. Not yet. People are wakening to the fact that great evil stalks this land." He glanced at Louise. "Where is your aerial machine berthed?"

She blushed. "I don't know. I've never been here before." She didn't like to admit that apart from accompanying Mother on a twice-yearly train trip to Boston for a clothes-buying spree she'd hardly ever ventured outside Cricklade's sprawling boundaries.

Carmitha pointed to a circular meadow half a mile outside

the town, with two modest hangars on the perimeter. "That's the aerodrome. And thank God it's on this side of the village."

"I suggest we make haste, lady," Titreano said.

Still not quite trusting him, Carmitha nodded reluctantly. "One minute." She stood up and hurried back into the caravan. Inside, it was a complete mess. All her possessions had been slung about by her madcap dash from Colsterworth, clothes, pots and pans, food, books. She sighed at the shards of broken blue and white china lying underfoot. Her mother always claimed the crockery had come with the family from Earth.

The heavy chest under her bed was one article which hadn't moved. Carmitha knelt down and spun the combination lock.

Louise gave the Romany woman an alarmed look when she emerged from the caravan. She was carrying a single-barrelled shotgun and a belt of cartridges.

"Pump action," Carmitha said. "It holds ten rounds. I've already loaded it for you. Safety's on. You hold it, get used to the weight."

"Me?" Louise gulped in surprise.

"Yes, you. Who knows what's waiting for us down there. You must have used a shotgun before?"

"Well, yes. Of course. But only on birds, and tree rats, and things. I'm not a very good shot, I'm afraid."

"Don't worry. Just point it in the general direction of any trouble, and shoot." She gave Titreano a dry grin. "I'd give it to you, but it's rather advanced compared to the kind of guns you had in your day. Better Louise carries it."

"As you wish, my lady."

Now that Duke was higher in the sky it was doing its best to burn away the red mist which hung over the land. Occasionally a beam of pure white sunlight would wash over the caravan, making all four of them blink from its glare. But for the most part, the veil remained unbroken.

The caravan reached the valley floor, and Carmitha urged the cob into a faster trot. Olivier did his best to oblige, but his reserves of strength were clearly ebbing.

As they drew nearer to the village they heard the church

bell tolling. It was no glad peal calling the faithful to morning service, just a monotonous strike. A warning.

"The villagers know," Titreano announced. "My kind are grouping together. They are stronger that way."

"If you know what they're doing, do they know about you?" Carmitha asked.

"Yes, lady, I would fear so."

"Oh, just wonderful." The road ahead was now angling away from the direction in which the aerodrome lay. Carmitha stood on the seat, and tried to work out where to turn off. The hedges and walls of the fields were spread out before her like a maze. "Bugger," she muttered under her breath. Both of the aerodrome's hangars were clearly visible about half a mile away, but you'd have to be a local to know how to get to them.

"Do they know we're with you?" Carmitha asked.

"Probably not. Not over such a distance. But when we are closer to the village, they will know."

Genevieve tugged anxiously at Titreano's sleeve. "They won't find us, will they? You won't let them?"

"Of course not, little one. I gave my word I will not abandon you."

"I don't like this at all," Carmitha said. "We're too visible. And when they realize there's four of us riding on it, your side is going to know you're travelling with non-possessed," she said accusingly to Titreano.

"We can't turn around now," Louise insisted, her voice high and strained. "We're so close. We'll never have another chance."

Carmitha wanted to add that there might not even be a pilot at the aerodrome; come to that she hadn't actually seen the distinctive shape of the aeroambulance itself yet. Could be in a hangar. But with the way their luck was turning out right now . . .

Both the sisters were obviously near the end of their tether. They looked dreadful, filthy and tired, close to breaking down in tears—for all Louise's outward determination.

Carmitha was surprised to realize just how much she had begun to respect the elder girl.

"You can't go back, no," Carmitha said. "But I can. If I take the caravan back to the woods the possessed will think we're all running away from Titreano here."

"No!" Louise said in shock. "We're together now. We've only got each other. There's only us left in the whole world."

"We are not all that's left. Don't ever think that. Outside Kesteven, people are going about their lives just like before. And once you get to Norwich, they'll be warned."

"No," Louise mumbled. But there was less conviction now.

"You know you have to go," Carmitha continued. "But me. Hell, I'll be a lot better off by myself. With my lore I can lose myself in the forests; the possessed will never find me. I can't do that with you three tagging along. You know us Romanies belong with the land, girl."

The corners of Louise's mouth turned down.

"Don't you?" Carmitha said sternly. She knew she was still being selfish; just plain didn't want to admit she couldn't stand seeing their delicate hopes burnt to cinders when they reached the aerodrome.

"Yes," Louise said docilely.

"Good girl. Okay, this section of road is wide enough to turn the caravan around. You three had better get down."

"Are you sure of this, lady?" Titreano asked.

"Absolutely. But I'm holding you to your promise of guarding these two."

He nodded sincerely and dropped down over the side.

"Genevieve?"

The little girl glanced up shyly, her lower lip pressed against her teeth.

"I know we didn't get on too well, and I'm sorry we didn't. But I want you to have this." Carmitha reached behind her neck and unfastened the pendant's chain. The silver bulb which glinted in the pink light was made from a fine mesh, much dinted now; but through the grid a filigree of thin brown twigs was just visible. "It used to be my grandma's; she gave it to me when I was about your age. It's a charm to ward off evil spirits. That's lucky heather inside, see? Genuine heather; it grew on Earth in the time before the armada storms. There's real earth magic stored in there."

Genevieve held the bauble up in front of her face, studying it intently. A fast smile lit up her delicate features, and she lunged forward to hug Carmitha. "Thank you," she whispered. "Thank you for everything." She climbed down into Titreano's arms.

Carmitha gave an edgy smile to Louise. "Sorry it turned out the way it did, girl."

"That's all right."

"Hardly. Don't lose faith in your father because of what I said."

"I won't. I love Daddy."

"Yes, I expect you do. That's good, something to hold on to. You are going to be facing a few more dark days yet, you know."

Louise started tugging at a ring on her left hand. "Here. It's not much. Not lucky, or anything special. But it is gold, and that's a real diamond. If you need to buy anything, it'll help."

Carmitha eyed the ring in surprise. "Right. Next time I need a mansion I'll remember."

They both grinned sheepishly.

"Take care, Carmitha. I want to see you when I come back, when all this is over." Louise twisted around, preparing to climb down.

"Louise."

There was such disquiet in the voice that Louise froze.

"There's something wrong about Titreano," Carmitha said quietly. "I don't know if I'm just being paranoid, but you ought to know before you go any further with him."

A minute later Louise clambered gingerly down the side of the caravan, keeping hold of the pump-action shotgun, the cartridge belt an uncomfortable weight around her hips. When she was on the dirt track she waved up at Carmitha. The Romany waved back and flicked the cob's reins.

Louise, Genevieve, and Titreano watched the caravan turn around and head back up the rucked road.

"Are you all right, Lady Louise?" Titreano asked courteously.

Her fingers tightened around the shotgun. Then she took a breath and smiled at him. "I think so."

They struck out for the aerodrome, scrambling through ditches and over hedges. The fields were mostly ploughed, ready for the second cereal crop, difficult to walk on. Dust puffed up from each footfall.

Louise glanced over at Genevieve, who was wearing Carmitha's pendant outside her torn and dusty blouse, one hand grasping the silver bulb tightly. "Not long now," she said.

"I know," Genevieve replied pertly. "Louise, will they have something to eat on the aeroambulance?"

"I expect so."

"Good! I'm starving." She trudged on for another few paces, then cocked her head to one side. "Titreano, you're not dirty at all," she exclaimed in a vexed tone.

Louise looked over. It was true; not a scrap of dirt or dust had adhered to his blue jacket.

He glanced down at himself, rubbing his hands along the seams of his trousers in a nervous gesture. "I'm sorry, little one, it must be the fabric. Although I do confess, I don't remember being immune to such depredations before. Perhaps I should bow to the inevitable."

Louise watched in some consternation as mud stains crept up from his ankles, discolouring his trousers below the knee. "You mean you can change your appearance whenever you want?" she asked.

"It would seem so, Lady Louise."

"Oh."

Genevieve giggled. "You mean you want to look all silly like that?"

"I find it . . . comfortable, little one. Yes."

"If you can change that easily, I think you ought to adopt something which will blend in a bit better," Louise said. "I mean, Gen and I look like a pair of tramps. And then there's you in all your strange finery. What would you think of us if you were one of the aeroambulance crew?"

"Finely argued, lady."

For the next five minutes as they crossed the fields Titreano went through a series of alterations. Genevieve and Louise kept up a stream of suggestions, arguing hotly, and explaining textures and styles to their mildly befuddled companion. When they finished he was dressed in the fashion of a young estate manager, with fawn cord trousers, calf-length boots, a tweed jacket, check shirt, and grey cap.

"Just right," Louise declared.

"I thank you, lady." He doffed his cap and bowed low.

Genevieve clapped delightedly.

Louise stopped at another of the interminable walls and found a gap in the stone to shove her boot toe in. Straddling the top of the wall she could see the aerodrome's perimeter fence two hundred yards away. "Almost there," she told the others cheerfully.

The Bytham aerodrome appeared to be deserted. Both hangars were closed up; nobody was in the control tower. Away on the other side of the mown field the row of seven cottages used by station personnel were silent and dark.

The only sound was the persistent clang of the church bell in the village. It hadn't stopped ringing the whole time they had walked across the fields.

Louise peered around the side of the first hangar, clutching at the shotgun. Nothing moved. A couple of tractors and a farm ranger were parked outside a small access door. "Are there any possessed here?" she whispered to Titreano.

"No," he whispered back.

"What about normal people?"

His brown face creased in concentration. "Several. I hear them over in yon houses. Five or six are malingering inside this second barn."

"Hangar," Louise corrected. "We call them hangars nowadays."

"Yes, lady."

"Sorry."

They swapped a nervous grin.

"I suppose we'd better go and see them, then," she said. "Come here, Gen." She pointed the shotgun at the ground and took her sister's hand as they walked towards the second hangar.

She really wished Carmitha hadn't given her the weapon. Yet at the same time it imbued her with an uncommon sense of confidence. Even though she doubted she could ever actually fire it at anyone.

"They have seen us," Titreano said quietly.

Louise scanned the corrugated panel wall of the hangar. A narrow line of windows ran the entire length. She thought she saw a shiver of motion behind one. "Hello?" she called loudly.

There was no reply.

She walked right up to the door and knocked firmly. "Hello, can you hear me?" She tried the handle, only to discover it was locked.

"Now what?" she asked Titreano.

"Hey!" Genevieve shouted at the door. "I'm hungry."

The handle turned, and the door opened a crack. "Who the hell are you people?" a man asked.

Louise drew herself up as best she could manage, knowing full well what she must look like to anyone inside. "I am Louise Kavanagh, the heir of Cricklade, this is my sister Genevieve, and William Elphinstone, one of our estate managers."

Genevieve opened her mouth to protest, but Louise nudged her with a toe.

"Oh, really?" came the answer from behind the door.

"Yes!"

"It is her," said another, deeper voice. The door opened wide to show two men gazing out at them. "I recognize her. I used to work at Cricklade."

"Thank you," Louise said.

"Until your father fired me."

Louise didn't know whether to burst into tears or just shoot him on the spot.

"Let them in, Duggen," a woman called. "The little girl looks exhausted. And this is no day to settle old grudges."

Duggen shrugged and moved aside.

A line of dusty windows was the sole source of illumination inside. The aeroambulance was a hulking dark presence in the middle of the concrete floor. Three people were standing below the plane's narrow, pointed nose; the woman who had spoken, and a pair of five-year-old twin girls. She introduced herself as Felicia Cantrell, her daughters were Ellen and Tammy; her husband Ivan was an aeroambulance pilot, the man who had opened the door. "And Duggen you already know, or at least he knows you."

Ivan Cantrell took a vigilant look out of the hangar door before closing it. "So would you like to tell us what you're doing here, Louise? And what happened to you?"

It took her over fifteen minutes to produce a patched-up explanation which satisfied them. All the time guarding her tongue from uttering the word possession, and mentioning who Titreano really was. As she realized, those two items would have got her ejected from the hangar in no time at all. Yet at the same time she was pleased with her white lies; the Louise who had woken to a normal world yesterday would have just blurted the truth and imperiously demanded they do something about it. This must be growing up, after a fashion.

"The Land Union with modern energy weapons?" Duggen mused sceptically when she was finished.

"I think so," Louise said. "That's what everyone said."

He looked as if he was about to object when Genevieve said: "Listen."

Louise couldn't hear a thing. "What?" she asked.

"The church bells, they've stopped."

Duggen and Ivan went over to the windows and looked out.

"Are they coming?" Louise mouthed to Titreano.

He nodded his head surreptitiously.

"Please," she appealed to Ivan. "You have to fly us out of here."

"I don't know about that, Miss Kavanagh. I don't have the authority. And we don't really know what's happening in the village. Perhaps I ought to check with the constable first."

"Please! If you're worried about your job, don't be. My family will protect you."

He sucked in his breath, blatantly unhappy.

"Ivan," Felicia said. She stared straight at him, pointing significantly to the twins. "Whatever is going on, this is no place for children to be. The capital will be safe if anywhere is."

"Oh, hell. All right, Miss Kavanagh. You win. Get in. We'll all go."

Duggen started to open the big sliding doors at the end of the hangar, allowing a thick beam of pink-tinted sunlight to strike the aeroambulance. The plane was an imported Kulu Corporation SCV-659 civil utility, a ten-seater VTOL supersonic with a near global range.

"It has the essence of a bird," Titreano murmured, his face gently intoxicated. "But with the strength of a bull. What magic."

"Are you going to be all right inside?" Louise asked anxiously.

"Oh, yes, Lady Louise. This is a voyage to be prized beyond mountains of gold. To be granted this opportunity I shall give full praise to the Lord tonight."

She coughed uncomfortably. "Right. Okay, we'd better get in; up that stairs on the other side, see?"

They followed Felicia and the twins up the airstairs. The plane's narrow cabin had been customized for its ambulance role, with a pair of stretchers and several cabinets of medical equipment. There were only two seats, which the twins used. Genevieve, Titreano, and Louise wound up sitting together on one of the stretcher couches. Louise checked the safety on the shotgun once again and wedged it below her feet. Surprisingly, no one had objected to her carrying it on board.

"This is all we need," Ivan called back from the pilot's seat as he started to run through the preflight checklist. "I've got half a dozen systems failures showing."

"Any critical?" Duggen asked as he closed the hatch.

"We'll survive."

Felicia opened one of the cabinets and handed Genevieve a bar of chocolate. The girl tore the wrapper off and sat munching it with a huge contented smile.

If she craned forwards, Louise could just see the windscreen beyond Ivan. The plane was rolling forwards out of the hangar.

"There are some houses on fire in the village," the pilot exclaimed. "And some people running down the road towards us. Hang on."

There was a sudden surge in the bee-hum from the fans, and the cabin rocked. They were airborne within seconds, climbing at a shallow angle. The only thing visible through the windscreen were daubs of insubstantial pink cloud.

"I hope Carmitha is all right down there," Louise said guiltily.

"I feel certain she will remain free from harm, lady. And it gladdens me that you resolved your quarrel with her. I admire you for that, my lady Louise."

She knew her cheeks would be blushing, she could feel the heat. Hopefully the smears of mud and dust would be veiling the fact. "Carmitha said something to me before she left. Something about you. It was a question. A good one."

"Ah. I did wonder what passed between you. If you care to ask, I will answer with such honesty as I own."

"She wanted me to ask where you really came from."

"But, Lady Louise, I have spoken nothing but the truth to you in this matter."

"Not quite. Norfolk is an English-ethnic planet; so we do learn something of our heritage in school. I know that the England of what you say is your time was a pure Anglo-Saxon culture."

"Yes?"

"Yes. And Titreano is not an English name. Not at that time. After that possibly, when immigration began in later centuries. But if you had been born in Cumbria in 1764 as you claim, that could not be your name."

"Oh, lady, forgive me any mistrust I have inadvertently caused you. Titreano is not the name I was born with. However, it is the one I lived with in my latter years. It is the closest rendering the island people I adopted could come to my family name."

"And that is?"

The dignity vanished from his handsome features, leaving only sorrow. "Christian, my lady Louise. I was baptized Fletcher Christian, and was proud to be named so. In that I must now be alone, for I have brought naught but shame to my family ever since. I am a mutineer, you see."

4

Ralph Hiltch was gratified and relieved by the speed with which Ombey's senior administration reacted to what they'd taken to calling the Mortonridge crisis. The people at Hub One were joined by the full complement of the Privy Council security committee. This time Princess Kirsten herself was sitting at the head of the table in the white bubble room, relegating Admiral Farquar to a position adjacent to her. The tabletop mutated into a detailed map showing the top half of Mortonridge; the four towns which the rogue Longhound bus had visited—Marble Bar, Rainton, Gaslee, and Exnall—glinted a macabre blood-red above the rumpled foothills. Flurries of symbols flickered and winked around each of them, electronic armies harassing their foes.

Once the last of Moyce's delivery lorries had been tracked down and eliminated, Diana Tiernan switched the entire capacity of the AIs to analysing vehicles that had left the four towns, and stopping them. In one respect they were fortunate: it was midnight along Mortonridge, the volume of traffic was much reduced from its daytime peak. Identification was reasonably easy. Deciding what to do about both cars and towns was less so.

It took twenty minutes of debate, arbitrated by the Princess, before they thrashed out an agreed policy. In the end, the deciding factor was Gerald Skibbow's completed personality debrief which was datavised down from Guyana. Dr Riley Dobbs appeared before the committee to testify its provenance; an apprehensive man, telling the planetary rulers that they were being assaulted by the dead reborn. But it did provide the justification, or spur, necessary for the kind of action which Ralph was pressing for. And even he sat through

Dobbs's report in a state of cold incredulity. If I'd made a mistake, shown a single gram of weakness . . .

The expanded security committee decided that all ground vehicles which had left the Mortonridge towns were to be directed to three separate holding areas established along the M6 by the police AT Squads. Refusal to comply would result in instantaneous SD fire. Once at the holding area, they would be required to wait in their vehicles until the authorities were ready to test them for possession. Failure to remain in the vehicle would result in the police AT Squads opening fire.

For the towns, a complete martial law curfew was to be effected immediately, no vehicular traffic or pedestrians allowed. Low orbit SD sensor satellites would scan the streets constantly in conjunction with the local police patrols. Anyone found disobeying the prohibition would be given exactly one opportunity to surrender. Weapons engagement authorization was granted to all the police personnel responsible for enforcing the curfew order.

At first light tomorrow the operation to evacuate the four towns would begin. Now that Diana Tiernan and the AIs were reasonably satisfied that no possessed were left anywhere else on the continent, Princess Kirsten agreed to dispatch marine troops from Guyana to assist with the evacuation. All Xingu police reserves would be called in, and together with the marines they would encircle the towns. Squads would then move in to conduct a house-to-house examination. Non-possessed members of the population were to be escorted out and flown on military transports to a Royal Navy ground base north of Pasto where they would be housed for the immediate future.

As for the possessed, they would be given a stark choice: release the body or face imprisonment in zero-tau. No exceptions.

"I think that covers everything," Admiral Farquar said.

"You'd better make it clear to the marine commanders that they're not to use assault mechanoids under any circumstances," Ralph said. "In fact, the more primitive the systems they deploy, the better."

"I don't know if we've got enough chemical projectile

weapons in store for everyone," the admiral said. "But I'll see that all our current stock is issued."

"It wouldn't be too difficult for Ombey's engineering factories to start production of new projectile rifles and ammunition," Ralph said. "I'd like to see what can be done in that direction."

"It would take at least a couple of days to set up," Ryle Thorne said. "Our current situation should have been settled by then."

"Yes, sir," Ralph said. "If we truly have got all the possessed trapped on Mortonridge this time. And if no more sneak on to the planet."

"Starship interception has been one hundred per cent throughout the Ombey system for the last five hours," Deborah Unwin said. "And you were the first ship to arrive from Lalonde, Ralph. I guarantee no more possessed will escape from orbit down to the planet."

"Thank you, Deborah," Princess Kirsten said. "I'm not doubting the competence of your officers, nor the efficiency of the SD network, but I have to say I think Mr Hiltch is correct in requesting contingency arrangements. What we've seen so far is simply the very first encounter with the possessed; and combating them is absorbing nearly all of our resources. We have to assume that other planets will not be as successful as us in containing the outbreaks. No, this problem is not one which is going to go away in the near or even midfuture. And, as is likely, it is proved beyond reasonable doubt that there is both an afterlife and an afterworld, the philosophical implications are quite extraordinary, and profoundly disturbing."

"Which brings us to our second problem," Ryle Thorne said. "What are we going to tell people?"

"Same as always," Jannike Dermot said. "As little as possible, certainly to start with. We really can't risk the prospect of a general panic right now. I would suggest we use the energy virus as a cover story."

"Plausible," Ryle Thorne agreed.

The Home Secretary, the Princess, and her equerry put together a statement for general release the next morning. It was instructive for Ralph to see the Saldana body politic at work in the flesh, as it were. There was no question of the Princess herself delivering the statement to the news companies. That was the job of the Prime Minister and the Home Secretary. A Saldana simply could not announce such appalling news. It was the function of royalty to offer comments of support and sympathy to the victims at a later date, and people were going to need all the comfort they could get when that byte of official news hit the communications net.

Thorne said, 'Your co... by then.

'Yes sir,' Ralton said. 'I... only have got all the possessed nanonic An Mortonridge this time. And if no more

•   •   •

The town of Exnall sat two hundred and fifty kilometres below the neck of Mortonridge, where the peninsula joined the main body of the continent. It had been founded thirty years ago, and had grown with confidence ever since. The soil around it was rich, the haunt of any number of aboriginal plant species, many of which were edible. Farmers came in the hundreds to cultivate the new species alongside terrestrial crops which thrived in the moist tropical climate. Exnall was a town dominated by agriculture; even the light industries attracted by the council produced and serviced farm machinery.

But by no means a hick town, Chief Inspector Neville Latham thought as his car drove along Maingreen, which ran straight through the centre. Exnall had amalgamated with the local harandrid forest instead of chopping it down to make way for buildings as other Mortonridge towns had done. Even twenty minutes after midnight Maingreen looked superb, the mature trees importing an air of rustic antiquity for the buildings, as if the two had been coexisting for centuries. Streetlights hanging from overhead cables cast a glareless haze of orange-white light, turning the harandrids' dripping leaves a spooky grey. Only a couple of bars and the all-nighter coffee shop were open; their liquid glass windows swirling in abstract patterns, making it impossible to see exactly what was happening inside. Not that anything wild ever did take place; Neville Latham knew that from his days as a patrol officer twenty years ago. Terminal drunks and stim victims slummed the bars, while night shift workers took refuge in the coffee shop, along with the duty police officers.

The car's drive processor datavised an update request, and

Neville directed it off Maingreen and into the police station's car park. Almost all of Exnall's twenty-five-strong police complement were waiting for him in the station's situation management room. Sergeant Walsh stood up as he entered, and the rest stopped talking. Neville took his place at the head of the room.

"Thank you all for coming in," he said briskly. "As you know from the level two security datavise you've received, the Prime Minister has decreed a continent-wide curfew to come into effect from one o'clock this morning. Now, I'm sure we've all accessed the rumours streaming the net today, so I'd like to clarify the situation for you. First the good news: I've been in communication with Landon McCullock who assures me that Ombey has not been contaminated by a xenoc biohazard as the media has been hinting. Nor are we under any sort of naval assault. However, it seems someone has released an extremely sophisticated sequestration technology down here on Xingu."

Neville watched the familiar faces in front of him register various levels of apprehension. The ever-dependable Sergeant Walsh remained virtually emotionless, the two detectives, Feroze and Manby, wary and working out angles, genuine disquiet among the junior patrol officers—who knew full well they'd have the dirty job of actually going out in their cars and enforcing the curfew order.

He waited a few moments for the grumbles to subside. "Unfortunately, the bad news is that the Privy Council security committee believes several examples of this technology may already be loose here in Exnall. Which means we are now under a full state of martial law. Our curfew has to be enforced one hundred per cent, no exceptions. I know this is going to be difficult for you, we've all got family and friends out there, but believe me the best way to help them now is to make sure the order holds. People must not come into contact with each other; which is how the experts think this technology spreads. Apparently it's very hard to spot anyone who has been sequestrated until it's too late."

"So we just sit in our homes and wait?" Thorpe Hartshorn asked. "For how long? For what?"

Neville held up a placatory hand. "I'm coming to that, Officer Hartshorn. Our efforts will be supported by a combined team of police and marines who are going to seal off the entire area. They should be here in another ninety minutes. Once they arrive all the houses in the town will be searched for any victims of the sequestration, and everyone else is going to be evacuated."

"The whole town?" Thorpe Hartshorn asked suspiciously.

"Everybody," Neville confirmed. "They're sending over a squadron of military transports to take us away. But it's going to take a few hours to organize, so it falls upon us to ensure that the curfew is maintained until then."

DataAxis, Exnall's sole news agency, was at the other end of Maingreen from the police station; a shabby, three-storey flat-roofed office module which made few creditworthy concessions to the sylvan character of the town. The agency itself was a typical small provincial outfit, employing five reporters and three communications technicians who between them combed the whole county for nuggets of information. Given the nature of the area their brief was wide-ranging, dealing in local human interest stories, official events, crime (such as it was), and the horrendously mundane crop price sheets which the office processors handled with little or no human supervision. Out of this fascinating assortment of articles they had managed to sell precisely four items to Ombey's major media companies in the last six weeks.

But that had certainly changed today, Finnuala O'Meara thought jubilantly as the desktop processor finished decrypting the level two security datavise from Landon McCullock to Neville Latham. She'd spent a solid ten hours fishing the net streams today, digesting every rumour since yesterday's Guyana alert. Thanks to the trivia and paranoid nightmares which every bulletin site geek on the planet had contributed she'd felt completely stimmed out and ready to pack it in. Then an hour ago things got interesting.

AT Squads had seen action in Pasto. Violent action by all accounts—and still no official media release on that from the police. The motorways were being shut down clean across the continent. Reports of SD fire on vehicles abounded, including a clear account of a runaway bus being vaporized not a hundred and fifty kilometres south of Exnall. And now, Xingu's police commissioner, in person, informing Neville Latham that an unknown, but probably xenoc, sequestration virus was loose in Exnall.

Finnuala O'Meara datavised a shutdown order into the desktop processor block and opened her eyes. "Bloody hell," she grunted.

Finnuala was in her early twenties, eleven months out of university in Atherstone. Her initial delight at landing a job within two days of qualifying, had, during the first quarter of an hour at the agency, turned into dismay. The Exnall agency didn't deal in news, it churned out anti-insomnia treatments. Dismay had slumped to surly anger. Exnall was everything which was rotten with small towns. It was run by a clique, a small elite group of councillors and businessmen and the richer local farmers, who made the decisions which counted at their dinner parties and out on their golf course.

It was no different from her own hometown, the one over on the Esparta continent where her parents never quite made the leap to real money contracts because they lacked the connections. Excluded, by class, by money.

She did nothing for half a minute after the decrypted datavise slipped from her mind, sitting staring at the desktop processor. Accessing the net's police architecture was illegal enough, owning a level two decryption program was grounds for deportation. But she couldn't ignore this. *Couldn't.* It was everything she'd become a reporter for.

"Hugh?" she called.

The communications technician sharing the graveyard shift with her cancelled the Jezzibella album he was running and gave her a disapproving look. "What?"

"How would the authorities announce a curfew to the general public, one where everyone is confined to their house? Specifically, a curfew here in Exnall."

"Are you having me on?"

"No."

He blinked away the figments of the flek and accessed a civil procedures file in his neural nanonics. "Okay, I've found it; it's a pretty simple procedure. The chief inspector will use his code rating to load a universal order into the town's net for every general household processor. The message will play as soon as the processor is accessed, no matter what function you asked for—you tell it to cook your breakfast or vacuum the floor, the first thing it will do is tell you about the curfew."

Finnuala patted her hands together, charting out options. "So people won't know about the curfew until tomorrow morning after they wake up."

"That's right."

"Unless we tell them first."

"Now you really are winding me up."

"No way." The smile on her face was carnivorous. "I know what that prat Latham is going to do next. He'll warn his friends before anyone else, he'll make sure they're ready to be evacuated first. It's his style, this whole bloody town's style."

"Don't be so paranoid," Hugh Rosler said edgily. "If the evacuation is under McCullock's command, nobody will be able to pull a fast one from this end."

Finnuala smiled sweetly and datavised an order into the desktop processor block. It accessed the net's police architecture again, and the monitor programs she designated went into primary mode.

The results simmered into Hugh's mind as a cluster of grey, dimensionless icons. Someone at the police station was datavising a number of houses in the town and outlying areas. They were personal calls, and the households they were being directed at were all depressingly familiar.

"He already is," Finnuala said. "I know these people as well as you do, Hugh. Nothing changes, not even when our planet is under threat."

"So what do you want to do?"

"What this agency is supposed to do: inform people. I'll assemble a package warning everyone about the sequestration, but instead of just releasing it on the media circuit I want you to program the agency processor to datavise it to everyone in Exnall right away, coded as a personal priority message. That way we'll all have an equal chance to get clear when the military transports arrive."

"I don't know about this, Finnuala. Maybe we ought to check with the editor first . . ."

"Bugger the editor," she snapped. "He already knows. Look who was seventh on Latham's list. Do you think his priority is to call us? Do you? Right now he's getting his fat wife and their backwards brat dressed ready to take off for the landing site. Are your wife and kids being told, Hugh? Are they being made safe?"

Hugh Rosler did what he always did and offered no resistance. "All right, Finnuala, I'll modify the processor's program. But by Christ, you'd better be right about this."

"I am." She stood up and pulled her jacket off the back of the chair. "I'm going down to the police station, see if I can get a personal comment from that good man Chief Inspector Latham on the crisis facing his little fiefdom."

"You're pushing it," Hugh warned.

"I know." She grinned sadistically. "Great, isn't it."

Ralph knew he didn't have anything to prove anymore. The AT Squads were alert to the terrible danger, they'd been fully blooded. So there was no practical reason for him to take a police hypersonic out to Mortonridge. Yet here he was with Cathal, Will, and Dean heading south at Mach five. His justification . . . well, the marine brigade coming down from the orbital bases would need to be brought up to speed. And he might have some advice invaluable to those on the ground.

In reality, he needed to see those towns cordoned off for himself. The threat contained, pinned down ready for extermination.

"It looks like your idea about zero-tau was on the ball," Roche Skark datavised. "All six prisoners we captured at Moyce's have now been placed in the pods shipped down from Guyana. Four of them fought like lunatics before the AT Squads could force them in. The other two were apparently cured before they went in. In both cases the possessors just gave up and left the bodies rather than undergo exposure to temporal stasis."

"That's about the best news I've had for ten hours," Ralph replied. "They can be beaten, squeezed out without killing the body they're possessing. It means we're not just fighting a holding action."

"Yes. Well, full credit to you for that one, Ralph. We still don't know why the possessed can't tolerate zero-tau, but no doubt the reason will turn up in debrief at some time."

"Are you shoving the cured prisoners into personality debrief?"

"We haven't decided. Although I think it's inevitable eventually. We must not get sidetracked from neutralizing the Mortonridge towns. Frankly, the science of it all can wait."

"What sort of state are the prisoners in?"

"Generally similar to Gerald Skibbow, disorientated and withdrawn, but their symptoms are nothing like as severe as his. After all they were only possessed for a few hours. Skibbow had been under Kingston Garrigan's control for several weeks. Certainly they're not classed as dangerous. But we're placing them in secure isolation wards for the moment, just in case. It's the first time I've agreed with Leonard DeVille all day."

Ralph snorted at the name. "I meant to ask you, sir. What is it with DeVille?"

"Ah, yes; sorry about him, Ralph. That's pure politics between us and our dear sister agency. DeVille is one of Jannike's puppets. The ISA keeps tabs on all major Kingdom politicians, and those who are squeaky clean are nudged forward. DeVille is obnoxiously pure in heart, if devious in mind. Jannike is grooming him as a possible replacement for Warren Aspinal as Xingu's Prime Minister. Ideally, she'd like him in charge of the hunt operation."

"Whereas you had the Princess appoint me as chief advisor . . ."

"Exactly. I'll have a word with Jannike about him. It's probably heretical of me, but I think the problem the possessed present us might be slightly more important than our little internal rivalries."

"Thank you, sir. It'd be nice to have him off my back."

"I doubt he'd be much more of a problem anyway. You've done some sterling work tonight, Ralph. Don't think it's gone unnoticed. You've condemned yourself to a divisional chief's desk for the rest of eternity now. I can assure you the boredom is quite otherworldly."

Ralph managed a contemplative smile in the half-light of the hypersonic's cabin. "Sounds attractive right now."

Roche Skark cancelled the channel.

With his mind free, Ralph datavised a situation update request to Hub One. The squadron of Royal Marine troop flyers were already halfway down from Guyana. Twenty-five police hypersonics carrying AT Squads were arrowing across the continent, converging on Mortonridge. All motorway traffic had now been shut down. An estimated eighty-five per cent of non-motorway vehicles had been located and halted. Curfew orders were going out to every general household processor in Xingu. Police in the four Mortonridge towns were preparing to enforce the martial law declaration.

It looked good. In the computer, it looked good. Secure. But there must be something we missed. Some rogue element. There always is. Someone like Mixi Penrice.

Someone . . . who abandoned the Confederation marines in Lalonde's jungle. Who left Kelven Solanki and his tiny, doomed command to struggle against the wave of possessed all alone.

All actions which were fully justifiable in the defence of the realm. Maybe I'm not so dissimilar to DeVille after all.

Twenty minutes after Neville Latham had issued his assignment orders, the station situation management room had settled down into a comfortable pattern. Sergeant Walsh and Detective Feroze were monitoring the movement of the patrol cars, while Manby was maintaining a direct link to the SD centre. Any sign of human movement along the streets should bring a patrol car response within ninety seconds.

Neville himself had taken part in issuing dispatch orders to the patrol officers. It felt good to be involved, to show his people the boss wasn't afraid of rolling up his sleeves and getting stuck in there. He'd quietly accepted the fact that for someone his age and rank Exnall was a dead end posting. Not that he was particularly bitter; he'd realized twenty-five years ago he wasn't cut out for higher office. And he fitted in well here with these people, the town was his kind of community. He understood it. When he retired he knew he would be staying on.

Or so he'd thought until today. Judging from some of the latest briefing updates he'd received from Pasto, after tomorrow there might not be much of Exnall left standing for him to retire to.

However, Neville was determined about one thing. Nonentity he might be, but Exnall was going to be protected to the best of his ability. The curfew would be carried out to the letter with a competence which any big city police commander would envy.

"Sir." Sergeant Walsh was looking up from the fence of stumpy AV pillars lining his console.

"Yes, Sergeant."

"Sir, I've just had three people datavise the station, wanting to know what's going on, and is the curfew some kind of joke."

Feroze turned around, frowning. "I've had five asking me the same thing. They all said they'd received a personal datavise telling them a curfew was being effected. I told them they should check their household processor for information."

"Eight people?" Neville queried. "All receiving personal messages at this time of night?"

Feroze glanced back at one of his displays. "Make that fifteen, I've got another seven incoming datavises stacked up."

"This is absurd," Neville said. "The whole point of my universal order was to explain what's happening."

"They're not bothering to access it," Feroze said. "They're calling us direct instead."

"Eighteen new datavises coming in," Walsh said. "It's going to hit fifty any minute."

"They can't be datavising warnings to each other this fast," Neville murmured, half to himself.

"Chief," Manby was waving urgently. "SD control reports that house lights are coming on all over town."

"What?"

"Hundred and twelve datavises, sir," Walsh said.

"Did we mess up the universal order?" Neville asked. At the back of his mind was the awful notion that the electronic warfare capability Landon McCullock warned him about had glitched the order.

"It was straight out of the file," Feroze protested.

"Sir, we're going to run out of net access channels at this rate," Walsh said. "Over three hundred datavises coming in now. Do you want to reprioritize the net management routines? You have the authority. We'd be able to re-establish our principle command channels if we shut down civilian data traffic."

"I can't—"

The door of the situation management room slid open.

Neville twisted around at the unexpected motion (the damn door was supposed to be codelocked!), only to gasp in surprise at the sight of a young woman pushing her way past a red-faced Thorpe Hartshorn. A characteristics recognition program in his neural nanonics supplied her name: Finnuala O'Meara, one of the news agency reporters.

Neville caught sight of a slender, suspicious-looking processor block which she was shoving back into her bag. A codebuster? he wondered. And if she has the nerve to use one inside a police station, what else has she got?

"Ms O'Meara, you are intruding on a very important official operation. If you leave now, I won't file charges."

"Recording and relaying, Chief," Finnuala said with a hint of triumph. Her eyes with their retinal implants were unblinking as they tracked him. "And I don't need to tell you this is a public building. Knowing what happens here is a public right under the fourth coronation proclamation."

"Actually, Miss O'Meara, if you bothered to fully access your legal file, you'd know that under martial law all proclamations are suspended. Leave now, please, and stop relaying at once."

"Does that same suspension give you the right to warn your friends about the danger of xenoc sequestration technology before the general public, Chief Inspector?"

Latham blushed. How the hell did the little bitch know that? Then he realized what someone with that kind of command access to the net could do. His finger lined up accusingly on her. "Have you datavised personal warnings to people in this town?"

"Are you denying you warned your friends first, Chief Inspector?"

"Shut up, you stupid cow, and answer me. Did you send out those personal alarm calls?"

Finnuala smirked indolently. "I might have done. Want to answer my question now?"

"God in Heaven! Sergeant Walsh, how many calls now?"

"One thousand recorded, sir, but that's all our channels blocked. It may be a lot more. I can't tell."

"How many did you send, O'Meara?" Neville demanded furiously.

She paled slightly, but stood her ground. "I'm just doing my job, Chief Inspector. What about you?"

"How many?"

She arched an eyebrow, aspiring to hauteur. "Everybody."

"You stupid—The curfew is supposed to be averting a panic; and it would have done just that if you hadn't interfered. The only way we're going to get out of this with our minds still our own is if people stay calm and follow orders."

"Which people?" she spat back. "Yours? The mayor's family?"

"Officer Hartshorn, get her out of here. Use whatever force is necessary, and some which isn't if you want. Then book her."

"Sir." A grinning Hartshorn caught Finnuala's arm. "Come along, miss." He held up a small nervejam stick in his free hand. "You wouldn't want me to use this."

Finnuala let Hartshorn tug her out of the situation management room. The door slid shut behind them.

"Walsh," Neville said. "Shut down the town's communications net. Do it now. Leave the police architecture functional, but all civil data traffic is to cease immediately. They mustn't be allowed to spread this damn panic any further."

"Yes, sir!"

The police hypersonic carrying Ralph had already started to descend over the town of Rainton when Landon McCullock datavised him.

"Some bloody journalist woman started a panic in Exnall, Ralph. The chief inspector is doing his best to damp it down, but I'm not expecting miracles at this point."

Ralph abandoned the hypersonic's sensor suite. The image he'd received of Rainton was all in the infrared spectrum, rectangles of luminous pink glass laid out over the black land.

Glowing dots converged in the air above it, marine troop flyers and police hypersonics ready to implement the isolation. Given they were the forces of salvation, their approach formation looked strangely like the circling of giant carrion birds.

"I suggest you or the Prime Minister broadcasts to them directly, sir. Appeal to them to follow the curfew order. Your word should carry more weight than some local dignitary. Tell them about the marines arriving; that way they'll also see that you're acting positively to help them."

"Good theory, Ralph. Unfortunately Exnall's chief inspector has shut down the town's net. Only the police architecture is functional right now. The only people we can broadcast to are the ones sitting in the patrol cars."

"You have to get the net back on-line."

"I know. But now it seems there's a problem with some of the local management processors."

Ralph squeezed his fists, not wanting to hear. "Glitches?"

"Looks like it. Diana is redirecting the AIs to interrogate Exnall's electronics. But there aren't nearly enough channels open for them to be as effective as they were in Pasto."

"Hellfire! Okay, sir, we're on our way." He datavised a quick instruction to the pilot, and the hypersonic rose above its spiralling siblings before streaking away to the south.

Two hundred and fifty kilometres above Mortonridge, the SD sensor satellite made its fourth pass over Exnall since the network had been raised to a code three alert status. Deborah Unwin directed its high-resolution sensors to scan the town. Several specialist teams of security council analysts and tactical advisors were desperate for information about the town's on-the-ground situation.

But they weren't getting the full picture. In several places the satellite images were fuzzy, edges poorly defined. Switching to infrared didn't help; red ripples swayed to and fro, never still.

"Just like the Quallheim Counties," Ralph concluded morosely when he accessed the data. "They're down there, all right. And in force."

"It gets worse," Deborah datavised. "Even in the areas relatively unaffected we still can't get a clear picture of what's going on below those damn harandrid trees. Not at night. All I can tell you is that there are a lot of people out on the streets."

"On foot?" Ralph queried.

"Yes. The AIs loaded travel proscription orders into all the processor controlled vehicles in the town. Some people will be able to break the order's code, of course. But basically the only mechanical transport left in Exnall right now are the bicycles."

"So where are all the pedestrians going?"

"Some are taking the main link road to the M6, but it looks like the majority are heading for the town centre. I'd say they're probably converging on the police station."

"Damn it, that's all we need. If they congregate in a crowd there's no way we'll be able to stop the possession from spreading. It'll be like a plague."

Frank Kitson was angry in a way he hadn't been for years. Angry, and just a bit alarmed, too. First, woken up in the dead of night by a priority message from some O'Meara woman he'd never heard of. Which turned out to be a paranoid fantasy about xenoc takeovers and martial law. Then when he tried to datavise the police station about it he couldn't get through to the duty officer. So he'd seen the lights on next door, and datavised old man Yardly to see if he knew what was going on. Yardly had received the same priority datavise, as had some of his family, and he couldn't get through to the police either.

Frank didn't want to make a fool of himself by appearing panicky, but something odd was definitely going down. Then the communications net crashed. When he accessed the general household processor for an emergency channel to the police station there was an official message in the processor's memory from Chief Inspector Latham announcing the curfew, setting out its rules, and assuring all the citizens they would be evacuated in the morning. Genuinely worried now, Frank told his little family to get ready, they were leaving right away.

The car processor refused to acknowledge his datavise.

When he switched the car to manual override, it still wouldn't function. That was when he set off to find a police officer and demand to be told just what the hell was going on. It was a few minutes short of one o'clock when the curfew was officially due to start. And in any case, he was an upstanding subject of the King, he had every right to be on the street. The curfew couldn't possibly apply to him.

A lot of other people seemed to have the same idea. Quite a group of them marched down the wide road out of their tranquil residential suburb heading for the town centre, shoulders set squarely against the night air. Some people had brought their kids, the children sleepy, their voices piping and full of queries. Comments were shouted back and forth, but no one had any answers to what was actually going on.

Frank heard someone call his name, and saw Hanly Nowell making his way towards him.

"Hell of a thing," he told Hanly. They worked for the same agrichemical company; different divisions, but they drank together some nights, and their two families went on joint outings occasionally.

"Sure." Hanly looked distracted. "Did your car pack up?"

Frank nodded, puzzled by how low Hanly was keeping his voice, almost as if he didn't want to be overheard. "Yes, some kind of official traffic division override in the processor. I didn't even know they could do that."

"Me neither. But I've got my four-wheeler. I can bypass the processor in that, go straight to manual drive."

They both stopped walking. Frank threw cautious glances at the rest of the loose group as they passed by.

"Room in it for you and the family," Hanly said when the stragglers had moved away.

"You serious?" Maybe it was the thick grey tree shadows which flapped across the street creating confusing movements of half-light, but Frank was sure Hanly's face was different somehow. Hanly always smiled, or grinned, forever happy with life. Not tonight, though.

Guess it's getting to him, too.

"Wouldn't have offered otherwise," Hanly said generously.

"God, thanks, man. It's not for me. I'm scared for the wife and Tom, you know?"

"I know."

"I'll go back and get them. We'll come around to your place."

"No need." And now Hanly was smiling. He put an arm around Frank's shoulders. "I'm parked just around the corner. Come on, we'll drive back to your house. Much quicker."

Hanly's big offroad camper was sitting behind a thick clump of ancient harandrids in a small park. Invisible from the street.

"You thought about where we can go to get clear?" Frank asked. He was keeping his own voice low now. There were still little groups of people walking about through the suburb, all making their way to the town centre. Most of them would probably appreciate a ride out, and wouldn't be too fussy how they got it. He was bothered by how furtive and uncharitable he'd become. Focusing on survival must do that to a man.

"Not really." Hanly opened the rear door and gestured Frank forwards. "But I expect we'll get there anyway."

Frank gave him a slightly stiff smile and climbed in. Then the door banged shut behind him, making him jump. It was pitch black inside. "Hey, Hanly." No answer. He pushed at the door, pumping the handle, but it wouldn't open. "Hanly, what the hell you doing, man?"

Frank had the sudden, awful realization that he wasn't alone inside the camper. He froze, spread-eagle against the door. "Who's there?" he whispered.

"Just us chickens, boss."

Frank whirled around as a fearsome green-white light bloomed inside the camper. Its intensity made him squeeze his eyes tight shut, fearing for his retinas. But not before he'd seen the sleek wolverine creatures launching themselves at him, their huge fangs dripping blood.

From his seat in the situation management room, Neville Latham could hear the crowd outside the police station. They produced an unpleasant ebb and flow of sound which lapped at the building, its angry tone plain for all to hear.

The final impossibility: a mob in Exnall! And while he was supposed to be enforcing a curfew. Dear Lord.

"You must disperse them," Landon McCullock datavised.

"They cannot be allowed to group together for any length of time, it would be a disaster."

"Yes, sir." How? he wanted to shout at his superior. I've only got five officers left in the station. "How long before the marines land?"

"Approximately four minutes. But, Neville, I'm not allowing them in to the town itself. Their priority is to establish a secure perimeter. I have to think of the whole continent. What's loose in Exnall cannot be allowed out."

"I understand." He glanced at the desktop processor's AV projector which was broadcasting Exnall's status display. The SD sensor satellite wasn't producing as many details as he would have liked, but the overall summary was accurate enough. Approximately six hundred people were milling along Maingreen outside the station, with dribs and drabs still arriving. Neville made his decision and datavised the communications block for a channel to each patrol car.

It was all over now, anyway: career, retirement prospects, probably his friends, too. Ordering the police to open fire with sonics on his own townsfolk wouldn't make the recriminations appreciably worse. And it would be helping them, even though they'd never appreciate the fact.

●   ●   ●

Eben Pavitt had arrived at the police station ten minutes ago, and still hadn't managed to get anywhere near the doors to make his complaint. Not that it would do him much good if he had got up there. He could see those at the front of the building hammering away at the thick glass doors to no avail. If that pompous dickbrain Latham was in there, he wasn't doing his duty and talking to the crowd.

It was beginning to look like his walk (two bloody kilometres, dressed in a thin T-shirt and shorts) had all been for nothing. How utterly bloody typical that Latham should bungle tonight. Ineffective warnings. Sloppy organization. Cutting people off from the net. The chief inspector was supposed to be helping the town, for crying out loud.

By God, my MP is going to hear about this.

If I get out in one piece.

Eben Pavitt glanced uneasily at his fellow townsfolk. There was a constant derisory shouting now. Several stones had been thrown at the police station. Eben disapproved of that, but he could certainly understand the underlying frustration.

Even Maingreen's overhead streetlights seemed to be sharing the town's malaise, they weren't as bright as usual. Away in the distance, above the fringes of the crowd, he could see several of them flickering.

He wasn't going to achieve anything here. Perhaps he should have hiked straight out of town? And it still wasn't too late, if he started now.

As he turned around and started to push his way through the press of aggrieved people, he thought he saw a large flyer curving through the sky above the western edge of town. Trees and the wayward streetlights swiftly cut it from his view, but there wasn't much else that gold-haze blob could be. And the size could only mean a military transport of some kind.

He grinned secretively. The government was doing something positive. Perhaps all was not lost after all.

Then he heard the sirens. Patrol cars were racing along Maingreen, approaching the crowd from both ends. Those people around him were straining to catch a glimpse of the latest distraction.

"LEAVE THE AREA," an amplified voice bellowed from the police station. "THE TOWN IS NOW UNDER MARTIAL LAW. RETURN HOME AND REMAIN THERE UNTIL YOU RECEIVE FURTHER INSTRUCTIONS."

Eben was sure the distorted voice belonged to Neville Latham.

The first patrol cars braked dangerously close to people on the edge of the main crowd, as if their safety systems had somehow become uncoupled. Several jumped clear hurriedly, two or three lost their footing and fell over. One man was struck by a patrol car, sending him cannoning into a woman. They both went sprawling.

A deluge of boos were directed at the patrol cars. Eben didn't like the mood which was emerging among his fellow citizens. These weren't the usual peaceable Exnall residents.

And the police reaction was unbelievably provocative. A life-long law abider, Eben was shocked by their actions.

"LEAVE THE AREA NOW. THIS IS AN ILLEGAL ASSEMBLY."

A single lump of stone tumbled through the air above the bobbing heads of the crowd. Eben never did see the arm which flung it. One thing remained certain, though, it was thrown with incredible force. When it hit the patrol car it actually managed to fracture the bonded silicon windscreen.

Several taunting cheers went up. Suddenly the air was thick with improvised missiles raining down on the patrol cars.

The response was predictable, and immediate. A couple of assault mechanoids emerged from the rear of each patrol car. Sense-overload ordnance shot out, red flares slicing brilliant ephemeral archways across the stars.

They should have been warning shots. The mechanoids had a direct-attack prohibition loaded into their processors which only Neville Latham could cancel.

The ordnance activated two metres above the compressed bustle of bodies at the heart of the crowd. The effect was almost as bad as if live ammunition had been fired straight at them.

Eben saw men and women keel over as though they'd been electrocuted. Then his eyes were streaming from intolerable light and wickedly acidic gas. Human screams vanished beneath a hyper-decibel whistle. His neural nanonics sensorium filter programs were unable to cope (as the ordnance designers intended), leaving him blind, deaf, and virtually insensate. Heavy bodies thudded into him, sending him spinning, stumbling for balance. Pinpricks of heat bloomed across his bare skin, turning to vicious stings. He felt his flesh ballooning, body swelling to twice, three times its normal size. Joints were seizing up.

Eben thought he was screaming. But there was no way to tell. The solid sensations, when they started to return, were crude ones. His bare legs scraping over damp grass. Limp arms banging against his side. He was being dragged along the ground by his collar.

When he'd regained enough rationality to look around, the scenes of suffering on Maingreen outside the police station made him want to weep with rage and helplessness. The crazed assault mechanoids were still pummelling people with their ordnance from point-blank range. A direct hit brought instant death, for those nearby the activation it was outright torture.

"Bastards," Eben rasped. "You bastards."

"Pigs are always the same."

He looked up at the man who was pulling him away from the melee. "Christ, thanks, Frank. I could have died if I'd stayed in there."

"Yeah, I suppose you could have," Frank Kitson said. "Lucky I came along, really."

The police hypersonic landed next to the five big marine troop flyers. They were strung out along the link road which connected Exnall to the M6; a quintet of dark, menacingly obese arachnids whose landing struts had dinted the carbon concrete. The start of the town's harandrid forest was two hundred metres away, a meticulous border where the aboriginal trees finished and the cultivated citrus groves began.

As he came down the hypersonic's airstairs, Ralph's suit sensors showed him the marine squads fanning out along the edge of the trees. Some kind of barrier had already been thrown across the road itself. So far a perfect deployment.

The marine colonel, Janne Palmer, was waiting for Ralph in the command cabin of her flyer. It was a compartment just aft of the cockpit with ten communications operatives, and three tactical interpretation officers. Even though it was inside and well protected, the colonel was wearing a lightweight armour suit like the rest of her brigade. Her shell helmet was off, showing Ralph a surprisingly feminine face. The only concession to military life appeared to be her hair, which was shaved down to a two-millimetre stubble of indeterminable colour. She gave him a fast nod of acknowledgement as he was escorted in by a young marine.

"I accessed a recording of the operation at Moyce's," she said. "These are one tough set of people we've got here."

"I'm afraid so. And it looks like Exnall is the worst infestation out of all the four Mortonridge towns."

She glanced into an AV pillar's projection. "Nice assignment. Let's hope my brigade can handle it. At the moment I'm trying to establish a circular perimeter roughly fifteen hundred metres outside the town. We should have it solid in another twenty minutes."

"Excellent."

"That forest's going to be a bitch to patrol. The SD sensor sats can't see shit below the trees, and you're telling me I can't rely on our usual observation systems."

" 'Fraid not."

"Pity. Aerovettes would be exceptionally handy in this case."

"I must advise against using them. The possessed can really screw our electronics. You're far better off without them. At least that way you know the information you're receiving is accurate, even though there isn't much of it."

"Interesting situation. Haven't handled anything like this since tac school, if then."

"Diana Tiernan told me the AIs have got very few datalinks left into Exnall. We've definitely lost most of the town's communications net. Even the police architecture has failed now. So the exact situation inside is unknown."

"There was some kind of fight outside the police station which finished a couple of minutes ago. But even if that crowd which gathered along Maingreen have all been possessed, that still leaves us with a lot of the population which have escaped so far. What do you want to do about them?"

"Same as we originally planned. Wait until dawn, and send in teams to evacuate everyone. But I wish to Christ that curfew had held. It did in all the other towns."

"Wishes always wind up as regrets in this game, I find."

Ralph gave her a speculative look, but she was concentrating on another AV projection. "I think our main concern right now is to contain the possessed in Exnall," he said. "When it's light we can start worrying about getting the rest out."

"Absolutely." Janne Palmer stared straight at the ESA operative, and gave him a regretful grin. "And come dawn I'm going to need the best information I can acquire. A lot of lives are going to depend on me getting it right. I don't have any special forces types in my brigade. This was a rush operation. But what I do have now is you and your G66 troops. I'd like you to go in and make that assessment for me. I believe you're the best qualified, in all respects."

"You don't happen to know Jannike Dermot, do you?"

"Not personally, no. Will you go in for me? I can't order you to; Admiral Farquar made it quite plain you're here to advise, and I have to take that advice."

"Considerate of him." Ralph didn't even need any time to decide. *I made that choice when I put the armour suit on again.* "Okay, I'll go and tell my people we're on line again. But I'd like to take a squad of your marines in with us. We might need some heavy-calibre firepower support."

"There's a platoon assembled and waiting for you in flyer four."

Finnuala O'Meara had passed simple frustration a long time ago. Over an hour, in fact. She had been sitting on a bunk in the police station's holding cell for an age. Nothing she did brought the slightest response from anyone, not datavises into the station processor, nor shouting, or thumping on the door. Nobody came. It must have been that prick Latham's orders. *Let her cool off for a few hours.* Jumped-up cretin.

But she could nail him. Anytime she wanted, now. He must know that. Which was probably why he'd kept her in here while the rest of *her* story played out, denying her a complete victory. If only her coverage had been complete she would have been able to dictate her own terms to a major.

She'd heard the noises from outside, the sound of a crowd gathering and protesting. A large crowd if she was any judge. Then the sirens of the patrol cars rushing along Maingreen. Speakers blaring a warning, pleas, and threats. Strange monotonous thumps. Screams, glass smashing.

It was awful. She belonged outside, drinking down the sight.

After the riot, or whatever, it had become strangely quiet. Finnuala had almost drifted off to sleep when the cell door did finally open.

"About bloody time," she said. The rest of the invective died in her throat.

A huge mummy shuffled laboriously into the cell, its bandages a dusty brown, with lime-green pustulant fluids weeping from its hands. It was wearing Neville Latham's immaculate peaked cap. "So sorry to keep you waiting," it apologized gruffly.

Colonel Palmer's field command officers informed Ralph's reconnaissance team about the woman as they were about to enter Exnall. Datavise bandwidth was being suppressed by the now-familiar electronic warfare field, preventing anything other than basic conversation. They certainly couldn't receive a full sensevise, or even a visual image, so they had to rely on a simple description instead.

As far as the SD sensor satellites could tell, the town's entire population had retreated back into the buildings. Earlier on there had been a considerable amount of movement under the umbrella of harandrids, blurred infrared smears skipping about erratically. Then as dawn rose even those beguiling traces vanished. The only things left moving in Exnall were the treetops swaying back and forth in the first morning zephyr. Roofs, and even entire streets, appeared blurred, as if a gentle rain was pattering on the satellite's lenses. Visually, the town was a complete hash, except for a solitary circle, fifteen metres across, in front of a diner which served the link road to the M6. And in the middle of that was the woman.

"She's just standing there," Janne Palmer datavised. "She'll be able to see anything approaching up the link road into town."

"Any weapons apparent?" Ralph asked. Along with the twelve-strong platoon the colonel had assigned him, he was crouched down at the side of the road, a hundred metres short of the first houses. They were using a small embankment for cover as they crept in towards the town.

His head was ringing with a mental version of tinnitus, which he suspected was due to the stimulants. After only two hours sleep in the last thirty-six he was having to use both chemical and software excitants to keep his edge. But he couldn't afford to relax his guard, not now.

"Definitely not," Janne Palmer told him. "At least not any heavy-calibre hardware, anyway. She's wearing a jacket, so she could be concealing a small pistol inside it."

"Not that it makes any difference if she's possessed. We've not seen them use a weapon yet."

"Quite."

"Dumb question, but is she alive?"

"Yes. We can see her chest moving when she breathes, and her infrared signature is optimum."

"She's some kind of bait, do you think?"

"No, too obvious. I'd guess some kind of sentry, except they must know we're here. Several squads have skirmished while we were setting up the perimeter."

"Hell, you mean they're loose in the woods?"

" 'Fraid so. Which means I can't confirm that all the possessed are inside the cordon. I've requested some more troops from Admiral Farquar to start searching the locality. The request is up before the security committee as we speak."

Ralph cursed silently. Possessed roaming around in this area would be nigh on impossible to track down. The Mortonridge countryside was a rugged nightmare. Pity we haven't got any affinity-bonded hounds, he thought. The ones he'd seen the settlement supervisors use back on Lalonde would have been perfect for the job. And I can just see Jannike Dermot's face if I make that suggestion to the security committee. But . . . hell, they're what we need.

"Ralph, one moment please," Colonel Palmer datavised. "We've run an ident check on our lady sentry. It's confirmed, she's Angeline Gallagher."

"Hell. That changes everything."

"Yes. Opinion here is that she's wanting to talk. She's not stupid. Allowing herself to be seen like this must be their equivalent of a white flag."

"I expect you're right." Ralph gave the platoon's lieutenant an order to halt their advance while the security committee came on line. The marines formed themselves into a defensive circle, scanning the trees and the nearby houses with their most basic sensors. Ralph let his automatic rifle hang at his side as he squatted in the middle of some thick marloop bushes. He had a terrible intimation that Gallagher (or rather her possessor) wasn't about to lay out some convenient terms of surrender. There never can be surrender between us, he acknowledged gloomily.

So what could she want to say?

"Mr Hiltch, we concur with Colonel Palmer that the woman wants to negotiate," Princess Kirsten datavised. "I know it's a lot to ask after all you've been through, but I'd like you to go in there and talk to her."

"We can set up SD ground-strike coverage to support you," Deborah Unwin datavised. "Put you in the eye of a hurricane, so to speak. Any tricks or attempts to overwhelm you, and we'll laser out a two-hundred-metre circle with you at the centre. We know they can't withstand the SD platform's power levels."

"It's all right," Ralph told his invisible audience. "I'll go in. After all, I was the one who brought her here."

Strangely enough, Ralph didn't think of very much at all when he was walking the last five hundred metres along the road. All he wanted to do now was get the job over. The road which had started at the mouth of a titanic river on a different, distant planet finished inside a pretty rural town on the rump of nowhere. If there was an irony to be had in those circumstances, Ralph couldn't taste it.

Angeline Gallagher's possessor waited calmly outside the cheap single-storey diner as he walked towards her. Dean, Will, and Cathal accompanied him for most of the way; then when they were still a hundred metres away from her he told them to wait and carried on alone. Nothing moved in any of the simple, elegant buildings which lined the link road. But he knew they were waiting behind the walls and blanked windows. The conviction grew inside him that they weren't showing themselves because it wasn't yet their time to do so. Their part in the drama would come later.

This was a surety he'd never known before, a kind of psychic upswelling. And with it his intimation of disaster grew ever stronger.

The closer he got to the woman, the less the electronic warfare field affected his implants and suit blocks. By the time he was five metres away, the security committee was receiving a full sensevise again.

He stopped. Squared his shoulders. Took off his shell helmet.

Her smile was almost pitying in its sparsity. "Looks like we've arrived at the crunch time," she said.

"Who are you?"

"Annette Ekelund. And you are Ralph Hiltch, the ESA's head of station on Lalonde. I might have known you would be the one they set on us. You've done quite a good job so far."

"Could we cut the bullshit? What do you want?"

"Philosophically, to live for ever. Practically, I want you to call off the police and marines you've got circling this town along with the other three we've managed to occupy. Right now."

"No."

"I see you've already learned not to make threats. No *or else*. No *if you don't you'll regret it*. That's good. After all, what can you threaten me with?"

"Zero-tau."

Annette Ekelund frowned as she considered the response. "Yes. Possibly. It is, I admit, certainly frightening enough for us. But there's no finality to that, not anymore. If we flee our possessed bodies to escape zero-tau, we can still return. There are already several million possessed walking upon the Confederation worlds. Within weeks, that number will be hundreds of millions, a few days later billions. I will always have a way back now. As long as a single human body is left alive my kind can resurrect me. Do you understand now?"

"I understand the zero-tau option works. We will put you in the pods; and we will keep putting you in the pods until there are no more of you left. Do you understand that?"

"I'm sorry, Ralph, but as I said, you simply cannot threaten me. Have you worked out why yet? Have you worked out the real reason I will win? It is because you will ultimately join me. You are going to die, Ralph. Today. Tomorrow. A year from now. If you're lucky, in fifty years time. It doesn't matter when. It is entropy, it is fate, it is the way the universe works. Death, not love, conquers all in the end. And when you die, you will find yourself in the beyond. That is when you and I will become brother and sister in the same fellowship. United against the living. Coveting the living."

"No."

"Do not speak about something you know nothing about."

"I still do not believe you. God is not that cruel. There will be more to death than this emptiness you found."

She laughed bitterly. "Fool. Know-nothing fool."

"But a living fool. A fool you have to contend with here and now."

"There is no such thing as God, Ralph. Only humans are stupid enough to create religions. Have you noticed that? None of the xenocs we've encountered need to bandage their insecurities and fears with promises of incorporeal glory that are every soul's due. Oh, no, Ralph; God is merely the term an ignorant primitive uses when he wants to say quantum cosmology. The universe is an entirely natural structure, one which is exceptionally vicious in its attitude to life. And now we have an opportunity to leave it for good, a chance of salvation. We're not going to let you stop us, Ralph."

"I can, and I will."

"Sorry, Ralph, but your intransigent belief in humanity is your principal weakness, one which you share with the rest of this Kingdom's devout population. We intend to exploit that to the full. What I'm about to say might seem inhuman, but then, that's what you think I am anyway. As I told you, the dead cannot lose this fight, for you have no lever on us. We cannot be threatened, coerced, nor pleaded with. Like death itself, we are an absolute."

"What is it you have to say?"

"Am I talking to this planet's authorities, the Saldana Princess?"

"Yes. She's on-line."

"Good. Then I say this: You almost managed to exterminate us last night, and if our fight continues along those same lines today then a great many people will be killed, a situation neither of us would welcome. Therefore I propose a standoff solution. We will keep Mortonridge for ourselves, and I pledge none of us will leave it. If you do not believe me, and I expect trust to be lacking on your part, you have the physical power to set up a blockade across the neck of this land where it joins the continent."

"No deal," Princess Kirsten datavised.

"The Kingdom will not abandon its subjects," Ralph said out loud. "You ought to know that by now."

"We acknowledge the Kingdom's strength," Annette Ekelund said. "And that is why we propose this ceasefire. The outcome of the struggle between the living and our kind will not be decided by what transpires here. We are too evenly matched. However, not every Confederation planet is as advanced or as competent as Ombey." She raised her head, closing her eyes as she did so, looking blindly up at the sky. "Out there is where both our fates are being decided right now. You, like I, will have to wait for the outcome to be determined by others. We know that we will triumph. Just as your misplaced faith tells you that the living will be victorious."

"So you're saying we should just sit it out on the sidelines?"

"Yes."

"I don't even have to ask the security committee for their opinion on that one. We're not the sideline, we're the front line, we are a major part of the struggle against you. If we can show other planets that it is possible to stop you from spreading, banish you from the bodies you've captured, then they will have faith in their own ability."

Annette Ekelund nodded sadly. "I understand. Princess Saldana, I have tried reason; now I must use something stronger to convince you."

"Ralph, our satellite sensors just came back on-line," Deborah Unwin reported. "We can see a lot of movement down there. Oh, Christ, they're swarming out of the houses. Ralph, get out of there. Now. Do it now! Run."

But he stood his ground. He knew the Ekelund woman wasn't threatening him personally. This was to be a demonstration. The one he'd anticipated, and dreaded all along.

"Do you want ground-strike support?" Admiral Farquar datavised.

"Not yet, sir." His enhanced retinas showed him doors opening all the way along the street, people emerging onto the pavements.

At Ekelund's invisible signal, the possessed were bringing out their hostages. The illusory bodies on display were deliberately gaudy, ranging from historical warlords to fictitious creatures, blighted monsters and necromantic demigods. Fantasies chosen to emphasise the impossible gulf between them and their frightened prisoners.

Each of the sorcerous apparitions was paired with one of Exnall's surviving non-possessed residents. Like their captors, they were a cross section of the community, young and old, male and female; dressed in nightgowns, pyjamas, hurriedly thrown on shirts, even naked. Some struggled, the diehards and the fatalists; but most had been tyrannized into obedience.

The possessed restrained them with the greatest of ease as they hustled them forwards, their energistic ability giving them a mechanoid's strength. Children wailed fearfully as they were gripped by hands and claws as hard as stone. Men grimaced in subdued fury.

A symphony of cries and hopeless shouts laid siege to Ralph's ears.

"What the hell are you doing?" he yelled at Ekelund. His arm swept around. "For Christ's sake, you're hurting them."

"This is not all," Annette Ekelund said impassively. "Tell your people to look four kilometres south-west of the town at a lake called Otsuo. There is an abandoned offroad camper there belonging to one of Exnall's residents."

"Hang on, Ralph," Deborah Unwin datavised. "We're scanning now. Yep, there's a vehicle parked there all right. Registered to a Hanly Nowell, he works at an agrichemical plant in the town's industrial precinct."

"Okay," Ralph said. "It's there. Now tell your people to ease off those hostages."

"No, Ralph," Annette Ekelund said. "They will not ease off. What I am trying to make clear to you is the fact that we have spread beyond this town. I could only know where the vehicle was if I ordered the driver to leave it there. And it is not the only one, not from this town nor the others. We have escaped the clutches of your marines, Ralph. I organized the four towns which the Longhound bus visited very carefully; we were busy last night while you were chasing after the possessed in Pasto. My followers spread out along the whole peninsula; on foot, on horseback, on bikes, in manual control vehicles. Even I don't know where they all are any more. The marines barricading the towns are worthless. Now you will have to block off Mortonridge in its entirety to prevent us from contaminating the rest of the continent."

"No problem."

"I'm sure. But you'll never retake this land from us, not now. You can't even claim back this single town, not without committing genocide. You've already seen what a single one of us can achieve when we have to defend ourselves. Imagine that destructive power focused with evil intent. Suburban fusion plants ruptured, hospitals incinerated, day clubs crashing down on their young occupants. So far we have never killed anyone, but if we chose to do so, if you leave us with no alternative, this planet will suffer enormously."

"Monster!"

"And I'll do it, Ralph. I'll give the order for my followers to start the campaign. It will come right after my order for every non-possessed in Exnall to be murdered. They're going to be killed right here on the streets in front of you, Ralph. We will crush their skulls, snap their necks, strangle them, cut their bellies open and leave them to bleed to death."

"I don't believe you."

"No, you don't want to believe me, Ralph. There is a difference." Her voice became smooth, taunting him. "What have we got to lose? These people you see around you will join us one way or the other. That is what I'm trying to tell you. Either their bodies will be possessed, or they will die and possess in turn. Please, Ralph, don't allow yourself and others to suffer because of your stupid beliefs. *We will win.*"

Ralph wanted to kill her, hating and fearing the serene way she talked about slaughter, knowing she wasn't bluffing. The most basic human urge, to wipe out your enemy hard and fast, came firing up from his subconscious. His neural nanonics had to reduce his heart rate. One hand moved fractionally towards the pistol holster on his belt.

And I can't do it. Can't kill her. Can't end it all with the one act of barbarism which we've always resorted to. Dear God, she's already dead.

Annette Ekelund's eyes followed the tiny motion of his hand. She smiled and turned to beckon one of the figures that had emerged from the diner.

Ralph watched numbly as a mummy wearing a peaked police cap shuffled forwards. The girl held in its solid embrace couldn't have been more than fifteen. All she wore was a long mauve T-shirt. Her bare legs were grazed and streaked with dirt. She'd been crying profusely. Now she could only whimper as she was dragged towards him.

"Nice-looking girl," Annette Ekelund said. "A fine body, if a little young. But I can alter that. You see, if you blow big chunks out of this body of Angeline Gallagher's, Ralph, the girl will become the one I possess next. My colleague here will break her bones, rape her, rip the skin from her face, hurt her so terribly she'll make a pact with Lucifer himself to make it stop. But it won't be Lucifer who answers her from the afterlife, only me. I shall come forth again; and you and I will be right back where we started, except that Gallagher's body will be dead. Will she thank you for that, do you think, Ralph?"

Nerve impulse overrides prevented Ralph's hands from tearing Ekelund's head from her shoulders. "What do you want me to say?" he datavised to the security committee.

"I don't think we have any choice," Princess Kirsten replied. "I cannot allow thousands of my people to be killed out of hand."

"If we leave, they'll be possessed," Ralph warned her. "Ekelund will do exactly what she described to this girl, and all the others. Not just here, but right along the whole length of Mortonridge."

"I know, but I have to consider the majority. If the possessed are outside the marine cordons, then we've already lost Mortonridge. I cannot lose Xingu, too."

"There are two million people living on Mortonridge!"

"I am aware of that. But at least if they're possessed they will still be alive. I think that Ekelund woman is right; the overall problem of possession isn't going to be solved here." There was a moment's pause. "We're cutting our losses, Ralph. Tell her she can have Mortonridge. For now."

"Yes, ma'am," he whispered.

Annette Ekelund smiled. "She agreed, didn't she?"

"You may have Mortonridge," Ralph relayed imperturbably as the Princess started to outline the conditions. "We will instigate an immediate evacuation procedure for people from areas you have not yet reached; any attempt to sabotage vehicles will result in SD strikes against areas where we know you are concentrated. If any of you try to pass the cordon we establish between Mortonridge and the main body of the continent you will be put into zero-tau. If any of you are found outside the cordon you will be put into zero-tau. If there is any terrorist assault against any Ombey citizen or building we will send in a punitive expedition and throw several hundred of you into zero-tau. If you attempt to communicate with other offplanet possessed forces, you will again be punished."

"Of course," Ekelund said mockingly. "I agree to your terms."

"And the girl comes with me," Ralph declared.

"Come come, Ralph, I don't believe the authorities actually said that."

"Try me," he challenged.

Ekelund glanced at the sobbing girl, then back to Ralph. "Would you have bothered if she was a wizened old grandmother?" she asked sarcastically.

"But you didn't choose a wizened old grandmother, did you? You chose her because you knew how protective we are towards the young. Your error."

Ekelund said nothing, but made a sharp irritated gesture to the mummy. It let the girl go. She floundered, trembling so badly she could hardly stand. Ralph caught her before she fell. He winced at the weight that put on his injured leg.

"I'll look forward to the day you join us, Ralph," Ekelund said. "However long it takes. You'll be quite an asset. Come and see me when your soul finally obtains a new body to live in."

"Fuck you." Ralph scooped the girl up and started to walk down the road. He ignored the hundreds of people standing in front of the prim buildings, the indifferent possessed and their wailing distraught victims, the ones he'd failed so completely. Staring resolutely ahead, concentrating on putting one foot in front of the other. He knew if he took it all in, acknowledged the magnitude of the disaster he'd wrought, he'd never be able to carry on.

"Enjoy your magnificent victory with the girl," Annette Ekelund called after him.

"This one is only the beginning," he promised grimly.

5

At a point in space four light-years distant from the star
around which Mirchusko orbited, the gravity density suddenly leapt upwards. The area affected was smaller than a
quark, at first. But once established, the warp rapidly grew
both in size and in strength. Faint strands of starlight curved
around the fringes, only to be sucked in towards the centre
as the gravity intensified further.

Ten picoseconds after its creation, the shape of the warp
twisted from a spherical zone to a two-dimensional disk. By
this time it was over a hundred metres in diameter. At the centre of one side, gravity fluctuated again, placing an enormous
strain on local space. A perfectly circular rupture appeared,
rapidly irising open.

A long grey-white fountain of gas spewed out from the epi-
centre of the wormhole terminus. The water vapour it contained immediately turned to minute ice crystals, spinning
away from the central plume, twinkling weakly in the sparse
starlight. Lumps of solid matter began to shoot out along the
gas jet, tumbling off into the void. It was a curious collection
of objects: sculpted clouds of sand, tufts of reed grass with
their roots wriggling like spider legs, small fractured den-
drites of white and blue coral, broken palm tree fronds, oscillating globules of saltwater, a shoal of frantic fish, their
spectacularly coloured bodies bursting apart as they underwent explosive decompression, several seagulls squirting
blood from beaks and rectums.

Then the crazy outpouring reduced drastically, blocked by
a larger body which was surging along the wormhole. *Udat*
slipped out into normal space, a flattened teardrop over a hundred and thirty metres long, its blue polyp hull enlivened with
a tortuous purple web. Straightaway the blackhawk changed

the flow of energy through the vast honeycomb of patterning cells which made up the bulk of its body, modifying its gravitonic distortion field. The wormhole terminus began to close behind it.

Almost the last object to emerge from the transdimensional opening was a small human figure. A woman: difficult to see because of the black SII spacesuit she wore, her limbs scrabbling futilely, almost as though she were clawing at the structure of space-time in order to pursue the big blackhawk as it drew away from her. Her movements slowly calmed as the suit's sensor collar revealed stars and distant nebulas again, replacing the menacingly insubstantial pseudofabric of the wormhole.

Dr Alkad Mzu felt herself shudder uncontrollably, the relief was so intoxicating. Free from the grip of equations become energy.

I understand the configuration of reality too well to endure such direct exposure. The wormhole has too many flaws, too many hidden traps. A quasi-continuum where time's arrow has to be directed by an artificial energy flow; the possible fates lurking within such a non-place would make you welcome death as the most beautiful of consorts.

The collar sensors showed her she had picked up a considerable tumble since losing her grip on the rope ladder. Her neural nanonics had automatically blocked the impulses from her inner ears as a precaution against nausea. There were also a number of analgesic blocks erected across the nerve paths from her forearms. A physiological status display showed her the damage inflicted on tendons and muscles as she'd forced herself to hang on as the *Udat* dived for safety. Nothing drastic, thankfully. Medical packages would be able to cope once she got the suit off.

"Can you retrieve me?" she datavised to the *Udat*'s flight computer. "I can't stop spinning." As if they couldn't see that. But the bitek starship was already seven hundred metres away, and still retreating from her. She wanted an answer, wanted someone to talk to her. Proof she wasn't alone. This predicament was triggering way too many thirty-year-old memories. Dear Mary, I'll be calling it déjà vu next. "Calling *Udat*, can you retrieve me?" Come on, answer.

On the *Udat*'s bridge Haltam was busy programming the medical packages which were knitting to the base of Meyer's skull. Haltam was the *Udat*'s fusion specialist, but doubled as ship's medical officer.

The captain was lying prone on his acceleration couch, unconscious. His fingers were still digging into the cushioning, frozen in a claw-like posture, nails broken by the strength he'd used to maul the fabric. Blood dribbling out of his nose made sticky blotches on his cheeks. Haltam didn't like to think of the whimpers coming from Meyer's mouth just before the blackhawk had swallowed out of Tranquillity, snatching Alkad Mzu away from the intelligence agents imprisoning her within the habitat. Nor did he like the physiological display he was accessing from Meyer's neural nanonics.

"How is he?" asked Aziz, the *Udat*'s spaceplane pilot.

"None too good, I think. He's suffered a lot of cerebral stress, which pushed him into shock. If I'm interpreting this display right, his neural symbionts were subjected to a massive trauma. Some of the bitek synapses are dead, and there's minor hemorrhaging where they interface with his medulla oblongata."

"Christ."

"Yeah. And we don't have a medical package on board which can reach that deep. Not that it would do us a lot of good if we had. You need to be a specialist to operate one."

"I cannot feel his dreams," *Udat* datavised. "I always feel his dreams. Always."

Haltam and Aziz exchanged a heavy glance. The bitek starship rarely used its link with the flight computer to communicate with any of the crew.

"I don't believe the damage is permanent," Haltam told the blackhawk. "Any decent hospital can repair these injuries."

"He will waken?"

"Absolutely. His neural nanonics are keeping him under for the moment. I don't want him conscious again until the packages have knitted. They ought to be able to help stabilize him, and alleviate most of the shock."

"Thank you, Haltam."

"Least I can do. And what about you? Are you all right?"

"Tranquillity was very harsh. My mind hurts. I have never known that before."

"What about your physical structure?"

"Intact. I remain functional."

A whistle of breath emerged from Haltam's mouth. Then the flight computer informed him that Alkad Mzu was datavising for help. "Oh, hell," he muttered. The coverage provided by the electronic sensor suite mounted around the outside of the starship's life support horseshoe was limited. Normally, *Udat*'s own sensor blisters provided Meyer with all the information he needed. But when Haltam accessed the suite, the infrared sweep found Mzu easily, spinning amid the thin cloud of dispersing debris which had been sucked into the wormhole with them.

"We've got you located," he datavised. "Stand by."

"*Udat*?" Aziz asked. "Can you take us over to her, please?"

"I will do so."

Haltam managed a nervous, relieved smile. At least the blackhawk was cooperating. The real big test would come when they wanted a swallow manoeuvre.

Udat manoeuvred itself to within fifty metres of Mzu, and matched her gentle trajectory. After that, Cherri Barnes strapped on a cold gas manoeuvring pack and hauled her in.

"We have to leave," Alkad datavised as soon as she was inside the airlock. "Immediately."

"You didn't warn us about your friends on the beach," Cherri answered reproachfully.

"You were told about the observation agents. I apologize if you weren't aware of how anxious they were to prevent me from escaping, but I thought that was implicit in my message. Now, please, we must perform a swallow manoeuvre away from here."

The airlock chamber pressurized as soon as the outer hatch closed, filling with a slightly chilled air. Cherri watched Mzu touch the seal catches on her worn old backpack with awkward movements. The small incongruous pack fell to the floor. Mzu's SII suit began flowing off her skin, its oil-like substance accumulating in the form of a globe hanging from the base of her collar. Cherri eyed their passenger curiously as her own suit reverted to neutral storage mode. The short black woman was shivering slightly, sweat coating her skin. Both hands were bent inward as though crippled with arthritis; twisted, swollen fingers unmoving.

"Our captain is incapacitated," Cherri said. "And I'm none too certain about *Udat* either."

Alkad grimaced, shaking her head. Oh, what an irony. Depending on the *Udat*'s goodwill, it of all starships. "Ships will be sent after us," she said. "If we remain in this location I will be captured, and you will probably be exterminated."

"Look, just what the hell did you do to get the Kingdom so pissed at you?"

"Better you don't know."

"Better I do, then I'll know what we're likely to be facing."

"Trouble enough."

"Try to be a little more specific."

"Very well: every ESA asset they can activate throughout the Confederation will be used to find me, if that makes you feel any happier. You really don't want to be around me for any length of time. If you are, you will die. Clear enough?"

Cherri didn't know how to answer. True, they'd known Mzu was some kind of dissident on the run, but not that she would attract this kind of attention. And why would Tranquillity, presumably in conjunction with the Lord of Ruin, help the Kulu Kingdom try to restrain her? Mzu was adding up to real bad news.

Alkad datavised the flight computer, requesting a direct link to the blackhawk itself. "*Udat*?"

"Yes, Dr Mzu."

"You must leave here."

"My captain is hurt. His mind has darkened and withered. I am in pain when I try to think."

"I'm sorry about Meyer, but we cannot stay here. The blackhawks at Tranquillity know where you swallowed to. The Lord of Ruin will send them after me. They'll take us all back."

"I do not wish to return. Tranquillity frightens me. I thought it was my friend."

"One swallow manoeuvre, that's all. A small one. Just a light-year will suffice, the direction is not important. No blackhawk will be able to follow us then. After that we can see what's to be done next."

"Very well. A light-year."

Cherri had already unfastened her spacesuit collar when she felt the familiar minute perturbation in apparent gravity which meant *Udat*'s distortion field was altering to open a wormhole interstice. "Very clever," she said sardonically to Mzu. "I hope to hell you know what you're doing. Bitek starships don't usually make swallows without their captain providing some supervision."

"That's a conceit you really ought to abandon," Alkad said tiredly. "Voidhawks and blackhawks are considerably more intelligent than humans."

"But their personalities are completely different."

"It's done now. And it would appear we are still alive. Were there any more complaints?"

Cherri ignored her and started to pull on a one-piece shipsuit.

"Could you sling my backpack over my shoulder, please?" Alkad asked. "I don't have the use of my hands at this moment. Our exit from Tranquillity was more precipitous than I imagined. And I'll need some medical packages."

"Fine. Haltam can apply the packages for you; he'll be on the bridge tending to Meyer. I'll take the backpack for you."

"No. Put it over my shoulder. I will carry it."

Cherri sighed through clenched teeth. She urgently wanted to see for herself how bad Meyer was. She was worried about the way *Udat* would react if the captain was unconscious for too long. She was coming down off the adrenaline high of the escape, which was like a hit of pure depression. And this small woman was about as safe as her own weight in naked plutonium.

"What have you got in it?"

"Do not concern yourself about that."

Cherri grabbed the backpack by its straps and held it up in front of Mzu's impassive face. There couldn't have been much in it, judging by the weight. "Now look——!"

"A great deal of money. And an even larger amount of information; none of which you would have the faintest comprehension of. Now, you are already harbouring me on board

which in itself is enough to get you killed if I'm discovered.
And if the agency knew you had physically held up the backpack containing the items it does, they would throw you
straight into personality debrief just to find out how much
those items weigh. Do you really want to compound matters
by taking a look inside?"

What Cherri wanted to do was swing the backpack at
Mzu's head. Meyer had made the worst error of judgement in
his life agreeing to this absurd rescue mission. All she could
do now was pray it turned out not to be a terminal mistake.

"As you wish," Cherri said with fragile calm.

•   •   •

San Angeles spaceport was situated on the southern rim of the
metropolis. A square ten kilometres to a side, a miniature city
chiselled from machinery. Vast barren swathes of carbon concrete had been poured over the levelled earth and then divided
up into roads, taxi aprons, and landing pads. Hundreds of line
company hangars and cargo terminals hosted a business
which accounted for a fifth of the entire planet's ground-to-
orbit traffic movements.

Among the numbingly constant lines of standardized com-
posite-walled hangars and office block cubes, only the main
passenger terminal had been permitted a flight of fancy architecture. It resembled the kind of starship which might have
been built if the practicalities of the ZTT drive hadn't forced
a uniform spherical hull on the astroengineering companies.
A soft-contoured meld between an industrial microgee refinery station and a hypersonic biplane, it dominated the skyline
with its imperious technogothic silhouette. On the long autoway ride out from the city it gave approaching drivers the
impression it was ready to pounce jealously on the tiny delta-
planform spaceplanes which scuttled underneath its sweeping
wings to embark passengers.

Jezzibella didn't bother looking at it. She sat in the car with
her eyes closed for the whole of the early morning journey,
not asleep, but brain definitely in neutral. Those kids from the
concert—whatever their names were—had proved worthless
last night, their awe of her interfering with their emotions.

Now she just wanted out. Out of this world. Out of this galaxy. Out of this universe. Forever living on the hope that the waiting starship would take her to a place where something new was happening. That the next stop would be different.

Leroy and Libby shared the car with her, silent and motionless. They knew the mood. Always the same when she was leaving a planet, and a fraction more intense every time.

Leroy was pretty sure the unspoken yearning was one reason she appealed to the kids; they identified with that integral sense of bewildered desperation and loss. Of course, it would have to be watched. Right now it was just an artist's essential suffering, a perverted muse. But eventually it could develop into full depression if he wasn't careful.

Another item to take care of. More stress. Not that he'd have it any other way.

The eleven cars which made up the Jezzibella tour convoy slid into the VIP parking slots below one of the terminal's flamboyant wings. Leroy had chosen such an early hour for the flight because it was the terminal's slackest time. They ought to be able to clear the official procedures without any problems.

Maybe that was the reason why none of the bodyguards sensed anything wrong. Always scanning for trouble with augmented senses, the absence of people was a relief rather than a concern.

It wasn't until Jezzibella asked: "Where the fuck are the reporters?" that Leroy noticed anything amiss. The terminal wasn't merely quiet, it was dead. No passengers, no staff, not even a sub-manager to greet Jezzibella. And certainly no sign of any reporters. That wasn't odd, that was alarming. He'd leaked their departure schedule to three reliable sources last night.

"Just fucking great, Leroy," Jezzibella growled as the entourage went through the entrance. "This exit is really up there in fucking mythland, isn't it? Because I certainly don't fucking believe it. How the hell am I supposed to make a fucking impression when the only things watching me leave are the fucking valeting mechanoids?"

"I don't understand it," Leroy said. The cavernous VIP

vestibule carried on the never-was illusion of the terminal building: ancient Egypt discovers atomic power. A marble fantasyville of obelisks, fountains, and outsize gold ornaments, where ebony sphinxes prowled around the walls. When he datavised the local net processor all he got was the *capacity engaged* response.

"What's to understand, dickbrain? You screwed up again." Jezzibella stomped off towards the wide wave-effect escalator which curved up towards one of the terminal's concourses. She could remember coming down it when she arrived, so it must be the way to the spaceplanes. The bastard local net processor wouldn't even permit her to access a floor plan. Cock-up planet!

She was five metres from the top (her retinue scurrying to catch up) when she saw the man standing waiting for her beside the arched entrance of the concourse. Some oaf in a terminal staff suit uniform, officious smile in place.

"I'm sorry, lady," he said, when she drew level with him. "You can't go any further."

Jezzibella said: "Oh, really?"

"Yes. We've got a priority flight operation in progress today, everything has been rescheduled."

Jezzibella smiled, her skin softening: a delectably young wide-eyed ingenue looking for a *real man* to guide her. "That's such a pity. I'm booked to leave this morning."

"I'm afraid there will be a short delay."

Still smiling, Jezzibella slammed her knee into his crotch.

Isaac Goddard had been pleased at his assignment. Putting the brakes on inconvenient civilians wandering through the terminal was an important task, Al Capone wouldn't give it to just anyone. And now it meant he got to meet this century's superstar, too. Lee Ruggiero, whose body he possessed, was full of admiration for Jezzibella. Looking at her up close, Isaac could see why. So sweet and vulnerable. Shame he had to use force to stop her. But the timing of the spaceplane flights was vital. Al had emphasised that often enough.

He was readying his energistic powers to deal with her bodyguards, who had now caught her up, when she did her level best to ram his testicles into his eye sockets via his intestinal tract.

The energistic power which was the inheritance of every possessed was capable of near-miraculous feats as it bent the fabric of reality to a mind's whim. As well as its destructive potential, items could be made solid at the flicker of a thought. It was also capable of reinforcing a body to resist almost any kind of assault as well as enhancing its physical strength. Wounds could be healed at almost the same rate they were inflicted.

But first the wish had to be formulated, the energistic flow regulated appropriately. Isaac Goddard never had a chance to wish for anything. A uniquely male agony blew apart every coherent thought current stealing through his captured brain. Pain was all that remained.

His face white, he slowly sank to the floor before Jezzibella. Tears trickled down his cheeks as his mouth laboured soundlessly.

"If it's all the same to you," Jezzibella said brightly, "I really would like to leave this shit tip of a planet right now." She strode away.

"Oh, hey, come on, Jez," Leroy called as he chased after her down the concourse, forcing himself into a fast waddle. "Give me a break. You can't go around doing things like that."

"Why not, for shit's sake? Worried this fucking great army of witnesses will all testify in court?"

"Look, you heard him. There's some kind of special flight schedule this morning. Why don't you wait here, and I'll find out what's going on. Huh? I won't be long."

"I'm the fucking special flight, shithead! *Me, me.*"

"Christ! Grow up, will you! I don't manage bloody teen-scream acts. I only do adults."

Jezzibella stopped in surprise. Leroy never shouted at her. She pouted prettily. "I've been bad."

"You got it."

"Forgive me. I was all worked up over Emmerson."

"I can understand that. But he's not coming on the starship with us. Panic over."

The mock smile faltered. "Leroy . . . Please, I just want to leave. I hate this fucking place. I'll behave, really. But you have got to get me away from here."

He rubbed his fat fingers over his face; sweat was making hair stick to his brow. "Okay. One miracle evacuation flight coming up."

"Thanks, Leroy. I don't have your defences, you know? The world's different for you. Hard and easy altogether."

Leroy tried to datavise a net processor. But he couldn't get a single response, the units were all inert. "What the hell is going on here?" he asked in annoyance. "If these flights were that big a deal, why weren't we informed?"

"Guess that's my fault," Al Capone told him.

Jezzibella and Leroy turned to see a group of ten men walking down the concourse towards them. They all wore double-breasted suits and carried machine guns. Somehow the idea of running from them seemed ludicrous. More gangsters were emerging from side corridors.

"You see, I don't want people informed," Al explained. "At least not for a while. After that, I'm gonna speak to this whole goddamn planet. Loud and clear."

Two of Jezzibella's bodyguards caught sight of the approaching gangsters. They began to run forwards, drawing their thermal induction pistols.

Al clicked his fingers. The bodyguards let out simultaneous yelps of pain as their pistols turned red hot. They dropped them fast. That was when a ripple of onyx flooring rose up and tripped them.

Jezzibella watched in astonishment as both bulky men went skidding into the wall. She looked from them back to Al, and grinned. *"Magnifico."*

She desperately wanted to record the scene, but her fucking neural nanonics were crashing. Fucking typical!

Al watched the beef boy back away fearfully. But the dame . . . she just stood there. This weird expression on her face, fascination and interest making her eyes narrow demurely. Interest in *him*, by damn! She wasn't afraid. She was pure class, this one. She was also one hell of a looker. Minx face, and a body the likes of which simply didn't exist in the twenties.

Lovegrove was itching for a peek at her, busy telling him who Jezzibella was. Some kind of hotshot nightclub singer. Except there was more to it than just singing and playing the ivories these days, a lot more.

"So what are you going to tell us?" Jezzibella asked, her voice husky.

"What?" Al asked.

"When you speak to the planet. What are you going to say?"

Al took his time lighting a cigar. Making her wait, showing exactly who was in control. "I'm gonna tell them that I'm in charge now. Number one guy on the planet. And you've all gotta do what I say. *Anything* I say." He winked broadly.

Jezzibella put on a disappointed expression. "Waste of talent."

"*What?*"

"You're the guys the police are calling Retros, right?"

"Yeah," Al said cautiously.

She flicked a casual finger towards her dazed bodyguards. "And you've got the balls and the power to take over a whole planet?"

"You catch on quick."

"So why waste it on this dump?"

"This *dump* has eight hundred and ninety million people living on it, lady. And I'm gonna be the fucking emperor of them all before the evening."

"My last album has sold over three billion so far, probably triple that number in bootlegs. Those people *want* me to be their empress. If you're going for broke, why not choose a decent planet? Kulu, or Oshanko, or even Earth."

Not taking his eyes off her, Al called over his shoulder: "Hey, savvy Avvy, get your crummy ass up here. Now!"

Avram Harwood scuttled forwards, his head bowed, shoulders drooping. Each step was obviously painful for him, he was favouring his right leg. "Yes, sir?"

"New California is the greatest goddamn planet in the Confederation, ain't that right?" Al asked.

"Oh, yes, sir. It is."

"Is your population bigger than Kulu?" Jezzibella asked in a bored tone.

Avram Harwood twitched miserably.

"Answer her," Capone growled.

"No, ma'am," Harwood said.

"Is your economy larger than Oshanko's?"

"No."

"Do you export as much as Earth?"

"No."

Jezzibella inclined her head contemptuously on one side, pushing her lips out towards Al. "Anything else you want to know?"

Her voice had suddenly become the same as a schoolteacher's. Al started to laugh in sincere admiration. "Goddamn! Modern women."

"Can you all do that heat trick with the fingers?"

"Sure can, honey."

"Interesting. So how is taking over this spaceport tied in with conquering the planet?"

Al's first instinct was to brag. About the synchronized flights up to the orbiting asteroids. About taking out the SD personnel. About using the SD network firepower to open up the whole planet to his Organization. But they were short on time. And this was no backwoods girl, she'd understand if he explained it. "Sorry, babe, but we're kinda in a hurry. It's been a ball."

"No it hasn't. If you'd had a ball with me, you'd know about it."

"Hot shit—"

"If it's tied in with spaceplane flights, you're either going up to starships or the orbiting asteroids. But if you're taking over the planet, it can't be the starships. So it has to be the asteroids. Let me guess, the Strategic Defence network." She watched the alarmed expressions light up on the faces of the gangsters. All except Mayor Harwood, but then he was already hopelessly adrift in some deep private purgatory. "How did I do?"

Al could only gawp. He'd heard of lady spiders like this; they knitted fancy webs or did hypnosis, or something. It ended up that the males just couldn't escape. Then they got screwed and eaten.

Now I know what they go through.

"You did pretty good." He was envious of her cool. Envious of a lot of things, actually.

"Al?" Emmet Mordden urged. "Al, we have to get going."

"Yeah, yeah. I ain't forgotten."

"We can send this group down to Luciano's people for possessing."

"Hey, who the fuck's in charge here?"

Emmet took a frightened pace backwards.

"In charge, but not in control," Jezzibella teased.

"Don't push it, lady," Al warned her sharply.

"True leaders simply tell people to do what they want to do anyway." She licked her lips. "Guess what I want to do?"

"Fuck this. Modern women. You're all like goddamn whores. I ain't never heard anything like it."

"The talk isn't all you've never had before."

"Holy Christ."

"So what do you say, Al?" Jezzibella switched her voice back to a liquid rumble. She almost didn't have to fake it. She was so turned on, excited, stimulated. You name it. Caught up in a terrorist hijack. And such strange terrorists, too. Wimps with a personal nuclear capability. Except the leader, he was massively focused. Not bad-looking, either. "Want me to tag along on your little coup d'état mission? Or are you going to spend the rest of every waking day wondering what it would have been like? And you will wonder. You know you will."

"We got a spare seat on the rocketship," Al said. "But you've got to do as you're told."

She batted her eyelashes. "That'll be a first."

Amazed at what he'd just said, Al tried to play back their conversation in his mind to see how he'd gotten to this point. No good, he couldn't figure it. He was acting on pure impulse again. And that felt first-class. Like the good old days. People never did know what he was going to do next. It kept them on edge, and him on top.

Jezzibella walked over to him and tucked her arm in his. "Let's go."

Al grinned around wolfishly. "Okay, wiseasses, you heard the lady. Mickey, take the rest of this bunch down to Luciano. Emmet, Silvano, take your boys to their spaceplanes."

"Leave me my manager, and the old woman, oh, and the band too," Jezzibella said.

"What the hell is this?" Al demanded. "I ain't got room in my Organization for freeloaders."

"You want me to look good. I need them."

"Je-zus, you're pushy."

"You want a girl who's a pushover, find yourself a teenage bimbo. Me, it's the whole package or nothing."

"Okay, Mickey, lay off the cornholers. But the rest of them get the full treatment." He shoved his hands out towards her, palms held up imploringly. "Good enough?" The sarcasm wasn't entirely feigned.

"Good enough," Jezzibella agreed.

They grinned knowingly at each other for a moment, then led the procession of gangsters down the concourse to the waiting spaceplanes.

•   •   •

The wormhole terminus opened smoothly six hundred and eighty thousand kilometres above Jupiter's equator, the absolute minimum permitted distance from the prodigious band of orbiting habitats. *Oenone* flew out of the circular gap, and immediately identified itself to the Jovian Strategic Defence network. As soon as their approach authorization had been granted, the voidhawk accelerated in towards the Kristata habitat at an urgent five gees. It was already asking the habitat to assemble a medical team to meet it as soon as it docked.

Of what nature? Kristata asked.

At which point Cacus, their medical officer, took over, using the voidhawk's affinity to relay a list of the grisly physical injuries inflicted on Syrinx by the possessed occupying Pernik island. **But most importantly we're going to need a psychological trauma team,** he said. **We put her in zero-tau for the flight, naturally. However, she did not respond to any level of mental communication after she was brought on board, other than a purely autonomic acknowledgement of *Oenone*'s contact. I'm afraid the intensity of the withdrawal is one which approaches catatonia.**

What happened to her? queried the habitat. It was unusual for a voidhawk to fly without its captain's guidance.

She was tortured.

Ruben waited until the medical discussion was under way before asking *Oenone* for an affinity link with Eden itself. Arriving at Jupiter he could actually feel his body relaxing in the bridge couch despite the acceleration pressure. The events which would play out over the next few hours were going to be strenuous, but nothing like as bad as Atlantis and the voyage to the Sol system.

Oenone's instinct had been to rush directly to Saturn and the Romulus habitat as soon as Oxley had brought Syrinx on board. The yearning to go *home* after such a tremendous shock was as much a voidhawk trait as a human one.

It had been down to Ruben to convince the frantic, frightened voidhawk that Jupiter would be preferable. Jovian habitats had more advanced medical facilities than those orbiting Saturn. And, of course, there was the Consensus to inform.

This was a threat which simply had to rank higher than individual concerns.

Then there was the flight itself. *Oenone* had never flown anywhere without Syrinx's subliminal supervision, much less performed a swallow manoeuvre. Voidhawks could fly without the slightest human input, of course. But as ever there was a big difference between theory and practice. They identified so much with the needs and wishes of their captains.

The crew's general affinity band had rung with a powerful cadence of relief when the first swallow manoeuvre passed off flawlessly.

Ruben knew he shouldn't have doubted *Oenone*, but his own mind was eddying with worry. The sight of Syrinx's injuries . . . And worse, her mind closed as if it were a flower at night. Any attempt to prise below her churning surface thoughts had resulted in a squirt of sickening images and sensations. Her sanity would surely suffer if she was left alone with such nightmares. Cacus had immediately placed her in zero-tau, temporarily circumventing the problem.

Hello, Ruben, Eden said. **It is pleasant to receive you again. Though I am saddened by the condition of Syrinx, and I sense that *Oenone* is suffering considerable distress.**

Ruben hadn't conversed directly with the original habitat for over forty years, not since his last visit. It was a trip which most Edenists made at some time in their life. Not a pilgrimage (they would hotly deny that) but paying their respects, acknowledging the sentimental debt to the founding entity of their culture.

That's why I need to speak with you, Ruben said. Eden, we have a problem. Would you call a general Consensus, please?

There was no hierarchy in Edenism, it was a society proud of its egalitarianism; he could have made the same request of any habitat. If the personality considered the request valid, it would be forwarded to the habitat Consensus, then if it passed that vote, a general Consensus would be called, comprising every single Edenist, habitat, and voidhawk in the Sol system. But for this issue, Ruben felt obliged to make his appeal direct to Eden, the first habitat.

He gave an account of what had happened on Atlantis, followed by the précis which was Laton's legacy. When he finished, the affinity band was silent for several moments.

I will call for a general Consensus, Eden said. The habitat's mental voice was uncharacteristically studious.

Relief mingled with a curious frisson of worry among Ruben's thoughts. At least the burden which *Oenone*'s crew had carried by themselves during the flight was to be shared and mitigated—the fundamental psychology of Edenism. But what amounted to the habitat's shock at the revelation of souls returning to possess the living was deeply unsettling. Eden had been germinated in 2075, making it the oldest living entity in the Confederation. If anything had the requisite endowment of wisdom to withstand such news then surely it must be the ancient habitat.

Disquieted by the habitat's response, and chiding himself for expecting miracles, Ruben settled back in the acceleration couch and used the voidhawk's sensor blisters to observe their approach flight. They were already twenty-five thousand kilometres from Europa, curving gently around its northern hemisphere. The moon's ice mantle glinted a grizzled oyster as distant sunlight skittered over its smooth surface, throwing off the occasional dazzling mirror-flash from an impact crater.

Behind the moon, Jupiter occluded half of the universe. They were close enough that the polar regions were invisible, distilling the planet to a simple flat barrier of enraged orange and white clouds. The gas giant was in one of its more active phases. Vast hurricane storm-spots geysered through the upper cloud bands, swirling mushroom formations bringing with them a multitude of darker contaminates from the lower levels. Colours fought like armies along frenzied boundaries of intricate curlicues, never winning, never losing. There was too much chaos for any one pattern or shade to gain the ultimate triumph of stability. Even the great spots, of which there were now three, had lifetimes measurable in mere millennia. But for raw spectacle they were unmatched. After five centuries of interstellar exploration, Jupiter remained one of the largest gas giants ever catalogued, honouring its archaic title as the father of gods.

A hundred thousand kilometres in from Europa, the habitats formed their own unique constellation around their lord, drinking down its magnetosphere energy, bathing in the tempestuous particle winds, listening to the wild chants of its radio voice, and watching the ever-changing panorama of the clouds. They could never live anywhere else but above such worlds; only the magnetic flux spun out by gas giants could generate the power levels necessary to sustain life within their dusky-crimson polyp shells. There were four thousand two hundred and fifty mature habitats in Jupiter orbit, nurturing a total Edenist population of over nine billion individuals. The second largest civilization in the Confederation—in numerical terms. Only Earth with its guesstimated population of thirty-five billion was bigger. But the *standard* of civilization, in both economic and cultural terms, was peerless. Jupiter's citizens had no underclass, no ignorance, no poverty, and no misfits, barring the one-in-a-million Serpent who rejected Edenism in its entirety.

The reason for such enviable social fortune was Jupiter itself. To build such a society, even with affinity-enhancing psychological stability, and bitek alleviating a great many mundane physical problems, required vast wealth. It came from helium$_3$, the principal fusion fuel used throughout the Confederation.

In comparison with other fuels, a mix of He$_3$ and deuterium produced one of the cleanest fusion reactions possible, resulting mainly in charged helium with an almost zero neutron emission. Such an end product meant that the generator systems needed little shielding, making them cheaper to build. Superenergized helium was also an ideal space drive.

The Confederation societies were heavily dependent on this form of cheap, low-pollution fusion to maintain their socioeconomic index. Fortunately deuterium existed in massive quantities; a common isotope of hydrogen, it could be extracted from any sea or glacial asteroid. He_3, however, was extremely rare in nature. The operation to mine it from Jupiter began in 2062 when the then Jovian Sky Power Corporation dropped its first aerostat into the atmosphere to extract the elusive isotope in commercial quantities. There were only minute amounts present, but minute is a relative term in the context of a gas giant.

It was that one tentative high-risk operation which had transformed itself, via political revolution, religious intolerance, and bitek revelation into Edenism. And Edenists continued to mine He_3 in every colonized star system which had a gas giant (with the notable exception of Kulu and its Principalities), although cloudscoops had replaced aerostats long ago as the actual method of collection. It was the greatest industrial enterprise in existence, and also the largest monopoly. And with the format for developing stage one colony worlds now institutionalized, it looked set to remain so.

Yet as any student of ekistics could have predicted, it was Jupiter which remained the economic heart of Edenism. For it was Jupiter which supplied the single largest consumer of He_3: Earth and its O'Neill Halo. Such a market required a huge mining operation, as well as its associated support infrastructure; and on top of that came their own massive energy requirements.

Hundreds of industrial stations flocked around every habitat, varying in size from ten-kilometre-diameter asteroidal mineral refineries to tiny microgee research laboratories. Tens of thousands of spaceships congested local space, importing and exporting every commodity known to the human and xenoc races of the Confederation—their assigned flight vectors weaving a sluggish, ephemeral DNA coil around the five-hundred-and-fifty-thousand-kilometre orbital band.

By the time *Oenone* was two thousand kilometres away from Kristata, the habitat was becoming visible to its optical sensors. It shone weakly of its own accord, a miniature galaxy with long, thin spiral arms. The habitat itself formed the glowing core of the nebula, a cylinder forty-five kilometres long, rotating gently inside a corona of Saint Elmo's fire sparked by the agitated particle winds splashing across its shell. Industrial stations glimmered around it, static flashing in crazed patterns over external girders and panels, their metallic structures more susceptible to the ionic squalls than bitek polyp. Fusion drives formed the spiral arms, Adamist starships and inter-orbit craft arriving and departing from the habitat's globe-shaped counter-rotating spaceport.

A priority flight path had been cleared through the other ships, allowing *Oenone* to race past them towards the docking ledges ringing Kristata's northern endcap, although the starship was actually decelerating now, pushing seven gees. Ruben observed the habitat expand rapidly, its central band of starscrapers coming into focus. It was virtually the only aspect of the external vista which had changed after travelling a hundred thousand kilometres from their swallow emergence point. Jupiter remained exactly the same. He couldn't even tell if they were closer to the gas giant or not, there were no valid reference points. It seemed as though *Oenone* were flying between two flat plains, one comprised of ginger and white clouds, the other a midnight sky.

They swept around the counter-rotating spaceport and headed in for the northern endcap. The violet haze of glowing particles was murkier here, disrupted by slithering waves of darkness as the energized wind broke and churned against the four concentric docking ledge rings. *Oenone* experienced a prickle of static across its blue polyp hull as it slipped over the innermost ledge at a shallow tangent; for a moment the tattered discharge mimicked the purple web pattern veining its hull surface. Then the bulky voidhawk was hovering directly above a docking pedestal, slowly twisting around until the feed tubes were aligned correctly. It settled on the pedestal with all the fuss of a falling autumn leaf.

A convoy of service vehicles rolled towards it. The ambulance was the first to reach the rim of the saucer-shaped hull, its long airlock tube snaking out to mate with the crew toroid. Cacus was still discussing Syrinx's status with the medical team as the zero-tau pod containing her body was rolled into the ambulance.

Ruben realized *Oenone* was hungrily ingesting nutrient fluid from the pedestal tubes. **How are you?** he asked the voidhawk belatedly.

I am glad the flight is over. Syrinx can begin to heal now. Kristata says all the damage can be repaired. Many doctors are part of its multiplicity. I believe what it says.

Yes, she'll heal. And we can help. Knowing you are loved is a great part of any cure.

Thank you, Ruben. I am glad you are my friend, and hers.

Rising from his acceleration couch, Ruben felt a flush of sentiment and admiration at the voidhawk's guileless faith. Sometimes its simple directness was like a child's honesty.

Edwin and Serina were busying themselves powering down the crew toroid's flight systems, and supervising the service vehicles as umbilicals were plugged into the ledge's support machinery. Tula was already conversing with a local cargo depot about storing the few containers remaining in the lower hull cradles. Everyone seemed to have acknowledged that they would be here for some time, even *Oenone*.

Ruben thought of her injuries again and shivered in the bridge's warm air. **I'd like to talk to Athene, please,** he asked the voidhawk. The final duty. Which he'd put off as long as possible, terrified Athene would pick up his shame. He felt so responsible for Syrinx. If I hadn't let her rush down there. If I'd gone with her . . .

Individuality is to be cherished, the voidhawk told him stiffly. **She decides for herself.**

He barely had time to form a rueful grin when he was aware of the voidhawk's potent affinity reaching out across the solar system to Saturn and the Romulus habitat.

It's all right, my dear, Athene told him as soon as they swapped identity traits. **She's alive, and she has *Oenone*. That is enough no matter what the damage those fiends inflicted. She will come back to us.**

You know?

Of course. I always know when one of *Iasius*'s children returns home, and *Oenone* informed me straightaway.

Since Eden called for a Consensus I've been listening to the details.

There will be a general Consensus?

Certainly.

Ruben felt the old voidhawk captain's lips assume an ironic smile.

You know, she said, we haven't called one since Laton destroyed Jantrit. And now he's back. I suppose there is a certain inevitability about it.

He was back, Ruben said. We really have seen the last of him now. It's funny, in a way I almost regret his suicide, however noble. I think we're going to need that kind of ruthlessness in the weeks ahead.

The general Consensus took several minutes to gather; people had to be woken, others had to stop work. All across the solar system Edenists merged their consciousness with that of their home habitats, which in turn linked together. It was the ultimate democratic government, in which everyone not only voted but also contributed to and influenced the formation of policy.

Oenone presented Laton's précis first, the message he had delivered to the Atlantean Consensus. He stood before them, a tall, handsome man with Asian-ethnic features and black hair tied back in a small ponytail; dressed in an unfussy green silk robe, belted at the waist, alone in a darkened universe. His studied attitude showed he knew they were his judges, and yet did not quite care.

"No doubt you have assimilated the account of events on Pernik island and what happened at Aberdale," he said. "As you can see this whole episode started with Quinn Dexter's sacrifice ritual. However, we can safely conclude that the breakthrough from beyond which occurred in the Lalonde jungle was unique. These idiot Satanists have been dancing through the woods at midnight for centuries, and they've never succeeded in summoning up the dead before. Had souls ever returned at any time in the past we would know about it; although I concede there have always been rumours of such incidents throughout human history.

"Unfortunately, I was never able to ascertain the exact cause of what I can only describe as a rupture between our dimension and this 'beyond' where souls linger after death. Something must have happened to make this ritual different from all the others. This is the area where you should concentrate your research effort. The spread of possession is not a threat which can be countered on an individual basis, though I'm sure Adamist populations will demand military action whenever it breaks out. Resist such futile actions. You must discover the root cause, close the dimensional rupture. Such a method is the only long-term chance for success you have. I believe that only Edenism has the potential to challenge this problem with the necessary commitment and resources. Your unity may be the only advantage which the living have. Use it.

"I assure you that though the possessed remain unorganized, they do have a common and overriding goal. They seek strength through numbers, and they will not rest until every living body is possessed. Now that you are warned you should be able to protect yourself from anything like Pernik happening again. Simple filtering sub-routines will safeguard the habitat multiplicities, and they in turn can detect possessed individuals claiming to be Edenists with a more detailed interrogation of personality traits.

"My last observation is more philosophical than practical, although equally important in the long run should you triumph. You are going to have to make considerable adjustments to your culture now you know humans have an immortal soul. In making this adaptation, I cannot overemphasise how important corporeal existence is. Do not think death is an easy escape option from suffering, or life as simply a phase of being, for when you die it is truly the end of a part of yourself. Nor would I want you to worry about being trapped in beyond for all of time, I doubt one in a billion Edenists ever would be. Think of what the returning souls are, who they are, and you will see what I mean. Ultimately you will know for yourself, as we all do. What I discovered on confronting the final reality is the belief that our culture is supreme among corporeal societies. I only wish I could have returned to it for just a little while longer knowing what I now know. Not that you would have me back, I suspect."

A final knowing smile, and he was gone for the last time.

First, Consensus decided, we must safeguard our own culture. Although we are relatively immune from infiltration, we must consider the longer term prospect of physical assault should the possessed gain control of a planetary system with military starships. Our protection will be achieved most effectively by supporting the Confederation, and preventing the spread of possession. To this end, all voidhawks will be recalled from civil flight activities to form an expanded defence force, one-third of which will be assigned to the Confederation Navy. Our scientific resources must be targeted as Laton suggested to discover the origin of the initial breakthrough, and achieve understanding of the energistic nature of the possessing souls. We must discover a permanent solution.

We acknowledge the views of those among us who favour a policy of isolation, and will retain it as an option should it appear the possessed are gaining the upper hand. But to be left alone in the universe after the possessed remove the Adamist planets and asteroids they have conquered is not a future we consider to be optimum. This threat must be faced in conjunction with the entire human race. We are the problem, we must cure ourselves.

* * *

Louise Kavanagh woke to the blessed smell of fresh clean linen, the pleasing sensation of crisp sheets pressing against her. When she opened her eyes the room she found herself in was even larger than her bedroom back at Cricklade. On the opposite wall, thick curtains were drawn across the windows, permitting very little light to enter. The gloomy chinks didn't even tell her what colour the light outside was. And that was tremendously important.

Louise pushed back the sheets and padded over the pile carpet to draw one of the high curtains. Duke's golden haze surged in. She studied the sky anxiously, but it was a clear day outside. There weren't even any rain clouds, and certainly none of the spirals of gauzy red mist. She had seen her fill of that banshee's breath yesterday as the aeroambulance flew across Kesteven, broad translucent whorls of it swirling above every town and village they passed. Streets, houses, and fields below the downy substance were all tarnished a lurid carmine.

They're not here yet, Louise thought in relief. But they'll come, sure as winter.

Norwich had been a city in panic when they arrived yesterday, though the authorities weren't entirely sure what they were panicking over. The only news which had reached the capital from islands afflicted by the relentless march of the possessed were muddled claims of uprisings and invasions by offworld forces carrying strange weapons. But the Confederation Navy squadron orbiting Norfolk assured the Prince and Prime Minister that no invasion had occurred.

Nonetheless a full mobilization of the Ramsey island militias had been ordered. Troops were digging in around the capital. Plans were being drawn up to free those islands like Kesteven which had been lost to the enemy.

Ivan Cantrell had been ordered to land his plane on a remote part of the city's aerodrome. Soldiers had surrounded the vehicle as they touched down, nervous men in ill-fitting khaki uniforms, squeezing the stocks of rifles which had been antique back in their grandfathers' time. But dotted among them were several Confederation Navy Marines, clad in sleek one-piece suits which seemed like an outgrowth of rubbery skin. And their dull black weapons were definitely not obsolete. Louise suspected a single shot from one of those blank muzzles would be quite capable of destroying the aeroambulance.

The soldiers had calmed considerably when the Kavanagh sisters had climbed down the plane's airstairs followed by Felicia Cantrell and her girls. Their commanding officer, a captain called Lester-Swindell, accepted that they were refugees, but it took another two hours of being questioned before they had been "cleared." At the end Louise had to call Aunt Celina to come and vouch for her and Genevieve. She really hadn't wanted to, but by that time there was little choice. Aunt Celina was Mother's elder sister, and Louise never could quite believe the two could be related: the woman was completely brainless, a simpering airhead concerned only with the season and shopping. But Aunt Celina was married to Jules Hewson, the Earl of Luffenham, and he was a senior advisor to the

Prince's court. If the Kavanagh name didn't carry quite the weight here on Ramsey which it did on Kesteven, his certainly did.

Two minutes after Aunt Celina had blustered and whined her way into the office, Louise and Genevieve were outside being bundled into her carriage. Fletcher Christian—*a Cricklade farmhand who helped us escape, Auntie*—was told to ride on the bench with the driver. Louise wanted to protest, but Fletcher gave her a wink and bowed deeply to Aunt Celina.

Louise dropped her gaze from the unblemished sky over Norwich. Balfern House was in the centre of Brompton, the most exclusive borough of the capital city, but even so it stood in its own extensive grounds. There had been two policemen on duty outside the iron gates as they drove in yesterday evening.

Safe for the moment, then, she told herself. Except she had brought one of the possessed right into the heart of the capital. Into the core of government, in fact.

But Fletcher Christian was her secret, hers and Genevieve's; and Gen wouldn't tell. It was funny, but she trusted Fletcher now, more so than the Earl and the Prime Minister. He had already proved he would and could protect her from the other possessed. And she in turn was charged with protecting Genevieve. Because Heaven knows the militia soldiers and Confederation marines couldn't, not against *them*.

She slumped her shoulders and walked the length of the room, pulling back the remaining curtains. What do I do next? Tell people the truth about what they're facing? I can just imagine Uncle Jules listening to that. He'll think I'm hysterical. Yet if they don't know, they'll never be able to protect themselves.

It was a horrible dilemma. And to think, she'd expected her problems to end once they reached the safety of the capital. That something would be done. That we could rescue Mummy and Daddy. A schoolgirl dream.

Carmitha's shotgun was resting against the side of the bed. Louise smiled fondly at the weapon. Aunt Celina had fussed so when she insisted on bringing it with them from the aerodrome, bleating that Young Ladies simply did not know about such things, let alone carry them on their person.

It was going to go hard on Aunt Celina when the possessed caught up with her. Louise's smile faded. *Fletcher*, she decided. I must ask Fletcher what to do next.

Louise found Genevieve sitting in the middle of her bed in the next room, knees tucked up under her chin, sulking silently. They both took one look at each other and burst out laughing. The maids, on Aunt Celina's strict instruction, had provided them with the most fanciful dresses, brightly coloured silk and velvet fabrics with huge ruffed skirts and puffball sleeves.

"Come on." Louise took her little sister's hand. "Let's get out of this madhouse."

Aunt Celina was taking breakfast in the long glass-walled morning room which looked out over the garden's lily ponds. She sat at the head of the teak table, an old world empress marshalling her troops of liveried manservants and starch-uniformed maids. A gaggle of overweight corgies snuffled hopefully around her chair to be rewarded with the odd tidbit of toast or bacon.

"Oh, that's so much better," she declared when the sisters were ushered in. "You did look simply awful yesterday. Why I barely recognized you. Those dresses are so much prettier. And your hair is so shiny now, Louise. You look a picture."

"Thank you, Aunt Celina," Louise said.

"Sit down, my dear, and do tuck in. Why you must be famished after such a terrible ordeal. Such dreadful things you've seen and endured, more than any gal I know. I gave thanks to God last night that you both reached us in one piece."

One of the maids put a plate of scrambled eggs in front of Louise. She felt her stomach curdle alarmingly. Oh, please Jesus, don't let me throw up now. "Just some toast, please," she managed to say.

"You remember Roberto, don't you, Louise?" Aunt Celina said. Her voice became slippery with pride. "My dear son, and such a strapping lad, too."

Louise glanced at the boy sitting at the other end of the table, munching his way through a pile of bacon, eggs, and kidneys. Roberto was a couple of years older than she was. They hadn't got on the last time he visited Cricklade. He never seemed to want to do anything. And now he'd put on at least another stone and a half, most of it around his middle.

Their eyes met. He was giving her what she now called the William Elphinstone look. And the dratted dress with its tight bodice flattered her figure.

She was rather surprised when her steely stare made him blush and shift his gaze hurriedly back to his plate. I've got to get out of here, she thought, out of this house, this city, away from these stupid bovine people, and most of all out of this bloody dress. I don't need Fletcher to tell me that.

"I never did know why your mother went to live on Kesteven," Aunt Celina said. "It's such a *wild* island. She should have stayed here in the city. Could have had her pick of the court, you know, your dear mother. Divine creature she was, simply divine when she was younger. Just like you two. And now who knows what dreadful things have happened to her in this horrid rebellion. I told her to stay, but she simply wouldn't listen. Wild, it is. Wild. I hope the navy squadron shoots every one of those savages. They should cleanse Kesteven, laser it clean right down to the bedrock. Then you two darlings can come and live here safely with me. Won't that be wonderful?"

"They'll come here, too," an indignant Genevieve said. "You can't stop them, you know. Nobody can."

Louise jabbed her with a toe and glared. Genevieve simply shrugged and tucked into her eggs.

Aunt Celina blanched theatrically, her handkerchief flapping in front of her face. "Why, my darling child, what a simply dreadful thing to say. Oh, your mother should never have left the capital. Gals are brought up properly here."

"I'm sorry, Aunt Celina," Louise said swiftly. "Neither of us is thinking straight right now. Not after . . . you know."

"Of course I understand. You must both visit a doctor. I should have summoned one last night. Goodness knows what you picked up tramping around the countryside for days on end."

"No!" A doctor would discover her pregnancy in minutes. And Heaven knows how Aunt Celina would react to that.

"Thank you, Aunt Celina. But really, it's nothing a few days rest won't cure. I was thinking, we could tour Norwich now we're here. It would be a real treat for us." She smiled winningly. "Please, Aunt Celina."

"Yes. Please may we?" Genevieve chipped in.

"I don't know," Aunt Celina said. "This is hardly the time for sightseeing, what with the militias forming up. And I promised Hermione I would attend the Red Cross meeting today. One must do what one can to support our brave menfolk in such times. I really can't spare the time to show you around."

"I could," Roberto said. "I'd enjoy it." His eyes were lingering on Louise again.

"Don't be silly, darling," Aunt Celina said. "You have school today."

"Fletcher Christian could chaperone us," Louise said quickly. "He's more than proved his worth. We'd be completely safe." From the corner of her eye she could see Roberto frowning.

"Well—"

"Please!" Genevieve wheedled. "I want to buy you some flowers, you've been so kind."

Aunt Celina clasped her hands together. "Oh, you are a little treasure, aren't you. I always wanted a little gal of my own, you know. Of course you can go."

Louise blew her cheeks out in thanks. She could just imagine what would have happened if they'd tried pulling that routine on Mother. Genevieve had gone back to her eggs, her face a perfect composure of purity.

At the other end of the table, Roberto was chewing thoughtfully on his third slice of toast.

The sisters found Fletcher Christian in the servants' quarters. With so many of Balfern House's staff called away to their militia regiments he had been put to work by the cook bringing sacks up from the storerooms.

He gave both girls a measured look as he lowered a big string bag of carrots onto the kitchen floor and bowed gracefully. "How splendid you look, my young ladies, so refined. I always imagined you more suited to finery such as this."

Louise gave him a *very* sharp stare. And then they were grinning at each other.

"Aunt Celina has lent us the use of a carriage," she said in her grandest tone. "And she's also given you leave to accompany us, my man. Of course, should you prefer to remain here doing what you seem to do so well . . ."

"Ah, my lady Louise, I see you are a cruel one. But justly do I deserve such mockery. It would be my honour to accompany you."

He picked up his jacket under the disapproving gaze of the cook, and followed Louise out of the kitchen. Genevieve picked up her skirt hems and ran on ahead of them through the house.

"The little one seems none the worse for all she has been through," Fletcher observed.

"Yes, thank the Lord. Was it truly awful for you last night?" Louise asked once they were out of earshot of the other servants.

"The room was dry and warm. I've made my bunk in sorrier circumstances."

"I apologize for bringing you here, I'd forgotten quite how bad Aunt Celina was. But I couldn't think of anyone else who could extract us from the aerodrome as quickly."

"Pay it no further heed, my lady. Your aunt is a model of enlightenment compared to some of the matrons I knew in my own youth."

"Fletcher." She put her hand on his arm and slowed their pace. "Are they here?"

His sturdy features turned melancholy. "Yes, my lady Louise. I can feel several dozen encamped throughout the city. And their numbers grow with every passing hour. It will take many days, perhaps a week. But Norwich will surely fall."

"Oh, dear Jesus, when will this ever end?"

She was aware of his arm around her as she trembled. Hating herself for being weak. Oh, where are you, Joshua? I *need* you.

"Speak not of evil, and it will pay you no heed," Fletcher said softly.

"Really?"

"So my mother assured me."

"Was she right?"

His fingers touched her chin, tilting her face up. "That was a long time ago, and far away. But today I think if we avoid their attentions, then you will remain out of harm's way for longer."

"Very well. I've been giving this some serious thought, you know; how to keep Genevieve and the baby truly safe. And there's only one way to do it."

"Yes, my lady?"

"Leave Norfolk."

"I see."

"It's not going to be easy. Will you help me?"

"You do not have to ask that of me, lady, you know I will offer you and the little one what aid I can."

"Thank you, Fletcher. The other thing was: Do you want to come with us? I'm going to try and reach Tranquillity. I know someone there who can help us." If anyone can, she added silently.

"Tranquillity?"

"Yes, it's a sort of palace in space, orbiting a star a long way away from here."

"Ah, lady, what a temptress you are. To sail the stars I once sailed by. How could I resist such a request?"

"Good," she whispered.

"I imply no criticism, Lady Louise. But do you really know how to prepare for such an endeavour?"

"I think so. There was one thing I learned from both Daddy and Joshua, Carmitha, too, in a way; and that is: Money makes everything possible."

Fletcher smiled respectfully. "A worthy saying. And do you have this money?"

"Not on me, no. But I'm a Kavanagh, I can get it."

6

Ione Saldana's palatial cliff-base apartment was empty now,
apart from herself; the guests from the Tranquillity Banking
Regulatory Council had been ushered out politely but insis-
tently. The convivial party most definitely over. And they
had known better than to argue. Unfortunately, they were
also astute enough to know they wouldn't be turned out unless it was a real crisis. Word would already be spreading
down the length of the giant habitat.

She had reduced the output of the ceiling's electrophorescent cells to a sombre starlight glimmer. It allowed her to see
out through the glass wall which held back the sea, revealing
a silent world composed entirely from shades of aquamarine.
And now even that was darkening as the habitat's light tube
allowed night to claim the interior. Fish were reduced to
stealthy shadows slithering among the prickly coral branches.

When Ione was younger she had spent hours staring out at
the antics of the fish and sand-crawling creatures. Now she sat
cross-legged on the apricot moss carpet before her private
theatre of life, Augustine nesting contentedly in her lap. She
stroked the little xenoc's velvety fur absently, eyes closed to
the world.

**We can still send a squadron of patrol blackhawks after
Mzu,** Tranquillity suggested. **I am aware of the _Udat_'s
wormhole terminus coordinate.**

So are the other blackhawks, she replied. **But it's their
crews I worry about. Once they're away from our SD platforms, there really is nothing we can do to enforce their
loyalty. Mzu would try to make a deal with them. She'd
probably succeed, too. She's proved astonishingly resourceful so far. Fancy even lulling us into complacency.**

I was not complacent, the habitat personality said irk-

somely. I was caught off guard by the method. Which in itself I find disturbing. It implies a great deal of thought
went into her escape. One wonders what her next move
will be.

I've got a pretty good idea, unfortunately. She'll go for
the Alchemist. There's no other reason for her to behave
like this. And after she's got it: Omuta.

Indeed.

So no, we don't send the blackhawks after her. She may
lead them to the Alchemist. That would give us an even
worse situation than the one we've got now.

In that case, what do you want to do about the intelligence agency teams?

I'm not sure. How are they reacting?

Lady Tessa, the head of the ESA's Tranquillity station, had
been badly frightened by the news of Alkad Mzu's escape, a
fact which she managed to conceal behind a show of pure
fury. Monica Foulkes stood in front of her in the starscraper
apartment which doubled as the ESA team's headquarters.
She had reported to Lady Tessa in person rather than use the
habitat's communications net. Not that Tranquillity was unaware (hardly!), but there were a great number of organiza-
tions and governments who knew nothing of Mzu's
existence, nor the implications arising from it.

It was twenty-three minutes since the physicist's escape,
and a form of delayed shock had begun to infiltrate Monica's
body as her subconscious acknowledged just how lucky she'd
been to avoid vanishing down the *Udat*'s wormhole. Her
neural nanonics were helpless to prevent the cold shivers
which spiralled their way around her limbs and belly muscles.

"I won't even dignify your performance by calling it a disaster," Lady Tessa stormed. "Great God Almighty, the principal reason we're here is to make sure she remained confined
to the habitat. Every agency endorses that policy, even the
bloody Lord of Ruin supports it. And you let her stroll out
right in front of you. I mean, Jesus Christ, what the hell were
you all doing on that beach? She stops to put on a spacesuit,
and you didn't even move in closer to investigate."

"It was not exactly a *stroll*, Chief. And I'd like to point out for the record that we are just an observation team. Our operation in Tranquillity has always been too small to guarantee Mzu remains inside should she make a determined effort to leave, or if someone uses force to extract her. If the agency wanted to be certain, it should have allocated a bigger team to monitor her."

"Don't datavise the rule flek at me, Foulkes. You're boosted, you've got weapons implants"—she flinched, and glanced up at the ceiling as though expecting divine censure—"and Mzu is in her sixties. There is no way she should have ever got near that bloody blackhawk, let alone have it snatch her away."

"The blackhawk tipped the physical balance heavily in her favour. It simply wasn't a contingency we allowed for. Tranquillity had two serjeants eliminated during our attempt to stop her boarding. Personally, I'm surprised the starship was allowed to swallow inside at all." Now Monica glanced guiltily around the naked polyp walls.

Lady Tessa's baleful expression didn't alter, but she did pause. "I doubt there was much it could do. As you say, that swallow manoeuvre was completely unprecedented."

"Samuel claimed that not many voidhawks could be that precise."

"Thank you. I'll be sure to include that most helpful unit of data in my report." She got up out of the chair and walked over to the oval window. The apartment was two thirds of the way down the StEtalia starscraper, where gravity was approaching Earth standard. It was a location which gave her a unimpeded view across the bottom of the vast curving burnt-biscuit-coloured habitat shell, with just a crescent of the counter-rotating spaceport showing beyond the rim as if it were a metallic moon rising. Today, as for the last four days, there were few starships arriving or departing from its docking bays. Big SD platforms glinted reassuringly against the backdrop of Mirchusko's darkside as they caught the last of the sunlight before Tranquillity sailed into the penumbra.

And what use would they be against the Alchemist? Lady Tessa wondered sagely. A doomsday device that's supposed to be able to kill stars . . .

"What's our next move?" Monica asked. She was rubbing

her arms for warmth in an attempt to stop the shaking. Grains of sand were still falling out of her sweater's sleeves.

"Informing the Kingdom is our primary responsibility now," Lady Tessa said in a challenging tone. There was no re-action from the AV pillar sticking up out of her desktop processor block. "But it's going to take time for them to re-spond and start searching. And Mzu will know that. Which means she's got two options, either she takes the *Udat* straight to the Alchemist, or she loses herself out there." She tapped a gold-chromed fingernail on the window as the myriad stars drifted past in slow arcs.

"If she was smart enough to get away from all the agency teams tagging her, she'll know that she'll never stay lost, not forever," Monica said. "Too many of us are going to be look-ing now."

"And yet the *Udat* doesn't have any special equipment rigged. I checked the CAB registry, it hasn't had any refit-ting for eight months. Sure, it has got standard interfaces for combat wasp cradles and heavy-duty close defence weapons. Almost every blackhawk has. But there was noth-ing unusual."

"So?"

"So if she does take *Udat* straight to the Alchemist, how will they fire it at Omuta's sun?"

"Do we know what equipment is necessary to fire it?"

"No," Lady Tessa admitted. "We don't even know if it does need anything special. But it was different, new, and unique; that means it's non-standard. Which may give us our one chance to neutralize this situation. If there is any hardware re-quirement involved, she's going to have to break cover and approach a defence contractor."

"She might not have to," Monica said. "She'll have friends, sympathisers; certainly in the Dorados. She can go to them."

"I hope she does. The agency has kept the Garissa sur-vivors under surveillance for decades, just in case any of them try to pull any stupid revenge stunts." She turned from the window. "I'm sending you there to brief their head of station. It's a reasonable assumption she'll turn up there eventually, and it may help having someone familiar with her on the ground."

Monica nodded in defeat. "Yes, Chief."

"Don't look so tragic. I'm the one who's going to have to report back to Kulu and tell the director we lost her. You're getting off lightly."

The meeting in the Confederation Navy Bureau on the forty-fifth floor of the StMichelle starscraper was synchronous with that of the ESA in both time and content. In the bureau it was an aghast Commander Olsen Neale who accessed the sensevise memory of Mzu's abrupt exit from the habitat as recorded by a thoroughly despondent Pauline Webb.

When the file ended he asked a few supplemental questions and came to the same conclusions as Lady Tessa. "We can assume she has access to the kind of money necessary to buy whatever systems she needs to use the Alchemist, and install them in a combat-capable ship," he said. "But I don't think it'll be the *Udat*; that's too high profile now. Every navy ship and government is going to be hunting it inside a week."

"Do you think the Alchemist really does exist then, sir?" Pauline asked.

"CNIS has always believed so, even though it could never track down any solid evidence. And after this, I don't think there can be any doubt. Even if it wasn't stored in zero-tau, don't forget she knows how to build another one. Another hundred, come to that."

Pauline hung her head. "Shit, but we screwed up big-time."

"Yes. I always thought we were a little overdependent on the Lord of Ruin's benevolence in keeping her here." He made a finger-fluttering gesture with one hand and muttered: "No offence."

The AV pillar on his desktop processor block sparkled momentarily. "None taken," said Tranquillity.

"We also got complacent with how static the whole situation had become. You were quite right when you said she'd fooled us for a quarter of a century. Bloody hell, but that is an awful long time to keep a charade going. Anyone who can hate for that long isn't going to be fooling around. She's gone because she thinks she has a good chance to use the Alchemist against Omuta."

"Yes, sir."

Olsen Neale made an effort to suppress his worry and formulate some kind of coherent response to the situation—one he didn't have a single contingency plan for. No one at CNIS ever believed she could actually escape. "I'll leave for Trafalgar right away. Our first priority is to inform Admiral Lalwani that Mzu's gone, so she can start activating our assets to find her. Then the First Admiral will have to beef up Omuta's defences. Damn, that's another squadron which the navy can't spare, not now."

"The Laton scare will make it difficult for her to travel," Pauline said.

"Let's hope so. But just in case, I want you to go to the Dorados and alert our bureau that she may put in an appearance soon."

Samuel, of course, didn't have to physically meet with the other three Edenist intelligence operatives in the habitat. They simply conferred with each other via affinity, then Samuel and a colleague called Tringa headed for the spaceport. Samuel chartered a starship to take him to the Dorados, while Tringa found one which would convey him to Jupiter so he could warn the Consensus.

The same scenario was played out by the other eight national intelligence agency teams assigned to watch Mzu. In each case, it was decided that alerting their respective directors was the primary requirement; three of them also dispatched operatives to the Dorados to watch for Mzu.

The spaceport charter agents who had been suffering badly from the lack of flights brought on by the Laton scare suddenly found business picking up.

So now you have to decide if you're going to allow them to inform their homeworlds, Tranquillity said. **For once the word gets out, you will be unable to control further events.**

I didn't really control events before. I was like an umpire insuring fair play.

Well now is your chance to get down off your stool and take part in the game.

Don't tempt me. I have enough problems right now with the Laymil's reality dysfunction. If dear Grandfather Michael was right, that may yet turn out to be a lot more trouble than Mzu's Alchemist.

I concede the point. But I do need to know if I am to permit the agency operatives to depart.

Ione opened her eyes to look through the window, but the water outside was sable-black now, there was nothing to see apart from a weak reflection of herself in the glass. For the first time in her life she began to understand what loneliness was.

You have me, Tranquillity assured her gently.

I know. But in a way you are a part of me. It would be nice to have someone else's shoulder to lean on occasionally.

A someone such as Joshua?

Don't be so bitchy.

I'm sorry. Why don't you ask Clement to come to the apartment? He makes you happy.

He makes me orgasm, you mean.

Is there a difference?

Yes, but don't ask me to explain it. It's just that I'm looking for more than physical contentment right now. These are big decisions I'm making here. They could affect millions of people, hundreds of millions.

You have known this time would come ever since you were conceived. It is what your life is for.

Most of the Saldanas, yes. They make a dozen decisions like this before lunch every day. Not me. I think the family's arrogance gene might be inactive in my case.

It is more likely to be a hormonal imbalance due to your pregnancy which is making you procrastinate.

She laughed out loud, the sound echoing around the vast room. You really don't understand the difference between your thought processes and mine, do you?

I believe I do.

Ione had the silliest vision of a two-kilometre-long nose sniffing disdainfully. Her laugh turned to a giggle. Okay, no more procrastination. Let's be logical. We blew it with safeguarding Mzu, and now she's presumably on her way to exterminate Omuta's star. And you and I certainly don't have the kind of resources available to the ESA and other agencies to track her down and stop her. Right?

An elegant summary.

Thank you. Therefore, the best chance to stop her will be to let the intelligence community off the leash.

Granted.

Then we let them out. At least that way Omuta stands a chance of survival. I don't think I really want a genocide on my conscience. Nor, I suspect, do you.

Very well. I will not restrict their starships from departing.

Which just leaves us with what's going to happen afterwards. If they do catch her, someone is going to wind up with the technology to build Alchemist devices. As Monica said on the beach, every government will want it to safeguard their own particular version of democracy.

Yes. The old term for a nation acquiring such an overwhelming military advantage is a "superpower." At the very least, the emergence of such a nation will result in an arms race as other governments try to acquire the Alchemist technology, which will not benefit the general Confederation economy. And if they succeed, the Confederation will be plunged into a deterrence cycle, a balance of terror.

And it was all my fault.

Not quite. Dr Alkad Mzu invented the Alchemist. From that moment on all subsequent events were inevitable. There is a saying that once you have released the genie from the bottle, he cannot be put back.

Maybe not. But it wouldn't hurt to have a go.

• • •

From the air Avon's capital, Regina, was almost indistinguishable from any big city on a fully developed and industrialized planet within the Confederation. A dark gritty stain of buildings which crept a little further outwards into the green countryside with every passing year. Only the steeper hill slopes and crinkled watercourses inconvenienced the encroachment to any degree, although in the central districts even they had been tamed with metal and carbon concrete. Again, as normal, a clump of skyscrapers occupied the very heart of the city, forming the commercial, financial, and government administration district. A lavish display of crystal spires, thick composite cylinders, and gloss-metal neo-modern towers, reflecting the planet's economic strength.

The one exception to the standard urban layout was a second, smaller cluster of silver and white skyscrapers occupying the shore of a long lake on the city's easternmost district. Like the Forbidden City of ancient Chinese Emperors, it existed aloof from the rest of Regina, yet it held sway over billions of lives. Home to one and a half million people, it was sixteen square kilometres of foreign diplomatic compounds, embassies, legal firms, multistellar corporation offices, navy barracks, executive agencies, media studios, and a thousand catering and leisure company franchises. This overcrowded, overpriced, bureaucratic mother-hive formed a protective ring around the Assembly building which straddled the lakeshore, itself looking more like a domed sports stadium than the very seat of the Confederation.

The stadium analogy was continued inside the main chamber, with tiered ranks of seats circling the central polity council table. First Admiral Samual Aleksandrovich always likened it to a gladiatorial arena, where the current polity council members had to present and defend their resolutions. It was ninety per cent theatre; but politicians, even in this day and age, clung to the public stage.

As one of the four permanent members of the polity council, the First Admiral had the right and authority to summon a full session of the Assembly. It was a right which earlier First Admirals had exercised only three times in the Confederation's history; twice to request additional vessels from member states to prevent inter-system wars, and once to ask for the resources to track down Laton.

Samual Aleksandrovich hadn't envisaged himself being

number four. But there really hadn't been time to consult with the President after the voidhawk from Atlantis arrived at Trafalgar. And after reviewing the report it carried, Samual Aleksandrovich was convinced that time was a crucial issue. Mere hours could make a colossal difference if the possessed were to be prevented from infiltrating unsuspecting worlds.

So now here he was in his dress uniform walking towards the polity council table under the bright lights shining out of a black marble ceiling, Captain Khanna on one side, Admiral Lalwani on the other. The chamber's tiers were full of diplomats and aides shuffling to their designated seats, their combined grumbling sounding like a couple of bulldozers attacking the foundations. A glance upwards showed him the media gallery was packed. Everybody wanted in on the phenomenon.

You wouldn't if you knew, he thought emphatically.

The President, Olton Haaker, wearing his traditional Arab robe, took his seat at the oaken horseshoe table along with the other members of the polity council. Samual Aleksandrovich thought Haaker looked nervous. It was a telling sign; the old Breznikan was a superb, not to mention wily, diplomat. This was his second five-year term of office; and only four of the last fifteen Presidents had managed to gain renomination.

Rittagu-FHU, the Tyrathca ambassador, walked imperiously across the chamber floor, minute particles of bronze-coloured powder shaking out of her scales to dust the tiles below her. She reached one end of the table and eased her large body onto a broad cradle arrangement. Her mate hooted softly at her from a similar cradle in the front tier.

Samual Aleksandrovich wished it were the Kiint who held the xenoc polity council seat this term. The two xenoc member races alternated every three years, although there were those in the Assembly who said that the xenocs should join the rota for the polity council seats like every human government had to.

The Assembly speaker called for silence, and announced that the First Admiral had been granted the floor under article nine of the Confederation Charter. As he got to his feet, Samual Aleksandrovich studied the blocks in the tiers which he would have to carry. The Edenists, of course, he already had. Earth's Govcentral would probably follow the Edenists, given their strong alliance. Other key powers were Oshanko, New Washington, Nanjing, Holstein, Petersburg, and, inevitably, the Kulu Kingdom, which probably had the most undue influence of all—and thank God the Saldanas were keen supporters of the Confederation.

In a way he was angry that an issue as vital as this (surely the most vital in human history?) would be dependent on who was speaking with whom, whose ideologies clashed, whose religions denounced the other. The whole point of ethnic streaming colonies, as Earth had painfully discovered centuries ago during the Great Dispersal, was that foreign cultures can live harmoniously with each other providing they didn't have to live jammed together on the same planet. And the Assembly allowed that wider spirit of cooperation to continue and flourish. In theory.

"I have asked for this session because I wish to call for a full state of emergency to be declared," Samual Aleksandrovich said. "Unfortunately, what started off as the Laton situation has now become immeasurably graver. If you would care to access the sensevise account which has just arrived from Atlantis." He datavised the main processor to play the recording.

Diplomats they might have been, but even their training couldn't help them maintain poker faces as the events of Pernik island unravelled inside their skulls. The First Admiral waited impassively as the gasps and grimaces appeared simultaneously throughout the chamber. It took a quarter of an hour to run, and many broke off during the playback to check the reactions of their colleagues, or perhaps even to make sure they were receiving the right recording, and not some elaborate horrorsense.

Olton Haaker got to his feet when it finished, and stared at Samual Aleksandrovich for a long time before speaking. The First Admiral wondered exactly how he was taking it, the President's Muslim faith was a strong one. Just what does he think about djinns coming forth?

"Are you certain this information is genuine?" the President asked.

Samual Aleksandrovich signalled Admiral Lalwani, the

CNIS chief, who was sitting in one of the chairs behind him. She got to her feet. "We vouch for its authenticity," she said, and sat down again.

A number of intense stares were directed at Cayeaux, the Edenist ambassador, who bore them stoically.

How typical to blame the messenger, the First Admiral thought.

"Very well, what exactly are you proposing we should do?" the President asked.

"Firstly, the vote for a state of emergency will provide a considerable reserve of national naval ships for the Confederation Navy," the First Admiral said. "We shall require all those national squadrons pledged to us to be transferred over to their respective Confederation fleets as soon as possible. Preferably within a week." That didn't go down well, but he was ready for it. "Combating the threat we now face cannot be achieved by confronting it in a piecemeal fashion. Our response has to be swift and overwhelming. That can only be achieved with the full strength of the navy."

"But to what end?" the Govcentral ambassador asked. "What possible solution can you provide for the dead coming back? You can't be considering killing those who are possessed."

"No, we cannot do that," the First Admiral acknowledged. "And unfortunately they know it, which will provide them with a huge advantage. We are faced with what is essentially the greatest hostage scenario ever. So I propose we do what we always do in such situations, and that is play for time while a genuine solution is found. While I have no idea what that will be, the overall policy we must adopt I consider to be very clear-cut. We must prevent the problem from spreading beyond those star systems in which it has already taken hold. To that end, I would ask for a further resolution requiring the cessation of all civil and commercial starflights, effective immediately. The number of flights has already been reduced sharply because of the Laton crisis; reducing it to zero should not prove difficult. Once a Confederation-wide quarantine is imposed, it will become easier to target our forces where they will be most effective."

"What do you mean, effective?" the President demanded. "You just said we cannot consider an armed response."

"No, sir, I said we cannot consider it as the ultimate solution. What it can, and must, be used for is to prevent the spread of possessed from star systems which they have infiltrated. If they ever manage to conquer an industrialized system, they will undoubtedly commit its full potential against us to further their aim; which, as Laton has told us, is total annexation. We have to be ready to match that, probably on several separate fronts. If we do not they will multiply at an exponential rate, and the entire Confederation will fall, every living human will become possessed."

"Are you saying we just abandon star systems that have been taken over?"

"We must isolate them until we have a solution which works. I already have a science team examining the possessed woman we hold in Trafalgar. Hopefully their research may produce some answers."

A loud murmur of consternation spiralled around the tiers at that disclosure.

"You have one captured?" the President inquired in surprise.

"Yes, sir. We didn't know exactly what she was until the voidhawk from Atlantis came. But now we do, our investigation can proceed along more purposeful lines."

"I see." The President seemed at a loss. He glanced at the speaker, who inclined his head.

"I second the motion of the First Admiral for a state of emergency," the President said formally.

"One vote down, eight hundred to go," Admiral Lalwani whispered.

The speaker rang the silver bell on the table in front of him. "As, at this time, there would seem little to add to the information the First Admiral has presented to us, I will now call upon those here present to cast their votes on the resolution before you."

Rittagu-FHU emitted a piping hoot and rose to her feet. Her thick head swung around to look at the First Admiral, a motion which sent the chemical program teats along her neck bobbling, delivering a leathery slapping sound. She worked her double lips elaborately, producing a prolonged gabble.

"Speaker statement not true," the translator block on the table said. "I have much to add. *Elemental* humans, dead humans; these are not part of Tyrathca nature. We did not know such things were possible for you. We impugn these assaults upon what is real today. If you all have this ability to become *elemental*, then you all threaten the Tyrathca. This is frightening for us. We must withdraw from contact with humans."

"I assure you, Ambassador, we did not know of this ourselves," the President said. "It frightens us as much as it does you. I would ask you to retain at least some lines of communication until this situation can be resolved."

Rittagu-FHU's fluting reply was translated as: "Who says this?"

Olton Haaker's weary face reflected his puzzlement. He flicked a glance at his equally uncertain aides. "I do."

"But who speaks?"

"I'm sorry, Ambassador, I don't understand."

"You say you speak. Who are you? I see Olton Haaker standing here today, as he has stood many times. I do not know if it is Olton Haaker. I do not know if it is an *elemental* human."

"I assure you I'm not!" the President spluttered.

"I do not know that. What is the difference?" She turned her gaze on the First Admiral, big glassy eyes displaying no emotions he could ever understand. "Is there a way of knowing?"

"There seems to be a localized disturbance of electronic systems in the presence of anyone possessed," he said. "That's the only method of detection we have now. But we're working on other techniques."

"You do not know."

"The possessions started on Lalonde. The first starship to reach here from that planet was *Ilex*, and it came directly. We can be safe in assuming that no one in the Avon system has been possessed yet."

"You do not know."

Samual Aleksandrovich couldn't answer. I'm sure, but the damn creature is right. Certainty is no longer possible. But then humans have never needed absolutes to convince themselves. The Tyrathca have, and it's a difference which divides us far greater than our biology.

When he appealed silently to the President, he met a blank face. Very calmly, he said: "I do not know."

There was a subliminal suggestion of a mass sigh from the tiers, maybe even resentment.

But I did what was right, I answered her on her own terms.

"I express gratitude that you speak the truth," Rittagu-FHU said. "Now I do what is my task in this place, and speak for my race. The Tyrathca this day end our contact with all humans. We will leave your worlds. Do not come to ours."

Rittagu-FHU stretched out a long arm, and a nine-fingered circular hand switched off her translator block. She hooted to her mate, and together they made their way to the exit.

The vast chamber was utterly silent as the door slid shut behind them.

Olton Haaker cleared his throat, squared his shoulders, and faced the Kiint ambassador who was standing passively in the bottom tier. "If you wish to leave us, Ambassador Roulor, then of course we shall provide every assistance in returning you and the other Kiint ambassadors to your homeworld. This is a human problem after all, we do not wish to jeopardize our fruitful relationship by endangering you."

One of the snow-white Kiint's tractamorphic arms uncurled to hold up a small processor block, its AV projection pillar produced a moiré sparkle. "Being alive is a substantial risk, Mr President," Roulor said. "Danger always balances enjoyment. To find one, you must face and know the other. And you are wrong in saying that it is a human problem. All sentient races eventually discover the truth of death."

"You mean you knew?" Olton Haaker asked, his diplomatic demeanour badly broken.

"We are aware of our nature, yes. We confronted it once, a great time ago, and we survived. Now you must do the same. We cannot help you in this struggle which you are facing, but we do sympathise."

•   •   •

Starflight traffic to Valisk was dropping off; ten per cent in two days. Even though Rubra's subsidiary thought routines managed the habitat's traffic control, the statistic hadn't registered with his principal personality. It was the economics of the shortfall which finally alerted him. The flights were all scheduled charters, bringing components to the industrial stations of his precious Magellanic Itg company. None of them were blackhawk flights from his own fleet, it was only Adamist ships.

Curious, he reviewed all the news fleks delivered by those starships which had arrived recently, searching for a reason, some crisis or emergency in another section of the Confederation. He drew a blank.

It was only when his principal personality routine made its weekly routine check on Fairuza that Rubra realized something was wrong inside the habitat as well. Fairuza was another of his protégés, a ninth-generation descendant who had showed promise from an early age.

Promise, as defined by Rubra, consisted principally of the urge to exert himself as leader of the other boys at the day club, snatching the biggest share, be it of sweets or game processor time, a certain cruel streak with regards to pets, contempt for his timid, loving parents. It marked him down as a greedy, short-tempered, bullying, disobedient, generally nasty little boy. Rubra was delighted.

When Fairuza reached ten years of age, the slow waves of encouragement began to twist their way into his psyche. Dark yearnings to go further, a feeling of righteousness, a sense of destiny, a quite insufferable ego. It was all due to Rubra's silent desires oozing continually into his skull.

The whole moulding process had gone wrong so often in the past. Valisk was littered with the neurotic detritus of Rubra's earlier attempts to create a dynamic ruthless personality in what he considered his own image. He wanted so much to forge such a creature, someone *worthy* to command Magellanic Itg. And for two hundred years he had endured the humiliation of his own flesh and blood failing him time and again.

But Fairuza had a resilient quality which was rare among his diverse family members. So far he had displayed few of the psychological weaknesses which ruined all the others. Rubra had hopes for him, almost as many hopes as he once had for Dariat.

However, when Rubra summoned the sub-routine which monitored the fourteen-year-old youth, nothing happened. A giant ripple of surprise ran down the entire length of the habitat's neural strata. Servitor animals flinched and juddered as it passed below them. Thick muscle rings regulating the flow of fluids inside the huge network of nutrient capillaries and water channels buried deep in the polyp shell spasmed, creating surges and swirls which took the autonomic routines over half an hour to calm and return to normal. All eight thousand of Rubra's descendants shivered uncontrollably, and for no reason they could understand, even the children who had no knowledge of their true nature yet.

For a moment, Rubra didn't know what to do. His personality was distributed evenly through the habitat's neural strata, a condition the original designers of Eden had called a homogenized presence. Every routine and sub-routine and autonomic routine was at once whole and separate. All perceptual information received by any sensitive cell was immediately disseminated for storage uniformly along the strata. Failure, *any* failure, was inconceivable.

Failure meant his own thoughts were malfunctioning. His mind, the one true aspect of self left to him, was flawed.

After surprise, inevitably, came fear. There could be few reasons for such a disaster. He might finally be succumbing to high-level psychological disorders. It was a condition the Edenists always predicted he would develop after enduring centuries of loneliness coupled with frustration at his inability to find a worthy heir.

He began to design a series of entirely new routines which would analyse his own mental architecture. Like undercover wraiths, these visitants flashed silently through the neural strata on their missions to spy on the performance of each sub-routine without it being aware, reporting back on his own performance.

A list of flaws began to emerge. They made a strange compilation. Some sub-routines, like Fairuza's monitor, were missing completely, others were inactive, then there were instances of memory dissemination being blocked. The lack of any logical pattern bothered him. Rubra didn't doubt that he was under attack, but it was a most peculiar method of assault.

However, one aspect of the attack was perfectly clear: whoever was behind the disruptions had a perfect understanding of both affinity and a habitat's thought routines. He couldn't believe it was the Edenists, not them with their repugnant superiority. They considered time to be their premier weapon against him; the Kohistan Consensus was of the opinion that he could not sustain himself for more than a few centuries. And a covert undeclared war on someone who didn't threaten them was an inconceivable breach of their culture's ethics. No, it had to be someone else. Someone more intimate.

Rubra reviewed the monitor sub-routines which had been rendered inactive. There were seven; six of them were assigned to ordinary descendants, all of them under twenty; as they weren't yet involved with Magellanic Itg they didn't require anything more than basic observation to keep an eye on them. But the seventh . . . Rubra hadn't bothered to examine him at any time during the last fifteen years of their thirty-year estrangement, his greatest ever failure: Dariat.

The intimation was profoundly shocking: that somehow Dariat had achieved a degree of control over the habitat routines. But then Dariat had managed to block all Rubra's attempts to gain access to his mind through affinity ever since that fateful day thirty years ago. Dariat, for all his massive imperfections, was unique.

Rubra reacted to the revelation by erecting safeguards all around his primary personality pattern; input filters which would scrutinize all the information reaching him for trojan viruses. He wasn't certain exactly what Dariat was trying to achieve by interfering with the sub-routines, but he knew the man still blamed him for Anastasia Rigel's death. Ultimately Dariat would try to extract his vengeance.

What remarkable determination. It actually rivalled his own.

Rubra hadn't been so stimulated for decades. Maybe he could still negotiate with Dariat; after all, the man was not yet fifty, there was another half century of useful life left in him. And if they couldn't come to an agreement, well . . . he could always be cloned. All Rubra needed for that was a single living cell.

With his mentality as secure as he could make it, he formed

a succession of new orders. Again, they were different from anything which existed in the neural strata before; fresh patterns, a modified routing hierarchy, invisible to anyone accustomed to the standard thought routines. The clandestine command went out to every optically sensitive cell, every affinity-capable descendant, every servitor animal: find a match for Dariat's visual image.

It took seven minutes. And it wasn't quite what Rubra was expecting.

A number of the observation routines on the eighty-fifth floor of the Kandi starscraper had been tampered with. The Kandi was used mainly by the less wholesome of Valisk's residents, which given the overall content of the population meant that the starscraper was just about the last resort for the real lowlife. It was in the apartment of Anders Bospoort, vice lord and semi-professional rapist, where the greatest anomaly was centred. One of the observation sub-routines had been altered to include a memory segment. Instead of observing the apartment, and feeding the processed image directly into a general event analysis routine it was simply substituting an old visualization of the rooms for the real-time picture.

Rubra solved the problem by wiping the old routine entirely and replacing it with a viable one. The apartment he was now looking around was a shambles, furniture out of place and smothered by every kind of male and female clothing, plates of half-eaten food discarded at random, empty bottles lying about. High-capacity Kulu Corporation processor blocks and dozens of technical encyclopedia fleks were piled up on the tables—not exactly Bospoort's usual bedtime material.

With the restoration of true sight and sound came an olfactory sense; a stiff price to pay: the feculent stink in the apartment was dreadful. The reason for that was simple: Dariat's obese corpse was lying slumped at the foot of the bed in the master bedroom. There was no sign of foul play, no bruising, no stab wounds, no energy beam charring. Whatever the cause, it had left an appallingly twisted grin scrawled across his chubby face. Rubra couldn't help but think that Dariat had actually enjoyed dying.

* * *

Dariat was inordinately happy with his new, captive body. He had quite forgotten what it was like to be skinny; to move fast, to slither adroitly between the closing doors of a lift, to be able to wear proper clothes instead of a shabby toga. And youth, of course, that was another advantage. A more *vital* physique, lean and strong. That Horgan was only fifteen years old was of no consequence, the energistic power made up for everything. He chose the appearance of a twenty-one-year-old, a male in his physical prime, his dark skin smooth and glossy; hair worn thick, long, and jet-black. His clothes were white, simple cotton pantaloons and shirt, thin enough to show off the panther flex of muscles. Nothing as gross-out as Bospoort's ridiculous macho frame which Ross Nash wore, but he'd certainly drawn the eye of several girls.

In fact, possession with all its glories was almost enough to make him renege on his task. Almost, but not quite. His agenda remained separate from the others', for unlike them he wasn't scared of death, of returning to the beyond. He believed in the spirituality Anastasia had preached, now as never before. The beyond was only part of the mystery of dying; God's creativity was boundless, of course more continua existed, an after-afterlife.

He pondered this as he walked with his fellow possessors towards the Tacoul Tavern. The others were all desperately intent on their mission, and so humourless.

The Tacoul Tavern was a perfect microcosm of life in Valisk. Its once stylish black and silver crystalline interior was a form now abandoned even by designers of retro chic; its food came out of packages where once its cuisine was prepared by chefs in a five-star kitchen; its waitresses were really too old for the short skirts they wore; and its clientele neither questioned nor cared about its inexorable decline. Like most bars it tended to attract one type of customer; in this case it was the starship crews.

There were a couple dozen people seated at the various rock mushroom tables when Dariat followed Kiera Salter inside. She sauntered over to the bar and ordered a drink for herself. Two men offered to buy it for her. While the charade played out, Dariat chose a table by the door and studied the big room. They'd done well; five of the drinkers had the tell-tale indigo eyes of Rubra's descendants, and all of them wore shipsuits with a silver star on the epaulet: blackhawk captains.

Dariat concentrated on the observation routines operating in the neural strata behind the tavern's walls, floor, and ceiling. Abraham, Matkin, and Graci, who also possessed affinity-capable bodies, were doing the same thing; all four of them were sending out a multitude of subversive commands to isolate the room and everything which happened in it from Rubra's principal personality.

He had taught them well. It took the foursome barely a minute to corrupt the simple routines, turning the Tacoul Tavern into a perceptual null zone. To complete the act, the muscle membrane door contracted quietly, its grey pumicelike surface becoming an intractable barrier, sealing everyone inside.

Kiera Salter stood up, dismissing her would-be suitors with a contemptuous gesture. When one of them rose and started to say something, she struck him casually, an openhanded slap across his temple. The blow sent him flailing backwards. He struck the polyp floor hard, yelling with pain. She laughed and blew him a kiss as he dabbed at the blood seeping from his nose. "No chance, lover boy." The long leather purse in her hand morphed into a pump-action shotgun. She swung it around to point towards the startled patrons, and blew one of the ceiling's flickering light globes to pieces.

Everyone ducked as splinters of pearl-white composite rained down. Several people were attempting to datavise emergency calls into the room's net processor. Electronics were the first thing the possessed had disabled.

"Okay, people," Kiera announced, with a grossly stressed American twang. "This is a stickup. Don't nobody move, and shove your valuables in this here sack."

Dariat sighed in contempt. It seemed altogether inappropriate that a complete bitch like Kiera should possess the body of such a physically sublime girl as Marie Skibbow. "There's no need for all this," he said. "We only came for the blackhawk captains. Let's just keep focused on that, shall we?"

"Maybe there's no need," she said, "but there's certainly plenty of want."

"You know what, Kiera, you really are a complete ass-hole."

"That so?" She flung a bolt of white fire at him.

Waitresses and customers alike shouted in alarm and dived for cover. Dariat just managed to deflect the bolt, thumping it aside with a fist he imagined as a fat table tennis bat. The white fire bounced about enthusiastically, careering off tables and chairs. But not before the strike gave him a vicious electric shock, jangling all the nerves in his arm.

"Give the lectures a rest, Dariat," Kiera said. "We do what we're driven to do."

"Nobody drove you to do that. It hurt."

"Oh, get real, you warped slob. You'd enjoy yourself a lot more if you didn't have that morals bug stuffed so far up your arse."

Klaus Schiller and Matkin sniggered at his discomfort.

"You're screwing up everything with this childishness," Dariat said. "If we are to acquire the blackhawks we cannot afford your indiscipline. The Lord Tarrug is making you dance to his tune. Contain yourself, listen to your inner music."

She shouldered the shotgun and levelled an annoyed finger at him. "One more word of that New Age bullshit, and I swear I'll take your head clean off. We brought you along so that you could deal with the habitat personality, that's all. I'm the one who lays down our goals. I have concrete bloody policies; policies which are going to help us come up trumps. Policies with attitude. What the fuck have you got to offer us, slob? Chop away at the habitat's floor for a century until we find this Rubra's brain, then stamp on it. Is that it? Is that your big, useful plan?"

"No," he said with wooden calm. "I keep telling you, Rubra cannot be defeated by physical means. This policy you have for taking over the habitat population isn't going to work until we've dealt with him. I think we're making a mistake with the blackhawks; not even their physical power can help us beat him. And if we start taking them over, we risk drawing attention to ourselves."

"As Allah wills," Matkin muttered.

"But don't you see?" Dariat appealed to him. "If we concentrate on annihilating Rubra and possessing the neural strata, then we can achieve anything. We'll be like gods."

"That is close to blasphemy, son," Abraham Canaan said. "You should have a little more care in what you say."

"Shit. Look, godlike, okay? The point is—"

"The *point*, Dariat," Kiera said, aligning the shotgun on him for emphasis, "is that you are steaming for vengeance. Don't try and plead otherwise, because you are even insane enough to kill yourself in order to achieve it. *We* know what we are doing, we are multiplying our numbers to protect ourselves. If you don't wish to do that, then perhaps you need a little more time in the beyond to set your mind straight."

Even as he gathered himself to argue, he realized he'd lost. He could see the blank expressions hardening around the other possessed, while his mind simultaneously perceived their emotions chilling. Weak fools. They really didn't care about anything other than the now. They were animals. But animals whose help he would ultimately need.

Kiera had won again, just as she had when she insisted on him proving his loyalty through self-sacrifice. The possessed looked to her for leadership, not him.

"All right," Dariat said. "Have it your way." For now.

"Thank you," Kiera said with heavy irony. She grinned, and sauntered over to the first blackhawk captain.

During the altercation, the patrons of the Tacoul Tavern had been as quiet as people invariably become when total strangers are discussing your fate two metres in front of you. Now the discussion was over. Fate decided.

The waitresses squealed, huddling together at the bar. Seven of the starship personnel made a break for the closed muscle-membrane door. Five actually launched themselves at the possessed, wielding whatever came to hand: fission blades (which malfunctioned), broken bottles, nervejam sticks (also useless), and bare fists.

White fire flared in retaliation: globes aimed at knees and ankles, disabling and maiming; whip tendrils which coiled around legs like scalding manacles.

With their victims thrashing about on the floor, and the stink of burnt flesh in the air, the possessed closed in.

Rocio Condra had been trapped in the beyond for five centuries when the time of miracles came. An existence of madness, which he could only liken to the last moment of smothering being drawn out and out and out . . . And always in total darkness, silence, numbness. His life had replayed itself a million times, but that wasn't nearly enough.

Then came the miracles, sensations leaking in from the universe outside. Cracks in the nothingness of the beyond which would open and shut in fractions of a second, akin to storm clouds of soot parting to let through the delicious golden sunlight of dawn. And every time, a single lost soul would fly into the blinding, deafening deluge of reality, out into freedom and beauty. Along with all the others left behind, Rocio would howl his frustration into the void. Then they would redouble their pleas and prayers and pledges to the obdurate, indifferent living, offering them salvation and ennoblement if they would just help.

Perhaps such promises actually worked. More and more of the cracks were appearing, so many that they had become a torment in their own right. To know there was a route out, and yet always denied.

Except now. *This time* . . . This time the glory arose all around Rocio Condra so loud and bright it nearly overwhelmed him. Furled with the torrent was someone crying for help, for the agony to stop.

"I'll help," Rocio lied perilously. "I'll stop it happening."

Pain flooded into him as the frantic thoughts clung to his false words. It was far, far more than the usual meshing of souls in search of bitter sustenance. He could feel himself gaining weight and strength as their thoughts entwined. And the pain surged towards ecstasy. Rocio could actually feel legs and arms jerking as agonizing heat played over skin, a throat which had been stung raw from screaming. It was all quite delicious, the kind of high a masochist would relish.

The man's thoughts were becoming weaker, smaller, as Rocio pushed and wriggled himself deeper into the brain's neural pathways. As he did so, more of the old human experiences made their eminently welcome return, the air rushing into his lungs, thud of a heart. And all the while his new host was diminishing. The way Rocio pushed him down, confining his soul, was almost instinctive, and becoming easier by the second.

He could hear the other lost souls of the beyond shrieking their outrage that he was the one to gain salvation. The bitter threats, the accusations of unworthiness.

Then there was just his host's feeble protests, and a second oddly distant voice begging to know what was happening to its beloved. He squeezed the host's soul away, expanding his own mind to fill the entire brain.

"That's enough," a woman's voice said. "We need you for something more important."

"Leave me!" he coughed. "I'm almost in, almost—" His strength was growing, the captive body starting to respond. Tear-drowned eyes revealed the wavery outline of three figures bending over him. Figures which must surely be angels. A gloriously pretty girl clad only in a resplendent white corona.

"No," she said. "Get into the blackhawk. Now."

There must have been some terrible mistake. Didn't they understand? This was the miracle. The redemption. "I'm in," Rocio told them. "Look, see? I'm in now. I've done it." He made one of his new hands rise, seeing blisters like big translucent fungi hanging from every finger.

"Then get out."

The hand disintegrated. Blood splattered across his face, obliterating his sight. He wanted to scream, but his vocal cords were too coarsened to obey.

"Get into the blackhawk, you little pillock, or we'll send you right back into the beyond again. And this time we'll never let you return."

Another burst of quite astonishing pain, followed by equally frightening numbness, told him his right foot had been destroyed. They were gnawing away at his beautiful new flesh, leaving him nothing. He raged barrenly at the unfairness of it all. Then strange echoey sensations blossomed into his mind.

See? Dariat asked. **It's simple, apply your thoughts like this.**

He did, and affinity opened, joining him with the *Mindor.*

What is happening? the frantic blackhawk asked.

Rocio's entire left leg was obliterated. White fire engulfed his groin and the stumpy remnant of his right leg.

Peran! the blackhawk called.

Rocio superimposed the captain's mind tone over his own thoughts. **Help me, *Mindor*.**

How? What is happening? I could not feel you. You closed yourself to me. Why? You have never done that before.

I'm sorry. It's the pain, a heart attack. I think I'm dying. Let me be with you, my friend.

Come. Hurry!

He felt the affinity link broaden, and the blackhawk was there waiting for its captain, its mind full of love and sympathy; a gentle and trusting creature for all its size and indomitable power. Kiera Salter exerted still more of her own particular brand of pressure.

With a last curse at the devils who left him no choice, Rocio abandoned that cherished human body, sliding himself along the affinity link. This transfer was different from the one which had brought him back from beyond. That had been a forced entry, this was a welcome embrace from an unsophisticated lover, drawing him in to secure him from harm.

The energistic nexus which his soul engendered established itself within the waiting neural cells at the core of the blackhawk, and the linkage which connected him to the captain's body snapped as the skull was smashed apart by Kiera's triumphant fist.

The *Mindor* sat on its pedestal on the second of Valisk's three docking ledges, patiently sucking nutrient fluid into its storage bladders. Beyond the eclipse of the habitat's non-rotating spaceport, the gas giant Opuntia was a pale cross-hatching of lime-green storm bands. The sight was a comforting one to the blackhawk. It had been birthed in Opuntia's rings, taking eighteen years to grow into the lengthy hundred-and-twenty-five-metre cone of its mature form. Even among blackhawks, whose profiles varied considerably from the standard voidhawk disk shape, it was an oddity. Its polyp hull was a dusky green speckled with purple rings; three fat finlike protuberances angled up out of its rear quarter. Given its squashed-missile appearance, the only option for the life support module was a swept-back teardrop, which sat like a metallic saddle over the midsection of its upper hull.

Like all blackhawks and voidhawks its distortion field was folded around the hull, barely operative while it was docked. A condition which ended as soon as Rocio Condra's soul invaded its neural cells. The number of neurones he now possessed was considerably larger than a human brain, increasing the amount of energistic power produced by the transdimensional twist. He extended himself out from the storage cluster *Mindor* had designated, breaking straight through the sub-routines designed to support him.

The startled blackhawk managed to ask: **Who are you?** before he vanquished its mind. But he couldn't assume control of a blackhawk's enormously complex functions as easily as he could a human body. There was no instinct to guide him, no old familiar nerve impulse sequences to follow. This was an alien territory, there hadn't been any starships at all during his life, let alone living ones.

The autonomic routines, those regulating the *Mindor*'s organs, were fine, he just left them operating. However, the distortion field was controlled by direct conscious thought.

A couple of seconds after he gained possession it was billowing outwards uncontrollably. The blackhawk tipped back, pulling the pedestal feed tubes from their orifices. Nutrient fluid fountained out, flooding across the ledge until the habitat hurriedly closed the muscle valves.

Mindor rocked forwards, then rose three metres above the mushroom-shaped pedestal as Rocio frantically tried to contain the oscillating fluxes running wild through his patterning cells. Unfortunately he couldn't quite coordinate the process. Mass detection, the blackhawk's primary sense, came from a sophisticated secondary manipulation of the distortion field. Rocio couldn't work out where he was, let alone how to return to where he'd been.

What the hell are you doing? an irate Rubra asked.

Mindor's stern swept around in a fast arc, lower fins almost scraping the ledge surface. The driver of a service vehicle slammed on the brakes, and reversed fast as the huge bitek starship swished past less than five metres in front of her cabin's bubble windscreen.

Sorry, Rocio said, frenziedly searching through the blackhawk's confined memories for some kind of command routine. **It's a power flux. I'll have it choked back in a second.**

Two more blackhawks had started similar gyrations as returned souls invaded their neurones. Rubra shot them vexed questions as well.

Rocio managed to regulate the field somewhat more effectively, and tie in the mass forms he was sensing to the images from the sensor blisters. His hull was slithering dangerously close to the rim of the docking ledge.

He reconfigured the distortion field to impel him in the other direction. Which was fine, until he realized exactly how fast he was heading for the shell wall. And another (non-possessed) blackhawk was sitting in the way.

Can't stop, he blurted at it.

It rose smooth and fast, shooting sixty metres straight up, protesting most indignantly. The *Mindor* skidded underneath, and just managed to halt before its rear fins struck Valisk's shell.

The remaining two blackhawk captains in the Tacoul Tavern were finally sacrificed to Kiera's strategy; and their ships shot off their respective pedestals like overpowered fireworks. Rubra and the other blackhawks fired alarmed queries after them. Three of the unpossessed blackhawks, thoroughly unnerved by their cousins' behaviour, also launched themselves from the ledge. A collision appeared imminent as the giant ships cavorted in the kilometre gap between the two ledges. Rubra began broadcasting flight vectors at them to try to steer them apart, demanding instant obedience.

By now, Rocio had mastered the basics of distortion field dynamics. He manoeuvred his prodigious bulk back towards the original pedestal. After five attempts, edging around in jerky spirals, he managed to settle.

If you've all *quite* finished, Rubra said as the agitated flock of blackhawks settled nervously.

Rocio sheepishly acquiesced to the admonishment. He and the other four possessed blackhawks exchanged private acknowledgements, swapping snippets of information on how to control their new bodies.

After experimenting for half an hour Rocio was pleasantly surprised with what he could see and feel. The gas giant environ was bloated with energy of many types, and a great deal of loose mass. There were overlapping tides of magnetic, electromagnetic, and particle energy. Twenty moons, hundreds of small asteroids. They all traced delicate lines across his consciousness, registering in a multitude of fashions: harmonics, colours, scents. He had far more sensations available than those produced by a human sensorium. And any sense at all was better than the beyond.

The affinity band fell into a subdued silence as they waited to see what would happen next.

7

The overloaded spaceplane ascended cleanly enough through Lalonde's stratosphere, racing away from Amarisk's mountainous eastern coastline. It wasn't until the craft reached an altitude of a hundred kilometres, where the ions had thinned out to little more than a static-congested vacuum, that Ashly Hanson had to switch from the induction rams to the reaction drive. That was when their problems began. He had to redline the twin rocket engines in the tail, shunting up the voltage from the power cells, boosting the plasma temperature to dangerous heights. Coolant shunts emitted caution warnings, which he balanced against the craft's performance, heeding some, ignoring others. The job was his personal milieu: true piloting, knowing just how far he could push the systems, when to take calculated risks.

Power reserves, fuel levels, and safety margins formed fabulously elaborate interacting multitextural graphics inside Ashly's mind as he continued the magic juggling act. The factors were slowly coming together, enabling him to decide on his best case option: escape velocity at a hundred and twenty kilometres altitude. In theory that would leave seven kilos of reaction mass in the tanks. "But not a nice height," he muttered to himself. Never mind, it gave them the ability to rendezvous with *Lady Mac*.

The reasons for the spaceplane's overstressed loading parameters, all twenty-nine of them, were chattering and whooping happily behind him, impervious to the efforts of Father Elwes and Kelly Tirrel to shush them. It wouldn't last, Ashly thought with an air of inevitable gloom, kids always threw up in zero-gee, especially the ones as young as these.

He datavised the flight computer for a channel to *Lady Mac*. It took a while for the communications processor to lock on to Lalonde's satellite, and even then the bandwidth was reduced. Sore evidence of the malicious forces swirling invisibly around the doomed planet.

"Joshua?"

"Tracking you, Ashly."

"You're going to have to manoeuvre to make rendezvous. I'm even having to expend my RC thruster reaction mass to achieve orbit. This is the vector." Ashly datavised over the file from the spaceplane's flight computer.

"Jesus, that's cutting it fine."

"I know. Sorry, but the kids weigh too much. And you're going to have to replace the reaction engines altogether when we reach port. I had to pump them over the safeties. A full structural stress test probably wouldn't hurt, either."

"Ah well, our no claims bonus got blown to shit in the battle anyway. Stand by for rendezvous in twelve minutes."

"Thank you, Joshua."

The contented babble coming from the spaceplane's cabin was quieting considerably. Acceleration had now declined to a twentieth of a gee as the orbital injection burn was finalized. Both rocket engines cut out. The flight computer reported four kilos of reaction mass were left in the tanks.

Then the first damp groan could be heard from the rear of the cabin. Ashly braced himself.

Acceleration warnings sounded in the *Lady Macbeth*'s cabins. The Edenists working under the direction of Sarha Mitcham and Dahybi Yadev to prepare for the influx of some thirty children hurried to the couches and temporary mattresses. They all wore variants of the same grey, haunted expression on their faces. Given what they'd been through in the last thirty hours, such consternation was understandable. The high-pitched hooting conjured up all the wrong associations.

"Don't worry," Joshua announced. "No killer gees this time, we're just manoeuvring."

He was alone on the bridge, lights reduced to a pink glimmer, sharpening the resolution of the console hologram displays and AV projections. Strangely enough, the solitude felt good. He was now what he had always wanted to be—or thought he did—a starship captain, devoid of any other responsibility. Overseeing the flight computer and simultaneously piloting the big vessel along their new course vector towards the inert spaceplane didn't leave him with much time to brood on the consequences of their recent actions: Warlow dead, the mercenary team lost, the planet conquered, the rescue fleet broken. The whole shabby disaster really wasn't one he wanted to reflect on, nor the wider implications of having the possessed loose in the universe. Better to function usefully, to lose oneself in the mechanics of the problem at hand.

In a way his emotional climb-down was akin to a sense of release. The battles which they'd personally fought in, they'd won. Then they'd rescued the Edenists, the children, and now Kelly. And in a little while they were going home.

At the end, what more could you ask?

The unsuppressible guilt was his silent answer.

Joshua stabilized *Lady Mac* a kilometre above the spaceplane, allowing orbital mechanics to bring the two together. Both craft had fallen into the penumbra, reducing the planet below to a featureless black smear. They were visually dead, only radar and infrared could distinguish between oceans and continents.

He ordered the flight computer to establish communications circuits with the small number of low-orbit observation satellites remaining. The image they provided built up quickly.

Amarisk had emerged completely into the daylight hemisphere now. He could see the continent was completely dominated by the huge red cloud. The vast patch must already cover nearly a quarter of the land; and it was expanding rapidly out from the Juliffe basin, its leading edges moving at hurricane velocities. Yet it still retained its silky consistency, a uniform sheet through which no glimpse of the ground below was possible. The grey blemish which had hung above the Quallheim Counties during the mercenaries' brief campaign had also vanished. Even the mountains where the Tyrathca lived proved no barrier; the cloud was bubbling around them, sealing over valleys. Only the very tallest peaks were left unclaimed, their jagged snow caps sticking up from the red veil, icebergs bobbing through a sea of blood.

The sight had repelled Joshua before. Now it frightened him. The sheer potency it intimated was appalling.

Joshua flicked back to the images coming in from the *Lady Mac*'s extended sensor clusters. The spaceplane was five hundred metres away, its wings already folded back. He played the starship's equatorial ion thrusters, and moved in, bringing the docking cradle around to engage the latches in the spaceplane's nose cone.

Sitting in his pilot's seat, watching the performance through the narrow windscreen, Ashly was, as ever, amazed by Joshua's ability to control the huge spherical starship's motions. The docking cradle which had telescoped out of the hangar bay swung around gracefully until it was head-on, then slid over the squashed-bullet nose. Naturally the alignment matched first time.

Various clunking sounds were transmitted through the stress structure, and the spaceplane was slowly drawn inside the *Lady Mac*'s narrow cylindrical hangar. Ashly shuddered as another warm, sticky, smelly globe of fluid landed on his ship-suit. He didn't make the mistake of trying to swat it, that just broke the larger portions into smaller ones. And you could inhale those.

"Eight of you are going to have to stay inside the spaceplane cabin," Sarha datavised as the hangar's airlock tube mated to the spaceplane.

"You're kidding me," a dismayed Ashly replied.

"Bad luck, Ashly. But we're maxing out our life support with so many people on board. I really need the spaceplane's carbon dioxide filters."

"Oh, God," he said miserably. "Okay. But send in some handheld sanitizer units, and quickly."

"They're already in the airlock waiting for you."

"Thanks."

"Send out the smallest children first, please. I'm going to cram them into the zero-tau pods."

"Will do." He datavised the flight computer to open the airlock hatch, then left his seat to talk with Father Elwes about which children should go where.

Lady Macbeth's two undamaged fusion drive tubes ignited as soon as the spaceplane was stowed inside the hull. She rose away from the planet at a steady one gee, heading up towards a jump coordinate which would align her on Tranquillity's star.

Far behind her, the middle section of the red cloud rippled and swirled in agitation. A tornado column swelled up from the centre, extending a good twenty kilometres above the twisting currents of cumulus. It flexed blindly for several minutes, like a beckoning—or clawing—finger. Then the *Lady Macbeth*'s sensor clusters and thermal dump panels began to retract into their jump positions below the hull. Her brilliant blue-white fusion exhaust shrank away, and she coasted onwards and upwards for a brief minute until an event horizon claimed her.

The questing finger of cloud lost its vigour, and slowly bowed over in defeat, its glowing vapour reabsorbed into the now quiescent centre of the shroud. The leading edges continued their advance.

*   *   *

The view from Monterey's Hilton was as spectacular as only a three-hundred-and-fifty-million-dollar building could provide. Al Capone loved it. The Nixon suite was on the bottom floor of the tower, giving it a standard gravity. New California glided slowly past the curving, radiation-shielded window which made up an entire wall of the master bedroom. The planet gleamed enticingly against the jet-black starfield. His one disappointment was that from here the stars didn't twinkle like they used to when he watched them at night above his summer retreat cottage at Round Lake. That aside, he felt like a king again.

The Hilton was a sixty-storey tower sticking out of the Monterey asteroid, orbiting a hundred and ten thousand kilometres above New California. Apart from Edenist habitat starscrapers (which it was modelled on), there were few structures like it in the Confederation. Tourists could rarely look down on terracompatible planets in such a fashion.

Which was stupid, Al thought, big business could make a packet out of hotels like the Hilton. But he couldn't spend all day looking at New California. He could sense his Organization's top lieutenants waiting patiently outside the suite. They'd learned quickly enough not to interrupt when he wanted his privacy. But they did need orders, to be kept on their toes. Al knew just how fast things would fall apart if he didn't ride them hard. The world might be different, but the nature of people didn't change.

As if on cue, Jezzibella purred, "Come back here, lover."

Well maybe some people did, women never acted like her back in the 1920s and thirties. Then, they were either whores or wives. But Al was beginning to suspect there weren't many girls quite like Jezzibella in this century, either.

One minute all cute and kittenish, the next an animal as strong and demanding as himself. Al had his energistic strength now, which meant he could do some pretty incredible things with his wang. Things which even Jezzibella hadn't known about. Performances which made him proud, for a while anyway, because they were the only times he could make her beg him for more, to keep going, tell him how stupendous he was. Most of the time it was the other way around. Shit, she even kissed like a boy. Trouble was, after he'd done all those fantastic things to her hot-rod body, she wanted them done again, and again, and again . . .

"Please, baby. I really liked the Egyptian position. Only you are big enough to make that work."

With a halfhearted sigh Al left the window and walked back to the sunken bed she was lying on. The oomph girl had no shame, she was absolutely naked.

He grinned and let the front of his white robe fall open. Jezzibella hooted and applauded as his erection rose. Then she flopped back, character shifting in an instant. Al looked down on a scared-for-her-cherry schoolgirl.

His entry was fierce, without any attempt at finesse. It made her cry out in disbelief, pleading for him to stop, to be kind. But she couldn't resist, no girl could, not a lover like him. In minutes his vigorous pumping had turned her cries to rolling moans of delight, her snarl to a smile. Her body was responding, the two of them moving in a slick acrobatic rhythm. He made no attempt to control himself, to wait for her, he climaxed when *he* was ready, oblivious to anything else.

When his drowsy eyes opened, he saw her staring drunkenly up at the ceiling, the tip of her tongue licking her lips. "That was a good fantasy fuck," she drawled. "We'll have to do that one again."

Al gave up. "I gotta get going. I gotta sort the boys out, you know how it is."

"Sure, baby. What are you going to get them to do?"

"Christ, you dumb broad. I'm running the whole fucking planet now. You think that just falls into place? I gotta million problems need looking at. Soldiers, they need orders or they go sour."

Jezzibella pouted, then rolled over to grab the processor block which lay on the side of the bed. She typed on it, and frowned. "Al, honey, you must pull in that field of yours."

"Sorry," he muttered, and made an effort to calm his thoughts. It was the best way to make the electric gadgets work.

Jezzibella whistled in appreciation as she read the data running down the block's screen (she'd long since given up trying to datavise when she was in Al's presence). According to the information assembled by Harwood's office, there were nearly forty million possessed on New California now. Hooking up with Al, that wild impulse back at the San Angeles spaceport, looked like being the smartest move she'd ever made. *This* was the anarchy ride she'd been hunting for most of her life. The buzz of power she got from being with Al— very literally one of life and death—stimmed her higher than any adulation the fans gave during a concert.

How could anyone know that a gangster from the past would have such a genius for assembling a power structure which could hold an entire planet in bondage? But that was what he'd done. "You just gotta know what strings to jerk," he'd told her on the flight up to the orbiting asteroids.

Of course all forty million possessed weren't perfectly loyal to him, they weren't even recruited into the Organization. But then neither had the vast majority of Chicago's citizens sworn fealty to him. Nonetheless, willing or not, they had been his vassals. "All we gotta do is have an Organization in place and ready when the possessed start to emerge," he explained. "Back in Chicago, they called me a mobster because there was another administration trying to run things parallel to mine: the government. I lost out because the fuckers were bigger and stronger. This time, I ain't making that mistake. This time there's only gonna be me from the word go."

And he'd been true to his word. She'd watched him at work that first day, just after they'd captured the orbiting asteroids and the SD network, sitting quietly in the background of the Monterey naval tactical operations room which the Organization soldiers had taken over as their headquarters. Watching and learning just what she'd gone and gotten herself involved in. And what she saw was the building of a pyramid, one constructed entirely from people. Without once losing his temper, Al issued orders to his lieutenants, who issued them to their seconds, and so on down the line. A pyramid which was constantly growing, absorbing new recruits at the bottom, adding to the height, to the power of the pinnacle. A pyramid whose hierarchy was established and maintained with the coldly ruthless application of force.

The first targets to be blasted into lava by the SD platforms had been government centres, everything from the Senate palace and the military bases right down to county police stations. (Al really hated the police. "Those cocksuckers murdered my brother," he'd growl darkly when she questioned him on it.) Even little town halls in country smallvilles were reduced to cinders after they opened for business in the morning. For eight hours, the platforms had fired energy pulses down on the hapless, helpless planet they had been constructed to defend. Any group who could organize resistance was systematically wiped out. After that, the possessed were free to sweep across the land.

But Al's Organization people were among them, directing the onwards march, finding out exactly who had returned from the beyond, when they came from, what they did in their first life. Their details would be sent up to the office which Avram Harwood had set up in Monterey, where they would be studied to gauge their potential usefulness. A select few would then be made an offer which—"They just can't refuse," Al chortled jubilantly.

They were a tiny minority, but that was all it ever took to govern. No rival could ever develop. Al had seen to that; he had the firepower to support his Organization if anyone stepped out of line. And when he captured the SD network, he acquired the ultra-hardened military communications net which went with it, the only one which had a chance of remaining functional in the territories of the possessed. So even if there were objectors among the newly emerged possessed (and there certainly were), they couldn't get in contact with others who thought along the same lines to create any decent kind of opposition.

In the end Jezzibella had felt privileged. It was a pivotal moment of history, like watching Eisenhower dispatching his D-day forces, or being with Richard Saldana as he organized the exodus from the New Kong asteroid to Kulu. Privileged and ecstatic.

More statistics ran down the processor block's screen. There were over sixteen million non-possessed left in the areas where the Organization ruled supreme. Harwood's office had declared they should be left alone to keep the utilities and services going, and by and large the Organization ensured they were left alone—for now. How long that would last, though, Jezzibella had her doubts.

Transport was also being orchestrated to invade the cities and counties which remained uncontaminated. According to the tactical estimates there would be a hundred million possessed living on New California by this time tomorrow. The Organization would achieve absolute control of the entire planet within a further three days.

And yesterday all she'd had to entertain her were a couple of fresh, gawky kids and the tiresome antics of the entourage.

"It's looking pretty fucking fantastic, Al," she said. "Guess you've got what it takes."

He slapped her buns playfully. "I always have. Things here ain't so different from Chicago. It's just a question of size; this is one fuck of a lot bigger, but I got savvy Avvy's boys to help sort out that side of things, keeping track and all. Avvy didn't get to be mayor of San Angeles the way Big Jim Thompson made it into city hall back in Chicago. No, sir, he's got a flair for paperwork."

"And Leroy Octavius, too."

"Yep. I see why you wanted to keep him now. I could do with a load more like him."

"To do what?"

"To keep going, of course. At least for a few days more." He slumped his shoulders and rubbed his face in his hands. "Then it's really gonna hit the fan. Most of the dumb asses down there want to do this magic disappearing act. Je-zus, Jez, I ain't so sure I can stop them." Eight times in the last day he'd ordered Emmet Mordden to use the SD platforms to sharpshoot buildings and city blocks over which the wisps of red cloud were forming. Each time the culprits had taken the hint, and the luminous swirl had vanished.

For the moment he was on top of things. But what was gonna happen after he'd won the planet was giving his brain a real hard time. It was going to be difficult stopping the possessed from vanishing inside the red cloud, because he was the only one among them who didn't want that to happen. Once he'd delivered the whole planet to them, they'd start looking around at what was stopping them from achieving their true goal. And some wiseass with an eye on the main chance would make his bid. Wouldn't be the first time.

"So give them something more to do," Jezzibella said.

"Sure, right, doll. Like after the entire fucking world, what else am I gonna give them, for Christ's sake?"

"Listen, you keep telling me this whole setup is going to end once the possessed pull New California out of the universe, right? Everyone's going to be equal and immortal."

"Yeah, that's about it."

"That means you'll be nothing, least nothing special."

"That's what I'm fucking telling *you*."

Jezzibella shifted again. This time she was like nothing he'd seen before: a librarian or schoolmarm. Not the remotest bit sexy. Al sucked some breath through his teeth, the way she did that was just plain unnerving—her not having the energistic power, and all.

She leaned over and put a hand on each of his shoulders, stern eyes inches from his. "When you're nothing, all your lieutenants and soldiers become nothing, too. Deep down they're not going to want that. You've got to find a reason— a fucking good reason—to keep the Organization intact. Once they grab that angle you can keep things humming along sweetly for quite a while yet."

"But we've won here. There isn't a single excuse to keep going the way we have."

"There are plenty," she said. "You simply don't know enough about the way the modern galaxy works to make any long-range plans, that's all. But I'm going to cure that, starting right here. Now listen closely."

New California's planetary government had always taken a progressive view on flinging tax dollars at the local defence establishment. Firstly, it provided a healthy primer for industry to pursue an aggressive export policy, boosting foreign earnings. Secondly, their navy's above-average size gave them an excellent heavyweight political stature within the Confederation.

Such enthusiasm for defence hardware had resulted in a superb C3 (command, control, and communication) setup, the core of which was Monterey's naval tactical operations centre. It was a large chamber drilled deep into the asteroid's rock, below the first biosphere cavern, and equipped with state-of-the-art AIs and communications systems, linked in to equally impressive squadrons of sensor satellites and weapons platforms. It was capable of coordinating the defence of the entire star system against anything from a full-scale invasion to a sneak attack by a rogue antimatter-powered starship. Unfortunately, no one had ever considered the consequences should it be captured and its firepower turned inwards on the planet and orbiting asteroids.

The Organization lieutenants had split into two fractions to run their operations centre. There was Avram Harwood's staff who dealt purely with the administration and management details of the Organization, essentially the new civil service. Then there were those, a smaller number, working under the auspices of Silvano Richmann and Emmet Mordden, who were operating the military hardware they'd captured. The law enforcers. Al's laws. He'd given that task to the possessed alone, just in case any non-possessed tried to be a hero.

When Al and Jezzibella walked into the centre the huge wall-mounted hologram screens were showing satellite views of Santa Volta. Grizzled spires of smoke were rising from several of the city's blocks. Graphic symbols were superimposed over the real-time layout as the organization advanced its troops. Silvano Richmann and Leroy Octavius stood in front of the colourful screens, heads together as they discussed the best strategy to crack open the population. Filling the eight rows of consoles behind them, the communications team was waiting patiently.

Everyone turned as Al strode forward. There were grins, smiles, whoops, sharp whistles. He did the rounds, pressing the flesh, joking, laughing, thanking, offering encouragement.

Jezzibella followed a pace behind him. She and Leroy quirked an eyebrow at each other.

"So how's it going?" Al asked a scrum of his senior lieutenants when he'd finished his processional.

"We're more or less sticking to the timetable," Mickey Pileggi said. "Some places put up a fight. Others just roll onto their backs and stick their legs in the air for us. We got no way of knowing in advance. Word's getting out that we aren't possessing everyone. It helps. Causes a shitload of confusion."

"Fine from my angle, too, Al," Emmet Mordden said. "Our sensor satellites have been monitoring some of the deep space message traffic. It's not easy, because most of it is directional tight beam. But it looks like the rest of the system knows we're here, and what we're doing."

"Is that going to be a problem?" Al asked.

"No, sir. We caught nearly forty per cent of New California's navy ships in dock when we took over the orbiting asteroids. They're still there, and another twenty per cent is on permanent assignment to the Confederation Navy fleets. That just leaves a maximum of about fifty ships left in the system who could cause us any grief. But I've got every SD platform on situation-A readiness. Even if the admirals out there get their act together, they know it would be suicide to attack us."

Al lit a cigar, and blew a stream of smoke towards the screen. The near-orbit tactical display, Emmet had called it yesterday. It looked pretty calm at the moment. "Sounds like you're handling your slice of the action, Emmet. I'm impressed."

"Thanks, Al." The nervous man bobbed in appreciation. "As you can see, there's no spacecraft activity within a million kilometres of the planetary surface, except for five void-hawks. They're holding themselves stable over the poles, seven hundred thousand kilometres out. My guess is they're just watching us to see what's happening."

"Spies?" Al inquired.

"Yes."

"We should blow them all to shit," Bernhard Allsop said loudly. "Ain't that right, Al? That'll give the rest of those frigging Commie Edenists the message: Don't spy on us, don't fuck with us or it's your ass."

"Shut up," Al said mildly.

Bernhard twitched apprehensively. "Sure, Al. I didn't mean nothing by it."

"Can you hit the voidhawks?" Jezzibella asked.

Emmet glanced from her to Al, and licked his suddenly sweaty lips. "It's difficult, you know? They chose those polar positions carefully. I mean, they're out of range of our energy weapons. And if we launch a combat wasp salvo at them, they'll just dive down a wormhole. But, hey ... they can't hurt us, either."

"Not this time," Al said. He chewed his cigar from the left side of his mouth to the right. "But they can see what we're about, and it'll frighten them. Pretty soon the whole goddamn Confederation is going to know what's happened here."

"I told you they'd be trouble, Al baby," Jezzibella said, on cue. Her voice had shunted down to a tart's whinny.

"Sure you did, doll," he said, not taking his eyes off the tactical display. "We're gonna have to do something about them," Al announced to the room at large.

"Well, hell, Al," Emmet said. "I'll give it a go, but I don't think ..."

"No, Emmet," Al said generously. "I ain't talking about five crappy little ships. I'm talking about what's lining up behind them."

"The Edenists?" Bernhard asked, hopefully.

"Partly, yeah. But they ain't the whole picture, are they, boy? You gotta think *big*, here. You're in a big universe now." He had their complete attention. Damn, but Jez had been right. Typical.

"The Edenists are gonna broadcast what we've done here

to the whole Confederation. Then what do you think is gonna happen, huh?" He turned a full circle, arms held out theatrically. "Any takers? No? Seems pretty goddamn obvious to me, guys. They're gonna come here with every fucking battleship they got, and grab the planet back off us."

"We can fight," Bernhard said.

"We'll lose," Al purred. "But that don't matter. Does it? Because I know what you're thinking. Every goddamned dumb-ass one of you. You're thinking: We won't be here. We're gonna be out of this stinking joint any day now, safe on the other side of the red cloud where there ain't no sky and there ain't no space, and nobody dies anymore. Ain't that right? Ain't that what's brewing inside those thick skulls of yours?"

Shuffled feet and downcast eyes was the only response he was offered. "Mickey, ain't that right?"

Mickey Pileggi developed an urgent wish to be somewhere else. He couldn't meet his boss's interrogatory stare. "Well, you know how it is, Al. That's a last resort, sure. But shit, we can do like Bernhard says and fight some first. I ain't afraid of fighting."

"Sure you ain't afraid. I didn't say you were afraid. I didn't insult you, Mickey, you rube goof. I'm saying you ain't thinking level. The Confederation Navy, they're gonna turn up here with a thousand, ten thousand starships, and you're gonna do the smartest thing you can do, and hide. Right? I would if they came at me with all pieces shooting."

The left side of Mickey's face began to tic alarmingly. "Sure, boss," he said numbly.

"So you think that's gonna make them give up?" Al asked. "Come on, all of you. I want to know. Who in this room believes the big government boys are just gonna give up if you make New California disappear? Huh? Tell me. They lose a planet with eight hundred million people on it, and the admiral in charge, he's just gonna shrug and say: Well fuck it, you can't win them all. And go home." Al stabbed a finger at the little purple stars of light representing the voidhawks on the tactical display screen. A slim bolt of white fire lashed out, striking the glass. Glowing droplets sprinkled out. A crater bowed inwards, distorting and magnifying the graphics below. "Is he FUCK," Al bellowed. "Open your goddamn eyes, shitheads! These people can fly among the stars for Christ's sake. They know everything there is to know about how energy works, they know all about quantum dimensions, hell they can even switch off time if they feel like it. And what they don't know, they can find out pretty fucking quick. They'll see what you've done, they'll follow where you take the planet. And they'll bring it back. Those cruddy longhairs will look at what happened, and they'll work on it, and they'll work on it. And they ain't never going to stop until they've solved the problem. I know the feds, the governments. Believe me, of all people, I fucking know. You ain't never safe from them. They don't ever fucking stop. Never! And it won't matter diddly how much you scream, and how much you cuss and rage. They'll bring you back. Oh, yeah, right back here under the stars and emptiness where you started from. Staring death and beyond in the face." He had them now, he could see the doubt blossoming, the concern. And the fear. Always the fear. The way right into a man's heart. The way a general jerked his soldiers' strings.

Al Capone grinned like the devil himself into the daunted silence. "There's only one fucking way to stop that from ever happening. Any of you cretins figured that out yet? No? Big surprise. Well, it's simple, assholes. You stop running scared like you have been all your life. You stop, you turn around to face what's scaring you, and you bite its fucking dick off."

• • •

For five centuries after the first successful ZTT jump, governments, universities, companies, and military laboratories throughout the Confederation had been researching methods of direct supralight communication. And for all the billions of fuseodollars poured into the various projects, no one had ever produced a valid theory let alone a practical system to surmount the problem. Starships remained the only method of carrying data between star systems.

Because of this, waves of information would spread out like ripples through the inhabited star systems within the Confederation. And as the stars were not arranged in a tidy geometrical lattice, such wavefronts became more and more distorted as time went on. News companies had long since refined a set of equations defining the most effective distribution procedure between their offices. On receiving a hot item (such as the appearance of Ione Saldana), an office would typically charter eight to twelve starships to relay the flek depending on when and where the story originated. Towards the end of the distribution coverage, the information could well arrive in one system from several directions over the course of a fortnight. The nature of the starships employed also had a strong influence on the timing, depending on the marque of ship used, how good the captain was, component malfunctions, a hundred diverse circumstances all contributing to the uncertainty.

Laton's appearance had naturally received an overriding precedence from all the Time Universe offices receiving Graeme Nicholson's flek. But Srinagar was over four hundred light-years away from Tranquillity. News of the *Yaku*'s existence, and who it was carrying, arrived several days after the *Yaku* itself had departed from Valisk.

Laton!

Rubra was astonished. They might have been fellow Serpents, but that hardly made them allies. So for the first time in a hundred and thirty years he expanded his affinity and grudgingly contacted the Edenist habitats orbiting Kohistan to tell them the starship had docked briefly.

But Laton did not come inside, he assured them. **Only three crew came through immigration: Marie Skibbow, Alicia Cochrane, and Manza Balyuzi.**

Skibbow was definitely sequestrated, and the other two are likely recipients, the Kohistan Consensus replied. **Where are they?**

I don't know. It was a humiliating, dismaying admission, especially to make to his former peers. But Rubra had immediately made the connection between Marie Skibbow and Anders Bospoort, in whose apartment Dariat's corpse had been found. Such a chain of events worried him enormously. But his supposedly infallible memory storage facility had failed him utterly. After Marie and Anders had gone down the starscraper that first time they had simply vanished from his perception; and the sub-routine in the starscraper hadn't noticed their absence. Nor could he locate them now, not even with his perception sub-routines expanded and upgraded with a new batch of safeguards.

Do you require our assistance? the Kohistan Consensus asked. Our neuropathologists may be able to analyse the nature of the distortion in your sub-routines.

No! You'd love that, wouldn't you? Getting into my mind again. Poking around to see what makes me pulse.

Rubra—

You shits don't ever give up, don't ever stop.

Given the circumstances, do you not think it would be sensible to put old antagonisms behind us?

I'll deal with it. By myself. They can only fuck with my peripheral routines. They can't touch *me*.

As far as you know.

I know! Believe me, I know. I'm me; same as I ever was.

Rubra, this is only the beginning. They will try to infiltrate your higher-order thought routines.

They won't succeed, not now I know what to watch for.

Very well. But we must recommend to the Srinagar system assembly that starships are prohibited from docking with you. We cannot risk the prospect of any contamination spreading.

Suits me fine.

Will you at least cooperate with us on that?

Yes, yes. But only until I've tracked down the three *Yaku* crew and exterminated them.

Please be careful, Rubra. Laton's proteanic virus is extremely dangerous.

So that's what you think I've got, why my routines are failing. Bastards!

It took several minutes for his anger to sink back into more rational, passive thought currents. By the time he was thinking logically again, Valisk's SD sensor network alerted him to five voidhawks emerging from their wormhole termini to take up station half a million kilometres away. Spies! They didn't trust him.

He had to find the three people from the *Yaku*, and those

members of his family whose monitor routines had been tampered with.

While the rest of the Srinagar system went to an agitated stage one military alert status, he tried again and again to scan his own interior for the renegades. Standard visual pattern recognition routines were useless. He upgraded and changed the perception interpretation routines several times. To no avail. He tried loading similar search orders into the servitors, hoping that they might succeed where the sensitive cells woven into every polyp surface had failed. He swept through entire starscrapers with his principal consciousness, certain that they still hadn't managed to infiltrate and corrupt his identity core. He found nothing.

After ten hours, the watching voidhawks were joined by three Srinagar navy frigates.

Inside the habitat, Time Universe played Graeme Nicholson's recording continuously, agitating the population badly. Opinions were divided. Some said Laton and Rubra were obviously colleagues, comrades in antagonism. Laton wouldn't hurt Valisk. Others pointed out that the two had never met, and had chosen very different paths through life.

There was unease, but no actual problems. Not for the first few hours. Then some idiot from the spaceport's civil traffic control centre leaked the news (actually he was paid two hundred thousand fuseodollars by Collins for the data) that the *Yaku* had docked at Valisk. Twenty starships immediately filed for departure flights, which Rubra refused.

Unease began to slip into resentment, anger, and alarm. Given the nature of the residents, they had no trouble asserting their feelings in a manner which the rentcops employed by Magellanic Itg had a hard time damping down. Riots broke out in several starscrapers. Localized 'councils' were formed, demanding the right to petition Rubra—who simply ignored them (after memorizing the ringleaders). More thoughtful and prudent members of the population started to hike out into the remoter sections of parkland, taking camping gear with them.

Such strife was almost designed to make Rubra's frantic search for the three *Yaku* crew members difficult verging on impossible.

Thirty-eight hours after Graeme Nicholson's flek arrived in

the Srinagar system, a voidhawk came from Avon, exposing the true nature of the threat the Confederation was facing. Such was the priority, it even beat the First Admiral's earlier communiqué warning of a possible energy virus.

In its wake all incoming starships were isolated and told to prepare for boarding and inspection by fully armed military teams. Civil starflight effectively shut down overnight. Proclamations were issued, requiring all newly arrived travellers to report to the police. Failure to comply was roughly equivalent to thumbprinting your own death warrant. Navy reserves were called in. Industrial astroengineering stations began producing combat wasps at full capacity.

In one respect, news of the possessed assisted Rubra. It seemed to shock Valisk's population out of their confrontational attitude. Rubra judged it an appropriate time to appeal to them for help. Every communications net processor, holoscreen, and AV pillar in the habitat relayed the same image of him: a man in his prime, handsome and capable, speaking calmly and authoritatively. Given that he'd had nothing to do with the general population for a century, it was an event unusual enough to draw everyone's attention.

"There are only three possessed at large in the habitat at this moment," he told his audience. "While they are certainly a cause for concern, they do not as yet present a threat to us. I have issued the police with the kind of heavy-calibre weapons necessary to surmount their energistic ability. And if circumstances warrant, several citizens have the kind of experience which might prove useful in a confrontation." An ironic, knowing curl of his lip brought an appreciative smile from many watchers. "However, their ability to alter their appearance means they are proving hard for me to track down. I'm therefore asking all of you to look out for them and inform me immediately. Don't trust people just because they look the same as they've always been; these bastards are probably masquerading as friends of yours. Another effect to watch for is the way they interfere with electronic equipment; if any of your processors start glitching, inform me immediately. There's a half-million-fuseodollar reward for the information which results in their elimination. Good hunting."

"Thank you, Big Brother." Ross Nash tipped his beer glass at the holoscreen over the Tacoul Tavern's bar. He looked away from the drastically wobbly picture of Rubra, and grinned at Kiera. She was sitting in one of the wall booths, talking in low intense tones with the small cadre she'd been building up; her staff officers, people joked. Ross was mildly bugged that she hadn't been including him in the consultation process recently. Okay, so he didn't have much in the way of technical knowledge, and this habitat was a far gone trip into future-world for a guy who was born in 1940 (and died in '89—bowel cancer); he kept expecting Yul Brynner to turn up in his black gunslinger outfit. But damn it, his opinion counted for something. She hadn't screwed with him for days either.

He glanced around the black and silver tavern, resisting the impulse to laugh. It was busier than it had been for years. Unfortunately for the owner, nobody was paying for their drinks and meals anymore. Not this particular clientele. Tatars and cyberpunks mixed happily with Roman legionaries and heavy-leather bikers, along with several rejects from the good Dr Frankenstein's assembly lab. Music was blasting out of a magnificent 1950s Wurlitzer, allowing a flock of seraphim to strut their stuff across the neon underlit floor. It was pure sensory overload after the deprivation of the beyond, nourishment for the mind. Ross grinned engagingly at his new buddies propping up the bar. There was poor old Dariat, also cut out of Kiera's elite command group and really pissed by that. Abraham Canaan, too, in full preacher's ensemble, scowling at the debauchery being practised all around. One thing about the possessed, Ross thought cheerfully, they knew how to party. And they could do it in perfect safety in the Tacoul Tavern; those who were affinity-capable had turned the joint into a safe enclave, completely reformatting the subroutines which operated in the neural strata behind the walls.

He gulped down the rest of his glass, then held it up in front of his nose and wished it full once again. The liquid which appeared in it really did look like gnat's piss. He frowned at it; a complicated process, coordinating that many facial muscles. For the last five hours he'd been delighted that possessing a body didn't prevent you from getting utterly smashed, now it seemed there were disadvantages. He chucked the glass over his shoulder. He was sure he'd seen shops out in the vestibule, some of them would stock a bottle or two of decent booze.

Rubra knew his thought processing efficiency was lower than optimum. The malaise was his own fault. He should be reviewing the search, reformatting sub-routines yet again. Now more than ever the effort should be made, now the true nature of his predicament was known. And it was a predicament. The possessed had conquered Pernik. Bitek was not invincible. He ought to divert every mental resource towards breaking the problem; after all, the possessed were physically present, there had to be some way of detecting them. Instead he brooded—something an Edenist habitat personality couldn't, or wouldn't, do.

Dariat. Rubra simply couldn't forget the insignificant little shit. Dariat was dead. But now death wasn't the end. And he died happy. That passive half smile seemed to flitter through the cells of the neural strata like a menacing ghost. Not such a stretched metaphor, now.

But to kill yourself just to return . . . No. He wouldn't.

But someone had taught the possessed how to glitch his thought routines. Someone very competent indeed.

That smile, though. Suppose, just suppose, he was *so* desperate for vengeance . . .

Rubra became aware of a disturbance in the Diocca starscraper, the seventeenth floor, a delicatessen. Some kind of attempted holdup. A sub-routine was attempting to call for the rentcops, but it kept misdirecting the information. The new safeguard protocols he'd installed were trying to compensate, and failing. They fell back on their third-level instructions, and alerted the principal personality pattern. And barely succeeded in that. Dozens of extremely potent subversive orders were operating within the Diocca starscraper's neural strata, virtually isolating it from Rubra's consciousness.

Elated and perturbed, he focused his full attention on it . . .

Ross Nash was leaning on the delicatessen's counter, pressing a very large pump-action shotgun into the face of the petrified manager. He clicked the fingers of his free hand, and a thousand-dollar bill flipped out of his cuff, just like the way he'd seen a magician do it in Vegas one time. The crisp note floated down to join the small pile on the counter.

"We got enough here yet, buddy?" Ross asked.

"Sure," the manager whispered. "That's fine."

"Goddamn bet your ass it is. Yankee dollar, best goddamn currency in the whole fucking world. Everybody knows that." He snatched up a bottle of Norfolk Tears from beside the bills.

Rubra focused on the shotgun, not entirely sure the seventeenth floor's perception interpretation routine was fully functional after all. The weapon seemed to be made of wood.

Ross grinned at the trembling manager. "I'll be back," he said, in a very heavy accent. He did an about-face and started to march away. The shotgun flickered erratically, competing with a broken chair leg to occupy the same space.

The manager snatched his shockrod from its clips under the counter and took a wild swing. It connected with the back of Ross's head.

Along with the manager, Rubra was amazed at the result of the simple blow.

As soon as the shockrod sparked across Ross's skin, his possessed body ignited with the pristine glory of a small solar flare. All colours in the shop vanished beneath the incandescent blaze, leaving only white and silver to designate rough shapes.

Nearby processors and sensors came back on-line. Thermal alerts flashed into Valisk's net, along with a security call. Ceiling-mounted fire suppression nozzles swivelled around, and squirted retardant foam at the blaze.

The thick streams made little difference. Ross's stolen body was dimming now, sinking to its charred knees, flakes of carbonated flesh crumbling away.

Rubra activated the audio circuit on in the shop's net processor. "Out!" he commanded.

The manager cringed at the shout.

"Move," Rubra said. "It's the possessed. Get out." He instructed all the net processors on the seventeenth floor to repeat the order. Analysis routines began correlating all the information from the starscraper's sensitive cells. Even with his principal personality pattern directing the procedure, he couldn't see what was happening inside the Tacoul Tavern.

Then bizarre figures started to emerge from the tavern's doorway into the vestibule.

He'd found them, the whole damnable nest.

White fireballs shot through the air, pursuing the terrorized delicatessen manager as he ran for the lifts. One of them caught him, clinging to his shoulder. He screamed as black, rancid smoke churned out of the wound.

Rubra immediately cancelled the floor's autonomic routines and shunted himself into the operating hierarchy. The vestibule's electrophorescent cells went dead, dropping the whole area into darkness, except for the confusing strobe of white fire. A muscle membrane door leading onto the stairwell snapped open, sending out a single fan of light. The manager altered course, put his head down, and charged straight at it.

Chips of polyp rained down on the vestibule floor. All across the ceiling the atmosphere duct tubules were splitting open as Rubra contracted and flexed the flow regulator muscles in directions they were never designed for. Thick white vapour poured out of the jagged holes. Warm, dank, and oily, it was the concentrated water vapour breathed out of a thousand lungs, which the tubules were supposed to extract from the air and pump into specialist refining organs.

The possessed wished it gone. And the muggy fog obeyed, rushing aside to let them pass. But not before it reduced their fireballs to impotent wispy swirls of fluorescing mist.

The manager reached the stairwell. Rubra closed the muscle-membrane door behind him, clenching it tight as several balls of white fire slammed into the surface, burrowing in like lava worms.

Kiera Salter ran out into the vestibule just as the last of the stinking mist vanished. Red emergency lights had come on, bringing an antagonistic moonlight glow to the broad chamber. She saw the stairwell's muscle-membrane door slap shut ahead of the vengeful mob.

"Stop!" she yelled.

Some did. Several threw white fire at the muscle membrane.

"Stop this right now," she said, this time there was an edge in her voice.

"Fuck you, Kiera."

"He zapped Ross, goddamnit."

"I'm gonna make him suffer."

"Maybe." Kiera strode into the centre of the vestibule and stood there, hands on her hips, staring around at her precariously allied colleagues. "But not like this." She gestured at the smoking muscle membrane door, which was still shut. The grey surface was visibly quivering. "He knows now." She tipped her head back, calling out at the ceiling. "Don't you, Rubra?"

The ceiling's electrophorescent cells slowly came back on, illuminating her upturned face. Lines of darkness flowed across them, taking shape. YES.

"Yes. See?" She dared any of the possessed to challenge her; a couple of her more powerful new lieutenants, Bonney Lewin and Stanyon, came forward to stand beside her for emphasis. "We're playing a different game now, no more skulking about. Now we take over the entire habitat."

NO, printed the ceiling.

"That wasn't a deal, Rubra," she shouted up at him. "I'm not offering to make you a partner. Got that? If you're real, *real* lucky, then you get to live on. That's all. If you don't piss me off. If you don't get in my way. Then maybe we'll have a use for your precious Valisk afterwards. But only if you behave. Because once I've taken over your population it's going to be easy to fly away. Only before we go, I'll use the starships to cut you into little pieces; I'll split your shell open, I'll bleed your atmosphere out, I'll freeze your rivers solid, I'll blast your digestive organs out of the endcap. It'll take a long time hurting for you to die completely. Decades, maybe. Who knows. You want to find out?"

YOU ARE COMPLETELY ALONE. POLICE AND COMBAT-BOOSTED MERCENARIES ON THEIR WAY. SURRENDER NOW.

Kiera laughed brutally. "No, we're not alone, Rubra. There are billions of us." She looked around at the possessed in the vestibule, not seeing any dissenters (except ones like Dariat and Canaan, who really didn't count). "Okay, people, as from now we're going overt. I want procedure five enacted this minute." A casual click of her fingers, designating tasks. "You

three, override the lift supervisor processors, have them ready
to take us up into the parkland. Bonney, track down that little
shit who wiped Ross, I want him creatively hurt. We'll set up
our command centre in Magellanic Itg's boardroom."

The first lift arrived at the seventeenth floor. Five of the
possessed hurried in, anxious to show Kiera their eagerness to
obey, anxious to reap the rewards. The doors slid shut. Rubra
overrode the starscraper's power circuit safeguards, and
routed eighty thousand volts through the metal tracks which
lined the lift shaft.

Kiera could hear the screams from inside the lift, feel the
agony of forced banishment. The silicon rubber seal between
the doors melted and burned, allowing the fearsome light of
the bodies' internecine flame to spew out of the crack.

NOT SO EASY, IS IT?

For about twenty seconds she stood absolutely still, face a
perfect cage around any emotion. Then her finger lined up on
a spindly youth in a baggy white suit. "You, open the muscle
membrane; we'll use the stairs."

"Told you so," the youth said. "We should have gone for
him first."

"Do it," Kiera snapped. "And the rest of you, Rubra's
demonstrated what he can do. It's not much compared to our
ability, but it's an irritant. We'll cut through the neural strata's
connections with the starscrapers eventually, but until then,
proceed with caution."

The muscle-membrane door parted smoothly, allowing the
now slightly subdued possessed to troop up the seventeen
flights of stairs to the parkland above.

It wasn't a pure affinity command, Rubra told the Kohistan Consensus. I felt what was almost like a power surge
through the neural cells around the muscle membrane. It
came in with the affinity command, just wiped all my routines completely. But it's localized, an area roughly five
metres in diameter; it can't reach into the main neural
strata.

Laton claimed that Lewis Sinclair had that same kind of
supercharged affinity when he took over Pernik island,
the Consensus replied. It works through brute strength, and
as such can be subverted. But should one of them suc-

ceed in transferring his personality into you, the energistic ability increases in proportion to the number of cells subsumed. You must not allow that to happen.

Fat chance. You know Valisk's neural cells were sequenced from my DNA, they will only process my thought routines. I guess that's similar to what Laton did to Pernik when he altered the island's neural strata with his proteanic virus. The affinity-capable possessed might be able to knock out some functions like the muscle membranes, but their personalities wouldn't function as independent entities in the neural strata, not unless they operate as a subsection of my pattern. I'd have to let them in.

Excellent news. But can you protect your general population from possession?

It's going to be tricky, Rubra admitted reluctantly. And I'll never save all of them, not even a majority. I'm going to have to take a whole load of internal damage, too.

We sympathise. We will help you rebuild afterwards.

If there is an afterwards.

8

Culey asteroid was an almost instinctive choice for André Duchamp. Located in the Dzamin Ude star system, a healthy sixty light-years from Lalonde, it acted as a ready haven for certain types of ships in certain circumstances. As if in reaction to its Chinese-ethnic ancestry, and all the clutter of authoritarian tradition which came with that, the asteroid was notoriously lax when it came to enforcing CAB regulations and scrutinizing the legitimacy of cargo manifests. Such an attitude hadn't done its economy any harm. Starships came for the ease of trading, and the astroengineering conglomerates came to maintain and support the ships, and where the majors went there followed a plethora of smaller service and finance companies. The Confederation Assembly subcommittee on smuggling and piracy might routinely condemn Culey's government and its policies, but nothing ever altered. Certainly in the fifteen years he'd been using it, André never had any trouble selling cargo or picking up dubious charters. The asteroid was virtually a second home.

This time, though, when the *Villeneuve's Revenge* performed its ZTT jump into the designated emergence zone, Culey spaceport was unusually reticent in granting docking permission. During the last three days the system had received first the reports of Laton's re-emergence, and secondly the warning from Trafalgar about possible energy virus contamination. Both designated Lalonde as the focus of the trouble.

"But I have a severely injured man on board," André protested as his third request to be allocated a docking bay was refused.

"Sorry, Duchamp," the port control officer replied. "We have no bays available."

"There's very little traffic movement around the port," Madeleine Collum observed; she'd accessed the starship's sensor suite, and was viewing the asteroid. "And most of that is personnel commuters and MSVs, no starships."

"I am declaring a first-degree emergency," André datavised to the port officer. "They have to take us now," he muttered to Madeleine. She simply grunted.

"Emergency declaration acknowledged, *Villeneuve's Revenge*," the port control officer datavised back. "We would advise you set a vector for the Yaxi asteroid. Their facilities are more appropriate to your status."

André glared at the almost featureless communications console. "Very well. Please open a channel to Commissioner Ri Drak for me."

Ri Drak was André's last card, the one he hadn't quite envisioned playing in a situation such as this, not over the fate of a crew member; the likes of Ri Drak were to be held in reserve until André's own neck was well and truly on the line.

"Hello, Captain," Ri Drak datavised. "We would seem to have a problem evolving here."

"Not for me," André answered. "No problems. Not like in the past, eh?"

The two of them switched to a high-order encryption program. Much to Madeleine's annoyance, she couldn't access the rest of the conversation. Whatever was said took nearly fifteen minutes to discuss. The only giveaway was André's clumsy face, registering a sneaky grin, intermingled with the sporadic indignant frown.

"Very well, Captain," Ri Drak said at last. "The *Villeneuve's Revenge* is cleared to dock, but at your own risk should you prove to be contaminated. I will alert the security forces to your arrival."

"Monsieur," André acknowledged gracelessly.

Madeleine didn't press. Instead she began datavising the flight computer for systems schematics, assisting the captain with the fusion drive's ignition sequence.

Culey's counter-rotating spaceport was a seven-pointed star, its unfortunate condition mirroring the asteroid's general attitude to spaceworthiness statutes. Several areas were in darkness: silver-white insulation blankets were missing from the surface, creating strange mosaic patterns, and at least three pipes were leaking, throwing up weak grey gas jets.

The *Villeneuve's Revenge* was assigned an isolated bay near one of the tips. That at least was fully illuminated, internal spotlights turning the steep-walled metal crater into a shadowless receptacle. Red strobes around the rim flashed in unison as the starship descended onto the extended cradle.

An armed port police squad were first through the airlock tube when it sealed. They rounded up André and the crew, detaining them on the bridge while a customs team examined the ship's life-support capsules from top to bottom. The search took two hours before clearance was granted.

"You put up a hell of a fight in here," the port police captain said as he slid through the open ceiling hatch into the lower deck lounge where the possessed had stormed aboard. The compartment was a shambles, fittings broken and twisted, blackened sections of composite melted into queer shapes, dark bloodstains on various surfaces starting to flake. Despite the best efforts of the straining environmental circuit there was a nasty smell of burnt meat in the air which refused to go away. Nine black body bags were secured to the hatch ladder by short lengths of silicon fibre. Stirred by the weak columns of air which was all the broken, vibrating conditioning duct could muster, they drifted a few centimetres above the scorched decking, bumping into each other and recoiling in slow motion.

"Erick and I saw them off," André said gruffly. It earned him a filthy glance from Desmond Lafoe, who was helping the spaceport coroner classify the bodies.

"You did pretty well, then," the captain said. "Lalonde sounds as if Hell has materialized inside the Confederation."

"It has," André said. "Pure hell. We were lucky to escape. I've never seen a space battle more ferocious than that."

The police captain nodded thoughtfully.

"Captain?" Madeleine datavised. "We're ready to take Erick's zero-tau pod down to the hospital now."

"Of course, proceed."

"We'll need you there to clear the treatment payment orders, Captain."

André's cheerfully chubby face showed a certain tautness.

"I will be along, we're almost through with the port clearance procedures."

"You know, I have several friends in the media who would be interested in recordings of your mission," the police captain said. "Perhaps you would care for me to put you in touch with them? There may even be circumstances where you wouldn't have to pay import duty; these matters are within my discretion."

André's malaised spirit lifted. "Perhaps we could come to some arrangement."

Madeleine and Desmond accompanied Erick's zero-tau pod to the asteroid's hospital in the main habitation cavern. Before the field was switched off, the doctors went through the flek Madeleine had recorded as she stabilized Erick.

"Your friend is a lucky man," the principal surgeon told them after the initial review.

"We know," Madeleine said. "We were there."

"Fortunately his Kulu Corporation neural nanonics are top of the range, very high capacity. The emergency suspension program he ran during the decompression event was correspondingly comprehensive; it has prevented major internal organ tissue death, and there's very little neural damage, the blood supply to his cranium was sustained almost satisfactorily. We can certainly clone and replace the cells he has lost. Lungs will have to be completely replaced, of course, they always suffer the most from such decompression. And quite a few blood vessels will need extensive repair. The forearm and hand are naturally the simplest operation, a straightforward graft replacement."

Madeleine grinned over at Desmond. The flight had been a terrific strain on everyone, not knowing if they'd used the correct procedures, or whether the blank pod simply contained a vegetable.

André Duchamp appeared in the private waiting room they were using, his smile so bright that Madeleine gave him a suspicious frown.

"Erick's going to be all right," she told him.

"*Très bon.* He is a beautiful *enfant.* I always said so."

"He can certainly be restored," the surgeon said. "There is the question of what kind of procedure you would like me to perform. We can use artificial tissue implants to return him to full viability within a few days, these we have in store. Following that we can begin the cloning operation and start to replace the AT units as his organs mature. Or alternatively we can simply take the appropriate genetic samples, and keep him in zero-tau until the new organs are ready to be implanted."

"Of course." André cleared his throat, not quite looking at his other two crew. "Exactly how much would these different procedures cost?"

The surgeon gave a modest shrug. "The cheapest option would just be to give him the artificial tissue and not bother with cloned replacements. AT is the technology which people use in order to boost themselves; the individual units will live longer than him, and they are highly resistant to disease."

"Magnifique." André gave a wide, contented smile.

"But we're not going to use that option, are we, Captain?" Madeleine said forcibly. "Because, as you said when Erick saved both your ship and your arse, you would buy him an entire new clone body if that's what it took. Didn't you? So how fortunate that you don't have to clone a new body, and all the expense that entails. Now all you are going to have to pay for is some artificial tissue and a few clones. Because you certainly don't want Erick walking around in anything less than a perfectly restored and natural condition. Do you, Captain?"

André's answering grin was a simple facial ritual. *"Non,"* he said. "How right you are, my dear Madeleine. As ever." He gave the surgeon a nod. "Very well, a full clone repair, if you please."

"Certainly, sir." The surgeon produced a Jovian Bank credit disk. "I must ask for a deposit of two hundred thousand fuseodollars."

"Two hundred thousand! I thought you were going to rebuild him, not rejuvenate him."

"Sadly, there is a lot of work to be done. Surely your insurance premium will cover it?"

"I'll have to check," André said heavily.

Madeleine laughed.

"Will Erick be able to fly after the artificial tissue has been implanted?" André asked.

"Oh, yes," the surgeon said. "I won't need him back here for the clone implants for several months."

"Good."

"Why? Where are we going?" Madeleine asked suspiciously.

André produced his own Jovian Bank disk, and proffered it towards the surgeon. "Anywhere we can get a charter for. Who knows, we might even avoid bankruptcy until we return. I'm sure that will make Erick very happy knowing what his recklessness has reduced me to."

* * *

Idria asteroid was on full Strategic Defence alert, and had been for three days. For the first forty-eight hours all the asteroid council knew was that *something* had taken over the New California SD network, and coincidentally knocked out (or captured) half of the planetary navy at the same time. Details were hazy. It was almost too much to believe that some kind of coup could be successful on a modern planet, but the few garbled reports which did get beamed out before the transmitters fell ominously silent confirmed that the SD platforms were firing at groundside targets.

Then a day ago the voidhawk messenger from the Confederation Assembly arrived in the system, and people understood what had happened. With understanding came terror.

Every settled asteroid in the Lyll belt was on the same maximum alert status. The Edenist habitats orbiting Yosemite had announced a two-million-kilometre emergence exclusion zone around the gas giant, enforced by armed voidhawks. Such New California navy ships as had escaped the planetary catastrophe were dispersed across several settled asteroids, while the surviving admirals gathered at the Trojan asteroid cluster trailing Yosemite to debate what to do. So far all they'd done was fall back on the oldest military maxim and send out scouts to fill in the yawning information gap.

Commander Nicolai Penovich was duty officer in Idria's SD command centre when the Adamist starships emerged three thousand kilometres away—five medium-sized craft, nowhere near the designated emergence zone. Sensors showed their infrared signature leap upwards within seconds of their appearance. Tactical programs confirmed a massive combat wasp launch. Targets verified as the asteroid's SD platforms, and supplementary sensor satellites.

Nicolai datavised the fire command computer to retaliate. Electron and laser beams stabbed out. The hastily assembled home defence force fleet—basically every ship capable of launching a combat wasp—was vectored onto the intruders. By the time most of them had got under way the attackers had jumped away.

Another four starships jumped in, released their combat wasps, and jumped out.

The assault was right out of the tactics flek, and there was nothing Nicolai could do about it. His sensor coverage had already degraded by forty per cent, and still more was dropping out as combat wasp submunitions stormed local space with electronic warfare pulses. Nuclear explosions were surrounding the asteroid with a scintillating veil of irradiated particles, almost completely wiping out the satellites' long-range scanner returns.

It was becoming increasingly difficult to direct the platforms' fire on incoming drones. He didn't even know how many surviving salvos there were anymore.

Two of the defending ships were struck by kinetic missiles, disintegrating into spectacular, short-lived streaks of stellar flame.

Nicolai and his small staff recalled the remainder of the fleet, trying to form them into an inner defensive globe. But his communications were as bad as the sensor coverage. At least three didn't respond. Two SD platforms dropped out of his command network. Victims of combat wasps, or electronic warfare? He didn't know, and the tactics program couldn't offer a prediction.

The platforms were never really intended to ward off a full-scale assault like this, he thought despairingly. Idria's real protection came from the system's naval alliance.

A couple of close-orbit detector satellites warned him of four starships emerging barely fifty kilometres from the asteroid. Frigates popped out, spraying combat wasps in all directions. Eight were aimed at Idria's spaceport, scattering shoals of submunitions as they closed at thirty-five gees. Nicolai didn't have anything left to stop them. Small explosions erupted right across the two-kilometre grid of metal and composite. Precisely targeted, they struck communications relays and sensor clusters.

Every input into the SD command centre went dead.

"Oh, shit almighty," Lieutenant Fleur Mironov yelled. "We're gonna die."

"No," Nicolai said. "They're softening us up for an assault." He called up internal structural blueprints, studying the horribly few options remaining. "I want whatever combat personnel we have positioned in the axial spindle tubes, they're to enforce a total blockade. And close down the transit tubes linking the caverns with the spaceport. Now. Whoever's left out there will just have to take their chances."

"Against the possessed?" Fleur exclaimed. "Why not just fling them out of an airlock?"

"Enough, Lieutenant! Now find me some kind of external sensor that's still functioning. I must know what's happening outside."

"Sir."

"We have to protect the majority of the population. Yreka and Orland will respond as soon as they see what's happened. And Orland had two navy frigates assigned to it. We only have to hold out for a couple of hours. The troops can manage that, surely. The possessed aren't that good."

"If Yreka and Orland haven't been attacked as well," Fleur said dubiously. "We only saw about a dozen ships. There were hundreds in the asteroids and low-orbit station docks when the possessed took over New California."

"Jesus, will you stop with the pessimism, already? Now where's my external sensor?"

"Coming up, sir. I got us a couple of thermo dump panel inspection mechanoids on microwave circuits. Guess the possessed didn't bother targeting those relays."

"Okay, let's have it."

The quality of the image which came foaming into his brain was dreadful: silver-grey smears drifting entirely at random against an intense black background, crinkled blue-brown rock across the bottom quarter of the picture. Fleur manipulated the mechanoids so that their sensors swung around to focus on the battered spaceport disk at the end of its spindle. The spaceport was venting heavily in a dozen places, girders had been mashed, trailing banners of tattered debris. Eight lifeboats were flying clear of the damaged sections. Nicolai Penovich didn't like to imagine how many people were crammed inside, nor how they could be rescued. Vivid white explosions shimmered into existence against the bent constellation of Pisces. Someone was still fighting out there.

A large starship slid smoothly into view, riding a lance of violet fusion fire. Definitely a navy craft of some kind, it was still in its combat configuration; short-range sensor clusters extended, thermo dump panels retracted. Steamy puffs of coolant gas squirted from small nozzles ringing its midsection. Hexagonal ports were open all around its front hull, too big for combat wasp launch tubes.

Scale was hard to judge, but Nicolai estimated it at a good ninety metres in diameter. "I think that's a marine assault ship," he said.

The main drive shut off, and blue ion thrusters fired, locking it in to position five hundred metres away from the spindle which connected the non-rotating spaceport with the asteroid.

"I've placed a couple of squads in the spindle," Fleur said. "They're not much, some port police and a dozen boosted mercenaries who volunteered."

"Horatio had it easy compared to them," Nicolai murmured. "But they should be able to hold. The possessed can't possibly mount a standard beachhead operation. Their bodies screw up electronics, they'd never be able to wear an SII suit, let alone combat armour. They're going to have to dock and try and fight their way along the transit tubes, that's going to cost them." He checked the external situation again, seeking confirmation of his assessment. The big ship was holding steady, with just intermittent orange fireballs spluttering out of the equatorial vernier thruster nozzles to maintain attitude.

"Get me access to sensor coverage of the spaceport, and check on our internal communications," Nicolai ordered. "We may be able to coordinate a running battle from here."

"Aye, sir." Fleur started to datavise instructions into the

command centre's computer, interfacing their communications circuits with the civil data channels which wove through the spaceport.

Shadows began to flicker inside the ship's open hatches. "What the hell have they got in there?" Nicolai asked.

The inspection mechanoids turned up their camera resolution. He saw figures emerging from the ship, hornets darting out of their nest. Dark outlines, hard to see with the mushy interference and low light level. But they were definitely humanoid in shape, riding manoeuvring packs that had enlarged nozzles for higher thrust. "Who are they?" he whispered.

"Traitors," Fleur hissed. "Those NC navy bastards must have switched sides. They never did support independent asteroid settlements. Now they're helping the possessed!"

"They wouldn't. Nobody would do that."

"Then how do you explain it?"

He shook his head helplessly. Outside the spindle, the fast, black hornets were burning their way in through the carbotanium structure. One by one, they flew into the ragged holes.

• • •

Louise was actually glad to return to the quiet luxury of Balfern House. It had been an extraordinary day, and a wearyingly long one, too.

In the morning she'd visited Mr Litchfield, the family's lawyer in the capital, to arrange for money from the Cricklade account to be made available to her. The transfer had taken hours; neither the lawyer nor the bank was accustomed to young girls insisting on being issued with Jovian Bank credit disks. She stuck to her guns despite all the obstacles; Joshua had told her they were acceptable everywhere in the Confederation. She doubted Norfolk's pounds were.

That part of the day had proved to be simplicity itself compared to finding a way off Norfolk. There were only three civil-registered starships left in orbit, and they were all chartered by the Confederation Navy to act as support ships for the squadron.

Louise, Fletcher, and Genevieve had taken their coach out to Bennett Field, Norwich's main aerodrome, to talk to a spaceplane pilot from the *Far Realm*, who was currently groundside. His name was Furay, and through him she had gradually persuaded the captain to sell them a berth. She suspected it was her money rather than her silver tongue which had eventually won them a cabin. Their fee was forty thousand fuseodollars apiece.

Her original hope of buying passage directly to Tranquillity had gone straight out of the window barely a minute after starting to talk to Furay. The *Far Realm* was contracted to stay with the squadron during its Norfolk assignment; when the ship did leave, it would accompany the navy frigates. No one knew when that would be anymore, the captain explained. Louise didn't care, she just wanted to get off the planet. Even floating around in low orbit would be safer than staying in Norwich. She would worry about reaching Tranquillity when the *Far Realm* arrived at its next port.

So the captain appeared to give in gracefully and negotiate terms. They were due to fly up tomorrow, where they would wait in the ship until the squadron's business was complete.

More delay. More uncertainty. But she'd actually started to accomplish her goal. Fancy, arranging to fly on a starship, all by herself. Fly away to meet Joshua.

And leave everyone else in the stew.

I can't take them all with me, though. I want to, dear Jesus, but I really can't. Please understand.

She tried not to let the guilt show as she led the maids through the house back to her room. They were carrying the parcels and cases Louise had bought after they'd left Bennett Field. Clothes more suitable to travelling on a starship (Gen had a ball choosing them), and other items she thought they might need. She remembered Joshua explaining how difficult and dangerous star travel could be. Not that it bothered him, he was so brave.

Thankfully Aunt Celina hadn't returned yet, even though it was now late afternoon. Explaining the baggage away would have been impossible.

After shooing the maids out of her room Louise kicked her shoes off. She wasn't used to high heels, the snazzy black leather was beginning to feel like some kind of torture implement. Her new jacket followed them onto the floor, and she pushed the balcony doors open.

Duke was low in the sky, emitting a lovely golden tint, which in turn made the gardens seem rich with colour. A cooling breeze was just strong enough to sway the branches on the trees. Out on the largest pond, black and white swans performed a detailed waltz around clumps of fluffy tangerine water lilies, while long fountains foamed quietly behind them. It was all so deceitfully tranquil; with the wall shielding the sound of the busy road outside she would never know she was in the heart of the largest city on the planet. Even Cricklade was noisier at times.

Thinking about her home made her skin cold. It was something she'd managed to avoid all day. I wonder what Mummy and Daddy are being made to do by their possessors? Evil, vile acts if that awful Quinn Dexter has any say in the matter.

Louise shivered, and retreated back into the room. Time for a long soak in the bath, then change for dinner. By the time Aunt Celina rose tomorrow morning, she and Gen would be gone.

She took off her new blouse and skirt. When she removed her bra she felt her breasts carefully. Were they more sensitive? Or was she just imagining it? Were they supposed to be sensitive this early in a pregnancy? She wished she'd paid more attention to the family planning lessons at school, rather than giggling with her friends at the pictures of men's privates.

"Looks like you're getting lonely, Louise; having to do that for yourself."

Louise yelped, grabbing up the blouse and holding it in front of her like a shield.

Roberto pushed aside the curtain at the far end of the room where he'd concealed himself and sauntered forward. His grin was arctic.

"Get out!" Louise screamed at him. The terrible first heat of embarrassment was turning to cold anger. "*Out*, you filthy fat oaf!"

"What you need is a close friend," Roberto gloated. "Someone who can do it for you. It's a lot better that way."

Louise took a step back, her body shaking with revulsion. "Get out, now," she growled at him.

"Or what?" His hand swept wide, the gesture taking in the pile of cases which the maids had left. "Going somewhere? What exactly have you been up to today?"

"How I spend my time is none of your business. Now go, before I ring for a maid."

Roberto took another step towards her. "Don't worry, Louise, I won't say anything to my mother. I don't rat on my friends. And we are going to be friends, aren't we? Real good friends."

She took a pace back, glancing around. The bell cord to summon a maid was on the other side of the bed, near him. She'd never make it. "Get away from me."

"I don't think so." He started to undo the buttons on his shirt. "See, if I have to leave now I might just tell the police about that so-called farmhand friend of yours."

"What?" she barked in shock.

"Yeah. Thought that might adjust your attitude. They make me do history at school, see. I don't like it, but I do know who Fletcher Christian was. Your friend is using a false name. Now why would he do that, Louise? In a bit of trouble back on Kesteven, was he? Bit of a rebel is he?"

"Fletcher is not in any trouble."

"Really? Then why don't I just go make that call?"

"No."

Roberto licked his lips. "Now that's a whole lot nicer, Louise. We're cooperating with each other. Aren't we?"

She just clutched the blouse closer to her, mind feverish.

"Aren't we?" he demanded.

Louise nodded jerkily.

"Okay, that's better." He peeled off his shirt.

Louise couldn't help the tears stinging her eyes. No matter what, she told herself, I won't let him. I'd sooner die; it would be cleaner.

Roberto unbuckled his belt, and started to take down his trousers. Louise waited until they were around his knees, then bolted for the bed.

"Shit!" Roberto yelled. He made a grab for her. Missed. Nearly toppled over as the trouser fabric tangled around his shins.

Louise flung herself on top of the bed and started to scurry over the blankets. She'd left it on the other side. Roberto was cursing behind her, grappling with his trousers. She reached the end of the bed and flopped down, hands reaching underneath.

"No you don't." Roberto grasped an ankle and started dragging her back.

Louise squealed, kicking backwards with her free foot.

"Bitch."

He landed on top of her, making her cry out at the pain of such a weight. She clawed desperately at the mattress, pulling both of them to the edge of the bed. Her hands could just reach the carpet. Roberto laughed victoriously at her ineffectual struggling, and shifted around until he was straddling her buttocks. "Going somewhere?" he taunted. Her head and shoulders hung over the edge of the bed, vast waves of hair flooding the sheets. He sat up, panting slightly, and brushed the hair off her back, enjoying the flawless skin which was exposed. Louise strained below him, as if she was still trying to wriggle free. "Stop fighting it," he told her. His cock was hugely erect. "It's going to happen, Louise. Come on, you'll love it when we get started. I'm going to last all night long with you." His hands pushed below her, reaching for her breasts.

Louise's desperate fingers finally found the cool, smooth shape of carved wood she was searching for under the bed. She grabbed at it, groaning in revulsion as Roberto's hands squeezed. But the feel of Carmitha's shotgun sent resolution surging through her veins, inflaming and chilling at the same time.

"Let me up," she begged. "Please, Roberto."

The obscene prowling hands were stilled. "Why?"

"I don't want it like this. Turn me over. Please, it'll make it easier for you. This hurts."

There was a moment's silence. "You won't struggle?" He sounded uncertain.

"I won't. I promise. Just not like this."

"I do like you, Louise. Really."

"I know."

The weight against the small of her back lifted. Louise tensed, gathering every ounce of strength. She pulled the shotgun clear from under the bed and twisted around, swinging it in a wide arc, trying to predict where his head would be.

Roberto saw it coming. He managed to bring his arms up in an attempt to ward off the blow, ducking to one side—

The shotgun barrel caught him a glancing blow above his left ear, the end of the pump mechanism thumping his guarding hand. Nothing like as devastating as Louise wanted it. But he cried out in pain and shock, clamping his hands over the side of his head. He started to keel over.

Louise tugged her legs out from under him and tumbled off the bed, almost losing hold of the shotgun. She could hear Roberto sob behind her. It was a sound which sent a frightening burst of glee into her head. It freed her from all that genteel refinement which Norfolk had instilled, put civilization aside.

She climbed to her feet, got a better grip on the shotgun, and brought it crashing down on the top of Roberto's skull.

The anxious knocking on the door was the next thing Louise was conscious of. For some inexplicable reason she'd sunk down onto the floor and started to weep. Her whole body was cold and trembling, yet her skin was prickled with perspiration.

The knock came again, more urgent this time. "Lady Louise?"

"Fletcher?" she gasped. Her voice was so weak.

"Yes, my lady. Are you all right?"

"I . . ." A giggle became choked in her throat. "One minute, Fletcher." She looked around, and gagged. Roberto was sprawled over the bed. Blood from his head wound had produced a huge stain over the sheet.

Dear Jesus, I've killed him. They'll hang me.

She stared at the body for a long, quiet moment, then got up and wrapped a towel around her nakedness.

"Is anyone with you?" she asked Fletcher.

"No, my lady. I am alone."

Louise opened the door, and he slipped inside. For some reason the sight of the corpse didn't seem to shake him.

"My lady." The voice was so soft with sympathy and concern. He opened his arms, and she pressed against him, trying not to cry again.

"I had to," she blurted. "He was going to . . ."

Fletcher's hand stroked her wild hair, smoothing and combing it with every stroke. Within a minute it was a dry, shiny cloak again. And somehow the pain inside was lessened.

"How did you know?" she murmured.

"I could sense your anguish. A mighty silent shout, it was."

"Oh." Now there was a strange notion, that the possessed could listen to your thoughts. There's so much badness inside my head.

Fletcher met her troubled gaze. "Did that animal violate you, my lady?"

She shook her head. "No."

"He is lucky. Had he done so, I would have dispatched him to the beyond myself. Nor would such a passage be pleasant for him."

"But, Fletcher, he is dead. I did it."

"No, lady, he lives."

"The blood . . ."

"A cut to the head always looks far worse than it is. Come now, I will have you shed no more tears for this beast."

"Oh, Lord, what a dreadful mess we're in. Fletcher, he suspects something about you. I can't just go to the police and file a rape charge. He'd tell them about you. Besides"—she drew an annoyed breath—"I'm not quite sure which of us Aunt Celina would believe."

"Very well. We shall have to leave now."

"But—"

"Can you think of another course to follow?"

"No," she said sadly.

"Then you must prepare; pack what you need. I shall go and tell the little one, also."

"What about him?" She indicated Roberto's unconscious form.

"Dress yourself, my lady. I will deal with him."

Louise picked through the boxes and went into the en suite bathroom. Fletcher was already leaning over Roberto.

She put on a pair of long dark blue trousers and a white T-shirt. Black sneakers completed the outfit: a combination unlike anything she'd ever worn before—unlike anything Mother had ever *allowed* her to wear. But practical, she decided. Just wearing such garments made her feel different. The rest of the things she needed went into one of the suitcases she'd bought. She was halfway through packing when she heard Roberto's frightened shout from the bedroom. It trailed off into a whimper. Her initial impulse was to rush in and find out what was happening. Instead, she took a deep breath, then looked in the mirror and finished tying back her hair.

When she did finally emerge back into the bedroom, Roberto had been trussed up with strips of blanket. He stared at her with wide, terrified eyes. The gag in his mouth muffled his desperate shouts.

She walked over to the bed and looked down at him. Roberto stopped trying to speak.

"I'm going to return to this house one day," she said. "When I do, I'll have my father and my husband with me. If you're smart, you won't be here when we arrive."

Duchess was already rising by the time they arrived at Bennett Field. Every aircraft on Norfolk had been pressed into military service (including the aeroambulance from Bytham), ready to fly the newly formed army out to the rebel-held islands. Over a third of them were parked in long ranks over the aerodrome's close-mown grass. There were a lot of khaki-uniformed troops milling around outside the hangars.

Three guards stood beside the entrance to the administration block, a sergeant and two privates. There hadn't been any at lunchtime when Louise had met Furay.

Genevieve climbed down out of the cab and gave them a sullen look. The young girl was becoming very short-tempered.

"Sorry, miss," the sergeant said. "No civilians permitted in here. The aerodrome is under army control now."

"We're not civilians, we're passengers," Genevieve said indignantly. She glared up at the big man, who couldn't help a grin.

"Sorry, love, but you still can't come in."

"She's telling the truth," Louise said. She fished a copy of their transport contract with the *Far Realm* out of her bag and proffered it to the sergeant.

He shrugged and flicked through the pages, not really reading it.

"The *Far Realm* is a military ship," Louise said hopefully.

"I'm not sure . . ."

"These two young ladies are the nieces of the Earl of Luffenham," Fletcher said. "Now surely your superior officer should be made aware of their travel documentation? I'm sure nobody would want the Earl to have to call the general commanding this base."

The sergeant nodded gruffly. "Of course. If you'd like to wait inside while I get this sorted out. My lieutenant is in the mess at the moment. It might take a while."

"You're very kind," Louise said.

The sergeant managed a flustered smile.

They were shown into a small ground-floor office overlooking the field. The privates brought their bags in for them, both smiling generously at Louise.

"Have they gone?" she asked after the door was closed.

"No, my lady. The sergeant is most discomforted by our presence. One of the privates has been left a few yards down the corridor."

"Damnation!" She went over to the single window. From her position she could see nearly a third of the field. If anything the planes seemed to be packed even tighter than this morning; there were hundreds of them. Squads of militia were marching along the grass roadways, shouted at by sergeant majors. A great many people were involved with loading big cargo planes. Flat-topped trucks trundled past the squads, delivering more matériel.

"I think the campaign must be starting," Louise said. Dear Jesus, they look so young. Just boys, my age. "They're going to lose, aren't they? They're all going to be possessed."

"I expect so, my lady, yes."

"I should have done something." She wasn't sure if she was speaking out loud or not. "Should have left Uncle Jules a letter. Warned them. I could have given them that much of my time, enough to write a few simple lines."

"There is no defence, dear lady."

"Joshua will protect us. He'll believe me."

"I liked Joshua," Genevieve said.

Louise smiled, and ruffed her sister's hair.

"If you had warned your family and the Prince's court, and they believed you, I fear you would not have been able to buy your passage on the *Far Realm*, lady."

"Not that it's done us much good, so far," she said in exasperation. "We should have gone up to the *Far Realm* as soon as Furay finalized the contract."

Genevieve gave her an anxious look. "We'll get up there, Louise. You'll see."

"Not very easily. I can't see the lieutenant allowing us on to the field on the strength of that contract, not when all the troops are taking off. At the very least he'll call Uncle Jules first. Then we'll really be in trouble."

"Why?" Genevieve asked.

Louise squeezed her sister's hand. "I had a bit of a quarrel with Roberto."

"Yuck! Mr Fatso. I didn't like him."

"Me neither." She glanced out of the window again. "Fletcher, can you tell if Furay is out there?"

"I will try, Lady Louise." He came over to stand beside her, putting both hands flat on the windowsill and bowing his head. He shut his eyes.

Louise and Genevieve swapped a glance. "If we can't get away into orbit, we'll have to go out onto the moors and camp there," Louise said. "Find somewhere isolated, like Carmitha did."

Genevieve put her arms around her big sister's waist and hugged. "You'll get us away, Louise. I know you will. You're so clever."

"Not really." She hugged the girl back. "But at least I got us into some decent clothes."

"Yes!" Genevieve smiled down approvingly at her jeans and sweatshirt, even though there was a horrid cartoon rabbit printed on the chest.

Fletcher's eyes flicked open. "He's here, Lady Louise.

Over yonder." He pointed out of the window in the direction of the central control tower.

Louise was fascinated by the wet palmprints he'd left on the sill. "Excellent. That's a start. Now all we have to do is work out how to get to the spaceplane." Her hand tightened on the new Jovian Bank credit disk in her trouser pocket. "I'm sure Mr Furay can be persuaded to take us up straightaway."

"There are also several possessed within the aerodrome perimeter." Fletcher gave a confused frown. "One of them is wrong."

"Wrong?"

"Odd."

"What do you mean?"

"I'm not quite sure, only that he is odd."

Louise glanced down at Genevieve, whose face had paled at the mention of the possessed. "They won't catch us, Gen. Promise."

"As do I, little one."

Genevieve nodded uncertainly, wanting to believe.

Louise looked from the girl to the soldiers marching about outside, and came to a decision. "Fletcher, can you fake one of the army uniforms?" she asked. "An officer, not too high-ranking. A lieutenant or captain, perhaps?"

He smiled. "A prudent notion, my lady." His grey suit shimmered, darkening to khaki, its surface roughening.

"The buttons are wrong," Genevieve declared. "They should be bigger."

"If you say so, little one."

"That'll do," Louise said after a minute, anxious that the sergeant would return before they were done. "Half of these boys have never seen uniforms before. They don't know if it's right or not. We're wasting time."

Genevieve and Fletcher pulled a face together at the reprimand. The girl giggled.

Louise opened the window and peered out. There was no one in the immediate vicinity. "Push the cases through first," she said.

They walked over to the nearest hangar as quickly as they could; Louise immediately regretted bringing their bags and cases. She and Fletcher were carrying two apiece, and they were heavy; even Genevieve had a big shoulder bag which she was wilting under. Any attempt to be inconspicuous was doomed from the start.

It was about two hundred yards to the hangar. When they got there, the central control tower didn't look any nearer. And Fletcher just said that Furay was "near there." The pilot could be well on the other side for all she knew.

The hangar was being used as a store depot by the army; long rows of wooden crates were lined up along the sides, arranged so that narrow alleyways branched off at right angles leading right back to the walls. Five forklift trucks were parked at the far end. There were no soldiers in sight. The doors at both ends were wide open, creating a gentle breeze along the main aisle.

"See if there's a farm ranger or something like it parked here," Louise said. "If not, we're going to have to dump the cases."

"Why?" Genevieve asked.

"They're too heavy, Gen, and we're in a hurry. I'll buy you some more, don't worry."

"Can you use such a contraption, my lady?" Fletcher asked.

"I've driven one before." Up and down Cricklade's drive. Once. With Daddy shouting instructions in my ear.

Louise let the bags fall to the floor and told Genevieve to wait by them.

"I will search around outside," Fletcher said. "My appearance will cause little concern. May I suggest you stay in here."

"Right. I'll check down there." She started walking towards the other end of the hangar. The ancient corrugated iron roof panels were creaking softly as they shed the heat of Duke-day.

She was about thirty yards from the open sliding doors when she heard Fletcher calling out behind her. He was running down the wide aisle formed by the crates, waving his arms urgently. Genevieve was chasing after him.

A jeep drove into the hangar. Two people were sitting in it. The one driving wore a soldier's uniform. The second, sitting in the back, was dressed all in black.

Louise turned to face them. I'll brazen it out; after all, that's what I've been doing all day.

Then she realized the man in black was a priest, she could see the dog collar. She breathed out a sigh of relief. He must be an army padre.

The jeep braked to a halt beside her.

Louise smiled winningly, the smile which always made Daddy say yes. "I wonder if you could help us, I'm a little bit lost."

"I doubt that, Louise," Quinn Dexter said. "Not someone as resourceful as you."

Louise started to run, but something cold and oily snaked around her ankles. She crashed down onto the timeworn concrete floor, grazing her hands and wrists.

Quinn stepped down out of the jeep. The mockery of a cassock swirled around his feet. "Going somewhere?"

She ignored her stinging hands and numbed knee, lifting her head to see him standing above her. "Devil! What have you done to Mummy?"

His dog collar turned a shiny scarlet, as though it were made from blood. "Such a fucking great hurry for knowledge. Well don't you worry, Louise, we're going to show you exactly what happened to *Mummy.* I'm going to give you a personal demonstration."

"Do not touch her, sir," Fletcher called as he came to a halt by the front of the jeep. "The lady Louise is my ward, under my protection."

"Traitor," Lawrence Dillon yelled. "You are one of the blessed ones. God's Brother allowed you back into this world to fight the legions of the false Lord. Now you defy the messiah chosen to lead the returned."

Quinn clicked his fingers, and Lawrence fell silent. "I don't know who you are, friend. But don't fuck with me or you'll die to regret it."

"I do not wish to draw swords with any man. So stand aside and we will go our separate ways."

"Arsehole. I'm stronger than you by myself; and there's two of us."

Fletcher smiled thinly. "Then why do you not take what you desire by your might? Could it be I would struggle? And that would draw the attention of the soldiers. Are you stronger than an entire army?"

"Don't push it," Quinn warned. "I'm off this shit tip planet today, and nobody's gonna stop that. Now I know this bitch from before, she's smart. She'll have a starship lined up to take her away, right?"

Louise glared up at him.

"Thought so," Quinn sneered. "Well, lover, you're gonna hand your tickets over to me. My need is one fuck of a lot greater than yours."

"Never!" She groaned as Lawrence Dillon grabbed her by the back of her neck and hauled her upright.

Fletcher made a start forwards, but stopped as Quinn pointed at Genevieve, who was cowering behind him.

"Dumb move," Quinn said. "I'll blow you back to the beyond if I have to. And then it'll go real bad for your little pal. You know I mean it. I won't possess her. I'll keep her for myself. Some nights I'll hand her over to Lawrence; he knows some real kinks now. I taught him myself."

"Sure did." Lawrence grinned wildly at Genevieve.

"You are inhuman." Fletcher put an arm instinctively around Genevieve.

"Wrong!" Quinn barked. His sudden fury made Fletcher take a half pace backwards.

"Banneth. Now she's inhuman. She did things to me . . ." Spittle appeared on Quinn's chin. He giggled, and wiped it away on the back of a trembling hand. "She did things, okay. And now. Now, I'm the one who's gonna do things right back to her. Things so sick she's never thought of them. God's Brother understands that, understands the need in me. I'm gonna let my serpent beast devour her and then spew out the bits. I'll turn my whole crusade on her if I have to. I'll use biowar bugs, I'll use nukes, I'll use antimatter. I don't fucking care. I'm gonna crack Earth wide open. And I'm gonna go down there, and I'm gonna take her. And nobody is going to stand in my way."

"Right on!" Lawrence shouted.

Quinn was breathing heavily, as if there were insufficient oxygen in the hangar. The cassock had returned to his original priest robe, tiny crackles of energy rippling along the voluminous fabric. Louise quailed before the expression on his face. There wasn't even any point in struggling.

Quinn smiled at her, enraptured; two drops of blood dripped off his vampire fangs, running down his chin.

"Sweet Jesus," Louise made the shape of the cross with her free hand.

"But," Quinn said, calm again, "right now, I'm only interested in you."

"Fletcher!" she wailed.

"I warn you, sir, do not touch her."

Quinn waved a dismissive hand. Fletcher doubled up as if a giant had slammed a fist into his stomach. Breath *oofed* out of his parted lips. With a look of horrified surprise, he was flung backwards, thin slivers of white fire crawling over him, slowly constricting. His uniform began to smoulder. Blood burst out of his mouth and nose, more began to stain his crotch. He screamed, bucking about helplessly, wrestling with the air.

"Nooo!" Louise implored. "Please stop. Stop!"

Genevieve had stumbled to her knees, white face staring brokenly.

Lawrence began to fumble at the collar of Louise's T-shirt, snickering eagerly. Then his hand froze, and he drew a breath in surprise.

Quinn was frowning, squinting along the length of the hangar.

Louise gulped, not understanding anything. But Fletcher had stopped his agonized contortions. A liquid dust, sparkling with rainbow colours, was slithering over him, and his clothes were slowly mending. He rolled around groggily and swayed up on his knees.

"What the fuck you doing here, man?" Quinn Dexter shouted.

Louise scanned the far end of the hangar. Duchess was shining directly through the wide-open doors, producing a brilliant scarlet rectangle set amid the funereal metal cavern. A blank, black human figure was silhouetted in the exact centre. It raised its arm, pointing.

A bullet bolt of white fire streaked down the hangar, almost too fast for the eye to follow. Louise saw huge shadows careering around at dizzying speeds. The bolt hit the iron roofing girder directly above Quinn Dexter. He flinched, ducking blindly as flakes of hot, tortured metal rained down. The whole roof creaked as the loading was redistributed.

"God's Brother, what the shit are you playing at?" Quinn raged.

A bass laugh rumbled down the hangar, distorted by the peculiar acoustics of the stacked crates.

Louise had time to flash one imploring look at Fletcher, who could only shrug in confusion before the strange figure spread both arms wide.

"Quinn?" Lawrence appealed. "Quinn, what the hell is happening?"

His answer was a rosette corona of white fire which burst out of the silhouette. The crates around the figure ignited in the eerily powerful topaz flame which the energistic ability always fanned. A dry wind rose from nowhere, sending Quinn's robe thrashing.

"Shit," Quinn gasped.

The flames were racing towards them, gorging on the crates, swirling around and around the aisle, faster and faster, the eye of a cyclonic inferno. Wood screeched and snapped as it was cremated, spilling the contents of the crates for the flames to consume, intensifying their strength.

Louise squealed as the awesome heat pummelled against her. Lawrence had let go of her, his arms waving frantically. In front of him the air was visibly flexing like a warped lens, a shield against the baneful radiance.

Fletcher scooped up Genevieve. Bending low, he scuttled towards the open door beyond the jeep. "Move, lady," he shouted.

Louise barely heard him above the roaring. Dull explosions sounded somewhere behind the leading edge of flame. Corrugated iron panels were taking flight, busting their rusty rivets to shoot off the roof, soaring high into the two-tone sky.

She staggered after Fletcher. Only when she was actually outside did she look around, just for a second.

The flames formed a furious rippling tunnel the entire length of the hangar. Dense black smoke churned out of the end. But the centre was perfectly clear.

Quinn stood before the conflagration, facing it down, arms raised to discharge his power, deflecting the devastating barrage of heat. Far ahead of him, the blank figure had adopted a similar pose.

"Who are you?" Quinn screamed into the holocaust. "Tell me!" A large wall of crates burst apart, sending a storm of sparks charging into the fray. Several roof girders buckled, sagging down, corrugated panels scythed into the flames. The tunnel began to twist, losing its stability. "Tell me. Show your face." Sirens were sounding, the shouts of men. And more of the ruined hangar collapsed. *"Tell me!"*

The rampaging flames obscured the impudent figure. Quinn let out a wordless howl of outrage. And then even he had to retreat as metal melted and concrete turned to sluggish lava. He and Lawrence together lurched out onto the withered grass. Men and fire engines swarmed around in chaos. It was easy to blend in and slink away. Lawrence said nothing as they made their way along a lane of parked aircraft, the darkness of Quinn's mind humbling him into silence.

Louise and Fletcher saw the first vehicles bumping over the grass, farm rangers painted military green and a couple of jeeps. A squad of militia were running around the rank of planes, urged on by their officer. Sirens were starting up in the distance. Behind her, the flames were crawling ever higher into the sky.

"Fletcher, your uniform," she hissed.

He glanced down. His trousers had become purple. A blink, and they were khaki again; his jacket lost its rumpled appearance. His bearing was impressively imperious.

Genevieve moaned in his arms, as if she were fighting a nightmare.

"Is she all right?" Louise asked.

"Yes, my lady. Simply a faint."

"And you?"

He nodded gingerly. "I survive."

"I thought . . . It was awful. That devil brute, Quinn."

"Never worry for me, lady. Our Lord has decreed some purpose for me, it will be revealed in time. I would not be here otherwise."

The first vehicles were nearly upon them. Louise could see

more soldiers on their way. It was going to be a complete madhouse; nobody would know what was going on, what was to be done.

"This could be our chance," she said. "We must be bold." She started waving at one of the farm rangers. "That's only a corporal driving. You outrank him."

"As always, lady, your ingenuity is matched only by your strength of spirit. What cruel fate that our true lives are separated by such a gulf of time."

She gave him a half-embarrassed, half-delighted smile. Then the farm ranger was pulling to a halt in front of them.

"You there," Fletcher snapped at the startled man. "Help me get this child away. She has been overcome by the fire."

"Yes, sir." The corporal rushed out of the driving seat to help Fletcher ease Genevieve onto the backseat.

"Our spaceplane is over by the tower," Louise said, fixing Fletcher with an emphatic stare. "It will have the medicine my sister requires. Our pilot is skilled in such matters."

"Yes, madame," Fletcher said. "The tower," he instructed the corporal.

The bewildered man looked from Louise to Fletcher, and decided not to question orders from an officer, no matter how bizarre the circumstances. Louise hopped in the back and cradled Genevieve's head as they drove away from the disintegrating hangar.

The corporal took ten minutes to find the *Far Realm*'s spaceplane, guided by Fletcher. Although she'd never seen one before, Louise could see how different it was from the aircraft it was parked among. A needle fuselage with sleek wings that didn't quite match, as if they'd come off another, larger craft.

Genevieve had recovered by the time they arrived, though she was very subdued, pressing into Louise's side the whole time. Fletcher helped her down out of the farm ranger, and she glanced mournfully over to where the stain of black smoke was spreading over the crimson horizon. One hand gripped the pendant which Carmitha had given her, knuckles white.

"It's over, now, all over," Louise said. "I promise, Gen." She ran her thumb over the Jovian Bank credit disk in her pocket as if it were a talisman as potent as Carmitha's charm. Thank heavens she'd kept hold of that.

Genevieve nodded silently.

"Thank you for your assistance, Corporal," Fletcher said. "Now I think you had better return to your commanding officer and see if you can help with the fire."

"Sir." He was dying to ask what was going on. Discipline defeated curiosity, and he flicked the throttle, driving off down the broad strip of grass.

Louise blew out a huge sigh of relief.

Furay waited for them at the bottom of the airstairs. A halfknowing smile in place; interested rather than apprehensive.

Louise looked straight at him, grinning in return—at their arrival, the state they were in. It was a relief that for once she didn't have to concoct some ludicrous story on the spot. Furay was too smart for that. Bluntness and a degree of honesty was all she needed here.

She held up her Jovian Bank disk. "My boarding pass."

The pilot cocked an eyebrow towards the smoke. "Anyone you know?"

"Yes. Just pray you never get to know them, too."

"I see." He took in Fletcher's uniform. When they'd met at lunchtime Fletcher had been in a simple suit. "I see you've made lieutenant in under five hours."

"I was once more than this, sir."

"Right." It wasn't quite the response Furay expected.

"Please," Louise said. "My sister needs to sit down. She's been through a lot."

Furay thought the little girl looked about dead on her feet. "Of course," he said sympathetically. "Come on. We've got some medical nanonics inside."

Louise followed him up the airstairs. "Do you think you could possibly lift off now?"

He eyed the ferocious blaze again. "Somehow, I just knew you were going to ask that."

Marine Private Shaukat Daha had been standing guard outside the navy spaceplane for six hours when the hangar caught fire on the other side of Bennett Field. The major in charge of his squad had dispatched half a dozen marines to assist, but the rest were told to stand firm. "It may just be a diversion," the major datavised.

So Shaukat could only watch the extraordinarily vigorous flames through enhanced retinas on full resolution. The fire engines which raced across the aerodrome were quite something, though, huge red vehicles with crews in silvery suits. Naturally this crazy planet didn't have extinguisher mechanoids. Actual people had to deploy the hoses. It was fascinating.

His peripheral senses monitor program alerted him to the two men approaching the spaceplane. Shaukat shifted his retinal focus. It was a couple of the locals, a Christian padre and an army lieutenant. Shaukat knew that technically he was supposed to take orders from Norfolk officers, but this lieutenant was ridiculously young, still a teenager. There were limits.

Shaukat datavised his armour suit communications block to activate the external speaker. "Gentlemen," he said courteously as they came up to him. "I'm afraid the spaceplane is a restricted zone. I'll have to see some identification and authorization before you come any closer."

"Of course," Quinn Dexter said. "But tell me, is this the frigate *Tantu*'s spaceplane?"

"It is, yes, sir."

"Bless you, my son."

Annoyed at the honorific, he tried to datavise a moderately sarcastic response into the communications block. His neural nanonics had shut down completely. The armour suit suddenly became oppressively constrictive, as if the integral valency generators had activated, stiffening the fabric. He reached up to tear the shell helmet off, but his arms wouldn't respond. A tremendous pain detonated inside his chest. Heart attack! he thought in astonishment. Allah be merciful, this cannot be, I'm only twenty-five.

Despite his disbelief the convulsion strengthened, jamming every muscle rock solid. He could neither move nor breathe. The padre was looking at him with a vaguely interested expression. Coldness bit into his flesh, fangs of ice piercing every pore. His guttural cry of anguish was stifled by the armour suit tightening like a noose around his throat.

Quinn watched the marine tremble slightly as he earthed

the man's body energy, snuffing out the chemical engines of life from every cell. After a minute he walked up to the dead statue and flicked it casually with a finger. There was a faint crystalline *ting* which faded quickly.

"Neat," Lawrence said in admiration.

"It was quiet," Quinn said with modest pride. He started up the spaceplane's airstairs.

Lawrence examined the armour suit closely. Tiny beads of pale hoarfrost were already forming over the dark leathery fabric. He whistled appreciatively and bounded up the airstairs after Quinn.

William Elphinstone rose up out of the diabolical cage of darkness at the center of his own brain into a riot of heat, light, sound, and almost intolerable sensation. His gasp of anguish at the traumatic rebirth was deafening to his sensitive ears. Air seemed to rasp over his skin, every molecule a saw tooth.

So long! So long without a single sense. Held captive inside himself.

His possessor had gone now. A departure which had freed his body. William whimpered in relief and fear.

There were fragments of memory left behind from the time he'd been reduced to a puppet. Of a seething hatred. Of a demonic fire let loose. Of satisfaction at confounding the enemy. Of Louise Kavanagh.

Louise?

William understood so very little. He was propped up against a chain-link fence, his legs folded awkwardly below him. In front of him were hundreds of planes lined up across a broad aerodrome. It wasn't a place he'd ever seen before.

The sound of sirens rose and fell noisily. When he looked around he saw a hangar which had been gutted by fire. Flames and smoke were still rising out of the blackened ruins. Silver-suited firemen were surrounding the building, spraying it with foam from their hoses. An awful lot of militia troops were milling around the area.

"Here," William cried to his comrades. "I'm over here." But his voice was a feeble croak.

A Confederation Navy spaceplane flew low over the field,

wobbling slightly as if it wasn't completely under control. He blinked at it in confusion. There was another memory associated with the craft. Strong yet elusive: a dead boy hanging upside down from a tree.

"And what do you think you're doing here?" The voice came from one of the two patrolling soldiers who were standing three yards away. One of them was pointing his rifle at William. The second was holding back a pair of growling Alsatians.

"I . . . I was captured," William Elphinstone said. "Captured by the rebels. But they're not rebels. Please, you must listen. They're devils."

Both soldiers exchanged a glance. The one with the rifle slung it over his shoulder and raised a compact communications block.

"You must listen," William said desperately. "I was taken over. Possessed. I'm a serving officer from the Stoke County militia. I order you to listen."

"Really, sir? Lost your uniform, did you?"

William looked at what he was wearing. It *was* his old uniform, but you had to look close to know. The shirt's original khaki colour had been superseded by a blue and red check pattern. From the thighs down his regulation trousers were now tough blue denim jeans. Then he caught sight of his hands. The backs of both were covered in black hair—and everyone always teased him about having delicate woman's hands.

He let out a little moan of dismay. "I'm telling you the truth. As God is my witness." Their blank, impersonal faces told him how useless it all was.

William Elphinstone remained slumped against the fence until the MPs came and took him off to Bennett Field's tiny police station. The detectives who arrived from Norwich's Special Branch division to interrogate him didn't believe his story either. Not until it was far too late.

• • •

The Nyiru asteroid orbited ninety thousand kilometres above Narok, one of the earliest Kenya-ethnic colony worlds. After it was knocked into position two centuries ago the construction company had sliced out a five-hundred-metre-diameter ledge for visiting bitek starships. Eager for the commerce they would bring, the asteroid council equipped the ledge with a comprehensive infrastructure; even a small chemical plant to provide the nutrient fluid the starships digested.

Udat complained it didn't taste right. Meyer wasn't up to arguing. With Haltam's best ministrations, it had taken him seven hours to recover consciousness after their escape from Tranquillity. Waking to find himself in interstellar space, with a worried, hurting blackhawk and an equally unsettled crew to placate did not help his frail mental state. They had flown directly to Narok, needing eleven swallows to cover the eighty light-years, where normally they would only use five.

In all that time he had seen Dr Alkad Mzu precisely twice. She kept to herself in her cabin for most of the trip. Despite analgesic blocks and the medical nanonic packages wrapped around her legs and arms, her injuries were causing some discomfort. Most curious of all she refused to let Haltam program the leg packages to repair an old knee injury. Neither of them had been in the mood to give ground. A few tersely formal words were exchanged; she apologised for his injuries and the vigour of the opposition, he filled her in on the flight parameters. And that was all.

After they arrived at Nyiru she paid the agreed sum without any quibble, added a five per cent bonus, and departed. Cherri Barnes did ask where she was headed, but the slight woman replied with one of her dead-eye smiles and said it was best nobody knew.

She vanished from their lives as much a mystery as when she entered it so dramatically.

Meyer spent thirty-six hours in the asteroid's hospital undergoing cranial deep-invasion procedures to repair the damage around his neurone symbionts. Another two days of recuperation and extensive checks saw him cleared to leave.

Cherri Barnes kissed him when he walked back onto the *Udat*'s bridge. "Nice to see you."

He winked. "Thanks. I was worried there for a while."

"*You* were worried?"

I was frightened, *Udat* said.

I know. But it's all over now. And by the way, I think you behaved commendably while I was out of it. I'm proud of you.

Thank you. I do not want to have to do that again, though.

You won't have to. I think we're finally through with trying to prove ourselves.

Yes!

He glanced inquiringly around at his three crew. "Anybody got any idea what happened to our weirdo passenger?"

" 'Fraid not," Aziz said. "I asked around the port, and all I could find out was that she's hired herself a charter agent. After that—not a byte."

Meyer eased himself down into his command couch. A small headache was still pulsing away behind his eyes. He was beginning to wonder if it was going to be permanent. The doctor had said most probably not. "No bad thing. I think Mzu was right when she said we'd be better off not knowing about her."

"Fine in theory," Cherri said irritably. "Unfortunately all those agency people saw it was us who lifted her from Tranquillity. If she's right about how dangerous she is, then we're in some sticky shit right now. They're going to want to ask us questions."

"I know," Meyer said. "God, targeted by the ESA at my age."

"We could just go straight to them," Haltam said. "Because, let's be real here, they're going to catch us if they want to. If we go to them, it ought to show we aren't at the heart of whatever it is she's involved in."

Cherri snorted in disgust. "Yeah, but running to the King's secret police . . . It ain't right. I've heard the stories, we all have."

"Too right," Haltam said. "They make bad enemies."

"What do you think, Meyer?" Aziz asked.

It wasn't something he wanted to think about. His nutrient levels had been balanced perfectly by the hospital while he was in recuperation therapy, but he still felt shockingly tired. Oh, for someone else to lift the burden from him, which of course was the answer, or at least a passable fudge.

Good idea, *Udat* commented. **She was nice.**

"There is somebody who might be able to help us," Meyer told them. "If she's still alive. I haven't seen her for nearly twenty years, and she was quite old then."

Cherri gave him a suspicious look. "Her?"

Meyer grinned. "Yeah. Her. A lady called Athene, she's an Edenist."

"They're worse than the bloody ESA," Haltam protested.

"Stop being so prejudiced. They have one quality above all else, they're honest. Which is a damn sight more than you can say for the ESA. Besides, Edenism is one culture the ESA can never subvert."

"Are you sure she'll help?" Cherri asked.

"No promises. All I can tell you is if she can, she will." He looked at each of them in turn. "Does anyone have an alternative?"

They didn't.

"Okay, Cherri, file a departure notice with the port, please. We've been here quite long enough."

"Aye, sir.

And, you, let's have a swallow sequence for the Sol system.

Of course, *Udat* said, then added rather wistfully: **I wonder if the** *Oenone* **will be at Saturn when we arrive?**

Who knows? But it would be nice to see how it developed.

Yes. As you say, it has been a long time.

The first swallow manoeuvre took them twelve light-years from Narok's star. The second added another fifteen light-years. Confident the blackhawk had recovered from its ordeal, Meyer told it to go ahead with the third swallow.

Empty space twisted apart under the immense distortion which the patterning cells exerted. *Udat* moved cleanly into the interstice it had opened, shifting the energy which chased through its cells in smaller, more subtle patterns to sustain the continuity of the pseudofabric that closed around the hull. Distance without physical length flowed past the polyp.

Meyer! Something is wrong!

The alarmed mental shout struck like a physical blow. **What do you mean?**

The terminus is retreating, I cannot match the distortion pattern to its coordinate.

Linked with the blackhawk's mentality he could actually feel the pseudofabric changing, twisting and flexing around the hull as if it were a tunnel of agitated smoke. *Udat* was unable to impose the stability necessary to maintain the wormhole's uniformity.

What's happening? he asked, equally panicked.

I don't understand. There is another force acting on the wormhole. It is interfering with my own distortion field.

Override it. Come on, get us out of here. He felt a burst of power surge through the blackhawk's cells, amplifying the distortion field. It simply made the interference worse. *Udat* could actually sense waves forming in the wormhole's pseudofabric. The blackhawk juddered as two of them rolled against its hull.

It doesn't work. I cannot support this energy output.

Keep calm, Meyer implored. **It might just be a temporary episode.** In his own mind he could feel the energy drain reach exorbitant levels. There was barely ninety seconds reserve left at this expenditure rate.

Udat reduced the strength of the distortion field, desperate to conserve its energy. A huge ripple ran down the wormhole, slapping across the hull. Loose items jumped and spun over the bridge. Meyer instinctively grabbed the couch arms even as the restraint webbing folded over him.

The flight computer datavised that a recorded message was coming on line. Meyer and the crew could only stare at the offending console in amazement as Dr Mzu's image invaded their neural nanonics. There was no background, she simply stood in the middle of a grey universe.

"Hello, Captain Meyer," she said. "If everything has gone according to plan you should be accessing this recording a few seconds before you die. This is just a slightly melodramatic gesture on my part to explain the how and why of your situation. The how is simple enough, you are now experiencing distortion feedback resonance. It's a spin-off discovery from my work thirty years ago. I left a little gadget in the life-support section which has set up an oscillation within the *Udat*'s distortion field. Once established, it is quite impossible to damp down; the wormhole itself acts as an amplifier. The resonance will not end while the distortion field exists, and without the field the wormhole will collapse back into its quantum state. A neat logic box you cannot escape from. You can now only survive as long as *Udat*'s patterning cells have energy, and that is depleting at quite a rate, I imagine.

"As to the why; I specifically chose you to extract me from Tranquillity because I always knew *Udat* was capable of pulling off such a difficult feat. I know because I've witnessed this blackhawk in action once before. Thirty years ago, to be precise. Do you remember, Captain Meyer? Thirty years ago, almost to the month, you were part of an Omuta mercenary squadron assigned to intercept three Garissan navy ships, the *Chengho*, the *Gombari*, and the *Beezling*. I was on the *Beezling*, Captain, and I know it was you in the Omuta squadron because after it was over I accessed the sensor recordings we made of the attack. The *Udat* is a most distinctive ship, both in shape, colouring, and agility. You are good, and because of that you won the battle. And don't we all know exactly what happened to my home planet after that."

The datavise ended.

Cherri Barnes looked over to Meyer, strangely placid. "Is she right? Was it you?"

All he could do was give her a broken smile. "Yes." **I'm sorry, my friend.**

I love you.

Three seconds later, the energy stored in the *Udat*'s patterning cells was exhausted. The wormhole, which was held open purely by the artificial input of the distortion field, closed up. A straight two-dimensional fissure, fifteen light-years in length, appeared in interstellar space. For an instant it spat out a quantity of hard radiation equal to the mass of the blackhawk. Then, with the universe returned to equilibrium, it vanished.

9

Nicolai Penovich tried not to show how outright shit-scared he was when the stern-faced gangsters ushered him into the Nixon suite. Not that the macho-routine facade would do a hell of a lot of good, they'd already let slip that the possessed could pretty much tell what was going on in your mind. But not read it direct, not pull out exact memories. And that was his ace. One memory, and a prayer.

As prayers went it was a goddamn feeble one to be gambling not just his life but also his life after death.

He was shown into a giant living room with a fluffy white shag carpet and pale pink furniture which resembled fragile glass balloons. There were several doors leading off to the rest of the suite, plain gold slabs three metres high. The far wall was a window looking down on New California. The view as the terracompatible planet slowly drifted past was magnificent.

One of the gangsters used his Thompson machine gun to prod Nicolai into the middle of the room. "Stand there. Wait," he grunted.

About a minute later one of the tall doors opened silently. A young girl walked out. Despite his predicament, Nicolai couldn't help staring. She was ravishing, a mid-teens face with every feature highlighted by the purest avian bones. All she wore was a long gossamer robe revealing an equally sublime physique.

When he thought about it, she was obscurely familiar. He couldn't imagine meeting her and not remembering, though.

She walked straight past him to a pile of travelling cases on the other side of the living room. "Libby, where's my red leather playsuit? The one with the silver chain collar. Libby!" Her foot stomped on the carpet.

"Coming, poppet." A harried woman shuffled into the lounge. "It's in the brown case, the one with your after-party informal collection."

"Which one's that?" the girl complained.

"This one, poppet. Honestly, you're worse now than when we were touring." She bent over to open the case.

Nicolai gave the nymphet a more intense scrutiny. It couldn't be . . .

Al Capone hurried in, followed by a number of cronies. And there was no doubt at all of his identity. A handsome man in his early twenties, with jet-black hair, slightly chubby cheeks which emphasised his near-permanent soft smile. His clothes were as antique (and as ridiculous to Nicolai's eyes) as the other gangsters', but he wore them with such panache it really didn't matter.

He took one glance at Jezzibella and grimaced. "Jez, I told you before, will you stop goddamn prancing around in front of the guys like this. You ain't wearing diddly."

She looked back over her shoulder, pouted, and twirled a lock of hair around one finger. "Oh, come on, Al baby, it gives you a kick. The boys can all see what it is you've got, and they can never have. Living proof you're top doggy."

"Jez-us." He raised his eyes heavenwards.

Jezzibella sauntered over to him and pecked him lightly on the cheek. "Don't be long, precious. I've got parts of me that need a serious seeing to." She beckoned Libby to follow, and made for the door. The woman walked after her, a garment made up from about five slender red leather straps draped over her arm.

Jezzibella treated Nicolai to a cutely bashful smile from the middle of a cloud of gold-blond curls. Then she was gone.

Al Capone was staring at him. "You got something on your mind, fella?"

"Yes, sir."

"And what's that?"

"I've got some information for you, Mr Capone. Something that could be very useful to your Organization."

Al nodded curtly. "Okay, you got through the door, that proves you got balls enough. Believe me not many get this far. So now you're here, make your pitch."

"I want to join your Organization. I hear you make room for non-possessed people with special talents."

Al pointed a thumb at Avram Harwood III who was standing among the little cluster of lieutenants. "Sure do. If savvy Avvy here says what you got is good news, then you're in."

"Is antimatter good news?" Nicolai asked. He caught the shudder of horror on the broken mayor's face.

Al rubbed a finger thoughtfully over his chin. "Could be. You got some?"

"I know where you can get it. And I can assist your starship fleet when it comes to handling the stuff. It's a tricky substance, but I've had the training."

"How come? You're a fed, or close to it; a G-man for sure. I thought it was illegal."

"It is. But Idria is a small asteroid sharing a star system with some powerful institutions. A lot of groundside politicos talk about strengthening our general assembly into a system-wide administration or union. Some of Idria's council and SD officers don't appreciate that kind of talk. It took us a long time to gain our independence from the founding company, and it wasn't easy. So we made preparations. Just in case. Several of our companies make components that can be used to build antimatter confinement systems and drives. Strategic Defence Command also established a link with a production station."

"So you can get it anytime you want?" Al asked.

"Yes, sir. I have the coordinate of the star which the station is orbiting. I can take you there."

"What makes you think I want this stuff?"

"Because you're in the same position Idria was. New California is big, but the Confederation is a lot bigger."

"You telling me I'm penny-ante?"

"You might wind up that way if the First Admiral comes knocking."

Al grinned broadly, he put his arm around Nicolai and patted his shoulders. "I like you, boy, you got what it takes. So here's the deal. You go sit in a corner with my friend Emmet Mordden, here, who is a real wiz with electric machines and stuff. And you tell him what you know, and if he says it checks out, you're in."

* * *

Al shut the door behind him and leaned against it, taking a moment out of life, that essential chunk of time alone in his head which allowed his worn-down resolution to build itself up again. *I never realized being me was so goddamn difficult.*

Jezzibella had shifted to the trim athlete persona again, strong and haughty. She lay on the bed, arms stretched above her head, one knee bent. The playsuit had gripped her breasts with tight silver chains, forcing hard dark nipples to point at the ceiling. Every time she breathed her whole body flexed with feline allure.

"Okay," Al said. "So tell me what the fuck is antimatter?"

She arched her back, glaring defiantly at him. "Never."

"Jez! Just tell me. I don't have time for this crap."

Her head was tossed from side to side.

"Goddamnit!" He strode over to the bed, grabbed her jaw, and forced her to face him. "I want to know. I gotta make decisions."

A hand came arching through the air to strike him. He managed to catch it just before it reached his face, but his pale grey fedora was knocked off. She started to struggle, pushing him aside.

"Games huh?" he shouted angrily. "You wanna play fucking games, bitch?" He grabbed both her arms, pinning them against the pillows. And the sight of her chest heaving below the playsuit's revealing confinement ignited the dragon's fire in his heart. He forced her further down into the mattress, gloating at the sight of her superb muscles straining helplessly. "Who's in charge now? Who fucking owns you?" He ripped the leather off her crotch and prised her legs apart. Then he was kneeling between her thighs, his clothes evaporating. She groaned, making one last desperate attempt to break free. Against him, she never stood a chance.

Somewhen later, his own fulfillment made him cry out in wonder. The orgasmic discharge from his body was primitive savagery, enrapturing every cell. He held himself rigid, prolonging the flow as long as he could bear before collapsing onto the rumpled silk sheets.

"That's better, baby," Jezzibella said as she stroked his shoulders. "I hate it when you're all uptight."

Al grinned languidly at her. She'd changed back into the teen-kitten again, all worshipful concern crowned by a frizz of golden curls. "No way, lady. No way are you human."

She kissed his nose. "About the antimatter," she said. "You need it, Al. If there's any chance at all, then grab it."

"I don't follow," he mumbled. "Lovegrove says it's just a different kind of bomb. And we got ourselves plenty of the atom explosives already."

"It's not just a better kind of bomb, Al; you can use it to power combat wasps and starships, too, bump up their performance by an order of magnitude. If you like, it's the difference between a rifle and a machine gun. They both fire bullets, but which would you prefer in a rumble?"

"Good point."

"Thanks. Now even with the asteroid campaign going well, we haven't got anything like numerical parity with the Confederation's conventional forces. However, antimatter is a superb force multiplier. If you've got some, they're going to think twice before launching any sort of offensive."

"Jeeze, you are a fucking marvel. I gotta get this organized with the boys." He swung his legs over the side of the bed, and started to reconstitute his clothes out of the magic realm where they'd been banished.

"Wait." She pressed up against his back, arms sliding around to hug. "Don't go rushing into this half-cocked, Al. We've got to think this through. You're going to have problems with antimatter, it's vicious stuff. And you don't help."

"What do you mean?" he bridled.

"The way your energistic ability gronks out electronics and power circuits, you just can't afford that with antimatter. Put a possessed anywhere near a confinement system and we're all going to be watching the last half of the explosion from the beyond. So . . . it will have to be the non-possessed who work with the stuff."

"Sheesh." Al scratched his mussed hair, desperately uncertain. His Organization was built along the principle of keeping the non-possessed in line, under his thumb. You had to have some group at the bottom who needed to be watched on a permanent basis, it kept the Organization soldiers busy, gave them a purpose. Made them take orders. But give the non-possessed antimatter . . . that would screw up the balance something chronic. "I ain't so sure, Jez."

"It's not that big a problem. You just have to make sure you've got a secure hold over anyone you assign to handle the stuff. Harwood and Leroy can fix that; they can arrange for you to hold their families hostage."

Al considered it. Hostages might just work. It would take a lot of effort to arrange, and the Organization soldiers would really have to be on the ball. Risky.

"Okay, we'll give it a shot."

"Al!" Jezzibella squealed girlishly and started kissing his throat exuberantly.

Al's half-materialized clothes vanished again.

The chiefs of staff's office was as extravagant as only senior government figures could get away with; its expensive, handcrafted furniture arranged around a long hardwood table running down the centre. One wall could be made transparent, giving the occupants a view out over the SD tactical operations centre.

Al sat himself down at the head of the table and acknowledged his senior lieutenants with a wave of his hand. There was no smile on his face, a warning that this was strictly business.

"Okay," he said. "So what's been happening? Leroy?"

The corpulent manager glanced along the table, a confident expression in place. "I've more or less kept to the original pacification schedule we drew up. Eighty-five per cent of the planet is now under our control. There are no industrial or military centres left outside our influence. The administrative structure Harwood has been building up seems to be effective. Nearly twenty per cent of the population is non-possessed, and they're doing what they're told."

"Do we need them?" Silvano Richmann asked Al, not even looking at Leroy.

"Leroy?" Al asked.

"For large urban areas, almost certainly," Leroy said. "The smaller towns and villages can be kept going with their possessed inhabitants providing a combined energistic operation. But cities still require their utilities to function, you just can't wish that much shit and general rubbish away. Apparently the possessed cannot create viable food out of inorganic compounds, so the transport network has to be maintained to keep edible supplies flowing in. At the moment that's just stock from the warehouses. Which means we'll have to come up with a basic economy of some sort to persuade the farms to keep supplying the cities. The problem with that is, the possessed who are living out in the rural areas aren't inclined to do too much work, and in any case I haven't got a clue what we could use for money—counterfeiting is too damn easy for you. We may just have to resort to barter. Another problem is that the possessed cannot manufacture items which have any permanence; once outside the energistic influence they simply revert to their component architecture. So a lot of factories are going to have to be restarted. As for the military arena, non-possessed are unquestionably necessary, but that's Mickey's field."

"Okay, you done good, Leroy," Al said. "How long before I'm in charge of everything down there?"

"You're in charge of everything that counts right now. But that last fifteen per cent is going to be a hard slog. A lot of the resistance is coming from the hinterland areas, farm country where they're pretty individual characters. Tough, too. A lot of them are holed up in the landscape with their hunting weapons. Silvano and I have been putting together hunter teams, but from what we've experienced so far it's going to be a long dirty campaign, on both sides. They know the terrain, our teams don't; it's an advantage which almost cancels out the energistic ability."

Al grunted sardonically. "You mean we gotta fight fair?"

"It's a level playing field," Leroy acknowledged. "But we'll win in the end, that's inevitable. Just don't ask me for a timetable."

"Fine. I want you to keep plugging away at that economy idea. We gotta maintain some kind of functioning society down there."

"Will do, Al."

"So, Mickey, how are you holding out?"

Mickey Pileggi scrambled to his feet, sweat glinting on his forehead. "Pretty good, Al. We broke forty-five asteroids with that first action. They're the big ones, with the most important industrial stations. So now we've got three times as many warships as when we started. The rest of the settlements are just going to be a mopping-up operation. There's nothing out there which can threaten us anymore."

"You got crews for all these new ships?"

"We're working on it, Al. It isn't as easy as the planet. There's a lot of distance involved here, our communications lines aren't so hot."

"Any reaction from the Edenists?"

"Not really. There were some skirmishes with armed void-hawks at three asteroids, we took losses. But no big retaliation attacks."

"Probably conserving their strength," Silvano Richmann said. "It's what I would do."

Al fixed Mickey with *the look* (God, the hours he'd spent practising that back in Brooklyn). And he hadn't lost it, poor old Mickey's tic started up like he'd thrown a switch. "When we've taken over all the ships docked at the asteroids, are we gonna be strong enough to bust the Edenists?"

Mickey's eyes performed a desperate search for allies. "Maybe."

"It's a question of how you want them, Al," Emmet Mordden said. "I doubt we could ever subdue them, not make them submit to possession, or hand the habitats over to the Organization's control. You'll just have to trust me on this, they're completely different from any kind of people you have ever met before. All of them, even the kids. You might be able to kill them, destroy their habitats. But conquest? I don't think so."

Al squeezed his lips together and studied Emmet closely. Emmet was nothing like Mickey; timid, yeah, but he knew his stuff. "So what are you saying?"

"That you've got to make a choice."

"What choice?"

"Whether to go for the antimatter. You see, Edenism has a monopoly on supplying He_3, and that's the fuel which all the starships and industrial stations run on, as well as the SD platforms, and we all know they have to be kept powered up. Now there's an awful lot of He_3 stored around the New California system, but ultimately it's going to run out. That means we must go to the source if we want to keep our starships going, and maintain our hold over the planet. Either that or use the alternative."

"Right," Al said reasonably. "You've been talking to this Nicolai Penovich character, Emmet, is he on the level?"

"As far as I can make out, yeah. He certainly knows a lot about antimatter. I'd say he can take us to this production station of his."

"We got ships which can handle that?"

Emmet gave an unhappy scowl. "Ships, yeah, no problem now. But, Al, starships and antimatter, it means using a lot of non-possessed to run them. Our energistic power, it's not good for space warfare, if anything it puts our ships at a disadvantage."

"I know," Al said smoothly. "But, shit, we can turn this in our favour if we handle it right. It'll prove that the non-possessed have got a part in the Organization just as much as anyone. Good publicity. Besides, those boosted guys, they helped out in the asteroids, right?"

"Yes," Silvano admitted reluctantly. "They're good."

"That's it then," Al said. "We'll give our ships a crack at the Edenists, for sure. See if we can snatch the helium mines they got. But in the meantime we take out a sweet little insurance policy. Emmet, start putting together the ships you'll need. Silvano, I want you and Avvy to work on who's gonna crew them. I only want you to use non-possessed who are family guys, catch? And before they leave for the station, I want those families up here in Monterey being given the holiday of a lifetime. Shift everyone out of the resort complex, and house them there."

Silvano produced a greedy smile. "Sure thing, Al, I'm on it."

Al sat back and watched as they started to implement his instructions. It was all going real smooth, which threw up its own brand of trouble. One which even Jez had overlooked— but then this was one field where he had a shitload more experience than she had. The lieutenants were getting used to

wielding power, they were learning how to pull levers. They
all had their own territories right now, but pretty soon they'd
start to think. And sure as chickens shat eggs, one of them
would try for it. He looked around the table and wondered
which it would be.

•   •   •

Kiera Salter sat down on the president's chair in Magellanic
Itg's boardroom and surveyed her new domain. The office
was one of the few buildings inside the habitat; a circular,
fifteen-storey tower situated at the foot of the northern endcap. Its windows gave her a daunting view down the interior. The shaded browns of the semi-arid desert were
directly outside, slowly giving way to the tranquil greens of
grassland and forest around the midsection, before finally
merging into the rolling grass plains, currently dominated by
some vivid pink xenoc plant. Moating that, and forming an
acute contrast, was the circumfluous sea; a broad band of
near-luminous turquoise shot through with wriggling scin-
tillations. High and serene above it all, the axial light tube
poured out a glaring noon-sun radiance. The only incon-
gruity amid the peaceful scene was the dozen or so clouds
which glowed a faint red as they drifted through the air.

There was little other evidence of the coup which she had
led, one or two small smudges of black smoke, a crashed rent-
cop plane in the parkland surrounding a starscraper lobby.
Most of the real damage had occurred inside the starscrapers;
but the important sections, the industrial stations and spaceport, had sustained only a modest amount of battering.

Her plan had been a good one. Anyone who came into contact with a possessed was immediately taken over, regardless
of status. A ripple effect spread out from the seventeenth floor
of the Diocca starscraper, slow at first, but gradually gaining
strength as the numbers grew. The possessed moved onto the
next starscraper.

Rubra warned people of course, told them what to look out
for, told them where the possessed were. He directed the rentcops and the boosted mercenary troops, ambushing the possessed. But good as they were, the troops he had at his

disposal were heavily dependent on their hardware. That gave the possessed a lethal advantage. Unless it was as basic as a chemical projectile weapon, technology betrayed them, failing at critical moments, producing false data. He didn't even attempt to take Valisk's small squad of assault mechanoids out of storage.

Out on the docking ridges, the polyp hulls of possessed starships began to swell below a shimmer of exotic light patterns, emerging from their convulsions as full-grown hellhawks. Fantastically shaped starships and huge harpies zoomed away from the habitat to challenge the voidhawks and Srinagar frigates that were edging in cautiously. The military ships had pulled back, abandoning their effort to assist the beleaguered population.

Kiera's authority now extended the length of the habitat, and encompassed a zone a hundred thousand kilometres in diameter outside the shell. All in all, not a bad little fiefdom for an ex-society wife from New Munich. She'd glimpsed it briefly once before, this position, the influence, importance, and respect which authority endowed. It could have been hers for the taking back then; she had the breeding and family money, her husband had the ambition and skill. By rights a cabinet seat awaited, and maybe even the chancellorship (so she dreamed and schemed). But he'd faltered, betrayed by his ambition and lack of patience, making the wrong deals in search of the fast track. A weak failure condemning her to sitting out her empty life in the grand old country house, working studiously for the right charities, pitied and avoided by the social vixens she'd once counted as her closest friends. Dying bitter and resentful.

Well, now Kiera Salter was back, younger and prettier than ever before. And the mistakes and weaknesses of yesteryear were not going to be repeated again. Not ever.

"We finished going through the last starscraper three hours ago," she told the council she'd assembled (oh-so-carefully selecting most of the members). "Valisk now effectively belongs to us."

That brought applause and some whistles.

She waited for it to die down. "Bonney, how many non-possessed are left?"

"I'd say a couple of hundred," the hunter woman said. "They're hiding out, with Rubra's help, of course. Tracking them down is going to take a while. But there's no way for them to get out; I'll find them eventually."

"Do they pose any danger?"

"The worst case scenario would be a few acts of sabotage; but considering we can all sense them if they get close enough to us, it would be very short-lived. No, I think the only one who could hurt us now would be Rubra. But I don't know enough about him and what his capabilities are."

Everyone turned to look at Dariat. Kiera hadn't wanted him on the council, but his understanding of affinity and the habitat routines was peerless. They needed his expertise to deal with Rubra. Despite that, she still didn't consider him a proper possessed; he was crazy, a very ruthless kind of crazy. His agenda was too different from theirs. A fact which to her mind made him a liability, a dangerous one.

"Ultimately, Rubra could annihilate the entire ecosystem," Dariat said calmly. "He has control over the environmental maintenance and digestive organs; that gives him a great deal of power. Conceivably he could release toxins into the water and food, replace the present atmosphere with pure nitrogen and suffocate us, even vent it out into space. He can turn off the axial light tube and freeze us, or leave it on and cook us. None of that would damage him in the long term; the biosphere can be replanted, and the human population replaced. He cares less for the lives of humans than we do, his only priority is himself. As I told you right at the start, everything else we achieve is completely pointless until he is eliminated. But you didn't listen."

"So, shitbrain, why hasn't he done any of that already?" Stanyon asked contemptuously.

Kiera put a restraining hand on his leg under the table. He was a good deputy for her, his intimidating strength accounting for a great deal of the obedience she was shown; he also made an excellent replacement for Ross Nash in her bed. However, vast intelligence was not one of his qualities.

"Yes," she said levelly to Dariat. "Why not?"

"Because we have one key element left to restrain him," Dariat said. "We can kill him. The hellhawks are armed with enough combat wasps to destroy a hundred habitats. We're in a deterrence situation. If we fight each other openly, we both die."

"Openly?" Bonney challenged.

"Yes. Right now, he will be conferring with the Edenist Consensus about methods of reversing possession. And as you know, I'm investigating methods of transferring my personality into the neural strata without him blocking it. That way I could assume control of the habitat and eliminate him at the same time."

Which isn't exactly the solution I want, Kiera thought.

"So why don't you just do it?" Stanyon asked. "Shove yourself in there and fight the bastard on his own ground. Don't you have the balls for it?"

"The neural strata cells will only accept Rubra's thought routines. If a thought routine is not derived from his own personality pattern it will not function in the neural strata."

"But you fucked with the routines before."

"Precisely. I made changes to what was there, I did not replace anything." Dariat sighed elaborately, resting his head in his hands. "Look, I've been working on this problem for nearly thirty years now. Conventional means were utterly useless against him. Then I thought I'd found the answer with affinity enhanced by this energistic ability. I could have used it to modify sections of the neural strata, force the cells to accept my personality routines. I was exploring that angle when that drunk cretin Ross Nash blew our cover. So we went overt and showed Rubra what we can do; fine, but by doing that we threw away our stealth advantage. He is on his guard like never before. I've had enough evidence of that over the last ten hours. If I try to convert a chunk of the neural strata ready to accept me, it drops out of the homogeneity architecture, and he does something to the cells' bioelectric component, too, which kills them instantly. Don't ask me what—breaks down the natural chemical regulators, or simply electrocutes them with nerve impulse surges. I don't know! But he's blocking me every step of the way."

"All very interesting," Kiera said coldly. "What we need to know, however, is can you beat him?"

Dariat smiled, his gaze unfocused. "Yes. I'll beat him, I feel the lady Chi-ri touching me. There will be a way, and I'll find it eventually."

The rest of the council exchanged irritated or worried glances; except for Stanyon who merely gave a disgusted groan.

"Can we take it then, that Rubra does not pose any immediate threat?" Kiera asked. She found Dariat's devotion to the Starbridge religion with its Lords and Ladies of the realms another indication of just how unstable he was.

"Yes," Dariat said. "He'll keep up the attrition, of course. Electrocution, servitor housechimps cracking rocks over your skull; and we'll have to abandon the tubes and starscraper lifts. It's an annoyance, but we can live through it."

"Until when?" Hudson Proctor asked. He was an ex-general Kiera had drafted in to her initial coterie to help plan their takeover strategy. "Rubra is in here with us, and the Edenists are outside. Both of them are doing their damnedest to push us back into the beyond. We have to stop that, we must fight back. I'm damned if I'm prepared to sit here and let them win." He glanced around the table, buoyed by the level of silent support shown by the council.

"Our hellhawks are easily a match for any voidhawk," Kiera said. "The Edenists cannot get inside Valisk, all they can do is sit at a safe distance and watch. I don't consider them a problem at all, let alone a threat."

"The hellhawks might be as good as a voidhawk in a fight, but what's to make them stay and guard us?"

"Dariat," Kiera said, irked at having to defer to him again. But he was the one who'd worked out how to keep the hellhawks loyal to Valisk.

"The souls possessing the hellhawks will help us for as long as we want," Dariat said. "We have something they ultimately want: human bodies. Rubra's descendants can all use their affinity to converse with Magellanic Itg's blackhawks. That means the souls can get out of the hellhawks and into those bodies the same way as they got in. During our takeover we captured enough of Rubra's descendants to provide each hellhawk possessor with a human body. They're all stored in zero-tau, waiting."

"Waiting for what?" Hudson Proctor asked. "This is what

gets me. I don't even know why we're bothering with this discussion in the first place."

"What do you suggest we should be doing, then?" Kiera asked.

"The blindingly obvious. Let's just go. Now! We know we can do it; together we have the power to lift Valisk clean out of this universe. We can create our own universe around us; one with new laws, a place where there's no empty eternity around us, and where we're safely sealed off from the beyond. We'll be safe there, from Rubra, from the Edenists, from everybody. Safe and immortal."

"Quite right," Kiera said. Most possessed had only been back for a few hours, but already the urge was growing. To run, to hide from the dreadful empty sky. Enclosed Valisk was better than a planet; but Kiera had hated the starscrapers with their windows showing the naked stars, always reminding her of the beyond. Yes, she thought, we will have to leave that sight eventually. But not yet. There were other, older instincts prising at her thoughts. For when Valisk departed to a universe where anything became possible to every individual, the need for leadership would fade away, lost among the dream of eternal sybaritic life into which they would all fall. Kiera Salter would cease to be anything special. Maybe it was inevitable, but there was no need to rush into it. "What about the threat from ourselves?" she asked them, a high note of curiosity in her voice. As if they'd already solved the obvious problem.

"What threat?" Stanyon asked.

"Think about it. How long are we intending to leave this universe for?"

"I wasn't planning on coming back," Hudson Proctor said caustically.

"Me neither. But eternity is rather a long time, isn't it? And those are the terms we're going to have to start thinking in nowadays."

"So?" he demanded.

"So how many people are there in Valisk right now? Stanyon?"

"Close to nine hundred thousand."

"Not quite nine hundred thousand people. And the purpose

of life, or the nearest definition I'll ever make, is to experience. Experience whatever you can for as long as you can." She gave the councillors a morbid smile. "That isn't going to change whatever universe we occupy. As it stands, there aren't enough of us; not if we want to keep providing ourselves with new and different experiences for all of eternity. We have to have variety to keep on generating freshness, otherwise we'll just be playing variants on a theme for ever. Fifty thousand years of that, and we'll be so desperate for a change that we'll even come back here just for the novelty." She'd won them; she could see and sense the doubt and insecurity fission in their minds.

Hudson Proctor sat back in his chair and favoured her with a languid smile. "Go on, Kiera, you've obviously thought this through. What's the solution?"

"There are two possibilities. First, we use the hellhawks to evacuate ourselves to a terracompatible world and begin the possession campaign all over again. Personally I'd hate to risk that. Srinagar's warships might not be able to break into Valisk, but if we tried to land on the planet it would be a shooting gallery. Alternatively, we can play it smart and gather people in to us. Valisk can support at least six or seven million, and that's without our energistic ability enhancing it. Six million should be enough to keep our society alive and fresh."

"You're joking. Bring in over five million people?"

"Yes. It'll take time, but it can be done."

"Bringing some people in, yes, but so many . . . Surely our population is going to grow anyway?"

"Not by five million it isn't. We'd have to make permanent pregnancy compulsory for every female for the next ten years. This council might be in command now, but try implementing that and see how long we last."

"I'm not talking about right now, I'm talking about after. We'll have children after we leave."

"Will we? These aren't our actual bodies, they'd never be *our* children. The biological imperative isn't driving us anymore; these bodies are sensory receptors for our consciousness, nothing else. I certainly don't intend to have any children."

"All right, even assuming you're right, and I'm not saying you are, how are you going to get that kind of influx, launch the hellhawks on pirate flights to capture people?"

"No," she said confidently. "Invite them. You've seen the Starbridge tribes. There are the disaffected just like them in every society throughout the Confederation. I know, one of the charities I used to work for helped rehabilitate youngsters who couldn't cope with modern life. Gather them all together, and you could fill twenty habitats this size."

"But how? What's going to make them want to come here, to Valisk?"

"We just have to find the right message, that's all."

•   •   •

Even by day, Burley Palace stood aloof from the city of Atherstone; surrounded by extensive parkland at the top of a small rise, it surveyed the sprawling lower districts with a suitably regal detachment. At night the isolation made it positively imperious. Atherstone's lights turned the motorways, boulevards, and grand squares into a gaudy mother-of-pearl blaze which shimmered as though it were alive. Right in the centre, however, the palace grounds were a lake of midnight darkness. And in the centre of that, Burley Palace shone brighter than it ever did under the noon sun, illuminated by a bracelet of five hundred spotlights. It was visible from almost anywhere in the city.

Ralph Hiltch observed it through the Royal Navy Marine flyer's sensor suite as they approached. It was a neoclassic building with innumerable wings slotting together at not quite geometrical angles, and five quadrangles enclosing verdant gardens. Even though it was nearly one o'clock in the morning, there were a lot of cars using the long drive which cut through the parkland, headlights creating a near-constant stream of white light. Although highly ornamental, the palace was the genuine centre of government; so given the planet's current state of alert, the activity was only to be expected.

The pilot brought the flyer down on one of the discreetly positioned rooftop pads. Roche Skark was waiting for Ralph

as he came down the airstairs, two bodyguards standing unobtrusively a few metres behind.

"How are you?" the ESA director asked.

Ralph shook his hand. "Still in one piece, sir. Unlike Mortonridge."

"That's a nasty case of guilt you've got there, Ralph. I hope
it's not clouding your judgement."

"No, sir. In any case, it isn't guilt. Just resentment. We
nearly had them, we were so close."

Roche gave the younger operative a sympathetic look. "I
know, Ralph. But you drove them out of Pasto, and that's got
to be a colossal achievement. Just think what would have happened if it had fallen to the likes of Annette Ekelund. Mortonridge multiplied by a hundred. And if they'd possessed that
many people they wouldn't have been content to stay put like
they are on the peninsula."

"Yes, sir."

They walked into the palace.

"This idea the pair of you came up with. Is it workable?"
Roche asked.

"I believe so, sir," Ralph said. "And I appreciate you allowing me to outline it to the Princess myself." The notion
had evolved from several strategy reviews he and Colonel
Palmer had held during the occasional lull in the frantic two
days of the Mortonridge evacuation. Ralph knew that it contained suggestions which had to be made to the Princess personally. He feared it being diluted by navy staff analysts and
tacticians if he routed it through the correct procedural channels. Smooth minds polishing away the raw substance to present a sleek concept, one that was politically acceptable. And
that wouldn't work, nothing short of hundred per cent adher-
ence to the proposal would produce success.

Sometimes when he stood back and observed this obses-
sional character he'd become he wondered if he wasn't simply overdosing on arrogance.

"Given the circumstances, it was the least we could do,"
Roche Skark said. "As I told you, your efforts have not gone
unnoticed."

Sylvester Geray was waiting for them in the decagonal reception room with its gleaming gold and platinum pillars. The

equerry in his perfect uniform gave Ralph's borrowed marine fatigues a reluctant appraisal, then opened a set of doors.

After the opulence of the state rooms outside, Princess Kirsten's private office was almost subdued, the kind of quietly refined study a noble landowner would run an estate from. He couldn't quite make the leap to accepting that the entire Ombey star system was ruled from this room.

He stepped up to the desk, feeling he ought to salute, but knowing it would appear ridiculous; he wasn't military. The Princess didn't look much different from her images on the news, a dignified lady who seemed to be locked in perpetual middle age. No amount of discipline was able to stop him checking her face. Sure enough, there was the classic Saldana nose, slender with a downturned end; which was almost her only delicate feature, she had an all-over robustness of a kind which made it impossible ever to imagine her growing into a frail old grandmother.

Princess Kirsten acknowledged him with a generous nod. "Mr Hiltch. In the flesh at last."

"Yes, ma'am."

"Thank you so much for coming. If you'd like to sit down, we can start."

Ralph took the chair next to Roche Skark, grateful for the illusion of protection his boss gave him. Jannike Dermot was eyeing him with what was almost a sense of amusement. The only other person in the room, apart from the equerry, was Ryle Thorne, who didn't appear to care about Ralph's presence one way or the other.

"We'll bring in Admiral Farquar now," Kirsten said. She datavised the desk's processor for a security level one sensenviron conference. The white bubble room emerged to claim them.

Ralph found he was sitting to the right of the admiral, down at the end of the table away from the Princess.

"If you'd like to summarize the current Mortonridge situation for us, Mr Hiltch," Kirsten said.

"Ma'am. Our principal evacuation operation is now finished. Thanks to the warnings we broadcast, we managed to lift out over eighteen thousand people with the planes and Royal Navy transport flyers. Another sixty thousand drove up the M6 and got out that way before the motorway failed. The sensor satellites show us that there are about eight hundred boats carrying refugees which are heading up to the main continent. Our priority at the moment is to try and take people off the smaller ones, which are desperately overcrowded."

"Which leaves us with close to two million people stranded in Mortonridge," Admiral Farquar said. "And not a damn thing we can do about it."

"We believe most of them are now possessed," Ralph said. "After all, Ekelund's people have had two days. And those that aren't possessed will be by tomorrow. We keep running into this exponential curve. It's a frightening equation when it's translated into real life."

"You're absolutely sure they are being possessed?" Princess Kirsten asked.

"I'm afraid so, ma'am. Our satellite images are being fudged, of course, right across the peninsula. But we can still use sections of the communications net. The possessed seem to have forgotten or ignored that. The AIs have been pulling what images they can from sensors and cameras. The overall pattern is constant. Non-possessed are tracked down, then systematically hurt until they submit to possession. They're fairly ruthless about it, though they do seem to be reticent with children. Most of those reaching the evacuation points now are under sixteen."

"Dear Heaven," the Princess muttered.

"Any of the possessed trying to get out?" Ryle Thorne asked.

"No, sir," Ralph said. "They seem to be sticking to the agreement as far as we can tell. The only anomaly at the moment is the weather. There's a considerable amount of unnatural cloud building up over Mortonridge, it started this morning."

"Unnatural cloud?" Ryle Thorne inquired.

"Yes, sir. It's an almost uniform blanket spreading up from the south, which doesn't appear to be affected by the wind. Oh, and it's starting to glow red. We believe it could be an additional form of protection from the sensor satellites. If it continues to expand at its current rate, Mortonridge will be completely veiled in another thirty-six hours. After that we'll only have the sensors hooked into the net, and I don't believe they'll overlook them for much longer."

"A red cloud? Is it poisonous?" Princess Kirsten asked.

"No, ma'am. We flew some drones through it, taking samples. It's just water vapour. But they're controlling it somehow."

"What about its potential as a weapon?"

"I don't see how it could be used aggressively. The amount of power necessary to generate it is quite impressive, but that's all. In any case, the border we've established at the top of Mortonridge is an effective block. The troops are calling it a firebreak. The SD lasers have cleared a two-kilometre-wide line of scorched earth straight across the neck. We're combining satellite observation with ground patrols to monitor it. If anything moves out there it'll be targeted immediately."

"What happens if the cloud tries to move over?"

"Then we'll attempt to burn it back with the SD lasers. If that doesn't work, then we'll need your authority to launch punitive strikes, ma'am."

"I see. How will you know how to target these punitive strikes if the red cloud covers all of Mortonridge?"

"Scout teams will have to go in, ma'am."

"Let us pray the cloud can be halted by the lasers, then."

"I can see you're geared up to prevent any attempt at a mass breakout," Ryle Thorne said. "What have you done to prevent individual possessed sneaking out among the refugees? We all know it only takes one to restart the whole nightmare. And I monitored aspects of the evacuation, it was rather chaotic at times."

"It was chaotic getting the refugees out, sir," Ralph said. "But the other end was more straightforward. Everyone was tested to see if they had this energistic effect. We didn't find anybody. Even if they did manage to get through, the refugees are all being held in isolation. We think the only possessed on Ombey are on Mortonridge."

"Good," Princess Kirsten said. "I know Roche Skark has already congratulated you, Mr Hiltch, but I'd like to express my own gratitude for the way you've handled this crisis. Your conduct has been exemplary."

"Thank you, ma'am."

"It galls me to say it, but I think that Ekelund woman was right. The final outcome isn't going to be decided here."

"Excuse me, ma'am, but I told Ekelund I thought that was incorrect, and I still believe that."

"Go on, Mr Hiltch," Kirsten told him cordially. "I don't bite, and I'd dearly love to be proved wrong in this instance. You have an idea?"

"Yes, ma'am. I think just waiting passively for this problem to be resolved somewhere else would be a vast mistake. For our own peace of mind, if nothing else, we have to know that the possessed can be beaten, can be made to give up what they've taken. We know zero-tau can force them to abandon the bodies they've stolen; and it may be that Kulu or Earth, or somewhere with real top-grade scientific resources, can find a quicker more effective method. But the point is, whatever solution we eventually come up with we still have to get out there on the ground and implement it."

"So you want to start now?" Admiral Farquar asked.

"The preparation stage, yes, sir. There is a lot of groundwork to be laid first. Colonel Palmer and myself believe the possessed have already made one critical mistake. By possessing everyone left in Mortonridge they have given up their blackmail weapon. They cannot threaten us with a massacre as they did in Exnall, not anymore, because they have no hostages left. There is only us and them now."

"Ralph, you've had firsthand experience of how hard they fight. It would cost us a couple of marines for every four or five possessed we captured. That's a bad ratio."

Ralph switched his attention to the Princess, wishing they were out of the sensenviron. He wanted physical eye contact, delivering her the truth of what he believed. "I don't believe we should use our own marines, sir. Not in the front line. As you say, they would be wiped out. We know the possessed have to be completely overwhelmed before they can be subdued, and those kinds of battles would demoralize the troops long before we made any real inroads."

"So what do you want to use?" Kirsten asked curiously.

"There is, ma'am, one technology which can function effectively around a possessed, and is also available in the kind of quantities necessary to liberate Mortonridge."

"Bitek," Kirsten said quickly, vaguely pleased at making the connection.

"Yes, ma'am." Ralph made an effort to rein in his surprise. "The Edenists could probably produce some kind of warrior construct which could do the job."

"There's even an appropriate DNA sequence which they could employ," she said, enjoying the game, her thoughts racing ahead, mapping our possibilities. "A Tranquillity serjeant. I've accessed sensevises of them. Nasty-looking brutes. And Ione is a cousin of ours, I'm sure acquisition wouldn't be a problem."

The rest of the security committee remained silent, startled by her apparent eagerness to discard taboos.

"We would still need a massive conventional army to occupy and hold the land we regained, and support the bitek constructs," Ralph said cautiously.

"Yes." The Princess was lost in thought. "You've certainly offered a valid proposal, Mr Hiltch. Unfortunately, as I'm sure you are aware, I could not conceivably approach the Edenists with such a request. The political implications of such an alliance would undermine some of the Kingdom's basic tenets of foreign policy, a policy which has been maintained for centuries."

"I see, ma'am," Ralph said stiffly.

"*I* can't petition them," Kirsten said, enjoying herself. "Only King Alastair can do that. So you'd better go and ask my big brother for me, hadn't you, Mr Hiltch?"

• • • •

As soon as New California fell to the Capone Organization the Consensus of the thirty habitats orbiting Yosemite started preparing for war. It was a situation which had never before occurred in the five centuries since Edenism was founded. Only Laton had ever threatened them in the past, but he was one man; the staggering pan-Confederation resources they had were adequate to deal with him (so they considered at the time). This was different.

Adamists throughout the Confederation nearly always allowed prejudice to contaminate their thinking towards the

Edenist culture. They assumed that as it was both wealthy and cloistered it would be if not decadent, then at least timorous. They were wrong. Edenists prided themselves in their rational approach to all facets of life. They might deplore violence, favouring endless diplomatic negotiations and economic sanctions to any form of conflict, but if there was no alternative, they would fight. And fight with a coldly logical precision which was frightening.

Once the decision was taken, Consensus began the job of coordinating the gas giant's resources and priorities. The extensive clusters of industrial stations which surrounded each habitat were immediately turned over in their entirety to armaments manufacture. Component production was integrated by Consensus, matching demand to capability within hours, then going on to harmonize final fabrication procedures. Barely four hours after the operation started, the first new combat wasps were emerging from their freshly allocated assembly bays.

After conquering New California itself, Capone began his campaign against the system's asteroid settlements. Consensus knew then it would only be a matter of time. Yosemite was the source of He_3 for the entire system, the strategic high ground.

Perhaps if Capone had ordered an all-out assault on Yosemite as his first action he might have been successful. Instead, taking over the asteroid settlements was a tactical error. It allowed the Consensus precious days to consolidate the gas giant's defences. Not even Emmet Mordden really grasped the awesome potential of an entire civilization converted to a war footing, especially one with Edenism's technological resources. How could he? It had never happened before.

Voidhawks hovering seven hundred thousand kilometres above New California's poles observed the three new squadrons being assembled among the fifty-three asteroids orbiting the planet. Their composition, numbers, and in some cases even the armament specifications were duly noted and relayed to Yosemite. Unknown to the Organization, the voidhawks were not the summation of the Edenist intelligence gathering operation, they simply coordinated the observation. Thousands of stealthed spy sensor globes the size of tomatoes were falling past the asteroids like a constant black snow. All the information they gathered was passed back to the void-hawks through affinity links with their bitek processors. The possessed couldn't detect affinity, nor was it susceptible to either conventional electronic warfare or the interference by the energistic ability, all of which allowed the spy globes to reveal a minute by minute account of the buildup.

Had anyone in the Organization realized just how detailed the Edenist knowledge was, they would never have dispatched the starships.

Thirty-nine hours after Capone had given the go-ahead to try to capture the Yosemite cloudscoops, two of the three squadrons of ships docked in the asteroids departed. Consensus knew both the vectors of the ships and their arrival time.

Yosemite orbited seven hundred and eighty-one million kilometres from the G5-type star of the New California system. At a hundred and twenty-seven thousand kilometres in diameter it was slightly smaller than Jupiter, although its storm bands lacked the vigour normally associated with such mass; even their coloration was uninspiring, streamers of sienna and caramel meandering among the pristine white upbursts of ammonia crystals.

The thirty Edenist habitats orbited sedately three-quarters of a million kilometres above the equator, their tracks perturbed only by gentle resonances with the eight large innermost moons. It was that radial band where the Consensus had concentrated its new defensive structure. Each of the habitats was englobed by beefed-up Strategic Defence platforms; but given the demonstrated ruthlessness of the attackers, Consensus was attempting to prevent any Organization ships getting near enough to launch a combat wasp salvo.

With the vectors identified and timed, Consensus redeployed twelve thousand of the combat wasps out of the total of three hundred and seventy thousand it had already seeded across the gas giant's equatorial zone. Their fusion drives ignited for a few minutes, putting them on a loose interception trajectory with the area of space the attackers were likely to emerge in. A hundred of the patrolling voidhawks were moved closer.

The first seven attackers to emerge, as per standard tactics programs, were all front-line navy rapid-response frigates. Their mission was to assess the level of opposition, and if necessary clear the incoming squadron's designated emergence zone of any hostile hardware. Even as their event horizons vanished, leaving them falling free, twenty-five voidhawks were accelerating towards them at ten gees. Distortion fields locked on, ruining the equilibrium of space around their hulls, preventing any of them from jumping clear. Combat wasps were already shooting over the intervening distance at twenty-five gees. The frigates immediately launched defensive salvos, but with their sensors hampered by the energistic flux of their own crews, the response was too slow in coming, and even when it did they were hopelessly outnumbered. Each of the frigates was the target of at least a hundred and fifty combat wasps, streaking in at them from every direction. At most, they could fire forty defenders. To have stood a good chance they would have needed close to five hundred apiece.

Within a hundred seconds all seven frigates were destroyed.

Ten minutes later, the rest of the Organization's starships started to emerge from their ZTT jumps. Their predicament was even worse. They were expecting the specialist frigates to have established a defensive perimeter. It took time for an ordinary Adamist starship to deploy its sensor clusters and scan local space for possible danger; time which in this case was lengthened by malfunctioning equipment. When the sensors finally did relay an image of the external arena, it seemed as though a small galaxy was on the move. Yosemite was almost invisible behind a sparkling nebula of fusion drives; thousands of combat wasps and tens of thousands of submunitions were generating a fraudulent dawn across half of the colossal planet's nightside. And the nebula was contracting, twin central whorls twisting lazily into two dense spires which were rising inexorably towards the emergence zones.

One by one, the Organization starships crashed against the terrible, moon-sized mountains of light, detonating into photonic avalanches which tumbled away into the yawning darkness.

* * *

Two hours later, the voidhawks on observation duty above New California reported that Capone's third squadron was leaving the orbital asteroids. When they were a quarter of a million kilometres above the planet, the starships activated their energy patterning nodes and vanished. Consensus was puzzled by the vector; they weren't aligned on any known inhabited world.

• • •

Not even the ending of the physical threat had brought any relief to the turmoil in Louise's head. They had flown all the way into orbit to dock with the *Far Realm* without any problem, although Furay had grumbled constantly about bits of machinery going wrong on the ascent.

The starship itself wasn't quite as impressive as she'd been expecting. The interior was like servants' quarters, except made out of metal and plastic. There were four spheres grouped together in a pyramid shape, which the crew called life-support capsules, and that was the total available living space; apparently the rest of the ship inside the hull was solid machinery. Everything was so dreadfully small—tables, chairs, bunks; and what wasn't being used had to be folded away. And to complete her misery, free fall was an utter nightmare.

It was ironic. As Genevieve had perked up during the spaceplane flight, so Louise had felt gradually worse. As soon as the rocket engines finally cut out, leaving them floating free, Genevieve had yelled delightedly, releasing her webbing and hurtling around the cabin, giggling as she bounced and somersaulted. Even Fletcher, after his initial alarm at the sensation, had relaxed, smiling cautiously as he attempted a few simple gymnast manoeuvres with Genevieve cheering him on.

But not her. Oh, no. She'd been wretchedly sick three times during the rendezvous, what with the spaceplane juddering around the whole time. It had taken her several tries to learn how to use the sanitation tube provided for such instances, much to the disgusted dismay of the others in the cabin.

She had then continued to be sick, or at least have the stomach spasms, after they floated through the airlock tube into the starship's tiny lounge. Endron, the ship's systems specialist who doubled as medical officer, had towed her into the sick bay cubicle. Twenty minutes later when the horrid warm itch inside her stomach faded, and some kind of cool fluid was sprayed into her mouth to rinse away the taste of vomit, she began to take stock for the first time. Her ears felt funny, and when she touched one she could feel something hard cupped around the back of it.

"That's a medical nanonic," Endron told her. "I've put one package behind each ear. Don't try and take them off, they've knitted with your inner ears. It ought to solve your balance problem."

"Thank you," she said meekly. "I'm sorry to be so much trouble."

"You're not. If only your sister was as quiet as you."

"Oh. I'm sorry. Is she being a nuisance?"

He laughed. "Not really. We're just not used to girls her age on board, that's all."

Louise stopped fingering the medical package. When she brought her hand away she saw a strange green bracelet on her wrist; it was made from a substance like lustreless polythene, an inch wide and about half an inch thick. There was no join, it was solid. On closer inspection she saw it had fused to her skin, yet it wasn't painful.

"Another package," Endron said dryly. "Again, don't touch it, please."

"Is it for my balance as well?"

"No. That one is for your other condition. It will keep your blood chemistry stable, and if it detects any metabolic problem starting from free-fall exposure it'll datavise a warning to me."

"Other condition?" she asked timidly.

"You did know you were pregnant, didn't you?"

She closed her eyes and nodded, too ashamed to look at him. A complete stranger knowing. How awful.

"You should have told Furay," he remonstrated gently. "Free fall exerts some strong physiological changes on a body, especially if you're unaccustomed to it. And in your state, you really should have been prepared properly before the spaceplane took off."

A warm tear squeezed out from under her eyelids. "It's all right, isn't it? The baby. Oh, please, I didn't know."

"Shush." Endron's hand stroked her forehead soothingly. "The baby is just fine. You're a very healthy young girl. I'm sorry if I frightened you; like I said, we're not used to passengers. I suppose it must be equally strange for you, too."

"It's all right, really?"

"Yes. And the nanonic will keep it that way."

"Thank you. You've been very kind."

"Just doing my job. I'll have to consult some files about your diet, though, and check what food stocks we've got on board. I'll get back to you on that one."

Louise opened her eyes, only to find the cabin blurred by liquid stretching across her irises. A lot of blinking cleared it.

"Let's get you mobile again," Endron said, and released the seal on the straps holding her down on the couch. "Though you're not to whizz about like your sister, mind."

His tone was identical to Mrs Charlsworth's. "I won't." The rest of the sentence died on her lips as she caught sight of him. Her first thought was that he was suffering some kind of terrible affliction.

Endron's head was ordinary enough. He was a man in his late fifties, she guessed, with a short crop of fading black, curly hair and cheeks which appeared almost bloated, eradicating wrinkles. However, his body ... He had very broad shoulders atop an inflated rib cage, she could actually see the lines of individual ribs under his glossy green ship-suit. She'd seen holograms of terrestrial sparrows at school, and the anatomical arrangement put her in mind of that puffed-out bird. His chest was huge, and very frail-looking.

"Not seen a Martian before, huh?" he asked kindly.

Furious with herself for staring, Louise turned her head away. "I'm not sure. Do all Martians look like you?"

"Yep. So you'd better get used to it. This is an SII line ship after all, the rest of the crew are the same as me. Except Furay of course; that's why he's on board. We couldn't fly the spaceplane down to terracompatible planets. Can't take the gravity."

"How . . ." She wasn't sure if this was really a fit subject to discuss so casually. It was almost as though they were talking about a terminal illness. "Why are you like that?"

"Geneering. It's very deliberate, dates back a while. Even with terraforming we don't have a standard atmosphere on Mars. Our ancestors decided to meet the problem halfway. As we're a Communist society, naturally everyone got the modification to expand our lung capacity; and that was on top of the earlier adaptations we made to ourselves to survive in the Moon's gravity field."

"The Moon?" Louise asked, trying to sort things out in her mind. "You lived on the Moon first?"

"It was the Lunar nation which terraformed Mars. Didn't they teach you that at school?"

"Uh, no. At least, we haven't got to it yet." She decided not to question him on the communism bit. Given Daddy's opinion on that topic, it would make life a little too complicated right now.

He was smiling gently at her. "I think that's enough history. It's nearing midnight, Norwich time. Perhaps you'd better get some sleep, yes?"

She gave him an eager nod.

Endron coached her in the elementary movements necessary to get about in free fall. Speed was not a requirement, he insisted, arriving safely and accurately at your destination was. And you must be careful of inertia, it creates huge bruises.

With his encouragement she made her way into the life support capsule they'd been allocated: a lounge five yards to a side, made from grubby pearl-grey composite walls which were inlaid with several instrument panels with tiny orange and green lights winking below their dark glass surfaces. Plastic doors which were like a kind of solidified liquid flowed apart to reveal three "cabins" for them to sleep in (the wardrobes she had in her Cricklade bedroom were larger). There was a bathroom in the upper deck at which Louise took one look and promptly recoiled, vowing not to go to the toilet again until they were safely back on a planet.

Genevieve shot up to embrace her as soon as she glided through the ceiling hatch. Fletcher smiled a welcome.

"Isn't this truly wondrous!" the little girl proclaimed. She was floating with her toes six inches off the decking, spinning like a ballerina. Two ponytails stood out at right angles from her head. When she spread her arms wide her speed slowed. A neat toe kick, too quick to follow, and she soared up to the ceiling, clasping a grab hoop to kill her movement. Enchanted eyes smiled at Louise. "Bet you I can do seven somersaults before I reach the floor."

"You probably can," Louise said wearily.

"Oh." Genevieve's face was instantly contrite. She levitated back to the decking until she was level with Louise. "I'm sorry. How are you feeling?"

"Fine now. And it's time for bed."

"Oww, Louise!"

"Now."

"All right."

Endron proffered the girl a squeeze bulb. "Here, it's a chocolate drink. Try it, I'm sure you'll like it."

Genevieve started sucking eagerly on the nozzle.

"You are recovered, lady?" Fletcher asked.

"Yes. Thank you, Fletcher."

They looked at each other for a long moment, unaware of Endron watching them.

One of the instrument panels let out a quiet bleep.

Endron scowled and drifted over to it, anchoring himself on a stikpad. "Shoddy components," he muttered.

Fletcher gave Louise an apologetic grimace, mildly embarrassed. "I can't stop it," he said in a whisper.

"Not your fault," she whispered back. "Don't worry. The ship still works."

"Yes, lady."

"That was nice," Genevieve announced. She held out the empty squeeze bulb and promptly burped.

"Gen!"

"Sorry."

With Endron showing her how the cabin fittings worked, Louise finally got Genevieve into bed; a heavily padded sleeping bag stuck to the decking. Louise tucked her sister's hair into the hood and kissed her gently. Genevieve gave her a drowsy smile and immediately closed her eyes.

"She'll sleep for a good eight hours now she's got that sedative in her," Endron said, holding up the empty squeeze bulb. "And when she wakes up she won't be anything like as hyper. Furay told me what she was like when you boarded the spaceplane. She was having a bounceback response to the hangar fire. In a way that kind of overreaction is as bad as depressive withdrawal."

"I see." There didn't seem anything to add. She glanced back at Genevieve before the funny door contracted. For one whole night there would be no possessed, no Roberto, and no Quinn Dexter.

I've done what I promised, Louise thought. Thank you, Jesus.

Despite how tired she was feeling, she managed a prideful smile. No longer the worthless, pampered landowner daughter Carmitha had such contempt for just scant days ago. I suppose I've grown up a bit.

"You should rest now, lady," Fletcher said.

She yawned. "I think you're right. Are you going to bed?"

For once Fletcher's sedate features showed a certain lightness. "I believe I will linger awhile longer." He indicated a holoscreen which was displaying the image from an external camera. Cloud-splattered landscape was rolling past, pastel greens, browns, and blues illuminated by Duke's radiance. "It is not often a mortal man is permitted to view a world over the shoulder of angels."

"Good night, Fletcher."

"Good night, lady. May the Lord guard your dreams from the darkness."

Louise didn't have time to dream. A hand pressing her shoulder woke her soon enough.

She winced at the light coming through the open door. When she tried to move, she couldn't, the sleeping bag held her too tight.

"What?" she groaned.

Fletcher's face was a few inches from hers, a gloomy frown spoiling his brow. "I apologise, lady, but the crew is in some confusion. I thought you should know."

"Are they on board?" she cried in dismay.

"Who?"

"The possessed."

"No, lady Louise. Be assured, we are perfectly safe."

"What then?"

"I think they are in another ship."

"All right, I'm coming." Her hand fumbled around until she found the seal catch inside the bag; she twisted it ninety degrees and the spongy fabric split open along its length. After she dressed she wrapped her hair into a single artless ponytail, and swam out into the tiny lounge.

Fletcher showed her the way to the bridge, wriggling along the tubular companionways which connected the life-support capsules, and through dimly lit decks which appeared even more cramped than their lounge. Louise's first sight of the bridge reminded her of the Kavanagh family crypt beneath the manor's chapel: a gloomy room with candlelike crystals sitting on top of instrument consoles, spilling out waves of blue and green light which crawled across the walls. Machinery, ribbed tubes, and plastic cables formed an untidy glyptic over most bulkheads. But most of all it came from the four crew members lying prone on their bulky acceleration couches; eyes closed, limbs immobile. A thin hexagonal web was stretched over them, holding them down on the cushioning.

Furay and Endron she recognised, but this was the first time she'd seen Captain Layia and Tilia, the *Far Realm*'s node specialist. Endron had been right, the other Martians had exactly the same anatomical features as himself. In fact there was very little difference between genders; Louise wasn't entirely sure the two women even had breasts. On top of that rib cage they would have been absurd.

"Now what?" she asked Fletcher.

"I am not sure, their repose refutes any disturbance."

"It's not sleep, they're datavising with the flight computer. Joshua told me that's what happens on a starship bridge. Um, I'll explain later." Louise blushed faintly; Joshua had become such a fixture in her life it was hard to remember who he actually was. She used some grab hoops to move herself over to Furay's couch, and tapped him experimentally on the shoulder. Somehow the thought of disturbing the others didn't arise, a child-fear of how those strange figures would respond.

Furay opened his eyes in annoyance. "Oh, it's you."

"I'm sorry. I wanted to know what was happening."

"Yeah, right. Hang on." The webbing peeled back and curled up, vanishing into the edge of the couch's cushioning. Furay pushed off, and slowly twisted his body around to the vertical, using a stikpad to anchor himself in front of Louise. "Nothing too good, I'm afraid. The navy squadron's commanding admiral has put every ship on condition amber, which is one stage short of an actual combat alert."

"Why?"

"The *Tantu* has dropped out of our communications net. They won't respond to any signals. She's worried that they might have been hijacked. Apparently there was some kind of garbled message a few minutes after the frigate's spaceplane docked, then nothing."

Louise flashed a guilty glance at Fletcher, who remained unperturbed. The action did not go unnoticed by Furay. "The *Tantu*'s spaceplane left Bennett Field about ten minutes after us. Care to comment?"

"The rebels were close behind us," Louise said quickly. "Perhaps they stowed away on the other spaceplane."

"And took over an entire frigate?" Furay said sceptically.

"They have energy weapons," Louise said. "I've seen them."

"Try waving a laser rifle around on the bridge of a Confederation Navy starship and the marines would cut you into barbecue ribs."

"I have no other explanation," she said earnestly.

"Hummm." His stare informed her he was having big second thoughts about bringing her on board.

"What remedial action does the admiral propose?" Fletcher asked.

"She hasn't decided yet. The *Serir* has been sent to rendezvous. The situation will be reviewed when they report."

"She?" Fletcher asked in surprise. "Your admiral is a lady?"

Furay pulled at his chin, trying to work out just what the hell he was dealing with.

"Yes, Fletcher," Louise hissed. "We don't have many female estate managers on Norfolk," she explained brightly to Furay. "We're not used to ladies holding important positions. Do excuse our ignorance."

"You don't strike me as unimportant, Louise," Furay said.

His tone was so muddled, silky, and scathing at the same time, she couldn't decide if he was making what Mrs Charlsworth called an overture, or just being plain sarcastic.

Furay suddenly stiffened. "It's moving."

"What is?"

"The *Tantu*. It's under way, heading up out of orbit. Your rebels must have hijacked it, there's no other reason."

"The ship is flying away?" Fletcher asked.

"That's what I just said!" Furay told him in irritation. "They must be heading up for a jump coordinate."

"What's the admiral doing about it?" Louise asked.

"I'm not sure. The *Far Realm* isn't a combat craft, we don't have access to the squadron's strategic communications."

"We must follow it," Fletcher announced.

"Pardon me?"

Louise glared at him with silent urgency.

"This ship must follow the frigate. People must be warned of what it carries."

"And just what does it carry?" Furay asked mildly.

"Rebels," Louise said hurriedly. "People who've looted and murdered, and will do so again if they aren't arrested. But I'm sure we can leave the administering of justice to the Confederation Navy, can't we, Fletcher?"

"Lady—"

"Exactly what has got you so all-fired het up?" Captain Layia asked. Her couch webbing peeled back allowing her to glide over towards the three of them.

Her face did have a few feminine qualities, Louise admitted, but not many; the shaven scalp was too unsettling—all ladies had long hair. The judgemental way Layia took in the scene betrayed her authority; that she was in command had never been in doubt from the moment she spoke, it had nothing to do with the silver star on her epaulette.

"I am concerned that we should follow the frigate, ma'am,"

Fletcher said. "The rebels on board cannot be allowed to spread their sedition any further."

"Nor will they be allowed to," Layia said patiently. "I can assure you the admiral does not regard the hijacking of a navy frigate lightly. However, it is a navy matter, and we are just a supply ship. It is not our problem."

"But they must be stopped."

"How? If you use combat wasps you'll kill everyone on board."

Fletcher appealed to Louise, who could only shrug, though the motion didn't quite come off in free fall.

"The admiral will send a ship to pursue them," Captain Layia said. "When it arrives in a star system it will simply broadcast the situation to the authorities. The *Tantu* will be unable to dock at any port, and eventually their consumables will run out, forcing them to negotiate."

"Those on board will not be allowed to disembark?" Fletcher asked apprehensively.

"Absolutely not," the captain assured him.

"Providing the pursuit ship manages to keep up with them through their ZTT jumps," Furay said pessimistically. "If *Tantu* programs for a sequential jump sequence, then anyone following will be in trouble, unless it's a voidhawk. Which it won't be, because the squadron doesn't have one." He trailed off under the captain's stare. "Sorry, but that's the normal method to avoid tracking, and every navy ship can perform sequential jumps. You know that."

"Ma'am, please," Fletcher entreated, "if there is any chance the rebels can escape, we have to fly after them."

"One, you're a passenger. I believe Mr Furay explained how we are obliged to stay in Norfolk orbit as long as the navy requires, and no amount of money can alter that. Two, if I broke orbit to chase the *Tantu*, then the admiral would have me brought back and relieved of my duty. Three, as you've been so helpfully informed, the *Tantu* can perform sequential jumps; if a top-line frigate can't follow them through those manoeuvres, then we certainly can't. And four, mister, if you don't get off my bridge *right now*, I'll sling you into a lifeboat and give you a one-way trip back down to the land you love so dearly. Have you got all that?"

"Yes, Captain," Louise said, feeling an inch small. "Sorry to bother you. We won't do it again."

"Aw shit," Endron called from his acceleration couch. "I'm getting multiple processor dropouts. Whatever this glitch is, it's multiplying."

Layia looked at Louise, and jabbed a finger at the hatch.

Louise grabbed Fletcher's arm and pushed off with her feet, trying to propel them towards the hatchway. She didn't like the expression of anguish on his face one bit. Her trajectory wasn't terribly accurate, and Fletcher had to flip them aside from one of the consoles.

"What are you trying to do?" Louise wailed when they were back in the lounge they'd been allocated. "Don't you understand how dangerous it is to antagonize the captain?" She caught herself and clamped a hand over her mouth, distraught at the gaffe. "Oh, Fletcher, I'm sorry. I didn't mean that."

"Yet you spoke the truth, lady. As always. It was foolish of me, I admit, aye, and reckless too. For you and the little one must remain safe up here." He turned and looked at the holo-screen. They were over the side of Norfolk which was turned to face Duchess, a harsh vista of reds and black.

"Why, Fletcher? What was so important about following Quinn Dexter? The navy can take care of him. Are you worried what'll happen if he gets loose on another planet?"

"Not exactly, lady. Alas, there are many possessed abroad in your fine Confederation now. No, I have seen into that man's heart, and he frightens me sorely, Lady Louise, a fright more profound than the hell of beyond. He is the strange one I felt earlier. He is not as other possessed. He is a monster, a bringer of evil. I have resolved this matter in my own mind, though it has taken many hours of struggle. I must become his nemesis."

"Dexter's?" she said weakly.

"Yes, my lady. I think he may be the reason Our Lord blessed me to return. I am vouchsafed a clarity in this regard I cannot in conscience ignore. I must raise the alarm before he can advance his schemes further to the misery of other worlds."

"But it's not possible for us to go after him."

"Aye, lady, such a conundrum has a fierce grip upon my

heart, borrowed though it be. It squeezes like a fire. To have been so close, and to lose the scent."

"We might not have lost him," Louise said, her thoughts aching they were spinning so fast.

"How so, lady?"

"He said he was going to Earth. To Earth so he could hurt someone . . . Banneth. He was going to hurt Banneth."

"Then Banneth must be warned. He will commit such terrible atrocities in pursuit of his devilsome aims. I can never purge what he said of the little one from my mind. To even think such filth. Only in his head do such ideas dwell."

"Well, we are going to Mars anyway. I expect there will be more ships flying to Earth than to Tranquillity. But I don't have a clue how you could find Banneth once you get there."

"Every voyage is divided into stages, lady. It is best to sail them one at a time."

She watched him for some while as the holoscreen's pallid light washing across his rapt face. "Why did you mutiny, Fletcher? Was it truly terrible on the *Bounty*?"

He gazed at her in surprise, then slowly smiled. "Not the conditions, lady, though I doubt you would much care for them. It was one man, my captain. He it was, the force moving my life towards the shore of destiny. William Bligh was my friend when the voyage started, strange though it is to recount such a fact now. But oh, how the sea changed him. He was embittered by his lack of promotion, fired by his notions of how a ship should be run. Never have I witnessed such barbarism from a man who claimed to be civilized, nor endured such treatment at his hands. I will spare you the anguish of detail, my fair lady Louise, but suffice it to say that all men have a breaking point. And mine was found during that long, dreadful voyage. However, I endure no shame over my actions. Many good and honest men were freed from his tyranny."

"Then you were in the right?"

"I believe so. If this day I were called before the captains in a court-martial, I could give a just account of my actions."

"Now you want to do something similar again. Freeing people, I mean."

"Yes, lady. Though I would endure a thousand voyages

with Bligh as my master in preference to one with Quinn Dexter. I had thought William Bligh versed in the ways of cruelty. I see now how mistaken I was. Now, to my horror, I have looked upon true evil. I will not forget the form it takes."

with Bligh as my master in preference to one with Quinn Dexter. I had thought William Bligh versed in the ways of cruelty; I see now how mistaken I was. Now, to my horror, I have looked upon true evil, and I shall not forget the form it takes.

10

The reporters had spent several days in prison, a phrase which their Organization captors studiously avoided; the preferred designation was house arrest, or protective confinement. They'd been singled out and spared when the possessed spread through San Angeles, then corralled with their families in the Uorestone Tower. Patricia Mangano who was in charge of the guard detail allowed the children to play in the opulent lounges while parents mixed freely, speculating on their circumstances and rehashing old gossip as only their profession knew how.

Five times in the last couple of days small groups had been taken out to tour the city, observing the steady falsification of buildings which was the hallmark of a land under possession. Once-familiar suburban streets had undergone timewarps overnight. It was as though some kind of dark architectural ivy were slowly creeping its way upwards, turning chrome-glass to stone, crinkling flat surfaces into arches, pillars, and statues. A plethora of era enclaves had emerged, ranging from 1950s New York avenues to timeless whitewashed Mediterranean villas, Russian dachas to traditional Japanese houses. All of them were ameliorated, more wistful renderings of real life.

The reporters recorded it all as faithfully as they could with their glitch-prone neural nanonic memory cells. This morning, though, was different. All of them had been summoned from their rooms, herded onto buses, and driven the five kilometres to City Hall. They were escorted from the buses by Organization gangsters and assembled on the sidewalk, forming a line between the autoway and the skyscraper's elaborate arched entrance. On Patricia's order the gangsters took several paces back, leaving the reporters to themselves.

Gus Remar found his neural nanonics coming back on-line, and immediately started to record his full sensorium, datavising his flek recorder block to make a backup copy. It had been a long time since he'd covered a story in the field. These days he was a senior studio editor at the city's Time Universe bureau, but the old skill was still there. He started to scan around.

There were no vehicles using the autoway, but crowds were lining the sidewalk, five or six deep at the barrier. When he switched to long-range focus he could see they stretched back for about three blocks. The possessed were a majority, easy to spot in their epoch garments: the outlandish and the tediously uninspired. They seemed to be mingling easily enough with the non-possessed.

A slight fracas two hundred metres away at the back of the crowd caught Gus's attention. His enhanced retinas zoomed in.

Two men were pushing at each other, faces red with anger. One was a dark, handsome youth, barely twenty with perfectly trimmed black hair; dressed in leather jacket and trousers. An acoustic guitar was slung over his back. The second was older, in his forties, and considerably fatter. His attire was the most bizarre Gus had yet seen on display; some kind of white suit, smothered in rhinestones, with trousers flaring over thirty centimetres around his ankles, and collars which looked like small aircraft wings. Large amber-tinted sunglasses covered a third of his puffed-out face. If it hadn't been for the circumstances, Gus would have said it was a father quarrelling with his son. He shunted his audio discrimination program into primary mode.

"Goddamn fake," the younger man shouted with a rich Southern drawl. "I was never *this*." Hands flicked insultingly over the front of the white costume, ruffling the fit. "You're what they squeezed me into. You ain't nothing but a sick disease the record companies cooked up to make money. I would never come back as you."

The larger man pushed him away. "Who are you calling a fake, son? I am the King, the one and only."

The shoving began in earnest; both of them trying to floor the other. Amber sunglasses went spinning. Organization gangsters moved in quickly to separate them, but not before the younger Elvis had unslung his guitar ready to brain the Vegas version.

Gus never saw the outcome. The crowd started cheering. A cavalcade had turned onto the autoway. Police motorcycles (Harley-Davidsons, according to Gus's encyclopedia memory file) appeared first, ten of them with blue and red lights flashing. They were followed by a huge limousine which crawled along at little more than walking pace: a 1920s Cadillac sedan which looked absurdly massive, fat tyres bulging from the weight of its armour plated bodywork. Glass that was at least five centimetres thick shaded the interior aquarium-green. There was one man sitting in the back, waving happily at the crowd.

The city was going wild for him. Al grinned around his cigar and gave them a thumbs-up. Je-zus, but it was like the good old days, riding around in this very same bulletproof Cadillac with the pedestrians staring openmouthed as he went past. In Chicago they'd known it contained a prince of the city. And now in San Angeles they goddamn well knew it again.

The Cadillac drew to a halt outside City Hall. A smiling Dwight Salerno came down the steps to open the door.

"Good to see you back, Al. We missed you."

Al kissed him on both cheeks, then turned to face the ecstatic crowd, clasping his hands together above his head like he was a prizefighter posing over a whipped opponent. They roared their approval. White fire cascaded and fizzed over the autoway as if Zeus were putting on a Fourth of July display.

"I love you guys!" Al bellowed at the faceless mass of chuckleheads. "Together ain't no miserable Confederation fucker gonna stop us doing what we wanna do."

They couldn't hear the words, not even those in the front rank. But the content was clear enough. The laudation increased.

With one hand still waving frantically, Al turned around and bounded up the stairs into City Hall. Always leave them wanting more, Jez said.

The conference was held in the lobby, a vaulting four-storey cavern that took up over half of the ground floor. An avenue of huge palm trees, cloned from California originals, stretched from the doors to the vast reception desk. Today their solartubes were diminished to an off-white fluorescence, their bowls of loam drying out. Other signs of neglect and hurried tidying were in evidence: defunct valet mechanoids lined up along one wall, emergency exit doors missing, scraps of rubbish swept into piles behind stilled escalators.

The reception desk had been completely cleared, and a row of chairs placed behind it. Al sat in the centre, with two lieutenants on either side. His chair had been raised slightly. He watched the nervous reporters being brought in and marshalled on the floor in front of him. When they'd shushed down he rose to his feet.

"My name is Al Capone, and I suppose you're all wondering why I asked you here," he said, and chuckled. Their answering grins were few and far between. Tight asses. "Okay, I'll lay it on the line for you; you're here because I want the whole Confederation to know what's been going down in these parts. Once they know and understand then that's gonna save everyone a shitload of grief." He took off his grey fedora and put it down carefully on the polished desk. "It's an easy situation. My Organization is now in charge of the whole New California system. We're keeping the planet and the asteroid settlements in order, no exceptions. Now we ain't out to harm anyone, we just use our clout to keep things flowing along as best they'll go, same as any other government."

"Are you running the Edenist habitats, too?" a reporter asked. The rest flinched, waiting for Patricia Mangano's retribution. It never came, though she looked far from happy.

"Smart of you, buddy," Al acknowledged with a grudging smile. "No, I ain't running the Edenist habitats. I could. But I ain't. Know why? Because we're about evenly matched, that's why. We could do a lot of damage to each other if we ever came to fighting. Too much. I don't want that. I don't want people sent into the beyond on account of some penny-ante dispute over territory. I've been there myself, it's worse than any fucking nightmare you can imagine; it shouldn't happen to anyone."

"Why do you think you've been returned from the beyond, Al? Has God passed judgement on you?"

"You got me there, lady. I don't know why any of this started. But I'll tell you guys this much: I never saw no angels or no demons while I was stuck in the beyond, none of us did. All I know is we're back. It ain't no one's fault, it just happened. And now we gotta make the best of what's a pretty shitty deal, that's what the Organization is for."

"Excuse me, Mr Capone," Gus said, encouraged by the response to earlier questions. "What's the point of your Organization? You don't need it. The possessed can do whatever they want."

"Sorry, buddy, you're way wrong there. Maybe we don't need quite the same government as we had before, not all that tax, and regulations, and ideology, and shit. But you've got to have order, and that's what I provide. I'm doing everyone a favour by taking charge like this. I'm protecting the possessed from attack by the Confederation Navy. I'm looking out for a whole load of non-possessed; because I'm telling you, without me you certainly wouldn't be standing here in charge of your own body. See, I'm providing for all kinds of people, even though half of them don't appreciate it right now. The possessed didn't have jack shit worked out about where they were going until I came along. Now we're all working together, making it happen. All because of me and the Organization. If I hadn't stepped in and kept things going the cities would have busted down, we would have had a whole flood of lost boys heading for the countryside. Listen, I've seen the Depression firsthand, I know what it's like for people who don't have a job or something to do. And that's what we were heading for here."

"So what are your long-range goals, Al? What's your Organization going to do next?"

"Smooth things out. No one is trying to deny things are still a little rough around the edges down here. We need to work on what kind of society we can build."

"Is it true you're planning to attack the Confederation?"

"That's pure bullshit, buddy. Je-zus, I don't know where you got that rumour from. No of course we're not going to attack anyone. But we can defend ourselves pretty good if the Confederation Navy tries any funny stuff, we sure got the ships for that. Hell, I don't want that to happen. We just want to be peaceable neighbours with everyone. I might even ask if we can join the Confederation." At the murmur of surprise echoing through the lobby he grinned around happily. "Yeah. Why the hell not? Sure we can ask to join. Maybe some good will come out of it, some kind of compromise that'll make everyone happy; a solution to all the souls that wanna come back. The Organization can pay Confederation longhairs to grow us all new bodies from scratch, something like that."

"You mean you'd give up your body if a clone was available?"

Al frowned as Emmet leaned over to murmur in his ear, explaining what a clone was. "Sure," he said. "Like I told you, we're all the victims of circumstance."

"You believe peaceful coexistence is possible?"

Al's jocularity darkened. "You'd better fucking believe it, buddy. We're back, and we're here to stay. Grab that? What I'm trying to convince you guys is that we ain't no end of the world threat, it's not us who's the riders of the Apocalypse. We've proved possessed and non-possessed can live together on this planet. Okay, so people out there are alarmed right now, that's only natural. But we're frightened too, you can't expect us to go back to the beyond. We've got to work together on this. I'm personally offering the Assembly President my hand in friendship. Now that's an offer he can't refuse."

The glowing red clouds had begun to grow, small ruby speckles blossoming right across Norfolk. Louise, Fletcher, and Genevieve spent their first day in orbit watching the images received by the *Far Realm*'s external cameras. Kesteven island was by far the worst. A solid crimson aureole had gathered to mask the land, its shape a distended mockery of the coastline it was obscuring. Strands of ordinary white cloud malingered around its disciplined edges, only to be rebuffed by invisible winds if they drifted too close.

Fletcher assured the girls that in itself the red cloud was harmless. "A simple manifestation of will," he proclaimed. "Nothing more."

"You mean it's just a wish?" Genevieve asked, intrigued. She had woken almost purged of her emotional turmoil; there were none of yesterday's periods of manic exuberance or haunted silences. Although she was quieter than usual; which Louise thought was about right. She didn't feel like talking much, either. Neither she nor Fletcher had mentioned the *Tantu*.

"Quite so, little one."

"But why are they wishing it?"

"So that they can seek refuge below it from the emptiness of the universe. Even this planet's sky, which has little night, is not a sight to cherish."

Over thirty islands now had traces of redness in the air. Louise likened it to watching the outbreak of some terrible disease, a swelling cancer gnawing away at the flesh of her world.

Furay and Endron had come down into the lounge a few times, keeping them informed of the navy squadron's actions, and the army's progress. Neither of which amounted to much. The army had landed on two islands, Shropshire and Lindsey, hoping to retake their capitals. But reports from the forwards units were confused.

"Same problem as we had with Kesteven," Furay confided when he brought them lunch. "We can't support the lads on the ground because we don't have any reliable targeting information. And that red cloud has got the admiral badly worried. None of the technical staff can explain it."

By midafternoon, ship's time, the army commanders had lost contact with half of their troops. The red cloud was visible over forty-eight islands, nine of which it covered completely. As Duke-day ended for Ramsey island slender wisps were located over a couple of villages. Teams of reserve soldiers were hurriedly flown in from Norwich. In both cases contact was lost within fifteen minutes of them entering the area.

Louise watched grimly as the coiling cloud thickened over each village. "I was right," she said miserably. "There's nothing anybody here can do. It's only a matter of time now."

• • •

Tolton made his way up the narrow creek, water from the narrow stream slopping over his glittery purple shoes. The top of the steep bank, a fringe of sandy grass, was several centimetres above his head. He couldn't see out onto the parkland, and nobody could see him—thankfully. Far overhead, Valisk's light tube gleamed. The intensity hurt Tolton's eyes. He was a night person, used to the clubs, bars, and vestibules of the starscrapers, delivering his poet sermons to the ship crew burnouts, bluesensers, stimmed-out wasters, and mercenaries who sprawled throughout the lower floors of the starscrapers. They tolerated him, those lost entities, listening to (or laughing at) his carefully crafted words, donating their own stories to his wealth of experiences. He moved among the descriptions of shattered lives as vagrants moved through the filthy refuse of a darkened cul-de-sac, forever picking, trying to understand what they said, to bestow some grace to their wizened dreams with his prose, to explain them to themselves.

One day, he told them, I will incorporate it all into an MF album. The galaxy will know of your plight, and liberate you.

They didn't believe him, but they accepted him as one of their own. It was a status which had saved him from many a bar fight. But now, in his hour of desperate need, they had failed him. However difficult it was to acknowledge, they had lost; the toughest bunch of bastards in the Confederation had been wiped out in less than thirty-six hours.

"Take the left hand channel at the next fork," the processor block clipped to his belt told him.

"Yes," he mumbled obediently.

And this was the greatest, most hurtful joke of all: him, the aspirant anarchist poet, pathetically grateful to Rubra, the super-capitalist dictator, for helping him.

Ten metres on two gurgling streams merged together. He turned left without hesitation, the foaming water splashing his knees. Fleeing from the starscraper, it was as though an insane montage of all the combat stories he'd ever been told had come scampering up out of his subconscious to torment him. Horror and laughter pursued him down every corridor, even the disused ones he thought only he walked. Only Rubra, a calm voice reeling off directions, had offered any hope.

Water made his black trousers heavy. He was cold, partly from the fright, partly cold turkey.

There had been no sign of pursuit for three hours now, though Rubra said they were still tracking him.

The narrow creek began to widen, its banks lowering. Tolton walked out into a tarn fifteen metres across with a crescent cliff cupping the rear half. Fat xenoc fish lumbered out of his way, apparently rolling along the bottom. There was no other exit, no feed stream.

"Now what?" he asked plaintively.

"There's an inlet at the far end," Rubra told him. "I've shut down the flow so you'll be able to swim through. It's only about five metres long, it bends, and there's no light; but it leads to a cave where you'll be safe."

"A cave? I thought caves were worn into natural rock over centuries."

"Actually, it's a surge chamber. I just didn't want to get technical on you, not with your artistic background."

Tolton thought the voice sounded tetchy. "Thank you," he said, and started to wade forwards towards the cliff. A couple more directions, and he dived under the surface. The inlet was easy to find, a nightmare-black hole barely a metre and a half wide. Knowing he would never be able to turn around or even back out, he forced himself to glide into the entrance, bubbles streaming behind him.

It couldn't have been five metres long, more like twenty or thirty. The curves were sharp, one taking him down, the other up. He broke surface with a frantic gasping cry. The cave was a dome shape, twenty metres across, every surface was coated in a film of water, thin ripples were still running down the walls. He had emerged in the pool at the centre. When he looked up there was a large hole at the apex, droplets splattered on his upturned face. A high ring of electrophorescent cells cast a weak pink-white glow into every cranny.

He paddled over to the side of the pool and pushed himself out onto the slippery floor. A bout of shivering claimed his limbs; he wasn't sure if it was from the cold water or the nagging feeling of claustrophobia. The surge chamber was horribly confined, and the fact that it was usually full of water didn't help.

"I'll have one of the housechimps bring you some dry clothes and food," Rubra said.

"Thank you."

"You should be safe here for a while."

"I . . ." He looked around apprehensively. Everyone always said Rubra could see everything. "I don't think I can stay very long. It's a bit . . . closed in."

"I know. Don't worry, I'll keep you moving, keep you ahead of them."

"Can I join up with anyone else? I need to be around people."

"There aren't that many of you left free, I'm afraid. And meeting up with them isn't a good idea, that would just make you easier to locate. I haven't quite worked out how they track the non-possessed yet; I suspect they've got some kind of esp ability. Hell, why not? They've got every other kind of magic."

"How many of us are there?" he asked, suddenly panicky.

Rubra considered giving him the truth, but Tolton wasn't the strongest of characters. "A couple of thousand," he lied. There were three hundred and seventy-one people left free within the habitat, and assisting all of them simultaneously was pure hell.

Even as he was reassuring Tolton he perceived Bonney Lewin stalking Gilbert Van-Riytell. The tough little woman had taken to dressing in nineteenth-century African safari gear, a khaki uniform with two crossed bandoleer straps holding polished brass cartridges in black leather hoops. A shiny Enfield .303 rifle was slung over her shoulder.

Gilbert was Magellanic Itg's old comptroller, and had never really stood a chance. Rubra had been trying to steer him along some service tunnels below a tube station, but Bonney and her co-hunters were boxing him in.

"There's an inspection hatch three metres ahead," Rubra datavised to Van-Riytell. "I want you to——"

Shadows lifted themselves off the service tunnel wall and grabbed the old man. Rubra hadn't even noticed them. His perception routines had been expertly circumvented.

Once again, he purged and reformatted local sub-routines. By the time he regained some observation ability Van-

Riytell's legs and arms were being tied around a long pole, ready to be carried away like a prize trophy. He wasn't even struggling anymore. Bonney was supervising the procedure happily.

One of her hunting team was standing back, watching aloofly; a tall young man in a simple white suit.

Rubra knew then. It had to be him.

Dariat!

The young man's head jerked up. For an instant the illusion flickered. Long enough for Rubra. Under the outline of the handsome youth lurked Horgan. Horgan with a shocked expression wrenching his thin face. Incontrovertible proof.

I knew it would be you, Rubra said. In a way the knowledge came almost as a relief.

Much good it will do you, Dariat answered. **Your awareness of anything is going to come to an end real soon now. And you won't even make it to the freedom of the beyond, I won't allow you that escape.**

You're amazing, Dariat. I mean that as a compliment. You still want me, don't you? You want revenge. It's all you've ever wanted, all that kept you alive these last thirty years. You still blame me for poor old Anastasia Rigel, even after all this time.

You got another suspect? If you hadn't driven me away, she and I would still be alive.

The pair of you would be dodging good old Bonney here, you mean.

Maybe so. But then maybe if I'd been happy I might have made something of my life. Ever think of that? I might have risen through the company hierarchy just like you always wanted. I could have made Magellanic Itg supreme; I could have turned Valisk into the kind of nation that would have had Tranquillity's plutocrats flocking to us in droves. There wouldn't be any of these misfits and losers who rally around your banner. King Alastair would have come here asking me for tips on how to run his Kingdom. Do you really think a shipload of fucking zombies could have walked in here past passport, customs, and immigration without anyone even noticing if

that kind of regime had been in place? Don't you dare try
and avoid facing up to what you've done.

Oh, really? Tell me: by misfits, and all the other trash
you'd fling out of the airlocks, do you include the kind of
girl you fell in love with?

"Bastard!" Dariat screamed. Everyone in the hunting party
stared at him, even Van-Riytell. "I'll find you. I'll get you. I'll
crush your soul to death." Rage distended his face. He flung
both arms out horizontally from his body, a magus Samson
thrusting against the temple pillars. White fire exploded from
his hands to chew into the tunnel walls. Polyp flaked and
cracked, black chips spinning away through the air.

Temper temper, Rubra mocked. I see that hasn't improved much over the years.

"Pack it in, you maniac!" Bonney yelled at him.

"Help me!" Dariat shouted back. The energistic hurricane
roaring through his body was turning his brain to white-hot
magma, wanting to burst clean out of his skull. "I'm going to
kill him. Help me, for Chi-ri's sake." White fire hammered at
the crumbling tunnel, desperate to reach the neural strata, to
reach the very substance of the mind, and burn and burn and
burn . . .

"Stop it, right now." Bonney aimed her Enfield at him, one
eyebrow cocked.

Dariat slowly allowed the white fire to sink back into the
passive energistic currents stirring the cells of his possessed
body. His shoulders hunched in as smoke from the scorched
polyp spun around him. He reverted to Horgan, even down to
the unwashed shirt and creased trousers. Hands were pressed
to his face as he resisted the onrush of tears. "I'll get him,"
Horgan's quavering, high-pitched voice proclaimed. "I'll
fucking have him. I'll roast him inside his shell like he was
some kind of lobster. You'll see. Thirty years I've waited.
Thirty! Thole owes me my justice. He *owes* me."

"Sure he does," Bonney said. "But just so you and I are
clear on this: pull another stunt like that, and you'll need a
new body to work out of." She jerked her head to the team
trussing up Van-Riytell. They lifted the old comptroller off the
ground and started off down the tunnel.

The hunter woman glanced back at Dariat's hunched figure, opened her mouth to say something, then thought better of it. She followed the rest of the hunters along the tunnel.

You frightened me so bad I'm trembling, Rubra sneered. Can you feel the quakes? I expect the sea is about to flood the parkland. How's about that for wetting yourself?

Laugh away, Dariat said shakily. Go right ahead. But I'm going to come for you one day. I'll crack your safeguards. They won't last forever, you know that. And forever is what I've got on my side now. Then when I've busted you, I'm going to come into that neural strata with you, I'm going to crawl into your mind like a maggot, Rubra. And like a maggot I'm going to gnaw away at you.

I always was right about you. You were the best. Who else could still burn so hot after thirty years? Damn, why did you ever have to meet her? Together we could have rebuilt the company into a galaxy challenger.

Such flattery. I'm honoured.

Don't be. Help me.

What? You have got to be fucking joking.

No. Together we could beat Kiera, purge the habitat of her cronies. You can rule Valisk yet.

The Edenists were right, you are insane.

The Edenists are frightened by my determination. You should know, you inherited that gene, it seems.

Yeah. So you know you can't deflect me. Don't even try.

Dariat, you're not one of them, boy, not one of the possessed. Not really. What can they possibly give you afterwards, huh? Ever thought of that? What sort of culture are they going to build? This is just an aberration of nature, a nonsense, and a transient one at that. Life has to have a purpose, and they're not alive. This energistic ability, the way you can create out of nothing, how can you square that with human behaviour? It's not possible, the two are not compatible, never will be. Look at yourself. If you want Anastasia back, bring her back. Find her in the beyond, get her back here. You can have everything now, remember? Kiera said so, did she not? Are you a part of that, Dariat? You have to decide, boy. Someday. If you don't, they'll do it for you.

"I can't bring her back," he whispered.

What's that?

I can't. You understand nothing.

Try me.

You, a confessor father? Never.

I always have been. I am the confessor for everyone inside me, you know that. I am the repository of everyone's secrets. Including those of Anastasia Rigel.

I know everything about Anastasia. We had no secrets. We were in love.

Really? She had a life before you met her, you know. Seventeen long years. And afterwards, too.

Dariat glanced around with cold anger, his appearance sliding back to the white-suited ascetic. There was no afterwards. She died! Because of you.

If you knew of her past, you would understand what I meant.

What secrets? he demanded.

Help me, and I'll show you.

You shit! I'm going to cremate you, I'll dance on your fragments—

Rubra's principal routine watched Dariat's rage run its course. He thought at one point that the man would revert to flailing at the tunnel walls with white fire again. But Dariat managed to hang on to that last shred of control—barely.

Rubra stayed silent. He knew it was too early to play his ace, the one final secret he had kept safe for the last thirty years. The doubt he had planted deep in Dariat's mind would have to be teased further, tormented into full-blown paranoia before the revelation was exposed.

•   •   •

Lady Macbeth's event horizon vanished, allowing her mushroom-shaped star trackers to rise out of their jump recesses and scan around. Fifteen seconds later the flight computer confirmed the starship had emerged fifty thousand kilometres above Tranquillity's non-rotational spaceport. By the time her electronic warfare sensors registered, eight of the habitat's Strategic Defence platforms had locked on to the hull, despite the fact their coordinate was smack in the centre of a designated emergence zone.

"Jesus," Joshua muttered sourly. "Welcome home, people, nice to see you again." He looked over to Gaura, who was lying on Warlow's acceleration couch. "Update Tranquillity on our situation, fast, please. It seems a little trigger-happy today." Combat sensors had located four blackhawks on interception trajectories, accelerating towards them at six gees.

Gaura acknowledged him with an indolent wrist flick. The Edenist's eyes were closed; he'd been communicating with the habitat personality more or less from the moment the starship had completed the ZTT jump. Even with affinity it was difficult to convey their situation in a single quick summary; explanations, backed up with full memory exposure, took several minutes. He detected more than one ripple of surprise within the personality's serene thoughts as the story of Lalonde unfolded in its mentality.

When he'd finished, Ione directed her identity trait at him in the Edenist custom. *That's some yarn you've got there,* she said. *Two days ago I wouldn't have believed a word of it, but as we've had warning fleks arriving from Avon on an almost hourly basis for the last day and a half all I can say is I'll grant you docking permission.*

Thank you, Ione.

However, you will all have to be checked for possession before I'll admit you into the habitat. I can hardly expose the entire population to the risk of contamination on the word of one man, even though you seem genuine.

Of course.

How's Joshua?

He is well. A remarkable young man.

Yes.

The flight computer's display showed the Strategic Defence platforms disengaging their weapons lock. Joshua received a standard acknowledgement from the spaceport's traffic control centre followed by a datavised approach vector.

"I need a docking bay which can handle casualties," he datavised back. "And put a pediatric team on alert status, as well as some biophysics specialists. These kids have had a real hard time on Lalonde, and that only finished when they got nuked."

"I am assembling the requisite medical teams now," Tranquillity replied. "They will be ready by the time you dock. I am also alerting a spaceport maintenance crew. Judging by the state of your hull, and the vapour leakages I can observe, I believe it would be appropriate."

"Thank you, Tranquillity. Considerate as ever." He waited for Ione to come on-line and say something, but the channel switched back to traffic control's guidance updates.

If that's the way she wants it . . . Fine by me. His features slumped into a grouch.

He ignited the *Lady Mac*'s two functional fusion tubes, aligning the ship on their approach vector. They headed in for Tranquillity at one and a half gees.

"They believe all that spiel about possession?" Sarha asked Gaura, a note of worried scepticism in her voice.

"Yes." He queried the habitat about the fleks from Avon. "The First Admiral's precautions have been endorsed by the Assembly. By now ninety per cent of the Confederation should be aware of the situation."

"Wait a minute," Dahybi said. "We only just got back here from Lalonde, and we didn't exactly hang around. How the hell could that navy squadron alert Avon two or three days ago?"

"They didn't," Gaura said. "The possessed must have got off Lalonde some time ago. Apparently Laton had to destroy an entire Atlantean island to prevent them from spreading."

"Shit," Dahybi grunted. "You mean they're loose in the Confederation already?"

"I'm afraid so. It looks like Shaun Wallace was telling Kelly the truth after all. I had hoped it was all some subtle propaganda on his part," the Edenist added sadly.

The news acted as a mood damper right through the starship. Their expected sanctuary wasn't so secure after all; they'd escaped a battle to find a war brewing. Not even an Edenist psyche could suppress that much gloom. The children from Lalonde (those not squeezed into the zero-tau pods) picked up on it, another emotional ricochet, though admittedly not as large as all the others they'd been through. The

happiness Father Horst had promised them waited at the end
of their journey was proving elusive. Even the fact the voyage
was ending didn't help much.

The damage *Lady Macbeth* had suffered in the fight above
Lalonde didn't affect her manoeuvrability, not with Joshua piloting. She closed in on her designated docking bay, CA 5-
099, at the very centre of the spaceport disk, precisely aligned
along the vector assigned by traffic control. There was no hint
that fifteen attitude control thrusters had been disabled, and
she was venting steadily from emergency dump valves as
well as a couple of fractured cryogenic feed pipes.

By that time almost a quarter of the habitat population was
accessing the spaceport's sensors, watching her dock. The
news companies had broken into their schedules to announce
that a single ship had made it back from Lalonde. Reporters
had been very quick off the mark in discovering the pediatric
teams were assembling in the bay. (Kelly's boss was making
frantic datavises to the incoming starship, to no avail.)

The space industry people, industrial station workers, and
ships' crews kicking their heels in the bars because of the
quarantine observed the approach with a sense of troubled
awe. Yes, Joshua had come through again, but the state of old
Lady Mac . . . Charred, flaking nultherm foam exposed sections of her hull which showed innumerable heat-stress ripples (a sure sign of energy beam strikes), melted sensor
clusters, only two fusion tubes functional. It must have been
one hell of a scrap. They all knew no one else would be returning. Knowledge that every friend, colleague, or vague ac-
quaintance who had accompanied Terrance Smith was either
radioactive dust or lost to possession was hard to accept.
Those starships were powerful, fast, and well armed.

The disembarkment process was, as expected, a shambles.
People kept emerging from the airlock tube as if *Lady Mac*
were the focus of some dimensional twist, her internal space
far larger than that which the hull enclosed. Edenists formed
a good percentage of the exiles, much to the surprise of the
rover reporters. They helped a horde of wondrously
senseogenic, scared-looking refugee kids in ragged clothes.
Pediatric nurses floated after them in the reception compart-

ment, while reporters dived like airborne sharks to ask the children how they felt/what they'd seen. Tears started to flow.

How the hell did they get in there? Ione asked the habitat. Serjeants launched themselves to intercept the reporters.

Jay Hilton hugged her legs to her chest as she drifted across the compartment, shivering unhappily. None of this was what she'd been expecting, not the starship voyage nor their arrival. She tried to catch sight of Father Horst amid the noisy swirl of bodies bouncing around the compartment, knowing that he had others to look out for and probably couldn't spare much time for her. In fact, she wouldn't be needed for anything much now there were plentiful adults around to take care of things again. Perhaps if she hunched up really small everyone would ignore her, and she'd be able to have a look at the habitat's park. Jay had heard stories of Edenist habitats and how beautiful they were; back in the arcology she'd often daydreamed that one day she'd visit Jupiter, despite everything Father Varhoos preached about the evils of bitek.

The opportunity to escape the melee never quite presented itself. A reporter soared past her, noticed she was the oldest kid in the compartment, and used a grab hoop to brake himself abruptly. His mouth split into a super-friendly smile, the kind his neural nanonics program advised was best to interface trustfully with Young Children. "Hi there. Isn't this atrocious? They should have organized things better."

"Yes," Jay said doubtfully.

"My name is Matthias Rems." The smile broadened further. "Jay Hilton."

"Well, hi there, Jay. I'm glad you've reached Tranquillity, you're quite safe here. From what we've heard it was nasty for all of you on Lalonde."

"Yes!"

"Really? What happened?"

"Well, Mummy got possessed the first night. And then—" A hand closed on her shoulder. She glanced around to see Kelly Tirrel giving Matthias Rems an aggressive stare.

"He wants to know what happened," Jay said brightly. She liked Kelly, admiring her right from the moment she arrived at the savanna homestead to rescue them. On the voyage to Tranquillity she'd secretly decided that she was going to be a tough, Confederation-roaming reporter like Kelly when she grew up.

"What happened is your story, Jay," Kelly said slowly. "It belongs to you; it's all you've got left. And if he wants to hear it he has to offer you a great deal of money for it."

"Kelly!" Matthias flashed her a slightly exasperated you-know-the-score grin.

It made no discernible impression on Kelly. "Pick on someone your own size, Matthias. Ripping off traumatized children is low even for you. I'm covering for Jay."

"Is that right, Jay?" he asked. "Did you thumbprint a contract with Collins?"

"What?" Jay glanced from one to the other, puzzled.

"Serjeant!" Kelly shouted.

Jay squeaked in alarm as a glitter-black hand closed around Matthias Rems's upper arm. The owner of the hand was a hard-skinned monster worse than any shape a possessed had ever worn.

"It's all right, Jay." Kelly grinned for the first time in days. "It's on our side. This is what Tranquillity uses for its police force."

"Oh." Jay swallowed loudly.

"I'd like to complain about an attempted violation of confidentiality copyright," Kelly told the serjeant. "Also, Matthias is breaking the sense-media ethics charter concerning the approach and enticement of minors in the absence of their parents or guardians."

"Thank you, Kelly," the serjeant said. "And welcome home, I offer my congratulations on your endurance through difficult times."

She grimaced numbly at the bitek servitor.

"Come along now, sir," the serjeant said to Matthias Rems. It pushed away from the compartment bulkhead with its stocky legs, the pair of them heading for one of the hatchways.

"Don't ever trust reporters, Jay," Kelly said. "We're not nice people. Worse than the possessed really; they only steal bodies, we steal your whole life and make a profit out of it."

"You don't," Jay said, shoving the full child-force of trusting worship behind the words. A belief which was a sheer impossibility for any adult to live up to.

Kelly kissed her forehead, emotions in a muddle. Kids today, so knowing, which only makes them even more vulnerable. She gently pushed Jay towards one of the pediatric nurses, and left them discussing what the little girl had eaten last, and when.

"Kelly, thank Christ!"

The familiar voice made her twitch, a movement which in free fall was like a ripple running from toe to crown. She held on to a grab hoop to steady herself.

Feetfirst, Garfield Lunde slid down into her vision field. Her direct boss, and the man who had authorized her assignment. A big gamble, as he told her at the time, this kind of fieldwork is hardly your forte. Putting her deeper in his debt; everything he did for his workforce was a favour, an against-the-rules kindness. He owed his position entirely to his mastery of office politics; sensevise talent and investigative ability never entered into it.

"Hello, Garfield," she said in a dull tone.

"You made it back. Great hairstyle, too."

Kelly had almost forgotten her hair, cut to a fine fuzz to fit her armour suit's skull helmet. Style, dress sense, cosmetic membranes: concepts which seemed to have dissolved clean out of her universe. "Well done, Garfield; I can see why your observational ability pushed you right the way up the seniority league."

He wagged a finger, almost catching his ponytail which was snaking around his neck. "Tough lady, at last. Looks like you lost your cherry on this assignment; touched a few corpses, wondered if you should have helped instead of recorded. Don't feel bad, it happens to us all."

"Sure."

"Is anyone else coming back, any other starships?"

"If they're not here by now, they won't be coming."

"Christ, this is getting better by the second. We've got us a total exclusive. Did you get down to the planet?"

"Yes."

"And is it possessed?"

"Yes."

"Magnificent!" He glanced contentedly around the reception chamber, watching children and Edenists in free-fall flight, their movements reminiscent of geriatric ballerinas. "Hey, where are the mercs you went with?"

"They didn't make it, Garfield. They sacrificed themselves so the *Lady Mac*'s spaceplane could lift the children off."

"Oh, my God. Wow! Sacrificed themselves for kids?"

"Yes. We were outgunned, but they stood their ground. All of them. I never expected . . ."

"Stunning. You got it, didn't you? For Christ's sake, Kelly, tell me you recorded it. The big fight, the last noble stand."

"I recorded it. What I could. When I wasn't so scared I couldn't think straight."

"Yes! I knew I made the right decision sending you. This is it, babe. Just watch our audience points go galactic. We're going to put Time Universe and the others out of business. Do you realize what you've done here? Shit, Kelly, you'll probably wind up as my boss, after this. Wonderful!"

Very calmly, Kelly let Ariadne's free-fall unarmed combat program shift into primary mode. Her sense of balance was immediately magnified, making her aware of every slight movement her body made in the minute air currents churning through the chamber. Her spacial orientation underwent a similar augmentation; distances and relative positions were *obvious*.

"Wonderful?" she hissed.

Garfield grinned proudly. "You bet."

Kelly launched herself at him, rotating around her centre of gravity as she did so. Her feet came around, seeking out his head, legs kicking straight.

Two of the serjeants had to pull her off. Luckily the pediatric team had some medical nanonic packages with them; they were able to save Garfield's eye; it would take a week before his broken nose knitted back into its proper shape, though.

All the passenger refugees had left *Lady Mac*. Overstressed environmental systems were calming. The docking bay's umbilicals sent a cool wind washing through the bridge, taking with it the air of the voyage; ugly air with its smell of human bodies, humidity, and heavy carbon dioxide. To Joshua's mind even the fans behind the grilles weren't whining so much. Perhaps it was his imagination.

Now there was only the crew left to soak up the luxuriously plentiful oxygen. The crew minus one. There hadn't been much time for Joshua to dwell on Warlow during the flight. Racing between jump coordinates, worrying about the energy patterning nodes holding out, the leakages, the damaged systems, children he had suddenly become responsible for, the desperate need to succeed.

Well, now he'd won, beaten the odds the universe had thrown at him. And it made him feel good, even though there was no happiness to accompany it. Self-satisfaction was a curious state, in this case roughly equivalent to fatigue-induced nirvana, he thought.

Ashly Hanson came up through the decking hatch and took a swift glance around the lethargic forms still encased by their acceleration couch webbing. "Flight's over, you know," he said.

"Yeah." Joshua datavised an instruction into the flight computer. Harlequin schematics of the starship's principal systems vanished from his mind, and the webbing peeled back.

"I think the cleaning up can wait until tomorrow," Dahybi said.

"Message received," Joshua said. "Shore leave is now granted, and compulsory."

Sarha glided over from her couch and gave Joshua a tiny kiss. "You were magnificent. After all this is over, we're going back to Aethra so we can tell him we escaped and got the children off."

"If he's there."

"He's there. You know he is."

"She's right, Joshua," Melvyn Ducharme said as he cancelled the neurographic visualization of *Lady Mac*'s power circuits. "He's there. And even if the transfer didn't work, his soul is going to be watching us right now."

"Jesus." Joshua shivered. "I don't even want to think about that."

"We don't have a lot of choice in the subject anymore."

"But not today," Ashly put in heavily. He held out an arm

to Sarha. "Come along, we'll leave these morbids to moan among themselves. I don't know about you, but I'm having one very stiff drink in Harkey's first, then it's bed for a week."

"Sounds good." She twisted her feet off the stikpad by Joshua's couch and followed the old time-hopper pilot through the hatch.

A vaguely nonplussed expression appeared on Joshua's face as they left together. None of your business, he told himself. Besides, there was Kelly to consider, though she'd been almost unrecognizable since returning from Lalonde. And then there was Louise. Ione, too.

"I think I'll skip the drink and go straight to bed," he announced to the other two.

They went out of the bridge hatch one at a time. It was only when they got to the airlock that they encountered the service company's systems specialist coming the other way. She wanted the captain's authority to begin assessing the ship so she could assemble a maintenance schedule. Joshua stayed behind to discuss priorities, datavising over the files on systems which had taken punishment above Lalonde.

There was nobody about when he finally left the starship. The circus in the reception chamber had ended. The reporters had packed up. There wasn't even a serjeant left to check him over for possession. Sloppy, he thought, not like Tranquillity at all.

A commuter lift took him along the spindle which connected the spaceport disk to the centre of the habitat's northern endcap. It deposited him in one of the ten tube stations which served the hub; deserted but for a single occupant.

Ione stood outside the waiting tube carriage, dressed in a sea-blue sarong and matching blouse. He smiled ruefully at the memory that evoked.

"I remember you," she said.

"Funny, I thought you'd forgotten."

"No. Not you, no matter what."

He stood in front of her, looking down at a face which owned far too much wisdom for such delicate features. "I was stupid," he confessed.

"I think you and I can withstand one argument, don't you?"

"I was stupid more than once."

"Tranquillity's been reviewing the memories of the Edenists you saved. I'm very proud of what you achieved on that flight, Joshua, and I don't just mean all that fancy flying. Very proud indeed."

All he could do was nod ineffectually. For a long time he'd dreamed about a reunion like this; going off after they'd had a fight had left too many things open-ended, too much unsaid. Now it was actually happening, his mind was slipping to Louise, who had also been left behind. It was all Warlow's fault, him and that damn promise to be a little less selfish with his girls.

"You look tired," Ione said, and held out her hand. "Let's go home."

Joshua looked down at her open hand, small and perfect. He twined his fingers through hers, rediscovering how warm her skin was.

* * *

Parker Higgens thought it must have been about twenty years since he last left Tranquillity, a short trip on an Adamist starship to a university on Nanjing so he could deliver a paper and assess some candidates for the Laymil project. He hadn't enjoyed the experience; free-fall nausea seemed capable of penetrating whatever defences his neural nanonics erected across his nerve pathways.

This time it was pleasantly different. The gravity in the blackhawk's life-support capsule never fluctuated, he had a comfortable cabin to himself, the crew were friendly, and his navy escort officer was a cultured lady who made an excellent travelling companion.

At the end of the flight he even accessed the blackhawk's electronic sensors to watch their approach to Trafalgar. Dozens of navy starships swarmed around its two large spaceport globes. Avon provided a sumptuous backdrop; the warm blues, whites, greens, and browns of a terracompatible planet were so much kinder than the abrasive storm bands of Mirchusko, he realized. Parker Higgens almost laughed at the stereotype image he presented as he gawped like some stupefied tourist: the dusty old professor finally discovers there is life outside the research centre.

Pity he didn't have time to enjoy it. The navy officer had been datavising Trafalgar constantly since their wormhole terminus closed behind them, outlining their brief and authenticating it with a series of codes. They'd been given a priority approach vector, allowing them to curve around one of the spaceports at an exhilarating speed before sliding into the huge crater which served as a docking ledge for bitek starships (they were the only blackhawk using it).

After that he'd had a couple of meetings with the First Admiral's staff officers, an exchange of information which chilled both sides. Parker found out about possession, they were given the data on the Laymil home planet, Unimeron. They decided there wasn't any room for doubt.

When he was shown into Samual Aleksandrovich's big circular office the first thing Parker Higgens felt was an obscure burst of jealousy. The First Admiral had a view out over Trafalgar's biosphere which was more impressive than the one in his own office back on the Laymil project campus. A true dedicated bureaucrat's reaction, he chided himself; prestige is everything.

The First Admiral came around from behind his big teak desk to greet Parker with a firm handshake. "Thank you for coming, Mr Director; and I'd also like to convey my gratitude to the Lord of Ruin as well for acting so promptly in this matter. It would appear she is a strong supporter of the Confederation; I just wish other heads of state followed her example."

"I'll be sure to tell her," Parker said.

The First Admiral introduced the others sitting around his desk: Admiral Lalwani, Captain Maynard Khanna, Dr Gilmore, and Mae Ortlieb, the President's science office liaison aide.

"Well the Kiint did warn us, I suppose," Admiral Lalwani said. "All races eventually face the truth about death. It would appear the Laymil lost their confrontation."

"They never said anything before," Parker said bitterly. "We have six Kiint assisting the project back at Tranquillity; I've worked with them for decades; they're helpful, cooperative, I even considered them as friends . . . And never once did they drop the slightest hint. Damn them! They knew all along why the Laymil killed themselves and their habitats."

"Ambassador Roulor did say it was something which we must come to terms with on our own."

"Very helpful," Dr Gilmore grunted. "I have to say it's a typical attitude to take given their psychology inclines towards the mystic."

"I think any race which has uncovered the secret of death and survived the impact is inevitably going to take a highly spiritual approach to life," the First Admiral said. "Don't begrudge them that, Doctor. Now then, Mr Director, it would appear that our possession and the Laymil reality dysfunction are one and the same thing, correct?"

"Yes, Admiral. In fact, in the light of what we know now, the Laymil shipmaster's reference to the Galheith clan's death essence makes perfect sense. Possession was spreading across Unimeron as he left orbit."

"I think I can confirm that," Admiral Lalwani said. She glanced at the First Admiral for permission. He inclined his head. "A voidhawk messenger has just returned from Ombey. Several possessed got loose there; fortunately the authorities were remarkably successful in hunting them down. However, despite that success, they've had to cede some ground to them. We have a recording of the phenomena."

Parker accessed the flek of images compiled by Ombey's Strategic Defence sensor satellites, seeing the remarkably smooth red cloud slowly sheathing Mortonridge. Time-lapse coverage showed the planet's terminator cruise in across the ocean. At night the peninsula's covering glowed a hostile cerise, its edges flexing in agitation over the crinkled coastline.

"Oh, dear," he said after he cancelled the visualization.

"They match," Dr Gilmore said. "Absolutely, the same event."

"Admittedly Laton was in a hurry and under a great deal of stress," Lalwani said. "But if we understand him correctly, once that red cloud envelops a world completely, the possessed can take it right out of the universe."

"Not outside, exactly," Dr Gilmore said. "If you can manipulate space-time to the extent they apparently can, then you should be able to format a favourable micro-continuum around a world. The surface simply won't be accessible through ordinary space-time. A wormhole might reach them, if we knew the correct quantum signature for its terminus."

"The Laymil homeworld wasn't destroyed," Parker said slowly. "Of that we are sure. We speculated that it could have been moved, but naturally we considered only physical movement through this universe."

"Then the possessed Laymil must have worked this vanishing trick," Lalwani said. "It really is possible."

"Dear God," the First Admiral murmured. "As if it wasn't enough trying to find a method of reversing possession, we now have to to consider how to bring back entire planets from some demented version of Heaven."

"And the Laymil in the spaceholms committed suicide rather than submit," Lalwani said bleakly. "The parallel between the Ruin Ring and Pernik island is one I find most disturbing. The possessed confront us with a single choice; surrender or die. And if we do die, we enhance their own numbers. Yet Laton chose death; indeed he seemed almost happy at the prospect. Right at the end he told Oxley he would begin what he named the great journey, though he never elaborated. But the intimation that he would not suffer in the beyond was a strong one."

"Unfortunately it's hardly something you can turn into a firm policy," Mae Ortlieb observed. "Nor one to reassure people with even if you did."

"I am aware of that," Lalwani told the woman coolly. "What this information can do is point us towards areas which should be investigated. From the result of those investigations, policies can then be formulated."

"Enough," the First Admiral said. "We are here to try and decide which is the most fruitful line of scientific inquiry. Given we now have a basic understanding of the problem confronting us I'd like some suggestions. Dr Gilmore?"

"We're continuing to examine Jacqueline Couteur to try and determine the nature of the energy which the possessing soul utilizes. So far we've had very little success. Our instruments either cannot read it, or suffer glitches produced by it. Either way, we cannot define its nature." He gave the First

Admiral a timorous glance. "I'd like your permission to move on to reactive tests."

Parker couldn't help the disapproving snort which escaped from his lips. Again reinforcing the persona of crusty old academic; but he deplored Gilmore's wholehearted right-wing militarism.

No one would think of it to look at him now, but Parker Higgens had done his stint for radicalism and its various causes during his student days. He wondered if that was on the file Lalwani must invariably keep on him, aging bytes in an obsolete program language detailing his protests over military development work carried out on the university campus. Had she accessed that before he'd been allowed in here, the heart of the greatest military force the human race had ever assembled? Perhaps she judged him safe these days. Perhaps she was even right in doing so. But people like Gilmore re-opened all the old contemptuous thoughts. Reactive tests, indeed.

"You have a problem with that, Mr Director?" Dr Gilmore asked with formal neutrality.

Parker let his gaze wander around the office's big holo-screens, watching the starships shoaling over Avon. Readying themselves for combat. For conflict. "I agree with the First Admiral," he said sorrowfully. "We must attempt to locate a scientific solution."

"Which is only going to happen if my research can proceed unhindered. I know what you're thinking, Mr Director, and I regret the fact that we're dealing with a live human here. But unless you can offer me a valid alternative we must use her to add to our knowledge base."

"I am aware of the argument about relative levels of suffering, Doctor. I just find it depressing that after seven centuries of adhering to the scientific method we haven't come up with a more humane principle. I find the prospect of experimenting on people to be abhorrent."

"You should review the file Lieutenant Hewlett made when his marine squad were sent on their capture mission to obtain Jacqueline Couteur. You'd see exactly who really practises abhorrent behaviour."

"Excellent argument. They do it to us, so we're fully justified doing it to them. We are all people."

"I'm sorry," the First Admiral interjected. "But we really
don't have time for the pair of you to discuss ethics and
morality. The Confederation is now officially in a state of
emergency, Mr Director. If that turns us into what you regard
as savages in order to defend ourselves, then so be it. We did
not initiate this crisis, we are simply reacting to it the only
way I know how. And I am going to use you as much as Dr
Gilmore will use the Couteur woman."

Parker straightened his spine, sitting up to stare at the First
Admiral. Somehow arguing with him as he had with the navy
scientist wasn't even an option. Lalwani was right, he acknowledged sorely. Student politics didn't stand much chance
against his adult survival instinct. We are what our genes
made us. "I don't think I would be much use to your endeavour, Admiral. I've made my contribution."

"Not so." He gestured to Mae Ortlieb.

"The Laymil must have tried to prevent possession from
engulfing their spaceholms before they committed suicide,"
she said. "I believe that is what the essencemasters were on
board the ship for."

"Yes, but it couldn't have worked."

"No." She gave him a heavily ironic smile. "So I'd like to
use the scientific method, Mr Director: eliminate the impossible and all you're left with is the possible. It would be a lot of
help to us if we knew what won't work against the possessed.
A great deal of time would be saved. And lives, too, I expect."

"Well yes, but our knowledge is extremely limited."

"I believe there are still many files in the Laymil electronics stack which have not been reformatted to human sense
compatibility?"

"Yes."

"Then that would be a good start. If you could return to
Tranquillity and ask Ione Saldana to initiate a priority search
for us, please."

"That was in hand when I left."

"Excellent. My office and the navy science bureau here in
Trafalgar can provide fresh teams of specialists to assist in the

analysis process. They'd probably be better qualified in helping to recognize any weapons."

Parker gave her an exasperated look. "The Laymil didn't work like that; weapons are not part of their culture. Their countermeasures would consist principally of psychological inhibitors distributed through the spaceholms' life-harmony gestalt. They would attempt to reason with their opponents."

"And when that failed, they might just have been desperate enough to try something else. The Laymil possessed weren't above using violence, we saw that in the recording. Their reality dysfunction was incinerating large portions of land."

Parker surrendered, even though he knew it was all wrong. These people could so easily believe in the concept of superweapons hidden amid the fractured debris of the Ruin Ring, a deus ex machina waiting to liberate the human race. The military mind! "Anything is possible," he said. "But I'd like to go on record as saying that in this case I strongly doubt it."

"Of course," the First Admiral said. "However, we do need to look, I'm sure you can appreciate that. May we send our specialists back with you?"

"Certainly." Parker didn't like to think what Ione Saldana would say about that. Her one principal limitation on the project was the right to embargo weapons technology. But these people had outmanoeuvred him with astonishing ease. An acute lesson in the difference between political manoeuvring practised on the Confederation capital and one of its most harmless outpost worldlets.

Samual Aleksandrovich watched the old director knuckle under, even feeling a slight sympathy. He really didn't like to invade the world of such a blatantly decent man of peace. The Parker Higgenses of this universe were what the Confederation existed to defend. "Thank you, Mr Director. I don't want to appear an ungracious host, but if you could be ready to leave within a couple of hours, please. Our people are already being assembled." He carefully avoided Higgens's sharp glance at that comment. "They can travel on navy voidhawks, which should provide you a suitable escort back to Tranquillity. I really can't run the risk of your mission being intercepted. You're too valuable to us."

"Is that likely?" Parker asked in concern. "An interception, I mean?"

"I would certainly hope not," the First Admiral said. "But the overall situation is certainly less favourable than I'd hoped. We didn't get our warnings out quite fast enough. Several returning voidhawks have reported that the possessed have gained an enclave on various worlds, and there are seven asteroid settlements we know of that have been taken over completely. Most worrying is a report from the Srinagar system that they have taken over the Valisk habitat, which means they have a fleet of blackhawks at their disposal. That gives them the potential to mount a substantial military operation to assist others of their kind."

"I see. I didn't realize the possessed had advanced so far. The Mortonridge recording is a distressing one."

"Precisely. So you can appreciate our hurry in acquiring what information we can from the Laymil recordings."

"I . . . I do, yes."

"Don't worry, Mr Director," Lalwani said. "Our advantage at the moment is that the possessed are all small individual groups, they lack coordination. It is only if they become organized on a multistellar level that we will be in real trouble. The Assembly's prohibition on commercial starflight should give us a few weeks grace. It will be difficult for them to spread themselves by stealth. Any interstellar movements they make from now on will have to be large scale, which gives us the ability to track them."

"That is where the navy will face its greatest challenge," the First Admiral said. "Also our greatest defeat. In space warfare there is no such thing as a draw, you either win or you die. We will be shooting at complete innocents."

"I doubt it will come to that," Mae Ortlieb said. "As you said, they are a disorganized rabble. We control interstellar communications, it should be enough to prevent them merging to form a genuine threat."

"Except . . ." Parker said, he caught himself, then gave a penitent sigh. "Some of our greatest generals and military leaders must be waiting in the beyond. They will understand just as much about tactics as we do. They'll know what they have to do in order to succeed."

"We'll be ready for them," the First Admiral said. He tried not to show any disquiet at Parker's suggestion. *Would I really be able to compete against an alliance between Napoleon and Richard Saldana?*

• • •

Dariat walked up the last flight of stairs into the foyer of the Sushe starscraper. None of the possessed used the lifts anymore—too dangerous, with Rubra still controlling the power circuits (and as for taking a tube carriage . . . forget it). The once-stylish circular foyer echoed a war zone, its glass walls cracked and tarnished with soot, furniture mashed and flung about, dripping with water and grubby grey foam from the ceiling fire sprinklers. Black soil from broken pot plants squelched messily underfoot.

He refused to say it to the others picking their way through the wreckage: *If you'd just listened to me.* They'd heard it from him so many times they didn't listen; besides, they followed Kiera slavishly now. He had to admit the council she'd put together was effective at maintaining control within the habitat. And precious little else. He found it a telling point that the possessed hadn't bothered using their energistic power to return the lobby to its original state; it wasn't as if they had to go around with a brush and sponge. Rubra's continuing presence and war-of-nerves campaign was taking its toll on morale.

He stepped through the twisted doors out onto the flagstones ringing the lobby building. The surrounding parkland had, at least, retained its bucolic appearance. Emerald grass, unblemished by a single weed, extended out to the rank of sagging ancient trees two hundred metres away, crisscrossed by hard-packed gravel paths leading off deeper into the habitat interior. Dense hemispherical bushes with dark violet leaves and tiny silver flowers were scattered about. Small reptilian birds that were little more than triangular wings of muscle, with scales coloured turquoise and amber, swooped playfully through the air overhead.

The corpse spoilt the idyll; lying with its legs across one of the gravel paths, one ankle twisted at an awkward angle.

There was no way of telling if it was male or female. Its head looked as if it had been shoved into a starship's fusion exhaust jet.

The remains of the perpetrators, a pair of servitor housechimps, were smouldering on the grass twenty metres away. One of them held a melted wand which Dariat recognized as a shockrod. A lot of the possessed had been caught unawares by the harmless-looking servitors. After a couple of days of unexpected, and unpredictable, attacks, most people simply exterminated them on sight now.

He walked past, wrinkling his nose at the smell. When he reached the trees he saw one of the triangular birds had alighted on the topmost branch. They eyed each other warily. It was a xenoc, so he was reasonably sure it wasn't affinitybonded. But with Rubra, you could never be certain. Now Dariat thought about it, the servitors would be an excellent way of keeping everyone under observation, circumventing the disruption he'd been inflicting on the neural strata's subroutines. He scowled up at the bird, which rippled its wings but didn't take off.

Dariat moved swiftly through the woods to a large glade which Kiera was using. Impressively tall trees with greygreen leaves formed a valley on either side of a wide stream, their black trunks host to a furry moss-analogue. Long grass fringed the water, littered with wild poppies.

Two groups of people were occupying the glade. One was comprised entirely of youngsters, couples in their late teens and early twenties; boys all with bare chests, wearing shorts or swimming trunks; girls in light summer dresses or bikinis, emphasising their femininity. Both genders had been chosen for their beauty. Four or five children milled about looking completely bored; girls in party frocks and ribbons in their hair, boys in shorts and smart shirts. Two of the under sevens were smoking.

At the other end of the glade four people in ordinary clothes stood in a group, talking in loud strained voices. Arms waved around as fingers jabbed for emphasis. Various electronic modules were scattered on the grass around their feet, the paraphernalia of a professional MF recording operation.

Dariat saw Kiera Salter was standing among the recording

team, and went over. She was wearing a white cotton camisole with tiny pearl buttons down the front, the top half undone to display her cleavage; and a thin white skirt showing tanned legs and bare feet. With her hair unbound over her shoulders the effect was awesomely sexy. It lasted right up until she turned her gaze on him. Marie Skibbow's body might be a male fantasy made flesh, but the maleficent intelligence now residing in her skull was instantly chilling.

"I hear you're losing it, Dariat," she said curtly. "I've been patient with you so far, because you've been very useful to us. But if there's another incident like the one in the service tunnel, then I shall consider that usefulness at an end."

"If you don't have me here to counter Rubra, then it's going to be you who'll wind up losing your temper. He'll blast every possessed back into the beyond if you let your guard down for a second. He doesn't care about the people whose bodies we've stolen."

"You are becoming a bore, Dariat. And from what I hear that wasn't a temper loss, more like a psychotic episode. You're a paranoid schizophrenic, and people find that unsettling. Now concentrate on how to flush Rubra out of the neural strata by all means, but stop trying to spread dissension or it's going to go hard on you. Clear?"

"As crystal."

"Good. I do appreciate what you're trying to do, Dariat. You're just going to have to learn a softer approach, that's all." She gave him a factory-issue sympathetic smile.

Dariat saw one of the xenoc triangle birds perched on a tree behind her, watching the scene in the glade. The smirk which rose on his real lips was hidden by the energistic mirage-form he cloaked himself with. "I expect you're right. I'll try."

"Good man. Look, I don't want to be forced out of Valisk by him any more than you do. We're both onto a good thing here, and we can both maintain our status providing we just keep calm. If this recording works we should have recruits flocking to join us. That way we can shift Valisk to a place where Rubra's neutered. Permanently. Just keep him from causing too much trouble before then, and leave the rest to me, okay?"

"Yeah, all right. I understand."

She nodded dismissal, then took a steadying breath and turned back to the recording team. "Are you ready yet?"

Khaled Jaros glared at the recalcitrant sensor block in his hand. "I think so, yes. I'm sure it will work this time. Ramon has reprogrammed it so that only the primary functions are left; we won't be able to get olfactory or thermal inputs, but the AV reception appears to be holding stable. With a bit of luck we can add some emotional activant patterns later."

"All right, we'll try again," she said loudly.

Under Khaled's directions the group of sybarite youths took up their positions once more. One couple started necking on the grass, another pair sported in the water. The little children stubbed their cigarettes out, then ran around in dizzy circles, giggling and shrieking. "Not so loud!" Khaled bellowed at them.

Kiera took up her own position leaning against the boulder at the side of the sparkling water. She cleared her throat, and forked her hair back with her left hand.

"Undo another couple more buttons, dear, please," Khaled instructed. "And bend your knees further." He was staring straight into an AV pillar on one of the blocks.

She paused irately, and thought about it. The solidity of the camisole buttons wavered, and the hoops fell off allowing the flimsy fabric to shift still further apart. "Is this quite necessary?" she asked.

"Trust me, darling. I've directed enough commercials in my time. Sex always sells: primary rule of advertising. And that's what this is, no matter what you want to call it. So I want legs and cleavage for the boys to drool over, and confidence to inspire the girls. That way we get them both feeding from our palm."

"Okay," she grumbled.

"Wait."

"*Now* what?"

He looked up from the AV pillar. "You're not distinctive enough."

Kiera glanced down at the slope of her breasts on show. "You are making a very bad joke."

"No no, not your tits, darling; they're just fine. No, it's the overall image, it's so passé." Fingers plucked at his lower lip.

"I know, let's be astonishingly bold. I want you lounging there, just as you are, but have a red scarf wrapped around your ankle."

Kiera stared at him.

"Please, love? Trust, remember?"

She concentrated again. The appropriate fabric materialized around her ankle, a silk handkerchief tied in a single knot. Blood red, and see if he caught the hint.

"That's wonderful. You look wild, gypsy exotic. I'm in love with you already."

"Can I start now?"

"Ready when you are."

Kiera took a moment to compose herself again, aiming for an expression which was the epitome of adolescent coyness. The water tinkled melodically beside her, other youths smiled and held each other close, children raced past her boulder. She grinned indulgently at them, and waved as they played their merry game. Then her head came around slowly to look straight at the sensor block.

"You know, they're going to tell you that you shouldn't be accessing this recording," she said. "In fact, they're going to get quite serious about that; your mum and dad, your big brother, the authorities in charge of wherever you live. Can't think why. Except, of course, I'm one of the possessed, one of the demons threatening 'the fabric of the universe,' your universe. I'm your enemy, apparently. I'm pretty sure I am, anyway; the Confederation Assembly says so. So . . . that must be right. Yes? I mean, President Haaker came here and looked me over, and talked to me, and found out all about me, what I want, what I hate, which is my favourite MF artist, what frightens me. I don't remember that time when I spoke to him. But it must have happened, because the ambassadors of every government in the Assembly voted that I'm officially to be denounced as a monster. They wouldn't do that, not all those bright, serious, wise people, unless they had all the facts at their disposal, now would they?

"Actually, the one lonely fact they had, and voted on, was that Laton killed ten thousand Edenists because they were possessed. You remember Laton. Some sort of hero a while back, I've been told, something about a habitat called Jantrit.

I wonder if he asked the individuals on Pernik island if they wanted to be exterminated. I wonder if they all said yes.

"They've done to us what they do to kids the universe over, lumped us together and said we're bad. One thug hits somebody, and every kid is a violent hooligan. You know that's truth, it happens all the time in your neighbourhood. You're never an individual, not to them. One wrong, all wrong. That's the way we're treated.

"Well, not here, not in Valisk. Maybe some possessed want to conquer the universe. If they do, then I hope the Confederation Navy fights them. I hope the navy wins. Those sort of possessed frighten me as much as they frighten you. That's not what we're about, it's so stupid, it's so obsolete. There's no need for that kind of behaviour, that kind of thinking, not anymore. Not now.

"Those of us here on Valisk have seen what the power which comes of possession can really do when it's applied properly. Not when it's turned to destruction, but when it's used to help people. That's what frightens President Haaker, because it threatens the whole order of his precious world. And if that goes, he goes, along with all his power and his wealth. Because that's what this is really all about: money. Money buys people, money lets companies invest and consolidate their markets, money pays for weapons, tax money pays for bureaucracy, money buys political power. Money is a way of rationing what the universe has to offer us. But the universe is infinite, it doesn't need to be rationed.

"Those of us who have emerged from the dead of night can break the restrictions of this corrupt society. We can live outside it, and flourish. We can burn your Jovian Bank ration cards and liberate you from the restrictions others impose on you." Her smile tilted towards shy impishness. She held a hand out towards the sensor block, palm open. Her fingers closed into a fist, then parted again. A pile of ice-blue diamonds glittered in her palm, laced with slim platinum chains.

She grinned back at the sensor block, then tipped them carelessly onto the grass. "You see, it's so simple. Items, objects, goods, the capitalist stockpile, exist only to give joy; for us living in Valisk they are an expression of emotion. Economics is dead, and true equality will rise out of the ashes.

We've turned our back on materialism, rejected it completely. It has no purpose anymore. Now we can live as we please, develop our minds not our finances. We can love one another without the barrier of fear now that honesty has replaced greed, for greed has died along with all the other vices of old. Valisk has become a place where every wish is granted, however small, however grand. And not just for those of us who have returned. To keep it to ourselves would be a cardinal act of greed. It is for everyone. For this aspect of our existence is the part which your society will despise the most, will curse us for. We are taking Valisk out of this physical dimension of the universe, launching it to a continuum where everyone will have our energistic power. It's a place where I can take on form, and return the body I have borrowed. All of us lost souls will be real people again, without conflict, and without the pain it takes for us to manifest ourselves here.

"And now I'll make our offer. We open Valisk to all people of goodwill, to those of a gentle disposition, to everyone sick of having to struggle to survive, and sick also of the petty limits governments and cultures place on the human heart. You are welcome to join us on our voyage. We shall be leaving soon, before the navy warships come and their bombs burn us for the crime of being what we are: people who embrace peace.

"I promise you that anyone who reaches Valisk will be granted a place among us. It will not be an easy journey for you, but I urge you to try. Good luck, I'll be waiting."

The white cotton changed, darkening into a swirling riot of colour, as if skirt and camisole were made from a thousand butterfly wings. Marie Skibbow's smile shone through, bringing a natural warmth all of its own to the watchers. Children flocked around her, giggling merrily, hurling poppy petals into the air so that when they fell they became a glorious scarlet snowstorm. She let them take her hands and hurry her forwards, eager to join their game.

The recording ended.

Despite being nearly fifty years old, the implant surgery care ward boasted an impressive array of contemporary equipment. Medicine, along with its various modern sidelines, was a profitable business in Culey asteroid.

The annex to which Erick Thakrar had been assigned (Duchamp hadn't paid for a private room) was halfway along the ward's main hall, a standardized room of pearl-white composite walls and glare-free lighting panels, the template followed by hospitals right across the Confederation. Patients were monitored by a pair of nurses at a central console just inside the door. They weren't strictly necessary, the hospital's sub-sentient processor array was a lot faster at spotting metabolic anomalies developing. But hospitals always adopted the person-in-the-loop philosophy; invalids wanted the human touch, it was reassuring. As well as being profitable, medicine was one of the last remaining labour-intensive industries, resisting automation with an almost Luddite zeal.

The operation to implant Erick's artificial tissue units had begun fifteen minutes after his removal from zero-tau. He'd been in surgery for sixteen hours; at one point he had four different surgical teams working on various parts of him. When he came out of theatre, thirty per cent of his body weight was accounted for by artificial tissue.

On the second day after his operation he had a visitor: a woman in her mid-thirties with unobtrusive Oriental features. She smiled at the ward's duty nurse, claiming she was Erick's second cousin, and could even have proved it with an ID card if she'd been pressed. The nurse simply waved her down the ward.

When she entered the annex two of the six beds were unoccupied. One had the privacy screen down to reveal an elderly man who gave her a hopeful talk-to-me-please look, the remaining three were fully screened. She smiled blandly at the lonely man, and turned to Erick's bed, datavising a code at the screen control processor. The screen split at the foot of the bed, shrinking back towards the walls. The visitor stepped inside, and promptly datavised a closure code at it.

She tried not to flinch when she saw the figure lying on the active shapeform mattress. Erick was completely coated in a medical package, as if the translucent green substance had been tailored into a skintight leotard. Tubes emerged from his neck and along the side of his ribs, linking him with a tall stack of medical equipment at the head of the bed, supplying the nanonics with specialist chemicals needed to bolster the traumatized flesh, and syphoning out toxins and dead blood cells.

Two bloodshot, docile eyes looked out at her from holes in the package smothering his face. "Who are you?" he datavised. There was no opening in the package for his mouth, only a ventlike aperture over his nose.

She datavised her identification code, then added: "Lieutenant Li Chang, CNIS. Hello, Captain, we received your notification code at the Navy Bureau."

"Where the hell have you people been? I sent that code yesterday."

"Sorry, sir, there's been a system-wide security flap for the last two days. It's kept us occupied. And your shipmates have been hanging around the ward. I judged it best that they didn't encounter me."

"Very smart. You know which ship I came in on?"

"Yes, sir, the *Villeneuve's Revenge*. You made it back from Lalonde."

"Just barely. I've compiled a report of our mission and what happened. It is vital you get this datapackage to Trafalgar. We're not dealing with Laton, this is something else, something terrible."

Li Chang had to order a neural nanonics nerve override to retain her impassive composure. After everything he'd been through to obtain this data . . . "Yes, sir; it's possession. We received a warning flek from the Confederation Assembly three days ago."

"You know?"

"Yes, sir, it appears the possessed left Lalonde before you got there, presumably on the *Yaku*. They're starting to infiltrate other planets. It was Laton who alerted us to the danger."

"Laton?"

"Yes, sir. He managed to block them on Atlantis, he warned the Edenists there before he kamikazed. The news companies are broadcasting the full story if you want to access it."

"Oh, shit." A muffled whimper was just audible from behind the package over his face. "Shit, shit, shit. This was all for nothing? I went through this for a story the news compa-

nies are shoving out? This?" An arm was raised a few centimetres from the mattress, shaking heavily as though the
package coating were too burdensome to lift.

"I'm sorry, sir," she whispered.

His eyes were watering. The facial package sucked the
salty liquid away with quiet efficiency. "There's some information left in the report. Important information. Vacuum can
defeat them. God, can it defeat them. The navy will need to
know that."

"Yes, sir, I'm sure they will." Li Chang hated how shallow
that sounded, but what else was there to say? "If you'd like to
datavise the report to me I'll include it on our next communiqué to Trafalgar." She assigned the burst of encrypted data
to a fresh memory cell.

"You'd better check my medical record," Erick said. "And
run a review on the team who operated on me. The surgeons
are bound to realize I was hardwired for weapons implants."

"I'll get on to it. We have some assets in the hospital staff."

"Good. Now for Heaven's sake, tell the head of station I
want taking off this bloody assignment. The next time I see
André Duchamp's face I'm going to smack his teeth so far
down his throat he'll be using them to eat through his arse. I
want the asteroid's prosecution office to formally charge the
captain and crew of the *Villeneuve's Revenge* with piracy and
murder. I have the appropriate files, it's all there, our attack on
the *Krystal Moon*."

"Sir, Captain Duchamp has some contacts of his own here,
political ones. That's how he circumvented the civil starflight
quarantine to dock here. We could probably have him arrested, but whoever that contact is, they aren't going to want
the embarrassment of a trial. He'd probably be allowed to
post bail, that's if he doesn't simply disappear quietly. Culey
asteroid is really not the kind of place to bring that kind of
charge against an independent trader. It's one of the reasons
so many of them use it, which is why CNIS has such a large
station here."

"You won't arrest him? You won't stop this madness? A fif-
teen-year-old girl was killed when we attacked that cargo
ship. Fifteen!"

"I don't recommend we arrest him here, sir, because he

wouldn't stay under arrest. If the service is to have any chance of nailing him, it ought to be done somewhere else." There was no answer, no response. The only clue she had that Erick was still alive came from the slow-blinking coloured LEDs on the medical equipment. "Sir?"

"Yes. Okay, I want him so bad I can even wait to be sure. You don't understand that people like him, ships like his, they've got to be stopped, and stopped utterly. We should fling every crew member from every independent trader down onto a penal planet, break the ships down for scrap and spare parts."

"Yes, sir."

"Go away, Lieutenant. Make arrangements to have me shipped back to Trafalgar. I'll do my convalescing there, thank you."

"Sir . . . Yes, sir. I'll relay the request. It might be some time before you can actually be transferred. As I said, there is a Confederation-wide quarantine order in effect. We could have you taken to a more private area and guarded."

Again there was a long interval. Li Chang bore it stoically.

"No," Erick datavised. "I will remain here. Duchamp is paying, perhaps my injuries along with the repairs his ship needs will be enough to bankrupt the bastard. I expect Culey's authorities regard bad debts as a serious crime, after all that's money which is at stake, not morality."

"Yes, sir."

"The first ship out of here, Lieutenant, I want to be on it."

"I'll set it up, sir. You can count on me."

"Good. Go now."

Feeling as guilty as she'd ever done in her life, she turned quickly and datavised the screen to open. One quick glance over her shoulder as she left—hoping to ease her conscience, hoping to see him relaxing into a peaceful sleep—showed his eyes were still open at the bottom of their green pits; a numbed angry stare, focused on nothing. Then the screen flowed shut.

• • • •

Alkad Mzu exited the Nyiru traffic control sensor display as soon as the wormhole interstice closed. At fifty thousand kilometres there hadn't been much of an optical-band return, the visualization was mostly graphics superimposed over enhanced pixel representations. But for all the lack of true visibility, there was no fooling them. *Udat* had departed.

She looked out through the observation lounge's giant window which was set in the rock wall just above the asteroid's docking ledge. A slender slice of stars were visible below the edge of the bulky non-rotational spaceport a kilometre and a half away. Narok itself drifted into view; seemingly smothered in white cloud, its albedo was sufficient to cast a frail radiance. Faint elongated shadows sprang up across the ledge, streaming away from the blackhawks and voidhawks perched on their docking pedestals. They tracked around over the smooth rock like a clock's second hand. Alkad waited until Narok vanished below the sharp synthetic horizon. The swallow manoeuvre would be complete now. One more, and the resonance device she had secreted on board would be activated.

There wasn't really any feeling of success, let alone happiness. A lone blackhawk and its greedy captain were hardly compensation for Garissa's suffering, the genocide of an entire people. It was a start, though. If nothing else, internal proof that she still retained the ardent determination of thirty years ago when she had kissed Peter goodbye. "*Au revoir*, only," he'd insisted. An insistence she'd willed herself to believe in.

Maybe the easy, simple heat of hatred had cooled over the decades. But the act remained, ninety-five million dead people dependent on her for some degree of justice. It wasn't rational, she knew, this dreadful desire for revenge. But it was so sadly human. Sometimes she thought it was all she had left to prove her humanity with, a single monstrously flawed compulsion. Every other genuine emotion seemed to have disappeared while she was in Tranquillity, suppressed behind the need to behave normally. As normal as anyone whose home planet has been destroyed.

The dusky shadows appeared again, odd outlines stroking

across the rock ledge, matching the asteroid's rotation. *Udat* would have performed its third swallow by now.

Alkad crossed herself quickly. "Dear Mother Mary, please welcome their souls to Heaven. Grant them deliverance from the crimes they committed, for we are all children who know not what we do."

What lies! But the Maria Legio Church was an ingrained and essential part of Garissan culture. She could never discard it. She didn't want to discard it, stupid as that paradox was for an unbeliever. There was so little of their identity left that any remnant should be preserved and cherished. Perhaps future generations could find comfort among its teachings.

Narok fell from sight again. Alkad turned her back on the starfield and walked towards the door at the back of the observation lounge; in the low gravity field her feet took twenty seconds to touch the ground between each step. The medical nanonic packages she wore around her ankles and forearms had almost finished their repair work now, making her lazy movements a lot easier.

Two of the *Samaku*'s crew were waiting patiently for her just inside the door, one of them an imposing-looking cosmonik. They fell in step on either side of her. Not that she thought she really needed bodyguards, not yet, but she wasn't willing to take the chance. She was hauling around too much responsibility to risk jeopardizing the mission over a simple accident, or even someone recognizing her (this was a Kenyan-ethnic star system, after all).

The three of them took a commuter lift along the spindle to the spaceport where the *Samaku* was docked. Chartering the Adamist starship had cost her a quarter of a million fuseodollars, a reckless sum of money, but necessary. She needed to get to the Dorados as quickly as possible. The intelligence agencies would be searching for her with a terrifying urgency now she'd evaded them on Tranquillity, and coincidentally proved they were right to fear her all along. *Samaku* was an independent trader; its military-grade navigational systems, and the bonuses she promised, would ensure a short voyage time.

Actually transferring over the cash to the captain had been the single most decisive moment for her; since escaping Tranquillity every other action had been unavoidable. Now, though, she was fully committed. The people she was scheduled to join in the Dorados had spent thirty years preparing for her arrival. She was the final component. The flight to destroy Omuta's star, which had started in the *Beezling* three decades ago, was about to enter its terminal phase.

• • •

The *Intari* started to examine the local space environment as soon as it slipped out of its wormhole terminus. Satisfied there was no immediate hazard from asteroidal rubble or high-density dust clouds it accelerated in towards Norfolk at three gees.

Norfolk was the third star system it had visited since leaving Trafalgar five days earlier, and the second to last on its itinerary. Captain Nagar had ambiguous feelings about carrying the First Admiral's warning of possession; in time-honoured fashion Adamists did tend to lay a lot of the blame on the messenger. Typical of their muddled thinking and badly integrated personalities. Nonetheless he was satisfied with the time *Intari* had made, few voidhawks could do better.

We may have a problem, *Intari* told its crew. The navy squadron is still in orbit, they have taken up a ground fire support formation.

Nagar used the voidhawk's senses to see for himself, his mind accepting the starship's unique perception. The planet registered as a steeply warped flaw in the smooth structure of space-time, its gravity field drawing in a steady sleet of the minute particles which flowed through the interplanetary medium. A clutter of small mass points were in orbit around the flaw, shining brightly in both the magnetic and electromagnetic spectrum.

They should have departed last week, he said rhetorically. At his silent wish *Intari* obligingly focused its sensor blisters on the planet itself, shifting its perceptive emphasis to the optical spectrum. Norfolk's bulk filled his mind, the twin sources of illumination turning the surface into two distinctly coloured hemispheres, divided by a small wedge of genuine night. The land which shone a twilight vermillion below

Duchess's radiance appeared perfectly normal, complying with *Intari*'s memory of their last visit, fifteen years ago. Duke's province, however, was dappled by circles of polluted red cloud.

They glow, *Intari* said, concentrating on the lone slice of night.

Before Nagar could comment on the unsettling spectacle, the communications console reported a signal from the squadron's commanding admiral, querying their arrival. When Nagar had confirmed their identity the admiral gave him a situation update on the hapless agrarian planet. Eighty percent of the inhabited islands were now covered by the red cloud, which seemed to block all attempts at communication. The planetary authorities were totally incapable of maintaining order in the affected zones; police and army alike had mutinied and joined the rebels. Even the navy marine squads sent in to assist the army had dropped out of contact. Norwich itself had fallen to the rebel forces yesterday, and now the streamers of red cloud were consolidating above the city. That substance more than anything had prevented the admiral from attempting any kind of retaliation using the starships' ground bombardment weapons. How, she asked, could the rebels produce such an effect?

"They can't," Nagar told her. "Because they're not rebels." He began datavising the First Admiral's warning over the squadron's secure communications channels.

Captain Layia remained utterly silent as the datavise came through. Once it was finished she looked round at her equally subdued crew.

"So now we know what happened to the *Tantu*," Furay said. "Hellfire, I hope the chase ship the admiral dispatched kept up with it."

Layia gave him an agitated glance, uncomfortable notions stirring in her brain. "You brought our three passengers up from the same aerodrome as the *Tantu*'s spaceplane, and at more or less the same time. The little girl was caught up in some sort of ruckus: a weird fire. You said so yourself. And they originally came from Kesteven island, where it all started."

"Oh, come on!" Furay protested. The others were all staring at him, undecided but definitely suspicious. "They fled from Kesteven. They bought passage on the *Far Realm* hours before the hangar fire."

"We're suffering from glitches," Tilia said.

"Really?" Furay asked scathingly. "You mean more than usual?"

Tilia glared at the pilot.

"Slightly more," Layia murmured seriously. "But nothing exceptional, I admit." The *Far Realm* might have been an SII ship, but that didn't mean the company necessarily operated an exemplary maintenance procedure. Cost cutting was a major company priority these days, not like when she started flying.

"They're not possessed," Endron said.

Layia was surprised by the soft authority in his voice, he sounded so certain. "Oh?"

"I examined Louise as soon as she came on board. The body sensors worked perfectly. As did the medical nanonics I used on her. If she was possessed the energistic effect the First Admiral spoke of would have glitched them."

Layia considered what he said, and gave her grudging agreement. "You're probably right. And they haven't tried to hijack us."

"They were concerned about the *Tantu*, as well. Fletcher hated those rebels."

"Yes. All right, point made. That just leaves us with the question of who's going to break the news to them, tell them exactly what's happened to their homeworld."

Furay found himself the centre of attention again. "Oh, great, thanks a lot."

By the time he'd drifted through the various decks to the lounge the passengers were using, the squadron admiral had begun to issue orders to the ships under her command. Two frigates, the *Ldora* and the *Levêque*, were to remain in Norfolk orbit where they could enforce the quarantine; any attempt to leave the planet, even in a spaceplane, was to be met with an instant armed response. Any commercial starship that arrived was to be sent on its way, again failure to comply was to be met with force. The *Intari* was to continue on its warning mission. The rest of the squadron was to return to 6th

Fleet headquarters at Tropea in anticipation of reassignment. *Far Realm* was released from its support duties and contract.

After a brief follow-on discussion with the admiral, Layia announced: "She's given permission for us to fly directly back to Mars. Who knows how long this emergency is going to last, and I don't want to be stranded in the Tropea system indefinitely. Technically, we're on military service, so the civil starflight proscription doesn't apply. At the worst case it'll be something for the lawyers to argue about when we get back."

With his mood mildly improved at the news they were going home, Furay slid into the lounge. He came through the ceiling hatch, head first, which inverted his visual orientation. The three passengers watched him flip around and touch his feet to a stikpad. He gave them an awkward grin. Louise and Genevieve were looking at him so intently, knowing something was wrong, yet still trusting. It wasn't a burden he was used to.

"First the good news," he said. "We're leaving for Mars within the hour."

"Fine," Louise said. "What's the bad news?"

He couldn't meet her questing gaze, nor that of Genevieve. "The reason we're leaving. A voidhawk has just arrived with an official warning from the First Admiral and the Confederation Assembly. They think . . . there's the possibility that people are being . . . possessed. There was a battle on Atlantis; someone called Laton warned us about it. Look, something strange is happening to people, and that's what they're calling it. I'm sorry. The admiral thinks that's what has been happening on Norfolk, too."

"You mean it's happening on other planets as well?" Genevieve asked in alarm.

"Yes." Furay frowned at her, goose bumps rising along his arms. There hadn't been the slightest scepticism in her voice. Children were always curious. He looked at Fletcher, then Louise. Both of them were concerned, yes, but not doubting. "You knew. Didn't you? You knew."

"Of course." Louise gave him a bashful smile.

"You knew all along. Holy Christ, why didn't you say

something? If we'd known, if the admiral . . ." He broke off, troubled.

"Quite," Louise said.

He was surprised by just how composed she was. "But—"

"You find it hard enough to accept an official warning from the Confederation Assembly. You would never have believed us, two girls and an estate worker. Now would you?"

Even though there was no gravity, Furay hung his head. "No," he confessed.

11

The heavily wooded valley was as wild and as beautiful as only an old habitat could be. Syrinx wandered off into the forest which came right up to the edge of Eden's single strip of town. She was heartened by just how many trees had survived from the habitat's early days. Their trunks might have swollen, and tilted over, but they were still alive. Wise ancient trees who several centuries ago had discarded the usual parkland concept of discreet order, becoming completely unmanageable, so the habitat didn't even try anymore.

She couldn't remember being happier; though the verdant surroundings were only one contributing factor.

"Separation generates anticipation," Aulie had told her with a mischievous smile as he kissed her goodbye just after lunch. He was probably right, his understanding of emotions was as extensive as his sexual knowledge. That was what made him such a *fabulous* lover, giving him complete control over her responses.

In fact, he was right, Syrinx admitted wistfully. They had only been parted for ninety minutes, and already her body missed him dreadfully. The very notion of what they'd do that night when she had him alone to herself again was glorious.

Their holiday visit to Eden was the talk of all her friends, and her family. She relished that aspect of their affair almost as much as the physical side. Aulie was forty-four, twenty-seven years older than she. In a culture which was too egalitarian and liberal to be shocked, she'd delighted in making a pretty good job of it so far.

There was the odd time when she was aware of the age gulf, this afternoon being one of them. Aulie had wanted to visit one of the caverns in the habitat's endcap which was full of late twenty-first century cybernetic machinery, kept working as a functional museum. Syrinx was hard put to think of anything more boring. Here they were in the first habitat ever grown, five hundred years old, the seat of their culture; and he wanted to take a look at antique robots?

So they'd parted company. Him to his steam engines, leaving her to explore the interior. Eden was much smaller than the other habitats, a cylinder eleven kilometres long, three in diameter; a prototype really. It didn't have starscrapers, the inhabitants lived in a small town ringing the northern endcap. Again, leftovers from a bygone age; simple, quick-to-assemble bungalows of metal and composite, laboriously preserved by their present occupants. Each of them had spruce handkerchief-sized gardens boasting ancient pure genotype plant varieties. The vegetation might not have the size or sharpness of colour owned by their modern descendants, but their context made them a visual treat. Living history.

She picked her way along what she thought were paths, dodging gnarled roots which knitted together at ankle height, ducking under loops of sticky vine. Moss and fungi had colonized every square centimetre of bark, giving each tree its own micro-ecology. It was hot among the trunks, the motionless air cloyingly humid. Her dress with its short skirt and tight top was intended purely to emphasise her adolescent figure for Aulie's benefit. In here it was totally impractical, damp fabric fighting every movement of her limbs. Her hair died within minutes, sodden strands flopping down to grease her shoulders. Green and brown smears multiplied over her arms and legs, nature's tribal war paint.

Despite the inconveniences she kept going forwards. The sensation of expectancy growing all the while, and nothing to do with Aulie anymore. This was something more ambivalent, a notion of approaching divinity.

She emerged from the jumbled trees into a glade which accommodated a calm lake that was almost sealed over with pink and white water lilies. Black swans drifted slowly along the few remaining tracts of open water. A bungalow sat on the marshy shore, very different from those in the town; it was built from stone and wood, standing on stilts above the reeds. A high, steeply curved blue slate roof overhung the walls, providing an all-round veranda, and giving the building an acutely Eastern aspect.

Syrinx walked towards it, more curious than apprehensive. The building was completely incongruous, yet apposite at the same time. Copper wind chimes, completely blue from age and exposure to the elements, tinkled softly as she climbed the rickety steps to the veranda which faced out over the lake.

Someone was waiting for her there, an old Oriental man sitting in a wheelchair, dressed in a navy-blue silk jacket, with a tartan rug wrapped around his legs. His face had the porcelain delicacy of the very old. Almost all of his hair had gone, leaving a fringe of silver strands at the back of his head, long enough to come down over his collar. Even the wheelchair was antique, carved from wood, with big thin wheels that had chrome spokes; there was no motor. It looked as though the man hadn't moved out of it for years; he blended into its contours perfectly.

An owl was perched on the veranda balcony, big eyes fixed on Syrinx.

The old man raised a hand with a thousand liver spots on its crinkled yellowing skin. He beckoned. **Come closer.**

Horribly aware of what a mess she looked, Syrinx took a hesitant couple of steps forwards. She glanced sideways, trying to see into the bungalow through its open windows. Empty blackness prowled behind the rectangles. Blackness which hid—

What is my name? the old man asked sharply.

Syrinx swallowed nervously. **You are Wing-Tsit Chong, sir. You invented affinity, and Edenism.**

Sloppy thinking, my dear girl. One does not invent a culture, one nurtures it.

I'm sorry. I can't . . . It's difficult to think. There were shapes flickering in the darkness, consolidating into outlines which she thought she recognized. The owl hooted softly. Guilty, Syrinx jerked her gaze back to Wing-Tsit Chong.

Why is it difficult for you to think?

She gestured to the window. **In there. People. I remember them. I'm sure I do. What am I doing here? I don't remember.**

There is no one inside. Do not allow your imagination

to fill the darkness, Syrinx. You are here for one reason only: to see me.

Why?

Because I have some very important questions to ask you.

Me?

Yes. What is the past, Syrinx?

The past is a summation of events which contribute to making the present everything which it is—

Stop. What is the past?

She shrugged her shoulders, mortified that here she was in front of the founder of Edenism, and couldn't answer a simple question for him. The past is a measure of entropic decay—

Stop. When did I die, what year?

Oh. Two thousand and ninety. She twitched a smile of relief.

And what year were you born?

Two thousand five hundred and eighty.

How old are you now?

Seventeen.

What am I when you are seventeen?

Part of Eden's multiplicity.

What components make up a multiplicity?

People.

No. Not physically, they don't. What are the actual components, name the process involved at death.

Transfer. Oh, memories!

So what is the past?

Memories. She grinned broadly, straightening her shoulders to say formally: The past is a memory.

At last, we achieve progress. Where is the only place your personal past can take form?

In my mind?

Good. And what is the purpose of life?

To experience.

This is so, though from a personal view I would add that life should also be a progression towards truth and purity. But then I remain an intransigent old Buddhist at heart, even after so long. This is why I could not refuse the request from your therapists to talk to you. Apparently I am an icon you respect. Humour quirked his lips for a moment. In such circumstances, for me to assist in your deliverance is an act of *dana* I could not possibly refuse.

Dana?

The Buddhist act of giving, a sacrifice which will allow the *dayaka*, the giver, a glimpse of a higher state, helping in transforming one's own mind.

I see.

I would be surprised if you did, at least fully. Edenism seems to have shied away from religion, which I admit I did not anticipate. However, our current problem is more immediate. We have established that you live to experience, and that your past is only a memory.

Yes.

Can it harm you?

No, she said proudly, the logical answer.

You are incorrect. If that were so you would never learn from mistakes.

I learn from it, yes. But I can't be hurt by it.

You can, however, be influenced by it. Very strongly. I believe we are debating how many angels dance on a pinhead, but influence can be harmful.

I suppose so.

Let me put it another way. You can be troubled by memories.

Yes.

Good. What effect does that have on your life?

If you are wise, it stops you from repeating mistakes, especially if they are painful ones.

This is so. We have established, then, that the past can control you, and you cannot control the past, yes?

Yes.

What about the future?

Sir?

Can the past control the future?

It can influence it, she said cautiously.

Through what medium?

People?

Good. This is karma. Or what Western civilization referred to as reaping the seeds you have sown. In simpler terms it is fate. Your actions in the present decide your future, and your actions are based on the interpretation of past experiences.

I see.

In that respect, what we have in your case is an unfortunate problem.

We do?

Yes. However, before we go any further, I would like you to answer a personal question for me. You are seventeen years old; do you now believe in God? Not some primitive concept as a Creator trumpeted by Adamist religions, but perhaps a higher force responsible for ordering the universe? Be honest with me, Syrinx. I will not be angry whatever the answer. Remember, I am probably the most spiritually inclined of all Edenists.

I believe ... I think ... No, I'm afraid that there might not be.

I will accept that for now. It is a common enough doubt among our kind.

It is?

Indeed. Now, I am going to tell you something about yourself in small stages, and I would like you to apply the most rigorous rational analysis to each statement.

I understand.

This is a perceptual reality, you have been brought here to help you overcome a problem. He smiled kindly, a gesture of his hand inviting her to continue.

If I am undergoing some form of treatment it can't be for physical injuries, I wouldn't need a perceptual reality for that. I must have had some kind of mental breakdown, and this is my therapy session. Even as she said it she could feel her heart rate increase, but the blood quickening in her veins only seemed to make her skin colder.

Very good. But, Syrinx, you did not have a breakdown, your own thought routines are quite exemplary.

Then why am I here?

Why indeed?

Oh, an outside influence?

Yes. A most unpleasant experience.

I've been traumatized.

As I said, your thought routines are impressive. Those of us running your therapy have temporarily blocked your access to your adult memories, thus avoiding contamination of those routines by the trauma. You can, for the moment, think without interference, even though this state does not permit your intellect to function at full capacity.

Syrinx grinned. I'm actually smarter than this?

I prefer the term swifter, myself. But what we have is adequate for our purpose.

The purpose being my therapy. With my adult mind traumatized I wouldn't listen. I was catatonic?

Partly; your withdrawal was within what the psychologist called a psychotic loop. Those responsible for hurting you were trying to force you to do something quite abhorrent. You refused, for love's sake. Edenists everywhere are proud of you for your resistance, yet that obstinacy has led to your current state.

Syrinx gave a downcast smile, not entirely perturbed. Mother always said I had a stubborn streak.

She was entirely correct.

So what must I do now?

You must face the root of what was done to you. The trauma can be overcome; not instantly, but once you allow yourself to remember what happened without it overwhelming you as it has done until now, then the auxiliary memories and emotions can be dealt with one at a time.

That's why you talked about the past, so I can learn to face my memories without the fear, because that's all they are, memories. Harmless in themselves.

Excellent. I will now make them available to you.

She steeled herself, foolish that it was, clenching her stomach muscles and fisting her hands.

Look at the owl, Wing-Tsit Chong instructed. Tell me its name.

The owl blinked at her, and half extended its wings. She stared at the flecked pattern of ochre and hazel feathers. They were running like liquid, becoming midnight-blue and purple.

"*Oenone!*" she shouted. Pernik island rushed towards her at a speed which made her grasp the balcony rail in fright.

Please don't, Syrinx, *Oenone* asked. The deluge of misery and longing entwined with that simple request made her eyes brim with tears. **Don't leave me again.**

Never. Never ever ever ever, beloved. Her whole body was trembling in reaction to the years of memory yawning open in her mind. And right at the end, the last before stinking darkness had grasped at her, most vivid of all, the dungeon and its torturers.

Syrinx?

I'm here, she reassured the voidhawk unsteadily. **It's okay, I'm fine.**

You saved me from them.

How could I not?

I love you.

And I you.

I was right, Wing-Tsit Chong said.

When Syrinx raised her head she saw the old man's face smiling softly, the multiplying wrinkles aging him another decade. **Sir?**

To do what I did all those centuries ago. To allow people to see the love and the sourness which lives in all of us. Only then can we come to terms with what we are. You are living proof of that, young Syrinx. I thank you for that. Now open your eyes.

They are open.

He sighed theatrically. **So pedantic. Then close them.**

Syrinx opened her eyes to look up at a sky-blue ceiling. The dark blobs around the edges of her vision field resolved into three terribly anxious faces bending over her.

"Hello, Mother," she said. It was very difficult to talk, and her body felt as though it were wrapped in a shrunken shiptunic.

Athene started crying.

• • •

There were fifteen holoscreens in the editing suite, arranged in a long line along one wall. All of them were switched on, and the variety of images they displayed was enormous, ranging from a thousand-kilometre altitude view of Amarisk with the red cloud bands mirroring the Juliffe tributary network, to the terrifyingly violent starship battle in orbit above Lalonde; and from Reza Malin's mercenaries flattening the village of Pamiers, to a flock of overexcited young children charging out of a homestead cabin to greet the arrival of the hovercraft.

Out of the five people sitting at the editing suite's table, four of them stared at the screens with the kind of nervous enthusiasm invariably suffered by voyeurs of suffering on a grand scale, where the sheer spectacle of events overcame the agony of any individual casualty. In the middle of her colleagues, Kelly regarded her work with a detachment which was mainly derived from a suppressor program her neural nanonics were running.

"We can't cut anything else," Kate Elvin, the senior news editor, protested.

"I don't like it," said Antonio Whitelocke. He was the head of Collins's Tranquillity office, a sixty-year career staffer who had plodded his way to the top from the Politics and Economics division. An excellent choice for Tranquillity, but hardly empathic with young rover reporters like Kelly Tirrel. Her Lalonde report scared him shitless. "You just can't have a three hour news item."

"Grow some bollocks," Kelly snapped. "Three hours is just dip-in highlights."

"Lowlights," Antonio muttered, glaring at his turbulent new megastar. Her skinhead hairstyle was devastatingly intimidating, and he'd heard all about poor Garfield Lunde. Marketing always complained about the use of non-mainstream image anchors. When he thought of that pretty, feminine young woman who used to present the breakfast round-up just last month he could only worry that one of the possessed had sneaked back from Lalonde after all.

"The balance is perfect," Kate said. "We've incorporated the fundamentals of the doomed mission, and even managed to end on an upbeat note with the rescue. That was a stroke of sheer brilliance, Kelly."

"Well, gee, thanks. I would never have gone with Horst and

the mercs back to the homestead unless it made a better report."

Kate sailed on serenely through the sarcasm; unlike Antonio she'd been a rover once, which had included a fair share of combat assignments. "This edit will satisfy both our corporate objectives, Antonio. First off, the rumour circuit has been overheating ever since *Lady Macbeth* came back; Marketing hasn't even needed to advertise our evening news slot. Everybody in Tranquillity is going to access us tonight—I've heard the opposition are just going to run soap repeats while Kelly's on. And once our audience access they aren't going to stop. We're not just giving them sensenviron impressions of a war, we've got a whole story to tell them here. That always hooks them. Our advertising premium for this is going to be half a million fuseodollars for a thirty-second slot."

"For one show," Antonio grumbled.

"More than one, that's the beauty. Sure, everyone is going to make a flek of tonight. But Kelly brought back over thirty-six hours of her own fleks, and *then* we've got the recordings taken from *Lady Macbeth*'s sensors from the moment they emerged in the Lalonde system. We can milk this for a month with specialist angle interviews, documentaries, and current affairs analysis panels. We've won the ratings war for the whole goddamn year, and we did it on the cheap."

"Cheap! Do you know what we paid that bloody Lagrange Calvert for those sensor recordings?"

"Cheap," Kate insisted. "Tonight alone is going to pay for those. And with universal distribution rights we'll quadruple Collins group profits."

"If we can ever get it distributed," Antonio said.

"Sure we can. Have you accessed the civil starflight prohibition order? It just prevents docking, not departure. Blackhawks can simply stay inside a planet's emergence zone and datavise a copy to our local office. We'll have to pay the captains a little more, but not much, because they're losing revenue sitting on the endcap ledges. This can work. It'll be head office seats for us after this."

"What, after this?" Kelly said.

"Come on, Kelly." Kate squeezed her shoulder. "We know it was rough, we felt it for ourselves. But the quarantine is going to stop the possessed from spreading, and now we're alert to the problem the security forces can contain them if there is an outbreak. They won on Lalonde because it's so damn backwards."

"Oh, sure." Kelly was operating on stimulant programs alone now, fatigue toxin antidote humming melodically in her head. "Saving the galaxy is a breeze now we know. Hell, it's only the dead we're up against after all."

"If you're not up to this, Kelly, then say so," Antonio said, then played his mastercard. "We can use another anchor. Kirstie McShane?"

"That bitch!"

"So we can go ahead as scheduled, can we?"

"I want to put in more of Pamiers, and Shaun Wallace. Those are the kind of events which will make people more aware of the situation."

"Wallace is depressing, he spent that entire interview telling you that the possessed couldn't be beaten."

"Damn right. Shaun's vital, he tells us what we really need to know, to face up to the real problem."

"Which is?"

"Death. Everyone's going to die, Antonio, even you."

"No, Kelly, I can't sanction this sort of slant. It's as bad as that Tyrathca Sleeping God ceremony you recorded."

"I shouldn't have let you cut that out. Nobody even knew the Tyrathca had a religion before."

"Xenoc customs are hardly relevant at a time like this," he said.

"Kelly, we can use that Tyrathca segment in a documentary at a later date," Kate said. "Right now we need to finalize the edit. Christ, you're on-line in another forty minutes."

"You want to keep me sweet, then put in all of Shaun's interview."

"We've got half of it," Antonio said. "All the salient points are covered."

"Hardly. Look, we have got to bring home to people what possession is really all about, the meaning behind the act," Kelly said. "So far all the majority of Confederation citizens have had is this poxy official warning from the Assembly. It's an abstract, a problem on another planet. People have to learn it's not that simple, that there's more to this disaster than simple physical security. We have to deal with the philosophical issues as well."

Antonio pressed the palm of his hand onto his brow, wincing.

"You don't get it, do you?" Kelly asked hotly. Her arm waved at the holoscreens with their damning images. "Didn't you access *any* of this? Don't you understand? We have to get this across to people. I can do that for you. Not Kirstie blowbrain McShane. I was there, I can make it more real for anyone who accesses the report."

Antonio looked at the holoscreen which showed Pat Halahan running through the smoky ruins of Pamiers, blasting his bizarre attackers to shreds of gore. "Great. Just what we need."

•   •   •

This just wasn't the way Ione had expected it to go. Joshua hadn't even looked at her bedroom door when they arrived back at the apartment, let alone show any eagerness. There had been times with him when she hadn't made it to the bed before her skirt was up around her waist.

Yet somehow she knew this wasn't entirely due to the traumas of the mission. He was intent and troubled, not frightened. Very unfamiliar territory as far as Joshua was concerned.

He'd simply had a shower and a light supper, then settled down in her big settee. When she sat beside him she was too uncertain about the reaction to even rest her hand on his arm.

I wonder if it's that girl on Norfolk? she asked dubiously.

He has endured some difficult times, Tranquillity answered. You must expect his usual behaviour to be toned down.

Not like this. I can see he's been shaken up, but this is more.

The human mind is constantly maturing. External events dictate the speed of the maturation. If he has begun to think harder for himself because of Lalonde, surely this is no bad thing?

Depends what you want from him. He was so perfect for me before. So very uncomplicated, the roguish charmer who would never try to claim me.

I believe you also mentioned something about sex on occasion.

Yeah, all right, that too. It was great, and completely guilt free. I picked him up, remember? What more could a girl with my kind of responsibilities want? He was someone who was never going to try and interfere with my duties as the Lord of Ruin. Politics simply didn't interest him.

A husband would be preferable to a casual lover. Someone who is always there for you.

You're my husband.

You love me, and I love you; it could never be anything else since I gave birth to you. But you are still human, you need a human companion. Look at voidhawk captains, the perfect example of mental symbiosis.

I know. Maybe I'm just feeling jealous.

Of the Norfolk girl? Why? You know how many lovers Joshua has had.

Not of her. Ione looked at Joshua's profile as he stared out of the living room's big window. Of me. Me a year ago. The old story, you never know what you have until it's gone.

He is right next to you. Reach out. I am sure he needs comfort as much as you.

He's not there, not anymore. Not my original Joshua. Did you see that flying he did? Gaura's memory of the Lagrange stunt nearly gave me a heart attack. I never realized just how good a captain he is. How could I ever take that away from him? He lives for space, for flying *Lady Mac* and what that can give him. Remember that last argument we had before he left for Lalonde? I think he was right. He's achieved his métier. Flying is sequenced into his genes the way dictatorship is in mine. I can't take that away from him any more than he could take you away from me.

I think you may be stretching the metaphor slightly.

Maybe. We were young, and we had fun, and it was lovely. I've got the memories.

He had fun. You are pregnant. He has responsibilities to the child.

Does he? I don't think mothers require a big tough hunter gatherer to support them nowadays. And monogamy becomes progressively more difficult the longer we live. Geneering has done more to change the old till death do us part concept than any social radicalism.

Doesn't your child deserve a loving environment?

My baby will have a loving environment. How can you even question that?

I do not question your intentions. I am simply pointing out the practicalities of the situation. At the moment you are unable to provide the child with a complete family.

That's very reactionary.

I admit I am arguing on the extreme. I am not a fundamentalist, I simply wish to concentrate your thoughts. Everything else in your life has been planned and accounted for, the child has not. Conception is something you have done all for yourself. I do not wish it to become a mistake. I love you too much for that.

Father had other children.

Who were given to the Edenists so that they would be brought up in the greatest possible family environment. A whole world of family.

She almost laughed out loud. Imagine that, Saldanas became Edenists. We made the transition in the end. Does King Alastair know about that?

You are ducking the issue, Ione. One child of the Lord of Ruin is brought up with me as a parental, the heir. The others are not. As a parent you have a responsibility to their future.

Are you saying I've been irresponsible conceiving this child?

Only you can answer that. Were you depending on Joshua to be a stay-at-home father? Even then you must have known how unlikely that was.

God, all this argument just because Joshua looks moody.

I am sorry. I have upset you.

No. You've done what you wanted to do, made me think. For some of us it's painful, especially if you're like me and hadn't really considered the consequences of your actions. It gets me all resentful and defensive. But I'll do the best for my child.

I know you will, Ione.

She blushed at the tenderness of the mental tone. Then she leaned against Joshua. "I was worried while you were gone," she said.

He took a sip of his Norfolk Tears. "You were lucky. I was scared shitless most of the time."

"Yes. Lagrange Calvert."

"Jesus, don't you start."

"If you didn't want the publicity, you shouldn't have sold *Lady Mac*'s sensor recordings to Collins."

"It's hard to say no to Kelly."

Ione squinted at him. "So I gather."

"I meant: it's hard to refuse that kind of money. Especially given my situation. The fee I got from Terrance Smith isn't going to cover *Lady Mac*'s repairs. And I can't see the Lalonde Development Company ever handing over the balance on our contract, given there isn't a Lalonde left to develop anymore. But the money I got from Collins will cover everything, and leave me happily in the black."

"Not forgetting the money you made on the Norfolk run."

"Yeah, that too. But I didn't want to break into that, it's kind of like a reserve I'm holding back for when everything settles down again."

"My hero optimist. Do you think the universe is going to settle down?"

Joshua didn't like the way the conversation was progressing. He knew her well enough now; she was steering, hoping to angle obliquely into the subject she wanted to discuss. "Who knows? Are we going to finish up talking about Dominique?"

Ione raised her head from his shoulder to give him a puzzled glance. "No. What made you ask that?"

"Not sure. I thought you wanted to talk about us, and what happens after. Dominique and the Vasilkovsky line played a heavy part in my original plans from here on in."

"There isn't going to be an after, Joshua, not in the sense of returning to the kind of existence we had before. Knowing there's an afterlife is going to tilt people's perception on life for ever."

"Yeah. It is pretty deep when you think about it."

"That's your considered in-depth analysis of the situation is it?" For a moment she thought she'd gone and wounded him. But he just gave a gaunt smile. Not angry.

"Yeah," he said, quiet and serious. "It's deep. I had three bloody narrow escapes inside two days on that Lalonde mission. If I'd made one mistake, Ione, just one, I'd be dead now. Only I wouldn't, as we now know, I'd be trapped in the beyond. And if Shaun Wallace was telling the truth—and I suspect he was—then I'd be screaming silently to be let back in no matter what the cost or who had to pay it."

"That's horrible."

"Yes. I sent Warlow to his death. I think I knew that even before he went out of the airlock. And now he's out there, or in there—somewhere, with all the other souls. He might even be watching us now, begging to be given sensation. The trouble with that is, I do owe him." Joshua put his head back on the silk cushions, staring up at the ceiling. "Do I owe him big enough for that, though? Jesus."

"If he was your friend, he wouldn't ask."

"Maybe."

Ione sat up and reached for the bottle to pour herself another measure of Norfolk Tears.

I'm going to ask him, she told Tranquillity.

Surely you are not about to ask for my blessing?

No. But I'd welcome your opinion.

Very well. I believe he has the necessary resources to complete the task; but then he always has. Whether he is the most desirable candidate still presents me with something of a dilemma. I acknowledge he is maturing; and he would not knowingly betray you. Impetuosity does weigh against him, however.

Yes. Yet I value that trait above all.

I am aware of this. I even accept it, when it applies to your first child and my future. But do you have the right to make that gamble when it concerns the Alchemist?

Maybe not. Although there might be a way around it. And I have simply got to do something. "Joshua?"

"Yeah. Sorry, didn't mean to go all moody on you."

"That's all right. I have a little problem of my own right now."

"You know I'll help if I can."

"That's the first part, I was going to ask you anyway. I'm not sure I can trust anyone else with this. I'm not even sure I can trust you."

"This sounds interesting."

She took a breath, committed now, and began: "Do you remember, about a year ago, a woman called Dr Alkad Mzu contacted you about a possible charter?"

He ran a quick check through his neural nanonics memory cells. "I got her. She said she was interested in going to the Garissa system. Some kind of memorial flight. It was pretty weird, and she never followed it up."

"No, thank God. She asked over sixty captains about a similar charter."

"Sixty?"

"Yes, Tranquillity and I believe it was an attempt to confuse the intelligence agency teams who keep her under observation."

"Ah." Instinct kicked in almost immediately, riding a wave of regret. This was big-time, and major trouble. It almost made him happy they hadn't leapt straight into bed, unlike the old days (a year ago, ha!). For him it was odd, but he was simply too ambivalent about his own feelings. And he could see how she'd been thrown by his just-old-friends approach, too.

Sex would have been so easy; he just couldn't bring himself to do it with someone he genuinely liked when it didn't mean what it used to. That would have been too much like betrayal. **I can't do that to her.** Which was a first.

Ione was giving him a cautious, inquiring look. In itself an offer.

I can stop it now if I want.

It was sometimes easy for him to forget that this blond twenty-year-old was technically an entire government, the repository of state, and interstellar, secrets. Secrets it didn't always pay to know about; invariably the most fascinating kind.

"Go on," Joshua said.

She smiled faintly in acknowledgement. "There are eight separate agencies with stations here; they have been watching Dr Mzu for nearly twenty-five years now."

"Why?"

"They believe that just before Garissa was destroyed she designed some kind of doomsday device called the Alchemist. Nobody knows what it is, or what it does, only that the Garissan Department of Defence was pouring billions into a crash-development project to get it built. The CNIS have been investigating the case for over thirty years now, ever since they first heard rumours that it was being built."

"I saw three men following her when she left Harkey's Bar that night," Joshua said, running a search and retrieval program through his neural nanonics. "Oh, hell, of course. The Omuta sanctions have been lifted; they were the ones who committed the Garissa genocide. You don't think she'd . . . ?"

"She already has. This is not for general release, but last week Alkad Mzu escaped from Tranquillity."

"Escaped?"

"Yes. She turned up here twenty-six years ago and took a job at the Laymil project. My father promised the Confederation Navy she would neither be allowed to leave nor pass on any technical information relating to the Alchemist to other governments or astroengineering conglomerates. It was an almost ideal solution; everyone knows Tranquillity has no expansionist ambitions, and at the same time she could be observed continually by the habitat personality. The only other alternative was to execute her immediately. My father and the then First Admiral both agreed the Confederation should not have access to a new kind of doomsday device; antimatter is quite bad enough. I continued that policy."

"Until last week."

"Yes. Unfortunately, she made total fools out of all of us."

"I thought Tranquillity's observation of the interior was perfect. How could she possibly get out without you knowing?"

"Your friend Meyer lifted her away clean. The *Udat* actually swallowed inside the habitat and took her on board. There was nothing we could do to stop him."

"Jesus! I thought my Lagrange point stunt was risky."

"Quite. Like I said, her escape leaves me with one hell of a problem."

"She's gone to fetch the Alchemist?"

"Hard to think of any other reason, especially given the timing. The only real puzzle about this is, if it exists, why hasn't it been used already?"

"The sanctions. No . . ." He started to concentrate on the problem. "There was only ever one navy squadron on blockade duties. A sneak raid would have a good chance of getting through. That's if one ship was all it took to fire it at the planet."

"Yes. The more we know about Dr Mzu, the less we understand the whole Alchemist situation. But I really don't think her ultimate goal can be in any doubt."

"Right. So she's probably gone to collect it, and use it. The *Udat* has a fair payload capacity; and Meyer's seen combat duty in his time, he can take a bit of heat." Except . . . Joshua knew Meyer, a wily old sod, for sure, but there was one hell of a difference between the occasional mercenary contract, and annihilating an entire planet of unsuspecting innocents. Meyer wouldn't do that, no matter how much money was offered. Offhand, Joshua couldn't think of many (or even any) independent trader captains who would. That kind of atrocity was purely the province of governments and lunatic fanatics.

"The use of it is what concerns me the most," Ione said. "Once it's been activated, governments will finally be able to see what it can actually do. From that, they'll deduce the principles. It'll be mass-produced, Joshua. We have to try and stop that. The Confederation has enough problems with antimatter, and now possession. We cannot allow another terror factor to be introduced."

"We? Oh, Jesus." He let his head flop back onto the cushions—if only there was a stone wall to thump his temple against instead. "Let me guess. You want me to chase after her. Right? Go up against every intelligence agency in the Confederation, not to mention the navy. Find her, tap her on the shoulder, and say nicely: All is forgiven, and the Lord of Ruin would really like you to come home, oh, and by the way, whatever your thirty-year plan—your *obsession*—was to screw up Omuta we'd like you to forget it as well. Jesus fucking Christ, Ione!"

She gave him an unflustered sideways glance. "Do you want to live in a universe where a super-doomsday weapon is available to every nutcase with a grudge?"

"Try not to weight your questions so much, you might drown."

"The only chance we have, Joshua, is to bring her back here. That or kill her. Now who are you going to trust to do that? More to the point, who can *I* trust? There's nobody, Joshua. Except you."

"Walk into Harkey's Bar any night of the week, there's a hundred veterans of covert operations who'll take your money and do exactly what you ask without a single question."

"No, it has to be you. One, because I trust you, and I mean really *trust* you. Especially after what you did back at Lalonde. Two, you've got what it takes to do the job, the ship and the contacts in the industry necessary to trace her. Three, you've got the motivation."

"Oh, yeah? You haven't said how much you'll pay me yet."

"As much as you want, I am the national treasurer after all. That is, until young Marcus takes over from me. Did you want to bequeath our son this problem, Joshua?"

"Shit, Ione, that's really—"

"Below the belt even for me? Sorry, Joshua, but it isn't. We all have responsibilities. You've managed to duck out of yours for quite a while now. All I'm doing is reminding you of that."

"Oh, great, now this is all my problem."

"No one else in the galaxy can make it your problem, Joshua, only you. Like I said, all I'm doing is making the data available to you."

"Nice cop-out. It's me that's going to be in at the shit end, not you." When Joshua looked over at her he expected to see her usual defiant expression, the one she used when she was powering up to out-stubborn him. Instead all he saw was worry and a tinge of sorrow. On a face that beautiful it was heartbreaking. "Look, anyway, there's a Confederation-wide quarantine in effect, I can't take *Lady Mac* off in pursuit even if I wanted to."

"It only applies to civil starflight. *Lady Macbeth* would be re-registered as an official Tranquillity government starship."

"Shit." He smiled up at the ceiling, a very dry reflex. "Ah well, worth a try."

"You'll do it?"

"I'll ask questions in the appropriate places, that's all, Ione. I'm not into heroics."

"You don't need to be, I can help."

"Sure."

"I can," she insisted, piqued. "For a start, I can issue you with some decent combat wasps."

"Great, no heroics please, but take a thousand megatonnes' worth of nukes with you just in case."

"Joshua . . . I don't want you to be vulnerable, that's all. There will be a lot of people looking for Mzu, and none of them are the type to ask questions first."

"Wonderful."

"I can send some serjeants with you as well. They'll be useful as bodyguards when you're docked."

He tried to think up an argument against that, but couldn't. "Fine. Unsubtle, but fine."

Ione grinned. She knew that tone.

"Everyone will just think they're cosmoniks," she said.

"Okay, that just leaves us with one minor concern."

"Which is?"

"Where the hell do I start looking? I mean, Jesus; Mzu's smart, she's not going to fly straight to the Garissa system to pick up the Alchemist. She could be *anywhere*, Ione; there are over eight hundred and sixty inhabited star systems out there."

"She went to the Narok system, I think. That's where the *Udat*'s wormhole was aligned, anyway. It makes sense, Narok is Kenyan-ethnic; she may be contacting sympathisers."

"How the hell do you know that? I thought only black-hawks and voidhawks could sense each other's wormholes."

"Our SD satellites have some pretty good sensors."

She was lying; he knew it right away. What was worse than the lie, he thought, was the reason behind it. Because he couldn't think of one, certainly not one that had to be kept from him, the only person she trusted to send on this job. She must be protecting something, a something more important than the Alchemist. Jesus. "You were right, you know that? The night we met at Dominique's party, you said something to me. And you were right."

"What was it?"

"I can't say no to you."

Joshua left an hour later to supervise the *Lady Mac*'s refit, and round up his crew. It meant he missed Kelly's report, which put him in a very small minority. Kate Elvin's earlier optimism had been well founded; the other news companies didn't even try to compete. Ninety per cent of Tranquillity's population accessed the sensevises Kelly had recorded on Lalonde. The impact was as devastating as predicted—though not at once. The editing was too good for that, binding segments together in a fast-paced assault on the sensorium. Only afterwards, when they could duck the all-out assault on their immediate attention, did the implications of possession begin to sink in.

The effect acted like a mild depressant program or a communal virus. Yes, there truly was life after corporeal death. But it seemed to be perpetual misery. Nor was there any sighting of God, any God, even the Creator's numerous prophets went curiously unseen; no pearly gates, no brimstone lakes, no judgement, no Jahannam, no salvation. There was apparently no reward for having lived a virtuous life. The best anybody now had to hope for after death was to come back and possess the living.

Having to come to terms with the concept of a universe besieged by lost souls was a wounding process. People reacted in different ways. Getting smashed, or stoned, or stimmed out was popular. Some found religion in a big way. Some became fervently agnostic. Some turned to their shrinks for reassurance. Some (the richer and smarter) quietly focused their attention (and funding) to zero-tau mausoleums.

One thing the psychiatrists did notice, this was a depression which drove nobody to suicide. The other constants were the slow decline in efficiency at work, increased lethargy, a rise in use of tranquilizer and stimulant programs. Pop psychology commentators took to calling it the rise of the why-bother psychosis.

The rest of the Confederation was swift to follow, and almost identical in its response no matter what ethnic culture base was exposed to the news. No ideology or religion offered much in the way of resistance. Only Edenism proved resilient, though even that culture was far from immune.

Antonio Whitelocke chartered twenty-five blackhawks and Adamist independent trader starships to distribute Kelly's fleks to Collins offices across the Confederation. Saturation took three weeks, longer than optimum, but the quarantine alert made national navies highly nervous. Some of the more authoritarian governments, fearful of the effect Kelly's recording would have on public confidence, tried to ban Collins from releasing it; an action which simply pushed the fleks underground whilst simultaneously boosting their credibility. It was an unfortunate outcome, because in many cases it clashed and interacted with two other information ripples expanding across the Confederation. Firstly there was the rapidly spreading bad news about Al Capone's takeover of New California, and secondly the more clandestine distribution of Kiera Salter's seductive recording.

* * *

The *Mindor* hit eight gees as soon as it cleared the wormhole terminus. Various masses immediately impinged on Rocio Condra's perception. The core of the Trojan point was twenty million kilometres in diameter, and cluttered with hundreds of medium-sized asteroids, tens of thousands of boulders, dust shoals, and swirls of ice pebbles, all of them gently resonating to the pull of distant gravity fields. *Mindor* opened its wings wide, and began beating them in vast sweeps.

Rocio Condra had chosen an avian form as the hellhawk's image. The three stumpy rear fins had broadened out, becoming thinner to angle back. Its nose had lengthened, creases and folds multiplying across the polyp, deepening, accentuating the creature's streamlining. Meandering green and purple patterns had vanished, washed away beneath a bloom of midnight-black. The texture was crinkly, delineating tight-packed leather feathers. He had become a steed worthy of a dark angel.

Loose streamers of inter-planetary dust were churned into erratic storms as he powered forwards in hungry surges. Radar and laser sensors began to pulse against his hull. It had taken Rocio Condra a long time experimenting with the energistic power pumping through his neural cells to maintain a viable operational level within the hellhawk's electronic systems, although efficiency was still well down on design specs. So long as he remained calm, and focused the power sparingly and precisely, the processors remained on-line. It helped that the majority of them were bitek, and military grade at that. Even so, combat wasps had to be launched with backup solid rockets, but once they were clear they swiftly recovered; leaving only a small window of vulnerability. Thankfully, his mass perception, a secondary effect of the distortion field, was unaffected. Providing he wasn't outnumbered by hostile voidhawks, he could give a good account of himself.

The beams of electromagnetic radiation directed at him were coming from a point ten thousand kilometres ahead: Koblat asteroid, a new and wholly unimportant provincial settlement in a Trojan cluster which after a hundred and fifteen years of development and investment had yet to prove its economic worth. There were thousands just like it scattered across the Confederation.

Koblat didn't even rate a navy ship from the Toowoomba star system's defence alliance. Its funding company certainly didn't provide it with SD platforms. The sole concession which the asteroid's governing council had made to "the emergency" was to upgrade their civil spaceflight sensors, and equip two inter-planetary cargo ships with a dozen combat wasps apiece, grudgingly donated by Toowoomba. It was, like every response to the affairs of the outside universe, a rather pathetic token.

And now a token which had just been exposed for what it was. The hellhawk's emergence, location, velocity, flight vector, and refusal to identify itself could only mean one thing: It was hostile. Both of the armed inter-planetary craft were dispatched on an interception vector, lumbering outwards at one and a half gees, hopelessly outclassed even before their fusion drives ignited.

Koblat beamed a desperate request for help to Pinjarra, the cluster's capital four million kilometres away, where three armed starships were stationed. The asteroid's inadequate internal emergency procedures were activated, sealing and isolating independent sections. Its terrified citizens rushed to designated secure chambers deep in the interior and waited for the attack to begin, dreading the follow on, the infiltration by possessed.

It never happened. All the incoming hellhawk did was open a standard channel and datavise a sensorium recording into the asteroid's net. Then it vanished, expanding a wormhole interstice and diving inside. Only a couple of optical sensors caught a glimpse of it, producing a smudgy image which nobody believed in.

When Jed Hinton finally got back from his designated safe shelter chamber, he almost wished the alert had kept going a few more hours. It was change, something new, different. A rare event in all of Jed's seventeen years of life.

When he returned to the family apartment, four rooms chewed out of the rock at level three (a two-thirds gravity field), his mum and Digger were shouting about something or other. The rows had grown almost continual since the warning from the Confederation Assembly had reached Koblat. Work shifts were being reduced as the company hedged its bets, waiting to see what would happen after the crisis was over. Shorter shifts meant Digger spending a lot more time at home, or up at the Blue Fountain bar on level five when he could afford it.

"I wish they'd stop," Gari said as more shouting sounded through the bedroom door. "I can't think right with so much noise." She was sitting at a table in the living room, trying to concentrate on a processor block. Its screen was full of text with several flashing diagrams, part of a software architecture course. The level was one his didactic imprints had covered five years ago; Gari was only three years younger, she should have assimilated it long ago. But then his sister had something in her genes which made it difficult for laser imprinters to work on her brain. She had to work hard at revising everything to make it stick.

"Girl's just plain arse backwards," Digger shouted some nights when he stumbled home drunk.

Jed hated Digger, hated the way he shouted at Mum, and hated the way he picked on Gari. Gari tried hard to keep up with her year, she needed encouraging. Not that there was anything to achieve in Koblat, he thought miserably.

Miri and Navar came in, and promptly loaded a games flek into the AV block. The living room immediately filled up with an iridescent laserlight sparkle. A flock of spherical, coloured-chrome chessboards swooped around Jed's head every time his eyes strayed towards the tall AV pillar. Both girls started yelling instructions at the block, and small figures jumped between the various spheres in strategic migrations, accompanied by a thumping music track. The projector was too damn large for a room this size.

"Come on, guys," Gari wailed. "I've got to get this stuff locked down ready for my assessment."

"So do it," Navar grunted back.

"Cow!"

"Dumb bitch!"

"Stop it! You played this all yesterday."

"And we haven't finished yet. If you weren't so *thick* you'd know that."

Gari appealed to Jed, chubby face quivering on the threshold of tears.

Miri and Navar were Digger's daughters (by different mothers), so if Jed lifted a finger to them Digger would hit him. He'd found that out months ago. They knew it too, and used the knowledge with tactical skill.

"Come on," he told Gari, "we'll go down to the day club."

Miri and Navar laughed jeeringly as Gari shut down her processor block and glared at them. Jed shoved the door open and faced his tiny worldlet.

"It's not any quieter at the club," Gari said as the door shut behind them.

Jed nodded dispiritedly. "I know. But you can ask Mrs Yandell if you can use her office. She'll understand."

"Suppose," Gari acknowledged brokenly. Not long ago her brother had been capable of putting the whole universe to rights. A time before Digger.

Jed set off down the tunnel. Only the floor had been covered in composite tiling, the walls and ceiling were naked rock lined with power cables, data ducts, and fat environmental tubes. He took the left turning at the first junction, not even thinking. His life consisted of walking the hexagonal weave of tunnels which circled the asteroid's interior; that entire topographic web existed only to connect two places: the apartment and the day club. There was nowhere else.

Tunnels with gloomy lighting, hidden machines that made every wall in Koblat thrum quietly; that was his environment now, a worldlet without a single horizon. Never fresh air and open spaces and plants, never *room*, not for his body or his mind. The first biosphere cavern was still being bored out (that was where Digger worked), but it was years behind schedule and ruinously over budget. At one time Jed had lived with the faith that it would provide him an outlet for all his crushed-up feelings of confinement and anger, allowing him to run wild over fresh-planted grass meadows. Not now. His mum and Digger along with all the rest of the adults were too stupid to appreciate what possession really meant. But he knew. Nothing mattered now, nothing you did, nothing you said, nothing you thought, nothing you wished for. Die now or die in a hundred years time, you still spent eternity with a sprained mind which was unable to extinguish itself. The final, absolute horror.

No, they didn't think about that. They were as trapped in this existence as the souls were in the beyond. Both of them trekking after the low income jobs, going where the companies assigned them. No choice, and no escape, not even for their children. Building a better future wasn't a concept which could run in their thought routines, they were frozen in the present.

For once the dreary tunnel outside the day club centre was enlivened with bustle. Kids hurried up and down, others clumped together to talk in bursts of high-velocity chatter. Jed frowned: this was wrong. Koblat's kids never had so much energy or enthusiasm. They came here to hang out, or access the AV projections which the company provided to absorb and negate unfocused teenage aggression. Travelling the same loop of hopelessness as their parents.

Jed and Gari gave each other a puzzled look, both of them sensitive to the abnormal atmosphere. Then Jed saw Beth winding through the press towards them, a huge smile on her narrow face. Beth was his maybe-girlfriend; the same age, and always trading raucous insults. He couldn't quite work out if that was affection or not. It did seem a solid enough friendship of some kind, though.

"Have you accessed it yet?" Beth demanded.

"What?"

"The sensevise from the hellhawk, cretin." She grinned and pointed to her foot. A red handkerchief was tied above her ankle.

"No."

"Come on then, mate, you're in for a swish-ride treat." She grabbed his hand and tugged him through the kids milling around the door. "The council tried to erase it, of course, but it was coded for open access. It got into every memory core in the asteroid. Nothing they could do about it."

There were three AV players in the day club centre, the ones Jed always used to access vistas of wild landscapes, his one taste of freedom. Even so he could only see and hear the wonderful xenoc planets; the AV projectors weren't sophisticated (i.e. expensive) enough to transmit activent patterns which stimulated corresponding tactile and olfactory sensations.

A dense sparkle-mist filled most of the room. Twenty people were standing inside it, their arms hanging limply by their sides, faces entranced as they were interacted with the recording. Curious now, Jed turned to face one of the pillars square on.

Marie Skibbow's tanned, vibrant body lounged back over a boulder five metres in front of him, all flimsy clothes and pronounced curves. It was a perfectly natural pose; such a Venus could only possibly belong in this paradisiacal setting with its warmth and light and rich vegetation. Jed fell in love, forgetting all about skinny, angular Beth with her hard-edge attitude. Until now girls such as Marie had existed only in adverts or AV dramas; they weren't real, *natural*, not like this. The fact that such a person actually lived and breathed somewhere in the Confederation gave him a kick higher than any of the floaters he scored.

Kiera Salter smiled at him, and him alone. "You know, they're going to tell you that you shouldn't be accessing this recording," she told him.

. . .

When it ended Jed stood perfectly still, feeling as though a piece of his own body had been stolen from him; certainly something was missing, and he was the poorer for it. Gari was at his side, her face forlorn.

"We have to go there," Jed said. "We have to get to Valisk and join them."

12

The hotel sat on its own plateau halfway up the mountainside, looking out across the deep bay. The only buildings to share the rocky amphitheatre with it were half a dozen weekend retreat villas belonging to old-money families.

Al could appreciate why the owners had made strenuous efforts to keep the developers out. It was a hell of a sight, an unspoilt beach which went on for miles, tiny fang rocks at the front of the headlands stirring up founts of spray, long lazy breakers rolling onto the sands. The only thing wrong about it was that he couldn't get down there to enjoy it. There was a lot of time pressure building up at the top of the Organization, dangerous amounts of work and too-tight schedules. Back in Brooklyn when he was a kid he'd sit on the docks and watch gulls pecking at dead things in the muddy shallows. One thing about those gulls, their necks never stayed still, peck peck peck all day long. Now he'd surrounded himself with people that took after them. Never ever did his senior lieutenants give him a break. Peck peck peck. "Al, we need you to settle a beef." Peck peck. "Al, what do we do with the navy rebels?" Peck peck. "Al, Arcata is pulling in the red cloud again, you want we should zap the bastards?" Peck peck.

Je-zus. In Chicago he had days off, months on holiday. Everyone knew what to do, things ran smoothly—well, kind of. Not here. Here, he didn't have a fucking minute to himself. His head was buzzing like a fucking hornets' nest he had to think so hard on the hoof.

"But you're loving it," Jezzibella said.

"Huh?" Al turned back from the window. She was lying across the bed, wrapped in a huge fluffy white robe, her hair lost beneath a towel turban. One hand held a slim book, the other was plucking Turkish delights out of a box.

"You're Alexander the Great and Jimi Hendrix all in one, you're having a ball."

"Dozy dame, who the hell is Jimi Hendrix?"

Jezzibella pouted crossly at the book. "Oh, he was the sixties, sorry. A real wildcat musician, everybody loved him. The thing I'm trying to say here is, don't knock what you've got, especially when you've got so much. Sure, things are a little rough at the start, they're bound to be. It just makes winning all the sweeter. Besides, what else have you got to do? If you don't give orders, you take orders. You told me that."

He grinned down at her. "Yeah. You're right." But how come she'd known what he was thinking? "You wanna come with me this time?"

"It's your shout, Al. I'll maybe go down to the beach later."

"Sure." He was beginning to resent these goddamn tours. San Angeles had been a beaut, but then everyone else wanted in on the act. This afternoon it was Ukiah, tomorrow morning it was Merced. Who gave a shit? Al wanted to get back up to Monterey where the action was at.

The silver and ivory telephone at the side of the bed rang. Jezzibella picked up the handset and listened for a moment. "That's good to hear, Leroy. Come on in; Al can give you ten minutes for news like that."

"What?" Al mouthed.

"He thinks he's cracked our money problem," she said as she replaced the handset.

Leroy Octavius and Silvano Richmann walked in, Leroy smiling effusively, Silvano managing a glimmer of enthusiasm as he greeted Al and ignored Jezzibella entirely. Al let the faint insult pass. Silvano was always on the level about how he hated the non-possessed, and there was no hint in Jez's mind that she'd taken offence.

"So what have you come up with?" Al asked as they sat in the chairs which gave them a splendid view out across the bay.

Leroy put a slim black case down on the coffee table in front of him, resting a proud hand on it. "I took a look at the basics of what money is all about, Al, and tried to see how it could apply to our situation."

"Money is just something you screw out of other people, right, Silvano?" Al laughed.

Leroy gave an indulgent smile. "That's about it, Al. Money is principally a fancy method of accounting, it shows you how much other people owe you. The beauty of it is you can use it to collect that debt in a thousand different ways, that's how come money always grows out of a barter economy. Individual currencies are just a measure of the most universal commodity. It use to be gold, or land, something which never changed. The Confederation uses energy, which is why the fuseodollar is the base currency, because it's linked to He_3 production, and those costs are fixed and universal."

Al sat back, materialized a Havana, and took a deep drag. "Thanks for the history lesson, Leroy. Get to the point."

"The method of accounting isn't so important, whether you use old-fashioned notes and coins or a Jovian Bank disk, it doesn't matter. What you must establish is the nature of the debt itself, the measure of what you owe. In this case it's so simple I could kick myself for not thinking of it straight off."

"Someone's gonna kick you, Leroy, for sure. And pretty quick. *What* debt?"

"An energistic one. An act of magic, you promise to pay someone whatever they want."

"For Christ's sake, that's crazy," Al said. "What's the sense in someone owing me a chunk of magic when I can work my own? The original New California economy went ass backwards in the first place because we got this ability."

Leroy's grin became annoyingly wide. Al let him get away with it because he could see how tight and excited the fat manager's thoughts were. He'd certainly convinced himself he was right.

"You can, Al," Leroy said. "But I can't. This is a not-so-rhetorical question, but how are you going to pay me for all this work I've been doing for you? Sure you've got the threat of possession to hold me with, but you need my talent, have me possessed and you don't get that. But put me on a salary and I'm yours for life. For a day's work you promise to do five minutes of magic for me; manifest a good suit or a copy of the Mona Lisa, whatever I ask for. But it doesn't have to be you who owes me for the day; I can take the token, or promise, or whatever, and go to any possessed for my magic to be performed."

Al chewed around his cigar. "Let me get this straight, here, Leroy. Any schmuck with one of your chocolate dime tokens can come along and ask me to make them a set of gold-plated cutlery anytime they want?"

"Not anytime, no, Al. But it's the simplest principle of all: you do something for me, I do something for you. Like I said, it's exchanging and redeeming debt. Don't think of it on such a personal level. We've been wondering how to keep the non-possessed working for the possessed, this is the answer: You'll pay them, but you pay them in whatever they want."

Al glanced over at Jezzibella, who shrugged. "I can't see a flaw in the idea," she said. "How are you going to measure it, Leroy? Surely the possessed will be able to counterfeit any currency?"

"Yes. So we don't use one." He opened his bag and took out a small processor block, matt-black with a gold Thompson sub-machine gun embossed on one side. "Like I said, money is all accounting. We use a computer memory to keep track of what's owed to whom. You want your magic doing for you, then the computer shows how much you're entitled to. Same for the reverse; if you're a possessed it shows how much work the non-possessed have been doing for you. We just set up a planetary bank, Al, keep a ledger on everyone."

"I must be crazy even listening to this. Me? You want me to run a bank? The First National Al Capone Bank? Jesus H Christ, Leroy!"

Leroy held up the black processor block to stress the argument. "That's the real beauty of it, Al. It makes the Organization utterly indispensable. The soldiers are the ones who are going to enforce and regulate payment on the ground. They make it fair, they make the whole economy slide along smoothly. We don't have to force or threaten anyone anymore, at least not on the scale we have been doing with the SD network. We don't put taxes on the economy, like other governments; we become the economy. And there's nothing to stop the possessed using the system themselves. There are a lot of jobs too big for one individual. It can work, Al. Really it can."

"I scratch your back, you scratch mine," Al said. He eyed the black processor block suspiciously. Leroy handed it over. "Did Emmet help with this accounting machine?" Al asked curiously. Apart from the gold emblem it could have been carved from a lump of coal for all he knew.

"Yes, Al, he designed it, and the ledger program. He says that the only way a possessed guy can tamper with it is if he gets into the computer chamber, which is why he wants to base it on Monterey. We're already making it the Organization headquarters; this will cement the deal."

Al scaled the electric gadget back on the table. "Okay, Leroy. I see you've busted your balls to do good work for me here. So I'll tell you what we'll do; I'll grab all my senior lieutenants for a meeting in Monterey in two days time, see what they make of it. If they buy it, I'm behind you all the way. How does that sound?"

"Achievable."

"I like you, Leroy. You setting up any more tours for me?"

Leroy flicked a fleeting glance at Jezzibella, who gave him a tiny shake of her head. "No, Al; Merced is the last for a while. It's more important you're up at Monterey for a while now, what with the next stage just about ready."

"Goddamn, am I glad to hear that."

Leroy smiled contentedly, and put the accountancy block back in his slim case. "Thanks for listening, Al." He stood.

"No problem. I'll just have a word with Silvano, here, then the pair of you can get back into space."

"Sure, Al."

"So?" Al asked when Leroy had left.

"It ain't my concern, Al," Silvano said. "If that's the way you wanna do it, then fine by me. I admit, we gotta have some kinda dough around here, else things are gonna start falling apart pretty damn fast. We can only keep people in line with the SD platforms for so long."

"Yeah, yeah." Al waved a discontented hand. Money for magic, Je-zus, even the numbers racket was more honest than that. He stared at his lieutenant; if it hadn't been for the ability to sense emotions there would have been no way for him to work out what was going on behind that Latino poker face.

But Silvano was eager about something. "So what do you want? And it better be good fucking news."

"I think it may be. Somebody came back from beyond who had some interesting information for us. He's an African type, name of Ambar." Silvan smiled at the memory. "He wound up in a blond Ivy League body, man was he pissed about that; it's taking up a lot of effort to turn himself into a true brother again."

"Now *there's* someone who could cash in a potload of Leroy's tokens," Jezzibella said innocently. She popped another Turkish delight in her mouth, and winked at Al as Silvano scowled.

"Right," Al chuckled. "What did he want to trade?"

"He's only been dead thirty years," Silvano said. "Came from a planet called Garissa, said it got blown away, the whole damn world. Some kind of starship attack that used antimatter. Don't know whether to believe him or not."

"You know anything about that?" Al asked Jezzibella.

"Sure, baby, I nearly did a concept album on the Garissa Genocide once. Too depressing, though. It happened all right."

"Sweet shit, a whole planet. And this Ambar guy was there?"

"So he says."

"Antimatter can really do that? Waste out an entire planet?"

"Yeah. But the thing is, Al, he says the Garissa government was working on their own weapon when they got wasted, something to fire at Omuta. The biggest weapon ever built, he swears. And he oughta know, he was some hotshot rocket scientist for their navy."

"Another weapon?"

"Yeah. They called it the Alchemist. Ambar said it got built, but never got used. Said the whole fucking Confederation would know if it had been, that mother's got some punch."

"So it's still around," Al said. "Let me guess: he'll lead us right to it."

"No. But he says he knows someone who can. His old college lecturer, a broad called Alkad Mzu."

Lady Macbeth was scheduled to depart in another eight hours, though no one would ever guess by looking at her. Twenty per cent of her hull was still open to space, exposing the hexagonal stress structure; engineers on waldo platforms had the gaps completely surrounded, working with methodical haste to integrate the new systems they had installed to replace battle-damaged units.

There was an equal amount of well-ordered effort going on inside the life-support capsules, as crews from five service and astroengineering companies laboured to bring the starship up to its full combat capable status. A status whose performance figures would surprise a lot of conventional warship captains. A status she hadn't truly enjoyed for decades. Her standard internal fittings were being stripped out, replaced by their military-grade equivalents.

Joshua wanted the old girl readied at peak performance, and as Ione was paying . . . The more he thought about what he'd agreed to do for her, the more he worried about it. Immersing himself in the details of the refit was an easy escape, almost as good as flying.

He had spent most of yesterday holding conferences with astroengineering company managers discussing how to compress a fortnight's work into forty-eight hours. Now he watched attentively as their technicians clustered around the consoles manipulating the cyberdrones and waldo arms enclosing *Lady Mac*.

A pair of legs slid through the control centre's hatch, wobbling about as though the owner wasn't quite accustomed to free-fall manoeuvring. Joshua hurriedly grabbed at the offending trousers, pulling the man to one side before his shoes caught one of the console operators behind her ear.

"Thank you, Joshua," a red-faced Horst Elwes said as Joshua guided him down onto a stikpad. He gave a watery blink, and peered out into the bay. "I was told I would find you here. I heard that you had found yourself a charter flight."

There was no detectable irony in the priest's tone, so Joshua said: "Yes, the Lord of Ruin contracted me to pick up some essential specialist components to enhance Tranquillity's defences. The industrial stations outside don't manufacture every component which goes into the SD platforms."

Joshua didn't actually hear anyone snigger, but there were definitely some sly grins flashing around the consoles. Nobody knew for sure what the flight was for, but they all had a good idea what it didn't entail. As an excuse the components charter was pretty feeble. Ione had reported that every intelligence agency in the habitat had taken a sudden interest in his impending departure.

"But they can manage to build combat wasps, apparently," Horst said with gentle amusement. Brackets on the bay walls held sixty-five combat wasps ready for loading into *Lady Macbeth*'s launch tubes.

"One of the reasons we won the contract, Father. *Lady Mac* can carry cargo and fight her way out of trouble."

"If you say so, young Joshua. But please, don't try that one on St Peter if you ever make it to those big white gates."

"I'll bear it in mind. Was there something you wanted?"

"Nothing important. I was gladdened to hear your starship was being repaired for you. *Lady Macbeth* sustained a lot of damage rescuing us. I understand how expensive such machinery is. I wouldn't want you to suffer a financial penalty for such a selfless act."

"Thank you, Father."

"The children would like to see you before you leave."

"Er . . . Why?"

"I believe they want to say thank you."

"Oh, yes." He glanced at Melvyn, who appeared equally discomforted. "I'll try, Father."

"I thought you could combine it with the memorial service. They will all be there for that."

"What memorial service?"

"Oh, dear, didn't Sarha tell you? The bishop has agreed that I can hold a service of commemoration to those who sacrificed themselves for the children. I think Mr Malin's team and Warlow deserve our prayers. It starts in three hours time."

Joshua's good humour drained away. *I do not want to think about death and after, not right now.*

Horst studied the young man's face, seeing both anxiety and guilt expressed in the carefully composed features. "Joshua," he said quietly. "There is more to death than the beyond. Believe me, I have seen how much more with my own two eyes. The recordings your friend Kelly made, while truthful, do not contain anything like the whole story. Do you think I could retain my faith in Our Lord if Shaun Wallace had been right?"

"What did you see?"

"The one thing which could convince me. For you, I expect it would be different."

"I see. We have to come to faith in our own way?"

"As always, yes."

Tranquillity's cathedral was modelled on the old European archetype. One of the few buildings inside the habitat, it grew up out of the parkland several kilometres away from the circle of starscraper lobbies halfway along the cylinder. The polyp walls were lily-white, with an arching ceiling ribbed by smooth polygonal ridges to give the appearance of a long-abandoned hive nest. Tall gashes in the wall had been sealed by traditional stained glass, with a huge circular rosette at the end of the nave overlooking the stone altar. The Virgin Mary, baby Jesus in arm, gazed down on the slab of granite which Michael Saldana had brought from Earth.

Joshua had been given a place in the front pew, sitting next to Ione. He hadn't had time to change out of his ship-suit, while she was dressed in some exquisitely elegant black dress complete with elaborate hat. At least the rest of the *Lady Mac*'s crew shared his sartorial manner.

The service was short, perhaps because of the children who fidgeted and whispered. Joshua didn't mind. He sang the hymns and listened to Horst's sermon, and joined in with the prayers of thanks.

It wasn't quite as cathartic as he wanted it to be, but there was some sense of relief. People congregating together to tell the dead of their gratitude. And just how did that ritual start, he wondered—have we always known they'd be watching?

Ione propelled him over to the knot of children after it was over. Father Horst and several pediatric nurses were trying to keep them in order. They looked different, Joshua decided. The gaggle which closed around him could have been any junior day club on an outing. Certainly none of them resembled that subdued, frightened group who had flooded on board *Lady Mac* barely a week ago.

As they giggled and recited their rehearsed thank yous he realized he was grinning back. Some good came out of the mission after all. In the background Father Horst was nodding approvingly. Wily old sod, Joshua thought, he set me up for this.

There were others filing out of the cathedral, the usual clutter of rover reporters, (surprisingly) the Edenists from Aethra, a large number of the clientele from Harkey's Bar and other space industry haunts, a few combat-boosted, Kelly Tirrel. Joshua excused himself from the children and caught up with her in the narthex.

"*Lady Mac* is departing this evening," he said lamely.

"I know."

"I caught some of the Collins news shows; you've done all right for yourself."

"Yes. Finally, I'm officially more popular than Matthias Rems." There was humour in her voice, but not her expression.

"There's a berth if you want it."

"No thanks, Joshua." She glanced over at Ione who was chatting to Horst Elwes. "I don't know what she's conned you into doing for her, but I don't want any part of it."

"It's only a charter to pick up components which—"

"Fuck off, Joshua. If that's all there is to it, why offer me a place? And why load *Lady Mac* full of top-grade combat wasps? You're heading straight back into trouble, aren't you?"

"I sincerely hope not."

"I don't need it, Joshua. I don't need the fame, I don't need the risk. For fuck's sake, do you know what's going to happen to you if you die? Didn't you access any of my recordings?" She almost seemed to be pleading with him.

"Yes, Kelly, I accessed some of them. I know what happens when you die. But you can't give up hope for something better. You can't stop living just because you're frightened. You kept going on Lalonde, despite everything the dead threw at you. And you triumphed."

"Ha!" She let out a bitter, agonized laugh. "I wouldn't call that triumph if I were you: thirty kids saved. That's the most pathetic defeat in history. Even Custer did better than that."

Joshua gazed at her, trying to understand where his Kelly had vanished. "I'm sorry you feel that way, really I am. I think we did okay at Lalonde, and a lot of other people share that opinion."

"Then they're stupid, and they'll grow out of it. Because everything now is temporary. Everything. When you're damned to exist for eternity, nothing you experience lasts for long."

"Quite. That's what makes living worthwhile."

"No." She gave him a fragile smile. "Know what I'm going to do now?"

"What?"

"Join Ashly, he's got the right idea about how to spend his time. I'm going to take million-year sojourns in zero-tau. I'm going to sleep away the rest of the universe's existence, Joshua."

"Jesus, that's dumb. What's the point?"

"The point is, you don't suffer the beyond."

Joshua grinned the infamous Calvert grin, then ducked forwards to give her a quick kiss. "Thanks, Kelly."

"What the hell for, bollockbrain?"

"It's a faith thing. You have to come to it by yourself . . . apparently."

"If you go on like this, Joshua, you're going to die young."

"And leave a beautiful corpse. Yeah, I know. But I'm still flying Ione's charter."

Her mournful eyes regarded him with hurt and the old pain of longing. But she knew the gulf was too wide now. They both did.

"I never doubted it." She kissed him back, so platonic it was almost formal. "Take care."

"It was fun while it lasted, though, wasn't it?" he inquired to her retreating back.

Her hand fluttered casually, a dismissive backwards wave.

"Sod it," he grunted.

"Ah, Joshua, good, I wanted to catch you."

He turned to face Horst. "Nice service, Father."

"Why, thank you. I got rather out of practice on Lalonde, nice to see the old art hasn't deserted me entirely."

"The children look well."

"I should hope so, the attention they're getting. Tranquillity is an extraordinary place for an old arcology dweller like me. You know, the Church really did get it wrong about bitek. It's a wonderful technology."

"Another cause, Father?"

Horst chuckled. "I have my hands full, thank you. Speaking of which—" He pulled a small wooden crucifix from his cassock pocket. "I'd like you to take this with you on your voyage. I had it with me the whole time on Lalonde. I'm not sure if it'll bring you good luck, but I suspect your need is greater than mine."

Joshua accepted the gift awkwardly, not quite sure whether to put it around his neck or stuff it in a pocket. "Thank you, Father. It'll come with me."

"Bon voyage, Joshua. May the Lord look after you. And do try and be good, this time."

Joshua grinned. "Do my best."

Horst hurried back to the children.

"Captain Calvert?"

Joshua sucked in a breath. Now what? "You got me." He was telling it to a gleaming brass breastplate, one with distinctly feminine contours. It belonged to a cosmonik that resembled some steam-age concept of a robot: solid metal bodywork and rubbery flexible joints. Definitely a cosmonik, Joshua determined after a quick survey, not combat boosted, there was too much finesse in the ancillary systems braceleting each of the forearms. This was a worker, not a warrior.

"My name is Beaulieu," she said. "I was a friend of Warlow's. If you are looking for a replacement for his post, I would like to be considered."

"Jesus, you're as blunt as he was, I'll give you that. But I don't think he ever mentioned you."

"How much of his past did he mention?"

"Yeah, not much."

"So?"

"I'm sorry?"

"So, do I have the post?" She datavised over her CV file.

The information matrix rotated slowly inside the confines of Joshua's skull. It competed for space with a sense of indignation that she should do this at Warlow's own memorial, coupled with a grudging acknowledgement that anyone this forthright probably had what it took, she wouldn't last long with an attitude that wasn't solidly backed up with competence.

Running a quick overview check on the file he saw she was seventy-seven years old. "You served with the Confederation Navy?"

"Yes, Captain. Thirty-two years ago; it qualifies me to maintain combat wasps."

"So I see. The navy issued an arrest warrant for me and *Lady Mac* at Lalonde."

"I'm sure they had their reasons. I only serve one captain at a time."

"Er, right. That's good." Joshua could see another three cosmoniks standing in the last pew, waiting to see what the outcome would be. He datavised the cathedral's net processor block. "Tranquillity?"

"Yes, Joshua."

"I've got three hours before we leave, and I don't have time for games. Is this Beaulieu on the level?"

"As far as I can ascertain, yes. She has been working in my spaceport for fifteen months, and has had no contact with any foreign agency operatives. Nor does she fraternize with the combat-boosted or the less savoury traders. She stays with her own kind; cosmoniks do tend to stick together. Warlow's outgoing nature was an exception rather than the rule."

"Outgoing?" Joshua's eyebrows shot up.

"Yes. Did you not find him so?"

"Thank you, Tranquillity."

"My pleasure to assist."

Joshua cancelled the datavise. "We're having to fly with one patterning node out until I can find a replacement, and there may be some trouble later on in the charter," he told Beaulieu. "I can't give you specifics."

"That does not concern me. I believe your ability will minimize any threat, Lagrange Calvert."

"Oh, Jesus. Okay, welcome aboard. You've got two hours to collect your gear and get it stowed."

The docking cradle gently elevated *Lady Macbeth* upwards out of bay CA 5-099. Several hundred people had accessed the spaceport's sensors to watch her departure; intelligence agency operatives, curious rumour-gorged space industry crews, news offices recording files for their library in case anything eventful did happen.

Ione saw the *Lady Macbeth*'s thermo dump panels slide out of their recesses, a parody of a bird's wings extending ready for flight. Tiny chemical verniers ignited around the starship's equator, lifting her smoothly from the cradle.

She used her affinity to receive a montage summary of the tired company engineering teams congratulating each other, traffic control officers coordinating the starship's vector, Kelly Tirrel alone in her room accessing the spaceport sensor image.

It is fortunate that Kelly Tirrel did not wish to go with him, Tranquillity said. **You would have had to stop her, which would have raised the flight's profile.**

Sure.

He will remain safe, Ione. We are there with him to provide assistance, and even in part to die to protect him.

Right.

The *Lady Macbeth*'s bright blue ion thrusters fired, washing out the bay's floodlights. Ione used the Strategic Defence platforms to track the starship as it flew in towards Mirchusko. Joshua piloted her into a perfectly circular one-hundred-and-eighty-five-thousand-kilometre orbit, cutting off the triple fusion drives at the precise moment of injection. The ion thrusters only fired twice more to fine-tune the trajectory before the thermo dump panels started to fold up.

Tranquillity sensed the gravitonic pulse as the starship's patterning nodes discharged. Then the tiny mote of mass was gone.

Ione turned back to her other problems.

Demaris Coligan thought he'd done okay with his suit, dreaming up a fawn-brown fabric with silvery pinstripes, and a neat cut that wasn't half as garish as some of the Organization lieutenants wore.

At the last minute he added a small scarlet buttonhole rose to his lapel, then nodded to the oily Bernhard Allsop who led him into the Nixon suite.

Al Capone was waiting for him in the vast lounge; his suit wasn't that different from Demaris's, it was just that Al wore it with such verve. Not even the equally snappy senior lieutenants flanking him could produce the same style.

The sight of so many heavyweights didn't do much to increase Demaris's level of confidence. But there was nothing he'd done wrong, he was sure of that.

Al gave him a broad welcoming smile, and clasped his hand in a warm grip. "Good to see you, Demaris. The boys here tell me you've been doing some good work for me."

"Do whatever I can, Al. And that's a fact. You and the Organization's been good to me."

"Mighty glad to hear that, Demaris. Come over here, got something to show you." Al draped his arm around Demaris's shoulder in a companionable fashion, guiding him over to the transparent wall. "Now ain't that a sight?"

Demaris looked out. New California itself was hidden behind the bulk of the asteroid, so he looked up. Crinkled sepia-coloured rock curved away to a blunt conical peak. Three kilometres away, hundreds of thermo dump panels the size of football fields hung down from the rock, forming a ruff collar right around the asteroid's neck. Beyond that was the non-rotating spaceport disk, which, like the stars, seemed to be revolving. An unnervingly large constellation of Adamist starships floated in a rigorously maintained lattice formation just past the edge of the disk. Demaris had spent the entire previous week helping to prep them for flight; and the constellation only represented thirty percent of the Organization's total warship fleet.

"It's, er . . . pretty fine, Al," Demaris said. He couldn't make out Al's thoughts too clearly, so he didn't know whether he was in the shit or not. But the boss seemed pleased enough.

"Pretty fine!" Al appeared to find this hilarious, roaring

with laughter. He slapped Demaris's back enthusiastically. The other lieutenants smiled politely.

"It's a fucking great ritzy miracle, Demaris. One hundred per cent proof. You know just one of those ships is packing enough firepower to blow the entire old U.S. Navy out of the water? Now that's the kinda thought makes you shit bricks, huh?"

"Right, Al."

"What you're seeing out there is something no one else has ever tried before. It's a fucking crusade, Demaris. We're gonna save the universe for people like us, put it to rights again. And you helped make it happen. I'm mighty grateful to you for that, yes, sir. Mighty grateful."

"Did what I could, Al. We all do."

"Yeah, but you helped with getting those star-rockets ready. That takes talent."

Demaris tapped the side of his head. "I possessed someone who knows; he don't hold nothing back." With great daring he gave a gentle punch to Al's upper arm. "Least, not if he knows what's good for him."

A split-second pause, then Al was laughing again. "Goddamn right. Gotta let em know who's calling the shots." A finger was raised in caution. "But, I gotta admit; I got one hell of a problem brewing here, Demaris."

"Well, Christ, Al, anything I can do to help, you know that."

"Sure, Demaris, I know that. The thing is, once we start the crusade they're gonna fight back, the Confederation guys. And they're bigger than we are."

Demaris dropped his voice an octave, glancing from side to side. "Well sure they are, Al; but we got the antimatter now."

"Yeah, that's right, we got that. But that don't make them any smaller, not numbers wise."

Demaris's smile was a little harder to maintain. "I don't see . . . What is it you want, Al?"

"This guy you're possessing—what's his name?"

"The goof calls himself Kingsley Pryor, he was a real hotshot engineer for the Confederation Navy, a lieutenant commander."

"That's right, Kingsley Pryor." Al pointed a finger at Leroy Octavius.

"Lieutenant Commander Kingsley Pryor," Leroy recited, glancing at the screen on his processor block. "Attended University of Columbus, and graduated 2590 with a degree in magnetic confinement physics. Joined Confederation Navy the same year, graduated from Trafalgar's officer cadet campus with a first. Took a doctorate in fusion engineering at Montgomery Tech in 2598. Assigned to 2nd Fleet headquarters engineering division. Rapid promotion. Currently working on the navy's project to reduce fusion rocket size. Married, with one son."

"Yeah," Demaris said cagily. "That's him. So?"

"So I got a job for him, Demaris," Al said. "A special job, see? I'm real sorry about that, but I can't see no way out of it."

"No need to be sorry, Al. Like I said, anything I can do."

Al scratched the side of his cheek, just above three thin white scars. "No, Demaris, you ain't listening. I fucking hate it when people do that. I got a job for *him* to do. Not you."

"Him? You mean Pryor?"

Al gave the ever-impassive Mickey a helpless grimace. "Je-zus, I'm dealing with fucking Einstein here. YES, shit-for-brains. Kingsley Pryor, I want him back. Now."

"But, but, Al, I can't give you him. I *am* him." Demaris thumped his chest frantically with both hands. "I ain't got anybody else to ride around in. You can't ask me to do that."

Al frowned. "Are you loyal to me, Demaris, are you loyal to the Organization?"

"What kind of a fucking question is that? Course I'm fucking loyal, Al. But it still don't mean you can ask that. You can't!" He whirled around as he heard the smooth *snik* of a Thompson being cocked. Luigi Balsmao was cradling one of the machine guns lightly, an affable smile on his thickset face.

"I am asking you, as a loyal member of my Organization, to give me back Kingsley Pryor. I'm asking you *nicely*."

"No. No fucking way, man!"

The scars on Al's reddening face were frost-white. "Because you acted loyal to me I give you the choice. Because we're gonna liberate every one of those ass-backwards planets out there, you're gonna have a zillion decent bodies to choose from. Because of this, I give you the opportunity to avoid zero-tau and prove your honour like a man. Now for the last goddamn time, read my lips: I want Pryor."

Kingsley Pryor didn't even know why he was crying like a baby. Because he was free? Because he'd been possessed? Because death wasn't final?

Whatever the reason, the emotional fallout was running through him like an electrical discharge. Control was impossible. However, he was fairly sure he was crying. Lying on cool silk sheets, a billowingly soft mattress below his spine. Knees hooked up under his chin with arms wrapped around his shins. And in darkness. Not the sensory deprivation of the mental imprisonment, but a wonderful genuine dusk, where a mosaic of grey on grey shadows delineated shapes. It was enough for a start. Had he been plunged directly into countryside on a sunny day he would probably have fried from sensory overload.

A swishing sound made him tighten his grip on himself. Currents of air stirred across his face as someone sat on the bed beside him.

"It's all right," a girl's melodic voice whispered. "The worst part's over now."

Fingers stroked the nape of his neck. "You're back. You're alive again."

"Did . . . Did we win?" he croaked.

"No. I'm afraid not, Kingsley. In fact, the real battle hasn't even begun yet."

He shivered uncontrollably. Too much. Everything was too much for him right now. He wanted, not to die (Gods no!) but just to be away. Alone.

"That's why Al let you out again. You have a part to play in the battle, you see. A very important part."

How could a voice so mellifluous carry such an intimation of catastrophe? He used his neural nanonics to retrieve a strong tranquillizer program and shunt it into primary mode. Sensations and palpitating emotions damped down. Something was not quite right about the neural nanonics function, but he couldn't be bothered to run a diagnostic.

"Who are you?" he asked.

A head was laid down on his shoulder, arms embracing him. For a moment he was reminded of Clarissa, the softness, the warmth, the female scent.

"A friend. I didn't want you to wake up with them taunting you. That would have been too horrible. You need my touch, my sympathy. I understand people like no other. I can prepare you for what is to come: the offer you can't refuse."

He slowly straightened himself and turned to look at her. The sweetest girl he'd ever seen, her age lost between fifteen and twenty-five, fair hair curling buoyantly around her face as she looked down at him in concern.

"You're beautiful," he told her.

"They've captured Clarissa," she said. "And dear little Webster, too. I'm sorry. We know how much you love them. Demaris Coligan told us."

"Captured?"

"But safe. Secure. Non-possessed. A child and a woman, they could not be hurt, not here. Al welcomes the non-possessed to his Organization. They'll have an honoured place, Kingsley. You can earn that for them."

He struggled to resolve the image which the name Al stirred in his mind. The fleshy-faced young man in a strange grey hat. "Earn it?"

"Yes. They can be safe forever, they need never die, never age, never endure pain. You can bring them that gift."

"I want to see them."

"You could." She kissed his brow, a tiny dry lick with her lips. "One day. If you do what we ask, you will be able to return to them. I promise that. Not as your friend. Not as your enemy. Just one human to another."

"When? When can I see them?"

"Hush, Kingsley. You're too tired now. Sleep. Sleep away all your anguish. And when you wake, you will learn of the fabulous destiny which is yours to fulfill."

Moyo watched Ralph Hiltch walk down the road out of Exnall, the girl lying in his arms. Together they made a classical image, the hero rescuing his damsel.

The other armour-suited troops closed around their leader, and together they slipped off the road, back into the cover of the trees. Not that the snarled-up trunks of the old forest could hide them; Ralph's fury acted like a magnesium flare to the strange senses which Moyo was only just accustoming himself to.

The ESA agent's anger was of a genus which perturbed Moyo deeply. The resolution behind it was awesome. After two centuries incarcerated in the beyond, Moyo had assumed he would be immune to any kind of threat ever again. That was why he had cooperated with Annette Ekelund's scheme, no matter how callous it was by the standards of the living. Possession, a return to the universe he had thought himself banished from, brought a different, darker slant on those things he had cherished and respected before—morality, honour, integrity. With such an outlook contaminating his thinking, he had considered himself invulnerable to fear, even aloof from it. Hiltch made him doubt the arrogance of his newfound convictions. He might have been granted an escape from the beyond, but remaining free was by no means guaranteed.

The boy whom Moyo held in front of him began to squirm again, crying out in anguish as Ralph Hiltch vanished from sight. His last hope dashed. He was about ten or eleven. The misery and terror whirling inside his head was so strong it was almost contagious.

His resolution fractured by Hiltch, Moyo began to feel shame at what he was doing. The craving which the lost souls in the beyond set up at the back of his mind was worse than any cold turkey, and it was relentless. They wanted what he had, the light and sound and sensation which dwelt so richly in the universe. They promised him fealty forever if he granted it to them. They cajoled. They insisted. They threatened. It would never end. A hundred billion imps of obligation and conscience whispering together were a voice more powerful than his.

He had no choice. While the living remained unpossessed,

they would fight to fling him back into the beyond. While souls dwelt in the beyond they would plague him to be given bodies. The equation was so horrifically simple, the two forces cancelling each other out. Providing he obeyed.

His rebirth was only a few hours old, and already independent destiny was denied him.

"Do you see what we can do?" Annette Ekelund shouted at the ranks of her followers. "The *Saldanas* reduced to bargaining with us, accepting our terms. That's the power we have now. And the first thing we must do is consolidate it. Everyone who was assigned to a vehicle, I want you ready to leave as soon as the marines withdraw; that should be in a quarter of an hour at the most, so be ready. If we even appear to lack the courage to go through with this, they'll unleash the SD platforms on us. You felt Hiltch's thoughts, you know it's true. Those of you holding a hostage, get them possessed right now. We need all the numbers we can muster. This isn't going to be easy, but we can capture this whole peninsula within a couple of days. After that we'll have the power to close the sky for good."

Moyo couldn't help but glance up. Dawn was strengthening above the barbed tree line, thankfully eradicating the stars and their hideous reminder of infinity. But even with daylight colours fermenting across the blackness the vista remained so empty, a void every bit as barren as the beyond. Moyo wanted nothing more than to seal it shut, to prevent the emptiness from draining his spirit once again.

Every mind around him had the same yearning.

Moans and shouting broke his introspection. The hostages were being dragged back inside the buildings. Nothing had been said about that, there was no prior arrangement. It was as though the possessed shared a communal unease at inflicting the necessary suffering in full view of each other and the low-orbit sensor satellites. Breaking a person's spirit was as private as sex.

"Come on," Moyo said. He picked the boy up effortlessly and went back into the wooden frame bungalow.

"Mummy!" the boy yelled. "Mummy help." He started weeping.

"Hey now, don't panic," Moyo said. "I'm not going to hurt

you." It didn't make any difference. Moyo went straight through into the living room, and opened the big patio doors. There was a lawn at the rear, extending back almost to the harandrid trees which encircled the town. Two horticultural mechanoids roamed anarchically over the trim grass, their mowing blades digging into the loamy soil as if they'd been programmed to plough deep furrows.

Moyo let go of the boy. "Go on," he said. "Run. Scoot."

Limpid eyes stared up at him, not understanding at all. "But my mummy . . ."

"She's not here anymore. She's not even her anymore. Now go on. The Royal Marines are out there in the forest. If you're quick, you'll find them before they leave. They'll look after you. Now *run*." He made it fiercer than he had to. The boy snatched a quick glance into the living room, then turned and shot off over the lawn.

Moyo waited to make sure he got through the hedge without any trouble, then went back inside. If it had been an adult he held hostage, there would have been no compunction, but a child . . . He hadn't abandoned all of his humanity.

Through the living-room window he could see vehicles rumbling down the road. It was a strange convoy which Annette Ekelund had mustered; there were modern cars, old models ranging across planets and centuries, mobile museums of military vehicles. Someone had even dreamed up a steam-powered traction engine which slowly clanked and snorted its way along, dripping water from leaky couplings. If he focused his thoughts, he could make out the profile of the actual cars and farm vehicles underneath the fanciful solid mirages.

There had been a coupe Moyo had always wanted back on Kochi, a combat wasp on wheels, its top speed three times the legal limit; but he never could quite manage to save enough for a deposit. Now though, it could be his for the price of a single thought. The concept depressed him, half of the coupe's attraction had been rooted in how unobtainable it was.

He spent a long time behind the window, wishing the procession of would-be conquerors well. He'd promised Annette Ekelund he would help, indeed he'd opened five of Exnall's residents for possession during the night. But now, contemplating the days which lay ahead, repeating that barbarity ten times an hour, he knew he wouldn't be able to do it. The boy had proved that to him. He would be a liability to Ekelund and her blitzkrieg coup. Best to stay here and keep the home fires burning. After the campaign, they would need a place to rest.

Breakfast was . . . interesting. The thermal induction panel in the kitchen went crazy as soon as he switched it on. So he stared at it, remembering the old range cooker his grandmother had in her house, all brushed black steel and glowing burner grille. When he was young she had produced the most magnificent meals on it, food with a tang and texture he'd never tasted since. The induction panel darkened, its outline expanding; the yellow composite cupboard unit it sat on merged into it—and the stove was there, radiant heat shining out of its grille as the charcoal blocks hissed unobtrusively. Moyo grinned at his achievement, and put the copper kettle on the hot plate. While it started to boil he searched around the remaining cupboards for some food. There were dozens of sachets, modern chemically nutritious food without any hint of originality. He tossed a couple into the iron frying pan, compelling the foil to dissolve, revealing raw eggs and several slices of streaky bacon (with the rind left on as he preferred). It began to sizzle beautifully just as the kettle started to whistle.

Chilled orange juice, light muesli flakes, bacon, eggs, sausages, kidneys, buttered wholemeal toast with thickly cut marmalade, washed down with cups of English tea—it was almost worth waiting two centuries for.

After he was finished eating, he tailored Eben Pavitt's sad casual clothes into the kind of expensive bright blue suit which the richer final year students had worn when he was a university freshman. Satisfied, he opened the bungalow's front door and stepped out into the street.

There had never been a town like Exnall on Kochi. Moyo found it pleasantly surprising. From the media company shows he had always imagined the Kulu Kingdom planets to have a society even more formal than his own Japanese-ethnic culture. Yet Exnall lacked any sort of disciplined layout. He wandered along its broad streets, sheltered by the lofty harandrids, enjoying what he found, the small shops, gleaming clean cafés, patisseries, and bars, the little parks, attractive houses, the snow-white wooden church with its bright scarlet tile roof.

Moyo wasn't alone exploring his new environment. Several hundred people had stayed behind after Annette Ekelund had left. Most of them, like himself, were ambling around, not quite meeting the eye of their fellow citizens. Everyone was party to the same guilty secret: what we did, what was done for us to return our souls into these bodies. The atmosphere was almost one of mourning.

The strollers were dressed in the clothes of their era and culture, solid citizens all. Those who favoured grotesquerie and mytho-beast appearances had departed with Ekelund.

He was delighted that several of the cafés were actually open, taken over by possessed proprietors who were industriously imagineering away the modern interiors, replacing them with older, more traditional decors (or in two cases retro-futuristic). Espresso machines gurgled and slurped enthusiastically, the smell of freshly baked bread wafted about. And then there was the doughnut machine. Set up in the window of one café, a beautiful antique contraption of dull polished metal with an enamel manufacturer's badge on the front, it was a couple of metres long, with a huge funnel at one end, filled with white dough. Raw doughnuts dropped out of a nozzle onto a metal grid conveyer belt which dunked them into a long vat of hot cooking oil where they fizzled away, effervescing golden bubbles until they rose out of the other side a rich brown in colour. After that they dropped off the end onto a tray of sugar. The smell they released into the crisp morning air was delectable. Moyo stood with his nose to the glass for a full minute, entranced by the parade of doughnuts trundling past while electric motors hummed and clicked, and the turquoise gas flames played underneath the oil. He had never guessed that anything so wondrously archaic could be found within the Confederation, so simple and so elaborate. He pushed the door open and went in.

The new proprietor was behind the counter, a balding man with a handkerchief knotted around his neck and wearing a blue and white striped apron. He was wiping the counter's shiny wooden top with a dishcloth. "Good morning, sir," he said. "And what can I get you?"

This is ridiculous, Moyo thought, we're both dead, we've been rescued by some weird miracle, and all he's interested in is what I want to eat. We should be getting to know each other, trying to understand what's happened, what this means to the universe. Then he sensed the alarm burbling up in the proprietor's thoughts, the man's terribly brittle nature.

"I'll have one of the doughnuts, of course, they look delicious. And have you got any hot chocolate?"

The proprietor gave a big smile of relief, sweat was prickling his forehead. "Yes, sir." He busied himself with the jugs and cups behind the counter.

"Do you think Ekelund will succeed?"

"I expect so, sir. She seems to know what she's doing. I did hear she came from another star. That's one resourceful lady."

"Yes. Where do you come from?"

"Brugge, sir. Back in the twenty-first century. A fine city it was in those days."

"I'm sure."

The proprietor put a mug of steaming hot chocolate on the counter along with a doughnut. Now what? Moyo wondered. I haven't got a clue what kind of coin to conjure up.

The whole situation was becoming more surreal by the second.

"I'll put it on your bill, sir," the proprietor said.

"Thank you." He picked up the mug and plate, glancing around. There were only three other people in the café. A young couple were oblivious to anything but each other. "Mind if I sit here?" he asked the third, a woman in her late twenties, making no attempt to cloak herself in any kind of image. Her head came up to show tear trails smearing chubby pale cheeks.

"I was just going," she muttered.

"Don't, please." He sat opposite her. "We ought to talk. I haven't talked to anyone for centuries."

Her eyes looked down at her coffee cup. "I know."

"My name's Moyo."

"Stephanie Ash."

"Pleased to meet you, Stephanie. I don't know what I

should be saying, half of me is terrified by what's happened, the other half is elated."

"I was murdered," she whispered. "He . . . he. He laughed when he did it, every time I screamed it just made him laugh louder. He enjoyed it." The tears were flowing openly again.

"I'm sorry."

"My children. I had three children, they were only little, the eldest was six. What kind of life would they have knowing what happened to me? And Mark, my husband, I thought I saw him once, later, much later. He was all broken down and old."

"Hey there, it's over now, finished," he said softly. "Me, I got hit by a bus. Which is a tricky thing to do in Kochi's capital city; there are barriers along the roads, and safety systems, all kinds of protective junk. But if you're real stupid, and loaded, and part of a group that's daring you to run the road, then you can jump in front of one before its brakes engage. Yeah, real tricky, but I managed it. So what use was my life? No girl, no kids; just Mum and Dad who would have been heartbroken. You had something, a family that loved you, kids you can be proud of. You were taken away from them, and that's a real evil, I'm not saying it isn't. But look at you now, you still love them after all this time. And I'll bet wherever they are, they love you. Compared to me, Stephanie, you're rich. You had it all, the whole life trip."

"Not anymore."

"No. But then this is a fresh start for all of us, isn't it? You can't allow yourself to grieve over the past. There's too much of it now. If you do that, then you'll never do anything else."

"I know. But it's going to take time, Moyo. Thank you, anyway. What were you, some kind of social worker?"

"No. I was at university studying law."

"You were young, then?"

"Twenty-two."

"I was thirty-two when it happened."

Moyo bit into his doughnut, which tasted as good as it looked. He grinned and gave the proprietor an appreciative thumbs up. "I can see I'll be coming back here."

"It seems silly to me," she confided.

"Me too. But it's the way he's chosen to anchor himself."

"Are you sure it was law, and not philosophy?"

He smiled around the doughnut. "That's better. Don't go for the big issues right away, you'll only get depressed, start small and work along to quantum metaphysics."

"You've lost me already, when I did work I was just a councillor at the local junior day club. I adored children."

"I don't think you were *just* anything, Stephanie."

She sat back in the chair, toying with the tiny coffee cup. "So what do we do now?"

"Generally speaking?"

"We have only just met."

"Okay, generally speaking, try and live the life we always wanted to. From now on, every day is going to be a summer's day you've taken off work so that you can go out and do the one thing you've always wanted to."

"Dance in the Rubix Hotel," she said quickly. "It had the most beautiful ballroom, the podium was big enough for a whole orchestra, and it looked out over the grounds to a lake. We never went to a function there; Mike always promised he'd take me. I wanted to wear a scarlet gown, with him in a dinner jacket."

"Not bad. You're a romantic, Stephanie."

She blushed. "What about you?"

"Oh, no. Mine are all pretty basic male daydreams. Tropical beaches and girls with perfect figures; that kind of thing."

"No, I don't believe that. There's more to you than simplistic clichés. And besides, I told you mine."

"Well . . . I suppose there is mountain gliding. It was a rich-kid sport on Kochi. The gliders were made out of linked molecule films, only weighed about five kilos, but they had a wingspan of about twenty-five metres. Then before you could even get in to one you had to have your retinas and cortical processor implants upgraded so that you could actually see air currents, determine their flow speed; the whole X-ray vision trip. That way you'd be able to pick out the wind stream which could carry you to the top.

"The clubs would set out courses over half a mountain range. I watched a race once. The pilots looked like they were lying in a torpedo-shaped bubble; the linked molecule film is so thin you can't even see it unless the sun catches it just right.

They were skiing on air, Stephanie, and they made it seem like the easiest thing in the world."

"I don't think either of us is going to be living our fantasies for a while."

"No. But we will, eventually, when Ekelund takes over Mortonridge. Then we'll have the power to indulge ourselves."

"That woman. God, she frightened me. I had to hold a man hostage while she spoke to the soldier. He was pleading and crying. I had to give him to someone else afterwards. I couldn't hurt him."

"I let mine go altogether."

"Really?"

"Yes. It was a boy. I think he got to the marines in time to be evacuated. Hope so, anyway."

"That was good of you."

"Yeah. I had the luxury this time. But if the Saldana Princess sends her troops in here to find us and claw us back, I'll fight. I'll do everything I can to stop them from evicting me from this body."

"I hear mine," Stephanie said. "She's inside me, lonely and afraid. She cries a lot."

"My host's called Eben Pavitt, he rages the whole time. But underneath he's scared."

"They're as bad as the souls in the beyond. Everyone is making demands on us."

"Ignore them. You can do it. Compared to the beyond, this is paradise."

"Not really. But it's a good first step."

He finished his chocolate, and smiled. "Do you want to come for a walk, see what our new town is like?"

"Yes. Thank you, Moyo, I think I would."

13

The Confederation Navy Intelligence Service had originally been formed with the intent of infiltrating the black syndicates that produced antimatter, and hunting down their production stations. Since those early days its activities had expanded along with those of the Confederation Navy as a whole. By the time Admiral Lalwani assumed command, one of its principal functions was to monitor, analyse, and assess the deplorable amount of new and ingenious weapons systems manufactured by governments and astroengineering companies across the Confederation, with emphasis on the more clandestine marques. To that end, the designers of the service's secure weapons technology laboratory complex were given a brief to contain just about any conceivable emergency, from biohazards to outbreaks of nanonic viruses, to small nuclear explosions.

There was only one entrance: a long corridor cut through the rock with two right-angle turns; it was wide and high enough to accommodate an outsize service truck or even a small flyer. Three separate doors were spaced along it, each built from a two-metre-thickness of carbotanium composite strengthened by molecular binding force generators. The first two slabs could only be opened by the security staff outside, while the third was operated from inside the facility.

Since the arrival of Jacqueline Couteur, Trafalgar's population had started calling it the demon trap.

Appropriate enough, Samual Aleksandrovich conceded as the final door swung upwards amid a hiss of pressure and loud mechanical whinings. Dr Gilmore was waiting on the other side to greet him and his entourage.

"I'm delighted I can actually offer you some good news for a change," Dr Gilmore said as he led the First Admiral up to the biological division's isolation facility. "We've all heard about New California. Is it really Al Capone leading them?"

"We don't have any evidence to the contrary," Lalwani said. "The Edenists in the system are monitoring news broadcasts. Capone appears very fond of publicity, he's been touring cities like some kind of medieval monarch. Pressing the flesh, he calls it. A number of reporters were left unpossessed purely so they could record the event."

"And this pre-starflight primitive had the ability to take over one of our most developed worlds?" Dr Gilmore inquired. "I find that hard to credit."

"Don't," Lalwani said. "We've been researching him. He's a genuine emperor genotype. People like him have an intuitive ability to format social structures which support their premiership, whatever their local environment, from street gangs to entire nations. Thankfully they don't occur very often, nor at such a high level; but when they do the rest of us need to watch out."

"Even so—"

"Obviously, he's getting advice on modern life. There will be an inner cabinet to help him, but he won't share the ultimate power. We don't believe he's psychologically capable of it. That could be a significant weakness given the sheer quantity of problems he must be facing in enforcing his rule."

"So far New California is the only planetary system we know of which has succumbed completely," the First Admiral said. "Seventeen more planets are suffering from large-scale incursions, and are doing their best to isolate the affected areas. Fortunately the legitimate authorities retained control of their SD networks. The worst casualties have been among the asteroid settlements; our last estimation was that we'd lost over a hundred and twenty Confederation-wide. If a possessed gets inside one, their success rate in taking it over is close to a hundred percent. It's proving difficult to fight them in such closed environments. Other planets have had trouble, but on a much smaller scale. Our warning seems to have had the required effect. It could have been a lot worse."

"Our main concern is that nobody attempts any foolhardy liberation missions," Lalwani said. "There would be few national navies capable of mounting a successful operation along those lines. At the moment any troops entering such an environment are liable to be possessed themselves."

"There will be political pressure on the military to act, though," the First Admiral said dourly. "So far our only notable public success has been the destruction of the *Yaku* in the Khabrat system. Trivial. What we need above all is some kind of weapon which is able to incapacitate the possessed. That or an effective method of exorcism. Preferably both." He gave Dr Gilmore a questing gaze.

"I believe we can now help you on the first count," the implant specialist said confidently. They stopped before the biological isolation facility, and he datavised his code at the door.

Euru's researchers had acted swiftly as soon as they'd obtained permission to advance their studies. The First Admiral flinched at the sight which greeted him within the examination room. On his side, the monitoring consoles were fully staffed; remorselessly obsessive scientists and technicians absorbed in the displays projected by AV pillars. A scene of brisk competence and scientific endeavour, as always reinforcing the concept of impersonal efficiency.

Samual Aleksandrovich doubted there was any other way the team could cope with their objective; it must act as a psychological buffer between them and the subject. *Subject*—he chided himself silently. Although he'd witnessed inhumanity on a far more brutal scale than this during his active service days.

With Captain Khanna at his side he walked hesitantly up to the transparent wall which cut the rock chamber in two, wondering if he should show signs of dismay or approval. In the end he settled for the same bleak acceptance which everyone else in the room had put on along with their baggy white lab overalls.

A naked and shaven Jacqueline Couteur had been immobilized on a surgical bed. Although wired into it would be a more honest evaluation, the First Admiral thought. Grey composite ribs formed a cage over the length of her body, supporting clamps which pressed pairs of large circular electrodes against her forearms, abdomen, and upper legs; clear jell was leaking out from beneath the silvery metal, ensuring better contact and conductivity. Two ceiling-mounted waldo arms had been equipped with sensor arrays, like bundles of fat white gun muzzles, which they were sweeping slowly and silently up and down the prone body. The thick circular brace which held her head fast looked as if it had melded with her skin. A plastic defecation tube had been inserted in her anus, while a free-fall toilet suction catheter adhered to her vagina. He couldn't decide if that was a civilized courtesy or the final humiliation.

Not that Couteur would care, not in her present condition.

Her entire musculature twitched and rippled in random spasms. The flesh quivering on her face made it seem as though she were enduring a ten-gee acceleration.

"What the hell are you doing to her?" Maynard Khanna asked in a guttural whisper.

It was the first time the First Admiral could ever remember the staff captain speaking before his superiors.

"Neutralizing her offensive potential," Dr Gilmore said with a tone of high satisfaction. "The report we received from Lalonde contained a reference from Darcy and Lori that electricity affects the possessed in an adverse fashion. We checked and discovered it's true. So we're running a current through her."

"Dear God, that's . . ." His face crunched up in a disgusted grimace.

Dr Gilmore ignored him, addressing himself solely to the First Admiral. "She is having to use her entire energistic ability to ward off the current. We experimented with the voltage level until we achieved this balance. Her physiological functions continue to operate normally, but she is completely incapable of manifesting any reality dysfunction effect. She can no longer distort matter, create illusions, or conjure up white fireballs. It means we are free to study her without any interference; even our electronic systems have recovered eighty-five per cent of their efficiency in her presence."

"So what have you learned?" the First Admiral asked.

"Please bear in mind we are on the threshold of a completely new field here."

"Doctor," the First Admiral cautioned.

"Of course. Firstly, we have developed a screening method which can pick out any possessed. There is a tiny but constant discharge of static electricity right across their bodies. We think it must be a by-product of their beyond continuum spilling into ours. Such an influx surge would also account for the energy they constantly have at their disposal."

"Static electricity?" a bemused Lalwani said.

"Yes, ma'am. It's beautiful: the sensors that will pick it up are cheap, easy to mass-produce, simple to use; and if they malfunction it's a certainty that a possessed is nearby anyway. Now we know what to look for they will find it impossible to hide in a crowd or infiltrate new areas."

"Excellent," the First Admiral said. "We'll have to see that this information is distributed as fast as our original warning." He moved right up to the transparent wall, seeing his breath mist the surface, and activated the intercom. "Do you remember me?" he asked.

Jacqueline Couteur took a long time to answer, her syllables maimed by the laboured gurgling of vocal cords not fully under control. "We know you, Admiral."

"Is she in communication with those in the beyond?" he asked Dr Gilmore quickly.

"I cannot give you an absolute, Admiral. However, I suspect not; at least nothing more than leaking a rudimentary form of contact back into her own continuum. Our Jacqueline is very fond of dominance games, and 'we' tends to sound impressive."

"If you are in pain," the First Admiral told her, "I apologize."

"Not as sorry as that shit's going to be when I catch up with him." Bloodshot eyes juddered around to focus on Dr Gilmore.

He responded with a thin superior smile.

"Exactly how much pain do you inflict on the mind of the body you have stolen?" Samual Aleksandrovich asked mildly.

"Touché."

"As you see, we are learning from you as I said we would." He gestured at the sensors which the waldo arms were sliding over her head and torso. "We know what you are, we know something of the suffering which awaits you back in the beyond, we understand why you are driven to do what you do. I would ask you to work with me in helping to solve this problem. I do not wish there to be conflict between us. We are one people, after all, albeit at different stages of existence."

"You will give us bodies? How generous." Somehow she managed to grin, lips wriggling apart to dribble saliva down her cheeks.

"We could grow bitek neural networks which you could inhabit. You would be able to receive the full range of human senses. After that they could be placed in artificial bodies, rather like a cosmonik."

"How very reasonable. But you forget that we are human, too; we want to live full human lives. For ever. Possession is only the beginning of our return."

"I am aware of your goals."

"Do you wish to help us?"

"Yes."

"Then terminate your life. Join us. Be on the winning side, Admiral."

Samual Aleksandrovich gave the vibrating, abused body a final, almost disgusted glance, and turned his back to the transparent wall.

"She says the same thing to us," Dr Gilmore said as if in apology. "Repeatedly."

"How much of what she says is the truth? For instance, do they really need human bodies? If not, we might just be able to force them into a compromise."

"Verification may be difficult," Euru said. "The electricity has contained the worst excesses of Couteur's reality dysfunction, but a personality debrief in these circumstances may prove beyond us. If the nanonics were to malfunction during axon interface they could cause a lot of damage to her brain."

"The possessed are certainly capable of operating within bitek neurone structures," Lalwani said. "Lewis Sinclair captured Pernik's neural strata; and we have confirmed that Valisk's blackhawks have also been captured."

"Physically they're capable of it, yes," Euru said. "But the problem is more likely to be psychological. As ex-humans, they want human bodies, they want the familiar."

"Acquire what information you can without risking the actual body itself," the First Admiral instructed. "In the meantime have you developed any method of subduing them?"

Dr Gilmore indicated the surgical table with a muddled gesture. "Electricity, Admiral. Equip our marines with guns that fire a dart that contains a small electron matrix cell and simply push a current into them. Such weapons were in widespread use from the mid-twentieth century right up until the twenty-third. We've already produced a modern chemical-powered design with a range over five hundred metres."

Samual Aleksandrovich didn't know whether to berate the implant specialist or commiserate with him. That was the trouble with laboratory types, all theory, no thought about how their gadgets would perform in the field. It was probably just the same in Couteur's time, he reflected. "And how far can they project their white fire?"

"It varies depending on the individual."

"And how will you determine what voltage to discharge from the electron matrix cell? Some will be stronger than Couteur, while others will be weaker."

Dr Gilmore glanced to Euru for support.

"Voltage regulation is a problem area," the suave, black-skinned Edenist said. "We are considering if a static scanner can determine the level in advance. It may be that the quantity of static exuded might indicate the individual's energistic strength."

"In here, possibly," the First Admiral said. "In combat conditions I very much doubt it. And even if it did work, what do you propose we should do with the captive?"

"Put them in zero-tau," Dr Gilmore said. "We know that method has enjoyed a hundred per cent success rate. They employed it on Ombey."

"Yes," the First Admiral acknowledged, recalling the file he'd accessed, the battle to capture the possessed inside the big department store. "And at what cost? I don't intend to be cavilling about your endeavours, Doctor, but you really need to bring some experienced combat personnel into your consultation process. Even conceding your stun gun could work, it would take two or three marines to subdue a possessed and place them in zero-tau. During which time those possessed remaining at liberty would have converted another five people. With that ratio we could never win. We must have a single weapon, a one-shot device which can rid a body of the possessing soul without harming it. Will electricity do that? Can you increase the voltage until the incursive soul is forced out?"

"No, Admiral," Euru said. "We have already tried with Couteur. The voltages necessary will kill the body. In fact we had to abandon the procedure for several hours to allow her to heal herself."

"What about other methods?"

"There will be some we can try, Admiral," Dr Gilmore insisted. "But we'll need to research her further. We have so little data at the moment. The ultimate solution will of course be to seal the junction between this universe and the beyond continuum. Unfortunately we still cannot locate the interface point. Those scanners we are operating in there are some of the most sensitive gravitonic distortion detectors ever built, yet there is no sign of any space-time density fluctuation in or around her. Which means the souls are not returning through a wormhole."

"Not wormholes as we understand them, anyway," Euru finished. "But then, given Couteur's existence, our whole conception of quantum cosmology is obviously seriously incomplete. Having the ability to travel faster than light isn't nearly as smart as we once thought it was."

* * * *

It had taken Quinn some time to modify the *Tantu's* bridge. It wasn't the look of the compartment which bothered him so much; the frigate was configured for high gee acceleration, its fittings and structure were correspondingly functional. He liked that inherent strength, and emphasised it by sculpting the surfaces with an angular matte-black bas-relief of the kind he imagined would adorn the walls of the Light Brother's supreme temple. Lighting panels were dimmed to a carmine spark, flickering behind rusty iron grilles.

It was the information he was presented with, or rather the lack of it, which displeased him, and consequently required the longest time to rectify. He had no neural nanonics, not that they would have worked even if he did have a set. Which meant he didn't know what was happening outside the ship. For all of *Tantu's* fabulous high-resolution sensor array, he was blind, unable to react, to make decisions. To have the external universe visible was his first priority.

Possessing the frigate's nineteen-strong crew had taken barely twenty minutes after he and Lawrence had docked. Initiating the returned souls into the sect, having them accept his leadership, had required another hour. Three times he had to discipline the faithless. He regretted the waste.

Those remaining had worked hard to build the displays he wanted; fitting holoscreens to the consoles, adapting the flight computer programs to portray the external environment in the simplest possible terms. Only then, with his confidence restored, had he ordered their departure from Norfolk orbit.

Quinn settled back in his regal, velvet-padded acceleration couch and gave the order to jump away. Twenty seconds after they completed the operation, the holoscreens showed him the little purple pyramid which represented the squadron's lone pursuit ship lit up at the centre of the empty cube. According to the scale, it was three thousand kilometres away.

"How do we elude them?" he asked Bajan.

Bajan was possessing the body of the *Tantu*'s erstwhile captain, the third soul to do so since the hijacking began. Quinn had been dissatisfied with the first two; they had both lived in pre-industrial times. He needed someone with a technological background, someone who could interpret the wealth of data in the captain's captive mind. A civil fusion engineer, Bajan had died only two centuries ago; starflight was a concept he understood. He also had a sleazy, furtive mind which promised instant obedience to both Quinn and the sect's doctrines. But Quinn didn't mind that, such weaknesses simply made him easier to control.

Bajan's fists squeezed, mimicking the pressure he was placing on the mind held within. "Sequential jumps. The ship can do it. That can throw off any pursuer."

"Do it," Quinn ordered simply.

Three jumps later, spanning seven light-years, they were alone in interstellar space. Four days after that, they jumped into a designated emergence zone two hundred thousand kilometres above Earth.

"Home," Quinn said, and smiled. The frigate's visible-spectrum sensors showed him the planet's nightside, a leaden blue-grey crescent which was widening slowly as the *Tantu*'s orbit inched them towards the edge of the penumbra. First magnitude stars blazed on the continents: the arcologies, silently boasting their vast energy consumption as the light from the streets, skyscrapers, stadiums, vehicles, parks, plazas, and industrial precincts merged into a monochrome blast of photons. Far above the equator, a sparkling haze band looped around the entire world, casting the gentlest reflection off the black-glitter oceans below.

"God's Brother, but it's magnificent," Quinn said. They hadn't shown him this view when he'd been brought up the Brazilian orbital tower on his way to exile. There were no ports in his deck of the lift capsule, nor on the sections of the mammoth docking station through which the Ivets had passed. He'd lived on Earth all his life, and never seen it, not as it should be seen. Exquisite, and tragically fragile.

In his mind he could see the dazzling lights slowly, torturously, snuffed out as thick oily shadows slid across the land, a tide which brought with it despair and fear. Then reaching out into space, crushing the O'Neill Halo, its vitality and power. No light would be left, no hope. Only the screams, and the Night. And Him.

Tears of joy formed fat distorting lenses across Quinn's eyeballs. The image, the conviction, was so strong. Total blackness, with Earth at its centre; raped, dead, frozen, entombed. "Is this my task, Lord? Is it?" The thought of such a privilege humbled him.

The flight computer let out an alarmed whistle.

Furious that his dreams should be interrupted, Quinn demanded: "What is it?" He had to squint and blink to clear his vision. The holoscreens were filling with tumbling red spiderwebs, graphic symbols flashed for attention. Five orange vector lines were oozing inwards from the edge of the display to intersect at the *Tantu*'s location. "What is happening?"

"It's some kind of interception manoeuvre," Bajan shouted. "Those are navy ships. And the Halo's SD platforms are locking on."

"I thought we were in a legitimate emergence zone."

"We are."

"Then what—"

"Priority signal for the *Tantu*'s captain from Govcentral Strategic Defence Command," the flight computer announced.

Quinn glowered at the AV projection pillar which had relayed the message. He snapped his fingers at Bajan.

"This is Captain Mauer, commander of the CN ship *Tantu*," Bajan said. "Can somebody tell me what the problem is?"

"This is SD Command, Captain. Datavise your ship's ASA code, please."

"What code?" Bajan mouthed, completely flummoxed.

"Does anybody know what it is?" Quinn growled. *Tantu* had already datavised its identification code as soon as the jump was completed, as per standard procedure.

"The code, Captain," SD Command asked again.

Quinn watched the fluorescent orange vectors of another two ships slide into the holoscreen display. Their weapons sensors focused on the *Tantu*'s hull.

"Computer, jump one light-year. Now," he ordered.

"No, the sensors . . ." Bajan exclaimed frantically.

His objection didn't matter. The flight computer was programmed to respond to Quinn's voice commands alone.

The *Tantu* jumped, its event horizon slicing clean through the carbon-composite stalks which elevated the various sensor clusters out of their recesses. Ten of them had deployed as soon as the starship emerged above Earth: star trackers, midrange optical sensors, radar, communications antennae.

All seven warships racing towards the *Tantu* saw it disappear behind ten dazzling white plasma spumes as its event horizon crushed the carbon molecules of the stalks to fusion density and beyond. Ruined sensor clusters spun out of the radioactive mist.

The SD Command centre duty officer ordered two of the destroyers to follow the *Tantu*, cursing his luck that the interception squadron hadn't been assigned any voidhawks. It took the two starships eleven minutes to match trajectories with the *Tantu*'s jump coordinate. Everybody knew that was too long.

Soprano alarms shrilled at painful volume, drowning out all other sounds on the *Tantu*'s bridge. The holoscreens which had been carrying the sensor images turned black as soon as the patterning nodes discharged, then flicked to ship schematic diagrams. Disturbing quantities of red symbols flashed for attention.

"Kill that noise," Quinn bellowed.

Bajan hurried to obey, typing rapidly on the keyboard rigged up next to his acceleration couch.

"We took four hull breaches," Dwyer reported as soon as the alarm cut off. He was the most ardent of Quinn's new apostles, a former black stimulant program pusher who was murdered at the age of twenty-three by a faster, more ambitious rival. His anger and callousness made him ideal for the cause. He'd even heard of the sects, dealing with them on occasion. "Six more areas have been weakened."

"What the fuck was that? Did they shoot at us?" Quinn asked.

"No," Bajan said. "You can't jump with sensors extended, the distortion effect collapses any mass caught in the field. Fortunately it's only a very narrow shell which covers the hull, just a few micrometers thick. But the atoms inside it get converted directly into energy. Most of it shoots outwards, but there's also some which is deflected right back against the hull. That's what hit us."

"How much damage did we pick up?"

"Secondary systems only," Dwyer said. "And we're venting something, too; nitrogen I think."

"Shit. What about the nodes? Can we jump again?"

"Two inoperative, another three damaged. But they're failsoft. I think we can jump."

"Good. Computer, jump three light-years."

Bajan clamped down on his automatic protest. Nothing he could do about the spike of anger and exasperation in his mind though, Quinn could perceive that all right.

"Computer, jump half a light-year."

This time the bridge lights sputtered almost to the point of extinction.

"All right," Quinn said as the gloomy red illumination grew bold again. "I want some fucking sensor visuals on these screens now. I want to know where we are, and if anyone followed us. Dwyer, start working around those damaged systems."

"Are we going to be okay, Quinn?" Lawrence asked. His energistic ability couldn't hide the sweat pricking his sallow face.

"Sure. Now shut the fuck up, let me think." He slowly unbuckled the straps holding him into his acceleration couch. Using the stikpads he shuffled on tiptoe over to Bajan's couch. His black robe swirled like bedevilled smoke around him, the hood deepening until his face was almost completely hidden. "What," he asked in a tight whisper, "is an ASA code?"

"I dunno, Quinn, honest," the agitated man protested.

"I know *you* don't know, dickhead. But the captain does. Find out!"

"Sure, Quinn, sure." He closed his eyes, concentrating on the captain's mind, inflicting as much anguish as he could dream of to wrest free the information. "It's an Armed Ship Authorization designation," he grunted eventually.

"Go on," Quinn's voice emerged from the shadows of his hood.

"Any military starship which jumps to Earth has to have one. There's so much industry in orbit, so many settled asteroids, they're terrified of the damage just one rogue ship could cause. So the captain of every Confederation government navy ship is given an ASA code to confirm they're legally entitled to be armed and that they're under official control. It acts as a fail-safe against any hijacking."

"It certainly does," Quinn said. "But it shouldn't have done. Not with us. You should have known."

Nobody else on the bridge was looking anywhere near Bajan, all of them hugely absorbed with their own tasks of stabilizing the damage. And Quinn, looming over him like some giant carrion creature.

"This Mauer is a tough mother, Quinn. He tricked me, that's all. I'll make him suffer for it, I swear. The Light Bringer will be proud of the way I let my serpent beast loose on him."

"There's no need," Quinn said genially.

Bajan let out a faltering whimper of relief.

"I shall supervise his suffering myself."

"But . . . how?"

In the absolute silence of the bridge, Lawrence Dillon sniggered.

"Leave us, Bajan, you little prick," Quinn ordered. "You have failed me."

"Leave? Leave what?"

"The body I provided for you. You don't deserve it."

"No!" Bajan howled.

"Go. Or I'll shove you into zero-tau."

With a last sob, Bajan let himself fall back into the beyond, the glories of sensation ripping out of his mind. His soul wept its torment as the crowded emptiness closed around him once again.

Gurtan Mauer coughed weakly, his body trembling. He had lurched from one nightmare to another. The *Tantu's* bridge had become an archaic crypt where technological artifacts protruded from whittled ebony, as if they were the foreign elements. A monk in midnight-black robes stood at the side of his couch, the hint of a face inside the voluminous hood indicated by the occasional carmine flicker striking alabaster skin. An inverted crucifix hung on a long silver chain around his neck; for some reason it wasn't drifting around as it ought in free fall.

"You didn't just defy me alone," Quinn said. "That I could almost accept. But when you held back that fucking ASA code you defied the will of God's Brother. Right now I should have been in the docking station, by morning I would have kissed the ground at the foot of the orbital tower. I was destined to carry the gospel of the Night to the whole motherfucking world! And you *fucked with me*, shithead. You!"

Mauer's ship-suit caught light. In free fall the flame was a bright indigo fluid, slithering smoothly across his torso and along his limbs. Scraps of charred fabric peeled off, exposing the charcoaled skin below. Fans whirred loudly behind the bridge's duct grilles as they attempted to suck the awful stench from the compartment's air.

Quinn ignored the agonized wailing muted by the captain's clamped mouth. He let his mind lovingly undress Lawrence.

The slight lad drifted idly in the centre of the bridge, smiling dreamily down at his naked body. He allowed Quinn to shape him, the young stable boy's skinny figure developing thick sinuous muscles, the width of his shoulders increasing. Clad only in a barbarian warrior garb of shiny leather strips, he began to resemble a dwarf addicted to bodybuilding.

The blue flame cloaking Mauer dribbled away as the last of the ship-suit was consumed. With a simple wave of his hand, Quinn healed the captain's burns, restoring skin, nails, hair to their former state. Mauer became a picture of vitality.

"Your turn," Quinn told Lawrence with a deviant laugh.

The pain-shocked, imprisoned captain could only stare upwards in terror as the freakishly hulking boy grinned broadly and glided in towards him.

• • •

Alkad Mzu accessed the *Samaku*'s sensor suite via the flight computer, allowing the picture to share her mind with a sense of benevolent dismay. This is what we fought over? This was what a planet died for? This? Dear Mary!

Like all starships jumping insystem, the *Samaku* had emerged a safe half-million kilometres above the plane of the eliptic. The star known as Tunja was an M4-type, a red dwarf. Bright enough from the starship's forty million kilometres distance, but hardly dazzling like a G-type, the primary of most terracompatible planets. From Alkad's excellent vantage point it hung at the centre of a vast disk of grizzled particles, extending over two hundred million kilometres in diameter.

The inner (annulet), surrounding Tunja out to about three million kilometres, was a sparsely populated region where the constant gale of solar wind had stripped away the smaller particles, leaving only tide-locked boulders and asteroid fragments. With their surfaces smoothed to a crystalline gloss by the incessant red heat, they twinkled scarlet and crimson as if they were a swarm of embers flung off by the dwarf's arching typhonic prominences. Further out, the disk's opacity began to build, graduating into a sheet of what looked like dense grainy fog; bright carmine at the inner fringe, shading away to a deep cardinal-red ninety million kilometres later. A trillion spiky shadows speckled the uniformity, cast by the larger chunks of rock and metal bobbing among the dust and slushy gravel.

No terracompatible planet was conceivable in such an environment. The star was barren except for a single gas giant, Duida, orbiting a hundred and twenty-eight million kilometres out. A couple of young Edenist habitats circled above it, but the main focus of human life was scattered across the disk.

A disk of such density was usually the companion of a newborn star, but Tunja was estimated to be over three billion years old. Confederation planetologists suspected the red dwarf's disk had its genesis in a spectacularly violent collision between a planet and a very large interstellar meteor. It was a theory which could certainly explain the existence of the Dorados themselves: three hundred and eighty-seven large asteroids with a near-pure metal content. Two-thirds of them were roughly spherical, permitting the strong conclusion that they were molten core magma material when the hypothetical collision took place. Whatever their origin, such abundant ore was an immensely valuable economic resource for the controlling government. Valuable enough to go to war over.

"Ayacucho's civil traffic control is refusing us docking permission," Captain Randol said. "They say all the Dorados are closed to civil starflight and we have to return to our port of origin."

Alkad exited the sensor visualization and stared across the *Samaku*'s bridge. Randol was wearing a diplomatically apologetic expression.

"Has this ever happened before?" she asked.

"No. Not that we've been to the Dorados before, but I've never heard of anything like it."

I have not waited this long, nor come so far, to be turned away by some bloody bureaucrat, Alkad thought. "Let me talk to them," she said.

Randol waved a hand, signalling permission. The *Samaku*'s flight computer opened a channel to Ayacucho asteroid's traffic control office.

"This is Immigration Service Officer Mabaki, how can I help you?"

"My name is Daphine Kigano," Alkad datavised back—she ignored the speculative gaze from Randol at the name on one of her passports. "I'm a Dorado resident, and I wish to dock. I don't see why that should be a problem."

"It isn't a problem, not under normal circumstances. I take it you haven't heard of the warning from the Confederation Assembly?"

"No."

"I see. One moment, I'll datavise the file over."

Alkad and the rest of the crew fell silent as they accessed the report. More than surprise, more than disbelief, she felt anger. Anger that this should happen *now*. Anger at the threat it posed to her mission, her life's duty. Mother Mary must have deserted the Garissan people long ago, leaving the universe to place so much heartbreak and malicious catastrophe in their path.

"I would still like to come home," she datavised when it was over.

"Impossible," Mabaki replied. "I'm sorry."

"I'm the only one who will enter the asteroid. Even if I were possessed I would present no threat. And I'm quite willing to be tested for possession, the Assembly warning says electronics malfunction in their presence. It should be simple enough."

"I'm sorry, we simply can't take the risk."

"How old are you, Officer Mabaki?"

"Excuse me?"

"Your age?"

"Is there some relevance to this?"

"Indeed there is."

"I'm twenty-six."

"Indeed? Well, Officer Mabaki, I am sixty-three."

"Yes?"

Alkad sighed quietly. Exactly what was included in the Dorados' basic history didactic courses? Did today's youth know nothing of their tragic past? "That means I was evacuated from Garissa. I survived the genocide, Officer Mabaki. If our Mother Mary had wanted me harmed, she would have done it then. Now, I am just an old woman who wishes to come home. Is that really so hard?"

"I'm sorry, really. But no civil starships can dock."

Suppose I really can't get in? The intelligence services will be waiting back at Narok, I can't return there. Maybe the Lord of Ruin would take me back. That would circumvent any personal disaster, not to mention personality debrief, but it would all be over then: the Alchemist, our justice.

She could see Peter's face that last time, still covered in a medical nanonic, but with his eyes full of trust. And that was the crux; too many people were relying on her; those treasured few who knew, and the blissfully ignorant masses who didn't.

"Officer Mabaki."

"Yes?"

"When this crisis is over, I will return home, will I not?"

"I shall look forward to issuing your ship docking permission personally."

"Good, because it will be the last docking authorization you ever do issue. The first thing I intend to do on my return will be to visit my close personal friend Ikela and tell him about this ordeal you have put me through." She held her breath, seemingly immersed in zero-tau. It was one lone name from the past flung desperately into the unknown. Mother Mary please let it strike its target.

Captain Randol gave a bass chuckle. "I don't know what you did, Alkad," he said loudly. "But they just datavised our docking authority and an approach vector."

* * * *

André Duchamp had long since come to the bitter realization that the lounge compartment would never be the same again. Between them, Erick and the possessed had wrought an appalling amount of damage, not just to the fittings, but the cabin systems as well.

The small utility deck beneath the lounge was in a similar deplorable state. And the spaceplane was damaged beyond repair. The loading clamps hadn't engaged, allowing it to twist about while the *Villeneuve's Revenge* was under acceleration. Structural spars had snapped and bent all along its sleek fuselage.

He couldn't afford to rectify half of the damage, let alone replace the spaceplane. Not unless he took on another mercenary contract. That prospect did not appeal, not after Lalonde. *I am too old for such antics,* he thought, *by rights I should have made a fortune to retire on by now. If it wasn't for those bastard anglo shipping cartels I would have the money.*

Anger gave him the strength to snap the last clip off the circulation fan unit he was working on; the little plastic star shattered from the pressure, chips spinning off in all directions. Bombarded by heat from a possessed's fireball, then subjected to hard vacuum for a week, the plastic had turned dismayingly brittle.

"Give me a hand, Desmond," he datavised. They had turned off the lounge's environmental circuit in order to dismantle it, which meant wearing his SII suit for the task. Without air circulating at a decent rate the smell in the compartment was unbearable. The bodies had been removed, but a certain amount of grisly diffusion had occurred during their flight from Lalonde.

Desmond left the thermal regulator power circuit he was testing and drifted over. They hauled the cylindrical fan unit out of the duct. It was clogged solid with scraps of cloth and spiral shavings of nultherm foam. André prodded at the grille with an anti-torque keydriver, loosening some of the mangled cloth. Tiny flakes of dried blood swirled out like listless moths.

"*Merde.* It'll have to be broken down and purged."

"Oh, come on, André, you can't use this again. The motor overloaded when Erick dumped the atmosphere. There's no telling what internal damage the voltage spike caused."

"Ship systems all have absurdly high performance margins. The motor can withstand a hundred spikes."

"Yeah, but the CAB . . ."

"To hell with them, data-constipated bureaucrats. They know nothing of operational flying."

"Some systems you don't take chances with."

"You forget, Desmond, this is my ship, my livelihood. Do you think I would risk that?"

"You mean, what's left of your ship, don't you?"

"What are you implying, that I am responsible for the souls

of humanity returning to invade us? Perhaps also it is my fault that the Earth is ruined, and the Meridian fleet never returned."

"You're the captain, you took us to Lalonde."

"On a legitimate government contract. It was honest money."

"Have you never heard of fool's gold?"

André's answer was lost as Madeleine opened the ceiling hatch and used the crumbling composite ladder to pull herself down into the lounge. "Listen, you two, I've seen . . . Yek!" She slapped a hand over her mouth and nose, eyes smarting from the unwholesome scents layering the atmosphere. In the deck above, an air contamination warning sounded. The ceiling hatch started to hinge down. "Christ, haven't the pair of you got this cycled yet?"

"*Non,*" André datavised.

"It doesn't matter. Listen, I've just seen Harry Levine. He was in a bar on the second residence level. I got out fast, I'm pretty sure he didn't see me."

"*Merde!*" André datavised the flight computer for a link into the spaceport's civil register, loading a search order. Two seconds later it confirmed the *Dechal* was docked, and had been for ten days. His SII suit's permeability expanded, allowing a sudden outbreak of sweat to expire. "We must leave. Immediately."

"No chance," Madeleine said. "The port office wouldn't even let us disengage the umbilicals, let alone launch, not with that civil starflight proscription order still in force."

"The captain's right, Madeleine," Desmond datavised. "There are only three of us left. We can't go up against Rawand's crew like this. We have to fly outsystem."

"Four!" she said through clenched teeth. "There are four of us left . . . Oh, mother of God, they'll go for Erick."

The fluid in Erick's inner ears began to stir, sending a volley of mild nerve impulses into his sleeping brain. The movement was so slight and smooth it made no impression on his quiescent mind. It did, however, register within his neural nanonics; the ever-vigilant basic monitor program noted the movement was consistent with a constant acceleration. Erick's body was being moved. The monitor program triggered a stimulant program.

Erick's hazy dream snuffed out, replaced by the hard-edged schematics of a personal situation display. Second-level constraint blocks were erected across his nerves, preventing any give-away twitches. His eyes stayed closed as he assessed what the hell was happening.

Quiet, easy hum of a motor. *Tap tap tap* of feet on a hard floor—an audio discrimination program went primary—two sets of feet, plus the level breathing of two people. Constant pulse of light pressure on the enhanced retinas below closed eyelids indicated linear movement, backed up by inner ear fluid motion; estimated at a fast walking pace. Posture was level: he was still lying on his bed.

He datavised a general query/response code, and received an immediate reply from a communications net processor. Its location was a corridor on the third storey of the hospital, already fifteen metres from the implant surgery care ward. Erick requested a file of the local net architecture, and found a security observation camera in the corridor. He accessed it to find himself with a fish-eye vantage point along a corridor where his own bed was sliding underneath the lens. Madeleine and Desmond were at either end of the bed, straining to supplement the motor as they hauled it along. A lift door was sliding open ahead of them.

Erick cancelled the constraint blocks and opened his eyes. "What the fuck's going on?" he datavised to Desmond.

Desmond glanced around to see a pair of furious eyes staring at him out of the green medical nanonic mask covering Erick's face. He managed a snatched, semi-embarrassed grin. "Sorry, Erick, we didn't dare wake you up in case someone heard the commotion. We had to get you out of there."

"Why?"

"The *Dechal* is docked here. But don't worry, we don't think Hasan Rawand knows about us. And we intend to keep it that way. André is working on his political contact to get us a departure authorization."

"For once he might make a decent job of it," Madeleine muttered as they steered Erick's bulky bed into the lift. "After all, it's his own neck on the block this time, not just ours."

Erick tried to rise, but the medical packages were too restrictive, he could only just get his head off the pillows, and that simple motion was tiring beyond endurance. "No. Leave me. You go."

Madeleine pushed him down gently as the lift started upwards. "Don't be silly. They'll kill you if they catch up with you."

"We'll see this through together," Desmond said, his voice full of sympathy and reassurance. "We won't desert you, Erick."

Encased in the protective, nurturing packages, Erick couldn't even groan in frustration. He opened a secure encrypted channel to the Confederation Navy Bureau. Lieutenant Li Chang responded immediately.

"You have to intercept us," Erick datavised. "These imbeciles are going to take me off Culey if no one stops them."

"Okay, don't panic, I'm calling in the covert duty squad. We can reach the spaceport in time."

"Do we have any assets in the flight control centre?"

"Yes, sir."

"Activate one; make sure whatever departure authorization Duchamp gets is invalidated. I want the *Villeneuve's Revenge* to stay locked tight in that bloody docking bay."

"I'm on it. And don't worry."

Desmond and Madeleine had obviously devoted considerable attention to planning their route in order to avoid casual observation. They took Erick straight up through the rock honeycomb which was Culey's habitation section, switching between a series of public utility lifts. When they were in the upper levels, where gravity had dropped to less than ten per cent standard, they left the bed behind and tugged him along a maze of simple passages bored straight through the rock. It was some kind of ancient maintenance or inspection grid, with few functional net processors. Lieutenant Li Chang had trouble tracking their progress.

Eighteen minutes after leaving the hospital they arrived at the base of the spaceport's spindle. Several intrigued sets of eyes followed their course as they floated across the big axial chamber to a vacant transit capsule.

"We're two minutes behind you," Li Chang datavised.

"Thank heavens they chose a devious route, it slowed you up."

"What about the departure authorization?"

"God knows how Duchamp did it, but Commissioner Ri Drak has cleared the *Villeneuve's Revenge* for departure. The Navy Bureau has lodged a formal protest with Culey's governing council. It should earn us a delay if not outright cancellation; Ri Drak's political opponents will use the complaint to make as much capital as they can."

The transit capsule took them to the bay containing the *Villeneuve's Revenge*. It was a tedious journey; like the rest of the structure the transit tubes were in need of refurbishment, if not outright replacement. The capsule juddered frequently as it ran through lengths of rail with no power, the light panels dimming, then brightening in sympathy. It paused at several junctions, as if the spaceport route management computer was unsure of the direction.

"Can you manoeuvre a bit now?" Madeleine asked Erick, hopeful that free fall would grant them some relief from straining at his mass. She was carrying two of the ancillary medical modules which were hooked up to his dermal armour of packages, feeding in a whole pharmacopoeia of nutrients to the new implants. The tubes were forever tangling around her limbs or snagging on awkward fixtures.

"Sorry. Tricky," he datavised back. It might earn them thirty seconds.

Madeleine and Desmond swapped a martyred glance, and bundled Erick out of the transit capsule. The hexagonal cross-section corridors that encircled the docking bay were white-walled composite, scuffed to a rusty grey by the boots of countless generations of crews and maintenance staff. The neat rows of grab hoops running along the walls had snapped off long ago, leaving only stumps. It didn't matter, the kind of people frequenting Culey spaceport were hardly novices. Madeleine and Desmond simply kept Erick in the middle of the corridor, imparting the odd gentle nudge to prevent him touching the walls as inertia slid him along.

Once the transit capsule door closed behind him, Erick lost his communications channel to Lieutenant Li Chang. He wished the packages didn't prevent him from sighing. Did nothing in this rat's arsehole of a settlement ever work? One of his medical support units emitted a cautionary bleep.

"Soon be over," Madeleine soothed, misinterpreting the electronic tone.

Erick blinked rapidly, the sole method of expression left to him. They were risking themselves to save him, while he would be turning them over to the authorities as soon as they docked at a civilized port. Yet he'd killed to protect them, leaving them free to commit murder and piracy in turn. Applying for a CNIS post had seemed such a prestigious step forwards at the time. How stupid his vanity appeared with hindsight.

His eye focused on a two-centimetre burn mark scoring the composite wall. Instinct or a well-written extended sensory analysis program, it was the result which mattered. That burn mark was on the cover of a net conduit inspection panel, and it was fresh. When he switched to infrared it still glowed a faint pink. With the spectrum active, other burns became apparent, a small ruddy constellation sprayed around the corridor walls, every glimmer corresponding to an inspection panel.

"Madeleine, Desmond, stop," he datavised. "Someone's deliberately screwed the net here."

Desmond halted his ponderous glide with a semi-automatic slap at the stump of a grab hoop. He reached out to brake Erick. "I can't even establish a channel to the ship," he complained.

"Do you think they got into the life-support capsules?" Madeleine asked. Her own enhanced retinas were scanning around the fateful inspection panels.

"They wouldn't get past Duchamp, not while his paranoia's roused. We'll be lucky if he even opens the airlock for us."

"They're armed, though; they could have cut their way in. And they're in front of us."

Desmond peered down the slightly curving corridor, alarmed and uncertain. There was a four-way junction ten metres in front of him, one of its branches leading directly to the docking bay's airlock. The only sounds he could hear were the rattly fans of the environmental maintenance system.

"Go back to the transit capsule," Erick datavised. "That has a working net processor, we can open a channel to the ship from there, even if we have to route it through the external antenna."

"Good idea." Madeleine braced her feet on a grab hoop stump, and gave Erick's shoulders a steady push, starting him off back down the corridor. Desmond was already slithering around them, lithe as a fish. When she looked back she could see shadows fluctuating within the junction. "Desmond!" She scrambled inside her jacket for the TIP pistol she was carrying. An elbow hit the corridor wall, setting her tumbling. She tried to damp her momentum with one hand clawing at the coarse composite, while still fumbling at the obstinate holster. Her feet caught Erick, sending him thudding against the wall. He bounced, trailing long confused spirals of tubing, ancillary modules flying free.

Shane Brandes, the *Dechal*'s fusion engineer, slid out of the corridor which led to the airlock; he was wearing the copper one-piece overall of the local spaceport services company. It took him a couple of seconds to recognize the frenetic woman four metres in front of him who was grappling with a gun caught up in her jacket. He gagged in astonishment.

"Don't move, ballhead!" Madeleine screeched, half in panic, half in exhilaration. She brought the TIP pistol around to point at the terrified man. Her body was still rebounding, which meant she had to keep tracking. Five separate combat programs went into primary mode; her thoughts were so churned up she'd simply designated the classification rather than individual files. Various options for combat wasp salvo attack formations skipped through her mind. She focused through the sleet of data and looping problematical high-gee vector lines to keep the nozzle trained on Brandes, who was doing a credible imitation of raising his hands in the air even though they were visually inverted.

"What do I do?" Madeleine yelled to Desmond. He was wrestling with Erick, trying to halt the injured man's cumbersome oscillations.

"Just keep him covered," Desmond shouted back.

"Okay." She squeezed the pistol grip in an effort to stop it shaking so much; her legs forked wide, stabilizing her against the corridor. "How many with you?" she asked Brandes.

"None."

Madeleine finally tamed her wayward programs. A blue neon targeting grid slid into place over her vision and locked. She aimed at a point ten centimetres to the side of Brandes's head and fired. Composite snapped and boiled, sending out a puff of unhealthy black smoke.

"*Jesus*. Nobody, I swear! I'm supposed to disable the starship's umbilical feeds, and smash this bay's net before . . ."

"Before what?"

Everybody had shunted an audio discrimination program into primary mode, so everybody heard the transit capsule door opening.

Desmond immediately activated a tactics program, and opened an encrypted channel to Madeleine. Their respective programs interfaced, coordinating their threat response. He turned to face the bright fan of light emerging from the door, his TIP pistol sliding around in a smooth program-controlled motion.

When Hasan Rawand came out of the commuter lift the exhilaration he was burning was hotter than any black-market stimulant program. He fancied himself as a hunting bird, power-diving on its unsuspecting prey.

The sharp reality of the corridor *hurt*. It was a situation so abrupt he was still smiling confidently as Desmond's TIP pistol nozzle was locked directly on his head. Stafford Charlton and Harry Levine almost cannoned into his back as they left the commuter lift; the four mercenaries hired to provide overwhelming firepower were considerably more controlled, reaching for their own weapons.

"Rawand, I've programmed in a dead man's trigger," Desmond said loudly. "If you shoot me, you still die."

The *Dechal*'s captain swore murderously. Behind him the mercenaries were having a lot of trouble deploying in the cramped corridor. Fast encrypted datavises assured him three of them were targeting the crewman from the *Villeneuve's Revenge*. Give the word, we can vaporize his pistol first. We're sure.

They weren't exactly the kind of odds Hasan Rawand was keen on. His eyes swept over the figure encased in medical nanonic packages. "Is that who I think it is?" he inquired.

"Not relevant," Desmond replied. "Now listen, nobody makes any sudden movements at all. Clear? That way no real untimely tragic accidents occur. This is what we have here: a standoff. With me so far? Nobody's going to win today, especially not if anyone starts shooting in here. So I'm calling time out, and we can both regroup and conspire to stab each other in the back some other happy time."

"I don't think so," Hasan said. "I don't have a quarrel with you, Lafoe, nor you, Madeleine. It's your captain I want, and that murdering bastard Thakrar. You two can leave anytime. Nobody's going to shoot you."

"You don't know shit about what we've been through," Desmond said, an anger which surprised him powering his voice. "I don't know about your ship, Rawand, but this isn't a crew which deserts each other the first second it hits the fan."

"Very noble," Hasan sneered.

"Okay, here's what's going to happen next. The three of us are going to back up into the *Villeneuve's Revenge*, and we'll take Brandes with us for insurance. One mistake on your part, and Madeleine fries him."

Hasan grinned rakishly. "So? He never was much use as a fusion engineer anyway."

"Rawand!" Shane screamed.

"Don't fuck with me!" Desmond shouted.

"Stafford, burn one of those medical modules our dear Erick is so attached to," Hasan ordered.

Stafford Charlton laughed, and shifted his maser pistol slightly. The module he chose let out a vicious crack as the lance of radiation pierced its casing. Boiling fluid shot out of blackened fissures as the internal reserve bladders were irradiated. Tubes broke free, chemicals spraying out of their melted ends, causing them to whip about with a serpent's ferocity.

Desmond didn't even have to datavise an order; acting on the evaluation of their combined programs, Madeleine fired her TIP pistol immediately. The pulse burned away half of the flesh covering Shane Brandes's left shin. He howled in agony, clutching at the mutilated limb. His voice subsided to a sob as his neural nanonics erected axon blocks against the pain.

Hasan Rawand narrowed his eyes, enhanced retinas absorbing the entire scene. He put a tactical analysis program into primary mode, which offered him two blunt options: retreat, or open fire. Estimated casualties on his side were fifty per cent, including Shane. When he added the secondary goal of successfully entering the *Villeneuve's Revenge* the only option was retreat and reorganize.

"Want to play double or quits?" Desmond asked calmly.

Hasan glared at him; being thwarted was bad enough, but being mocked was almost intolerable.

The transit capsule doors opened again. A fist-sized sphere emitting intolerable white light soared into the corridor. Hasan Rawand and his accomplices were closest to it, receiving the full impact of the photonic blitz. Two of the mercenaries who had their retinal sensitivity cranked up wide were instantly blinded as the implants burnt out. For the others it was as though the terrible light were boring right through their eye sockets and into the soft tissue of the brain. Instinct and situation analysis response programs fused into a simple protective act: eyelids slammed shut and hands jammed over eyes.

Unseen in the glare, the three members of the CNIS covert duty squad dived out into the corridor, following Lieutenant Li Chang. Dressed in smooth neutral-grey armour suits, their active optical sensors were filtered for the intensity of the quasar grenade.

"Break through Rawand's people, snatch Erick," Li Chang ordered. She fired another quasar grenade from her forearm magazine, aiming along the corridor at Desmond. It never reached its intended goal, one of the blinded mercenaries struck it as he thrashed about.

The mercenaries had linked combat programs, coordinating their response. Guidance and orientation programs allowed them to fix an accurate line on the transit capsule door and bring their weapons to bear. Thermal induction pulses discharged, maser beams slashed about.

The dissipation layers on the suits which Li Chang's squad wore deflected or absorbed most direct hits. The composite walls of the tunnel had no such protection. Flames squirted out amid fountains of smoking composite. Fire alarms screeched in warning. Turbulent jets of thick grey extinguisher gas roared into the air, turning to blobs of oily turquoise liquid as soon as the substance came into contact with any flame, smearing the combustible surface. Huge bubbling clumps congealed around the quasar grenades, smothering them.

Answering shots from Li Chang's squad eliminated three mercenaries straightaway. But their bodies formed a formidable tangled obstacle blocking off the corridor, as well as contriving a shield against further energy weapon fire. Behind it, Hasan and his remaining active cohorts rallied hurriedly.

Li Chang fought her way through the swirling extinguisher gas to grapple with one of the corpses. Her armour suit gauntlets couldn't get a decent grip on anything. The gas had slicked every damn surface. Two maser beams struck her chest and shoulder as she attempted to force her way forwards. She could actually see the gas crystallizing in long straight lines marking out the beams. One of the covert squad members was beside her, clawing at the dead man's neck. The body was bucking fitfully between them, its mass impeding every move.

Another TIP shot struck her armour, diffracting. A wide splash of skin on the dead man veered to a rancid bruise-brown as the energy punched it. His clothes were smouldering, drawing the extinguisher gas like a condensing dew.

Her neural nanonics had to activate a nausea suppressor program. "Use the smarts," she said, formulating search hunt parameter patterns. A volley of centimetre-long darts slid out of the cartridges on her belt. Miniature programmable missiles with a tiny ionic exhaust. They curved and rolled through the seething air, sliding around the awkward contours of the lifeless mercenaries, and accelerated down the corridor.

Li Chang heard a savage firecracker barrage as over two hundred diminutive EE warheads detonated in the space of three seconds. Sharp flickering fingers of blue-white light stabbed back past the floating bodies. Ripples of purple static surfed along the composite walls towards her. There was a sudden surge of air, sucking her towards the source of the light and sound. The three battered corpses began to move. A pressure drop warning sounded, its metallic whistle dopplering as the pressure thinned out fast. Emergency hatches were sliding out of the corridor walls, sealing off the damaged section.

"Captain Thakrar?" she datavised. "Sir, are you there?"

Scrambling after the corpses she could see the butchery which the smart darts had inflicted. A galaxy of blood globules spun around the ripped torsos of Hasan Rawand and the others. She assumed there were four in total. It was hard to tell.

Chunks of gore were splatting against the cracks in the wall, producing temporary seals which would shake and wobble under pressure, before being sucked through. Holding her breath—which was ridiculous as the suit provided her with a full oxygen supply—Li Chang flung herself through the centre of the bloody pulp, flinching every time the suit's tactile sensors faithfully reported an *object* slithering down her side.

The corridor beyond was empty. An emergency hatch had cut off the junction. Li Chang hauled her way along to it. The wind was abating now, almost all of the air had gone.

A small transparent port was set in the centre of the hatch. When Li Chang pressed her shell helmet sensors against it, all she could see was more hatches closed across the other corridors. Captain Thakrar and the crew members from the *Villeneuve's Revenge* were nowhere to be seen.

That was when a new sound was added to the fading clamour of the various alarms: a deep bass rumble which she could feel through the structure as much as hear. The light panels flickered, then went out. Small blue-white backup globes came on.

"Oh, God, no," she whispered to herself inside the helmet. "I promised him, I said he'd be safe now."

The *Villeneuve's Revenge* was launching from inside its docking bay. André had released the cradle hold-down latches, but without the bay manager to assist there was nothing he could do about the umbilical couplings and airlock tube. Secondary drive tubes ignited, power from the main generators vaporising hydrogen at barely sub-fusion temperatures. Clouds of searing blue ions billowed out around the spherical starship as it rose laboriously. Hoses and cables jacked into their sockets on the lower hull tore and snapped; streams of coolant fluid, water, and cryogenic fuel sluiced around the cylindrical bay. Once the starship was above the cradle the drive exhaust played directly over the girders, reducing them to garish slag in seconds. The airlock tube stretched and flexed to its limit, then ripped free of the docking ring, pulling spars, data cables, and locking pins with it.

"What the fuck are you doing, Duchamp?" an enraged traffic control broadcast at the rogue starship. "Turn your drive off now."

The *Villeneuve's Revenge* was rising out of the bay on a pillow of radiant ions. Walls and support girders marked its progress by melting and sagging.

André was only dimly aware of the massive damage his departure was causing. Flying the starship alone required his full concentration. Culey's SD platforms had lock-on, but he knew they would never fire, not while he was still so close. Frantically, he ordered all the open access hatches to close.

A ring of cryogenic storage tanks around the rim of the bay finally detonated under the unceasing blast of the starship's exhausts. It was a chain reaction, sending out vast plumes of white vapour and spinning chunks of debris. The entire docking bay structure began to crumple under the force of the multiple explosions. Momentum damping mechanisms in the spaceport spindle bearings veered towards overload as the impulse juddered its way through the framework.

The wave front from the tank explosions struck the *Villeneuve's Revenge*, fragments of wreckage puncturing the dark silicon hull in a dozen places. The starship was buffeted violently. An event horizon sealed over the hull, then shrank to nothing.

• • •

It was Gerald Skibbow's third trip to the lounge: a spacious semicircular room cut into Guyana's rock, with wide sliding-glass doors leading out onto a veranda that gave an excellent view down the interior of the asteroid's second habitation cavern. Despite the apparent easygoing nature, the lounge was at the centre of the navy's secure medical sanatorium, although the security measures were deliberately unobtrusive. Staff and patient-inmates mingled openly, producing what the doctors hoped was a casual atmosphere. It was intended to redevelop the social interactivity skills of the inmates who had been bruised by traumas, stress, and, in several cases, stringent interrogation. Anyone was free to come and go as they pleased; sit in the big spongy chairs and contemplate the view, have a drink and a snack, or play the simple games provided.

Gerald Skibbow didn't like the lounge at all. The artificial asteroid cavern was too removed from his experience. Its cyclorama landscape unsettled him, and the lounge's expensive modern setting reminded him of the arcology he'd yearned to escape from. He didn't want memories. His family dwelt in memories, the only place they did live now.

For the first few days after his personality debrief he had begged and pleaded with his captors to end those memories with their clever devices (that or death). The nanonics were still entombed within his skull, it would take so little effort on their part to cleanse him, a purge of fiery impulses and his past would be gone. But Dr Dobbs had smiled kindly and shaken his head, saying they wanted to cure him, not persecute him further.

Gerald had come to despise that mild smile, the utter intransigence it fronted. It condemned him to live amid a swirl of wondrously awful images: those of the savannah, the shared laughter, the tired happiness which had come at the end of each day, the days themselves, filled with simple achievement. In short, happiness. And in knowing it, he knew all he had lost, and was never to regain. He convinced himself the Kulu military people were deliberately submerging him in his own recollections as a punishment for his involvement in Lalonde and the outbreak of possession. There was no other reason for them to refuse him help. They blamed him, and wanted him to remember that. Memories emphasised that he had nothing, that he was worth nothing, that he had failed the only people he'd ever loved. Memories which kept him permanently looped in his failure.

His other wounds, physical ones from the encounter with Jenny Harris's team, had been treated efficiently and effectively by medical packages. His face and head sported fresh scars from the time a few days ago when he'd tried to claw the lovely smiling faces from within his brain; fingernails tearing at the skin to let him get at the bone of the skull and prise it open so that his darling family could escape and unfetter him. But the strong medical orderlies had jumped on him, and Dr Dobbs's smile had become sad. There had been fresh batches of chemicals to make him drowsy, and extra sessions when he had to lie on the psychiatrist's comfy couch and tell everyone how he felt. It hadn't done any good. How could it?

Gerald sat on one of the tall stools at the lounge's bar and asked for a cup of tea. The steward smiled and said: "Yessir. I'll get you some biscuits, too."

His tea and biscuits arrived on a tray. He poured, concentrating hard. These days his reactions weren't too sharp and his vision seemed to lack any real depth perception. Flat and unresponsive; so perhaps it was the world at fault, not him.

He rested his elbows on the polished wood of the bar, and cradled the cup in his hands, sipping slowly. His eyes scanned the ornamental plates and cups and vases in the showcase behind the bar. Not interested, but at least it kept him from looking out of the veranda windows and receiving the wickedly vertiginous view of the cavern. The first time they'd brought him into the lounge he'd tried to jump over the veranda. It was a hundred and fifty metres above the ground, after all. Two of the other inmates had actually cheered and laughed as he hurdled over the metal railing. But there was a net to snag him. Dr Dobbs had smiled tolerantly after it had stopped bouncing and winched him in.

At the far end of the bar, a holoscreen was switched to a news show (presumably censored—they wouldn't give inmates anything too contentious). Gerald shifted along a couple of stools so he could hear the commentary. The presenter was a handsome, silver-haired man speaking in level, measured tones. And smiling—naturally. The image changed to a low-orbit shot of Ombey, focusing on the Xingu continent. A curious appendicular finger glowed crimson amid the dour browns and greens of the earth, prodding out from the bottom of the main land mass. It was, Gerald heard, the latest anomaly to engulf Mortonridge. Unfortunately it meant that no one was able to see what was happening beneath. Royal Kulu

Navy sources confirmed it matched the reality dysfunction effect observed on the Laymil homeworld; but emphasised that whatever mischief the possessed were cooking up below it there was no possibility of them removing Ombey from the universe. There simply weren't enough of them; they didn't have the strength. And the red cloud had been halted at the firebreak. After two laser shots from a low-orbit SD platform the cloud's leading edge had recoiled, yielding to the negotiated boundary.

The disconcerting image of cloud was replaced by a sequence of fast pictures of big government buildings and uniformed officials with grim faces bustling through their doors and ignoring shouted questions. Gerald found the report hard to follow, although it seemed to be hinting that the Mortonridge situation was going to be "resolved," that "certain" plans were being "initiated."

Fools. They didn't realize. Not even sucking out every piece of knowledge in his brain had brought them understanding.

He sipped some more of his tea, thoughts calming to a more contemplative mood. Perhaps if he was lucky the possessed would begin another offensive; that way his misery would be extinguished for good as he was crushed back into the numbing darkness.

Then came the report about yesterday's hellhawk incursion. Five of them had emerged into the Ombey system; two of their number skipping high above the planet, three jumping about between the system's handful of settled asteroids. Always maintaining their distance, keeping well outside the range of SD platforms, and sliding back into wormholes as soon as Royal Navy ships were dispatched to interdict. Apparently their missions were to datavise a sensorium recording coded for open access into every communications net they could establish a channel with.

Leonard DeVille appeared to say how unfortunate the recording was, and that he hoped people would be sensible enough to see it for the crude propaganda it represented. In any case, he added contemptuously, with the civil starflight proscription in force, anyone sad enough to succumb would be safe from Kiera Salter's clutches. They would simply be unable to reach Valisk.

"There now follows," said the handsome anchorman, "a brief extract of the recording; though we are voluntarily complying with government wishes and not playing it in full."

The holoscreen showed a beautiful teenage girl whose flimsy clothes were virtually falling off her.

Gerald blinked. His vision was deluged by a dizzy rush of memories, the pictures more vivid than anything his eyes provided. Past and present wrestled for dominance.

"You know, they're going to tell you that you shouldn't be accessing this recording," the girl said. "In fact, they're going to get quite serious about that—"

Her voice: a harmony which threaded through every memory. Gerald's teacup hit the top of the bar and spun away, flinging the hot liquid over his shirt and trousers.

"—your mum and dad, your big brother, the authorities in charge of wherever you live. Can't think why. Except, of course, I'm one of the possessed—"

"Marie?" His throat was so clogged he could barely whisper. Two of the inmate supervision staff sitting at a table behind him exchanged a troubled look.

"—one of the demons—"

"Marie." Tears brimmed up in Gerald's eyes. "Oh, my God. Darling!"

The two supervision staff rose to their feet, one of them datavising an alert code into the sanatorium's net. Other inmates in the lounge had begun to notice Gerald's behaviour. Grins zipped around: the loony's at it again.

"You're alive!" He shoved both hands palm-down on the top of the bar and tried to vault over. *"Marie!"* The steward ran towards him, an arm outstretched. "Marie! Darling, baby." With his wobbly senses, Gerald completely misjudged his leap and went crashing onto the floor behind the bar. The steward had time for a fast yelp of shock as his flying feet tangled with Gerald's sprawled body and sent him tumbling to smack painfully into the base of the bar. A flailing arm sent a cascade of glasses smashing down on the hard tiles.

Gerald shook the glass splinters from his hair and jerked

his head back. Marie was still there above him, still smiling coyly and invitingly. At him. She wanted Daddy back.

"MARIE." He surged up at the same time the two supervisors arrived at the bar. The first snatched hold of Gerald's shirt, tugging him away from the holoscreen. Gerald spun around to face this new impediment, roared in rage, and swung a violent punch. The supervisor's unarmed combat program could barely cope with the suddenness of the attack. Muscles bunched under the orders of abrupt override impulses, twisting him away from the fist. The response wasn't quite good enough. Gerald caught him a glancing blow on the side of his head. Behind that strike was the force of a body hardened by months of tough physical labour. The supervisor stumbled back into his partner, the two of them swaying desperately for balance.

Cheers and raucous whoops of encouragement were hurled from all across the lounge. Someone picked up one of the big potted plants and threw it at a distracted nurse. An alarm shrilled. The staff began to draw their nervejam sticks.

"Marie! Baby, I'm here." Gerald had finally reached the holoscreen, thrusting his face against the cool plastic. His nose was squashed almost flat. She grinned and flirted mere centimetres away, her figure composed from a compact cellular array of small glowing spheres. "Marie! Let me in, Marie." He started to thump on the screen. "Marie!"

She vanished. The handsome anchorman smiled out. Gerald shrieked in anguish, and started pummelling the holoscreen with all his strength. "Marie. Come back. Come back to me." Smears of blood from torn knuckles dribbled down the anchorman's tanned features.

"Oh, Christ," the first supervisor grunted. He aimed a nervejam stick at Gerald's back and fired. Gerald froze, then his limbs started to quake fiercely. A long wretched wail fluted out of his lips as he crumpled onto the floor. He managed to gasp one last piteous "Marie" before unconsciousness claimed him.

14

Given the propensity for mild paranoia among Tranquillity's plutocrats, medical facilities were always one aspect of the habitat never short of investment and generous charitable donations. Consequentially, and in this case fortuitously, there was always a degree of overcapacity. After twenty years of what amounted to chronic underuse, the Prince Michael Memorial Hospital's pediatric ward was now chock full. A situation which produced a permanent riot along its broad central aisle during the day.

When Ione called in, half of the kids from Lalonde were chasing each other over beds and around tables, yelling ferociously. The game was possessed and mercenaries, and mercenaries always won. The two rampaging teams charged past Ione, neither knowing nor caring who she was (her usual escort of serjeants had been left outside). A harassed Dr Giddings, the head of the pediatric department, caught sight of his prestigious visitor and hurried over. He was in his late twenties, effusiveness and a lanky frame marrying to produce a set of hectic, rushed mannerisms whenever he spoke. His face inclined towards chubby, which gave him an engagingly boyish appearance. Ione wondered if he'd undergone cosmetic tailoring; that face would be so instantly trustworthy to children, a big brother you could always confide in.

"Ma'am, I'm so sorry," he blurted. "We had no idea you were coming." He tried to reseal the front of his white house tunic, glancing around fretfully at the ward. Cushions and bedclothes were scattered everywhere, colourful animatic dolls waddled around, either laughing or repeating their catch phrases. (Probably wasted, Ione thought, none of these children would recognize the idols from this season's AV shows.)

"I don't think I'd be very popular if you made them clean

up just for me," Ione said with a smile. "Besides, I've been watching them for the last few days. I'm really only here to confirm they're adapting properly."

Dr Giddings gave her a careful glance, using his fingers to comb back some of his floppy ginger hair. "Oh, yes, they're adapting all right. But then children are always easy to bribe. Food, toys, clothes, trips into the parkland, every kind of outdoor game they can play. Never fails. This is Heaven's holiday camp as far as they're concerned."

"Aren't they homesick?"

"Not really. I'd describe them as parent-sick more than anything. Separation causes some psychological problems, naturally." He gestured around. "But as you can see, we're doing our best to keep them busy, that way they don't have time to think about Lalonde. It's easier with the younger ones. Some of the older ones are proving recalcitrant; they can be prone to moodiness. But again, I don't think it's anything serious. Not in the short term."

"And in the long term?"

"Long term, the only real cure is to get them back to Lalonde and their parents."

"That's going to have to wait, I'm afraid. But you've certainly done a wonderful job with them."

"Thank you," Dr Giddings murmured.

"Is there anything else you need?" Ione asked.

Dr Giddings pulled a face. "Well, medically they're all fine now apart from Freya and Shona; and the nanonic packages are taking good care of those two. They should be healed within a week. So, as I said, what the rest could really do with right now is a strong, supportive family environment. If you were to appeal for foster families, I'm sure we'd have enough volunteers."

"I'll have Tranquillity put out an announcement, and make sure the news studios mention it."

Dr Giddings grinned in relief. "That's very kind, thank you. We were worried people might not come forwards, but I'm sure that if you back the appeal personally . . ."

"Do my best," she said lightly. "Do you mind if I wander around?"

"Please." He half bowed, half stumbled.

Ione walked on down the aisle, stepping around a thrilled three-year-old girl who was dancing with, and cuddling, a fat animatic frog in a bright yellow waistcoat.

The twin rows of beds had channelled an avalanche of toys along the main aisle. Holomorph stickers were colonizing the walls and even some of the furniture, their cartoon images swelling up from the surface to run through their cycle, making it appear as if the polyp were flexing with rainbow diffraction patterns. A blue-skinned imp appeared to be the favourite; picking its nose, then flicking disgusting tacky yellow bogies at anyone passing by. No medical equipment was actually visible, it was all built unobtrusively into the walls and bedside cabinets.

The far end opened up into a lounge section, with a big table where they all sat around for meals. Its curving wall had two large oval windows which provided a panoramic view out past the curving habitat shell. Right now Tranquillity was above Mirchusko's nightside, but the rings glinted as if they were arches of frosted glass, and the smooth beryl orb of Falsia shone with a steady aquamarine hue. The stars continued their eternal orbit around the habitat.

A girl had made a broad nest of cushions in front of a window, snuggling down in them to watch the astronomical marvels roll past her. According to the neural strata's local memory, she'd been there for a couple of hours—a ritual practised every day since *Lady Mac* had arrived.

Ione hunched down beside her. She looked about twelve, with short-cropped hair so blond it was almost silver.

What's her name? Ione asked.

Jay Hilton. She's the oldest of the group, and their leader. She is one of the moody ones Dr Giddings mentioned.

"Hello, Jay."

"I know you." Jay managed an aslant frown. "You're the Lord of Ruin."

"Oh, dear, you've found me out."

"Thought so. Everyone said my hair is the same as yours."

"Hum, they're almost right; I'm growing mine a bit longer these days."

"Father Horst cut mine."

"He did a good job."

"Of course he did."

"Cutting hair isn't the only thing he did right by all accounts."

"Yes."

"You're not joining in with the games much, are you?"

Jay wrinkled her nose up contemptuously. "They're just kids' games."

"Ah. You prefer the view then?"

"Sort of. I've never seen space before. Not real space, like this. I thought it was just empty, but this is always different. It's so pretty with the rings and everything. So's the parkland, too. Tranquillity's nice all over."

"Thank you. But wouldn't you be better off in the parkland? It's healthier than sitting here all day long."

"Suppose so."

"Did I say something wrong?"

"No. It's just . . . I think it's safer here, that's all."

"Safer?"

"Yes. I talked to Kelly on the flight here, we were in the spaceplane together. She showed me all the recordings she'd made. Did you know the possessed were frightened of space? That's why they make the red cloud cover the sky, so they don't have to see it."

"I remember that part, yes."

"It's sort of funny if you think about it, the dead scared of the dark."

"Thank heavens they're scared of something, I say. Is that why you like sitting here?"

"Yes. This is like the night; so I'll be safe from them here."

"Jay, there are no possessed in Tranquillity, I promise."

"You can't promise that. Nobody can."

"Okay. Ninety-nine per cent, then. How's that sound?"

"I believe that." Jay smiled sheepishly.

"Good. You must be missing your family?"

"I miss Mummy. We went to Lalonde so we could get away from the rest of our family."

"Oh."

"I miss Drusilla, too. She's my rabbit. And Sango; he was Mr Manani's horse. But he's dead anyway. Quinn Dexter shot him." The tenuous smile faded, and she glanced back at the stars in a hunt for reassurance.

Ione studied the young girl for a moment. She didn't think a foster family would be much use in this case, Jay was too clued up to accept a substitute for anything. However, Dr Giddings had mentioned bribes . . . "There's someone I'd like you to meet, I think you'll get on very well with her."

"Who?" Jay asked.

"She's a friend of mine, a very special friend. But she doesn't come down into the starscrapers; it's tricky for her. You'll have to come up and visit her in the park."

"I ought to wait for Father Horst. We normally have lunch together."

"I'm sure he won't mind just this once. We can leave a message."

Jay was obviously torn. "I suppose so. I don't know where he's gone."

To see Tranquillity's bishop, but Ione didn't say it.

* * *

"I wonder why you saw the demon as red?" the bishop was asking as the two of them walked the old-fashioned grounds of the cathedral with its century-old yew hedges, rose beds, and stone-lined ponds. "It does seem somewhat classical. One can hardly credit that Dante did actually get shown around Hell."

"I think demon might be a simplistic term in this instance," Horst replied. "I've no doubt that it was some kind of spiritual entity; but given the clarity of hindsight, it seemed to be more curious than malevolent."

"Remarkable. To come face-to-face with a creature not of this realm. And you say it first appeared before the Ivets performed their dark mass?"

"Yes. Hours before. Though it was definitely present at the mass; right there when possession started."

"It was the instigator, then?"

"I don't know. But I hardly think its presence can be a coincidence. It was certainly involved."

"How strange."

Horst was disturbed by how melancholic the old man sounded. Joseph Saro was far removed from the tough realist of a bishop Horst had served with back at the arcology; this was a genteel jolly man, whose subtlety was perfectly suited to an undemanding diocese like Tranquillity. With his almost-white beard and crinkled ebony skin, he had evolved a cosy dignity. More of a social figure than religious leader.

"Your grace?" Horst prompted.

"Strange to think that it is two thousand six hundred years since Our Lord walked the earth, the last time of miracles. We are, as you said earlier, so used to dealing in the concept of faith rather than fact. And now here we are again, surrounded by miracles, although of a singularly dark countenance. The Church no longer has to teach people and then pray that they come to believe in their own way; all we have to do today is point. Who can refute what the eye beholds, even though it doth offend." He finished with a lame smile.

"Our teachings still have purpose," Horst said. "More so than ever now. Believe me, your grace, the Church has endured for millennia so that people alive today can know Christ's message. That is a tremendous achievement, one we can all draw comfort from. So much has been endured, schism from within, conflict and assaults from outside. All so His word can be heard in the darkest hour."

"Which word?" Joseph Saro asked quietly. "We have so many true histories now; old orthodoxies, revelationist scrolls, revisionist teachings; Christ the pacifist, Christ the warrior. Who knows what was really said, what was altered to appease Rome? It was so long ago."

"You're wrong, your grace. I'm sorry, but the details of that time are irrelevant. That He existed is all we need to know. We carried the essence of Our Lord across the centuries, it is that which we've kept alive for so long, ready for this day. Christ showed us the human heart has dignity, that everyone can be redeemed. If we have faith in ourselves, we cannot fail. And that is the strength we must gather if we are to confront the possessed."

"I'm sure you're right; it's just that such a message seems, well . . . "

"Simplistic? Fundamentals are always simple. That is why they endure for so long."

Joseph Saro patted Horst's shoulder. "Ah, my boy, I envy your faith, I really do. My task would be so much easier if I believed with your fervour. That we have souls is of no doubt to me; though we can be assured our scientist brethren will seek a solid rationale among the grubby shadows of quantum cosmology. Who knows, perhaps they will even find it. Then what? If our very souls are given a scientific basis, what use will people have for the Church?"

"I don't believe the Church's ethos can change simply because we have learned more of ourselves. The love of Christ will be no less valid for us now than it has been for the billions of past believers who lived in ignorance. His message uplifts the spirit, no matter what the substance of that spirit is revealed to be. If anything, the message becomes more important. We must have some hope as we face the beyond."

"Ah yes, the beyond. Purgatory indeed. It frightens people, Horst. It certainly frightens me."

"It shouldn't, your grace. There is more than purgatory awaiting us. Much more."

"Goodness me, you believe that as well?"

"Yes." Horst half smiled, as though he had only just realized it himself. "We can't pick and choose what parts of Christ's teachings to believe in; those sections which are convenient, or comforting, and disregard the rest. Above everything, he gave us the hope of redemption. I believe in that. Completely."

"Then the heavenly city awaits?"

"Some version of it, some sheltered haven for our souls where we can be at peace with our new existence."

"Did any of the lost souls you talked to happen to mention seeing such a place?"

"No." Horst smiled. "To demand proof is to lack faith."

The bishop laughed heartily. "Oh, well done, my boy. Teach the master what he once taught. Very good." He sobered. "So how do you explain the different faiths? Their myriad versions of the afterlife, and reincarnation, and spiritual development. You are going to have to think of that now. God knows, others will. Now spirituality is real, religion—all religion—will come in for scrutiny as never before. What of the others who claim theirs is the true path to God in his Heaven? What of the Muslims, the Hindus, the Buddhists, the Sikhs, the Confucians, the Shintoists, even the Starbridge tribes, not to mention all those troublesome cultists?"

"The origin of each is identical, that's what's important. The notion that we are something more than flesh and mind alone. People must have faith. If you believe in your God, you believe in yourself. There is no greater gift than that."

"Such murky waters we are adrift in," Joseph Saro murmured. "And you, Horst, you have grown into a man with the clearest of visions. I'm humbled, and even a little frightened by you. I must have you deliver the sermon next Sunday; you'll bring them flocking in. You may very well be the first of the Church's new evangelists."

"I don't think so, your grace. I've simply passed through the eye of the needle. The Lord has tested me, as He will test all of us in the months ahead. I regained my faith. For that I have the possessed to thank." Unconsciously, his hand went to his throat, sensitive fingertips feeling the tiny scars left over from when invisible fingers had clawed at him.

"I do hope Our Lord doesn't set me too hard a test," Joseph Saro said in a forlorn tone. "I'm far too old and comfortable in my ways to do what you did on Lalonde. That's not to say I'm not proud of you, for I certainly am. You and I are strictly New Testament priests, yet you were set a decidedly Old Testament task. Did you really perform an exorcism, my boy?"

Horst grinned. "Yes, I really did."

●　●　●

Captain Gurtan Mauer was still dry retching as the lid of the zero-tau pod closed over him, blackness suspending him from time. The tortures and obscenities might have wrecked his dignity, the pitiful pleas and promises were proof of that, but he was still cold sober sane. Quinn was quite determined in that respect. Only sane, rational people were able to appreciate the nuances of their own suffering. So the pain and barbarism was always pitched a degree below the level which would tip the *Tantu*'s ex-captain into the refuge of insanity. This way he could hold out for days, or even weeks. And zero-tau would hold him ready for when Quinn's wrath rose again; for him there would be no periods of relief, just one long torment.

Quinn smiled at the prospect. His robe and hood shrank to more manageable proportions, and he pushed off from the decking. He'd needed the interlude to regain his own equilibrium after the disaster in Earth orbit, the humiliation of retreat. Gurtan Mauer provided him with a valid focus for his anger. He could hardly use the starship's crew; there were only fifteen of them left now, and few were inessential.

"Where are we going, Quinn?" Lawrence asked as the two of them drifted through the companionway to the bridge.

"I'm not sure. I'll bet most of the Confederation knows about possession now, it'll make life fucking difficult." He wriggled through the hatch to the bridge, and checked around to see what was being done.

"We're almost finished, Quinn," Dwyer said. "There wasn't too much damage, and this is a warship, so most critical systems have backups. We're flight-ready again. But people are going to know we've been in some sort of scrap. No way could we go outside to repair the hull. Spacesuits won't work on us."

"Sure, Dwyer. You've done good."

Dwyer's grin was avaricious.

They were all waiting for Quinn to tell them where he wanted to go next. And the truth was, he wasn't entirely sure he knew. Earth was his goal, but perhaps he'd been too ambitious trying for it first. It was the old problem: to charge in with an army of disciples, or to stealthily rot the structure from within. After the dreariness of Norfolk, the prospect of action had excited him. It still did, but he obviously didn't have enough forces to break through Earth's defences. Not even the Royal Kulu Navy could do that.

He needed to get there on a different ship, one which wouldn't cause such a heated response. After he'd docked at the orbital tower station he could get down to the planet. He knew that.

But where to get another ship from? He knew so little about

the Confederation worlds. Only once during his twenty years on Earth had he met anyone from offworld.

"Ah." He grinned at Lawrence. "Of course, Banneth's colleague."

"What?"

"I've decided where we're going." He checked the bridge displays; their cryogenic fuel reserves could fly them another four hundred light years. More than enough. "Nyvan," he announced. "We're going to Nyvan. Dwyer, start working out a vector."

"What's Nyvan?" Lawrence asked.

"The second planet anyone ever found which was good enough to live on. Everyone used to flock there from the arcologies. They don't now."

* * *

Nova Kong has always boasted that it is the most beautiful city to be found within the Confederation. Wisely, few challenged the claim.

No other Adamist society had the kind of money which had been lavished on the city ever since the day Richard Saldana first stepped down out of his spaceplane and (according to legend) said: "This footstep will not depart in the sands of time."

If he did say it, he was certainly right. The capital city of the Kulu Kingdom was a memorial which no one who saw it would ever be likely to forget. Right from the start, aesthetics was a paramount factor in planning, and pretty grandiose aesthetics at that. It had no streets, only flamboyant boulevards, greenway avenues, and rivers (half of them artificial); all powered ground traffic used the labyrinth of underground motorways. Commemorative monuments and statues dominated the junctions; the Kingdom's heroic history was celebrated in hundreds of artistic styles from megalithic to contemporary.

Although it had a population of nineteen million, the building density regulations meant it was spread out over five hundred square kilometres, with Touchdown plaza at its centre. Every conceivable architectural era was to be found among

the public, private, and commercial buildings so carefully
sprinkled across the ground, with the exception of prefab concrete, programmable silicon, and composite ezystak panels
(anything built in Nova Kong was built to last). Seventeen
cathedrals strove for attention against neo-Roman government offices. Gloss-black pyramid condominiums were as
popular as Napoleonic apartment blocks with conservatory
roofs arching over their central wells. Sir Christopher Wren
proved a heavy influence on the long curving terraces of
snow-white stone town houses, while Oriental and Eastern
designs appeared to be favoured among the smaller individual
residences.

Chilly autumn air was gusting along the boulevards when
Ralph Hiltch flew in over the clean spires and ornate belfries.
His vantage point was a privilege not awarded to many peo-
ple. Commercial overflights were strictly forbidden; only
emergency craft, police, senior government officials, and the
Saldanas were ever permitted this view.

He couldn't have timed his arrival better, he thought. The
trees which filled the parks, squares, and ornamental water-
ways below were starting to turn in the morning frosts. Green
leaves were fading to an infinite variety of yellows, golds,
bronzes, and reds, a trillion flecks of rusty colour glinting in
the strong sunlight. Soggy auburn mantles were already expanding across the damp grass, while thick dunes snuggled up
in the sheltered lees of buildings. Nova Kong's million strong
army of utility mechanoids were programmed to go easy on
the invasive downfall, allowing the rustic image to prevail.

Today though, the refined perfection of the city was marred
by twisters of smoke rising from several districts. As they
passed close to one, Ralph accessed the flyer's sensor suite to
obtain a better view of a Gothic castle made from blocks of
amber and magenta glass which seemed to be the source. The
smoke was a dense billow pouring out from the stubby remains of a smashed turret. Fires were still flickering inside the
main hall. Over twenty police and Royal Marine flyers had
landed on the parkland outside; figures in active armour suits
walked through the castle's courtyards.

Ralph knew that depressing scene well enough. Although
in his heart he'd never expected to see it here, not Nova Kong,

the very nucleus of the Kingdom. He'd been born on the Principality of Jerez, and this was his first visit to Kulu. One part of his mind wryly acknowledged he would always retain a hint of the provincial attitude. Nova Kong was the capital, it ought to remain impervious to anything, any form of attack, physical or subversive. That was the reason his job, his agency, existed: the first line of defence.

"How many of these incursions have there been?" he asked the Royal Navy pilot.

"A couple of dozen in the last three days. Tough bastards to beat, I can tell you. The marines had to call down SD fire support a couple of times. We haven't seen any new ones for eleven hours now, thank Christ. That means we've probably got them all. City's under martial law, every transport route on the planet has shut down, and the AIs are sweeping the net for any sign of activity. Nowhere the possessed can hide anymore, and they certainly can't run."

"Sounds like you people were on the ball. We did much the same thing on Ombey."

"Yeah? You beat them there?"

"Almost."

The ion field flyer lined up on Apollo Palace. Awe and nerves squeezed Ralph's heart, quickening its pulse. Physically this was the middle of the city, politically the hub of an interstellar empire, and home to the most notorious family in the Confederation.

Apollo Palace was a small town in its own right, albeit contained under a single roof. Every wing and hall interlocked, their unions marked by rotundas and pagodas. Sumptuous stately homes, which in centuries past must have been independent houses for senior courtiers, had been now incorporated in the overall structure, ensnared by the flourishing webbing of stone cloisters which had gradually crept out from the centre. The family chapel was larger than most of the city's cathedrals, and more graceful than all.

A hundred quadrangles containing immaculate gardens flashed past underneath the flyer's fuselage as it descended. Ralph shunted a mild tranquillizer program into primary mode. Turning up electronically stoned before your sovereign probably went against every written and unwritten court protocol in existence. But, damn it, he couldn't afford a slip due to nerves now—the Kingdom couldn't afford it.

Eight armed Royal Marines were waiting at the foot of the airstairs when they landed in an outer quadrangle. Their captain clicked his heels together and saluted Ralph.

"Sorry, sir, but I must ask you to stand still."

Ralph eyed the chemical projectile guns trained on him. "Of course." Cold air turned his breath to grey vapour.

The captain signalled one of the marines who came forward holding a small sensor pad. She touched it to Ralph's forehead, then went on to his hands.

"Clear, sir," she barked.

"Very good. Mr Hiltch, would you please datavise your ESA identification code, and your martial law transport authority number." The captain held up a processor block.

Ralph obliged the request.

"Thank you, sir."

The marines shouldered their weapons. Ralph whistled silent relief, happy at how seriously they were taking the threat of possession, but at the same time wishing he wasn't on the receiving end.

A tall, middle-aged man stepped out of a nearby doorway and walked over. "Mr Hiltch, welcome to Kulu." He put his hand out.

That he was a Saldana was not in doubt; his size, poise, and that distinct nose made it obvious for anyone to see. Trouble was, there were so many of them. Ralph ran an identity check through his neural nanonics, the file was in his classified section: the Duke of Salion, chairman of the Privy Council's security commission, and Alastair II's first cousin. One of the most unobtrusive and powerful men in the Kingdom.

"Sir. Thank you for meeting me."

"Not at all." He guided Ralph back through the door. "Princess Kirsten's message made it clear she considers you important. I have to say we're all extremely relieved to hear Ombey has survived a not inconsiderable assault by the possessed. The Principality does lack the resources available to the more developed worlds of the Kingdom."

"I saw the smoke as I flew down. It seems nowhere is immune."

A lift was waiting for them just inside the building. The Duke datavised an order into its processor. Ralph felt it start off, moving downwards, then horizontally.

"Regrettably so," the Duke admitted. "However, we believe we have them contained here. And preliminary indications from the other Principalities are that they've also been halted. Thankfully, it looks like we're over the worst."

"If I might ask, what was the sensor that marine used on me?"

"You were being tested for static electricity. The Confederation Navy researchers have found the possessed carry a small but permanent static charge. It's very simple, but so far it's proved infallible."

"Some good news, that makes a change."

"Quite." The Duke gave him a sardonic smile.

The lift opened out into a long anteroom. Ralph found it hard not to gape; he'd thought Burley Palace was opulent. Here the concept of ornamentation and embellishment had been taken to outrageous heights. Marble was drowning under arabesque patterns of platinum leaf; the church-high ceiling was adorned with frescoes of unusual xenocs which were hard to see behind the glare of galactic chandeliers. Arched alcoves were inset with circular windows of graduated glass, each fashioned after a different flower. Trophy heads were mounted on the wall, jewelled armour helmet effigies of fantasy creatures; dragons wrought in curving jade panes inlaid with rubies, unicorns in alabaster and emeralds, hobgoblins in onyx and diamonds, mermaids in aquamarine and sapphires.

Courtiers and civil servants were walking about briskly, their footfalls completely silent on the Chinese carpet. The Duke strode diagonally across the room, with everyone melting out of his way. Ralph hurried to keep up.

Double doors opened into a library of more manageable proportions. Then Ralph was through into a snug oak-panelled study with a log fire burning eagerly in the grate and frost-rimed French windows presenting a view out into a quadrangle planted with ancient chestnuts. Five young children were scampering about on the lawn, dressed against the cold in colourful coats, woollen bobble hats, and leather gloves. They were flinging sticks and stones into the big old trees, trying to bring down the prickly burrs.

King Alastair II stood before the fire, rubbing his hands together in front of the flames. A bulky camel's hair coat was slung over a high-backed leather chair. Damp footprints on the carpet indicated he'd just come in from the quadrangle.

"Good afternoon, Mr Hiltch."

Ralph stood to attention. "Your Majesty." Despite the fact he was in the presence of his King, Ralph could only stare at the oil painting on the wall. It was the Mona Lisa. Which was impossible. The French state of Govcentral would never let *that* out of the Paris arcology. Yet would the King of Kulu really have a copy on his wall?

"I reviewed the report which came with you, Mr Hiltch," the King said. "You've had a busy few weeks. I can see why my sister valued your counsel so highly. One can only hope all my ESA officers are so efficient and resourceful. You are a credit to your agency."

"Thank you, Your Majesty."

The Duke shut the study door as the King used an iron poker to stir the fire.

"Do stand easy, Mr Hiltch," Alastair said. He put the poker back in the rack and eased himself down in one of the leather chairs which ringed the hearth rug. "Those are my grandchildren out there." A finger flicked towards the quadrangle. "Got them here at the palace while their father's off with the Royal Navy. Safest place for them. Nice to have them, too. That lad in the blue coat, being pushed around by his sister, that's Edward; your future king, in fact. Although I doubt you'll be around when he ascends the throne. God willing, it won't be for another century at least."

"I hope so, Your Majesty."

"Course you do. Sit down, Mr Hiltch. Thought we'd have an informal session to start with. Gather you've something controversial to propose. This way if it is too controversial, well . . . it'll simply never have happened. Can't have the monarch exposed to controversy, now can we?"

"Certainly not," the Duke said with a modest smile as he sat between the two of them.

An arbitrator, or a buffer? Ralph mused. He sat in the remaining leather chair, mildly relieved that he wasn't having to look up at the two men anymore. Both of them were half a head taller than he (another Saldana trait). "I understand, Your Majesty."

"Good man. So what hot little mess is dear Kirsten dropping in my lap this time?"

Ralph upped the strength of his tranquillizer program and started to explain.

When he finished, the King rose silently and dropped a couple of logs on the fire. Flames cast a shivering amber light across his face. At seventy-two he had acquired a dignity that went far beyond the superficial physical countenance provided by his genes; experience had visibly enriched his personality. The King, Ralph decided, had become what kings were supposed to be, someone you could trust. All of which made his troubled expression more worrying than it would be on any normal politician.

"Opinion?" Alastair asked the Duke, still gazing at the fire.

"It would appear to be an evenhanded dilemma, sir. Mr Hiltch's proposal is tenable, certainly. Reports we have received show the Edenists are more than holding their own against the possessed; only a handful of habitats have been penetrated, and I believe all the insurgents were rounded up effectively. And using bitek constructs as front line troops would reduce our losses to a minimum if you commit an army to liberating Mortonridge. Politically, though, Princess Kirsten is quite right; such a course of action will mean a complete reversal of a foreign policy which has stood for over four hundred years, and was actually instigated by Richard Saldana himself."

"For good reasons at the time," the King ruminated. "Those damn atheists with their Helium$_3$ monopoly have so much power over us Adamists. Richard knew being free of their helping hand was the only road to true independence. It might have been ruinously expensive to build our own cloudscoops in those days, but by God look at what we've achieved with that freedom. And now Mr Hiltch here is asking me to become dependent on those same Edenists."

"I'm suggesting an alliance, Your Majesty," Ralph said. "Nothing more. A mutually advantageous military alliance in time of war. And they will benefit from the liberation of Mortonridge just as much as we will."

"Really?" the King asked; he sounded sceptical.

"Yes, Your Majesty. It has to be done. We have to prove to ourselves, and every other planet in the Confederation, that the possessed can be driven back into the beyond. I expect such a war might well take decades; and who would ever agree to start it if they didn't know victory was possible? Whatever the outcome, we have to try."

"There has to be another solution," said the King, almost inaudibly. "Something easier, a more final way of ridding ourselves of this threat. Our navy scientists are working on it, of course. One can only pray for progress, though so far it has been depressingly elusive." He sighed loudly. "But one cannot act on wishes. At least not in my position. I have to respond to facts. And the fact is that two million of my subjects have been possessed. Subjects I am sworn before God to defend. So something must be done, and you, Mr Hiltch, have offered me the only valid proposal to date. Even if it is only related to the physical."

"Your Majesty?"

"One isn't criticising. But I have to consider what the Ekelund woman said to you. Even if we win and banish them all from living bodies, we are still going to wind up joining them eventually. Any thoughts on how to solve that little conundrum, Mr Hiltch?"

"No, Your Majesty."

"No. Of course not. Forgive me, I'm being dreadfully unfair. But never fear; you're not alone on that one, I'm sure. We can dump it off on the bishop for the moment, though ultimately it will have to be addressed. And addressed thoroughly. The prospect of spending eternity in purgatory is not one I naturally welcome. Yet at the moment it seems one to which we are all destined." The King smiled wanly, glancing out of the French windows at his grandchildren. "I can only hope Our Lord will eventually show us some of His mercy. But for now, the problem at hand: liberating Mortonridge, and the political fallout from asking the Edenists to help. Simon?"

The Duke deliberated on his answer. "As you say, sir, the situation today is hardly the same as when Richard Saldana founded Kulu. However, four centuries of discord has entrenched attitudes, particularly that of the average middle-Kulu citizen. The Edenists aren't seen as demons, but neither are they regarded with any geniality. Of course, as Mr Hiltch has said, in times of war allies are to be found in the most unusual places. I don't believe an alliance in these circumstances would damage the monarchy. Certainly a successful conclusion to a liberation campaign would prove your decision to be justified. That is assuming the Edenists will agree to come to our aid."

"They'll help, Simon. We might snub them for the benefit of the public, but they are not stupid. Nor are they dishonourable. Once they see I am making a genuine appeal they will respond."

"The Edenists, yes. But the Lord of Ruin? I find it hard to believe the Princess suggested we ask her for the DNA sequence of Tranquillity's serjeants, no matter how good they would be as soldiers."

The King gave a dry laugh. "Oh, come now, Simon, where's your sense of charity? You of all people should know how accommodating Ione is when it comes to the really important problems faced by the Confederation. She's proved her worth in the political arena with the Mzu woman; and she is family, after all. I'd say it was far less galling for me to request her help than it is making any approach to the Edenists."

"Yes, sir," the Duke said heavily.

Alastair tutted in bogus dismay. "Never mind, Simon, it's your job to be paranoid on my behalf." He turned his gaze back to Ralph Hiltch. "My decision, though. As always."

Ralph tried to appear resolute. It was quite extraordinary to witness the use of power at such a level. The thoughts and words formulated in this room would affect literally hundreds of worlds, maybe even a fate greater than that. He wanted to scream at the King to say yes, that it was bloody obvious what he should decide. Yes. Yes. YES. Say it, damn you.

"I'll give my authority to initiate the project," Alastair said. "That's all for now. We will ask the Edenists if they can assist us. Lord Mountjoy can sound out their ambassador to the court, that's what he's good at. While you, Mr Hiltch, will go directly to the Admiralty and begin a detailed tactical analysis

of the Mortonridge Liberation. Find out if it really is possible.
Once I've seen how these two principal factors mature, the
proposal will be brought before the Privy Council for consid-
eration."

"Thank you, Your Majesty."

"It's what I'm here for, Ralph." His stately smile became
artful. "I think you can cancel your tranquillizer program
now."

• • •

"Oh, Lord, now what's he up to?" Staff Nurse Jansen Kovak
asked as soon as he accessed the ceiling sensors in Gerald
Skibbow's room. All the medical facility's inmates were reviewed on a regular basis; with troublesome ones like Skibbow a check was scheduled every twenty minutes.

The room had modest furnishings. A single bed and a deep
settee had puffed themselves up out of the floor, ready to retract if an inmate tried to injure himself against them. All the
services were voice-activated. There was nothing to grab hold
of, no loose items lying around which could weight a fist.

Gerald was kneeling beside the bed as if in prayer, his
hands hidden from the ceiling sensors. Jansen Kovak
switched cameras, using one incorporated in the floor, giving
him a mouse-eye view.

The image showed Gerald was holding a spoon with both
hands. Slowly and relentlessly he was flexing it, bending the
stem just below the scoop. It was made of a strong composite, but Jansen Kovak could see the tiny white stress fractures
crinkling the surface. Another minute and the spoon would
break, leaving Gerald with a long spike which although not
exactly sharp could certainly harm anyone caught on the end
of a lunge.

"Dr Dobbs," Jansen datavised. "I think we have a problem
with Skibbow."

"What now?" Dobbs asked. He had only just caught up on
his appointments; yesterday's episode with Skibbow in the
lounge had wrecked his schedule. Skibbow had been recover-
ing well up until that point. Bad luck his daughter had turned
up again—certainly the timing, anyway. Although the fact she

was still alive could eventually be worked into his therapy, give him a long-term achievement goal.

"He's smuggled a spoon out of the lounge. I think he's going to use it as a weapon."

"Oh, great, just what I need." Riley Dobbs hurriedly finished with the patient he was counselling, and accessed the facility's AI. He retrieved the interpretation routine which could make sense of Skibbow's unique thought patterns and opened a channel to the debrief nanonics. This kind of grubby mental spying was totally unethical; but then he had discarded the constraints of the General Medical Council all those years ago when he came to work for the Royal Navy. Besides, if he was to effect any kind of cure on Skibbow, he needed to know exactly what kind of demons were driving the man. Resorting to a weapon, however feeble, seemed extreme for Skibbow.

The images were slow to form in Dobbs's mind. Gerald's thoughts were in turmoil, fast-paced, flicking between present reality and extrapolated fantasies.

Dobbs saw the pale blue wall of the bedroom, fringed with the redness which came from squinted eyes. Feeling the spoon in his hands, the friction heat building up in its stem. Tired arm muscles as they pushed and pulled at the stubborn composite. "And they'll regret getting in my way. God will they ever."

Image shift to—a corridor. Kovak screaming in pain as he sinks to his knees, the spoon handle jutting out of his white tunic. Blood spreading over his chest, drops splattering on the floor. Dr Dobbs was already sprawled facedown on the corridor floor, his whole body soaked in glistening blood. "Which is less than he deserves." Kovak emitted a last gurgle and died. Gerald pulled the Weapon of Vengeance from his chest and carried on down the corridor. Sanatorium staff peered fearfully out of doors, only to shrink back when they saw who was coming. As well they might; they knew who had Right and Justice on his side.

Shifting back—to the bedroom, where the damn spoon still hadn't snapped. His breath was becoming ragged now. But still he persevered. A soundless mutter of: "Come on. Please!"

Shifting—to the journey through Guyana, a confused blur of rock walls. Not actually knowing the geometry of the asteroid; but he'd find a way. Asteroid spaceports were always attached up at the axis. There would be trains, lifts . . .

Back—when the spoon finally snaps, making his taut arms judder. "Now I can begin. I'm coming for you, darling. Daddy's coming."

To—fly through space. Stars streaking into blue-white lightning outside the ship's hull as he rushes to the strange distant habitat. And there's Marie waiting for him at the end of the voyage, adrift in space, clad in those fragile white swirls of gauze, luscious hair blown back by the breeze. Where she says to him: "They'll tell you that you shouldn't have come, Daddy."

"Oh, but I should," he replies. "You need me, darling. I know what you're going through. I can drive the demon out. You'll feel nothing as I push you into zero-tau." And so he lays her gently down into the plastic coffin and closes the lid. Blackness eclipses her, then ends to show her face smiling up at him, twinkling tears of gratitude slipping from her eyes.

Which is why he's standing up now, slipping the jagged spoon handle into his sleeve. Calm. Take deep calming breaths now. There's the door. Daddy's coming to rescue you, baby. He is.

Riley Dobbs cancelled the interpretation routine. "Oh, bugger." He ordered Gerald's debrief nanonics to induce somnolence within the fevered brain.

Nerves and courage fired up, Gerald was reaching for the bedroom door when a wave of tiredness slapped into him with an almost physical force. He sagged, swaying on his feet as muscles became too exhausted to carry him. The bed loomed before him, and he was toppling towards it as darkness and silence poured into the room.

"Jansen," Riley Dobbs datavised. "Get in there and take the spoon away, and any other implements you can find. Then I want him transferred to a condition three regime; twenty-four-hour observation, and a softcare environment. He's going to be a dangerous pain until we can wean him off this new obsession."

Kiera Salter had dispatched fifteen hellhawks to the Oshanko sector of the Confederation to seed dissent into the communications nets of the Imperium's worlds and asteroid settlements. That was three days ago.

Now, Rubra observed eleven wormhole termini blink open to disgorge the survivors. Two bloated warplanes, and a sinister featureless black aeromissile-shape kept a loose formation with eight Olympian-sized harpies who flapped their way back towards Valisk's docking ledges with lethargic, defeated wing strokes.

I see the Emperor's navy has lived up to its top gun reputation, Rubra remarked in a tone of high spirits. **Just how is troop morale coming along these days? That's the eighth of Kiera's little jaunts in which your hellhawks have taken a beating from unfriendly natives. Any grumblings of rebellion at the new regime yet? A few discreet suggestions that priorities ought to be altered?**

Screw you, Dariat retorted. He was sitting on a small riverbank of crumbling earth, dark water flowing swiftly below his dangling feet. Occasionally he caught sight of a big garpike slithering past on the way to its spawning ground upriver. Five hundred metres away in the other direction the water tipped over a shallow cliff to splatter down into the circumfluous saltwater reservoir ringing the endcap. Out here among the habitat's low rolling hills the eight separate xenoc grasses waged a continual war for primacy. As they all came to seed at different times of the year none ever won an outright victory. Right now it was a salmon-pink Tallok-aboriginal variety which was flourishing, its slender corkscrew blades tangling in a dense blanket of dry candyfloss which matted the ground. Back along the cylindrical habitat, Dariat could see the broad rosy bracelet fading to emerald around the midsection where the starscraper lobbies were; and in turn that rich terrestrial vegetation eventually petered away into the ochre scrub desert which occupied the far end. The bands of colour were as striking as they were regular; it was as if someone had sprayed them on while Valisk turned on a lathe.

Of course, you wouldn't actually know much about what's happening to the subjects of Kiera's politburo dictatorship these days, Rubra continued pleasantly. **You**

being a loner now. Did you know dear old Bonney was shouting for you yesterday? I whisked one of the non-possessed away from her clutches, put him on a tube carriage, and shot him off to one of my safe areas. I don't think she was very happy about it. Your name came up several times.

Sarcasm is a pitiful form of wit.

Absolutely, my boy. So you won't be letting it get to you, will you?

No.

Mind you, Kiera is having some success. The second hellhawk full of kids arrived this morning, looking for that bright new world she promised in her recording. Two dozen of them; the youngest was only nine. Would you like to see what was done to them so they could be possessed? I have all the memories, nobody tried to block my perception from that ceremony.

Shut up.

Oh, dear, is that a twang of conscience I detect?

As you well know, I don't care what happens to the morons who get suckered here. All I'm interested in is how badly I'm going to fuck you up.

I understand. But then I know you better than Kiera does. It's a pity you don't understand me.

Wrong. I know you completely.

You don't, my boy. You don't know what I'm holding secret. Anastasia would thank me for what I'm doing, the protection I'm extending you.

Dariat growled, sinking his head into his hands. He had chosen this spot for the seclusion it offered from Kiera's merry band of maniacs. He wanted somewhere quiet to meditate. Free from distractions he could try to formulate a mental pattern which had the ability to penetrate the neural strata. But he wasn't free of distractions, he never could be. For Rubra would never tire of playing his game; the insinuations, the doubts, the dark hints.

During the last thirty years, Dariat thought he'd perfected patience to an inhuman degree. But now he was finding that a different kind of patience was required. Despite a herculean resolution he was beginning to question if Rubra really did have any secrets. It was stupid, of course, because Rubra was bluffing, running an elaborate disinformation campaign. However, if Anastasia did have some secret, some legacy, the only entity who would know was Rubra.

Yet if it did exist, why hadn't Rubra used it already? Both of them knew this was a struggle to the bitterest of ends.

Anastasia could never have done anything which would make him betray himself. Not sweet Anastasia, who had always warned him about Anstid. Her Lord Thoale made sure she knew the consequences of every action. Anastasia understood destiny. Why did I never listen to her?

Anastasia left nothing for me, he said.

Oh, yeah? In that case, I'll do a deal with you, Dariat.

Not interested.

You should be. I'm asking you to join me.

What?

Join me, here in the neural strata. Transfer yourself over like a dying Edenist. We can become a duality.

You have got to be fucking joking.

No. I have been considering this for some time. Our current situation is not going to end well, not for either of us. Both of us are at odds with Kiera; that will never change. But together we could beat her easily, purge the habitat of her cronies. You can rule Valisk yet.

You used to control a multistellar industrial empire, Rubra. Now look what you're reduced to. You're pathetic, Rubra. Contemptible. And the best thing is, you know it.

Rubra shifted his principal focus from the linen-suited young man, withdrawing to contemplate a general perception of the habitat. Bonney Lewin was missing again. That damn woman was getting too good at foxing his observation routines. He automatically expanded the secondary routines surrounding and protecting the remaining non-possessed. She'd show up near one of them soon enough.

He didn't agree, Rubra said to the Kohistan Consensus.

That is unfortunate. Salter is expending a great deal of effort to collect her Deadnight followers.

Her what?

Deadnight is the name which her subversive recording

has acquired. Unfortunately a great many young Adamists are finding it seductive.

Don't I know it. You should see what she does to them when they get here. Those hellhawks should never have been allowed to collect them.

There is little we can do. We do not have the capability to shadow every hellhawk flight.

Pity.

Yes. The hellhawks are causing us some concern. So far they have not been used in an aggressor role. If they were deployed in combat with Valisk's armament resources behind them, they would pose a formidable problem.

So you keep telling me. Don't say you've finally come to a decision?

We have. With your permission we would like to remove their threat potential.

Do as you would be done by, and do it first. Well, well, you've finally started thinking like me. There's hope for all of you yet. Okay, go ahead.

Thank you, Rubra. We know this must be difficult for you.

Just make damn sure you don't miss. Some of my industrial stations are very close to my shell.

Rubra had always maintained an above-average number of Strategic Defence platforms around Valisk. Given his semi-paranoid nature it was inevitable he should want to make local space as secure as possible. Forty-five weapons platforms covered a bubble of space fifty thousand kilometres in diameter with the habitat and its comprehensive parade of industrial stations at the centre. They were complemented by two hundred sensor satellites, sweeping both inwards and outwards. No one had ever attempted an act of aggression within Valisk's sphere of interest—a remarkable achievement considering the kind of ships which frequented the spaceport.

Magellanic Itg had manufactured the network, developing indigenous designs and fabricating all the components itself. A policy which had earned the company a healthy quantity of export orders. It also enabled Rubra to install his personality as the network's executive. He certainly wasn't about to trust any of his woefully ineffectual descendants with his own defence.

That arrangement had come to an abrupt end with the emergence of the possessed. His control over the network was via affinity with bitek management processors that were integrated into every platform's command circuitry. He hadn't even realized he'd lost control of the platforms until he'd attempted to interdict the hellhawks when they first revealed themselves. Afterwards, he'd worked out that somebody— that little shit Dariat, no doubt—had subverted his SD governor thought routines long enough to load powerdown orders into every platform.

With the power off, there was no way of regaining control through the bitek processors. Every platform would have to be reactivated manually. Which was exactly what Kiera had done. Spacecraft had rendezvoused with the platforms and taken out Rubra's bitek management processors, replacing them with electronic processors and new fire authority codes.

A new SD Command centre was established in the counter-rotating spaceport, outside Rubra's influence. He couldn't strike at that like he could the starscrapers. The possessed technicians who reactivated the network were convinced they had made it independent, a system which only Kiera and her newly installed codes could control.

What neither they nor Dariat quite appreciated were the myriad number of physical interfaces between the neural strata and Valisk's communications net. The tube trains and the starscraper lifts were the most obvious examples, but every mechanical and electronic utility system had a similar junction, a small processor nodule which converted fibre optic pulses to nerve impulses and vice versa. And Magellanic Itg not only built Valisk's communications net, it also supplied ninety per cent of the counter-rotating spaceport's electronics. A fact which even fewer people were aware of was that every company processor had a back-door access function hardwired in, to which Rubra alone had the key.

Within seconds of the possessed establishing their new SD command channels he was in the system. A delicious irony, he felt, a ghost in the ghosts' machinery. The devious interface circuits he'd established to gain entry couldn't support anything like the data traffic necessary to give him full control of the platforms once more, but he could certainly do unto others what they'd done to him.

On the ready signal from the Kohistan Consensus, Rubra immediately sent a squall of orders out to the SD platforms. Command codes were wiped and replaced, safety limiters were taken off line, fusion generator management programs were reformatted.

In the commandeered spaceport management office used to run the habitat's SD network, every single alarm tripped at once. The whole room was flooded with red light from AV projectors and holoscreens. Then the power went off, plunging the crew into darkness.

"What the holy fuck is happening?" the recently appointed network captain shouted. A bright candle flame ignited at the tip of his index finger, revealing equally confounded faces all around him. He reached for his communications block to call Kiera Salter, dreading what she would say. But his hand never made it.

"Oh, shit, *look*," someone cried.

Severe white light began to flood in through the office's single port.

In forty-five fusion generators the plasma jet had become unstable, perturbed by rogue manipulations in the magnetic confinement field. Burnthrough occurred, plasma striking the confinement chamber walls, vaporizing the material, which increased the pressure a thousandfold. Forty-five fusion generators ruptured almost simultaneously, tearing apart the SD platforms in a burst of five million degree shrapnel and irradiated gas.

You're clear, Rubra told the waiting fleet.

Three hundred wormhole termini opened, englobing the habitat. Voidhawks shot out. Two hundred were designated to eradicate the industrial stations, depriving Kiera of their enormous armament manufacturing base. The bitek starships immediately swooped around onto their assault vectors. Kinetic missiles flashed out of their launch cradles, closing on the stations at sixteen gees. Each salvo was aimed so that the impact blast would kick the debris shower away from the habitat, minimizing the possibility of collision damage to the polyp shell.

The remaining hundred voidhawks were given suppression duties. Flying in ten-strong formations they broadcast affinity warnings to the thoroughly disconcerted hellhawks sitting on the docking ledges, ordering them to remain where they were. Sharp ribbons of ruby-red light from targeting lasers made the ledge polyp shimmer like black ice speared by an early morning sun. Refracted beams twisted around the alien shapes perched on the pedestals as the voidhawks strove to match their discordant vectors with the habitat's rotation.

Closer to the habitat, cyclones of shiny debris were churning out from the ruined industrial stations. Victorious voidhawks dived and spun above the metallic constellations, racing away ahead of the perilous wavefront of sharp high-velocity slivers. The hellhawks sat on their pedestals, observing the carnage with mute impotence.

Exemplary shooting, Rubra told the Kohistan Consensus. **Just remember when this is all over, you're paying Magellanic Itg's compensation claim.**

Three hundred wormhole interstices opened. The voidhawks vanished in an extraordinary display of synchronization. Elapsed time of the attack was ninety-three seconds.

Even in the heat of passion Kiera Salter could sense nearby minds starting to flare in alarm. She tried to dislodge Stanyon from her back and rise to her feet. When he resisted, tightening his grip, she simply smacked an energistic bolt into his chest. He grunted, the impact shoving him backwards.

"What the fuck are you playing at, bitch?" he growled.

"Be silent." She stood up, her wishes banishing the soreness and rising bruises. Sweat vanished, her hair returned to a neatly brushed mane. A simple, scarlet summer dress materialized over her skin.

On the other side of the endcap, the hellhawks were seething with resentment and anger. Beyond them was a haze of life which gave off a scent of icy determination. And Rubra, the ever-present mental background whisper, was radiating satisfaction. "Damn it!"

Her desktop processor block started shrilling. Data scrawled over its screen. A Strategic Defence alert, and red systems failure symbols were flashing all over the network schematic.

The high-pitched sound started to cut off intermittently, and the screen blanked out. The more she glared at the block, the worse the glitches became.

"What's happening?" Erdal Kilcady asked. Her other bedroom fancy—a gormless twenty-year-old who as far as she could determine had only one use.

"We're being attacked, you fool," she snapped. "It's those fucking Edenists." Shit, and her schemes had been progressing beautifully up until now. The idiot kids believed her recording; they were starting to arrive. Another couple of months would have seen the habitat population rise to a decent level.

Now this. The constant hellhawk flights must have frightened the Edenists into taking action.

The burn mark on Stanyon's chest healed over. Clothes sprang up to conceal his body. "We'd better get along to the SD control centre and kick some butt," he said.

Kiera hesitated. The SD centre was in the counter-rotating spaceport. She was certain the habitat itself would be safe from attack. Rubra would never allow that, but the spaceport might be a legitimate target.

Just as she took a reluctant first step towards the door the black bakelite telephone on her bedside table started to ring. The primitive communications instrument was one which worked almost infallibly in the energistic environment exuded by the possessed. She picked it up and pressed the handset to her ear. "Yes?"

"This is Rubra."

Kiera stiffened. She'd thought this room was outside of his surveillance. Exactly how many of their systems were exposed to him? "What do you want?"

"I want nothing. I'm simply delivering a warning. The voidhawks from Kohistan are currently eliminating the habitat's industrial production capability. There will be no more combat wasps to arm the hellhawks. We don't like the threat they present. Do not attempt to resupply from other sources or it will go hard on you."

"You can do nothing to us," she said, squeezing some swagger into her voice.

"Wrong. The Edenists respect life, which is why no hellhawks were destroyed this time. However, I can guarantee you the next voidhawk strike will not be so generous. I have eliminated the habitat's SD platforms so that in future it won't even be as difficult for them as today's strike. You and the hellhawks will sit out the rest of the conflict here. Is that understood?" The phone went dead.

Kiera stood still, her whitened fingers tightening around the handset. Little chips of bakelite sprinkled down onto the carpet. "Find Dariat," she told Stanyon. "I don't care where he is, find him and bring him to me. Now!"

* * *

Chaumort asteroid in the Châlons star system. Not a settlement which attracted many starships; it had little foreign exchange to purchase their cargoes of exotica, and few opportunities for export charters. Attendant industrial stations were old, lacking investment, their products a generation out-of-date; their poor sales added to the downwards cycle of the asteroid's economy. Ten per cent of the adult population was unemployed, making qualified workers Chaumort's largest (and irreplaceable) export. The fault lay in its leadership of fifteen years ago, who had been far too quick to claim independence from the founding company. Decline had been a steady constant from that carnival day onwards. Even as a refuge for undesirables, it was close to the bottom of the list.

But it was French-ethnic, and it allowed certain starships to dock despite the Confederation's quarantine edict. Life could have been worse, André Duchamp told himself, though admittedly not by much. He sat out at a table in what qualified as a pavement café, watching what there was of the worldlet passing by. The sheer rock cliff of the biosphere cavern wall rose vertically behind him, riddled with windows and balconies for its first hundred metres. Out in the cavern the usual yellow-green fields and orchards of spindly trees glimmered under the motley light of the solartubes which studded the axis gantry.

The view was acceptable, the wine passable, his situation if not tolerable then stable—for a couple of days. André took another sip and tried to relax. It was a pity his initial thought of selling combat wasps (post-Lalonde, fifteen were still languishing in the starship's launch tubes) to Chaumort's government had come to nothing. The asteroid's treasury didn't have the funds, and three inter-planetary ships had already been placed on defence contract retainers. Not that the money would have been much use here; the two local service companies which operated the spaceport had a very limited stock of spare parts. Of course, it would have come in useful to pay his crew. Madeleine and Desmond hadn't actually said anything, but André knew the mood well enough. And that bloody *anglo* Erick—as soon as they'd docked Madeleine had hauled him off to the local hospital. Well, those thieving doctors would have to wait.

He couldn't actually remember a time when there had been so few options available. In fact, he was down to one slender possibility now. He'd found that out as soon as he'd arrived (*this time* checking the spaceport's register for ships he knew). An unusually large number of starships were docked, all of them arriving recently. In other words, after the quarantine had been ratified and instituted by the Châlons system congress.

The Confederation Assembly had demonstrated a laudable goal in trying to stop the spread of the possessed, no one disputed that. However, the new colony planets and smaller asteroids suffered disproportionately from the lack of scheduled flights; they needed imported high-technology products to maintain their economies. Asteroid settlements like Chaumort, whose financial situation was none too strong to start with, were going to shoulder a heavy cost for the crisis not of their making. What most of these backwater communities shared was their remoteness; so if say an *essential* cargo were to arrive on a starship, then it was not inconceivable that said starship would be given docking permission. The local system congress wouldn't know, and therefore wouldn't be able to prevent it. That cargo could then (for a modest charter fee) be distributed to help other small disadvantaged communities by inter-planetary ships, whose movements were not subject to any Confederation proscription.

Chaumort was quietly establishing itself as an important node in a whole new market. The kind of market starships such as the *Villeneuve's Revenge* were uniquely qualified to exploit.

André had spoken to several people in the bars frequented by space industry crews and local merchants, voicing his approval for this turn of events, expressing an interest in being able to help Chaumort and its people in these difficult times. In short, becoming known. It was a game of contacts, and André had been playing it for decades.

Which was why he was currently sitting at a table waiting for a man he'd never seen before to show up. A bunch of teenagers hurried past, one of the lads snatching a basket of bread rolls from the café's table. His comrades laughed and cheered his bravado, and then ran off before the patron discovered the theft. André no longer smiled at the reckless antics of youth. Adolescents were a carefree breed; a state to which he had long aspired, and which his chosen profession had singularly failed to deliver. It seemed altogether unfair that happiness should exist only at one end of life, and the wrong end at that. It should be something you came in to, not left further and further behind.

A flash of colour caught his eye. All the delinquents had tied red handkerchiefs around their ankles. What a stupid fashion.

"Captain Duchamp?"

André looked up to see a middle-aged Asian-ethnic man dressed in a smart black silk suit with flapping sleeves. The tone and the easy body posture indicated an experienced negotiator; too smooth for a lawyer, lacking the confidence of the truly wealthy. A middleman.

André tried not to smile too broadly. The bait had been swallowed. Now for the price.

The medical nanonic around Erick's left leg split open from crotch to ankle, sounding as though someone were ripping strong fabric. Dr Steibel and the young female nurse slowly teased the package free.

"Looks fine," Dr Steibel decided.

Madeleine grinned at Erick and pulled a disgusted face. The leg was coated in a thin layer of sticky fluid, residue of the package unknitting from his flesh. Below the goo, his skin was swan-white, threaded with a complicated lacework of blue veins. Scars from the burns and vacuum ruptures were patches of thicker translucent skin.

Now the package covering his face and neck had been removed, Erick sucked in a startled breath as cool air gusted over the raw skin. His cheeks and forehead were still tingling from the same effect, and they'd been uncovered two hours ago.

He didn't bother looking at the exposed limb. Why bother? All it contained was memories.

"Give me nerve channel access, please," Dr Steibel asked. He was looking into an AV pillar, disregarding Erick completely.

Erick complied, his neural nanonics opening a channel directly into his spinal cord. A series of instructions were datavised over, and his leg rose to the horizontal before flexing his foot about.

"Okay." The doctor nodded happily, still lost in the information the pillar was directing at him. "Nerve junctions are fine, and the new tissue is thick enough. I'm not going to put the package back on, but I do want you to apply the moisturizing cream I'll prescribe. It's important the new skin doesn't dry out."

"Yes, Doc," Erick said meekly. "What about . . . ?" He gestured at the packages enveloping his upper torso and right arm.

Dr Steibel flashed a quick smile, slightly concerned at his patient's listless nature. " 'Fraid not. Your AT implants are integrating nicely, but the process isn't anywhere near complete yet."

"I see."

"I'll give you some refills for those support modules you're dragging around with you. These deep invasion packages you're using consume a lot of nutrients. Make sure the reserves don't get depleted."

He picked up the support module which Madeleine had repaired and glanced at the pair of them. "I'd strongly advise no further exposure to antagonistic environments for a while, as well. You can function at a reasonably normal level now, Erick, but only if you don't stress your metabolism. Do not ignore warnings from your metabolic monitor program. Nanonic packages are not to be regarded as some kind of infallible safety net."

"Understood."

"I take it you're not flying away for a while."

"No. All starship flights are cancelled."

"Good. I want you to keep out of free fall as much as possible, it's a dreadful medium for a body to heal in. Check in to a hotel in the high gravity section while you're here." He datavised a file over. "That's the exercise regime for your legs. Stick to it, and I'll see you again in a week."

"Thanks."

Dr Steibel nodded benevolently at Madeleine as he left the treatment room. "You can pay the receptionist on your way out."

The nurse began to spray a soapy solution over Erick's legs, flushing away the mucus. He used a neural nanonic override to stop a flinch when she reached his genitals. Thank God they hadn't been badly injured, just superficial skin damage from the vacuum.

Madeleine gave him an anxious glance over the nurse's back. "Have you got much cash in your card?" she datavised.

"About a hundred and fifty fuseodollars, that's all," he datavised back. "André hasn't transferred this month's salary over yet."

"I've got a couple of hundred, and Desmond should have some left. I think we can pay."

"Why should we? Where the hell is Duchamp? He should be paying for this. And my AT implants were only the first phase."

"Busy with some cargo agent, so he claimed. Leave it with me, I'll find out how much we owe the hospital."

Erick waited until she'd left, then datavised the hospital's net processor for the Confederation Navy Bureau. The net management computer informed him there was no such eddress. He swore silently, and accessed the computer's directory, loading a search order for any resident Confederation official. There wasn't one, not even a CAB inspector, too few ships used the spaceport to warrant the expense.

The net processor opened a channel to his neural nanonics.

"Report back to the ship, please, *mon enfant* Erick," André datavised. "I have won us a charter."

If his neck hadn't been so stiff, Erick would have shaken his head in wonder. A charter! In the middle of a Confederation quarantine. Duchamp was utterly unbelievable. His trial would be the shortest formality on record.

Erick swung his legs off the examination table, ignoring the nurse's martyrdom as her spray hoses were dislodged. "Sorry, duty calls," he said. "Now go and find me some trousers, I haven't got all day."

The middleman's name was Iain Girardi. André envied him his temperament; nothing could throw him, no insult, no threat. His cool remained in place throughout the most heated of exchanges. It was just as well; André's patience had long since been exhausted by his ungrateful crew.

They were assembled in the day lounge of the *Villeneuve's Revenge*, the only place André considered secure enough to discuss Girardi's proposition. Madeleine and Desmond had their feet snagged by a stikpad on the decking, while Erick was hanging on to the central ladder, his medical support modules clipped on to the composite rungs. André floated at Iain Girardi's side, glowering at the three of them.

"You've got to be fucking joking!" Madeleine shouted. "You've gone too far this time, Captain. Too bloody far. How can you even listen to this bastard's offer? God in Heaven, after all we went through at Lalonde. After all Erick did. Look at this ship! They did that to it, to you."

"That's not strictly accurate," Iain Girardi said, his voice tactfully smooth and apologetic.

"Shut the fuck up!" she bawled. "I don't need you to tell me what's been happening to us."

"Madeleine, please," André said. "You are hysterical. No one is forcing you to take part. I will not hold you to your contract if that is your wish."

"Damn right it's my wish. And nowhere does it say in my crew contract that I fly for the possessed. You pay me my last two months in full, plus the Lalonde combat bonus you owe me, and I'm out of here."

"If that is what you want."

"You've got the money?"

"*Oui.* But of course. Not that it is any of your business."

"Bastard. Why did you leave us to pay for Erick's treatment, then?"

"I am only a captain, I do not claim to perform miracles. My account has only just been credited. Naturally it is my pleasure to pay for dear Erick's treatment. It is a matter of honour for me."

"Just been . . ." Madeleine glanced from André to Iain Girardi, then back again. Understanding brought outraged astonishment. "You accepted a retainer from him?"

"*Oui,*" André snapped.

"Oh, Jesus." The shock of his admission silenced her.

"You spoke about Lalonde," Iain Girardi said. "Did the Confederation Navy rush to your aid while you were there?"

"Do not speak about an event of which you know nothing," Desmond growled.

"I know something about it. I've accessed Kelly Tirrel's report. Everybody has."

"And we have all accessed Gus Remar's report from New California. The possessed have conquered that world. By rights we ought to sign on with the Confederation Navy and help eradicate every one of them from this universe."

"Eradicate them how? This is a dreadful calamity which has befallen the human race, both halves of it. Dropping nukes on millions of innocent people is not going to bring about a resolution. Sure it was chaos at Lalonde, and I'm sorry you were hit with the worst of it. Those possessed were a disorganized terrified rabble, lashing out blindly to protect themselves from the mercenary army you carried. But the Organization is different. For a start we're proving that possessed and non-possessed can live together."

"Yeah, while we're convenient," Madeleine said. "While you need us to run the technology and fly starships. After that it's going to be a different bloody story."

"I can appreciate your bitterness, but you are wrong. Al Capone has taken the first steps to solving this terrible dilemma; he's proposing a joint research project to find a solution. All the Confederation Navy is doing is working on methods of blowing the possessed back into the beyond. I don't know about you, but I certainly don't want them to tri-umph."

Desmond bunched his fist, one toe coming off the stikpad, ready to launch himself at the man. "You traitorous little shit."

"You're going to die," Iain Girardi said remorselessly. "You, me, everyone on board this ship, everyone in Chau-mort. All of us die. It can't be helped, you can't reverse en-tropy. And when you die, you're going to spend eternity in the beyond. Unless something is done about it, unless you can find a living neurone structure which will host you. Now I ask again, do you want Al Capone's project to fail?"

"If all Capone is interested in is spreading happiness across the galaxy, why does he want to hire a combat-capable star-ship?" Madeleine asked.

"Protection in the form of deterrence. There are Organiza-tion representatives like me in dozens of asteroids looking to sign up combat-capable starships. The more we have in orbit above New California, the more difficult it will be for anyone to launch a strike force against it. The Confederation Navy is going to attack New California's Strategic Defence network. Everyone knows that. The First Admiral has got the Assem-bly screaming at him for some kind of positive action. If he can crack the SD network open, he's cleared the way for an invasion; have the marines round up all the bad guys and shove them into zero-tau." Iain Girardi let out a heartfelt pained breath. "Can you imagine the bloodshed that'll cause? You have seen firsthand how hard the possessed can fight when they're cornered. Imagine the conflict in your lower lounge multiplied by a billion. That's what it will be like." He gave Erick a sympathetic glance. "Is that what you want?"

"I'm not fighting for the possessed," Madeleine muttered sullenly. She hated the way Iain Girardi could turn her words, make her doubt her convictions.

"Nobody is asking the *Villeneuve's Revenge* to fight," Iain Girardi said earnestly. "You are there for show, that's all. Perimeter defence patrol, where you're visible, a demonstra-tion of numerical strength. Hardly an onerous duty. And you get paid full combat rates, with a guaranteed six-month con-tract; in addition to which I have a discretionary retainer fee to offer. Obviously for a prime ship like the *Villeneuve's Re-*

venge it will be a substantial one. You will be able to afford to have the worst of the damage repaired here at Chaumort, plus Erick can receive the best medical treatment available. I can even arrange for a brandnew spaceplane on very favourable terms; New California astroengineering companies make the best models."

"You see?" André said. "This is the kind of charter to be proud of. If the Organization is right we will have helped to secure the future of the entire human race. How can you object?"

"No, Captain," Madeleine said. "I'm not sharing the life-support capsules with the possessed. Not ever. Period."

"Nobody is suggesting you do." Girardi sounded shocked. "Obviously we understand there is a lot of suspicion at the moment. The Organization is working hard at breaking down those old prejudicial barriers. But until more trust is built up, then obviously you will have your own crew and no one else. In a way, that's part of establishing trust. The Organization is prepared to accept an armed ship crewed by non-possessed orbiting the planet providing you are integrated into its SD command network."

"Shit," Madeleine hissed. "Erick?"

He knew it was some kind of trap. And yet . . . it was hard to see how the possessed proposed to hijack the ship. This was one crew totally aware of the danger in letting even one of the bastards on board. Iain Girardi might have made a major mistake in approaching André.

The CNIS could undoubtedly use firsthand intelligence data on the disposition of ships around New California, which the *Villeneuve's Revenge* would be ideally placed to gather. And he could always jump the ship away when the data was collected, no matter what objections Duchamp raised. There were items stowed in his cabin which could overcome the rest of the crew.

Which just left personal factors. *I don't want to go into the front line again.*

"It's an important decision," he muttered.

André gave him a puzzled look. Naturally he was pleased some of the (diabolically expensive) medical nanonic packages were off, but obviously the poor boy's brain still hadn't completely recovered from decompression. And Madeleine was asking him to decide. *Merde.* "We know that, Erick. But I don't want you to worry. All I need to know is which of my crew is loyal enough to come with me. I have already decided to take my ship to New California."

"What do you mean, loyal enough?" Madeleine asked hotly.

André held his hand up in a pleading gesture. "What does Erick have to say, eh?"

"Will we be docking with anything in the New California system? Do you expect us to take on any extra crew, for example?"

"Of course not," Girardi said. "Fuel loading doesn't require anyone coming into the life-support capsules. And if the unlikely event does arise, then obviously you'll have a full veto authority over anyone in the airlock tube. Whatever precautions you want, you can have."

"Okay," Erick said. "I'll come with you, Captain."

• • • • • •

"Yeah?"

. . .

"Fuck, I might have guessed, who else is going to call this time of night. Don't you people ever sleep?"

. . .

"Everybody wants favours. I don't do them anymore. I'm not so cheap these days."

. . .

"Yeah? So you go run and tell my comrades; what use will I be to you then?"

. . .

"Mother Mary! You've got to be . . . Alkad Mzu? Shit, that's a name I didn't expect to hear ever again."

. . .

"Here? In the Dorados? She wouldn't dare."

. . .

"You're sure?"

. . .

"No, of course nobody's said anything. It's been months

since the partizans even bothered having a meeting. We're all too busy doing charity work these days."

"Mother Mary. You believe it, don't you? Ha! I bet you lot are all pissing yourselves. How do you like it for a change, arsehole? After all these years waiting, us poor old wanderers have gone and got us some real sharp teeth at last."

. . .

"You think so? Maybe I just resigned from your agency. Don't forget what the issue is here. I was born on Garissa."

. . .

"Fuck you, don't you fucking dare say that to me, you bastard. You even so much as look at my family, you little shit, and I'll fire that fucking Alchemist at your home planet myself."

. . .

"Yeah, yeah. Right, it's a sorry universe."

. . .

"I'll think about it. I'm not promising you anything. Like I said, there are issues here. I have to talk to some people."

• • •

The party was being thrown on the eve of the fleet's departure. It had taken over the entire ballroom of the Monterey Hilton, and then spread out to occupy a few suites on the level below. The food was real food; Al had been insistent about that, drunk possessed could never keep the illusion of delicacies going. So the Organization had run search programs through their memory cores and hauled in anyone who listed their occupation as chef, possessed or non-possessed. Skill was all that counted, not its century of origin. The effort was rewarded in a formal eight-course banquet, whose raw materials had been ferried up to the asteroid in seven spaceplane flights, and resulted in Leroy Octavius handing out eleven hundred hours worth of energistic credits to farmers and wholesalers.

After the meal Al stood on the top table and said: "We're gonna have a bigger and better ball when you guys come back safe, and you got Al Capone's word on that."

There was a burst of tumultuous applause, which only ended when the band struck up. Leroy and Busch had auditioned over a hundred musicians, whittling the numbers down to an eight-strong jazz band. Some of them were even genuine twenties musicians, or so they claimed. They certainly sounded and looked the part when they got up onstage to play. Nearly three hundred people were out on the dance floor jiving away to the old honky-tonk tunes which Al loved best.

Al himself led the way, hurling a laughing Jezzibella about with all the energy and panache he'd picked up at the Broadway Casino back in the old days. The rest of the guests soon picked up the rhythm and the moves. Men, Al insisted, wore their tuxes or, if they were serving in the fleet, a military uniform; while the women were free to wear their own choice of ball gowns, providing the styles and fabrics weren't anything too modern. With the decorations of gossamer drapes and giant swans created out of fresh-cut flowers the overall effect was of a grand Viennese ball, but a damn sight more fun.

Possessed and non-possessed rubbed shoulders harmoniously. Wine flowed, laughter shook the windows, some couples snuck off to be by themselves, a few fights broke out. By any standard it was a roaring success.

Which was why at half past two in the morning Jezzibella was puzzled to find Al all by himself in one of the lower level suites, leaning against its huge window, tie undone, brandy glass in one hand. Outside, star-points of light moved busily through space as the last elements of the fleet manoeuvred into their jump formation.

"What's the matter, baby?" Jezzibella asked quietly. Soft arms circled around him. Her head came to rest on his shoulder.

"We'll lose the ships."

"Bound to lose some, Al honey. Can't make an omelette without breaking eggs."

"No, I mean, they're gonna be in action light-years away. What's to make them do as I say?"

"Command structure, Al. The fleet is a mini-version of the Organization. The soldiers at the bottom do what the lieutenants at the top tell them. It's worked in warships for centuries. When you're in battle you automatically follow orders."

"So what if that piece of shit Luigi takes it into his head to dump me and set up all on his own in Arnstadt?"

"He won't. Luigi is loyal."

"Right." He chewed at a knuckle, thankful he was facing away from her.

"This bothers you, doesn't it?"

"Yeah. It's a goddamn problem, okay? That fleet is one fuck of a lot of power to hand over to one guy."

"Send two others."

"What?"

"Put a triumvirate in charge."

"What?"

"Easy, lover; if there's three of them in charge of the fleet, then each of them is going to be busting his balls to prove how loyal he is in front of the others. And let's face it, the fleet's only going to be away for a week at the most. It takes a hell of a lot longer than that to get a conspiracy up and running successfully. Besides, ninety per cent of those soldiers are loyal to you. You've given them everything, Al; a life, a purpose. Don't sell yourself short, what you've done with these people is a miracle, and they know it. They cheer your name. Not Luigi's, not Mickey, not Emmet. You, Al."

"Yeah." He nodded, drawing his confidence back together. What she said made a lot of sense. It always did.

Al looked at her in the drizzle of starlight. The personas were combined tonight: a feminine athlete. Her dress of sparkling pearl-coloured silk hinted at rather than revealed her figure. The allure she exerted was terrifying. Al had been hard put to control his temper that evening as he picked up the swell of hunger and lust from the other men on the dance floor every time she glided past.

"Goddamn," he whispered. "I ain't never done anything to deserve a reward as big as you."

"I think you have," she murmured back. Their noses touched again, arms moving gently into an embrace. "I've got a present for you, Al. We've been saving it up as a treat, and I think the time's right."

His hold around her tightened. "I got the only treat I need."

"Flatterer."

They kissed.

"It can wait till the morning," Jezzibella decided.

The lift opened onto a section of Monterey Al didn't recognize. An unembellished rock corridor with an air duct and power cables clinging to the ceiling. The gravity was about half-strength. He pulled a face at that, free fall was the one thing about this century he really hated. Jez kept trying to get him to make out with her in one of the axis hotel cubicles, but he wouldn't. Just thinking about it made his stomach churn.

"Where are we?" he asked.

Jezzibella grinned. She was the knowing and carefree girl-about-town persona this morning, wearing a snow-white ship-suit which stretched around her like rubber. "The docking ledges. They've not been used much since you took over. Not until now."

Al let her lead him along the corridor and into an observation lounge. Emmet Mordden, Patricia Mangano, and Mickey Pileggi were waiting in front of the window wall. All of them smiled proudly, an emotion reflected in their thought currents. Al played along with the game as Jez tugged him over to the window.

"We captured this mother on one of the asteroids a couple of weeks back," Mickey said. "Well, its captain was possessed, actually. Then we had to persuade the soul to transfer down the affinity link. Jezzibella said you'd like it."

"What is this shit, Mickey?"

"It's our present to you, Al baby," Jezzibella said. "Your flagship." She smiled eagerly, and gestured at the window.

Al walked over and looked out. Buck Rogers's very own rocketship was sitting on the rock shelf below him. It was a beautiful scarlet torpedo with yellow fins sprouting from the sides, and a cluster of copper rocket engine tubes at the rear.

"That's for me?" he asked in wonder.

The rocketship's interior was fully in keeping with its external appearance, the pinnacle of 1930s engineering and decor. Al felt more at home than any time since he had emerged from the beyond. This was his furniture, his styling. A little chunk of his home era.

"Thank you," he said to Jezzibella.

She kissed him on the tip of his nose, and they linked arms.

"It's a blackhawk," she explained. "The possessing soul is called Cameron Leung; so you be nice to him, Al. I said you'd find him a human body when the universe calms down a little."

"Sure."

An iron spiral stair led up to the promenade deck. Al and Jezzibella settled back on a plump couch of green leather where they could see out of the long curving windows and along the rocket's nose cone. He put his fedora down on a cane table at the side of the couch and draped an arm around her shoulders. Prince of the city again, full-time.

"Can you hear me, Cameron?" Jezzibella inquired.

"Yes," came the reply from a silver tannoy grille set in the wall.

"We'd like to see the fleet before it leaves. Take us over please."

Al winced, grabbing hold of the couch's flared arms. More fucking spaceflight! But there was none of the rush of acceleration he'd braced himself for. All that happened was the view changed. One minute the spherical silver-white grid of Monterey's spaceport was rotating slowly in front of them, the next it was sliding to one side and racing past overhead.

"Hey, I can't feel nothing," Al whooped. "No acceleration, none of that free-fall crap. Hot damn, now this is the way to travel."

"Yes." Jezzibella clicked her fingers smartly, and a small boy hurried forwards. He was dressed in a white high-collar steward's uniform, and his hair had been parted in the centre and slicked back with cream. "A bottle of Norfolk Tears, I think," she told him. "This is definitely celebration time. I think we might make a toast, too. Make sure you chill the glasses."

"Yes, miss," he piped.

Al frowned after him. "Kinda young to be doing that, ain't he?"

"It's Webster Pryor," she said sotto voce. "Sweet boy."

"Kingsley's son?"

"Yes. Thought it best we keep him close to hand the whole time. Just in case."

"I see. Sure."

"You're right about the ship, Al. Bitek is the only way to travel. My media company was always too miserly to let me have one for touring. Blackhawks make the best warships, too."

"Yeah? So how many have we got?"

"Three, counting this one. And we only got those because their captains were coldfooted when we snatched the asteroids."

"Pity."

"Yes. But we're hoping to get luckier this time."

Al grinned out of the window as the luscious crescent of New California swung into view, and settled back to enjoy the ride.

Cameron Leung accelerated away from Monterey at two gees, curving down towards the planet a hundred and ten thousand kilometres below. Far ahead of the blackhawk's sharp emerald aerospike, the Organization's fleet was sliding along its five-thousand-kilometre orbit, a chain of starships spaced a precise two kilometres apart. Sunlight bounced and sparkled off foil-coated machinery as they emerged from the penumbra; a silver necklace slowly threading itself around the entire planet.

It had taken two days for all of them to fly down from their assembly points at the orbiting asteroids, jockeying into their jump formation under the direction of Emmet Mordden and Luigi Balsmao. The *Salvatore* was the lead vessel, an ex-New California navy battle cruiser, and now Luigi Balsmao's command ship.

Two million kilometres away, hanging over New California's south pole, the voidhawk *Galega* had observed the fleet gathering. The swarm of stealthed spy globes it showered around the planet had monitored the starships manoeuvring into their designated slot in the chain, intercepting their command communications. Given the two-degree inclination of the fleet's orbital track, *Galega* and its captain, Aralia, had calculated the theoretical number of jump coordinates. Fifty-two stars were possible targets.

The Yosemite Consensus had dispatched voidhawks to warn the relevant governments, all of whom had been extremely alarmed by the scale of the potential threat. Other than that there was little the Edenists could do. Attack was not a viable option. The Organization fleet was under the shield of New California's SD network, and its own offensive potential was equally formidable. If it was to be broken up, then it would have to be intercepted by a fleet of at least equal size. But even if the Confederation Navy did assemble a task force large enough, the admirals were then faced with the problem of where to deploy it: a fifty-two to one chance of getting the right system.

Galega watched Capone's scarlet and lemon blackhawk race down from Monterey to hold station fifty kilometres away from the *Salvatore*. A spy globe fell between the two. The intelligence-gathering staff in the voidhawk's crew toroid heard Capone say: "How's it going, Luigi?"

"Okay, boss. The formation's holding true. They'll all hit the jump coordinate."

"Goddamn, Luigi, you should see what you guys look like from here. It's a powerhouse of a sight. I tell you, I wouldn't want to wake up in the morning and find you in my sky. Those jerkhead krauts are gonna crap themselves."

"Count on it, Al."

"Okay, Luigi, take it away, it's all yours. You and Patricia and Dwight take care now, you hear? And Jez says good luck. Go get 'em."

"Thank the little lady for us, boss. And don't worry none, we'll deliver for you. Expect some real good news a week from now."

The *Salvatore*'s heat dump panels and sensor clusters began to retract down into their jump recesses, taking a long while to do so. Several times they seemed to stick or judder. The second ship in the formation began to configure itself for a jump, then the third.

For another minute nothing happened, then the *Salvatore* vanished inside its event horizon.

Aralia and *Galega* were instinctively aware of its spatial location, and with that the jump coordinate alignment could have only one solution. **It's Arnstadt,** Aralia told the Yosemite Consensus. **They're heading for Arnstadt.**

Thank you, Aralia, Consensus replied. **We will dispatch a voidhawk to alert the Arnstadt government. It will take the Organization fleet at least two days to reach the system. The local navy forces will have some time to prepare.**

Enough?

Possibly. It depends on the Organization's actual goal.

When Aralia reviewed the images from the spy globes, another twelve ships had already followed the *Salvatore*. A further seven hundred and forty were gliding inexorably toward the Arnstadt jump coordinate.

• • •

"No, Gerald," Jansen Kovak said. The tone was one which parents reserved for particularly troublesome children. His hand tightened around Gerald's upper arm.

He and another supervisory nurse had walked Gerald to the sanatorium's lounge where he was supposed to eat his lunch. Once they reached the door, Gerald had glanced furtively down the corridor, muscles tensing beneath his baggy sweatshirt.

Kovak was familiar with the signs. Gerald could drop into a frenzy at the slightest provocation these days; anything from an innocuous phrase to the sight of a long corridor which he assumed led directly to the outside world. When it happened, he'd lash out at his supervisors and anyone else who happened to be in the way, before making yet another run for it. The concept of codelocked doors seemed utterly beyond him.

The corner of Gerald's lip spasmed at the stern warning, and he allowed himself to be led into the lounge. The first thing he did was glance at the bar to see if the holoscreen was on. It had been removed altogether (much to the annoyance of other inmates). Dr Dobbs wasn't going to risk triggering another incident of that magnitude.

Privately, Jansen Kovak considered that they were wasting their time in trying to rehabilitate Skibbow. The man had obviously tipped right over the edge and was now free-falling into his own personal inferno. He should be shipped off to a long-term care institution for treatment and maybe some selective memory erasure. But Dr Dobbs insisted the psychosis could be treated here; and Gerald was technically an ESA internee, which brought its own complications. It was a bad duty.

The lounge fell silent when the three of them came in. Not that there were many people using it; four or five inmates and a dozen staff. Gerald responded to the attention with a frightened stare, checking faces. He frowned in puzzlement as one woman with Oriental features and vivid copper hair gave him a sympathetic half smile.

Jansen quickly steered him over to a settee halfway between the window and the bar and sat him down. "What would you like to eat, Gerald?"

"Um . . . I'll have the same as you."

"I'll get you a salad," Kovak said, and turned to go over to the bar. Which was his first mistake.

Something smashed into the middle of his back, knocking him forwards completely off balance. He went crashing painfully onto the ground. Auto-balance and unarmed combat programs went primary, interfacing to roll him smoothly to one side. He regained his feet in a fluid motion.

Gerald and the other nurse were locked together, each trying to throw the other to the ground. Jansen selected an option from the neural nanonics menu. His feet took a pace and a half forwards, and his weight shifted. One arm came around in a fast arc. The blow caught Gerald on his shoulder, which toppled him sideways. Before he could compensate, the back of his legs came into contact with Jansen's outstretched leg. He tripped, the weight of the other supervisory nurse quickening his fall.

Gerald yelled in pain as he landed on his elbow, only to be smothered below the bulk of the other nurse. When he raised his head the lounge door was five metres away. So close!

"Let me go," he begged. "She's my daughter. I have to save her."

"Shut up you prize pillock," Jansen grunted.

"Now that's not nice."

Jansen spun around to see the redheaded woman standing

behind him. "Er . . . I. Yes." Shame was making his face became uncomfortably warm. It also seemed to be enervating his neural nanonics display. "I'm sorry, it was unprofessional. He's just so annoying."

"You should try being married to him for twenty years."

Jansen's face registered polite incomprehension. The woman wasn't an inmate. She was wearing a smart blue dress, civilian clothing. But he didn't remember her on the staff.

She smiled briskly, grabbed hold of the front of his tunic, and threw him six metres clean through the air. Jansen's scream was more of shock than of pain. Until he hit the ground. That impact was pure agony, and his neural nanonics had shut down, allowing every volt of pain to flow cleanly through his nerves.

The other nurse who was still wrapped around Gerald managed to get out one dull grunt of surprise before the woman hit him. Her fist shattered his jaw, sending a spurt of blood splashing across Gerald's hair.

By that time one of the other sanatorium staff in the lounge had enough presence of mind to datavise an alarm code at the room's net processor. Sirens started wailing. A grid of metal bars started to slide up out of the floor, sealing off the open balcony doors.

Three burly nurses were closing on the red-haired woman as Gerald blinked up at her in amazement. She winked at him and raised an arm high, finger pointing to the ceiling. A bracelet of white fire ignited around her wrist.

"Shit," the leader of the three nurses yelped. He nearly pitched over as he tried desperately to reverse his headlong rush.

"It's a fucking possessed."

"Back! Get back!"

"Where the hell did she come from?"

"Go for it, babe," one of the inmates roared jubilantly.

A rosette of white fire exploded from her hand, dissolving into a hundred tiny spheres almost as soon as it appeared. They smashed into the ceiling and walls and furniture. Sparks cascaded down as small plumes of black smoke squirted out. Flames began to take hold. Fire alarms added their clamour to the initial alert. Then the lights went out and the alarms were silenced.

"Come on, Gerald," the woman said. She pulled him to his feet.

"No," he squeaked in terror. "You're one of them. Let me go, please. I can't be one of you again. I can't take that again. Please, my daughter."

"Shut up, and get a move on. We're going to find Marie."

Gerald gaped at her. "What do you know of her?"

"That she needs you, very badly. Now come on!"

"You know?" he snivelled. "How can you know?"

"Come on." She tugged at him as she started towards the lounge door. It was as if the grapple arm of a heavy-load cargo mechanoid had attached itself to him.

The steward raised his head above the bar to see what was happening. Various inmates and staff had dived for cover behind the furniture. The terrifying possessed woman was striding purposefully for the door, hauling a cowering Skibbow along. He datavised a codelock order at the door, then opened an emergency channel to the net processor. It didn't respond. His hand curled around the nervejam stick, ready to—

"Hey you!" called the woman.

A streamer of white fire smacked straight into his forehead.

"Naughty," she said grimly.

Gerald gibbered quietly as the steward slumped forwards, smoke rising from the shallow crater in his temple. "Oh, dear God, what are you?"

"Don't blow it for me now, Gerald." She stood in front of the door. The room's air rushed past her, ruffling her long copper tresses. Then the air flow reversed, turning to a howling hurricane with a solid core. It smashed into the door, buckling the reinforced composite.

She stepped through the gap, pulling Gerald after her. "Now we run," she told him happily.

As the sanatorium was operated by the Royal Navy the guards were armed. It didn't make any difference, they weren't front-line combat troops. Whenever one of them got near to Gerald and the woman she would use her white fire to devastating effect. The asteroid's internal security centre could trace her position purely because of the wave of destruction she generated around herself. All electronics and power circuits were ruptured by flares of white fire, doors were simply ripped apart, environmental ducts were battered and split, mechanoids reduced to slag. She did it automatically, a defensive manoeuvre burning clean any conceivable threat in front of her. Crude but effective.

The asteroid went to an immediate status two defence alert. Royal Marines were rushed from their barracks to the sanatorium.

But as with all asteroid settlements, everything was packed close together, and made as compact as possible. It took the woman and Gerald ninety seconds to get from the lounge to the sanatorium's nearest entrance. Sensors and cameras in the public hall caught her emerging from the splintered door. Terrified pedestrians sprinted from the vicious tendrils of white fire she unleashed; it was almost as though she were using them as whips to drive people away from her. Then the images vanished as she hammered at the net processors and sensors.

The Royal Marine commander coordinating the emergency at least had the presence of mind to shut down the lifts around the hall. If she wanted out, she'd have to walk. And when she did, she'd run smack into the marines now deploying in a pincer movement around her.

Both squads were edging cautiously down the public hall, hurrying civilians out of the way. They approached the sanatorium's wrecked entrance from opposite directions, chemical projectile rifles held ready, electronic warfare blocks alert for any sign of the distortion pattern given off by a possessed. When they came into view of each other they froze, covering the length of the hall with their rifles. No one was left between them.

The squad captain of one side shouldered his weapon. "Where the fuck did she go?"

"I knew they'd stop the lifts," the redhead said in satisfaction. "Standard tactics for dealing with the possessed is to block all nearby transport systems to prevent us from spreading. Bloody good job they were on the ball today."

Gerald agreed, but didn't say anything. He was concentrating on the rungs in front of his face, not daring to look down.

The possessed woman might have smashed open all the doors in the medical facility, but once they were out in the hall she had stood in front of the lift doors and made a parting motion with her hands. The lift doors had obeyed, sliding open silently. After that they had started to climb down the ladder set in the wall of the shaft. There wasn't much light to see where he was putting his hands and feet, just some sort of bluish radiance coming from the woman above him. Gerald didn't want to see how she was making it.

It was cold in the shaft, the air tasting both wet and metallic. And silent, too, the darkness above and below swallowing all sounds. Every minute or so he could just make out another door in the shaft wall; the buzz of conversation and tiny slivers of light oozing around the seals.

"Careful," she said. "You're near the bottom now. Ten more rungs."

The light increased, and he risked a glance down. A metal grid slicked with condensation glinted dully at the foot of the ladder. Gerald stood on it, shivering slightly and rubbing his arms. Mechanical clunks started to rumble down from above.

The possessed woman jumped nimbly past the last two rungs and gave him an enthusiastic smile. "Stand still," she said, and put her hands on either side of his head, spreading her fingers over his ears.

Gerald quivered at her touch. Her hands were starting to glow. This was it. The start of the pain. Soon he would hear the demented whispers emerging from the beyond, and one of *them* would pour into his body again. All hope would die then. I might as well refuse, and let her torture kill me. Better that than . . .

She took her hands away, their internal glimmer fading away. "I think that should do it. I've broken down the debrief nanonics. The doctors and police would only use you to see where we were and what we were doing, then they'd send you to sleep."

"What?" He started to probe his skull with cautious fingers. It seemed intact. "Is that all you did?"

"Yes. Not so bad was it?" She beckoned. "There's a hatch

here which leads to the maintenance tunnels. It's only got a mechanical lock, so we won't trigger any processors."

"Then what?" he asked bleakly.

"Why, we get you off Guyana and on your way to Valisk to find Marie, of course. What did you think, Gerald?" She grasped the handle on the metre-high hatch and shoved it upwards. The hatch swung open, revealing only more darkness behind.

Gerald felt like crying. His head was all funny, hot and light, which made it very hard for him to think. "Why? Why are you doing this? Are you just playing with me?"

"Of course I'm not playing, Gerald. I want Marie back to normal more than anything. She's all we have left now. You know that. You saw the homestead."

He sank to his knees, looking up at her flat-featured face and immaculate hair, trying desperately to understand. "But why? Who are you to want this?"

"Oh, dearest Gerald, I'm sorry. This is Pou Mok's body. It takes up far too much concentration to maintain my own appearance, especially with what I was doing up there."

Gerald watched numbly as the copper hair darkened and the skin of her face began to flow into new features. No, not new. Old. So very very old. "Loren," he gasped.

15

After five centuries of astounding technological endeavour and determined economic sacrifice by the Lunar nation, the God of War, Mars, had finally been pacified. The hostile red gleam which had so dominated Earth's night skies for millennia was extinguished. Now the planet had an atmosphere, complete with vast swirls of white and grey clouds; blooms of vegetation were expanding across the deserts, patches of sepia and dark green vegetation staining the tracts of rust-red soil. To an approaching starship it seemed, at first, almost identical to any other terracompatible planet to be found within the Confederation's boundaries. Disparities became apparent only when the extent of the remaining deserts was revealed, accounting for three-fifths of the surface; and there was a definite sparsity of free water. Although there were thousands of individual crater lakes, Mars had only one major body of water, the Lowell Sea, a gently meandering ribbon which wrapped itself around the equator. Given the scale involved it appeared as though a wide river were flowing constantly around the planet. Closer inspection showed that circumnavigation would be impossible. The Lowell Sea had formed as water collected in the hundreds of large asteroid-impact craters which pocked the planet's equator in an almost straight line.

Population, too, was one of the planet's quirks: a phenomenon which was also visible from orbit, provided you knew what to look for. Anyone searching the nightside for the usual sprawling iridescent patches of light which marked the kind of vigorous human cities normally present after five centuries of colonization would be disappointed; only six major urban areas had sprung up so far. Towns and villages were also present amid the rolling steppes, but in total the number of people living on the surface didn't exceed three million. Phobos and Deimos were heavily industrialized, providing homes for a further half-million workers and their families. They at least followed a standard development pattern.

Apart from stage one colony planets in their formative years, Mars had the smallest human population of any world in the Confederation. However, that was where comparisons ended. The Martian technoeconomy was highly developed, providing its citizens with a reasonable standard of living, though nothing like the socioeconomic index enjoyed by Edenists or the Kulu Kingdom.

One other aspect of mature Confederation societies missing from Mars was a Strategic Defence network. The two asteroid moons were defended, of course; both of them were important SII centres with spaceports boasting a high level of starship traffic. But the planet was left open; there was nothing of any value on its surface to threaten or hold hostage or steal. The trillions of fuseodollars poured into the terraforming project were dispersed evenly throughout the new biosphere. Oxygen and geneered plants were not the kinds of targets favoured by pirates. Mars was the most expensive single project ever undertaken by the human race, yet its intrinsic value was effectively zero. Its real value was as the focus of aspirations for a whole nation of exiles, to whom it had become the modern promised land.

None of this was readily apparent to Louise, Genevieve, and Fletcher as they observed the planet growing in the lounge's holoscreen. The difference from Norfolk was apparent (Genevieve said Mars looked worn-out rather than brand-new) but none of them knew how to interpret what they were seeing in geotechnical terms. All they cared about was the lack of glowing red cloud.

"Can you tell if there are any possessed down there?" Louise asked.

"Alas no, Lady Louise. The planet lies far outside my second sight. All I can feel is the shape of this doughty ship. We could be alone in the universe for all the perception I have."

"Don't say that," Genevieve said. "We've come here to get away from horrible things."

"And away from them we certainly are, little one."

Genevieve spared a moment from watching the holoscreen to grin at him. The voyage had calmed her considerably. With very little to do for any of the passengers during the flight, the novelty of bouncing around in free fall had soon worn off, and she had swiftly learned how to access the flight computer. Furay had brought some old voice-interactive tutorial programs on-line for her, and she had been engrossed ever since with AV recordings of children's stories, educational files, and games. Genevieve adored the games, spending hours in her cabin, surrounded by a holographic haze, fighting off fantasy creatures, or exploring mythological landscapes, even piloting ships to the galactic core.

Louise and Fletcher had used the same programs to devour history encyclopedia files, reviewing the major events which had shaped human history since the mid 1800s. Thanks to Norfolk's restrictive information policies, most of it was as new to her as it was to him. The more she reviewed, the more ignorant she felt. Several times she had been obliged to ask Furay if a particular incident was genuinely true; the information in the *Far Realm*'s memory was so different from that which she'd been taught. Invariably, the answer was yes; though he always tempered it by saying that no one viewed anything in the same context. "Interpretation through the filters of ideology has always been one of our race's curses."

Even that cushion didn't make her any happier. The teachers at school hadn't exactly been lying to her, censorship was hardly practical given the number of starship crews who visited at midsummer; but they'd certainly sheltered her from an awful lot of unsavoury truths.

Louise ordered the flight computer to show a display of their approach vector. The holoscreen image shifted, showing them the view from the forward sensor clusters overlaid with orange and green graphics. Phobos was falling towards the horizon, a darkened star embedded at the heart of a large scintillating wreath of industrial stations. They watched it expand as the *Far Realm* matched orbits at a tenth of a gee. Inhabited for over five centuries, it had a weighty history. No other settled asteroid/moon of such a size orbited so close to an inhabited planet. But its proximity made it ideal to provide raw material for the early stages of the terraforming project. Since

those days it had reverted primarily to being an SII manufacturing centre and fleet port. The spin imparted to provide
gravity within its two biosphere caverns had flung off the last
of the surface dust centuries ago. Naked grey-brown rock was
all that faced the stars now; large areas had a marbled finish
where mining teams had removed protrusions to enhance the
symmetry, and both ends had been sheared flat. With its cylindrical shape and vast encrustations of machinery capping
each end its genealogy appeared to be midway between ordinary asteroid settlements and an Edenist habitat.

Captain Layia slotted the starship into the spaceport approach vector which traffic control assigned her, then spent a
further twenty minutes datavising the SII fleet operations office, explaining why their scheduled return flight from Norfolk had been delayed.

"You didn't mention our passengers then?" Tilia said when
the exchange was over.

"Life is complicated enough right now," Layia retorted.
"Explaining to the operations office why they're on board,
and the financial circumstances, isn't going to make a good
entry on anyone's record. Agreed?"

She received a round of apathetic acknowledgements from
the other crew members.

"None of them have passports," Furay commented. "That
might be a problem when we dock."

"We could get them to register as refugees," Endron said.
"Under Confederation law the government is obliged to accept them."

"The first thing they would have to do is explain how they
got here," Layia said. "Come on, think. We've got to off load
them somehow, and without any comebacks."

"They're not listed on our manifest," Tilia said. "So no
one's going to be looking for them. And if the port Inspec-
torate does decide to give us a customs check we can just
move them around the life-support capsules to keep them out
of sight of their team. Once our port clearance comes through
we can sneak them into the asteroid without any difficulty."

"Then what?"

"They don't want to stay here," Furay said. "They just want
to find a ship which will take them to Tranquillity."

"You heard traffic control," Layia said. "All civil flights have ended. The only reason our Defence Command didn't swarm all over us is because we still have a Confederation Navy flight authorization."

"There might not be any flights to Tranquillity from Mars, but if anyone in this system is going there, it'll be from Earth. Getting them to the O'Neill Halo shouldn't be too difficult, there are still plenty of inter-orbit flights, and Louise has enough money. She was talking about chartering the entire ship, remember?"

"That could work," Layia said. "And if we can acquire some passports for them first, then nobody in the Halo will ask how they got to Mars. From that distance, everything at this end will appear perfectly legitimate."

"I might know someone who can fix passports for them," Tilia volunteered.

Layia snorted. "Who doesn't?"

"He's not cheap."

"Not our problem. All right, we'll try it. Endron, tell them the way it is. And make certain they cooperate."

The *Far Realm* settled lightly on a docking cradle. Umbilical hoses snaked up to jack into the lower hull. Genevieve watched the operation on the lounge's holoscreen, fascinated by all the automated machinery.

"We'd best not tell Daddy we came here, had we?" she said without looking up.

"Why not?" Louise asked. She was surprised; it was the first time Gen had mentioned either of their parents since they'd left Cricklade. *But then, neither have I.*

"Mars has a Communist government. The computer said so. Daddy hates them."

"I think you'll find the Martians are a bit different from the people Daddy's always moaning about. In any case, he'll be glad we came here."

"Why?"

"Because he'll be glad we got away. The route we travel isn't really important, just that we get safely to our destination."

"Oh. I suppose you're right." Her face became solemn for

a moment. "What do you think he's doing right now? Will that nasty knight man be making him do things he doesn't want to?"

"Daddy isn't doing anything for anyone. He's just stuck inside his own head, that's all. It's the same as being in prison. He'll be thinking a lot, he's perfectly free to do that."

"Really?" Genevieve looked at Fletcher for confirmation.

"Indeed, little one."

"I suppose that's not so bad then."

"I know Daddy," Louise said. "He'll be spending the whole time worrying about us. I wish there were some way we could tell him we're all right."

"We can when it's all over. And Mummy, too. It is going to be all over, isn't it, Louise?"

"Yes. It's going to end; someday, somehow. And when we get to Tranquillity, we can stop running and do whatever we can to help."

"Good." She smiled primly at Fletcher. "I don't want you to go, though."

"Thank you, little one." He sounded ill at ease.

Endron came gliding through the ceiling hatch, head first. He twisted neatly around the ladder and touched his feet to a stikpad beside the holoscreen.

Fletcher kept very still. Now that she knew what to look for, Louise could see how hard he was concentrating. It had taken several days of intense practice for him to learn how to minimise the disruption his energistic effect exerted on nearby electronics. In the end it had paid off; it had been fifty hours since the last time any of the *Far Realm*'s crew had come flashing through the life-support capsule searching for an elusive glitch in the starship's systems.

"We made it home," Endron started off blithely. "But there is a small problem with your legal status. Mainly the fact you don't have a passport between you."

Louise deliberately avoided glancing at Fletcher. "Is there a Norfolk Embassy here? They may be able to issue us with some documentation."

"There will be a legal office to handle Norfolk's diplomatic affairs, but no actual embassy."

"I see."

"But you have a solution," Fletcher said. "That is why you are here, is it not?"

"We have a proposal," Endron said edgily. "There is an unorthodox method of acquiring a passport for the three of you; it's expensive but has the advantage of not involving the authorities."

"Is it illegal?" Louise asked.

"What we have here is this: Myself and the rest of the crew have rather a lot of Norfolk Tears on board which we can sell to our friends, so we really don't want to draw too much official attention to ourselves right now."

"Your government wouldn't send us back, would they?" Genevieve asked in alarm.

"No. Nothing like that. It's just that this way would be easier all around."

"We'll get our passports the way you suggested," Louise said hurriedly. She felt like hugging the genial payload officer; it was exactly what she had been nerving herself up to ask him.

* * *

Moyo didn't exactly sleep, there were too many pressures being applied against his mind for that, but he did rest for several hours each night. Eben Pavitt's body wasn't in the best condition, nor was he in the first flush of youth. Of course, Moyo could use his energistic power to enhance any physical attribute such as strength or agility, but as he stopped concentrating he could feel the enervation biting into his stolen organs. Tiredness became an all-over ache.

After a couple of days he had learned the limits pretty well, and took care to respect them. He was lucky to have obtained this body; it would be the direst of follies to lose it by negligence. Another might not be so easy to come by. The Confederation was larger now than when he had been alive, but the number of souls back in the beyond was also prodigious. There would never be enough bodies to go around.

The slim blades of light which dawn drove through the loose bamboo blind were an unusually intense crimson. They shifted the bedroom from a familiar collection of grisaille outlines to a strong two-tone portrait of red and impenetrable black. Despite the macabre perspective, Moyo was imbued by a feeling of simple contentment.

Stephanie stirred on the mattress next to him, then sat up frowning. "Your thoughts look indecently happy to me all of a sudden. What is it?"

"I'm not sure." He got up and padded over to the window. His fingers pressed the slim tubes of bamboo down. "Ah. Come and look."

The sky above Exnall was clotting with wisps of cloud, slowly condensing into a broad disk. And they glowed a muted red. Dawn's corona was rising up to blend with them. Only in the west was there a dark crescent of night, and that was slowly being squeezed to extinction.

"The stars will never rise here again," Moyo said happily.

There was a power thrumming through the land now, one which he could feel himself responding to, contributing a little of himself towards maintaining the whole. A vast conjunction of will, something he suspected was akin to an Edenist Consensus. Annette Ekelund had won, converting the peninsula to a land where the dead walked free once more. Now two million of them were marrying their energistic power at a subconscious level, bringing about the overriding desire which also dwelt within the latent mind.

Several shadows flittered across the bottom of the garden where the overhanging boughs granted immunity against the spreading red light. The horticultural mechanoids had long since cranked to a halt, though not before wrecking most of the flower beds and small shrubs. When he opened his mind to the dark area he found several nervous bundles of thought. It was the kids left over from the possession again. He hadn't been alone in letting one go. Unfortunately the Royal Marines had executed a fast, efficient retreat.

"Damn. They're back for the food again."

Stephanie sighed. "They've had all of the sachets in the kitchen. What else can we give them?"

"There are some chickens in one of the houses opposite; we could always cook them and leave the meat out."

"Poor little mites. They must be frozen sleeping out there.

Could you go and fetch some chickens, please? I'll get the range cooker hot, we'll cook them in the oven."

"Why bother? We can just turn them straight into roasts."

"I'm not convinced about that; and I don't want them to catch anything from food that hasn't been cooked properly."

"If you just zap the chickens they'll be cooked properly."

"Don't argue. Just go and get them." She turned him around and gave him a push. "They'll need plucking, as well."

"All right, I'm going." He laughed as his clothes formed around him. Argument would be pointless. It was one of the things he enjoyed about her. She didn't have many opinions, but those she did have . . . "By the way, what are *we* going to do for food? There's none left in the bungalow, and people have been helping themselves to the stocks in the stores on Maingreen." After some experimenting he'd found his energistic power wasn't quite as omnipotent as he'd first thought. He could cloak anything in an illusion, and if the wish was maintained for long enough the matter underneath would eventually flow into the shape and texture which he was visualizing. But the human body needed to ingest specific proteins and vitamins. A lump of wood that looked, tasted, and smelt like salmon was still just a lump of wood when it was in his stomach. Even with real food he had to be sensible. Once he'd actually thrown up after transforming sachets of bread into chocolate gateau—he hadn't removed the foil wrapping first.

"That's something we can start thinking about later," she said. "If necessary we can move out of the town and set ourselves up in one of the farms."

He didn't like the idea—he'd lived all his life in cities—but didn't say anything out loud.

Someone knocked on the front door before he got to it. Pat Staite, their neighbour, was standing outside dressed in elaborate blue and grey striped baseball gear.

"We're looking for people to help make up the teams," he said hopefully.

"It's a little early in the day for me."

"Absolutely. Terribly sorry. If you're free this afternoon . . . ?"

"Then I'll come along, certainly."

Pat was one of Exnall's growing band of sports enthusiasts who seemed intent on playing every ball game ever devised by the human race. They had already taken over two of the town's parks.

"Thanks," Staite said, not registering the irony in Moyo's voice or thoughts. "There's an ex-Brit living in the street now. He said he'd teach us how to play cricket."

"Fabulous."

"Is there anything you used to play?"

"Strip poker. Now if you'll excuse me, I have to go and catch some chickens for my breakfast."

The chickens had broken out of their coop, but they were still pecking and scratching around the garden. They were a geneered variety, plump, with rusty yellow feathers. They were also remarkably quick.

Moyo's first couple of attempts at catching one ended with him falling flat on his stomach. When he climbed to his feet the second time, the whole flock was squawking in alarm and vanishing fast into the shrubbery. He glared at them, banishing the mud caking his trousers and shirt, and pointed a finger. The tiny bolt of white fire caught the chicken at the base of its neck, sending out a cloud of singed feathers and quite a lot of blood. It must have looked ludicrous, he knew, using his power for this. But, if it got the job done . . .

When he'd finished blasting every chicken he could see, he walked over to the nearest corpse. And it started running away from him, head flopping down its chest on the end of a flaccid strip of skin. He stared at it disbelievingly; he'd always thought that was an urban myth. Then another of the corpses sprinted for freedom. Moyo pushed his sleeves up and summoned a larger bolt of white fire.

There were voices drifting through the open kitchen door when he returned to the bungalow. He didn't even have to use his perception to know who was in there with her.

Under Stephanie's control the range cooker was radiating waves of heat. Several children were warming themselves around it, holding big mugs of tea. They all stopped talking as he walked in.

Stephanie's bashful welcoming smile was transformed to

an astonished blink as she saw the smoking remnants of chicken he was carrying. A couple of the children started giggling.

"Into the lounge everyone," Stephanie ordered the kids. "Go on, I'll see what I can salvage."

Once they had left he asked: "What the hell are you doing?"

"Looking after them, of course. Shannon says she hasn't had a meal ever since the possessed arrived."

"But you can't. Suppose—"

"Suppose what? The *police* come?"

He dropped the burnt carcasses onto the tile worktop next to the range cooker. "Sorry."

"We're responsible only to ourselves now. There are no laws, no courts, no rights and wrongs. Only what feels good. That's what this new life is for, isn't it? Indulgence."

"I don't know. It might be."

She leaned against him, arms encircling his waist. "Look at it selfishly. What else have you got to do today?"

"And there I was thinking I was the one who'd adjusted best to this."

"You did, at first. I just needed time to catch up."

He peered through the door at the children. There were eight of them bouncing around on the lounge furniture, none over twelve or thirteen. "I'm not used to children."

"Nor chickens by the look of things. But you managed to bring them back in the end, didn't you?"

"Are you sure you want to do this? I mean, how long do you want to look after them for? What's going to happen when they grow up? Do they hit sixteen and get possessed? That's an awful prospect."

"That won't happen. We'll take this world out of the reach of the beyond. We're the first and the last possessed. This kind of situation won't arise again. And in any case, I wasn't proposing to bring them up in Exnall."

"Where then?"

"We'll take them up to the end of Mortonridge and turn them over to their own kind."

"You're kidding me." A pointless statement; he could sense the determination in her thoughts.

"Don't tell me you want to stay in Exnall for all of eternity?"

"No. But the first few weeks would be fine."

"To travel is to experience. I won't force you, Moyo, if you want to stay here and learn how to play cricket, that's okay by me."

"I surrender." He laughed, and kissed her firmly. "They won't be able to walk, not all that way. We'll need some sort of bus or truck. I'd better scout around and see what Ekelund left us."

. . .

It was the eighth time Syrinx had walked to Wing-Tsit Chong's odd house on the side of the lake. For some of these meetings it would be just the two of them sitting and talking, on other occasions they would be joined by therapists and Athene and Sinon and Ruben for what amounted to a joint session. But today it was only the pair of them.

As ever, Wing-Tsit Chong was waiting in his wheelchair on the veranda, a tartan rug tucked around his legs. **Greetings, my dear Syrinx. How are you today?**

She bowed slightly in the Oriental tradition, a mannerism she had taken up after the second session. **They took the nanonic packages off my feet this morning. I could barely walk, the skin was so tender.**

I hope you did not chastise the medical team for this minor discomfort.

No. She sighed. **They have done wonders with me. I'm grateful. And the pain will soon be gone.**

Wing-Tsit Chong smiled thinly. **Exactly the answer you should give. If I were a suspicious old man . . .**

Sorry. But I really have accepted the physical discomfort as transitory.

How fortunate, the last chain unshackled.

Yes.

You will be free to roam the stars again. And if you were to fall into their clutches once more?

She shivered, giving him a censorious glance as she leaned

on the veranda rail. I don't think I'm cured enough to want to think about that.

Of course.

All right, if you really want to know. I doubt I'll venture out of *Oenone*'s crew toroid quite so readily now. Certainly not while the possessed are still loose in the universe. Is that wrong for someone of my situation? Have I failed?

Answer yourself.

I still have some nightmares.

I know. Though not as many; which we all know is a good sign of progress. What other symptoms persist?

I want to fly again. But . . . it's difficult to convince myself to do it. I suppose the uncertainty frightens me. I could meet them again.

The uncertainty or the unknown?

You're so fond of splitting hairs.

Indulge an old man.

Definitely the uncertainty. The unknown used to fascinate me. I loved exploring new planets, seeing wonders.

Your pardon, Syrinx, but you have never done these things.

What? She turned from the railing to stare at him, finding only that annoying, passive expression. *Oenone* and I spent years doing exactly that.

You spent years playing tourist. You admired what others had discovered, what they had built, the way they lived. The actions of a tourist, Syrinx, not an explorer. *Oenone* has never flown to a star which has not been catalogued; your footprint has never been the first upon a planet. You have always played safe, Syrinx. And even that did not protect you.

Protect me from what?

Your fear of the unknown.

She sat on the wickerwork chair opposite him, deeply troubled. You believe that of me?

I do. I want you to feel no shame, Syrinx, all of us have weaknesses. Mine, I know, are more terrible than you would ever believe me capable of.

If you say so.

As always, you remain stubborn to the last. I have not yet decided if this is a weakness or a strength.

Depends on the circumstances, I guess. She flashed a mischievous smile.

He inclined his head in acknowledgement. As you say. In these two circumstances, it must therefore count as a weakness.

You would rather I had surrendered myself and *Oenone*?

Of course not. And we are here to deal with the present, not dwell on what was.

So you see this alleged fear of mine to be a continuing problem?

It inhibits you, and this should not be. Your mind should not be caged, by your own bars or anyone else's. I would like you and *Oenone* to face the universe with determination.

How? I mean, I thought I was just about cured. I've been through all my memories of the torture and the circumstances around it with the therapists; we broke up each and every black spectre with rigorous logic. Now you tell me I have this deep-seated flaw. If I'm not ready now, I doubt I ever will be.

Ready for what?

I don't know exactly. Do my bit, I suppose. Help protect Edenism from the possessed, that's what all the other voidhawks are doing right now. I know *Oenone* wants to be a part of that.

You would not make a good captain at this point, not if you were to take an active part in the conflict. The unknown would always cast its shadow of doubt over your actions.

I know all about the possessed, believe me.

Do you? Then what will you do when you join them?

Join them? Never!

You propose to avoid dying? I will be interested to hear the method you plan for this endeavour.

Oh. Her cheeks reddened.

Death is always the great unknown. And now we know more of it the mystery only deepens.

How? How can it deepen when we know more?

Laton called it the great journey. What did he mean? The Kiint said they have confronted the knowledge and come to terms with it. How? Their understanding of reality cannot be so much greater than ours. Edenists transfer their memories into the neural strata when their bodies die. Does their soul also transfer? Do these questions not bother you? That such philosophical abstracts should attain a supreme relevance to our existence is most disturbing to me.

Well, yes, they are disturbing if you lay them out in clinical detail like that.

And you have never considered them?

I have considered them, certainly. I just don't obsess on them.

Syrinx, you are the one Edenist still with us who has come closest to knowing the truth of any of these. If it affects any of us, it affects you.

Affect, or hinder?

Answer yourself.

I wish you'd stop saying that to me.

You know I never will.

Yes. Very well, I've thought about the questions; as to the answers, I don't have a clue. Which makes the questions irrelevant.

Very good, I would agree with that statement.

You would?

With one exception. They are irrelevant only for the moment. Right now, our society is doing what it always does in times of crisis, and resorting to physical force to defend itself. Again I have no quarrel with this. But if we are to make any real progress in this arena these questions must be examined with a degree of urgency so far lacking. For answer them we must. This is not a gulf of knowledge the human race can survive. We must deliver—dare I call it—divine truth.

You expect that out of a *therapy* session?

My dear Syrinx, of course not. What sloppy thinking. But I am disappointed the solution to our more immediate problem has eluded you.

Which problem? she asked in exasperation.

Your problem. He snapped his fingers at her with some vexation, as if she were a miscreant child. **Now concentrate please. You wish to fly, but you retain a perfectly understandable reticence.**

Yes.

Everyone wishes to know the answer to those questions I asked, yet they do not know where to look.

Yes.

One race has those answers.

The Kiint? I know, but they said they wouldn't help.

Incorrect. I have accessed the sensevise recording of the Assembly's emergency session. Ambassador Roulor said the Kiint would not help us in the struggle we faced. The context of the statement was somewhat ambiguous. Did the ambassador mean the physical struggle, or the quest for knowledge?

We all know that the Kiint would not help us to fight. QED the ambassador was referring to the afterlife.

A reasonable assumption. One hopes the future of the human race does not rest on a single misinterpreted sentence.

So why haven't you asked the Kiint ambassador to Jupiter to clarify it?

I doubt that even a Kiint ambassador has the authority to disclose the kind of information we now search for, no matter what the circumstances.

Syrinx groaned in understanding. **You want me to go to the Kiint homeworld and ask.**

How kind of you to offer. You will embark on a flight with few risks involved, and you will also be confronting the unknown. Sadly your latter task will be conducted on a purely intellectual level, but it is an honourable start.

And good therapy.

A most fortuitous combination, is it not? If I were not a Buddhist I would be talking about the killing of two birds.

Assuming the Jovian Consensus approves of the flight.

An amused light twinkled in the deeply recessed eyes.

Being the founder of Edenism has its privileges. Not even the Consensus would refuse one of my humble requests.

Syrinx closed her eyes, then looked up at the vaguely puzzled face of the chief therapist. She realized her lips were parted in a wide smile.

Is everything all right? he asked politely.

Absolutely. Taking a cautious breath, she eased her legs off the side of the bed. The hospital room was as comfortable and pleasant as only their culture could make it. But it would be nice to have a complete change.

Oenone.

Yes?

I hope you've enjoyed your rest, my love. We have a long flight ahead of us.

At last!

• • •

It had not been an easy week for Ikela. The Dorados were starting to suffer from the civil and commercial starflight quarantine. All exports had halted, and the asteroids had only a minuscule internal economy, which could hardly support the hundreds of industrial stations that refined the plentiful ore. Pretty soon he was going to have to start laying off staff in all seventeen of the T'Opingtu company's foundry stations.

It was the first setback the Dorados had ever suffered in all of their thirty-year history. They had been tough years, but rewarding for those who had believed in their own future and worked hard to attain it. People like Ikela. He had come here after the death of Garissa, like so many others tragically disinherited from that world. There had been more than enough money to start his business in those days, and it had grown in tandem with the system's flourishing economy. In three decades he had changed from bitter refugee to a leading industrialist, with a position of responsibility in the Dorados' governing council.

Now this. It wasn't financial ruin, not by any means, but the social cost was starting to mount up at an alarming rate. The Dorados were used only to expansion and growth. Unemployment was not an issue in any of the seven settled asteroids. People who found themselves suddenly without a job and regular earnings were unlikely to react favourably to the council washing their hands of the problem.

Yesterday, Ikela had sat in on a session to discuss the idea of making companies pay non-salaried employees a retainer fee to tide them through the troubles; which had seemed the easy solution until the chief magistrate started explaining how difficult that would be to implement legally. As always the council had dithered. Nothing had been decided.

Today Ikela had to start making his own decisions along those same lines. He knew he ought to set an example and pay some kind of reduced wage to his workforce. It wasn't the kind of decision he was used to making.

He strode into the executive floor's anteroom with little enthusiasm for the coming day. His personal secretary, Lomie, was standing up behind her desk, a harassed expression on her face. Ikela was mildly surprised to see a small red handkerchief tied around her ankle. He would never have thought a levelheaded girl like Lomie would pay any attention to that Deadnight nonsense which seemed to be sweeping through the Dorados' younger generation.

"I couldn't stonewall her," Lomie datavised. "I'm sorry, sir, she was so forceful, and she did say she was an old friend."

Ikela followed her gaze across the room. A smallish woman was rising from one of the settees, putting her cup of coffee down on the side table. She clung to a small backpack which was hanging at her side from a shoulder strap. Few Dorados residents had skin as dark as hers, though it was extensively wrinkled now. Ikela guessed she was in her sixties. Her features were almost familiar, something about them agitating his subconscious. He ran a visual comparison program through his neural nanonics personnel record files.

"Hello, Captain," she said. "It's been a while."

Whether the program placed her first, or the use of his old title triggered the memory, he never knew. "Mzu," he choked. "Dr Mzu. Oh, Mother Mary, what are you doing here?"

"You know exactly what I'm doing here, Captain."

"Captain?" Lomie inquired. She looked from one to the other. "I never knew . . ."

Keeping his eyes fixed on Mzu as if he expected her to leap for his throat, Ikela waved Lomie to be silent. "I'm taking no appointments, no files, no calls, nothing. We're not to be interrupted." He datavised a code at his office door. "Come through, Doctor, please."

The office had a single window, a long band of glass which looked down on Ayacucho's biosphere cavern. Alkad gave the farms and parks an appreciative glance. "Not a bad view, considering you've only had thirty years to build it. The Garissans seem to have done well for themselves here. I'm glad to see it."

"This cavern's only fifteen years old, actually. Ayacucho was the second Dorado to be settled after Mapire. But you're right, I enjoy the view."

Alkad nodded, taking in the large office; its size, furnishings, and artwork chosen to emphasise the occupant's status rather than conforming to any notion of aesthetics. "And you have prospered, too, Captain. But then, that was part of your mission, wasn't it?"

She watched him slump down into a chair behind the big terrestrial-oak desk. Hardly the kind of dynamic magnate who could build his T'Opingtu company into a multistellar market leader in the fabrication of exotic alloy components. More like a fraud whose bluff had just been called.

"I have some of the resources we originally discussed," he said. "Of course, they are completely at your disposal."

She sat on a chair in front of the desk, staring him down. "You're straying from the script, Captain. I don't want resources, I want the combat-capable starship we agreed on. The starship you were supposed to have ready for me the day the Omuta sanctions ended. Remember?"

"Look, bloody hell it's been decades, Mzu. Decades! I didn't know where the hell you were, even if you were still alive. Mother Mary, things change. Life is different now. Forgive me, I know you are supposed to be here at this time, I just never expected to see you. I didn't think . . ."

A chilling anger gained control of Alkad's thoughts, unlocked from that secret centre of motivation at the core of her brain. "Have you got a starship which can deploy the Alchemist?"

He shook his head before burying it in his hands. "No."

"They slaughtered ninety-five million of us, Ikela, they wrecked our planet, they made us breathe radioactive soot until our lungs bled. Genocide doesn't even begin to describe what was done to us. You and I and the other survivors were a mistake, an oversight. There's no life left for us in this universe. We have only one purpose, one duty. Revenge, vengeance, and justice, our three guiding stars. Mother Mary has given us this one blessing, providing us with a second chance. We're not even attempting to kill the Omutans. I would never use the Alchemist to do that; I'm not going to become as they are, that would be their ultimate victory. All we're going to do is make them suffer, to give them a glimpse, a pitiful glimmer of the agony they've forced us to endure every waking day for thirty years."

"Stop it," he shouted. "I've made a life for myself here, we all have. This mission, this vendetta, what would it achieve after so much time? Nothing! We would be the tainted ones then. Let the Omutans carry the guilt they deserve. Every person they talk to, every planet they visit, they'll be cursed to carry the weight of their name with them."

"As we suffer pity wherever we go."

"Oh, Mother Mary! Don't do this."

"You will help me, Ikela. I am not giving you a choice in this. Right now you've allowed yourself to forget. That will end. I will make you remember. You've grown old and fat and comfy. I never did, I never allowed myself that luxury. They didn't allow me. Ironic that, I always felt. They kept my angry spirit alive with their eternal reminder, their agents and their discreet observation. In doing so, they also kept their own nemesis alive."

His face lifted in bewilderment. "What are you talking about? Have the Omutans been watching you?"

"No, they're all locked up where they belong. It's the other intelligence agencies who have discovered who I am and what I built. Don't ask me how. Somebody must have leaked the information. Somebody weak, Ikela."

"You mean, they know you're here?"

"They don't know exactly where I am. All they know is I escaped from Tranquillity. But now they'll be looking for me.

And don't try fooling yourself, they'll track me down eventually. It's what they're good at, very good. The only question now is which one will find me first."

"Mother Mary!"

"Exactly. Of course, if you had prepared the starship for me as you were supposed to, this wouldn't even be a problem. You stupid, selfish, petty-minded bastard. Do you realize what you've done? You have jeopardized everything we ever stood for."

"You don't understand."

"No, I don't; and I won't dignify you by trying to. I'm not even going to listen to any more of your pitiful whining. Now tell me, where are the others? Do we even have a partizan group anymore?"

"Yes. Yes, we're still together. We still help the cause whenever we can."

"Are all the originals here?"

"Yes, we're all still alive. But the other four aren't in Ayacucho."

"What about other partizans, do you have a local leadership council?"

"Yes."

"Then call them to a meeting. Today. They will have to be told what's happening. We need nationalist recruits for a crew."

"Yes," he stammered. "Yes, all right."

"And in the meantime, start looking for a suitable starship. There ought to be one in dock. It's a shame I let the *Samaku* go. It would have suited us."

"But there's a Confederation-wide quarantine . . ."

"Not where we're going there isn't. And you're a member of the Dorados council, you can arrange for the government to authorize our departure."

"I can't do that!"

"Ikela, look at me very closely. I am not playing games with you. You have endangered both my life and the mission you swore to undertake when you took the oath to serve your naval commission. As far as I am concerned, that amounts to treason. Now if an agency grabs me before I can retrieve the Alchemist, I am going to make damn sure they know where the money came from to help you start up T'Opingtu all those years ago. I'm sure you remember exactly what the Confederation law has to say about antimatter, don't you?"

He bowed his head. "Yes."

"Good. Now start datavising the partizans."

"All right."

Alkad regarded him with a mixture of contempt and worry. That the others would falter had never occurred to her. They were all Garissan navy. Thirty years ago she had secretly suspected that if anyone was destined to be the weak link it would be her.

"I've been moving around a lot since I docked," she said. "But I'll spend the rest of the afternoon in your apartment. I need to clean up, and that's the one place I can be sure you won't tip anyone off about. There'd be too many questions."

Ikela recouped some of his old forcefulness. "I don't want you there. My daughter's living with me."

"So?"

"I don't want her involved."

"The sooner you get my starship prepared, the sooner I'll be gone." She hoisted the backpack's strap over her shoulder and went out into the anteroom.

Lomie glanced up from behind her desk, curiosity haunting her narrow features. Alkad ignored her, and datavised the lift processor for a ride to the lobby. The doors opened, revealing a girl inside. She was in her early twenties, a lot taller than Mzu, with a crown of short dreadlocks at the top of a shaven skull. First impression was that someone had attempted to geneer an elf into existence her torso was so slim, her limbs were disproportionately long. Her face could have been pretty if her personality wasn't so stern.

"I'm Voi," she said after the doors shut.

Alkad nodded in acknowledgement, facing the doors and wishing the lift could go faster.

All movement stopped, the floor indicator frozen between four and three.

"And you're Dr Alkad Mzu."

"There's a nervejam projector in this bag, and its control processor is activated."

"Good. I'm glad you're not walking around unprotected."

"Who are you?"

"I'm Ikela's daughter. Check my public record file, if you like."

Alkad did, datavising the lift's net processor for a link to Ayacucho's civil administration computer. If Voi was some kind of agency plant, they'd made a very good job of ghosting details. Besides, if she was from an agency, the last thing they'd be doing was talking. "Restart the lift, please."

"Will you talk to me?"

"Restart the lift."

Voi datavised the lift's control processor, and they started to descend. "We want to help you."

"Who's we?" Alkad asked.

"My friends; there are quite a few of us now. The partizans you belong to have done nothing for years. They are soft and old and afraid of making waves."

"I don't know you."

"Was my father helpful?"

"We made progress."

"They won't help you. Not when it comes to action. We will."

"How did you find out who I am?"

"From my father. He shouldn't have told me, but he did. He's so weak."

"How much do you know?"

"That the partizans were supposed to prepare for you. That you were bringing something to finally give us our revenge against Omuta. Logically it has to be some kind of powerful weapon. Possibly even a planet-buster. He was always afraid of you, they all were. Have they made the proper preparations? I bet they haven't."

"As I said, I don't know you."

Voi leaned over her, furiously intent. "We have money. We're organized. We have people who aren't afraid. We won't let you down. We'd never let you down. Tell us what you want, we'll provide it."

"How did you know I was seeing your father?"

"Lomie, of course. She's not one of us, not a core member, but she's a friend. It's always useful for me to know what my father is doing. As I said, we're properly organized."

"So are children's day clubs." For a moment Alkad thought the girl was going to strike her.

"All right," Voi said with a calm that could only have been induced by neural nanonic overrides. "You're being sensible, not trusting a stranger with the last hope our culture owns. I can accept that. It's rational."

"Thank you."

"But we can help. Just give us the chance. Please." And *please* was obviously not a word which came easy from that mouth.

The lift doors opened. A lobby of polished black stone and curving white metal glinted under large silver light spires. A thirty-year-old unarmed combat program reviewed the image from Alkad's retinal implants, deciding nobody was lurking suspiciously. She looked up at the tall, anorexically proportioned girl, trying to decide what to do. "Your father invited me to stay at his apartment. We can talk more when we get there."

Voi gave a shark's smile. "It would be an honour, Doctor."

* * *

It was the woman sitting up at the bar wearing a red shirt who caught Joshua's attention. The red was very red, a bright, effervescent scarlet. And the style of the shirt was odd, though he'd be hard pressed to define exactly what was wrong with the cut, it lacked . . . smoothness. The clincher was the fact it had buttons down the front, not a seal.

"Don't look," he murmured to Beaulieu and Dahybi. "But I think she's a possessed." He datavised his retinal image file to them.

They both turned and looked. In Beaulieu's case it was quite a performance, twisting her bulk around in the too-small chair, streamers of light slithering around the contours of her shiny body.

"Jesus! Show some professionalism."

The woman gave the three of them a demurely inquisitive glance.

"You sure?" Dahybi asked.

"Think so. There's something wrong with her, anyway."

Dahybi said nothing; he'd experienced Joshua's intuition at work before.

"We can soon check," Beaulieu said. "Go over to her and see if any of our blocks start glitching."

"No." Joshua was slowly scanning the rest of the teeming bar. It was a wide room cut square into the rock of Kilifi asteroid's habitation section, with a mixed clientele mostly taken from ships' crews and industrial station staff. He was anonymous here, as much as he could be (five people had so far recognized "Lagrange Calvert"). And Kilifi had been a good cover, it manufactured the kind of components he was supposed to be buying for Tranquillity's defences. Sarha and Ashly were handling the dummy negotiations with local companies; and so far no one had questioned why they'd flown all the way to Narok rather than a closer star system.

He saw a couple more suspicious people drinking in solitude, then another three crammed around a table with sullen sly expressions. I'm getting too paranoid.

"We have to concentrate on our mission," he said. "If Kilifi isn't enforcing its screening procedures properly, that's their problem. We can't risk any sort of confrontation. Besides, if the possessed are wandering around this freely it must mean their infiltration is quite advanced."

Dahybi hunched his shoulders and played with his drink, trying not to look anxious. "There are navy ships docked here, and most of the independent traders are combat-capable. If the asteroid falls, the possessed will get them."

"I know." Joshua met the node specialist's stare, refusing to show weakness. "We cannot cause waves."

"Sure, you said: Don't draw attention to yourself, don't talk to the natives, don't fart loudly. What the hell are we doing here, Joshua? Why are you so anxious to trace Meyer?"

"I need to talk to him."

"Don't you trust us?"

"Of course I do. And don't try such cheap shots. You know I'll tell all of you as soon as I can. For now, it's best you don't know. You trust me, don't you?"

Dahybi put his lips together in a tired grin. "Cheap shot."

"Yeah."

The waitress brought another round of drinks to their alcove. Joshua watched her legs as she wriggled away through the crowd. A bit young for him, mid-teens. Louise's age. The thought warmed him briefly. Then he saw she was wearing a red handkerchief around her ankle. Jesus, I don't know which is worse, the horrors of possession or the pathetic dreams of the Deadnights.

He'd received one hell of a shock the first time he accessed the recording from Valisk. Marie Skibbow possessed and luring naive kids to their doom. She'd been a lovely girl, beautiful and smart, with thoughts as hard as carbotanium composite. If she could be caught, anyone could. Lalonde strummed out far too many resonances.

"Captain," Beaulieu warned.

Joshua saw Bunal approaching their alcove. He sat down and smiled. There wasn't the slightest sign of nerves. But then as Joshua had discovered while asking around his fellow captains, Bunal was overfamiliar with this kind of transaction.

"Good afternoon, Captain," Bunal said pleasantly. "Have you managed to acquire your cargo yet?"

"Some of it," Joshua said. "I'm hoping you were successful with the rest."

"Indeed I was. Most of the information was quite simple to obtain. However, I am nothing if not assiduous in any freelance work I undertake. I discovered that, sadly, what you actually need falls outside our original agreement."

Dahybi gave the man a hateful glare. He always despised bent civil servants.

"And will cost . . . ?" Joshua inquired, unperturbed.

"An additional twenty thousand fuseodollars." Bunal sounded sincerely regretful. "I apologize for the cost, but times are hard at the moment. I have little work and a large family."

"Of course." Joshua held up his Jovian Bank credit disk.

Bunal was surprised by the young captain's swift concession. It took him a moment to produce his own credit disk. Joshua shunted the money over.

"You were right," Bunal said. "The *Udat* did come to this star system. It docked at the Nyiru asteroid. Apparently its captain was hurt when they arrived, he spent almost four days in hospital undergoing neural trauma treatment. When it was complete, they filed a flight plan for the Sol system, and left."

"Sol?" Joshua asked. "Are you sure?"

"Positive. However—and this is where the twenty thousand comes in—their passenger, Dr Alkad Mzu, didn't go with them. She hired an independent trader called the *Samaku*, and departed an hour later."

"Flight plan?"

"Filed for a Dorado asteroid, Ayacucho. I even checked traffic control's sensor data for the flight. They were definitely aligned for Tunja when they jumped."

Joshua resisted the impulse to swear. Ione was right, Mzu was running to the last remnants of her nation. She must be going for the Alchemist. He flicked another glance at the girl in the red shirt, her head tipped back elegantly as she drank her cocktail. Jesus, as if we don't have enough problems right now. "Thank you."

"My pleasure. You should also know, for no extra charge, that I'm not the only one to be asking these questions. There are three access requests logged on the Civil Spaceflight Department computer for the same files. One request was made only twenty minutes before mine."

"Oh, Jesus."

"Bad news?"

"Interesting news," Joshua grunted. He rose to his feet.

"If there is anything else I can obtain for you, Captain, please call."

"Sure thing." Joshua was already walking for the door, Dahybi and Beaulieu a couple of steps behind.

Before he reached the exit, people watching the AV pillar behind the bar were gasping in shock; agitated murmurs of conversation rippled down the length of the room. Perfect strangers asking each other: *Did you access that?* the way they always did with momentous news.

Joshua focused on the AV pillar's projection, allowing the hazy laserlight sparkle to form its picture behind his eyes. A planet floated below him, its geography instantly familiar. No real continents or oceans, just winding seas and thousands of medium-sized islands. Patches of glowing red cloud squatted over half of the islands, concentrated mainly in the tropic zones—though on this world tropic was a relative term.

". . . Confederation Navy frigate *Levêque* confirmed that all inhabited islands on Norfolk have now been covered by the reality dysfunction cloud," the news commentator said. "All contact with the surface has been lost, and it must be assumed that the majority, if not all, of the population has been possessed. Norfolk is a pastoral planet with few spaceplanes available to the local government; because of this no attempt was made to evacuate any inhabitants to the navy squadron before the capital Norwich fell. A statement from Confederation Navy headquarters at Trafalgar said that the *Levêque* would remain in orbit to observe the situation, but no offensive action was being considered at this time. This brings to seven the number of planets known to have been taken over by the possessed."

"Oh, Jesus, Louise is down there." The AV image broke up as he turned his head away from the pillar, seeing Louise running over the grassy wolds in one of those ridiculous dresses, laughing over her shoulder at him. And Genevieve, too, that irritating child who was either laughing or sulking. Marjorie, Grant (it would go worse for him, he would resist as long as possible), Kenneth, and even that receptionist at Drayton's Import. "Goddamnit. No!" I should have been there. I could have got her away.

"Joshua?" Dahybi asked in concern. "You okay?"

"Yeah. Did you catch that piece about Norfolk?"

"Yes."

"She's down there, Dahybi. I left her there."

"Who?"

"Louise."

"You didn't leave her there, Joshua. It's her home, it's where she belongs."

"Right." Joshua's neural nanonics were plotting a course from Narok to Norfolk. He didn't remember requesting it.

"Come on, Captain," Dahybi said. "We've got what we came for. Let's go."

Joshua looked at the woman in the red shirt again. She was staring at the AV pillar, abstract pastel streaks from the projection glinting dully on her ebony cheeks. A delighted smile flourished on her lips.

Joshua hated her, her invincibility, the cool arrogance sitting among her enemies. Queen of the bitch demons come to taunt him. Dahybi's hand tightened around his arm.

"Okay, we're gone."

• • •

"Here we are, home at last," Loren Skibbow said with a histrionic sigh. "Not that we can stay for long. They'll tear Guyana apart to find us now."

The apartment was on the highest level of the biosphere's habitation complex, where gravity was only eighty per cent standard. The penthouse of some Kingdom aristocrat, presumably, furnished with dark active-contour furniture and large hand-painted silk screens; every table and alcove shelf were littered with antiques.

Gerald felt it was a somewhat bizarre setting to wind up in considering the day's events. "Are you creating this?" When they lived in the arcology, Loren had always badgered him for what she termed a "grander" apartment.

She looked around with a rueful smile and shook her head. "No. My imagination isn't up to anything so gaudy. This is Pou Mok's place."

"The woman you're possessing? The redhead?"

"That's right." Loren smiled and took a step towards him.

Gerald stiffened. Not that she needed any physical signs; his mind was foaming with fear and confusion. "Okay, Gerald, I won't touch you. Sit down, we have a lot to talk about. And this time I mean talk, not just you telling me what you've decided is best for us."

He flinched. Everything she did and said triggered memories. The unedited past seemed to have become his curse in life.

"How did you get here?" he asked. "What happened, Loren?"

"You saw the homestead, what that bastard Dexter and his Ivets did to us." Her face paled. "To Paula."

"I saw."

"I tried, Gerald. Honestly, I tried to fight back. But it all happened so fast. They were crazy brutes; Dexter killed one of his own just because the boy would slow them down. I wasn't strong enough to stop it."

"And I wasn't there."

"They'd have killed you, too."

"At least . . ."

"No, Gerald. You would have died for nothing. I'm glad you escaped. This way you can help Marie."

"How?"

"The possessed can be beaten. Individually, in any case. I'm not so sure about overall. But that's for others to fight over, planetary governments and the Confederation. You and I have to rescue our daughter, allow her to have her own life. No one else will."

"How?" This time it was a shout.

"The same way you were freed: zero-tau. We have to put her in zero-tau. The possessed can't endure it."

"Why not?"

"Because we're conscious the whole time. Zero-tau suspends normal energy wave functions, but our souls are still connected to the beyond somehow, that makes us aware of time passing. But only time, nothing else. It is the ultimate sensory deprivation, actually worse than the beyond. At least in the beyond souls have the memories of other souls to feed on, and some perception of the real universe."

"That's why," Gerald murmured. "I knew Kingsford Garrigan was scared."

"Some can hold out longer than others, it depends on how strong their personality is. But in the end, everyone retreats from the body they possess."

"There is hope, then."

"For Marie, yes. We can save her."

"So that she can die."

"Everybody dies, Gerald."

"And goes on to suffer in the beyond."

"I'm not sure. If it hadn't been for you and Marie, I don't think I would have remained with all the other souls."

"I don't understand."

Loren gave him a hapless smile. "I was worried about the

two of you, Gerald, I wanted to make sure you were all right. That's why I stayed."

"Yes but . . . where else could you go?"

"I'm not certain that question applies. The beyond is strange, there are no separate places within it, not like this universe."

"So how could you leave?"

"I wouldn't leave it . . ." She fluttered her hands in exasperation as she struggled with the concept. "I just wouldn't be in the same part of it as the rest of them."

"You said there were no different parts."

"There aren't."

"So how—"

"I don't pretend to understand, Gerald. But you can leave the others behind. The beyond isn't necessarily the torment everyone is making it out to be."

Gerald studied the pale salmon carpet, shamed at being unable to look at his own wife. "And you came back for me."

"No, Gerald." Her voice hardened. "We might be husband and wife, but my love isn't that blind. I came back principally for Marie's sake. If it had just been you, I don't think I would have had the courage. I endured the other souls devouring my memories for her sake. Did you know you can see out of the beyond? Just. I watched Marie, and that made the horror tolerable. I hadn't seen her since that day she walked out on us. I wanted to know she was alive and safe. It wasn't easy; I almost abandoned my vigil, then she was possessed. So I stayed, waiting for an opportunity to help, for someone close to you to be possessed. And here I am."

"Yes. Here you are. Who is Pou Mok? I thought the Principality had defeated the possessed, confined them all to Mortonridge."

"They have, according to the news reports. But the three who arrived here on the *Ekwan* with you got to Pou Mok before they left the asteroid. They were smart choosing her; she supplies illegal stimulant programs to the personnel up here, among other things. That's why she can afford this place. It also means she's not included on any file of Guyana's inhabitants, so she never got hauled in to be tested like everyone else. The idea was that even if the three from the *Ekwan* got caught on the planet, Pou Mok's possessor would be safe to begin the process all over again. In theory, she was the perfect provocateur to leave behind. Unfortunately for the three of them, I was the one who came forwards from the beyond. I don't care about their goals, I'm only interested in Marie."

"Was I wrong taking her to Lalonde?" Gerald asked remotely. "I thought I was doing the best possible thing for her, for all of you."

"You were. Earth's dying; the arcologies are old, worn out. There's nothing there for people like us; if we'd stayed, Marie and Paula would have had lives no different from us, or our parents, or any of our ancestors for the last ten generations. You broke the cycle for us, Gerald. We had the chance to take pride in what our grandchildren would become."

"What grandchildren?" He knew he was going to start crying any minute. "Paula's dead; Marie hated our home so much she ran away at the first opportunity."

"Good thing she did, Gerald, wasn't it? She was always headstrong, and she's a teenager. Teenagers can never look and plan ahead; having a good time is the only thing they can think of. All she knew was that two months of her life weren't as comfy as the ones which went before, and she had to do some work for the first time as well. Small surprise she ran away. It was a premature taste of adulthood that scared her off, not us being bad parents.

"You know, I perceived her before she was possessed. She'd found herself a job in Durringham, a good job. She was doing all right for herself, better than she could ever do on Earth. Knowing Marie, she didn't appreciate it."

When Gerald found the nerve to glance up, he saw Loren's expression was a twin to his own. "I didn't tell you before. But I was so frightened for her when she ran away."

"I know you were. Fathers always think their daughters can't take care of themselves."

"You were worried, too."

"Yes. Oh, yes. But only that fate would throw something at her she couldn't survive. Which it has. She would have done all right if this curse hadn't been unleashed."

"All right," he said shakily. "What do we do about it? I just wanted to go to Valisk and help her."

"That's my idea, too, Gerald. There's no big plan, though I do have some of the details sorted out. First thing we need to do is get you on the *Quadin*, it's one of the few starships still flying. Right now the Kingdom is busy selling weapons components to its allies. The *Quadin* is departing for Pinjarra asteroid in seven hours with a cargo of five-gigawatt maser cannons for their SD network."

"Just me?" he asked in alarm. "Where are you going?"

"To Valisk, eventually. But we can't travel together, it's too risky."

"I can't go alone. Really, I can't. I don't know how to, not anymore. I can't think right, not now. I want you to come with me, Loren. Please."

"No, Gerald. You must do this by yourself."

"It . . . it's hard. There are other things in my head."

"We're the only chance Marie has. Focus on that, Gerald."

"Yes. Yes, I will." He gave her a grave smile. "Where is Pinjarra?"

"It's in the Toowoomba star system, which is Australian-ethnic. The Kingdom is anxious to keep them locked in to its diplomatic strategy. Their asteroid settlements aren't very well defended, so they're being offered upgrades on favourable financial terms."

Gerald fidgeted with his fingers. "But how do I get on board? We'd never make it into the spaceport, never mind a starship. Maybe if we just asked Ombey's government if we can go to Valisk. They'll know we're telling the truth about wanting to help Marie. And that information about zero-tau would be useful. They'd be grateful."

"Bloody hell." Loren regarded the pathetically hopeful smile on his face more with astonishment than contempt. He had always been the forceful one, the go-getter. "Oh, Gerald, what have they done to you?"

"Remember." He hung his head, probing at his temples in a vain attempt to alleviate some of the sparkling pain inside. "They made me remember. I don't want that. I don't want to remember, I just want to forget it all."

She came over and sat beside him, her arm going around his shoulder the way she used to do with her daughters when they were younger. "Once we free Marie, all this will be over. You can think of other things again, new things."

"Yes." He nodded vigorously, speaking with the slow surety of the newly converted. "Yes, you're right. That's what Dr Dobbs told me, too; I have to formulate relevant goals for my new circumstances, and concentrate on achieving them. I must eject myself from the failings of the past."

"Good philosophy." Her eyebrows rose in bemusement. "Firstly we have to buy you passage on the *Quadin*. The captain has supplied Pou Mok with various fringe-legal fleks before, which can be used to lever him into taking you. If you're firm enough with him, Gerald. Are you going to manage that?"

"Yes. I can do that." He grasped his hands together, squeezing. "I can tell him anything if it will help Marie."

"Just don't be too aggressive. Stay polite and calmly determined."

"I will."

"Fine. Now money isn't a problem, obviously, I can give you a Jovian Bank credit disk with about half a million fuseodollars loaded in. Pou Mok also has half a dozen blank passport fleks. Our real problem is going to be your appearance, every sensor in the asteroid is going to be programmed for your features now. I can change the way you look, but only while I'm near you, which is no use at all. They can detect me easily in public places, especially if I'm using my energistic ability. So we're going to have to give you a permanent alteration."

"Permanent?" he asked uneasily.

"Pou Mok has a set of cosmetic adaptation packages. She used to keep changing her own face in case the asteroid police became too familiar with it—she's not even a natural redhead. I think I know enough to program the control processor manually. If I don't get too close, the packages should be able to give you a basic makeover. It ought to be enough."

Loren took him through into one of the apartment's bedrooms and told him to lie down. The cosmetic adaptation packages were similar to nanonic medical packages but with warty bubbles on the outside, holding reserves of collagen ready to be implanted, firming up new contours. Gerald felt the furry inner surface knitting to his skin, then his nerves went dead.

It took a lot of effort on Gerald's part not to shy away from the ceiling-mounted sensors in the public hall. He still wasn't convinced about the face which appeared each time he looked in the mirror. Ten years younger, but with puffy cheeks and drooping laughter lines, skin a shade darker with an underlying red flush; a face which conveyed his internal worry perfectly. His hair had been trimmed to a centimetre fuzz and coloured a light chestnut—at least there were no silver strands any more.

He walked into the Bar Vips and ordered a mineral water, asking the barman where he could find Captain McRobert.

McRobert had brought two of his crew with him, one of whom was a cosmonik with a body resembling a mannequin: jet-black with no features at all, not even on the head; he was an impressive two hundred and ten centimetres tall.

Gerald tried to retain an impassive expression as he sat at their table, but it wasn't easy. Their steely presence was conjuring up memories of the squad which had captured Kingsford Garrigan in Lalonde's jungle. "I'm Niall Lyshol; Pou Mok sent me," he stuttered.

"If she hadn't, we wouldn't be here," McRobert said curtly. "As it is . . ." He gave the cosmonik a brief signal.

Gerald was offered a processor block.

"Take it," McRobert instructed.

He tried, but the huge black hand wouldn't let go.

"No static charge," the cosmonik said. "No glitches." The block was withdrawn.

"All right, Niall Lyshol," McRobert said. "You're not a possessed, so what the fuck are you?"

"Someone who wants a flight out of here." Gerald exhaled softly, reminding himself of the relaxation exercises Dr Dobbs urged him to employ: cycle down the body and the brain waves will follow. "As someone else who deals with Pou Mok, Captain, you should appreciate the need to keep moving on before people start to take an interest in you."

"Don't pull that bullshit pressure routine on me, boy. I'm not taking anyone who's hot, not with the way things are right now. I don't even know if we're going to leave Guyana, the code two defence alert still hasn't been lifted. Traffic control is hardly going to clear anyone for flight while one of those bastards is running loose up here."

"I'm not hot. Check the bulletins."

"I have."

"So you'll take me when the code two is lifted?"

"You're a complication, Lyshol. I can't take passengers because of the quarantine, which means you'd have to be listed as crew. You haven't got neural nanonics, which means the line company would start asking me questions. I don't like that."

"I can pay."

"Be assured: you will."

"And you'll have Pou Mok's gratitude. For what it's worth."

"Less than she likes to think. What are you running from?"

"People. Not the authorities. There's no official trouble."

"One hundred thousand fuseodollars, and you spend the whole voyage in zero-tau. I'm not having you throwing up all over the life-support capsule."

"Agreed."

"Too quickly. A hundred thousand is an awful lot of money."

Gerald wasn't sure how much longer he could keep this up; slow thoughts echoed in his skull, telling him that the sanatorium had been a much kinder environment than this. If I went back, Dr Dobbs would understand, he'd make sure the police didn't punish me. If it wasn't for Marie . . . "You can't have it both ways. If I stay here then a lot of secrets are going to get spilt. You probably wouldn't be able to fly to any of the Kingdom systems again. I think that would bother the line company more than taking on a crewman without neural nanonics; not that they'll know I don't have neural nanonics unless you tell them."

"I don't like being threatened, Lyshol."

"I'm not threatening you. I'm asking for help. I need your help. Please."

McRobert glanced at his companions. "All right. The *Quadin* is docked at bay 901-C, we're scheduled to depart in three hours. Like I said, I can't guarantee that time with the code two, but if you're not there I'm not waiting."

"I'm ready now."

"No baggage? You surprise me. Very well, you can pay me when we get on board. And, Lyshol, don't expect any crew salary."

When the four of them came out of Bar Vips, Gerald gave what he believed to be a surreptitious glance along the public hall. There weren't many people about, the code two alert had hauled in all the asteroid's off-duty military and civil service personnel.

Loren watched him go, hunched up and tragic between his three escorts. They stepped into a lift, and the door closed behind them. She walked the other way down the public hall, a smile playing over her illusory lips.

After seven and a half hours with over a hundred false alerts and not one genuine sighting, Admiral Farquar was considering running a suppressor program through his neural nanonics. He hated the artificial calm the software brought, but the tension and depression were getting to him. The hunt for the possessed woman was being run from the Royal Navy tactical operations centre. It wasn't quite the operation envisaged while it was being built, but its communications were easily reconfigured to probe the asteroid's net, and its AI had been loaded with the tracker programs developed by Diana Tiernan to hunt possessed across Xingu. Given the size of Guyana, and the density of electronic systems spread throughout the interior, they should have had a result within minutes.

But the woman had eluded them. In doing so, she had forced him to admit to Princess Kirsten that if one could, so could more. There might be any number running around Guyana. For all he knew the entire navy staff could have been possessed, which was why the operations centre kept saying they couldn't find her. He didn't believe it himself (he'd visited the centre personally) but no doubt it was an option the cabinet had to consider. Even he must be considered suspect, though they'd been tactful enough not to say so.

As a result, Guyana had handed over Ombey's Strategic

Defence network command to a Royal Navy base in Atherstone. A complete quarantine of the asteroid had been quietly enforced under the guise of the code two defence alert.

So far it had all been for nothing.

The office management computer datavised him that Captain Oldroyd, his staff security officer, and Dr Dobbs were requesting an interview. He datavised an acknowledgement, and his office dissolved into the white bubble room of a sensenviron conference room.

"Have you made any progress finding her?" Dobbs asked.

"Not yet," Farquar admitted.

"That ties in," the doctor said. "We've been running analysis scenarios based on the information we've collated so far; and based on that I believe I've come up with a rationale for her actions. Extracting Skibbow from our medical facility was slightly puzzling behaviour. It was an awful risk even for a possessed. If the marines had been thirty seconds faster she would never have made it. She must have had an extremely good reason."

"Which is?"

"I think she's Loren Skibbow, Gerald's wife. If for no other reason than what she said to Jansen Kovak: You should try being married to him for twenty years. I checked our file, they were married for twenty years."

"His wife?"

"Exactly."

"Okay, I've heard stranger." The admiral faced Captain Oldroyd. "I hope you've got some evidence to back up this theory."

"Yes, sir. Assuming she is who we suspect, her behavioural profile certainly fits her actions to date. First of all, we believe she's been in Guyana for some time, possibly right from the beginning when the *Ekwan* docked. She has obviously had enough time to learn how to move around without activating any of our tracer programs. Secondly, if she can do that, why hasn't she launched the kind of takeover effort we saw on Xingu? She's held back for a reason."

"Because it doesn't fit in with her plans," Dr Dobbs said eagerly. "If the whole asteroid became possessed, her peers would be unlikely to allow Gerald his freedom. This is all personal, Admiral, it's not part of what's happening to Mortonridge or New California. She's completely on her own. I don't believe she's any real danger to the Kingdom's security at all."

"Are you telling me we've shifted the Principality to a code two alert because of a *domestic* matter?" Admiral Farquar asked.

"I believe so," Dr Dobbs said apologetically. "The possessed are people, too. We've had ample proof that they retain a nearly complete range of human emotions. And, er . . . we did put Gerald through quite an ordeal. If what we suspect is true, it would be quite reasonable to assume Loren would do her best to take him away from us."

"Dear God. All right, so now what? How does this theory help us deal with her?"

"We can negotiate."

"To what end? I don't care that she's a loving wife. She's a bloody possessed. We can't have the pair of them living happily ever after up here."

"No. But we can offer to take better care of Gerald. From her viewpoint, of course," Dr Dobbs added quickly.

"Maybe." The admiral would have dearly loved to have found a flaw in the reasoning, but the facts did seem to fit together with uncomfortable precision. "So what do you recommend?"

"I'd like to broadcast over Guyana's net, load a message into every personal communications processor, blanket the news and entertainment companies. It'll only be a matter of time before they access it."

"If she answers she'll give away her location. She'll know that."

"We'll find her eventually, I'll make that quite clear. What I can offer is a solution she can accept. Do I have your permission? It will need to be a genuine offer. After all, the possessed can read the emotional content of minds. She'll know if I'm telling the truth."

"That's a pretty broad request, Doctor. What exactly do you want to offer her?"

"Gerald to be taken down to the planet and given an Ombey citizenship. We provide full financial compensation for what we put him through, complete his counselling and therapy. And finally, if this crisis is resolved, we'll do whatever we can to reunite him with his daughter."

"You mean that Kiera girl in Valisk?"

"Yes, Admiral."

"I doubt my authority runs to that . . ." He broke off as the office management computer datavised a change in Guyana's status. The operations centre had just issued a full combat alert.

The admiral opened a channel to the duty officer. "What's happening?" he datavised.

"The AI has registered an anomaly, sir. We think it could be her. I've dispatched a Royal Marine squad."

"What sort of anomaly?"

"A camera in the spaceport spindle entrance chamber registered a man getting into a transit capsule. When the capsule stopped at section G5 a woman got out. The capsule never stopped at any other section."

"What about processor glitches?"

"The AI is analysing all the electronics around her. There are some efficiency reductions, but well below the kind of disturbance which we were getting from the possessed down in Xingu."

The admiral requested a schematic of the spaceport. Section G5 was the civil spaceplane and ion field flyer dock. "Dear God, Dr Dobbs, I think you might have been right after all."

Loren floated along the brightly lit tubular corridor towards the airlock. According to the spaceport register, a Kulu Corporation SD2002 spaceplane was docked to it, a thirty-seater craft owned by the Crossen company who used it to ferry staff up to their microgee industrial stations. One of the smallest spaceplanes at Guyana, it was exactly the kind of craft a pair of fairly ignorant desperadoes would try to steal if they wanted to get down to the planet.

There was nobody about. The last person she'd seen had been a maintenance engineer who'd boarded the transit capsule she'd arrived in. She toyed with the idea of letting her energistic ability flare out and mess up some of the electronics in the corridor. But that might make them suspicious, she'd controlled herself for so long that any change now would cause questions. She'd just have to hope that their security programs and sensors would catch her. The change of image was a subtle enough betrayal, providing their monitor routines were good enough.

The airlock tube was five metres long, and narrower than the corridor, barely two metres wide. She manoeuvred herself into it, only to find the hatch at the far end was shut.

At last, an excuse to use the energistic ability.

There was a surge of electricity around the hatch. She could sense the main power cables behind the azure blue composite walls, thick lines that burnt with an ember glow of current. There were other cables too, smaller and dimmer. It was one of those which had come alive, connected to a small communications block set into the rim of the hatch.

"It's Loren, isn't it?" a voice from the block asked. "Loren Skibbow, I'm sure it's you. My name is Dr Riley Dobbs. I was treating Gerald before you took him away."

She stared at the block in shock. How the bloody hell had he figured that out?

The power flowed through her body, twisting up from the beyond like a hot spring; she could feel it squirting through every cell. Her mind shaped it as it rose inside her, transforming it into the pattern she wanted, a pattern which matched her dreamy wish. It began to superimpose itself over reality. Sparks shivered over the surface of the hatch.

"Loren, I want to help, and I've been given the authority which will allow me to help. Please listen. Gerald is my patient, I don't want him harmed. I believe the two of us agree on that."

"Go to hell, Doctor. Better still, I'll take you there personally. You damaged my husband's mind. I'm not going to forget that."

There were noises in the corridor behind her, soft scraping, clinking sounds. When she focused, she could perceive the minds of the marines closing on her. Cold and anxious, but very determined.

"Gerald was damaged by the possession," Dobbs said. "I was trying to cure him. I want to continue that process."

The sparks had begun to swirl around the composite of the airlock tube, penetrating below the surface as if they were swimming through the material.

"Under the muzzle of a gun?" she asked scathingly. "I know they're behind me."

"The marines won't shoot. I promise that, Loren. It would be pointless. Shooting would just cost the life of the person you've possessed. Nobody wants that. Please, come and talk to me. I've already obtained huge concessions from the authorities. Gerald can be taken down to the planet. He'll be looked after properly, I'll continue his therapy. Perhaps someday he can even see Marie again."

"You mean Kiera. That bitch won't let my daughter go."

"Nothing is certain. We can discuss this. Please. You can't leave on the spaceplane. Even if you get in you can hardly pilot it down through the SD network. The only way Gerald can get down to the planet is if I take him."

"You won't touch him again. He's safe in my hiding place now, and you never found me, not in all the time I was there."

The airlock walls gave out a small creak. All the sparks had blurred together to form a glowing ring of composite encircling her. She smiled tightly. The subterfuge was nearly complete. Dobbs's intervention had turned out to be a beautiful bonus.

Loren could sense the marines holding back just past the edge of the airlock tube. She took a deep breath, attempting to deflect the knowledge of what was about to come. White fire burst out of her feet with a terrible screeching sound. It fountained into the corridor and broke apart into an avalanche of individual fireballs which careered into the waiting marines.

"No, Loren, don't, I can help. Please—"

She exerted herself to the full. Dobbs's voice fractured into a brassy caterwaul before vanishing altogether as the energistic effect crashed every processor within twenty-five metres.

"Don't," Pou Mok pleaded from the heart of Loren's mind. "I won't tell them where he is. I promise. They'll never know. Let me live."

"I can't trust the living," Loren told her.

"Bitch!"

The wall of the airlock tube gleamed brighter than the fireballs, then the composite vaporised. Loren flew out of the widening gap, impelled by the blast of air which stampeded away into the vacuum.

"Dear God," Admiral Farquar grunted. The spaceport's external sensors showed him the jet of air diminishing. Three marines had followed Loren Skibbow out into space. Their armour suits would provide some protection against decompression, and they had a small oxygen reserve. The duty officer had already dispatched some MSVs to chase after them.

Loren Skibbow was a different matter. For a while she had glowed from within, a fluorescent figure spinning around and around as she left the ruptured dock behind. Now the glow was fading. After a couple of minutes it winked out. The body exploded far more violently than it should have done.

"Locate as much as you can of her, and bring the pieces back," Admiral Farquar told the duty officer. "We can take a DNA sample; the ISA ought to be able to identify her for us."

"But why?" Dr Dobbs asked, mortified. "What the hell made her do that?"

"Perhaps they don't think quite like us, after all," the admiral said.

"They do. I know they do."

"When we find Skibbow, you can ask him."

It was a task which proved harder than expected. There was no response from his debrief nanonics, so the Royal Navy began a physical search of Guyana, monitored by the AI. No room, no service tunnel, and no storage chamber was overlooked. Any space larger than a cubic metre was examined.

It took two and a half days. Pou Mok's room was opened and searched thirty-three hours after it began. Because it was listed as being rented (currently unoccupied) by someone on Ombey, and the diligent search turned up nothing, it was closed up and codelocked.

The cabinet meeting which followed the end of the search decided that one missing mental patient could not justify keeping the navy's premier defence base isolated, nor could Ombey do without the products of Guyana's industrial stations. The asteroid was stood down to a code three status, and the problem of the woman's identity and Skibbow's where-abouts handed over to a joint ISA ESA team.

Three and a half days after its original departure time, the *Quadin* left for Pinjarra. Gerald Skibbow wasn't aware of it, he had been in zero-tau an hour before Loren's final diversion.

16

The Bar KF-T wasn't up to much, but after a fifty-hour trip
squashed into the two-deck life support capsule of an inter-
orbit cargo tug with just the captain's family to talk to, Monica Foulkes wasn't about to closet herself away in a barren
hotel room. *A drink and some company, that's what I need.*
She sat on a stool up at the bar sipping an imported beer while
Ayacucho's meagre nightlife eddied around her. The economic
downturn from the quarantine was affecting every aspect of
Dorados life, even here. It was ten-thirty P.M. local time and
only five couples were braving the dance floor, there were
even some tables free. But the young men were still reassuringly on the prowl; she'd already had three offers of a drink.

The only cause for concern was how many of them were
wearing red handkerchiefs around their ankles, boys and girls.
She couldn't be entirely sure if they wanted to seduce her or
simply convert her. Deadnight was becoming an alarming
trend; the ESA's head of station in Mapire estimated twenty
per cent of the Dorados' teenage population was getting
sucked in. Monica would have put it nearer to fifty per cent.
Given the blandness of existence among the asteroids she was
surprised it wasn't even higher.

Her extended sensory analysis program plotted the tall
man's approach, only alerting her to his existence when he was
two metres away and his destination obvious.

"Can I get you another bottle?"

Her intended reply perished as soon as she saw the too-long
greying hair flopping over his brow. "Sure," she said, grinning
whimsically.

He sat on the empty stool beside her and signalled the barmaid for a couple of bottles. "Now this is far more stylish than
our last encounter."

"True. How are you, Samuel?"

"Overworked and underpaid. Government employees get the same deal the Confederation over."

"You forgot unappreciated."

"No I didn't," he said cheerfully. "That's the benefit of Edenism, everyone contributes to the greater good, no matter what area we excel in."

"Oh, God." She accepted her new beer from the barmaid. "An evangelical Edenist. Just my luck."

"So, what are you doing here?"

"Negotiating armament manufacturing contracts; it actually says I'm a rep for Octagon Exports on my passport."

"Could be worse." Samuel tried his beer, and frowned at the bottle with some dismay. "Take me, I'm supposed to be part of the delegation from this system's Edenist habitats, discussing mutual defence enhancement arrangements. I specialize in internal security procedures."

Monica laughed, and tipped her bottle at the middle-aged Edenist. "Good luck." The humour ended. "You must have seen them?"

"Yes. I'm afraid the possessed are definitely inside the barricades."

"Shit! I meant the Deadnight kids."

"Ah. Monica, please take care. Our . . . examination of the Dorados has shown up several cadres of possessed. They're here, and they are expanding. I do not advise you return to Mapire. Our estimation is that it will fall within another three days, probably less."

"Did you tell the governing council?"

"No. We decided it would cause too much panic and disorder. The council would institute quite draconian measures, and be completely unable to enforce them, which would only worsen the situation. The Dorados do not have the usual civil government structure; for all their size and economic importance, they remain company towns, without adequate law enforcement personnel. In short, the possessed will take over here anyway. We need time to search in peace before they do. I'm afraid Mzu comes before everything, including alerting the population."

"Oh. Thanks for the warning."

"My pleasure. Have your assets located Daphine Kigano yet?"

Monica crinkled her face up in distaste. I shouldn't be discussing this, not with him. Standard agency doctrine. But the universe wasn't exactly standard anymore. And the ESA didn't have too many resources here. "No. But we know it's her."

"Yes. That's what we concluded."

"A chartered starship carrying one passenger was rather unsubtle. Our station accessed the Department of Immigration's file on the *Samaku*'s docking: one hundred per cent visual confirmation. God knows what she was doing in the Narok system, though."

"Just trading ships, we hope. An interdiction order has gone out for the *Samaku*, all voidhawks and Confederation Navy ships are alert for it."

"Good. Look, Samuel, I don't know what your orders are—"

"Originally: find Mzu, prevent her from handing over the Alchemist to the Garissan partizan movement, retrieve the Alchemist. That's the soft option. If we can't do that, then I was instructed to terminate her and destroy her neural nanonics. If we don't get the Alchemist, no one else must have it."

"Yeah. Pretty much the same as mine. Personally I think the second option would be best all round."

"Possibly. I must admit that even after seventy-five years in the job I am reluctant to kill in cold blood. A life is a life."

"For the greater good, my friend."

Samuel smiled sadly. "I know both the arguments and the stakes involved. However, there is also a new factor to consider. We absolutely cannot allow her or it to fall into the hands of the possessed."

"God, I know that. Capone with antimatter is bad enough; give him the Alchemist and the Confederation Navy might not be able to contain him."

"Which means, we really don't want to expedite option two, do we?"

Facing him was the same as receiving a stern glance from a loving grandfather who was dispensing homely wisdom. How infuriating that she had to have the obvious pointed out to her in such a fashion. "How can I argue against that?" She grunted miserably.

"Just as long as you appreciate all the factors."

"Sure. Consider my wrist firmly smacked. What have your lot got planned for her, then?"

"Following acquisition, Consensus recommended placing her in zero-tau. At the very least until the possessed situation is resolved. Possibly longer."

"How long?" Monica almost didn't want to ask, or know.

"Consensus thought it prudent that she remains there until we have a requirement for the Alchemist. It is a large galaxy, after all; there may be other, more hostile xenocs than the Kiint and Tyrathca out there."

"I was wrong, you're not an evangelist, you're a paranoid."

"A pragmatist, I sincerely hope; as are all Edenists."

"Okay, Samuel, so pragmatically, what do you want to do next? And please bear in mind that I am a loyal subject of my King."

"Concentrate on finding her first, then get her away from the Dorados. The argument over custody can come later."

"Nine-tenths of the law," she muttered. "Are you offering me a joint operation?"

"Yes, if you're willing. We have more resources here, I think, which gives us the greater chance of launching a successful extraction mission. But neither of us can afford to dismiss any avenue which will locate her. I am sure your Duke of Salion would approve of any action which guaranteed her removal from the scene right now. You can accompany her on our evacuation flight; and afterwards we would allow a joint custody to satisfy the Kingdom we have not acquired Alchemist technology. Is that reasonable?"

"Yeah, very. We have a deal."

They touched bottles.

"The local partizan leadership has been called to a meeting here tonight," she said. "Unfortunately, I don't know exactly where that is in the asteroid. I'm waiting for our asset to get in touch as soon as it's over."

"Thank you, Monica. We don't know where it is, either. But we're assuming she will be there."

"Can you track any of the partizans?"

"It is not easy. But we'll certainly make every effort."

* * *

For three days the rented office suite which had become the new Edenist intelligence service headquarters in Ayacucho had been the centre of a remarkable breeding program. When the agents of the "defence delegation" team arrived they brought with them seventy thousand geneered spider eggs. Every arachnid was affinity-capable, and small enough to clamber through grilles and scurry through the vast mechanical plexus of lift shafts, maintenance passages, environmental ducts, cable conduits, and waste disposal pipes which knitted the asteroid's rooms and public halls together into a functional whole.

For over seventy hours the tiny infiltrators were coaxed and manipulated along black pipes and through chinks in the rock, slipping around cracks in badly fitted composite panels. Thousands never made it to their required destination. Victims of more predatory creatures, of working insect grids, of security barriers (most common in the corporate areas), sluices of strange liquids, smears of sticky fluids, and the most common failing of all: being lost.

But for every one which didn't make it, five did. At the end of the deployment period the Edenists had visual coverage of sixty-seven per cent of Ayacucho's interior (which was how Samuel found Monica Foulkes so easily). The three void-hawks perched on Ayacucho's docking ledges, along with the ten armed voidhawks holding station inside Tunja's particle disk, and the agents reviewed the spiders on a snapshot rotor, managing a complete sweep every four hours. As a method of locating one individual it was horribly inefficient. Samuel knew that it would only be pure chance if Mzu was spotted during one of the sweeps. It was up to the agents on the ground to lower the odds by procedural work; their dull routine of researching public files, bullying assets, bribing officialdom, and on occasion outright blackmail.

For thirty years the Garissan partizan movement had pursued a course of consistently lacklustre activity. It funded several anti-Omuta propaganda campaigns to keep the hatred alive among the first of a new generation born to the refugees. Mercenaries and ex-Garissan navy marines were recruited and sent on sabotage missions against any surviving Omutan interests. There were even a couple of attempts to fly into the Omuta system and attack asteroid settlements, both of which were snuffed by CNIS before the starships ever left dock. But for the last decade the leadership had done little except talk. Membership had dropped away steadily, as had funding, along with any real enthusiasm.

With such shoddy organization and defunct motivation it was inevitable that any intelligence agency which had ever shown an interest in the partizans had collated files on every person who had been a member, or even attended a fringe meeting. Their leadership was perfectly documented, long since consigned to the semi-crank category and downgraded to intermittent monitoring. A status which was now abruptly reversed.

There were five people making up the executive of Ayacucho's partizan group. In keeping with the movement's deterioration none of them followed the kind of security procedures they had obeyed so rigorously in the early days. That sloppiness in conjunction with an encyclopedic knowledge of their daily activity patterns allowed the Edenists to position spiders where they could provide a comprehensive coverage of the leadership's movements in the hours leading up to the meeting.

Samuel and the voidhawks were presented with eyeblink pictures of the partizan leaders making their way through the asteroid. Respectable middle-age professionals now, they all had escorts of bodyguards, keen for any sign of trouble. These entourages were unmistakable, making them easy to follow.

"It looks like either level three or four in section twelve," Samuel told Monica.

She datavised her processor block for a schematic of the asteroid. "It's all offices there, corporate country. That makes sense, it's more secure, and they are all rich. It wouldn't be suspicious for them to be there together."

"Unfortunately it makes life complicated for us. We're having trouble infiltrating that area." He was watching an inverted image of Ikela walking along a corridor at the centre of five boosted bodyguards. They were approaching a junction. A fast check with the voidhawks revealed that there were no more spiders left ahead. He ordered the one he was using to scuttle along the ceiling after Ikela.

There are UV lights ahead, a voidhawk warned. **The spider is approaching a grade-five clean environment.**

I know, but I need to see which way he turns. It was a strange viewpoint; to Samuel the corridor wasn't particularly large, to the spider it was vast. The two visual interpretations tended to clash confusingly inside Samuel's cortex unless he maintained a high level of concentration. Drab whiteness slid smoothly past galloping legs. Far above him was the sky of hazel carpet. Footsteps crashed against the spider's pressure-sensitive cells. Stalactite mountains clad in expensive black silk marched on in front of the racing arachnid, becoming difficult to resolve as they approached the fork. He just needed a hint . . .

The affinity link vanished amid a violet flash. *Damnation!* A further review showed Samuel no spiders had managed to penetrate the area.

"What is it?" Monica asked as he flinched in annoyance.

"We just lost them."

"So now what?"

He looked around at the other agents in the office suite. "Kit up and move out. We'll cover as many approaches as we can. Monica, are you sure your asset is reliable?"

"Don't fret; we've got him hoisted by the short and curlies. He won't be able to datavise during the meeting, but as soon as it's over we'll know where it was and if she's there. Did any of your infiltration systems see her going in?"

"No," he admitted. "Not even a fifty per cent characteristics match."

"I'm not surprised."

The Edenist agents were putting on slim equipment belts and strapping up shoulder holsters. Monica checked her own maser pistol and ran a diagnostic program through her implants.

"Monica," Samuel said.

She caught the tone. "I know: I'm not in your command network, I'd be in the way if I try to front-line. It's all yours, Samuel."

"Thank you." **Stand by,** he told the voidhawks waiting on

the docking ledge, **if we do grab her we'll need to exit fast.**
He led the team out.

There were only five people in the Tunja system who knew the
real reason for forming the Garissan partizan movement. None
of them lived on the same asteroid, so that if disaster did strike
the others would be there to carry on with the plan.

In Ayacucho it was Ikela, the nominal head of the original
five. It suited him to be one of the partizan group's executives
rather than the leader. This way he kept up-to-date on the
movement's activities while staying out of the limelight. His
position was due principally to his financial support rather than
any active participation. Again, according to plan.

Dan Malindi, the Ayacucho group's leader, was the first to
arrive at the secure conference office of Laxa and Ahmad, the
legal firm they were using as cover. He gave Ikela a puzzled,
vaguely annoyed glance as he entered. No one knew why Ikela
had demanded the meeting at seven hours notice. And the executive weren't people used to being kept in ignorance, not by
one of their own. The sight of the normally composed industrialist sitting mutely at the table looking as if he were suffering some kind of fever with the way he was sweating did
nothing to ease the tension.

Kaliua Lamu was the second to arrive; a financier who
made little secret about his growing ambivalence to the movement. Partizan membership didn't sit well alongside his newfound respectability.

Feira Ile and Cabral arrived together, the most senior rank-
ing figures in the Dorados administration. Feira Ile had been
an admiral in the Garissan navy and was now Ayacucho's SD
chief, while Cabral had built himself the largest media group
in the Dorados. His company's growth and popularity were
due to the tabloid nationalism of its editorial policy, which
made him a natural choice for the partizans. Most of the executive staff suspected his support was strictly for appearance
sake.

Bodyguards and assistants left the room. Dan Malindi
glared at the small woman sitting quietly behind Ikela, who
obstinately refused to be intimidated into moving.

"She's with me," Ikela said.

Dan Malindi grunted in dissatisfaction and activated the office's security screen. "All right, Ikela, what the hell is this about?"

Ikela gave the woman a respectful gesture, and she stood up, walking to the end of the table opposite Dan Malindi. "My name is Dr Alkad Mzu, I'm here to finish our war with Omuta."

Dan Malindi and Kaliua Lamu both gave her a nonplussed glance. Cabral frowned, ordering a neural nanonics file search. But it was Feira Ile who produced the strongest reaction; he half rose to his feet, openly astonished. "The Alchemist," he murmured. "You built the Alchemist. Holy Mary."

"The what?" Cabral asked.

"The Alchemist," Alkad told them. "It was our super-weapon. I was its designer."

"Feira?" Cabral prompted.

"She's right," the old ex-admiral said. "I was never given any details, the project was classified way above my security rating. But the navy built this . . . thing, whatever it is, just before the genocide. We were going to use it against Omuta." He drew a long breath and looked at the diminutive physicist. "What happened?"

"Our flight was intercepted by blackhawks hired by Omuta," Alkad said. "We never got there. The Alchemist was never used."

"No way," Dan Malindi said. "This is complete bullshit. You appear on the scene thirty years after the event and spin some crap about a missing legend you heard about in some bar. I bet the next stage is asking us for money to search for this Alchemist. In fact, I bet it's going to take a lot of money to find it, right?" He was sneering contemptuously at her when he finished, but somehow her cold smile managed to rob his anger.

"I don't need to search. I know exactly where it is."

"It wasn't lost?" Kaliua Lamu asked. His enthusiasm bought him a disgusted look from Dan Malindi.

"No, it's never been lost. It's been kept safe."

"Where?"

Alkad merely smiled.

"Maybe it does exist," Cabral said. "And our illustrious ad-

miral here was right saying someone called Alkad Mzu built it.
How do we know you're her? We can't make the decisions we
need to make on the word of some stranger who turns up out
of the blue, especially not at this precise time."

Alkad raised an eyebrow. "Captain?"

"I can vouch for her," Ikela said softly. "This is Dr Alkad
Mzu."

"Captain?" Dan Malindi asked. "What does she mean?"

Ikela cleared his throat. "It was my rank in the Garissan
navy. I used to be captain of the frigate *Chengho*. We were flying escort duty on the Alchemist deployment mission. That's
how I know."

"Datavise your command authority code," Feira Ile said
sternly.

Ikela nodded reluctantly, and retrieved the code from its
memory cell.

"It would appear our colleague is telling the truth," Feira Ile
told the silent office.

"Mother Mary," Cabral muttered, glancing at the man he
thought he'd known for the last thirty years. "Why didn't you
tell us?"

Ikela sank his head into his hands. "The plan operates on a
need to know basis only. Up until today you didn't need to
know."

"What plan?" Feira Ile snapped.

"To deploy the Alchemist," Alkad said. "After the original
mission was crippled, Ikela and four other officers were detailed to sell the antimatter we were carrying. They were supposed to invest that money so there would be sufficient funds
to hire a combat-capable starship and equip it to fire the Alchemist once the sanctions were lifted and the Confederation
Navy squadron assigned to blockade duties returned home.
The only reason you partizans exist is to provide me with a
crew that will not flinch from the job that needs to be done."
She stared at Ikela. "And now I'm here, on schedule, and I find
no ship, and no crew."

"I told you," Ikela shouted. "You can have your ship if that's
still what we want. I have more than enough money. Anyone
of us in this room has enough money to provide a starship for

you. I have never failed my duty to my people. Don't you ever say that. But things have changed."

"Looks like you've failed to me," Cabral said briskly. "Looks like you've failed a lot of people."

"Think!" Ikela stormed. "Think for the love of Mary what she is proposing. What will the Confederation do to us if we blow up Omuta's star? What revenge will they take?"

"It can do that?" a startled Kaliua Lamu asked. "The Alchemist will destroy their star?"

"On one setting, yes," Alkad said. "I don't intend using that. I propose to simply extinguish the star. No one will die, but their planet and asteroid settlements will have to be evacuated and abandoned. They will become a broken homeless people, as we are. That's fitting, surely?"

"Well yes . . ." He searched around the table for support, finding only uneasy confusion. "But I don't understand. If you survived the blackhawk attack, why didn't you continue with the mission? Why wait thirty years?"

"There were complications," Alkad said tonelessly. "By the time we were in any position to function again the sanctions had been imposed, and the blockade squadron was in place. It was decided to wait until these obstructions were removed, which would give us a much greater chance of success. We did not have limitless government resources anymore, and we only have one chance to get it right. This is the optimum time to strike. We won't have another chance; the intelligence agencies are pursuing me. And they will find me."

Dan Malindi groaned. "Intelligence agencies? Holy Mary, they'll find out where you've been."

"Oh, yes, they'll know you're involved. Does that bother you?"

"Bother me? You bitch! I have a family."

"Yes. I've heard this argument already today. It is beginning to bore me. I have lived the reality of the genocide for thirty years. You, all of you, have just been playing patriot. Each of you has profited in your own field by chanting the cry of nationalism. Well, my being here has put an end to your pathetic game."

"Are you threatening us?" Cabral asked.

"I have always been a threat to your cosy life, even though you never knew I existed."

"What exactly do you want?" Feira Ile asked.

"Two things. A combat-capable starship with a decent crew of committed nationalists. And a secure environment for myself while you prepare them. Do not underestimate the agencies. They now know for certain that the Alchemist is real, which means they will go to any lengths to acquire me."

Ikela stood up, placing his hands on the table and leaning forwards. "I say we cannot do this. Mother Mary, we're sitting here talking about wrecking an entire star system as if it were some kind of difficult business venture. Times have changed, we are not Garissans anymore. I'm sorry if that is painful for you to hear, Doctor, but we're not. We have to look to the future, not the past. This is madness."

"And that is treachery," Cabral said.

"Treachery to what? To a planet that was killed thirty years ago? If that's what it is, then fine, I'm a traitor to it. I don't care."

"Other people might when they get to hear."

"Ikela, I really don't think you're in any position to back out now," Feira Ile said. "Given your mission, you are still a serving officer. That means you are required to discharge your obligations."

"Then I quit, I resign my commission."

"Very well. In that case, I must ask you to hand over the T'Opingtu company to me."

"*What?*"

"I believe we just heard that it was founded on money provided by the Garissan navy. That means it doesn't belong to you."

"Go fuck yourself."

"Listen, we can't make a snap judgement over this," Kaliua Lamu said. "Ikela's right, we're talking about wiping out an entire solar system."

"I might have known you'd take that attitude," Dan Malindi said.

"Excuse me?"

"You heard. I'm willing to provide as much help as Dr Mzu

wants. What the hell is the Confederation going to do to us if we're armed with Alchemists?"

"There is only one," Alkad said.

"You can build more, can't you?"

She hesitated uncomfortably. "If there was a requirement, it could be duplicated."

"There you are then. You can't leave what's left of the Garissan nation and culture unprotected, can you?"

"You want to start a damn arms race as well?" Ikela yelled. "You're as mad as she is."

"Curb your language. Have you forgotten the possessed?"

"In Mary's name what have they got to do with this?"

"If we were armed with Alchemists, that bastard Capone would think twice before sending his fleet here."

"And who precisely is going to be in charge of these Alchemists?"

"The Dorados council, of course," Dan Malindi said scornfully.

"Exactly, and we all know how much influence you have there."

"Enough!" Alkad slammed her fist down. "I will not supply Alchemists to anyone. You have no conception of what it is capable of. It is not some bigger and better bomb you can use for political advantage. It was built for one purpose, to destroy the people who threatened our world. It will be used for one purpose, our revenge against them." She looked at each of them in turn, furious and sickened that this was all that remained of the planet she was once so proud of. Where was their dignity, their resolution? Could none of them perform one single act of remembrance? "I will give you thirty minutes to debate this. After that you will tell me which of you support me, and which do not."

"I certainly support you," Kaliua Lamu said loudly, but he was talking to her back as she limped away.

The shouting had already begun again before the door closed behind her. All the bodyguards and aides in the anteroom stared; Alkad barely saw them. If she had just known or anticipated the shambles which the partizans had become, then she would have been mentally geared up.

"Alkad?" Voi was bending down, giving the smaller woman an anxious look.

"Don't mind me, I'll be all right."

"Please, I have something to show you. Now."

The girl took Alkad's arm, hustling her across the room and out into the corridor. Alkad couldn't be bothered to protest, although force of habit made her activate a threat analysis program. Her enhanced retinas began scanning the length of the corridor.

"Here," Voi said triumphantly. She opened her palm to reveal a tiny squashed spider.

"Mother Mary! Have you completely flipped?"

"No, listen. You know you said you thought the intelligence agencies were following you."

"I should never have told you that. Voi, you don't know what you're getting involved with."

"Oh, yes I do. We started checking the spaceport log. There's a delegation of Edenists here to discuss strengthening our defences. Three voidhawks brought thirty of them."

"Yes?"

"Mapire only rated one voidhawk, and six Edenists to discuss our mutual defence with the council. It should be the other way around, the capital should have got the larger delegation, not Ayacucho."

Alkad glanced at the little brown blob in the girl's hand, a bad feeling sinking through her. "Go on."

"So we thought about how Edenists would search the asteroid for you. Adamists would use spylenses and hack into the communications net to get at public monitor security cameras. Edenists would use bitek systems, either simulants or affinity-bonded animals. We started looking. And here they are. Spiders. They're everywhere, Alkad. We checked. Ayacucho is totally infested."

"That doesn't necessarily prove—" she said slowly.

"Yes it does." The hand with the crushed blob was shaken violently. "This is from the *Lycosidae* family. Ayacucho's ecologists never introduced any *Lycosidaes* into the biosphere. Check the public records if you don't believe me."

"All sorts of things can get through bio-quarantine; irradiation screening isn't perfect."

"Then why are they all male? We haven't found a single female, not one. It's got to be so they can't mate, they won't reproduce. They'll die off without causing any sort of ecological imbalance. Nobody will ever notice them."

Strangely enough, Alkad was almost impressed. "Thank you, Voi. I'd better go back in there and tell them I need more security."

"Them?" Voi was utterly derisory. "Did they leap to help you? No. Of course not. I said they wouldn't."

"They have what I need, Voi."

"They have nothing we don't. Nothing. Why don't you trust us? Trust me? What does it take to make you believe in us?"

"I do believe in your sincerity."

"Then come with me!" It was an agonized plea. "I can get you out of here. They don't even have any way to get you out of the office without the spiders seeing."

"That's because they don't know about them."

"They don't know, because they're not concerned about security. Look at them, they've got enough bodyguards in there to form a small army. Everybody in the asteroid knows who they are."

"Truthfully?"

"All right, not everybody. But certainly every reporter. The only reason they don't say anything is because of Cabral. Anyone coming to the Dorados who really wanted to make contact with the partizan movement wouldn't need more than two hours to find a name."

"Mary be damned!" Alkad glanced back at the door to the anteroom, then at the tall girl. Voi was everything her father was not: dedicated, determined, hurting to help. "You have some kind of safe route out of here?"

"Yes!"

"Okay. You can take me out of this section. After that I'll get in touch with your father again, see what they're going to do for me."

"And if they won't help?"

"Then it looks like you're on."

"Yeah? So, I'm late. Sue me. Listen, this meeting caused me a shitload of grief. I don't need no lecture from the ESA on contact procedures right now."

 . . .

"Yeah, she's here all right, in the flesh. Mother Mary, she's really got the Alchemist stashed away somewhere. She's not kidding. I mean, shit, she really wants to take out Omuta's star."

 . . .

"Course I don't know where it is, she wouldn't say. But, Mary, Ikela used to be a frigate captain in the Omuta navy. He flew escort on the Alchemist mission. I never knew. Twenty years we've been plotting away together, and I never knew."

 . . .

"Sure you want to know where we are. Look, you're going to come in here shooting, right? I mean, how do I know you're not going to snuff me? This is serious heavy-duty shit."

 . . .

"All right, but if you're lying you'd better make sure you finish me. I'll have you if you don't, no matter what it costs. And hey, even if you do kill me, I can come back and get you that way. Yeah. So you'd better not be fucking me over."

 . . .

"Oh, absolutely. I always believe every word you people say. Okay, listen, we're in Laxa and Ahmad's conference office. The bodyguards are all in the anteroom. Tell your people to be fucking careful when they come in. You let them know I'm on your side, yeah?"

 . . .

"No, she's out in the anteroom. She went out there twenty minutes ago so we could argue about what to do. The vote was three to two for wasting Omuta's star. Guess how I voted."

"Laxa and Ahmad, the conference office," Monica said. "Mzu's in the anteroom along with the bodyguards."

Go, Samuel ordered.

The twenty Edenist agents closed on the Laxa and Ahmad offices. Floor plans were pulled from the asteroid's civil engineering memory cores. Entry routes and tactics were formulated and finalized while they jogged towards their target, the general affinity band thick with tense exchanges.

Monica kept three paces behind Samuel the whole way. It irked her, and she wasn't looking forwards to her debrief, either. Teaming up with Edenists! But at least this way the Alchemist would be neutered. Providing Samuel kept his part of the agreement. Which she was sure he would do. Although high politics could still screw everything up. God!

It took them four minutes to reach Laxa and Ahmad. One featureless corridor after another. Thankfully there were few people about, with only a handful of workaholics left. They barged past an old man carrying several flek cases, a man and a woman who looked so guilty they were obviously having an affair, a pair of teenage girls, one very tall and skinny and black, the other small and white, both wearing red handkerchiefs around their ankles.

When she reached Laxa and Ahmad the Edenist team was already inside. Two agents stood guard out in the corridor. Monica stepped wearily through the crumpled door, drawing her pistol.

Samuel drew his breath sharply. "Damnation."

"What?" she asked. By then they had reached the conference office anteroom. The partizan bodyguards were all sprawled on the floor with limbs twitching erratically. Six Edenists stood over them, their TIP pistols pointing down. Three scorch lines slashed the walls where laser fire had burned the composite. A pair of spent nerve short-out grenades rolled around on the carpet.

"Where's Mzu?" Monica asked.

Samuel beckoned her into the conference office. The partizan leadership had been caught by the nerve short-out pulses, but the door and security screening had saved them from the worst effects. They were still conscious. Four of them. The fifth was dead.

Monica grimaced when she saw the broad char mark on the side of Ikela's skull. The beam had fractured the bone in several places, roasting the brain to a black pulp. Someone had made very sure his neural nanonics were ruined. "God, what happened here?"

Two Edenist agents were standing behind Feira Ile, their pistol muzzles pressed into his neck. His wrists had been secured in a composite zipcuff behind his back. Crumbs of vomit were sticking to his lip; he was sweating profusely from the grenade assault, but otherwise defiant. A laser pistol was lying on the table in front of him.

"He shot Ikela," Samuel said in bewildered dismay. He squatted down beside Ikela's chair. "Why? What was the point? He was one of yours."

Feira Ile grinned savagely. "My last duty for the Garissan navy."

"What do you mean?"

"Ikela flew escort duty on the Alchemist. He probably knew where it is. Now he can't tell you."

Monica and Samuel swapped a grim glance.

"She's gone, hasn't she?" Monica said bitterly.

"It would seem so."

"Fuck it!" She stamped over to Kaliua Lamu, who had an agent holding him upright in his chair. "Where did Mzu go?" Monica asked.

"Screw you."

Monica gave an amused glance at the other partizans around the table. "Oh, come on, Kaliua," she said sweetly. "You were eager enough to tell us this meeting's location."

"Liar!"

She took out a Royal Kulu Bank credit disk. "A hundred thousand pounds, wasn't it?"

"Bitch whore! I never," he shouted at his comrades. "It wasn't me. For Mary's sake, it wasn't."

Monica grabbed his chin, and slowly exerted her boosted grip. Kaliua Lamu gagged fearfully at the force which threatened to shatter his jawbone.

"You said I'd better be certain when I finish you. Well, I intend to be extremely thorough extinguishing your life unless I know where she went."

"I don't know."

"Debrief nanonics would be the pleasant option, but we don't have time for that. Fortunately, old-fashioned pain can still produce some pretty impressive results during field interrogation. And they trained me very well, Kaliua." She pushed her face centimetres from his bugging eyes. "Would you like to try calling my bluff? Or perhaps you think you're strong enough to resist me for a couple of hours after I've fused your neural nanonics into ash? Once they're dead you can't block the pain. And the field way to fuse neural nanonics is with electrodes. Crude, but it works. Guess where they're applied."

"No. Please! Don't." His eyes were watering as he started shaking.

"Where then?"

"I don't know. I promise. She was gone when we finished. I told you she was supposed to be waiting outside for us to finish. But she wasn't there."

"Then who did she leave with?"

"It was a girl, my bodyguard said. Ikela's daughter, Voi. She's tall, young. They were talking together and never came back. *Honestly*, that's all I know."

Monica let go of his chin. He slumped back in the chair, trembling in relief.

"A tall girl," Monica whispered. She was looking at Samuel in dawning dismay as the memory blossomed. She hurriedly accessed the neural nanonics memory cell she'd kept running to record the operation.

In the corridor on the way up. Two girls, one tall and black, the other white and small. Pressed against the wall in alarm as she and Samuel ran past. The memory cell image froze. Green neon grid lines closed around the smaller girl, calculating her height. It matched Mzu's. So did the approximated weight.

A backpack fitted with a long shoulder strap hung at the girl's side.

Monica had seen that backpack once before. Never in her life would she need help from neural nanonics to remember that time. The backpack had been flapping behind a small spacesuit-clad figure who was clinging desperately to a rope ladder.

"Dear God, we walked right bloody past her," she told an aghast Samuel. "The bitch is wearing a chameleon suit."

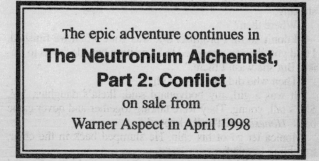

The epic adventure continues in

**The Neutronium Alchemist,
Part 2: Conflict**

on sale from

Warner Aspect in April 1998

TIMELINE

2020 . . . Cavius base established. Mining of Lunar subcrustal resources starts.

2037 . . . Beginning of large-scale geneering on humans; improvement to immunology system, eradication of appendix, organ efficiency increased.

2041 . . . First deuterium-fuelled fusion stations built; inefficient and expensive.

2044 . . . Christian reunification.

2047 . . . First asteroid capture mission. Beginning of Earth's O'Neill Halo.

2049 . . . Quasi-sentient bitek animals employed as servitors.

2055 . . . Jupiter mission.

2055 . . . Lunar cities granted independence from founding companies.

2057 . . . Ceres asteroid settlement founded.

2058 . . . Affinity symbiont neurons developed by Wing-Tsit Chong, providing control over animals and bitek constructs.

2064 . . . Multinational industrial consortium (Jovian Sky Power Corporation) begins mining Jupiter's atmosphere for He_3 using aerostat factories.

2064 . . . Islamic secular unification.

2067 . . . Fusion stations begin to use He_3 as fuel.

2069 . . . Affinity bond gene spliced into human DNA.

2075 . . . JSKP germinates Eden, a bitek habitat in orbit around Jupiter, with UN Protectorate status.

2077 . . . New Kong asteroid begins FTL stardrive research project.

2085 . . . Eden opened for habitation.

2086 . . . Habitat Pallas germinated in Jupiter orbit.

2090 . . . Wing-Tsit Chong dies, and transfers memories to Eden's neural strata. Start of Edenist culture. Eden and Pallas declare independence from UN. Launch buyout of JSKP shares. Pope Eleanor excommunicates all Christians with affinity gene. Exodus of affinity capable humans to Eden. Effective end of bitek industry on Earth.

2091 . . . Lunar referendum to terraform Mars.

2094 . . . Edenists begin exowomb breeding programme coupled with extensive geneering improvement to embryos, tripling their population over a decade.

2103 . . . Earth's national governments consolidate into Govcentral.

2103 . . . Thoth base established on Mars.

2107 . . . Govcentral jurisdiction extended to cover O'Neill Halo.

2115 . . . First instantaneous translation by New Kong spaceship, Earth to Mars.

2118 . . . Mission to Proxima Centauri.

2123 . . . Terracompatible plant found at Ross 154.

2125 . . . Ross 154 planet named Felicity, first multiethnic colonists arrive.

2125–2130 . . . Four new terracompatible planets discovered. Multiethnic colonies founded.

2131 . . . Edenists germinate Perseus in orbit around Ross 154 gas giant, begin He_3 mining.

2131–2205 . . . One hundred and thirty terracompatible planets discovered. Massive starship building programme initiated in O'Neill Halo. Govcentral begins large-scale enforced outshipment of surplus population, rising to 2 million a week in 2160: Great Dispersal. Civil conflict on some early multiethnic colonies. Individual Govcentral states sponsor ethnic-streaming colonies. Edenists expand their He_3 mining enterprise to every inhabited star system with a gas giant.

2139 . . . Asteroid Braun impacts on Mars.

2180 . . . First orbital tower built on Earth.

2205 . . . Antimatter production station built in orbit around sun by Govcentral in an attempt to break the Edenist energy monopoly.

2208 . . . First antimatter-drive starships operational.

2210 . . . Richard Saldana transports all of New Kong's industrial facilities from the O'Neill Halo to an asteroid orbiting Kulu. He claims independence for the Kulu star system, founds Christian-only colony, and begins to mine He_3 from the system's gas giant.

2218 . . . First voidhawk gestated, a bitek starship designed by Edenists.

2225 . . . Establishment of a hundred voidhawk families. Habitats Romulus and Remus germinated in Saturn orbit to serve as voidhawk bases.

2232 . . . Conflict at Jupiter's trailing Trojan asteroid cluster between belt alliance ships and an O'Neill Halo company hydrocarbon refinery. Antimatter used as a weapon; twenty-seven thousand people killed.

2238 . . . Treaty of Deimos; outlaws production and use of antimatter in the Sol system; signed by Govcentral, Lunar nation, asteroid alliance, and Edenists. Antimatter stations abandoned and dismantled.

2240 . . . Coronation of Gerrald Saldana as King of Kulu. Foundation of Saldana dynasty.

2267–2270 . . . Eight separate skirmishes involving use of antimatter among colony worlds. Thirteen million killed.

2271 . . . Avon summit between all planetary leaders. Treaty of Avon, banning the manufacture and use of antimatter throughout inhabited space. Formation of Human

Confederation to police agreement. Construction of Confederation Navy begins.

2300 . . . Confederation expanded to include Edenists.

2301 . . . First Contact. Jiciro race discovered, a pre-technology civilization. System quarantined by Confederation to avoid cultural contamination.

2310 . . . First ice asteroid impact on Mars.

2330 . . . First blackhawks gestated at Valisk, independent habitat.

2350 . . . War between Novska and Hilversum. Novska bombed with antimatter. Confederation Navy prevents retaliatory strike against Hilversum.

2356 . . . Kiint homeworld discovered.

2357 . . . Kiint join Confederation as "observers."

2360 . . . A voidhawk scout discovers Atlantis.

2371 . . . Edenists colonize Atlantis.

2395 . . . Tyrathca colony world discovered.

2402 . . . Tyrathca join Confederation.

2420 . . . Kulu scoutship discovers Ruin Ring.

2428 . . . Bitek habitat Tranquillity germinated by Crown Prince Michael Saldana, orbiting above Ruin Ring.

2432 . . . Prince Michael's son, Maurice, geneered with affinity. Kulu abdication crisis. Coronation of Lukas Saldana. Prince Michael exiled.

2550 . . . Mars declared habitable by Terraforming office.

2580 . . . Dorado asteroids discovered around Tunja, claimed by both Garissa and Omuta.

2581 . . . Omuta mercenary fleet drops twelve antimatter planet-busters on Garissa, planet rendered uninhabitable. Confederation imposes thirty-year sanction against Omuta, prohibiting any interstellar trade or transport. Blockade enforced by Confederation Navy.

2582 . . . Colony established on Lalonde.

"A space opera that is big, boisterous, and has something for everyone. . . . Hamilton's universe will not fit into a single volume. There are just too many heroes to love, villains to hate, and worlds to explore. . . . His imagination knows no bounds!"
—*Science Fiction Weekly*

"ABSOLUTELY VINTAGE SCIENCE FICTION. . . . HAMILTON PUTS [SF] BACK INTO INTERSTELLAR OVERDRIVE. An intergalactic adventure story laced with ironies, insights, and held together by a transcending central plot."
—*The Times* (London)

"A hugely rich . . . mystery on a grand scale. . . . The kind of book that's so good you wish it would go on forever. . . . A masterful job of storytelling."
—Amazon.com

"SUPER-INTELLIGENT SPACE OPERA, WROUGHT BY AN AUTHOR WHO KNOWS HIS STUFF . . . AND IT'S A RATTLING PAGE-TURNER TOO. . . . An astonishing read crammed with golden-age wonders, but all depicted with an intellectual toughness that marks this as a landmark work for the 1990s."
—Stephen Baxter, author of *The Time Ships*

more . . .

"ELOQUENT AND INGENIOUS. . . . A host of believable characters deploy against rich descriptions of worlds and living starships. Horror and heroism and even the humor are convincing. . . . Special effects run riot. . . . It all hangs together compulsively."
—*Daily Telegraph* (London)

"IF ANY BOOK DESERVES A RECOMMENDATION 'DO NOT MISS,' IT IS THIS."
—*Critical Wave*

"BRASH, BROAD SPACE OPERA WITH MILITARY HARDWARE GALORE. FAST MOVEMENT AND DAZZLING INVENTION. MASSIVE!"
—Gregory Benford, author of *Timescape*

"PAINTED ON THE VAST CANVAS OF CLASSIC SPACE OPERA."
—*SFX*